Mary Roberts Rinehart

best novels

In this book:

Locked Doors

The Circular Staircase

The Breaking Point

The Case of Jennie Brice

Mary Roberts Rinehart (1876 – 1958) was an American writer, often called the American Agatha Christie, although her first mystery novel was published 14 years before Christie's. She is considered the source of the phrase "The butler did it", although she did not actually use the phrase. She is considered to have invented the "Had-I-But-Known" school of mystery writing. She also created a costumed supercriminal called "the Bat", who was cited by Bob Kane as one of the inspirations for his "Batman."

In this book:

Locked Doors

I

"You promised," I reminded Mr. Patton, "to play with cards on the table."

"My dear young lady," he replied, "I have no cards! I suspect a game, that's all."

"Then—do you need me?"

The detective bent forward, his arms on his desk, and looked me over carefully.

"What sort of shape are you in? Tired?"

"No."

"Nervous?"

"Not enough to hurt."

"I want you to take another case, following a nurse who has gone to pieces," he said, selecting his words carefully. "I don't want to tell you a lot—I want you to go in with a fresh mind. It promises to be an extraordinary case."

"How long was the other nurse there?"

"Four days."

"She went to pieces in four days!"

"Well, she's pretty much unstrung. The worst is, she hasn't any real reason. A family chooses to live in an unusual manner, because they like it, or perhaps they're afraid of something. The girl was, that's sure. I had never seen her until this morning, a big, healthy-looking young woman; but she came in looking back over her shoulder as if she expected a knife in her back. She said she was a nurse from St. Luke's and that she'd been on a case for four days. She'd left that morning after about three hours' sleep in that time, being locked in a room most of the time, and having little but crackers and milk for food. She thought it was a case for the police."

"Who is ill in the house? Who was her patient?"

"There is no illness, I believe. The French governess had gone, and they wished the children competently cared for until they replaced her. That was the reason given her when she went. Afterward she—well, she was puzzled."

"How are you going to get me there?"

He gathered acquiescence from my question and smiled approval.

"Good girl!" he said. "Never mind how I'll get you there. You are the most dependable woman I know."

"The most curious, perhaps?" I retorted. "Four days on the case, three hours' sleep, locked in and yelling 'Police'! Is it out of town?"

"No, in the heart of the city, on Beauregard Square. Can you get some St. Luke's uniforms? They want another St. Luke's nurse."

I said I could get the uniforms, and he wrote the address on a card.

"Better arrive about five," he said.

"But—if they are not expecting me?"

"They will be expecting you," he replied enigmatically.

"The doctor, if he's a St. Luke's man——"

"There is no doctor."

3

It was six months since I had solved, or helped to solve, the mystery of the buckled bag for Mr. Patton. I had had other cases for him in the interval, cases where the police could not get close enough. As I said when I began this record of my crusade against crime and the criminal, a trained nurse gets under the very skin of the soul. She finds a mind surrendered, all the crooked little motives that have fired the guns of life revealed in their pitifulness.

Gradually I had come to see that Mr. Patton's point of view was right; that if the criminal uses every means against society, why not society against the criminal? At first I had used this as a flag of truce to my nurse's ethical training; now I flaunted it, a mental and moral banner. The criminal against society, and I against the criminal! And, more than that, against misery, healing pain by augmenting it sometimes, but working like a surgeon, for good.

I had had six cases in six months. Only in one had I failed to land my criminal, and that without any suspicion of my white uniform and rubber-soled shoes. Although I played a double game no patient of mine had suffered. I was a nurse first and a police agent second. If it was a question between turpentine compresses—stupes, professionally—and seeing what letters came in or went out of the house, the compress went on first, and cracking hot too. I am not boasting. That is my method, the only way I can work, and it speaks well for it that, as I say, only one man escaped arrest—an arson case where the factory owner hanged himself in the bathroom needle shower in the house he had bought with the insurance money, while I was fixing his breakfast tray. And even he might have been saved for justice had the cook not burned the toast and been obliged to make it fresh.

I was no longer staying at a nurses' home. I had taken a bachelor suite of three rooms and bath, comfortably downtown. I cooked my own breakfasts when I was off duty and I dined at a restaurant near. Luncheon I did not bother much about. Now and then Mr. Patton telephoned me and we lunched together in remote places where we would not be known. He would tell me of his cases and sometimes he asked my advice.

I bought my uniforms that day and took them home in a taxicab. The dresses were blue, and over them for the street the St. Luke's girls wear long cloaks, English fashion, of navy blue serge, and a blue bonnet with a white ruching and white lawn ties. I felt curious in it, but it was becoming and convenient. Certainly I looked professional.

At three o'clock that afternoon a messenger brought a small box, registered. It contained a St. Luke's badge of gold and blue enamel.

At four o'clock my telephone rang. I was packing my suitcase according to the list I keep pasted in the lid. Under the list, which was of uniforms, aprons, thermometer, instruments, a nurse's simple set of probe, forceps and bandage scissors, was the word "box." This always went in first—a wooden box with a lock, the key of which was round my neck. It contained skeleton keys, a small black revolver of which I was in deadly fear, a pair of handcuffs, a pocket flashlight, and my badge from the chief of police. I was examining the revolver nervously when the telephone rang, and I came within an ace of sending a bullet into the flat below.

Did you ever notice how much you get out of a telephone voice? We can dissemble with our faces, but under stress the vocal cords seem to draw up tight and the voice comes thin and colorless. There's a little woman in the flat beneath—the one I nearly bombarded—who sings like a bird at her piano half the day, scaling vocal heights that make me dizzy. Now and then she has a visitor, a nice young man, and she disgraces herself, flats F, fogs E even, finally takes cowardly refuge in a wretched mezzo-soprano and cries herself to sleep, doubtless, later on.

The man who called me had the thin-drawn voice of extreme strain—a youngish voice.

"Miss Adams," he said, "this is Francis Reed speaking. I have called St. Luke's and they referred me to you. Are you free to take a case this afternoon?"

I fenced. I was trying to read the voice.

4

"This afternoon?"

"Well, before night anyhow; as—as early this evening as possible."

The voice was strained and tired, desperately tired. It was not peevish. It was even rather pleasant.

"What is the case, Mr. Reed?"

He hesitated. "It is not illness. It is merely—the governess has gone and there are two small children. We want some one to give her undivided attention to the children."

"I see."

"Are you a heavy sleeper, Miss Adams?"

"A very light one." I fancied he breathed freer.

"I hope you are not tired from a previous case?" I was beginning to like the voice.

"I'm quite fresh," I replied almost gayly. "Even if I were not, I like children, especially well ones. I shan't find looking after them very wearying, I'm sure."

Again the odd little pause. Then he gave me the address on Beauregard Square, and asked me to be sure not to be late.

"I must warn you," he added; "we are living in a sort of casual way. Our servants left us without warning. Mrs. Reed has been getting along as best she could. Most of our meals are being sent in."

I was thinking fast. No servants! A good many people think a trained nurse is a sort of upper servant. I've been in houses where they were amazed to discover that I was a college woman and, finding the two things irreconcilable, have openly accused me of having been driven to such a desperate course as a hospital training by an unfortunate love affair.

"Of course you understand that I will look after the children to the best of my ability, but that I will not replace the servants."

I fancied he smiled grimly.

"That of course. Will you ring twice when you come?"

"Ring twice?"

"The doorbell," he replied impatiently.

I said I would ring the doorbell twice.

The young woman below was caroling gayly, ignorant of the six-barreled menace over her head. I knelt again by my suitcase, but packed little and thought a great deal. I was to arrive before dusk at a house where there were no servants and to ring the doorbell twice. I was to be a light sleeper, although I was to look after two healthy children. It was not much in itself, but, taken in connection with the previous nurse's appeal to the police, it took on new possibilities.

At six I started out to dinner. It was early spring and cold, but quite light. At the first corner I saw Mr. Patton waiting for a street car, and at his quick nod I saw I was to get in also. He did not pay my fare or speak to me. It was a part of the game that we were never seen together except at the remote restaurant I mentioned before. The car thinned out and I could watch him easily. Far downtown he alighted and so did I. The restaurant was near. I went in alone and sat down at a table in a recess, and very soon he joined me. We were in the main dining room but not of it, a sop at once to the conventions and to the necessity, where he was so well known, for caution.

"I got a little information—on—the affair we were talking of," he said as he sat down. "I'm not so sure I want you to take the case after all."

"Certainly I shall take it," I retorted with some sharpness. "I've promised to go."

"Tut! I'm not going to send you into danger unnecessarily."

"I am not afraid."

"Exactly. A lot of generals were lost in the Civil War because they were not afraid and wanted to lead their troops instead of saving themselves and their expensive West Point training by sitting back in a safe spot and directing the fight. Any fool can run into danger. It takes intellect to keep out."

I felt my color rising indignantly.

"Then you brought me here to tell me I am not to go?"

"Will you let me read you two reports?"

"You could have told me that at the corner!"

"Will you let me read you two reports?"

"If you don't mind I'll first order something to eat. I'm to be there before dark."

"Will you let me——"

"I'm going, and you know I'm going. If you don't want me to represent you I'll go on my own. They want a nurse, and they're in trouble."

I think he was really angry. I know I was. If there is anything that takes the very soul out of a woman, it is to be kept from doing a thing she has set her heart on, because some man thinks it dangerous. If she has any spirit, that rouses it.

Mr. Patton quietly replaced the reports in his wallet and his wallet in the inside pocket of his coat, and fell to a judicial survey of the menu. But although he did not even glance at me he must have felt the determination in my face, for he ordered things that were quickly prepared and told the waiter to hurry.

"I have wondered lately," he said slowly, "whether the mildness of your manner at the hospital was acting, or the chastening effect of three years under an order book."

"A man always likes a woman to be a sheep."

"Not at all. But it is rather disconcerting to have a pet lamb turn round and take a bite out of one."

"Will you read the reports now?"

"I think," he said quietly, "they would better wait until we have eaten. We will probably both feel calmer. Suppose we arrange that nothing said before the oysters counts?"

I agreed, rather sulkily, and the meal went off well enough. I was anxious enough to hurry but he ate deliberately, drank his demi-tasse, paid the waiter, and at last met my impatient eyes and smiled.

"After all," he said, "since you are determined to go anyhow, what's the use of reading the reports? Inside of an hour you'll know all you need to know." But he saw that I did not take his teasing well, and drew out his pocketbook.

They were two typewritten papers clamped together.

They are on my desk before me now. The first one is indorsed:

Statement by Laura J. Bosworth, nurse, of St. Luke's Home for Graduate Nurses.

Miss Bosworth says:

I do not know just why I came here. But I know I'm frightened. That's the fact. I think there is something terribly wrong in the house of Francis M. Reed, 71 Beauregard Square. I think a crime of some sort has been committed. There are four people in the family, Mr. and Mrs. Reed and two children. I was to look after the children.

I was there four days and the children were never allowed out of the room. At night we were locked in. I kept wondering what I would do if there was a fire. The telephone wires are cut so no one can call the house, and I believe the doorbell is disconnected too. But that's fixed now. Mrs. Reed went round all the time with a face like chalk and her eyes staring. At all hours of the night she'd unlock the bedroom door and come in and look at the children.

6

Almost all the doors through the house were locked. If I wanted to get to the kitchen to boil eggs for the children's breakfast—for there were no servants, and Mrs. Reed was young and didn't know anything about cooking—Mr. Reed had to unlock about four doors for me.

If Mrs. Reed looked bad, he was dreadful—sunken eyed and white and wouldn't eat. I think he has killed somebody and is making away with the body.

Last night I said I had to have air, and they let me go out. I called up a friend from a pay-station, another nurse. This morning she sent me a special-delivery letter that I was needed on another case, and I got away. That's all; it sounds foolish, but try it and see if it doesn't get on your nerves.

Mr. Patton looked up at me as he finished reading.

"Now you see what I mean," he said. "That woman was there four days, and she is as temperamental as a cow, but in those four days her nervous system went to smash."

"Doors locked!" I reflected. "Servants gone; state of fear—it looks like a siege!"

"But why a trained nurse? Why not a policeman, if there is danger? Why any one at all, if there is something that the police are not to know?"

"That is what I intend to find out," I replied. He shrugged his shoulders and read the other paper:

Report of Detective Bennett on Francis M. Reed, April 5, 1913:

Francis M. Reed is thirty-six years of age, married, a chemist at the Olympic Paint Works. He has two children, both boys. Has a small independent income and owns the house on Beauregard Square, which was built by his grandfather, General F. R. Reed. Is supposed to be living beyond his means. House is usually full of servants, and grocer in the neighborhood has had to wait for money several times.

On March twenty-ninth he dismissed all servants without warning. No reason given, but a week's wages instead of notice.

On March thirtieth he applied to the owners of the paint factory for two weeks' vacation. Gave as his reason nervousness and insomnia. He said he was "going to lay off and get some sleep." Has not been back at the works since. House under surveillance this afternoon. No visitors.

Mr. Reed telephoned for a nurse at four o'clock from a store on Eleventh Street. Explained that his telephone was out of order.

Mr. Patton folded up the papers and thrust them back into his pocket. Evidently he saw I was determined, for he only said:

"Have you got your revolver?"

"Yes."

"Do you know anything about telephones? Could you repair that one in an emergency?"

"In an emergency," I retorted, "there is no time to repair a telephone. But I've got a voice and there are windows. If I really put my mind to it you will hear me yell at headquarters."

He smiled grimly.

II

The Reed house is on Beauregard Square. It is a small, exclusive community, the Beauregard neighborhood; a dozen or more solid citizens built their homes there in the early 70's, occupying large lots, the houses flush with the streets and with gardens behind. Six on one street, six on another, back to back with the gardens in the center, they occupied the whole block. And the gardens were not fenced off, but made a sort of small park unsuspected from the streets. Here and there bits of flowering shrubbery sketchily outlined a property, but the general impression was of lawn and trees, free of access to all the owners. Thus with the square in front and the gardens in the rear, the Reed house faced in two directions on the early spring green.

In the gardens the old tar walks were still there, and a fountain which no longer played, but on whose stone coping I believe the young Beauregard Squarites made their first climbing ventures.

The gardens were always alive with birds, and later on from my windows I learned the reason. It seems to have been a custom sanctified by years, that the crumbs from the twelve tables should be thrown into the dry basin of the fountain for the birds. It was a common sight to see stately butlers and *chic* little waitresses in black and white coming out after luncheon or dinner with silver trays of crumbs. Many a scrap of gossip, as well as scrap of food, has been passed along at the old stone fountain, I believe. I know that it was there that I heard of the "basement ghost" of Beauregard Square—a whisper at first, a panic later.

I arrived at eight o'clock and rang the doorbell twice. The door was opened at once by Mr. Reed, a tall, blond young man carefully dressed. He threw away his cigarette when he saw me and shook hands. The hall was brightly lighted and most cheerful; in fact the whole house was ablaze with light. Certainly nothing could be less mysterious than the house, or than the debonair young man who motioned me into the library.

"I told Mrs. Reed I would talk to you before you go upstairs," he said. "Will you sit down?"

I sat down. The library was even brighter than the hall, and now I saw that although he smiled as cheerfully as ever his face was almost colorless, and his eyes, which looked frankly enough into mine for a moment, went wandering off round the room. I had the impression somehow that Mr. Patton had had of the nurse at headquarters that morning—that he looked as if he expected a knife in his back. It seemed to me that he wanted to look over his shoulder and by sheer will-power did not.

"You know the rule, Miss Adams," he said: "When there's an emergency get a trained nurse. I told you our emergency—no servants and two small children."

"This should be a good time to secure servants," I said briskly. "City houses are being deserted for country places, and a percentage of servants won't leave town."

He hesitated.

"We've been doing very nicely, although of course it's hardly more than just living. Our meals are sent in from a hotel, and—well, we thought, since we are going away so soon, that perhaps we could manage."

The impulse was too strong for him at that moment. He wheeled and looked behind him, not a hasty glance, but a deliberate inspection that took in every part of that end of the room. It was so unexpected that it left me gasping.

The next moment he was himself again.

"When I say that there is no illness," he said, "I am hardly exact. There is no illness, but there has been an epidemic of children's diseases among the Beauregard Square children and we are keeping the youngsters indoors."

"Don't you think they could be safeguarded without being shut up in the house?"

He responded eagerly

"If I only thought——" he checked himself. "No," he said decidedly; "for a time at least I believe it is not wise."

I did not argue with him. There was nothing to be gained by antagonizing him. And as Mrs. Reed came in just then, the subject was dropped. She was hardly more than a girl, almost as blond as her husband, very pretty, and with the weariest eyes I have ever seen, unless perhaps the eyes of a man who has waited a long time for deathly tuberculosis.

I liked her at once. She did not attempt to smile. She rather clung to my hand when I held it out.

"I am glad St. Luke's still trusts us," she said. "I was afraid the other nurse—— Frank, will you take Miss Adams' suitcase upstairs?"

She held out a key. He took it, but he turned at the door:

"I wish you wouldn't wear those things, Anne. You gave me your promise yesterday, you remember."

"I can't work round the children in anything else," she protested.

"Those things" were charming. She wore a rose silk negligee trimmed with soft bands of lace and blue satin flowers, a petticoat to match that garment, and a lace cap.

He hesitated in the doorway and looked at her—a curious glance, I thought, full of tenderness, reproof—apprehension perhaps.

"I'll take it off, dear," she replied to the glance. "I wanted Miss Adams to know that, even if we haven't a servant in the house, we are at least civilized. I—I haven't taken cold." This last was clearly an afterthought.

He went out then and left us together. She came over to me swiftly.

"What did the other nurse say?" she demanded.

"I do not know her at all. I have not seen her."

"Didn't she report at the hospital that we were—queer?"

I smiled.

"That's hardly likely, is it?"

Unexpectedly she went to the door opening into the hall and closed it, coming back swiftly.

"Mr. Reed thinks it is not necessary, but—there are some things that will puzzle you. Perhaps I should have spoken to the other nurse. If—if anything strikes you as unusual, Miss Adams, just please don't see it! It is all right, everything is all right. But something has occurred—not very much, but disturbing—and we are all of us doing the very best we can."

She was quivering with nervousness.

I was not the police agent then, I'm afraid.

"Nurses are accustomed to disturbing things. Perhaps I can help."

"You can, by watching the children. That's the only thing that matters to me—the children. I don't want them left alone. If you have to leave them call me."

"Don't you think I will be able to watch them more intelligently if I know just what the danger is?"

I think she very nearly told me. She was so tired, evidently so anxious to shift her burden to fresh shoulders.

"Mr. Reed said," I prompted her, "that there was an epidemic of children's diseases. But from what you say——"

But I was not to learn, after all, for her husband opened the hall door.

"Yes, children's diseases," she said vaguely. "So many children are down. Shall we go up, Frank?"

The extraordinary bareness of the house had been dawning on me for some time. It was well lighted and well furnished. But the floors were innocent of rugs, the handsome furniture was without arrangement and, in the library at least, stood huddled in the center of the room. The hall and stairs were also uncarpeted, but there were marks where carpets had recently lain and had been jerked up.

The progress up the staircase was not calculated to soothe my nerves. The thought of my little revolver, locked in my suitcase, was poor comfort. For with every four steps or so Mr. Reed, who led the way, turned automatically and peered into the hallway below; he was listening, too, his head bent slightly forward. And each time that he turned, his wife behind me turned also. Cold terror suddenly got me by the spine, and yet the hall was bright with light.

(Note: Surely fear is a contagion. Could one isolate the germ of it and find an antitoxin? Or is it merely a form of nervous activity run amuck, like a runaway locomotive, colliding with other nervous activities and causing catastrophe? Take this up with Mr. Patton. But would he know? He, I am almost sure, has never been really afraid.)

I had a vision of my oxlike predecessor making this head-over-shoulder journey up the staircase, and in spite of my nervousness I smiled. But at that moment Mrs. Reed behind me put a hand on my arm, and I screamed. I remember yet the way she dropped back against the wall and turned white.

Mr. Reed whirled on me instantly.

"What did you see?" he demanded.

"Nothing at all." I was horribly ashamed. "Your wife touched my arm unexpectedly. I dare say I am nervous."

"It's all right, Anne," he reassured her. And to me, almost irritably:

"I thought you nurses had no nerves."

"Under ordinary circumstances I have none."

It was all ridiculous. We were still on the staircase.

"Just what do you mean by that?"

"If you will stop looking down into that hall I'll be calm enough. You make me jumpy."

He muttered something about being sorry and went on quickly. But at the top he went through an inward struggle, evidently succumbed, and took a final furtive survey of the hallway below. I was so wrought up that had a door slammed anywhere just then I think I should have dropped where I stood.

The absolute silence of the house added to the strangeness of the situation. Beauregard Square is not close to a trolley line, and quiet is the neighborhood tradition. The first rubber-tired vehicles in the city drew up before Beauregard Square houses. Beauregard Square children speak in low voices and never bang their spoons on their plates. Beauregard Square servants wear felt-soled shoes. And such outside noises as venture to intrude themselves must filter through double brick walls and doors built when lumber was selling by the thousand acres instead of the square foot.

Through this silence our feet echoed along the bare floor of the upper hall, as well lighted as belowstairs and as dismantled, to the door of the day nursery. The door was locked—double locked, in fact. For the key had been turned in the old-fashioned lock, and in addition an ordinary bolt had been newly fastened on the outside of the door. On the outside! Was that to keep me in? It was certainly not to keep any one or anything out. The feeblest touch moved the bolt.

We were all three outside the door. We seemed to keep our compactness by common consent. No one of us left the group willingly; or, leaving it, we slid back again quickly. That was my impression, at least. But the bolt rather alarmed me.

"This is your room," Mrs. Reed said. "It is generally the day nursery, but we have put a bed and some other things in it. I hope you will be comfortable."

I touched the bolt with my finger and smiled into Mr. Reed's eyes.

"I hope I am not to be fastened in!" I said.

He looked back squarely enough, but somehow I knew he lied.

"Certainly not," he replied, and opened the door.

If there had been mystery outside, and bareness, the nursery was charming—a corner room with many windows, hung with the simplest of nursery papers and full of glass-doored closets filled with orderly rows of toys. In one corner a small single bed had been added without spoiling the room. The window-sills were full of flowering plants. There was a bowl of goldfish on a stand, and a tiny dwarf parrot in a cage was covered against the night air by a

10

bright afghan. A white-tiled bathroom connected with this room and also with the night nursery beyond.

Mr. Reed did not come in, I had an uneasy feeling, however, that he was just beyond the door. The children were not asleep. Mrs. Reed left me to let me put on my uniform. When she came back her face was troubled.

"They are not sleeping well," she complained. "I suppose it comes from having no exercise. They are always excited."

"I'll take their temperatures," I said. "Sometimes a tepid bath and a cup of hot milk will make them sleep."

The two little boys were wide awake. They sat up to look at me and both spoke at once.

"Can you tell fairy tales out of your head?"

"Did you see Chang?"

They were small, sleek-headed, fair-skinned youngsters, adorably clean and rumpled.

"Chang is their dog, a Pekingese," explained the mother. "He has been lost for several days."

"But he isn't lost, mother. I can hear him crying every now and then. You'll look again, mother, won't you?"

"We heard him through the furnace pipe," shrilled the smaller of the two. "You said you would look."

"I did look, darlings. He isn't there. And you promised not to cry about him, Freddie."

Freddie, thus put on his honor, protested he was not crying for the dog.

"I want to go out and take a walk, that's why I'm crying," he wailed. "And I want Mademoiselle, and my buttons are all off. And my ear aches when I lie on it."

The room was close. I threw up the windows, and turned to find Mrs. Reed at my elbows. She was glancing out apprehensively.

"I suppose the air is necessary," she said, "and these windows are all right. But—I have a reason for asking it—please do not open the others."

She went very soon, and I listened as she went out. I had promised to lock the door behind her, and I did so. The bolt outside was not shot.

After I had quieted the children with my mildest fairy story I made a quiet inventory of my new quarters. The rough diagram of the second floor is the one I gave Mr. Patton later. That night, of course, I investigated only the two nurseries. But, so strangely had the fear that hung over the house infected me, I confess that I made my little tour of bathroom and clothes-closet with my revolver in my hand!

I found nothing, of course. The disorder of the house had not extended itself here. The bathroom was spotless with white tile, the large clothes-closet which opened off the passage between the two rooms was full of neatly folded clothing for the children. The closet was to play its part later, a darkish little room faintly lighted by a ground glass transom opening into the center hall, but dependent mostly on electric light.

Outside the windows Mrs. Reed had asked me not to open was a porte-cochère roof almost level with the sills. Then was it an outside intruder she feared? And in that case, why the bolts on the outside of the two nursery doors? For the night nursery, I found, must have one also. I turned the key, but the door would not open.

I decided not to try to sleep that night, but to keep on watch. So powerfully had the mother's anxiety about her children and their mysterious danger impressed me that I made frequent excursions into the back room. Up to midnight there was nothing whatever to alarm me. I darkened both rooms and sat, waiting for I know not what; for some sound to show that the house stirred, perhaps. At a few minutes after twelve faint noises penetrated to my room from the hall, Mr. Reed's nervous voice and a piece of furniture scraping over the floor. Then silence again for half an hour or so.

Then—I was quite certain that the bolt on my door had been shot. I did not hear it, I think. Perhaps I felt it. Perhaps I only feared it. I unlocked the door; it was fastened outside.

There is a hideous feeling of helplessness about being locked in. I pretended to myself at first that I was only interested and curious. But I was frightened; I know that now. I sat there in the dark and wondered what I would do if the house took fire, or if some hideous tragedy enacted itself outside that locked door and I were helpless.

By two o'clock I had worked myself into a panic. The house was no longer silent. Some one was moving about downstairs, and not stealthily. The sounds came up through the heavy joists and flooring of the old house.

I determined to make at least a struggle to free myself. There was no way to get at the bolts, of course. The porte-cochère roof remained and the transom in the clothes-closet. True, I might have raised an alarm and been freed at once, but naturally I rejected this method. The roof of the porte-cochère proved impracticable. The tin bent and cracked under my first step. The transom then.

I carried a chair into the closet and found the transom easy to lower. But it threatened to creak. I put liquid soap on the hinges—it was all I had, and it worked very well—and lowered the transom inch by inch. Even then I could not see over it. I had worked so far without a sound, but in climbing to a shelf my foot slipped and I thought I heard a sharp movement outside. It was five minutes before I stirred. I hung there, every muscle cramped, listening and waiting. Then I lifted myself by sheer force of muscle and looked out. The upper landing of the staircase, brilliantly lighted, was to my right. Across the head of the stairs had been pushed a cotbed, made up for the night, but it was unoccupied.

Mrs. Reed, in a long, dark ulster, was standing beside it, staring with fixed and glassy eyes at something in the lower hall.

III

Some time after four o'clock my door was unlocked from without; the bolt slipped as noiselessly as it had been shot. I got a little sleep until seven, when the boys trotted into my room in their bathrobes and slippers and perched on my bed.

"It's a nice day," observed Harry, the elder. "Is that bump your feet?"

I wriggled my toes and assured him he had surmised correctly.

"You're pretty long, aren't you? Do you think we can play in the fountain to-day?"

"We'll make a try for it, son. It will do us all good to get out into the sunshine."

"We always took Chang for a walk every day, Mademoiselle and Chang and Freddie and I."

Freddie had found my cap on the dressing table and had put it on his yellow head. But now, on hearing the beloved name of his pet, he burst into loud grief-stricken howls.

"Want Mam'selle," he cried. "Want Chang too. Poor Freddie!"

The children were adorable. I bathed and dressed them and, mindful of my predecessor's story of crackers and milk, prepared for an excursion kitchenward. The nights might be full of mystery, murder might romp from room to room, but I intended to see that the youngsters breakfasted. But before I was ready to go down breakfast arrived.

Perhaps the other nurse had told the Reeds a few plain truths before she left; perhaps, and this I think was the case, the cloud had lifted just a little. Whatever it may have been, two rather flushed and blistered young people tapped at the door that morning and were admitted, Mr. Reed first, with a tray, Mrs. Reed following with a coffee-pot and cream.

The little nursery table was small for five, but we made room somehow. What if the eggs were underdone and the toast dry? The children munched blissfully. What if Mr. Reed's face was still drawn and haggard and his wife a limp little huddle on the floor? She sat with her head against his knee and her eyes on the little boys, and drank her pale coffee slowly. She was very tired, poor thing. She dropped asleep sitting there, and he sat for a long time, not liking to disturb her.

It made me feel homesick for the home I didn't have. I've had the same feeling before, of being a rank outsider, a sort of defrauded feeling. I've had it when I've seen the look in a man's eyes when his wife comes-to after an operation. And I've had it, for that matter, when I've put a new baby in its mother's arms for the first time. I had it for sure that morning, while she slept there and he stroked her pretty hair.

I put in my plea for the children then.

"It's bright and sunny," I argued. "And if you are nervous I'll keep them away from other children. But if you want to keep them well you must give them exercise."

It was the argument about keeping them well that influenced him, I think. He sat silent for a long time. His wife was still asleep, her lips parted.

"Very well," he said finally, "from two to three, Miss Adams. But not in the garden back of the house. Take them on the street."

I agreed to that.

"I shall want a short walk every evening myself," I added. "That is a rule of mine. I am a more useful person and a more agreeable one if I have it."

I think he would have demurred if he dared. But one does not easily deny so sane a request. He yielded grudgingly.

That first day was calm and quiet enough. Had it not been for the strange condition of the house and the necessity for keeping the children locked in I would have smiled at my terror of the night. Luncheon was sent in; so was dinner. The children and I lunched and supped alone. As far as I could see, Mrs. Reed made no attempt at housework; but the cot at the head of the stairs disappeared in the early morning and the dog did not howl again.

I took the boys out for an hour in the early afternoon. Two incidents occurred, both of them significant. I bought myself a screw driver—that was one. The other was our meeting with a slender young woman in black who knew the boys and stopped them. She proved to be one of the dismissed servants—the waitress, she said.

"Why, Freddie!" she cried. "And Harry too! Aren't you going to speak to Nora?"

After a moment or two she turned to me, and I felt she wanted to say something, but hardly dared.

"How is Mrs. Reed?" she asked. "Not sick, I hope?"

She glanced at my St. Luke's cloak and bonnet.

"No, she is quite well."

"And Mr. Reed?"

"Quite well also."

"Is Mademoiselle still there?"

"No, there is no one there but the family. There are no maids in the house."

She stared at me curiously.

"Mademoiselle has gone? Are you cer—— Excuse me, Miss. But I thought she would never go. The children were like her own."

"She is not there, Nora."

She stood for a moment debating, I thought. Then she burst out:

"Mr. Reed made a mistake, miss. You can't take a houseful of first-class servants and dismiss them the way he did, without half an hour to get out bag and baggage, without making talk. And there's talk enough all through the neighborhood."

"What sort of talk?"

"Different people say different things. They say Mademoiselle is still there, locked in her room on the third floor. There's a light there sometimes, but nobody sees her. And other folks say Mr. Reed is crazy. And there is worse being said than that."

But she refused to tell me any more—evidently concluded she had said too much and got away as quickly as she could, looking rather worried.

I was a trifle over my hour getting back, but nothing was said. To leave the clean and tidy street for the disordered house was not pleasant. But once in the children's suite, with the goldfish in the aquarium darting like tongues of flame in the sunlight, with the tulips and hyacinths of the window-boxes glowing and the orderly toys on their white shelves, I felt comforted. After all, disorder and dust did not imply crime.

But one thing I did that afternoon—did it with firmness and no attempt at secrecy, and after asking permission of no one. I took the new screw driver and unfastened the bolt from the outside of my door.

I was prepared, if necessary, to make a stand on that issue. But although it was noticed, I knew, no mention of it was made to me.

Mrs. Reed pleaded a headache that evening, and I believe her husband ate alone in the dismantled dining room. For every room on the lower floor, I had discovered, was in the same curious disorder.

At seven Mr. Reed relieved me to go out. The children were in bed. He did not go into the day nursery, but placed a straight chair outside the door of the back room and sat there, bent over, elbows on knees, chin cupped in his palm, staring at the staircase. He roused enough to ask me to bring an evening paper when I returned.

When I am on a department case I always take my off-duty in the evening by arrangement and walk round the block. Some time in my walk I am sure to see Mr. Patton himself if the case is big enough, or one of his agents if he cannot come. If I have nothing to communicate it resolves itself into a bow and nothing more.

I was nervous on this particular jaunt. For one thing my St. Luke's cloak and bonnet marked me at once, made me conspicuous; for another, I was afraid Mr. Patton would think the Reed house no place for a woman and order me home.

It was a quarter to eight and quite dark before he fell into step beside me.

"Well," I replied rather shakily; "I'm still alive, as you see."

"Then it is pretty bad?"

"It's exceedingly queer," I admitted, and told my story. I had meant to conceal the bolt on the outside of my door, and one or two other things, but I blurted them all out right then and there, and felt a lot better at once.

He listened intently.

"It's fear of the deadliest sort," I finished.

"Fear of the police?"

"I—I think not. It is fear of something in the house. They are always listening and watching at the top of the front stairs. They have lifted all the carpets, so that every footstep echoes through the whole house. Mrs. Reed goes down to the first door, but never alone. To-day I found that the back staircase is locked off at top and bottom. There are doors."

I gave him my rough diagram of the house. It was too dark to see it.

"It is only tentative," I explained. "So much of the house is locked up, and every movement of mine is under surveillance. Without baths there are about twelve large rooms, counting the third floor. I've not been able to get there, but I thought that to-night I'd try to look about."

"You had no sleep last night?"

"Three hours—from four to seven this morning."

We had crossed into the public square and were walking slowly under the trees. Now he stopped and faced me.

"I don't like the look of it, Miss Adams," he said. "Ordinary panic goes and hides. But here's a fear that knows what it's afraid of and takes methodical steps for protection. I didn't want you to take the case, you know that; but now I'm not going to insult you by asking you to give it up. But I'm going to see that you are protected. There will be some one across the street every night as long as you are in the house."

"Have you any theory?" I asked him. He is not strong for theories generally. He is very practical. "That is, do you think the other nurse was right and there is some sort of crime being concealed?"

"Well, think about it," he prompted me. "If a murder has been committed, what are they afraid of? The police? Then why a trained nurse and all this caution about the children? A ghost? Would they lift the carpets so that they could hear the specter tramping about?"

"If there is no crime, but something—a lunatic perhaps?" I asked.

"Possibly. But then why this secrecy and keeping out the police? It is, of course, possible that your respected employers have both gone off mentally, and the whole thing is a nightmare delusion. On my word it sounds like it. But it's too much for credulity to believe they've both gone crazy with the same form of delusion."

"Perhaps I'm the lunatic," I said despairingly. "When you reduce it like that to an absurdity I wonder if I didn't imagine it all, the lights burning everywhere and the carpets up, and Mrs. Reed staring down the staircase, and I locked in a room and hanging on by my nails to peer out through a closet transom."

"Perhaps. But how about the deadly sane young woman who preceded you? She had no imagination. Now about Reed and his wife—how do they strike you? They get along all right and that sort of thing, I suppose?"

"They are nice people," I said emphatically. "He's a gentleman and they're devoted. He just looks like a big boy who's got into an awful mess and doesn't know how to get out. And she's backing him up. She's a dear."

"Humph!" said Mr. Patton. "Don't suppress any evidence because she's a dear and he's a handsome big boy!"

"I didn't say he was handsome," I snapped.

"Did you ever see a ghost or think you saw one?" he inquired suddenly.

"No, but one of my aunts has. Hers always carry their heads. She asked one a question once and the head nodded."

"Then you believe in things of that sort?"

"Not a particle—but I'm afraid of them."

He smiled, and shortly after that I went back to the house. I think he was sorry about the ghost question, for he explained that he had been trying me out, and that I looked well in my cloak and bonnet.

"I'm afraid of your chin generally," he said; "but the white lawn ties have a softening effect. In view of the ties I have almost the courage——"

"Yes?"

"I think not, after all," he decided. "The chin is there, 31 ties or no ties. Good-night, and—for heaven's sake don't run any unnecessary risks."

The change from his facetious tone to earnestness was so unexpected that I was still standing there on the pavement when he plunged into the darkness of the square and disappeared.

At ten minutes after eight I was back in the house. Mr. Reed admitted me, going through the tedious process of unlocking outer and inner vestibule doors and fastening them again behind me. He inquired politely if I had had a pleasant walk, and without waiting for my reply fell to reading the evening paper. He seemed to have forgotten me absolutely. First he scanned the headlines; then he turned feverishly to something farther on and ran his fingers down along a column. His lips were twitching, but evidently he did not find what he expected—or feared—for he threw the paper away and did not glance at it again. I watched him from the angle of the stairs.

Even for that short interval Mrs. Reed had taken his place at the children's door.

She wore a black dress, long sleeved and high at the throat, instead of the silk negligee of the previous evening, and she held a book. But she was not reading. She smiled rather wistfully when she saw me.

"How fresh you always look!" she said. "And so self-reliant. I wish I had your courage."

"I am perfectly well. I dare say that explains a lot. Kiddies asleep?"

"Freddie isn't. He has been crying for Chang. I hate night, Miss Adams. I'm like Freddie. All my troubles come up about this time. I'm horribly depressed."

Her blue eyes filled with tears.

"I haven't been sleeping well," she confessed.

I should think not!

Without taking off my things I went down to Mr. Reed in the lower hall.

"I'm going to insist on something," I said. "Mrs. Reed is highly nervous. She says she has not been sleeping. I think if I give her an opiate and she gets an entire night's sleep it may save her a breakdown."

I looked straight in his eyes, and for once he did evade me.

"I'm afraid I've been very selfish," he said. "Of course she must have sleep. I'll give you a powder, unless you have something you prefer to use."

I remembered then that he was a chemist, and said I would gladly use whatever he gave me.

"There is another thing I wanted to speak about, Mr. Reed," I said. "The children are mourning their dog. Don't you think he may have been accidentally shut up somewhere in the house in one of the upper floors?"

"Why do you say that?" he demanded sharply.

"They say they have heard him howling."

He hesitated for barely a moment. Then:

"Possibly," he said. "But they will not hear him again. The little chap has been sick, and he—died to-day. Of course the boys are not to know."

No one watched the staircase that night. I gave Mrs. Reed the opiate and saw her comfortably into bed. When I went back fifteen minutes later she was resting, but not asleep. Opiates sometimes make people garrulous for a little while—sheer comfort, perhaps, and relaxed tension. I've had stockbrokers and bankers in the hospital give me tips, after a hypodermic of morphia, that would have made me wealthy had I not been limited to my training allowance of twelve dollars a month.

"I was just wondering," she said as I tucked her up, "where a woman owes the most allegiance—to her husband or to her children?"

"Why not split it up," I said cheerfully, "and try doing what seems best for both?"

"But that's only a compromise!" she complained, and was asleep almost immediately. I lowered the light and closed the door, and shortly after I heard Mr. Reed locking it from the outside.

With the bolt off my door and Mrs. Reed asleep my plan for the night was easily carried out. I went to bed for a couple of hours and slept calmly. I awakened once with the feeling that some one was looking at me from the passage into the night nursery, but there was no one there. However, so strong had been the feeling that I got up and went into the back room. The children were asleep, and all doors opening into the hall were locked. But the window on to the porte-cochère roof was open and the curtain blowing. There was no one on the roof.

It was not twelve o'clock and I still had an hour. I went back to bed.

At one I prepared to make a thorough search of the house. Looking from one of my windows I thought I saw the shadowy figure of a man across the street, and I was comforted. Help was always close, I felt. And yet, as I stood inside my door in my rubber-soled shoes, with my ulster over my uniform and a revolver and my skeleton keys in my pockets, my heart was going very fast. The stupid story of the ghost came back and made me shudder, and the next instant I was remembering Mrs. Reed the night before, staring down into the lower hall with fixed glassy eyes.

My plan was to begin at the top of the house and work down. The thing was the more hazardous, of course, because Mr. Reed was most certainly somewhere about. I had no excuse for being on the third floor. Down below I could say I wanted tea, or hot water—anything. But I did not expect to find Mr. Reed up above. The terror, whatever it was, seemed to lie below.

Access to the third floor was not easy. The main staircase did not go up. To get there I was obliged to unlock the door at the rear of the hall with my own keys. I was working in bright light, trying my keys one after another, and watching over my shoulder as I did so. When the door finally gave it was a relief to slip into the darkness beyond, ghosts or no ghosts.

I am always a silent worker. Caution about closing doors and squeaking hinges is second nature to me. One learns to be cautious when one's only chance of sleep is not to rouse a peevish patient and have to give a body-massage, as like as not, or listen to domestic troubles—"I said" and "he said"—until one is almost crazy.

So I made no noise. I closed the door behind me and stood blinking in the darkness. I listened. There was no sound above or below. Now houses at night have no terror for me. Every nurse is obliged to do more or less going about in the dark. But I was not easy. Suppose Mr. Reed should call me? True, I had locked my door and had the key in my pocket. But a dozen emergencies flew through my mind as I felt for the stair rail.

There was a curious odor through all the back staircase, a pungent, aromatic scent that, with all my familiarity with drugs, was strange to me. As I slowly climbed the stairs it grew more powerful. The air was heavy with it, as though no windows had been opened in that part of the house. There was no door at the top of this staircase, as there was on the second floor. It opened into an upper hall, and across from the head of the stairs was a door leading into a room. This door was closed. On this staircase, as on all the others, the carpet had been newly lifted. My electric flash showed the white boards and painted borders, the carpet tacks, many of them still in place. One, lying loose, penetrated my rubber sole and went into my foot.

I sat down in the dark and took off the shoe. As I did so my flash, on the step beside me, rolled over and down with a crash. I caught it on the next step, but the noise had been like a pistol shot.

Almost immediately a voice spoke above me sharply. At first I thought it was out in the upper hall. Then I realized that the closed door was between it and me.

"Ees that you, Meester Reed?"

Mademoiselle!

"Meester Reed!" plaintively. "Eet comes up again, Meester Reed! I die! To-morrow I die!"

She listened. On no reply coming she began to groan rhythmically, to a curious accompaniment of creaking. When I had gathered up my nerves again I realized that she must be sitting in a rocking chair. The groans were really little plaintive grunts.

By the time I had got my shoe on she was up again, and I could hear her pacing the room, the heavy step of a woman well fleshed and not young. Now and then she stopped inside the door and listened; once she shook the knob and mumbled querulously to herself.

I recovered the flash, and with infinite caution worked my way to the top of the stairs. Mademoiselle was locked in, doubly bolted in. Two strong bolts, above and below, supplemented the door lock.

Her ears must have been very quick, or else she felt my softly padding feet on the boards outside, for suddenly she flung herself against the door and begged for a priest, begged piteously, in jumbled French and English. She wanted food; she was dying of hunger. She wanted a priest.

And all the while I stood outside the door and wondered what I should do. Should I release the woman? Should I go down to the lower floor and get the detective across the street to come in and force the door? Was this the terror that held the house in thrall—this babbling old Frenchwoman calling for food and a priest in one breath?

Surely not. This was a part of the mystery, not all. The real terror lay below. It was not Mademoiselle, locked in her room on the upper floor, that the Reeds waited for at the top of the stairs. But why was Mademoiselle locked in her room? Why were the children locked in? What was this thing that had turned a home into a jail, a barracks, that had sent away the servants, imprisoned and probably killed the dog, sapped the joy of life from two young people? What was it that Mademoiselle cried "comes up again"?

I looked toward the staircase. Was it coming up the staircase?

I am not afraid of the thing I can see, but it seemed to me, all at once, that if anything was going to come up the staircase I might as well get down first. A staircase is no place to meet anything, especially if one doesn't know what it is.

I listened again. Mademoiselle was quiet. I flashed my light down the narrow stairs. They were quite empty. I shut off the flash and went down. I tried to go slowly, to retreat with dignity, and by the time I had reached the landing below I was heartily ashamed of myself. Was this shivering girl the young woman Mr. Patton called his right hand?

I dare say I should have stopped there, for that night at least. My nerves were frayed. But I forced myself on. The mystery lay below. Well, then, I was going down. It could not be so terrible. At least it was nothing supernatural. There must be a natural explanation. And then that silly story about the headless things must pop into my head and start me down trembling.

The lower rear staircase was black dark, like the upper, but just at the foot a light came in through a barred window. I could see it plainly and the shadows of the iron grating on the bare floor. I stood there listening. There was not a sound.

It was not easy to tell exactly what followed. I stood there with my hand on the rail. I'd been very silent; my rubber shoes attended to that. And one moment the staircase was clear, with a patch of light at the bottom. The next, something was there, half way down—a head, it seemed to be, with a pointed hood like a monk's cowl. There was no body. It seemed to lie at my feet. But it was living. It moved. I could tell the moment when the eyes lifted and saw my feet, the slow back-tilting of the head as they followed up my body. All the air was squeezed out of my lungs; a heavy hand seemed to press on my chest. I remember raising a shaking hand and flinging my flashlight at the head. The flash clattered on the stair tread harmless. Then the head was gone and something living slid over my foot.

I stumbled back to my room and locked the door. It was two hours before I had strength enough to get my aromatic ammonia bottle.

It seemed to me that I had hardly dropped asleep before the children were in the room, clamoring.

"The goldfish are dead!" Harry said, standing soberly by the bed. "They are all dead with their stummicks turned up."

I sat up. My head ached violently.

"They can't be dead, old chap." I was feeling about for my kimono, but I remembered that when I had found my way back to the nursery after my fright on the back stairs I had lain down in my uniform. I crawled out, hardly able to stand. "We gave them fresh water yesterday, and——"

I had got to the aquarium. Harry was right. The little darting flames of pink and gold were still. They floated about, rolling gently as Freddie prodded them with a forefinger, dull eyed, pale bellies upturned. In his |39| cage above the little parrot watched out of a crooked eye.

I ran to the medicine closet in the bathroom. Freddie had a weakness for administering medicine. I had only just rescued the parrot from the result of his curiosity and a headache tablet the day before.

"What did you give them?" I demanded.

"Bread," said Freddie stoutly.

"Only bread?"

"Dirty bread," Harry put in. "I told him it was dirty."

"Where did you get it?"

"On the roof of the porte-cochère!"

Shade of Montessori! The rascals had been out on that sloping tin roof. It turned me rather sick to think of it.

Accused, they admitted it frankly.

"I unlocked the window," Harry said, "and Freddie got the bread. It was out in the gutter. He slipped once."

"Almost went over and made a squash on the pavement," added Freddie. "We gave the little fishes the bread for breakfast, and now they're gone to God."

The bread had contained poison, of course. Even the two little snails that crawled over the sand in the aquarium were motionless. I sniffed the water. It had a slightly foreign odor. I did not recognize it.

Panic seized me then. I wanted to get away and take the children with me. The situation was too hideous. But it was still early. I could only wait until the family roused. In the meantime, however, I made a nerve-racking excursion out on to the tin roof and down to the gutter. There was no more of the bread there. The |40| porte-cochère was at the side of the house. As I stood balancing myself perilously on the edge, summoning my courage to climb back to the window above, I suddenly remembered the guard Mr. Patton had promised and glanced toward the square.

The guard was still there. More than that, he was running across the street toward me. It was Mr. Patton himself. He brought up between the two houses with absolute fury in his face.

"Go back!" he waved. "What are you doing out there anyhow? That roof's as slippery as the devil!"

I turned meekly and crawled back with as much dignity as I could. I did not say anything. There was nothing I could bawl from the roof. I could only close and lock the window and hope that the people in the next house still slept. Mr. Patton must have gone shortly after, for I did not see him again.

I wondered if he had relieved the night watch, or if he could possibly have been on guard himself all that chilly April night.

Mr. Reed did not breakfast with us. I made a point of being cheerful before the children, and their mother was rested and brighter than I had seen her. But more than once I found her staring at me in a puzzled way. She asked me if I had slept.

"I wakened only once," she said. "I thought I heard a crash of some sort. Did you hear it?"

"What sort of a crash?" I evaded.

The children had forgotten the goldfish for a time. Now they remembered and clamored their news to her.

"Dead?" she said, and looked at me.

"Poisoned," I explained. "I shall nail the windows over the porte-cochère shut, Mrs. Reed. The boys got out there early this morning and picked up something—bread, I believe. They fed it to the fish and—they are dead."

All the light went out of her face. She looked tired and harassed as she got up.

"I wanted to nail the window," she said vaguely, "but Mr. Reed—— Suppose they had eaten that bread, Miss Adams, instead of giving it to the fish!"

The same thought had chilled me with horror. We gazed at each other over the unconscious heads of the children and my heart ached for her. I made a sudden resolution.

"When I first came," I said to her, "I told you I wanted to help. That's what I'm here for. But how am I to help either you or the children when I do not know what danger it is that threatens? It isn't fair to you, or to them, or even to me."

She was much shaken by the poison incident. I thought she wavered.

"Are you afraid the children will be stolen?"

"Oh, no."

"Or hurt in any way?" I was thinking of the bread on the roof.

"No."

"But you are afraid of something?"

Harry looked up suddenly.

"Mother's never afraid," he said stoutly.

I sent them both in to see if the fish were still dead.

"There is something in the house downstairs that you are afraid of?" I persisted.

She took a step forward and caught my arm.

"I had no idea it would be like this, Miss Adams. I'm dying of fear!"

I had a quick vision of the swathed head on the back staircase, and some of my night's terror came back to me. I believe we stared at each other with dilated pupils for a moment. Then I asked:

"Is it a real thing?—surely you can tell me this. Are you afraid of a reality, or—is it something supernatural?" I was ashamed of the question. It sounded so absurd in the broad light of that April morning.

"It is a real danger," she replied. Then I think she decided that she had gone as far as she dared, and I went through the ceremony of letting her out and of locking the door behind her.

The day was warm. I threw up some of the windows and the boys and I played ball, using a rolled handkerchief. My part, being to sit on the floor with a newspaper folded into a bat and to bang at the handkerchief as it flew past me, became automatic after a time.

As I look back I see a pair of disordered young rascals in Russian blouses and bare round knees doing a great deal of yelling and some very crooked throwing; a nurse sitting tailor fashion on the floor, alternately ducking to save her cap and making vigorous but ineffectual passes at the ball with her newspaper bat. And I see sunshine in the room and the dwarf parrot eating sugar out of his claw. And below, the fish in the aquarium floating belly-up with dull eyes.

Mr. Reed brought up our luncheon tray. He looked tired and depressed and avoided my eyes. I watched him while I spread the bread and butter for the children. He nailed shut the windows that opened on to the porte-cochère roof and when he thought I was not looking he examined the registers in the wall to see if the gratings were closed. The boys put the dead fish in a box and made him promise a decent interment in the garden. They called on me for an epitaph, and I scrawled on top of the box:

These fish are dead
Because a boy called Fred
Went out on a porch roof when he should
Have been in bed.

I was much pleased with it. It seemed to me that an epitaph, which can do no good to the departed, should at least convey a moral. But to my horror Freddie broke into loud wails and would not be comforted.

It was three o'clock, therefore, before they were both settled for their afternoon naps and I was free. I had determined to do one thing, and to do it in daylight—to examine the back staircase inch by inch. I knew I would be courting discovery, but the thing had to be done, and no power on earth would have made me essay such an investigation after dark.

It was all well enough for me to say to myself that there was a natural explanation; that this had been a human head, of a certainty; that something living and not spectral had slid over my foot in the darkness. I would not have gone back there again at night for youth, love or money. But I did not investigate the staircase that day, after all.

I made a curious discovery after the boys had settled down in their small white beds. A venturesome fly had sailed in through an open window, and I was immediately in pursuit of him with my paper bat. Driven from the cornice to the chandelier, harried here, swatted there, finally he took refuge inside the furnace register.

Perhaps it is my training—I used to know how many million germs a fly packed about with it, and the generous benevolence with which it distributed them; I've forgotten—but the sight of a single fly maddens me. I said that to Mr. Patton once, and he asked what the sight of a married one would do. So I sat down by the register and waited. It was then that I made the curious discovery that the furnace belowstairs was burning, and burning hard. A fierce heat assailed me as I opened the grating. I drove the fly out of cover, but I had no time for him. The furnace going full on a warm spring day! It was strange.

Perhaps I was stupid. Perhaps the whole thing should have been clear to me. But it was not. I sat there bewildered and tried to figure it out. I went over it point by point:

The carpets up all over the house, lights going full all night and doors locked.

The cot at the top of the stairs and Mrs. Reed staring down.

The bolt outside my door to lock me in.

The death of Chang.

Mademoiselle locked in her room upstairs and begging for a priest.

The poison on the porch roof.

The head without a body on the staircase and the thing that slid over my foot.

The furnace going, and the thing I recognized as I sat there beside the register—the unmistakable odor of burning cloth.

Should I have known? I wonder. It looks so clear to me now.

I did not investigate the staircase, for the simple reason that my skeleton key, which unfastened the lock of the door at the rear of the second-floor hall, did not open the door. I did not understand at once and stood stupidly working with the lock. The door was bolted on the other side. I wandered as aimlessly as I could down the main staircase and tried the corresponding door on the lower floor. It, too, was locked. Here was an *impasse* for sure. As far as I could discover the only other entrance to the back staircase was through the window with the iron grating.

As I turned to go back I saw my electric flash, badly broken, lying on a table in the hall. I did not claim it.

The lower floor seemed entirely deserted. The drawing room and library were in their usual disorder, undusted and bare of floor. The air everywhere was close and heavy; there was not a window open. I sauntered through the various rooms, picked up a book in the library as an excuse and tried the door of the room behind. It was locked. I thought at first that something moved behind it, but if anything lived there it did not stir again. And yet I had a vivid impression that just on the other side of the door ears as keen as mine were listening. It was broad day, but I backed away from the door and out into the wide hall. My nerves were still raw, no doubt, from the night before.

I was to meet Mr. Patton at half after seven that night, and when Mrs. Reed relieved me at seven I had half an hour to myself. I spent it in Beauregard Gardens, with the dry fountain in the center. The place itself was charming, the trees still black but lightly fringed with new green, early spring flowers in the borders, neat paths and, bordering it all, the solid, dignified backs of the Beauregard houses. I sat down on the coping of the fountain and surveyed the Reed house. Those windows above were Mademoiselle's. The shades were drawn, but no light came through or round them. The prisoner—for prisoner she was by every rule of bolt and lock—must be sitting in the dark. Was she still begging for her priest? Had she had any food? Was she still listening inside her door for whatever it was that was "coming up"?

In all the other houses windows were open; curtains waved gently in the spring air; the cheerful signs of the dinner hour were evident near by—moving servants, a gleam of stately shirt bosom as a butler mixed a salad, a warm radiance of candle-light from dining room tables and the reflected glow of flowers. Only the Reed house stood gloomy, unlighted, almost sinister.

Beauregard Place dined early. It was one of the traditions, I believe. It liked to get to the theater or the opera early, and it believed in allowing the servants a little time in the evenings. So, although it was only something after seven, the evening rite of the table crumbs began to be observed. Came a colored butler, bowed to me with a word of apology, and dumped the contents of a silver tray into the basin; came a pretty mulatto, flung her crumbs gracefully and smiled with a flash of teeth at the butler.

Then for five minutes I was alone.

It was Nora, the girl we had met on the street, who came next. She saw me and came round to me with a little air of triumph.

"Well, I'm back in the square again, after all, miss," she said. "And a better place than the Reeds. I don't have the doilies to do."

"I'm very glad you are settled again, Nora."

She lowered her voice.

"I'm just trying it out," she observed. "The girl that left said I wouldn't stay. She was scared off. There have been some queer doings—not that I believe in ghosts or anything like that. But my mother in the old country had the second-sight, and if there's anything going on I'll be right sure to see it."

It took encouragement to get her story, and it was secondhand at that, of course. But it appeared that a state of panic had seized the Beauregard servants. The alarm was all belowstairs and had been started by a cook who, coming in late and going to the basement to prepare herself a cup of tea, had found her kitchen door locked and a light going beyond. Suspecting another maid of violating the tea canister she had gone soft-footed to the outside of the house and had distinctly seen a gray figure crouching in a corner of the room. She had called the butler, and they had made an examination of the entire basement without result. Nothing was missing from the house.

"And that figure has been seen again and again, miss," Nora finished. "McKenna's butler Joseph saw it in this very spot, walking without a sound and the street light beyond there shining straight through it. Over in the Smythe house the laundress, coming in late and going down to the basement to soak her clothes for the morning, met the thing on the basement staircase and fainted dead away."

I had listened intently.

"What do they think it is?" I asked.

She shrugged her shoulders and picked up her tray.

"I'm not trying to say and I guess nobody is. But if there's been a murder it's pretty well known that the ghost walks about until the burial service is read and it's properly buried."

She glanced at the Reed house.

"For instance," she demanded, "where is Mademoiselle?"

"She is alive," I said rather sharply. "And even if what you say were true, what in the world would make her wander about the basements? It seems so silly, Nora, a ghost haunting damp cellars and laundries with stationary tubs and all that."

"Well," she contended, "it seems silly for them to sit on cold tombstones—and yet that's where they generally sit, isn't it?"

Mr. Patton listened gravely to my story that night.

"I don't like it," he said when I had finished. "Of course the head on the staircase is nonsense. Your nerves were ragged and our eyes play tricks on all of us. But as for the Frenchwoman——"

"If you accept her you must accept the head," I snapped. "It was there—it was a head without a body and it looked up at me."

We were walking through a quiet street, and he bent over and caught my wrist.

"Pulse racing," he commented. "I'm going to take you away, that's certain. I can't afford to lose my best assistant. You're too close, Miss Adams; you've lost your perspective."

"I've lost my temper!" I retorted. "I shall not leave until I know what this thing is, unless you choose to ring the doorbell and tell them I'm a spy."

He gave in when he saw that I was firm, but not without a final protest.

"I'm directly responsible for you to your friends," he said. "There's probably a young man somewhere who will come gunning for me if anything happens to you. And I don't care to be gunned for. I get enough of that in my regular line."

"There is no young man," I said shortly.

"Have you been able to see the cellars?"

"No, everything is locked off."

"Do you think the rear staircase goes all the way down?"

"I haven't the slightest idea."

"You are in the house. Have you any suggestions as to the best method of getting into the house? Is Reed on guard all night?"

"I think he is."

"It may interest you to know," he said finally, "that I sent a reliable man to break in there last night quietly, and that he—couldn't do it. He got a leg through a cellar window, and came near not getting it out again. Reed was just inside in the dark." He laughed a little, but I guessed that the thing galled him.

"I do not believe that he would have found anything if he had succeeded in getting in. There has been no crime, Mr. Patton, I am sure of that. But there is a menace of some sort in the house."

"Then why does Mrs. Reed stay and keep the children if there is danger?"

"I believe she is afraid to leave him. There are times when I think that he is desperate."

"Does he ever leave the house?"

"I think not, unless——"

"Yes?"

"Unless he is the basement ghost of the other houses."

He stopped in his slow walk and considered it.

"It's possible. In that case I could have him waylaid tonight in the gardens and left there, tied. It would be a hold-up, you understand. The police have no excuse for coming in yet. Or, if we found him breaking into one of the other houses we could get him there. He'd be released, of course, but it would give us time. I want to clean the thing up. I'm not easy while you are in that house."

We agreed that I was to wait inside one of my windows that night, and that on a given signal I should go down and open the front door. The whole thing, of course, was contingent on Mr. Reed leaving the house some time that night. It was only a chance.

"The house is barred like a fortress," Mr. Patton said as he left me. "The window with the grating is hopeless. We tried it last night."

VI

I find that my notes of that last night in the house on Beauregard Square are rather confused, some written at the time, some just before. For instance, on the edge of a newspaper clipping I find this:

"Evidently this is the item. R—— went pale on reading it. Did not allow wife to see paper."

The clipping is an account of the sudden death of an elderly gentleman named Smythe, one of the Beauregard families.

The next clipping is less hasty and is on a yellow symptom record. It has been much folded—I believe I tucked it in my apron belt:

"If the rear staircase is bolted everywhere from the inside, how did the person who locked it, either Mr. or Mrs. Reed, get back into the body of the house again? Or did Mademoiselle do it? In that case she is no longer a prisoner and the bolts outside her room are not fastened.

"At eleven o'clock tonight Harry wakened with earache. I went to the kitchen to heat some mullein oil and laudanum. Mrs. Reed was with the boy and Mr. Reed was not in sight. I slipped into the library and used my skeleton keys on the locked door to the rear room. It was empty even of furniture, but there is a huge box there, with a lid that fastens down with steel hooks. The lid is full of small airholes. I had no time to examine further.

"It is one o'clock. Harry is asleep and his mother is dozing across the foot of his bed. I have found the way to get to the rear staircase. There are outside steps from the basement to the garden. The staircase goes down all the way to the cellar evidently. Then the lower door in the cellar must be only locked, not bolted from the inside. I shall try to get to the cellar."

The next is a scrawl:

"Cannot get to the outside basement steps. Mr. Reed is wandering round lower floor. I reported Harry's condition and came up again. I must get to the back staircase."

I wonder if I have been able to convey, even faintly, the situation in that highly respectable old house that night: The fear that hung over it, a fear so great that even I, an outsider and stout of nerve, felt it and grew cold; the unnatural brilliancy of light that bespoke dread of the dark; the hushed voices, the locked doors and staring, peering eyes; the babbling Frenchwoman on an upper floor, the dead fish, the dead dog. And, always in my mind, that vision of dread on the back staircase and the thing that slid over my foot.

At two o'clock I saw Mr. Patton, or whoever was on guard in the park across the street, walk quickly toward the house and disappear round the corner toward the gardens in the rear. There had been no signal, but I felt sure that Mr. Reed had left the house. His wife was still asleep across Harry's bed. As I went out I locked the door behind me, and I took also the key to the night nursery. I thought that something disagreeable, to say the least, was inevitable, and why let her in for it?

The lower hall was lighted as usual and empty. I listened, but there were no restless footsteps. I did not like the lower hall. Only a thin wooden door stood between me and the rear staircase, and any one who thinks about the matter will realize that a door is no barrier to a head that can move about without a body. I am afraid I looked over my shoulder while I unlocked the front door, and I know I breathed better when I was out in the air.

I wore my dark ulster over my uniform and I had my revolver and keys. My flash, of course, was useless. I missed it horribly. But to get to the staircase was an obsession by that time, in spite of my fear of it, to find what it guarded, to solve its mystery. I worked round the house, keeping close to the wall, until I reached the garden. The night was the city night, never absolutely dark. As I hesitated at the top of the basement steps it seemed to me that figures were moving about among the trees.

The basement door was unlocked and open. I was not prepared for that, and it made me, if anything, more uneasy. I had a box of matches with me, and I wanted light as a starving man wants food. But I dared not light them. I could only keep a tight grip on my courage and go on. A small passage first, with whitewashed stone walls, cold and scaly under my hand; then a large room, and still darkness. Worse than darkness, something crawling and scratching round the floor.

I struck my match, then, and it seemed to me that something white flashed into a corner and disappeared. My hands were shaking, but I managed to light a gas jet and to see that I was in the laundry. The staircase came down here, narrower than above, and closed off with a door.

The door was closed and there was a heavy bolt on it but no lock.

And now, with the staircase accessible and a gaslight to keep up my courage, I grew brave, almost reckless. I would tell Mr. Patton all about this cellar, which his best men had not been able to enter. I would make a sketch for him—coal-bins, laundry tubs, everything. Foolish, of course, but hold the gas jet responsible—the reckless bravery of light after hideous darkness.

So I went on, forward. The glow from the laundry followed me. I struck matches, found potatoes and cases of mineral water, bruised my knees on a discarded bicycle, stumbled over a box of soap. Twice out of the corner of my eye and never there when I looked I caught the white flash that had frightened me before. Then at last I brought up before a door and stopped. It was a curiously barricaded door, nailed against disturbance by a plank fastened across, and, as if to make intrusion without discovery impossible, pasted round every crack and over the keyhole with strips of strong yellow paper. It was an ominous door. I wanted to run away from it, and I wanted also desperately to stand and look at it and imagine what might lie beyond. Here again was the strange, spicy odor that I had noticed in the back staircase.

I think it is indicative of my state of mind that I backed away from the door. I did not turn and run. Nothing in the world would have made me turn my back to it.

Somehow or other I got back into the laundry and jerked myself together.

It was ten minutes after two. I had been just ten minutes in the basement!

The staircase daunted me in my shaken condition. I made excuses for delaying my venture, looked for another box of matches, listened at the end of the passage, finally slid the bolts and opened the door. The silence was impressive. In the laundry there were small, familiar sounds—the dripping of water from a faucet, the muffled measure of a gas meter, the ticking of a clock on the shelf. To leave it all, to climb into that silence——

Lying on the lower step was a curious instrument. It was a sort of tongs made of steel, about two feet long, and fastened together like a pair of scissors, the joint about five inches from the flattened ends. I carried it to the light and examined it. One end was smeared with blood and short, brownish hairs. It made me shudder, but—from that time on I think I knew. Not the whole story, of course, but somewhere in the back of my head, as I climbed in that hideous quiet, the explanation was developing itself. I did not think it out. It worked itself out as, step after step, match after match, I climbed the staircase.

Up to the first floor there was nothing. The landing was bare of carpet. I was on the first floor now. On each side, doors, carefully bolted, led into the house. I opened the one into the hall and listened. I had been gone from the children fifteen minutes and they were on my mind. But everything was quiet.

The sight of the lights and the familiar hall gave me courage. After all, if I was right, what could the head on the staircase have been but an optical delusion? And I was right. The evidence—the tongs—was in my hand. I closed and bolted the door and felt my way back to the stairs. I lighted no matches this time. I had only a few, and on this landing there was a little light from the grated window, although the staircase above was in black shadow.

I had one foot on the lowest stair, when suddenly overhead came the thudding of hands on a closed door. It broke the silence like an explosion. It sent chills up and down my spine. I could not move for a moment. It was the Frenchwoman!

I believe I thought of fire. The idea had obsessed me in that house of locked doors. I remember a strangling weight of fright on my chest and of trying to breathe. Then I started up the staircase, running as fast as I could lift my weighted feet, I remember that, and getting up perhaps a third of the way. Then there came a plunging forward into space, my hands out, a shriek frozen on my lips, and——quiet.

I do not think I fainted. I know I was always conscious of my arm doubled under me, a pain and darkness. I could hear myself moaning, but almost as if it were some one else. There were other sounds, but they did not concern me much. I was not even curious about my location. I seemed to be a very small consciousness surrounded by a great deal of pain.

Several centuries later a light came and leaned over me from somewhere above. Then the light said:

"Here she is!"

"Alive?" I knew that voice, but I could not think whose it was.

"I'm not—— Yes, she's moaning."

They got me out somewhere and I believe I still clung to the tongs. I had fallen on them and had a cut on my chin. I could stand, I found, although I swayed. There was plenty of light now in the back hallway, and a man I had never seen was investigating the staircase.

"Four steps off," he said. "Risers and treads gone and the supports sawed away. It's a trap of some sort."

Mr. Patton was examining my broken arm and paid no attention. The man let himself down into the pit under the staircase. When he straightened, only his head rose above the steps. Although I was white with pain to the very lips I laughed hysterically.

"The head!" I cried. Mr. Patton swore under his breath.

They half led, half carried me into the library. Mr. Reed was there, with a detective on guard over him. He was sitting in his old position, bent forward, chin in palms. In the blaze of light he was a pitiable figure, smeared with dust, disheveled from what had evidently been a struggle. Mr. Patton put me in a chair and dispatched one of the two men for the nearest doctor.

"This young lady," he said curtly to Mr. Reed, "fell into that damnable trap you made in the rear staircase."

"I locked off the staircase—but I am sorry she is hurt. My—my wife will be shocked. Only I wish you'd tell me what all this is about. You can't arrest me for going into a friend's house."

"If I send for some member of the Smythe family will they acquit you?"

"Certainly they will," he said. "I—I've been raised with the Smythes. You can send for any one you like." But his tone lacked conviction.

Mr. Patton made me as comfortable as possible, and then, sending the remaining detective out into the hall, he turned to his prisoner.

"Now, Mr. Reed," he said. "I want you to be sensible. For some days a figure has been seen in the basements of the various Beauregard houses. Your friends, the Smythes, reported it. Tonight we are on watch, and we see you breaking into the basement of the Smythe house. We already know some curious things about you, such as dismissing all the servants on half an hour's notice and the disappearance of the French governess."

"Mademoiselle! Why, she——" He checked himself.

"When we bring you here tonight, and you ask to be allowed to go upstairs and prepare your wife, she is locked in. The nurse is missing. We find her at last, also locked away and badly hurt, lying in a staircase trap, where some one, probably yourself, has removed the steps. I do not want to arrest you, but, now I've started, I'm going to get to the bottom of all this."

Mr. Reed was ghastly, but he straightened in his chair.

"The Smythes reported this thing, did they?" he asked. "Well, tell me one thing. What killed the old gentleman—old Smythe?"

"I don't know."

"Well, go a little further." His cunning was boyish, pitiful. "How did he die? Or don't you know that either?"

Up to this point I had been rather a detached part of the scene, but now my eyes fell on the tongs beside me.

"Mr. Reed," I said, "isn't this thing too big for you to handle by yourself?"

"What thing?"

"You know what I mean. You've protected yourself well enough, but even if the—the thing you know of did not kill old Mr. Smythe you cannot tell what will happen next."

"I've got almost all of them," he muttered sullenly. "Another night or two and I'd have had the lot."

"But even then the mischief may go on. It means a crusade; it means rousing the city. Isn't it the square thing now to spread the alarm?"

Mr. Patton could stand the suspense no longer.

"Perhaps, Miss Adams," he said, "you will be good enough to let me know what you are talking about."

Mr. Reed looked up at him with heavy eyes.

"Rats," he said. "They got away, twenty of them, loaded with bubonic plague."

I went to the hospital the next morning. Mr. Patton thought it best. There was no one in my little flat to look after me, and although the pain in my arm subsided after the fracture was set I was still shaken.

He came the next afternoon to see me. I was propped up in bed, with my hair braided down in two pigtails and great hollows under my eyes.

"I'm comfortable enough," I said, in response to his inquiry; "but I'm feeling all of my years. This is my birthday. I am thirty today."

"I wonder," he said reflectively, "if I ever reach the mature age of one hundred, if I will carry in my head as many odds and ends of information as you have at thirty!"

"I?"

"You. How in the world did you know, for instance, about those tongs?"

"It was quite simple. I'd seen something like them in the laboratory here. Of course I didn't know what animals he'd used, but the grayish brown hair looked like rats. The laboratory must be the cellar room. I knew it had been fumigated—it was sealed with paper, even over the keyhole."

So, sitting there beside me, Mr. Patton told me the story as he had got it from Mr. Reed—a tale of the offer in an English scientific journal of a large reward from some plague-ridden country of the East for an anti-plague serum. Mr. Reed had been working along bacteriological lines in his basement laboratory, mostly with guinea pigs and tuberculosis. He was in debt; the offer loomed large.

"He seems to think he was on the right track," Mr. Patton said. "He had twenty of the creatures in deep zinc cans with perforated lids. He says the disease is spread by fleas that infest the rats. So he had muslin as well over the lids. One can had infected rats, six of them. Then one day the Frenchwoman tried to give the dog a bath in a laundry tub and the dog bolted. The laboratory door was open in some way and he ran between the cans, upsetting them. Every rat was out in an instant. The Frenchwoman was frantic. She shut the door and tried to drive the things back. One bit her on the foot. The dog was not bitten, but there was the question of fleas.

"Well, the rats got away, and Mademoiselle retired to her room to die of plague. She was a loyal old soul; she wouldn't let them call a doctor. It would mean exposure, and after all what could the doctors do? Reed used his serum and she's alive.

"Reed was frantic. His wife would not leave. There was the Frenchwoman to look after, and I think she was afraid he would do something desperate. They did the best they could, under the circumstances, for the children. They burned most of the carpets for fear of fleas, and put poison everywhere. Of course he had traps too.

"He had brass tags on the necks of the rats, and he got back a few—the uninfected ones. The other ones were probably dead. But he couldn't stop at that. He had to be sure that the trouble had not spread. And to add to their horror the sewer along the street was being relaid, and they had an influx of rats into the house. They found them everywhere in the lower floor. They even climbed the stairs. He says that the night you came he caught a big fellow on the front staircase. There was always the danger that the fleas that carry the trouble had deserted the dead creatures for new fields. They took up all the rest of the carpets and burned them. To add to the general misery the dog Chang developed unmistakable symptoms and had to be killed."

"But the broken staircase?" I asked. "And what was it that Mademoiselle said was coming up?"

"The steps were up for two reasons: The rats could not climb up, and beneath the steps Reed says he caught in a trap two of the tagged ones. As for Mademoiselle the thing that was coming up was her temperature—pure fright. The head you saw was poor Reed himself, wrapped in gauze against trouble and baiting his traps. He caught a lot in the neighbors' cellars and some in the garden."

"But why," I demanded, "why didn't he make it all known?"

Mr. Patton laughed while he shrugged his shoulders.

"A man hardly cares to announce that he has menaced the health of a city."

"But that night when I fell—was it only last night?—some one was pounding above. I thought there was a fire."

"The Frenchwoman had seen us waylay Reed from her window. She was crazy."

"And the trouble is over now?"

"Not at all," he replied cheerfully. "The trouble may be only beginning. We're keeping Reed's name out, but the Board of Health has issued a general warning. Personally I think his six pets died without passing anything along."

"But there was a big box with a lid——"

"Ferrets," he assured me. "Nice white ferrets with pink eyes and a taste for rats." He held out a thumb, carefully bandaged. "Reed had a couple under his coat when we took him in the garden. Probably one ran over your foot that night when you surprised him on the back staircase."

I went pale. "But if they are infected!" I cried; "and you are bitten——"

"The first thing a nurse should learn," he bent forward smiling, "is not to alarm her patient."

"But you don't understand the danger," I said despairingly. "Oh, if only men had a little bit of sense!"

"I must do something desperate then? Have the thumb cut off, perhaps?"

I did not answer. I lay back on my pillows with my eyes shut. I had given him the plague, had seen him die and be buried, before he spoke again.

"The chin," he said, "is not so firm as I had thought. The outlines are savage, but the dimple—— You poor little thing; are you really frightened?"

"I don't like you," I said furiously. "But I'd hate to see any one with—with that trouble."

"Then I'll confess. I was trying to take your mind off your troubles. The bite is there, but harmless. Those were new ferrets; had never been out."

I did not speak to him again. I was seething with indignation. He stood for a time looking down at me; then, unexpectedly, he bent over and touched his lips to my bandaged arm.

"Poor arm!" he said. "Poor, brave little arm!" Then he tiptoed out of the room. His very back was sheepish.

The Circular Staircase

CHAPTER I

I TAKE A COUNTRY HOUSE

This is the story of how a middle-aged spinster lost her mind, deserted her domestic gods in the city, took a furnished house for the summer out of town, and found herself involved in one of those mysterious crimes that keep our newspapers and detective agencies happy and prosperous. For twenty years I had been perfectly comfortable; for twenty years I had had the window-boxes filled in the spring, the carpets lifted, the awnings put up and the furniture covered with brown linen; for as many summers I had said good-by to my friends, and, after watching their perspiring hegira, had settled down to a delicious quiet in town, where the mail comes three times a day, and the water supply does not depend on a tank on the roof.

And then—the madness seized me. When I look back over the months I spent at Sunnyside, I wonder that I survived at all. As it is, I show the wear and tear of my harrowing experiences. I have turned very gray—Liddy reminded me of it, only yesterday, by saying that a little bluing in the rinse-water would make my hair silvery, instead of a yellowish white. I hate to be reminded of unpleasant things and I snapped her off.

"No," I said sharply, "I'm not going to use bluing at my time of life, or starch, either."

Liddy's nerves are gone, she says, since that awful summer, but she has enough left, goodness knows! And when she begins to go around with a lump in her throat, all I have to do is to threaten to return to Sunnyside, and she is frightened into a semblance of cheerfulness,— from which you may judge that the summer there was anything but a success.

The newspaper accounts have been so garbled and incomplete—one of them mentioned me but once, and then only as the tenant at the time the thing happened—that I feel it my due to tell what I know. Mr. Jamieson, the detective, said himself he could never have done without me, although he gave me little enough credit, in print.

I shall have to go back several years—thirteen, to be exact—to start my story. At that time my brother died, leaving me his two children. Halsey was eleven then, and Gertrude was seven. All the responsibilities of maternity were thrust upon me suddenly; to perfect the profession of motherhood requires precisely as many years as the child has lived, like the man who started to carry the calf and ended by walking along with the bull on his shoulders. However, I did the best I could. When Gertrude got past the hair-ribbon age, and Halsey asked for a scarf-pin and put on long trousers—and a wonderful help that was to the darning.—I sent them away to good schools. After that, my responsibility was chiefly postal, with three months every summer in which to replenish their wardrobes, look over their lists of acquaintances, and generally to take my foster-motherhood out of its nine months' retirement in camphor.

I missed the summers with them when, somewhat later, at boarding-school and college, the children spent much of their vacations with friends. Gradually I found that my name signed to a check was even more welcome than when signed to a letter, though I wrote them at stated intervals. But when Halsey had finished his electrical course and Gertrude her boarding-school, and both came home to stay, things were suddenly changed. The winter Gertrude came out was nothing but a succession of sitting up late at night to bring her home from things, taking her to the dressmakers between naps the next day, and discouraging ineligible youths with either more money than brains, or more brains than money. Also, I acquired a great many things: to say lingerie for under-garments, "frocks" and "gowns" instead of dresses, and that beardless sophomores are not college boys, but college men. Halsey required less personal supervision, and as they both got their mother's fortune that winter, my responsibility became purely moral. Halsey bought a car, of course, and I learned how to tie over my bonnet a gray baize veil, and, after a time, never to stop to look at the dogs one has run down. People are apt to be so unpleasant about their dogs.

The additions to my education made me a properly equipped maiden aunt, and by spring I was quite tractable. So when Halsey suggested camping in the Adirondacks and Gertrude wanted Bar Harbor, we compromised on a good country house with links near, within motor distance of town and telephone distance of the doctor. That was how we went to Sunnyside.

We went out to inspect the property, and it seemed to deserve its name. Its cheerful appearance gave no indication whatever of anything out of the ordinary. Only one thing seemed unusual to me: the housekeeper, who had been left in charge, had moved from the house to the gardener's lodge, a few days before. As the lodge was far enough away from the house, it seemed to me that either fire or thieves could complete their work of destruction undisturbed. The property was an extensive one: the house on the top of a hill, which sloped away in great stretches of green lawn and clipped hedges, to the road; and across the valley, perhaps a couple of miles away, was the Greenwood Club House. Gertrude and Halsey were infatuated.

"Why, it's everything you want," Halsey said "View, air, good water and good roads. As for the house, it's big enough for a hospital, if it has a Queen Anne front and a Mary Anne back," which was ridiculous: it was pure Elizabethan.

Of course we took the place; it was not my idea of comfort, being much too large and sufficiently isolated to make the servant question serious. But I give myself credit for this: whatever has happened since, I never blamed Halsey and Gertrude for taking me there. And another thing: if the series of catastrophes there did nothing else, it taught me one thing—that somehow, somewhere, from perhaps a half-civilized ancestor who wore a sheepskin garment and trailed his food or his prey, I have in me the instinct of the chase. Were I a man I should be a trapper of criminals, trailing them as relentlessly as no doubt my sheepskin ancestor did his wild boar. But being an unmarried woman, with the handicap of my sex, my first acquaintance with crime will probably be my last. Indeed, it came near enough to being my last acquaintance with anything.

The property was owned by Paul Armstrong, the president of the Traders' Bank, who at the time we took the house was in the west with his wife and daughter, and a Doctor Walker, the Armstrong family physician. Halsey knew Louise Armstrong,—had been rather attentive to her the winter before, but as Halsey was always attentive to somebody, I had not thought of it seriously, although she was a charming girl. I knew of Mr. Armstrong only through his connection with the bank, where the children's money was largely invested, and through an ugly story about the son, Arnold Armstrong, who was reported to have forged his father's name, for a considerable amount, to some bank paper. However, the story had had no interest for me.

I cleared Halsey and Gertrude away to a house party, and moved out to Sunnyside the first of May. The roads were bad, but the trees were in leaf, and there were still tulips in the borders around the house. The arbutus was fragrant in the woods under the dead leaves, and on the way from the station, a short mile, while the car stuck in the mud, I found a bank showered with tiny forget-me-nots. The birds—don't ask me what kind; they all look alike to me, unless they have a hall mark of some bright color—the birds were chirping in the hedges, and everything breathed of peace. Liddy, who was born and bred on a brick pavement, got a little bit down-spirited when the crickets began to chirp, or scrape their legs together, or whatever it is they do, at twilight.

The first night passed quietly enough. I have always been grateful for that one night's peace; it shows what the country might be, under favorable circumstances. Never after that night did I put my head on my pillow with any assurance how long it would be there; or on my shoulders, for that matter.

On the following morning Liddy and Mrs. Ralston, my own housekeeper, had a difference of opinion, and Mrs. Ralston left on the eleven train. Just after luncheon, Burke, the butler, was taken unexpectedly with a pain in his right side, much worse when I was within hearing distance, and by afternoon he was started cityward. That night the cook's sister had a baby—the cook, seeing indecision in my face, made it twins on second thought—and, to be short, by noon the next day the household staff was down to Liddy and myself. And this in a house with twenty-two rooms and five baths!

Liddy wanted to go back to the city at once, but the milk-boy said that Thomas Johnson, the Armstrongs' colored butler, was working as a waiter at the Greenwood Club, and might come back. I have the usual scruples about coercing people's servants away, but few of us have any conscience regarding institutions or corporations—witness the way we beat railroads and street-car companies when we can—so I called up the club, and about eight o'clock Thomas Johnson came to see me. Poor Thomas!

Well, it ended by my engaging Thomas on the spot, at outrageous wages, and with permission to sleep in the gardener's lodge, empty since the house was rented. The old man—he was white-haired and a little stooped, but with an immense idea of his personal dignity—gave me his reasons hesitatingly.

"I ain't sayin' nothin', Mis' Innes," he said, with his hand on the door-knob, "but there's been goin's-on here this las' few months as ain't natchal. 'Tain't one thing an' 'tain't another—it's jest a door squealin' here, an' a winder closin' there, but when doors an' winders gets to cuttin' up capers and there's nobody nigh 'em, it's time Thomas Johnson sleeps somewhar's else."

Liddy, who seemed to be never more than ten feet away from me that night, and was afraid of her shadow in that great barn of a place, screamed a little, and turned a yellow-green. But I am not easily alarmed.

It was entirely in vain; I represented to Thomas that we were alone, and that he would have to stay in the house that night. He was politely firm, but he would come over early the next morning, and if I gave him a key, he would come in time to get some sort of breakfast. I stood on the huge veranda and watched him shuffle along down the shadowy drive, with mingled feelings—irritation at his cowardice and thankfulness at getting him at all. I am not ashamed to say that I double-locked the hall door when I went in.

"You can lock up the rest of the house and go to bed, Liddy," I said severely. "You give me the creeps standing there. A woman of your age ought to have better sense." It usually braces Liddy to mention her age: she owns to forty—which is absurd. Her mother cooked for my grandfather, and Liddy must be at least as old as I. But that night she refused to brace.

"You're not going to ask me to lock up, Miss Rachel!" she quavered. "Why, there's a dozen French windows in the drawing-room and the billiard-room wing, and every one opens on a porch. And Mary Anne said that last night there was a man standing by the stable when she locked the kitchen door."

"Mary Anne was a fool," I said sternly. "If there had been a man there, she would have had him in the kitchen and been feeding him what was left from dinner, inside of an hour, from force of habit. Now don't be ridiculous. Lock up the house and go to bed. I am going to read."

But Liddy set her lips tight and stood still.

"I'm not going to bed," she said. "I am going to pack up, and to-morrow I am going to leave."

"You'll do nothing of the sort," I snapped. Liddy and I often desire to part company, but never at the same time. "If you are afraid, I will go with you, but for goodness' sake don't try to hide behind me."

The house was a typical summer residence on an extensive scale. Wherever possible, on the first floor, the architect had done away with partitions, using arches and columns instead. The effect was cool and spacious, but scarcely cozy. As Liddy and I went from one window to another, our voices echoed back at us uncomfortably. There was plenty of light—the electric plant down in the village supplied us—but there were long vistas of polished floor, and mirrors which reflected us from unexpected corners, until I felt some of Liddy's foolishness communicate itself to me.

The house was very long, a rectangle in general form, with the main entrance in the center of the long side. The brick-paved entry opened into a short hall to the right of which, separated only by a row of pillars, was a huge living-room. Beyond that was the drawing-room, and in the end, the billiard-room. Off the billiard-room, in the extreme right wing, was a den, or card-room, with a small hall opening on the east veranda, and from there went up a narrow circular staircase. Halsey had pointed it out with delight.

"Just look, Aunt Rachel," he said with a flourish. "The architect that put up this joint was wise to a few things. Arnold Armstrong and his friends could sit here and play cards all night and stumble up to bed in the early morning, without having the family send in a police call."

Liddy and I got as far as the card-room and turned on all the lights. I tried the small entry door there, which opened on the veranda, and examined the windows. Everything was secure, and Liddy, a little less nervous now, had just pointed out to me the disgracefully dusty condition of the hard-wood floor, when suddenly the lights went out. We waited a moment; I think Liddy was stunned with fright, or she would have screamed. And then I clutched her by the arm and pointed to one of the windows opening on the porch. The sudden change threw the window into relief, an oblong of grayish light, and showed us a figure standing close, peering in. As I looked it darted across the veranda and out of sight in the darkness.

CHAPTER II
A LINK CUFF-BUTTON

Liddy's knees seemed to give away under her. Without a sound she sank down, leaving me staring at the window in petrified amazement. Liddy began to moan under her breath, and in my excitement I reached down and shook her.

"Stop it," I whispered. "It's only a woman—maybe a maid of the Armstrongs'. Get up and help me find the door." She groaned again. "Very well," I said, "then I'll have to leave you here. I'm going."

She moved at that, and, holding to my sleeve, we felt our way, with numerous collisions, to the billiard-room, and from there to the drawing-room. The lights came on then, and, with the long French windows unshuttered, I had a creepy feeling that each one sheltered a peering face. In fact, in the light of what happened afterward, I am pretty certain we were under surveillance during the entire ghostly evening. We hurried over the rest of the locking-up and got upstairs as quickly as we could. I left the lights all on, and our footsteps echoed cavernously. Liddy had a stiff neck the next morning, from looking back over her shoulder, and she refused to go to bed.

"Let me stay in your dressing-room, Miss Rachel," she begged. "If you don't, I'll sit in the hall outside the door. I'm not going to be murdered with my eyes shut."

"If you're going to be murdered," I retorted, "it won't make any difference whether they are shut or open. But you may stay in the dressing-room, if you will lie on the couch: when you sleep in a chair you snore."

She was too far gone to be indignant, but after a while she came to the door and looked in to where I was composing myself for sleep with Drummond's Spiritual Life.

"That wasn't a woman, Miss Rachel," she said, with her shoes in her hand. "It was a man in a long coat."

"What woman was a man?" I discouraged her without looking up, and she went back to the couch.

It was eleven o'clock when I finally prepared for bed. In spite of my assumption of indifference, I locked the door into the hall, and finding the transom did not catch, I put a chair cautiously before the door—it was not necessary to rouse Liddy—and climbing up put on the ledge of the transom a small dressing-mirror, so that any movement of the frame would send it crashing down. Then, secure in my precautions, I went to bed.

I did not go to sleep at once. Liddy disturbed me just as I was growing drowsy, by coming in and peering under the bed. She was afraid to speak, however, because of her previous snubbing, and went back, stopping in the doorway to sigh dismally.

Somewhere down-stairs a clock with a chime sang away the hours—eleven-thirty, forty-five, twelve. And then the lights went out to stay. The Casanova Electric Company shuts up shop and goes home to bed at midnight: when one has a party, I believe it is customary to fee the company, which will drink hot coffee and keep awake a couple of hours longer. But the lights were gone for good that night. Liddy had gone to sleep, as I knew she would. She was a very unreliable person: always awake and ready to talk when she wasn't wanted and dozing off to sleep when she was. I called her once or twice, the only result being an explosive snore that threatened her very windpipe—then I got up and lighted a bedroom candle.

My bedroom and dressing room were above the big living-room on the first floor. On the second floor a long corridor ran the length of the house, with rooms opening from both sides. In the wings were small corridors crossing the main one—the plan was simplicity itself. And just as I got back into bed, I heard a sound from the east wing, apparently, that made me stop, frozen, with one bedroom slipper half off, and listen. It was a rattling metallic sound, and it reverberated along the empty halls like the crash of doom. It was for all the world as if something heavy, perhaps a piece of steel, had rolled clattering and jangling down the hard-wood stairs leading to the card-room.

In the silence that followed Liddy stirred and snored again. I was exasperated: first she kept me awake by silly alarms, then when she was needed she slept like Joe Jefferson, or Rip,—they are always the same to me. I went in and aroused her, and I give her credit for being wide awake the minute I spoke.

"Get up," I said, "if you don't want to be murdered in your bed."

"Where? How?" she yelled vociferously, and jumped up.

"There's somebody in the house," I said. "Get up. We'll have to get to the telephone."

"Not out in the hall!" she gasped; "Oh, Miss Rachel, not out in the hall!" trying to hold me back. But I am a large woman and Liddy is small. We got to the door, somehow, and Liddy held a brass andiron, which it was all she could do to lift, let alone brain anybody with. I listened, and, hearing nothing, opened the door a little and peered into the hall. It was a black void, full of terrible suggestion, and my candle only emphasized the gloom. Liddy squealed and drew me back again, and as the door slammed, the mirror I had put on the transom came down and hit her on the head. That completed our demoralization. It was some time before I could persuade her she had not been attacked from behind by a burglar, and when she found the mirror smashed on the floor she wasn't much better.

"There's going to be a death!" she wailed. "Oh, Miss Rachel, there's going to be a death!"

"There will be," I said grimly, "if you don't keep quiet, Liddy Allen."

And so we sat there until morning, wondering if the candle would last until dawn, and arranging what trains we could take back to town. If we had only stuck to that decision and gone back before it was too late!

The sun came finally, and from my window I watched the trees along the drive take shadowy form, gradually lose their ghostlike appearance, become gray and then green. The Greenwood Club showed itself a dab of white against the hill across the valley, and an early robin or two hopped around in the dew. Not until the milk-boy and the sun came, about the same time, did I dare to open the door into the hall and look around. Everything was as we had left it. Trunks were heaped here and there, ready for the trunk-room, and through an end window of stained glass came a streak of red and yellow daylight that was eminently cheerful. The milk-boy was pounding somewhere below, and the day had begun.

Thomas Johnson came ambling up the drive about half-past six, and we could hear him clattering around on the lower floor, opening shutters. I had to take Liddy to her room up-stairs, however,—she was quite sure she would find something uncanny. In fact, when she did not, having now the courage of daylight, she was actually disappointed.

Well, we did not go back to town that day.

The discovery of a small picture fallen from the wall of the drawing-room was quite sufficient to satisfy Liddy that the alarm had been a false one, but I was anything but convinced. Allowing for my nerves and the fact that small noises magnify themselves at night, there was still no possibility that the picture had made the series of sounds I heard. To prove it, however, I dropped it again. It fell with a single muffled crash of its wooden frame, and incidentally ruined itself beyond repair. I justified myself by reflecting that if the Armstrongs chose to leave pictures in unsafe positions, and to rent a house with a family ghost, the destruction of property was their responsibility, not mine.

I warned Liddy not to mention what had happened to anybody, and telephoned to town for servants. Then after a breakfast which did more credit to Thomas' heart than his head, I went on a short tour of investigation. The sounds had come from the east wing, and not without some qualms I began there. At first I found nothing. Since then I have developed my powers of observation, but at that time I was a novice. The small card-room seemed undisturbed. I looked for footprints, which is, I believe, the conventional thing to do, although my experience has been that as clues both footprints and thumb-marks are more useful in fiction than in fact. But the stairs in that wing offered something.

At the top of the flight had been placed a tall wicker hamper, packed, with linen that had come from town. It stood at the edge of the top step, almost barring passage, and on the step below it was a long fresh scratch. For three steps the scratch was repeated, gradually diminishing, as if some object had fallen, striking each one. Then for four steps nothing. On the fifth step below was a round dent in the hard wood. That was all, and it seemed little enough, except that I was positive the marks had not been there the day before.

It bore out my theory of the sound, which had been for all the world like the bumping of a metallic object down a flight of steps. The four steps had been skipped. I reasoned that an iron bar, for instance, would do something of the sort,—strike two or three steps, end down, then turn over, jumping a few stairs, and landing with a thud.

Iron bars, however, do not fall down-stairs in the middle of the night alone. Coupled with the figure on the veranda the agency by which it climbed might be assumed. But—and here was the thing that puzzled me most—the doors were all fastened that morning, the windows unmolested, and the particular door from the card-room to the veranda had a combination lock of which I held the key, and which had not been tampered with.

I fixed on an attempt at burglary, as the most natural explanation—an attempt frustrated by the falling of the object, whatever it was, that had roused me. Two things I could not understand: how the intruder had escaped with everything locked, and why he had left the small silver, which, in the absence of a butler, had remained down-stairs over night.

Under pretext of learning more about the place, Thomas Johnson led me through the house and the cellars, without result. Everything was in good order and repair; money had been spent lavishly on construction and plumbing. The house was full of conveniences, and I had no reason to repent my bargain, save the fact that, in the nature of things, night must come again. And other nights must follow—and we were a long way from a police-station.

In the afternoon a hack came up from Casanova, with a fresh relay of servants. The driver took them with a flourish to the servants' entrance, and drove around to the front of the house, where I was awaiting him.

"Two dollars," he said in reply to my question. "I don't charge full rates, because, bringin' 'em up all summer as I do, it pays to make a special price. When they got off the train, I sez, sez I, 'There's another bunch for Sunnyside, cook, parlor maid and all.' Yes'm—six summers, and a new lot never less than once a month. They won't stand for the country and the lonesomeness, I reckon."

But with the presence of the "bunch" of servants my courage revived, and late in the afternoon came a message from Gertrude that she and Halsey would arrive that night at about eleven o'clock, coming in the car from Richfield. Things were looking up; and when Beulah, my cat, a most intelligent animal, found some early catnip on a bank near the house and rolled in it in a feline ecstasy, I decided that getting back to nature was the thing to do.

While I was dressing for dinner, Liddy rapped at the door. She was hardly herself yet, but privately I think she was worrying about the broken mirror and its augury, more than anything else. When she came in she was holding something in her hand, and she laid it on the dressing-table carefully.

"I found it in the linen hamper," she said. "It must be Mr. Halsey's, but it seems queer how it got there."

It was the half of a link cuff-button of unique design, and I looked at it carefully.

"Where was it? In the bottom of the hamper?" I asked.

"On the very top," she replied. "It's a mercy it didn't fall out on the way."

When Liddy had gone I examined the fragment attentively. I had never seen it before, and I was certain it was not Halsey's. It was of Italian workmanship, and consisted of a mother-of-pearl foundation, encrusted with tiny seed-pearls, strung on horsehair to hold them. In the center was a small ruby. The trinket was odd enough, but not intrinsically of great value. Its interest for me lay in this: Liddy had found it lying in the top of the hamper which had blocked the east-wing stairs.

That afternoon the Armstrongs' housekeeper, a youngish good-looking woman, applied for Mrs. Ralston's place, and I was glad enough to take her. She looked as though she might be equal to a dozen of Liddy, with her snapping black eyes and heavy jaw. Her name was Anne Watson, and I dined that evening for the first time in three days.

CHAPTER III
MR. JOHN BAILEY APPEARS

I had dinner served in the breakfast-room. Somehow the huge dining-room depressed me, and Thomas, cheerful enough all day, allowed his spirits to go down with the sun. He had a habit of watching the corners of the room, left shadowy by the candles on the table, and altogether it was not a festive meal.

Dinner over I went into the living-room. I had three hours before the children could possibly arrive, and I got out my knitting. I had brought along two dozen pairs of slipper soles in assorted sizes—I always send knitted slippers to the Old Ladies' Home at Christmas—and now I sorted over the wools with a grim determination not to think about the night before. But my mind was not on my work: at the end of a half-hour I found I had put a row of blue scallops on Eliza Klinefelter's lavender slippers, and I put them away.

I got out the cuff-link and went with it to the pantry. Thomas was wiping silver and the air was heavy with tobacco smoke. I sniffed and looked around, but there was no pipe to be seen.

"Thomas," I said, "you have been smoking."

"No, ma'm." He was injured innocence itself. "It's on my coat, ma'm. Over at the club the gentlemen—"

But Thomas did not finish. The pantry was suddenly filled with the odor of singeing cloth. Thomas gave a clutch at his coat, whirled to the sink, filled a tumbler with water and poured it into his right pocket with the celerity of practice.

"Thomas," I said, when he was sheepishly mopping the floor, "smoking is a filthy and injurious habit. If you must smoke, you must; but don't stick a lighted pipe in your pocket again. Your skin's your own: you can blister it if you like. But this house is not mine, and I don't want a conflagration. Did you ever see this cuff-link before?"

No, he never had, he said, but he looked at it oddly.

"I picked it up in the hall," I added indifferently. The old man's eyes were shrewd under his bushy eyebrows.

"There's strange goin's-on here, Mis' Innes," he said, shaking his head. "Somethin's goin' to happen, sure. You ain't took notice that the big clock in the hall is stopped, I reckon?"

"Nonsense," I said. "Clocks have to stop, don't they, if they're not wound?"

"It's wound up, all right, and it stopped at three o'clock last night," he answered solemnly. "More'n that, that there clock ain't stopped for fifteen years, not since Mr. Armstrong's first wife died. And that ain't all,—no MA'M. Last three nights I slep' in this place, after the electrics went out I had a token. My oil lamp was full of oil, but it kep' goin' out, do what I would. Minute I shet my eyes, out that lamp'd go. There ain't no surer token of death. The Bible sez, LET YER LIGHT SHINE! When a hand you can't see puts yer light out, it means death, sure."

The old man's voice was full of conviction. In spite of myself I had a chilly sensation in the small of my back, and I left him mumbling over his dishes. Later on I heard a crash from the pantry, and Liddy reported that Beulah, who is coal black, had darted in front of Thomas just as he picked up a tray of dishes; that the bad omen had been too much for him, and he had dropped the tray.

The chug of the automobile as it climbed the hill was the most welcome sound I had heard for a long time, and with Gertrude and Halsey actually before me, my troubles seemed over for good. Gertrude stood smiling in the hall, with her hat quite over one ear, and her hair in every direction under her pink veil. Gertrude is a very pretty girl, no matter how her hat is, and I was not surprised when Halsey presented a good-looking young man, who bowed at me and looked at Trude—that is the ridiculous nickname Gertrude brought from school.

"I have brought a guest, Aunt Ray," Halsey said. "I want you to adopt him into your affections and your Saturday-to-Monday list. Let me present John Bailey, only you must call him Jack. In twelve hours he'll be calling you 'Aunt': I know him."

We shook hands, and I got a chance to look at Mr. Bailey; he was a tall fellow, perhaps thirty, and he wore a small mustache. I remember wondering why: he seemed to have a good mouth and when he smiled his teeth were above the average. One never knows why certain men cling to a messy upper lip that must get into things, any more than one understands some women building up their hair on wire atrocities. Otherwise, he was very good to look at, stalwart and tanned, with the direct gaze that I like. I am particular about Mr. Bailey, because he was a prominent figure in what happened later.

Gertrude was tired with the trip and went up to bed very soon. I made up my mind to tell them nothing; until the next day, and then to make as light of our excitement as possible. After all, what had I to tell? An inquisitive face peering in at a window; a crash in the night; a scratch or two on the stairs, and half a cuff-button! As for Thomas and his forebodings, it was always my belief that a negro is one part thief, one part pigment, and the rest superstition.

It was Saturday night. The two men went to the billiard-room, and I could hear them talking as I went up-stairs. It seemed that Halsey had stopped at the Greenwood Club for gasolene and found Jack Bailey there, with the Sunday golf crowd. Mr. Bailey had not been hard to persuade—probably Gertrude knew why—and they had carried him off triumphantly. I roused Liddy to get them something to eat—Thomas was beyond reach in the lodge—and paid no attention to her evident terror of the kitchen regions. Then I went to bed. The men were still in the billiard-room when I finally dozed off, and the last thing I remember was the howl of a dog in front of the house. It wailed a crescendo of woe that trailed off hopefully, only to break out afresh from a new point of the compass.

At three o'clock in the morning I was roused by a revolver shot. The sound seemed to come from just outside my door. For a moment I could not move. Then—I heard Gertrude stirring in her room, and the next moment she had thrown open the connecting door.

"O Aunt Ray! Aunt Ray!" she cried hysterically. "Some one has been killed, killed!"

"Thieves," I said shortly. "Thank goodness, there are some men in the house to-night." I was getting into my slippers and a bath-robe, and Gertrude with shaking hands was lighting a lamp. Then we opened the door into the hall, where, crowded on the upper landing of the stairs, the maids, white-faced and trembling, were peering down, headed by Liddy. I was greeted by a series of low screams and questions, and I tried to quiet them.

Gertrude had dropped on a chair and sat there limp and shivering.

I went at once across the hall to Halsey's room and knocked; then I pushed the door open. It was empty; the bed had not been occupied!

"He must be in Mr. Bailey's room," I said excitedly, and followed by Liddy, we went there. Like Halsey's, it had not been occupied! Gertrude was on her feet now, but she leaned against the door for support.

"They have been killed!" she gasped. Then she caught me by the arm and dragged me toward the stairs. "They may only be hurt, and we must find them," she said, her eyes dilated with excitement.

I don't remember how we got down the stairs: I do remember expecting every moment to be killed. The cook was at the telephone up-stairs, calling the Greenwood Club, and Liddy was behind me, afraid to come and not daring to stay behind. We found the living-room and the drawing-room undisturbed. Somehow I felt that whatever we found would be in the card-room or on the staircase, and nothing but the fear that Halsey was in danger drove me on; with every step my knees seemed to give way under me. Gertrude was ahead and in the card-room she stopped, holding her candle high. Then she pointed silently to the doorway into the hall beyond. Huddled there on the floor, face down, with his arms extended, was a man.

Gertrude ran forward with a gasping sob. "Jack," she cried, "oh, Jack!"

Liddy had run, screaming, and the two of us were there alone. It was Gertrude who turned him over, finally, until we could see his white face, and then she drew a deep breath and dropped limply to her knees. It was the body of a man, a gentleman, in a dinner coat and white waistcoat, stained now with blood—the body of a man I had never seen before.

CHAPTER IV
WHERE IS HALSEY?

Gertrude gazed at the face in a kind of fascination. Then she put out her hands blindly, and I thought she was going to faint.

"He has killed him!" she muttered almost inarticulately; and at that, because my nerves were going, I gave her a good shake.

"What do you mean?" I said frantically. There was a depth of grief and conviction in her tone that was worse than anything she could have said. The shake braced her, anyhow, and she seemed to pull herself together. But not another word would she say: she stood gazing down at that gruesome figure on the floor, while Liddy, ashamed of her flight and afraid to come back alone, drove before her three terrified women-servants into the drawing-room, which was as near as any of them would venture.

Once in the drawing-room, Gertrude collapsed and went from one fainting spell into another. I had all I could do to keep Liddy from drowning her with cold water, and the maids huddled in a corner, as much use as so many sheep. In a short time, although it seemed hours, a car came rushing up, and Anne Watson, who had waited to dress, opened the door. Three men from the Greenwood Club, in all kinds of costumes, hurried in. I recognized a Mr. Jarvis, but the others were strangers.

"What's wrong?" the Jarvis man asked—and we made a strange picture, no doubt. "Nobody hurt, is there?" He was looking at Gertrude.

"Worse than that, Mr. Jarvis," I said. "I think it is murder."

At the word there was a commotion. The cook began to cry, and Mrs. Watson knocked over a chair. The men were visibly impressed.

"Not any member of the family?" Mr. Jarvis asked, when he had got his breath.

"No," I said; and motioning Liddy to look after Gertrude, I led the way with a lamp to the card-room door. One of the men gave an exclamation, and they all hurried across the room. Mr. Jarvis took the lamp from me—I remember that—and then, feeling myself getting dizzy and light-headed, I closed my eyes. When I opened them their brief examination was over, and Mr. Jarvis was trying to put me in a chair.

"You must get up-stairs," he said firmly, "you and Miss Gertrude, too. This has been a terrible shock. In his own home, too."

I stared at him without comprehension. "Who is it?" I asked with difficulty. There was a band drawn tight around my throat.

"It is Arnold Armstrong," he said, looking at me oddly, "and he has been murdered in his father's house."

After a minute I gathered myself together and Mr. Jarvis helped me into the living-room. Liddy had got Gertrude up-stairs, and the two strange men from the club stayed with the body. The reaction from the shock and strain was tremendous: I was collapsed—and then Mr. Jarvis asked me a question that brought back my wandering faculties.

"Where is Halsey?" he asked.

"Halsey!" Suddenly Gertrude's stricken face rose before me the empty rooms up-stairs. Where was Halsey?

"He was here, wasn't he?" Mr. Jarvis persisted. "He stopped at the club on his way over."

"I—don't know where he is," I said feebly.

One of the men from the club came in, asked for the telephone, and I could hear him excitedly talking, saying something about coroners and detectives. Mr. Jarvis leaned over to me.

"Why don't you trust me, Miss Innes?" he said. "If I can do anything I will. But tell me the whole thing."

I did, finally, from the beginning, and when I told of Jack Bailey's being in the house that night, he gave a long whistle.

"I wish they were both here," he said when I finished. "Whatever mad prank took them away, it would look better if they were here. Especially—"

"Especially what?"

"Especially since Jack Bailey and Arnold Armstrong were notoriously bad friends. It was Bailey who got Arnold into trouble last spring—something about the bank. And then, too—"

"Go on," I said. "If there is anything more, I ought to know."

"There's nothing more," he said evasively. "There's just one thing we may bank on, Miss Innes. Any court in the country will acquit a man who kills an intruder in his house, at night. If Halsey—"

"Why, you don't think Halsey did it!" I exclaimed. There was a queer feeling of physical nausea coming over me.

"No, no, not at all," he said with forced cheerfulness. "Come, Miss Innes, you're a ghost of yourself and I am going to help you up-stairs and call your maid. This has been too much for you."

Liddy helped me back to bed, and under the impression that I was in danger of freezing to death, put a hot-water bottle over my heart and another at my feet. Then she left me. It was early dawn now, and from voices under my window I surmised that Mr. Jarvis and his companions were searching the grounds. As for me, I lay in bed, with every faculty awake. Where had Halsey gone? How had he gone, and when? Before the murder, no doubt, but who would believe that? If either he or Jack Bailey had heard an intruder in the house and shot him—as they might have been justified in doing—why had they run away? The whole thing was unheard of, outrageous, and—impossible to ignore.

About six o'clock Gertrude came in. She was fully dressed, and I sat up nervously.

"Poor Aunty!" she said. "What a shocking night you have had!" She came over and sat down on the bed, and I saw she looked very tired and worn.

"Is there anything new?" I asked anxiously.

"Nothing. The car is gone, but Warner"—he is the chauffeur—"Warner is at the lodge and knows nothing about it."

"Well," I said, "if I ever get my hands on Halsey Innes, I shall not let go until I have told him a few things. When we get this cleared up, I am going back to the city to be quiet. One more night like the last two will end me. The peace of the country—fiddle sticks!"

Whereupon I told Gertrude of the noises the night before, and the figure on the veranda in the east wing. As an afterthought I brought out the pearl cuff-link.

"I have no doubt now," I said, "that it was Arnold Armstrong the night before last, too. He had a key, no doubt, but why he should steal into his father's house I can not imagine. He could have come with my permission, easily enough. Anyhow, whoever it was that night, left this little souvenir."

Gertrude took one look at the cuff-link, and went as white as the pearls in it; she clutched at the foot of the bed, and stood staring. As for me, I was quite as astonished as she was.

"Where did—you—find it?" she asked finally, with a desperate effort at calm. And while I told her she stood looking out of the window with a look I could not fathom on her face. It was a relief when Mrs. Watson tapped at the door and brought me some tea and toast. The cook was in bed, completely demoralized, she reported, and Liddy, brave with the daylight, was looking for footprints around the house. Mrs. Watson herself was a wreck; she was blue-white around the lips, and she had one hand tied up.

She said she had fallen down-stairs in her excitement. It was natural, of course, that the thing would shock her, having been the Armstrongs' housekeeper for several years, and knowing Mr. Arnold well.

Gertrude had slipped out during my talk with Mrs. Watson, and I dressed and went down-stairs. The billiard and card-rooms were locked until the coroner and the detectives got there, and the men from the club had gone back for more conventional clothing.

I could hear Thomas in the pantry, alternately wailing for Mr. Arnold, as he called him, and citing the tokens that had precursed the murder. The house seemed to choke me, and, slipping a shawl around me, I went out on the drive. At the corner by the east wing I met Liddy. Her skirts were draggled with dew to her knees, and her hair was still in crimps.

"Go right in and change your clothes," I said sharply. "You're a sight, and at your age!"

She had a golf-stick in her hand, and she said she had found it on the lawn. There was nothing unusual about it, but it occurred to me that a golf-stick with a metal end might have been the object that had scratched the stairs near the card-room. I took it from her, and sent her up for dry garments. Her daylight courage and self-importance, and her shuddering delight in the mystery, irritated me beyond words. After I left her I made a circuit of the building. Nothing seemed to be disturbed: the house looked as calm and peaceful in the morning sun as it had the day I had been coerced into taking it. There was nothing to show that inside had been mystery and violence and sudden death.

In one of the tulip beds back of the house an early blackbird was pecking viciously at something that glittered in the light. I picked my way gingerly over through the dew and stooped down: almost buried in the soft ground was a revolver! I scraped the earth off it with the tip of my shoe, and, picking it up, slipped it into my pocket. Not until I had got into my bedroom and double-locked the door did I venture to take it out and examine it. One look was all I needed. It was Halsey's revolver. I had unpacked it the day before and put it on his shaving-stand, and there could be no mistake. His name was on a small silver plate on the handle.

I seemed to see a network closing around my boy, innocent as I knew he was. The revolver—I am afraid of them, but anxiety gave me courage to look through the barrel—the revolver had still two bullets in it. I could only breathe a prayer of thankfulness that I had found the revolver before any sharp-eyed detective had come around.

I decided to keep what clues I had, the cuff-link, the golf-stick and the revolver, in a secure place until I could see some reason for displaying them. The cuff-link had been dropped into a little filigree box on my toilet table. I opened the box and felt around for it. The box was empty—the cuff-link had disappeared!

CHAPTER V
GERTRUDE'S ENGAGEMENT

At ten o'clock the Casanova hack brought up three men. They introduced themselves as the coroner of the county and two detectives from the city. The coroner led the way at once to the locked wing, and with the aid of one of the detectives examined the rooms and the body. The other detective, after a short scrutiny of the dead man, busied himself with the outside of the house. It was only after they had got a fair idea of things as they were that they sent for me.

I received them in the living-room, and I had made up my mind exactly what to tell. I had taken the house for the summer, I said, while the Armstrongs were in California. In spite of a rumor among the servants about strange noises—I cited Thomas—nothing had occurred the first two nights. On the third night I believed that some one had been in the house: I had heard a crashing sound, but being alone with one maid had not investigated. The house had been locked in the morning and apparently undisturbed.

Then, as clearly as I could, I related how, the night before, a shot had roused us; that my niece and I had investigated and found a body; that I did not know who the murdered man was until Mr. Jarvis from the club informed me, and that I knew of no reason why Mr. Arnold Armstrong should steal into his father's house at night. I should have been glad to allow him entree there at any time.

"Have you reason to believe, Miss Innes," the coroner asked, "that any member of your household, imagining Mr. Armstrong was a burglar, shot him in self-defense?"

"I have no reason for thinking so," I said quietly.

"Your theory is that Mr. Armstrong was followed here by some enemy, and shot as he entered the house?"

"I don't think I have a theory," I said. "The thing that has puzzled me is why Mr. Armstrong should enter his father's house two nights in succession, stealing in like a thief, when he needed only to ask entrance to be admitted."

The coroner was a very silent man: he took some notes after this, but he seemed anxious to make the next train back to town. He set the inquest for the following Saturday, gave Mr.

Jamieson, the younger of the two detectives, and the more intelligent looking, a few instructions, and, after gravely shaking hands with me and regretting the unfortunate affair, took his departure, accompanied by the other detective.

I was just beginning to breathe freely when Mr. Jamieson, who had been standing by the window, came over to me.

"The family consists of yourself alone, Miss Innes?"

"My niece is here," I said.

"There is no one but yourself and your niece?"

"My nephew." I had to moisten my lips.

"Oh, a nephew. I should like to see him, if he is here."

"He is not here just now," I said as quietly as I could. "I expect him—at any time."

"He was here yesterday evening, I believe?"

"No—yes."

"Didn't he have a guest with him? Another man?"

"He brought a friend with him to stay over Sunday, Mr. Bailey."

"Mr. John Bailey, the cashier of the Traders' Bank I believe." And I knew that some one at the Greenwood Club had told. "When did they leave?"

"Very early—I don't know at just what time."

Mr. Jamieson turned suddenly and looked at me.

"Please try to be more explicit," he said. "You say your nephew and Mr. Bailey were in the house last night, and yet you and your niece, with some women-servants, found the body. Where was your nephew?"

I was entirely desperate by that time.

"I do not know," I cried, "but be sure of this: Halsey knows nothing of this thing, and no amount of circumstantial evidence can make an innocent man guilty."

"Sit down," he said, pushing forward a chair. "There are some things I have to tell you, and, in return, please tell me all you know. Believe me, things always come out. In the first place, Mr. Armstrong was shot from above. The bullet was fired at close range, entered below the shoulder and came out, after passing through the heart, well down the back. In other words, I believe the murderer stood on the stairs and fired down. In the second place, I found on the edge of the billiard-table a charred cigar which had burned itself partly out, and a cigarette which had consumed itself to the cork tip. Neither one had been more than lighted, then put down and forgotten. Have you any idea what it was that made your nephew and Mr. Bailey leave their cigars and their game, take out the automobile without calling the chauffeur, and all this at—let me see certainly before three o'clock in the morning?"

"I don't know," I said; "but depend on it, Mr. Jamieson, Halsey will be back himself to explain everything."

"I sincerely hope so," he said. "Miss Innes, has it occurred to you that Mr. Bailey might know something of this?"

Gertrude had come down-stairs and just as he spoke she came in. I saw her stop suddenly, as if she had been struck.

"He does not," she said in a tone that was not her own. "Mr. Bailey and my brother know nothing of this. The murder was committed at three. They left the house at a quarter before three."

"How do you know that?" Mr. Jamieson asked oddly. "Do you KNOW at what time they left?"

"I do," Gertrude answered firmly. "At a quarter before three my brother and Mr. Bailey left the house, by the main entrance. I—was—there."

"Gertrude," I said excitedly, "you are dreaming! Why, at a quarter to three—"

"Listen," she said. "At half-past two the downstairs telephone rang. I had not gone to sleep, and I heard it. Then I heard Halsey answer it, and in a few minutes he came up-stairs and knocked at my door. We—we talked for a minute, then I put on my dressing-gown and slippers, and went down-stairs with him. Mr. Bailey was in the billiard-room. We—we all talked together for perhaps ten minutes. Then it was decided that—that they should both go away—"

"Can't you be more explicit?" Mr. Jamieson asked. "WHY did they go away?"

"I am only telling you what happened, not why it happened," she said evenly. "Halsey went for the car, and instead of bringing it to the house and rousing people, he went by the lower road from the stable. Mr. Bailey was to meet him at the foot of the lawn. Mr. Bailey left—"

"Which way?" Mr. Jamieson asked sharply.

"By the main entrance. He left—it was a quarter to three. I know exactly."

"The clock in the hall is stopped, Miss Innes," said Jamieson. Nothing seemed to escape him.

"He looked at his watch," she replied, and I could see Mr. Jamieson's snap, as if he had made a discovery. As for myself, during the whole recital I had been plunged into the deepest amazement.

"Will you pardon me for a personal question?" The detective was a youngish man, and I thought he was somewhat embarrassed. "What are your—your relations with Mr. Bailey?"

Gertrude hesitated. Then she came over and put her hand lovingly in mine.

"I am engaged to marry him," she said simply.

I had grown so accustomed to surprises that I could only gasp again, and as for Gertrude, the hand that lay in mine was burning with fever.

"And—after that," Mr. Jamieson went on, "you went directly to bed?"

Gertrude hesitated.

"No," she said finally. "I—I am not nervous, and after I had extinguished the light, I remembered something I had left in the billiard-room, and I felt my way back there through the darkness."

"Will you tell me what it was you had forgotten?"

"I can not tell you," she said slowly. "I—I did not leave the billiard-room at once—"

"Why?" The detective's tone was imperative. "This is very important, Miss Innes."

"I was crying," Gertrude said in a low tone. "When the French clock in the drawing-room struck three, I got up, and then—I heard a step on the east porch, just outside the card-room. Some one with a key was working with the latch, and I thought, of course, of Halsey. When we took the house he called that his entrance, and he had carried a key for it ever since. The door opened and I was about to ask what he had forgotten, when there was a flash and a report. Some heavy body dropped, and, half crazed with terror and shock, I ran through the drawing-room and got up-stairs—I scarcely remember how."

She dropped into a chair, and I thought Mr. Jamieson must have finished. But he was not through.

"You certainly clear your brother and Mr. Bailey admirably," he said. "The testimony is invaluable, especially in view of the fact that your brother and Mr. Armstrong had, I believe, quarreled rather seriously some time ago."

"Nonsense," I broke in. "Things are bad enough, Mr. Jamieson, without inventing bad feeling where it doesn't exist. Gertrude, I don't think Halsey knew the—the murdered man, did he?"

But Mr. Jamieson was sure of his ground.

"The quarrel, I believe," he persisted, "was about Mr. Armstrong's conduct to you, Miss Gertrude. He had been paying you unwelcome attentions."

And I had never seen the man!

When she nodded a "yes" I saw the tremendous possibilities involved. If this detective could prove that Gertrude feared and disliked the murdered man, and that Mr. Armstrong had been annoying and possibly pursuing her with hateful attentions, all that, added to Gertrude's confession of her presence in the billiard-room at the time of the crime, looked strange, to say the least. The prominence of the family assured a strenuous effort to find the murderer, and if we had nothing worse to look forward to, we were sure of a distasteful publicity.

Mr. Jamieson shut his note-book with a snap, and thanked us.

"I have an idea," he said, apropos of nothing at all, "that at any rate the ghost is laid here. Whatever the rappings have been—and the colored man says they began when the family went west three months ago—they are likely to stop now."

Which shows how much he knew about it. The ghost was not laid: with the murder of Arnold Armstrong he, or it, only seemed to take on fresh vigor.

Mr. Jamieson left then, and when Gertrude had gone up-stairs, as she did at once, I sat and thought over what I had just heard. Her engagement, once so engrossing a matter, paled now beside the significance of her story. If Halsey and Jack Bailey had left before the crime, how came Halsey's revolver in the tulip bed? What was the mysterious cause of their sudden flight? What had Gertrude left in the billiard-room? What was the significance of the cuff-link, and where was it?

CHAPTER VI
IN THE EAST CORRIDOR

When the detective left he enjoined absolute secrecy on everybody in the household. The Greenwood Club promised the same thing, and as there are no Sunday afternoon papers, the murder was not publicly known until Monday. The coroner himself notified the Armstrong family lawyer, and early in the afternoon he came out. I had not seen Mr. Jamieson since morning, but I knew he had been interrogating the servants. Gertrude was locked in her room with a headache, and I had luncheon alone.

Mr. Harton, the lawyer, was a little, thin man, and he looked as if he did not relish his business that day.

"This is very unfortunate, Miss Innes," he said, after we had shaken hands. "Most unfortunate—and mysterious. With the father and mother in the west, I find everything devolves on me; and, as you can understand, it is an unpleasant duty."

"No doubt," I said absently. "Mr. Harton, I am going to ask you some questions, and I hope you will answer them. I feel that I am entitled to some knowledge, because I and my family are just now in a most ambiguous position."

I don't know whether he understood me or not: he took of his glasses and wiped them.

"I shall be very happy," he said with old-fashioned courtesy.

"Thank you. Mr. Harton, did Mr. Arnold Armstrong know that Sunnyside had been rented?"

"I think—yes, he did. In fact, I myself told him about it."

"And he knew who the tenants were?"

"Yes."

"He had not been living with the family for some years, I believe?"

"No. Unfortunately, there had been trouble between Arnold and his father. For two years he had lived in town."

"Then it would be unlikely that he came here last night to get possession of anything belonging to him?"

"I should think it hardly possible," he admitted.

"To be perfectly frank, Miss Innes, I can not think of any reason whatever for his coming here as he did. He had been staying at the club-house across the valley for the last week, Jarvis tells me, but that only explains how he came here, not why. It is a most unfortunate family."

He shook his head despondently, and I felt that this dried-up little man was the repository of much that he had not told me. I gave up trying to elicit any information from him, and we went together to view the body before it was taken to the city. It had been lifted on to the billiard-table and a sheet thrown over it; otherwise nothing had been touched. A soft hat lay beside it, and the collar of the dinner-coat was still turned up. The handsome, dissipated face of Arnold Armstrong, purged of its ugly lines, was now only pathetic. As we went in Mrs. Watson appeared at the card-room door.

"Come in, Mrs. Watson," the lawyer said. But she shook her head and withdrew: she was the only one in the house who seemed to regret the dead man, and even she seemed rather shocked than sorry.

I went to the door at the foot of the circular staircase and opened it. If I could only have seen Halsey coming at his usual hare-brained clip up the drive, if I could have heard the throb of the motor, I would have felt that my troubles were over.

But there was nothing to be seen. The countryside lay sunny and quiet in its peaceful Sunday afternoon calm, and far down the drive Mr. Jamieson was walking slowly, stooping now and then, as if to examine the road. When I went back, Mr. Harton was furtively wiping his eyes.

"The prodigal has come home, Miss Innes," he said. "How often the sins of the fathers are visited on the children!" Which left me pondering.

Before Mr. Harton left, he told me something of the Armstrong family. Paul Armstrong, the father, had been married twice. Arnold was a son by the first marriage. The second Mrs. Armstrong had been a widow, with a child, a little girl. This child, now perhaps twenty, was Louise Armstrong, having taken her stepfather's name, and was at present in California with the family.

"They will probably return at once," he concluded "sad part of my errand here to-day is to see if you will relinquish your lease here in their favor."

"We would better wait and see if they wish to come," I said. "It seems unlikely, and my town house is being remodeled." At that he let the matter drop, but it came up unpleasantly enough, later.

At six o'clock the body was taken away, and at seven-thirty, after an early dinner, Mr. Harton went. Gertrude had not come down, and there was no news of Halsey. Mr. Jamieson had taken a lodging in the village, and I had not seen him since mid-afternoon. It was about nine o'clock, I think, when the bell rang and he was ushered into the living-room.

"Sit down," I said grimly. "Have you found a clue that will incriminate me, Mr. Jamieson?"

He had the grace to look uncomfortable. "No," he said. "If you had killed Mr. Armstrong, you would have left no clues. You would have had too much intelligence."

After that we got along better. He was fishing in his pocket, and after a minute he brought out two scraps of paper. "I have been to the club-house," he said, "and among Mr. Armstrong's effects, I found these. One is curious; the other is puzzling."

The first was a sheet of club note-paper, on which was written, over and over, the name "Halsey B. Innes." It was Halsey's flowing signature to a dot, but it lacked Halsey's ease. The ones toward the bottom of the sheet were much better than the top ones. Mr. Jamieson smiled at my face.

"His old tricks," he said. "That one is merely curious; this one, as I said before, is puzzling."

The second scrap, folded and refolded into a compass so tiny that the writing had been partly obliterated, was part of a letter—the lower half of a sheet, not typed, but written in a cramped hand.

"——by altering the plans for——rooms, may be possible. The best way, in my opinion, would be to——the plan for——in one of the——rooms——chimney."

That was all.

"Well?" I said, looking up. "There is nothing in that, is there? A man ought to be able to change the plan of his house without becoming an object of suspicion."

"There is little in the paper itself," he admitted; "but why should Arnold Armstrong carry that around, unless it meant something? He never built a house, you may be sure of that. If it is this house, it may mean anything, from a secret room—"

"To an extra bath-room," I said scornfully. "Haven't you a thumb-print, too?"

"I have," he said with a smile, "and the print of a foot in a tulip bed, and a number of other things. The oddest part is, Miss Innes, that the thumb-mark is probably yours and the footprint certainly."

His audacity was the only thing that saved me: his amused smile put me on my mettle, and I ripped out a perfectly good scallop before I answered.

"Why did I step into the tulip bed?" I asked with interest.

"You picked up something," he said good-humoredly, "which you are going to tell me about later."

"Am I, indeed?" I was politely curious. "With this remarkable insight of yours, I wish you would tell me where I shall find my four-thousand-dollar motor car."

"I was just coming to that," he said. "You will find it about thirty miles away, at Andrews Station, in a blacksmith shop, where it is being repaired."

I laid down my knitting then and looked at him.

"And Halsey?" I managed to say.

"We are going to exchange information," he said "I am going to tell you that, when you tell me what you picked up in the tulip bed."

We looked steadily at each other: it was not an unfriendly stare; we were only measuring weapons. Then he smiled a little and got up.

"With your permission," he said, "I am going to examine the card-room and the staircase again. You might think over my offer in the meantime."

He went on through the drawing-room, and I listened to his footsteps growing gradually fainter. I dropped my pretense at knitting and, leaning back, I thought over the last forty-eight hours. Here was I, Rachel Innes, spinster, a granddaughter of old John Innes of Revolutionary days, a D. A. R., a Colonial Dame, mixed up with a vulgar and revolting crime, and even attempting to hoodwink the law! Certainly I had left the straight and narrow way.

I was roused by hearing Mr. Jamieson coming rapidly back through the drawing-room. He stopped at the door.

"Miss Innes," he said quickly, "will you come with me and light the east corridor? I have fastened somebody in the small room at the head of the card-room stairs."

I jumped! up at once.

"You mean—the murderer?" I gasped.

"Possibly," he said quietly, as we hurried together up the stairs. "Some one was lurking on the staircase when I went back. I spoke; instead of an answer, whoever it was turned and ran up. I followed—it was dark—but as I turned the corner at the top a figure darted through this door and closed it. The bolt was on my side, and I pushed it forward. It is a closet, I think." We were in the upper hall now. "If you will show me the electric switch, Miss Innes, you would better wait in your own room."

Trembling as I was, I was determined to see that door opened. I hardly knew what I feared, but so many terrible and inexplicable things had happened that suspense was worse than certainty.

"I am perfectly cool," I said, "and I am going to remain here."

The lights flashed up along that end of the corridor, throwing the doors into relief. At the intersection of the small hallway with the larger, the circular staircase wound its way up, as if it had been an afterthought of the architect. And just around the corner, in the small corridor, was the door Mr. Jamieson had indicated. I was still unfamiliar with the house, and I did not remember the door. My heart was thumping wildly in my ears, but I nodded to him to go ahead. I was perhaps eight or ten feet away—and then he threw the bolt back.

"Come out," he said quietly. There was no response. "Come—out," he repeated. Then—I think he had a revolver, but I am not sure—he stepped aside and threw the door open.

From where I stood I could not see beyond the door, but I saw Mr. Jamieson's face change and heard him mutter something, then he bolted down the stairs, three at a time. When my knees had stopped shaking, I moved forward, slowly, nervously, until I had a partial view of what was beyond the door. It seemed at first to be a closet, empty. Then I went close and examined it, to stop with a shudder. Where the floor should have been was black void and darkness, from which came the indescribable, damp smell of the cellars.

Mr. Jamieson had locked somebody in the clothes chute. As I leaned over I fancied I heard a groan—or was it the wind?

CHAPTER VII
A SPRAINED ANKLE

I was panic-stricken. As I ran along the corridor I was confident that the mysterious intruder and probable murderer had been found, and that he lay dead or dying at the foot of the chute. I got down the staircase somehow, and through the kitchen to the basement stairs. Mr. Jamieson had been before me, and the door stood open. Liddy was standing in the middle of the kitchen, holding a frying-pan by the handle as a weapon.

"Don't go down there," she yelled, when she saw me moving toward the basement stairs. "Don't you do it, Miss Rachel. That Jamieson's down there now. There's only trouble comes of hunting ghosts; they lead you into bottomless pits and things like that. Oh, Miss Rachel, don't—" as I tried to get past her.

She was interrupted by Mr. Jamieson's reappearance. He ran up the stairs two at a time, and his face was flushed and furious.

"The whole place is locked," he said angrily. "Where's the laundry key kept?"

"It's kept in the door," Liddy snapped. "That whole end of the cellar is kept locked, so nobody can get at the clothes, and then the key's left in the door? so that unless a thief was as blind as—as some detectives, he could walk right in."

"Liddy," I said sharply, "come down with us and turn on all the lights."

She offered her resignation, as usual, on the spot, but I took her by the arm, and she came along finally. She switched on all the lights and pointed to a door just ahead.

"That's the door," she said sulkily. "The key's in it."

But the key was not in it. Mr. Jamieson shook it, but it was a heavy door, well locked. And then he stooped and began punching around the keyhole with the end of a lead-pencil. When he stood up his face was exultant.

"It's locked on the inside," he said in a low tone. "There is somebody in there."

"Lord have mercy!" gasped Liddy, and turned to run.

"Liddy," I called, "go through the house at once and see who is missing, or if any one is. We'll have to clear this thing at once. Mr. Jamieson, if you will watch here I will go to the lodge and find Warner. Thomas would be of no use. Together you may be able to force the door."

"A good idea," he assented. "But—there are windows, of course, and there is nothing to prevent whoever is in there from getting out that way."

"Then lock the door at the top of the basement stairs," I suggested, "and patrol the house from the outside."

We agreed to this, and I had a feeling that the mystery of Sunnyside was about to be solved. I ran down the steps and along the drive. Just at the corner I ran full tilt into somebody who seemed to be as much alarmed as I was. It was not until I had recoiled a step or two that I recognized Gertrude, and she me.

"Good gracious, Aunt Ray," she exclaimed, "what is the matter?"

"There's somebody locked in the laundry," I panted. "That is—unless—you didn't see any one crossing the lawn or skulking around the house, did you?"

"I think we have mystery on the brain," Gertrude said wearily. "No, I haven't seen any one, except old Thomas, who looked for all the world as if he had been ransacking the pantry. What have you locked in the laundry?"

"I can't wait to explain," I replied. "I must get Warner from the lodge. If you came out for air, you'd better put on your overshoes." And then I noticed that Gertrude was limping—not much, but sufficiently to make her progress very slow, and seemingly painful.

"You have hurt yourself," I said sharply.

"I fell over the carriage block," she explained. "I thought perhaps I might see Halsey coming home. He—he ought to be here."

I hurried on down the drive. The lodge was some distance from the house, in a grove of trees where the drive met the county road. There were two white stone pillars to mark the entrance, but the iron gates, once closed and tended by the lodge-keeper, now stood permanently open. The day of the motor-car had come; no one had time for closed gates and lodge-keepers. The lodge at Sunnyside was merely a sort of supplementary servants' quarters: it was as convenient in its appointments as the big house and infinitely more cozy.

As I went down the drive, my thoughts were busy. Who would it be that Mr. Jamieson had trapped in the cellar? Would we find a body or some one badly injured? Scarcely either. Whoever had fallen had been able to lock the laundry door on the inside. If the fugitive had come from outside the house, how did he get in? If it was some member of the household, who could it have been? And then—a feeling of horror almost overwhelmed me. Gertrude! Gertrude and her injured ankle! Gertrude found limping slowly up the drive when I had thought she was in bed!

I tried to put the thought away, but it would not go. If Gertrude had been on the circular staircase that night, why had she fled from Mr. Jamieson? The idea, puzzling as it was, seemed borne out by this circumstance. Whoever had taken refuge at the head of the stairs could scarcely have been familiar with the house, or with the location of the chute. The mystery seemed to deepen constantly. What possible connection could there be between Halsey and Gertrude, and the murder of Arnold Armstrong? And yet, every way I turned I seemed to find something that pointed to such a connection.

At the foot of the drive the road described a long, sloping, horseshoe-shaped curve around the lodge. There were lights there, streaming cheerfully out on to the trees, and from an upper room came wavering shadows, as if some one with a lamp was moving around. I had come almost silently in my evening slippers, and I had my second collision of the evening on the road just above the house. I ran full into a man in a long coat, who was standing in the shadow beside the drive, with his back to me, watching the lighted windows.

"What the hell!" he ejaculated furiously, and turned around. When he saw me, however, he did not wait for any retort on my part. He faded away—this is not slang; he did—he absolutely disappeared in the dusk without my getting more than a glimpse of his face. I had a vague impression of unfamiliar features and of a sort of cap with a visor. Then he was gone.

I went to the lodge and rapped. It required two or three poundings to bring Thomas to the door, and he opened it only an inch or so.

"Where is Warner?" I asked.

"I—I think he's in bed, ma'm."

"Get him up," I said, "and for goodness' sake open the door, Thomas. I'll wait for Warner."

"It's kind o' close in here, ma'm," he said, obeying gingerly, and disclosing a cool and comfortable looking interior. "Perhaps you'd keer to set on the porch an' rest yo'self."

It was so evident that Thomas did not want me inside that I went in.

"Tell Warner he is needed in a hurry," I repeated, and turned into the little sitting-room. I could hear Thomas going up the stairs, could hear him rouse Warner, and the steps of the chauffeur as he hurriedly dressed. But my attention was busy with the room below.

On the center-table, open, was a sealskin traveling bag. It was filled with gold-topped bottles and brushes, and it breathed opulence, luxury, femininity from every inch of surface. How did it get there? I was still asking myself the question when Warner came running down the stairs and into the room. He was completely but somewhat incongruously dressed, and his open, boyish face looked abashed. He was a country boy, absolutely frank and reliable, of fair education and intelligence—one of the small army of American youths who turn a natural aptitude for mechanics into the special field of the automobile, and earn good salaries in a congenial occupation.

"What is it, Miss Innes?" he asked anxiously.

"There is some one locked in the laundry," I replied. "Mr. Jamieson wants you to help him break the lock. Warner, whose bag is this?"

He was in the doorway by this time, and he pretended not to hear.

"Warner," I called, "come back here. Whose bag is this?"

He stopped then, but he did not turn around.

"It's—it belongs to Thomas," he said, and fled up the drive.

To Thomas! A London bag with mirrors and cosmetic jars of which Thomas could not even have guessed the use! However, I put the bag in the back of my mind, which was fast becoming stored with anomalous and apparently irreconcilable facts, and followed Warner to the house.

Liddy had come back to the kitchen: the door to the basement stairs was double-barred, and had a table pushed against it; and beside her on the table was most of the kitchen paraphernalia.

"Did you see if there was any one missing in the house?" I asked, ignoring the array of sauce-pans rolling-pins, and the poker of the range.

"Rosie is missing," Liddy said with unction. She had objected to Rosie, the parlor maid, from the start. "Mrs. Watson went into her room, and found she had gone without her hat. People that trust themselves a dozen miles from the city, in strange houses, with servants they don't know, needn't be surprised if they wake up some morning and find their throats cut."

After which carefully veiled sarcasm Liddy relapsed into gloom. Warner came in then with a handful of small tools, and Mr. Jamieson went with him to the basement. Oddly enough,

I was not alarmed. With all my heart I wished for Halsey, but I was not frightened. At the door he was to force, Warner put down his tools and looked at it. Then he turned the handle. Without the slightest difficulty the door opened, revealing the blackness of the drying-room beyond!

Mr. Jamieson gave an exclamation of disgust.

"Gone!" he said. "Confound such careless work! I might have known."

It was true enough. We got the lights on finally and looked all through the three rooms that constituted this wing of the basement. Everything was quiet and empty. An explanation of how the fugitive had escaped injury was found in a heaped-up basket of clothes under the chute. The basket had been overturned, but that was all. Mr. Jamieson examined the windows: one was unlocked, and offered an easy escape. The window or the door? Which way had the fugitive escaped? The door seemed most probable, and I hoped it had been so. I could not have borne, just then, to think that it was my poor Gertrude we had been hounding through the darkness, and yet—I had met Gertrude not far from that very window.

I went up-stairs at last, tired and depressed. Mrs. Watson and Liddy were making tea in the kitchen. In certain walks of life the tea-pot is the refuge in times of stress, trouble or sickness: they give tea to the dying and they put it in the baby's nursing bottle. Mrs. Watson was fixing a tray to be sent in to me, and when I asked her about Rosie she confirmed her absence.

"She's not here," she said; "but I would not think much of that, Miss Innes. Rosie is a pretty young girl, and perhaps she has a sweetheart. It will be a good thing if she has. The maids stay much better when they have something like that to hold them here."

Gertrude had gone back to her room, and while I was drinking my cup of hot tea, Mr. Jamieson came in.

"We might take up the conversation where we left off an hour and a half ago," he said. "But before we go on, I want to say this: The person who escaped from the laundry was a woman with a foot of moderate size and well arched. She wore nothing but a stocking on her right foot, and, in spite of the unlocked door, she escaped by the window."

And again I thought of Gertrude's sprained ankle. Was it the right or the left?

CHAPTER VIII
THE OTHER HALF OF THE LINE

"Miss Innes," the detective began, "what is your opinion of the figure you saw on the east veranda the night you and your maid were in the house alone?"

"It was a woman," I said positively.

"And yet your maid affirms with equal positiveness that it was a man."

"Nonsense," I broke in. "Liddy had her eyes shut—she always shuts them when she's frightened."

"And you never thought then that the intruder who came later that night might be a woman—the woman, in fact, whom you saw on the veranda?"

"I had reasons for thinking it was a man," I said remembering the pearl cuff-link.

"Now we are getting down to business. WHAT were your reasons for thinking that?"

I hesitated.

"If you have any reason for believing that your midnight guest was Mr. Armstrong, other than his visit here the next night, you ought to tell me, Miss Innes. We can take nothing for granted. If, for instance, the intruder who dropped the bar and scratched the staircase—you see, I know about that—if this visitor was a woman, why should not the same woman have come back the following night, met Mr. Armstrong on the circular staircase, and in alarm shot him?"

"It was a man," I reiterated. And then, because I could think of no other reason for my statement, I told him about the pearl cuff-link. He was intensely interested.

"Will you give me the link," he said, when I finished, "or, at least, let me see it? I consider it a most important clue."

"Won't the description do?"

"Not as well as the original."

"Well, I'm very sorry," I said, as calmly as I could, "I—the thing is lost. It—it must have fallen out of a box on my dressing-table."

Whatever he thought of my explanation, and I knew he doubted it, he made no sign. He asked me to describe the link accurately, and I did so, while he glanced at a list he took from his pocket.

"One set monogram cuff-links," he read, "one set plain pearl links, one set cuff-links, woman's head set with diamonds and emeralds. There is no mention of such a link as you describe, and yet, if your theory is right, Mr. Armstrong must have taken back in his cuffs one complete cuff-link, and a half, perhaps, of the other."

The idea was new to me. If it had not been the murdered man who had entered the house that night, who had it been?

"There are a number of strange things connected with this case," the detective went on. "Miss Gertrude Innes testified that she heard some one fumbling with the lock, that the door opened, and that almost immediately the shot was fired. Now, Miss Innes, here is the strange part of that. Mr. Armstrong had no key with him. There was no key in the lock, or on the floor. In other words, the evidence points absolutely to this: Mr. Armstrong was admitted to the house from within."

"It is impossible," I broke in. "Mr. Jamieson, do you know what your words imply? Do you know that you are practically accusing Gertrude Innes of admitting that man?"

"Not quite that," he said, with his friendly smile. "In fact, Miss Innes, I am quite certain she did not. But as long as I learn only parts of the truth, from both you and her, what can I do? I know you picked up something in the flower bed: you refuse to tell me what it was. I know Miss Gertrude went back to the billiard-room to get something, she refuses to say what. You suspect what happened to the cuff-link, but you won't tell me. So far, all I am sure of is this: I do not believe Arnold Armstrong was the midnight visitor who so alarmed you by dropping—shall we say, a golf-stick? And I believe that when he did come he was admitted by some one in the house. Who knows—it may have been—Liddy!"

I stirred my tea angrily.

"I have always heard," I said dryly, "that undertakers' assistants are jovial young men. A man's sense of humor seems to be in inverse proportion to the gravity of his profession."

"A man's sense of humor is a barbarous and a cruel thing, Miss Innes," he admitted. "It is to the feminine as the hug of a bear is to the scratch of—well;—anything with claws. Is that you, Thomas? Come in."

Thomas Johnson stood in the doorway. He looked alarmed and apprehensive, and suddenly I remembered the sealskin dressing-bag in the lodge. Thomas came just inside the door and stood with his head drooping, his eyes, under their shaggy gray brows, fixed on Mr. Jamieson.

"Thomas," said the detective, not unkindly, "I sent for you to tell us what you told Sam Bohannon at the club, the day before Mr. Arnold was found here, dead. Let me see. You came here Friday night to see Miss Innes, didn't you? And came to work here Saturday morning?"

For some unexplained reason Thomas looked relieved.

"Yas, sah," he said. "You see it were like this: When Mistah Armstrong and the fam'ly went away, Mis' Watson an' me, we was lef' in charge till the place was rented. Mis' Watson, she've bin here a good while, an' she warn' skeery. So she slep' in the house. I'd bin havin' tokens—I tol' Mis' Innes some of 'em—an' I slep' in the lodge. Then one day Mis' Watson, she came to me an' she sez, sez she, 'Thomas, you'll hev to sleep up in the big house. I'm too nervous to do it any more.' But I jes' reckon to myself that ef it's too skeery fer her, it's too skeery fer me. We had it, then, sho' nuff, and it ended up with Mis' Watson stayin' in the lodge nights an' me lookin' fer work at de club."

"Did Mrs. Watson say that anything had happened to alarm her?"

"No, sah. She was jes' natchally skeered. Well, that was all, far's I know, until the night I come over to see Mis' Innes. I come across the valley, along the path from the club-house, and I goes home that way. Down in the creek bottom I almost run into a man. He wuz standin' with his back to me, an' he was workin' with one of these yere electric light things that fit in yer pocket. He was havin' trouble—one minute it'd flash out, an' the nex' it'd be gone. I hed a view of 'is white dress shirt an' tie, as I passed. I didn't see his face. But I know it warn't Mr. Arnold. It was a taller man than Mr. Arnold. Beside that, Mr. Arnold was playin' cards when I got to the club-house, same's he'd been doin' all day."

"And the next morning you came back along the path," pursued Mr. Jamieson relentlessly.

"The nex' mornin' I come back along the path an' down where I dun see the man night befoh, I picked up this here." The old man held out a tiny object and Mr. Jamieson took it. Then he held it on his extended palm for me to see. It was the other half of the pearl cuff-link!

But Mr. Jamieson was not quite through questioning him.

"And so you showed it to Sam, at the club, and asked him if he knew any one who owned such a link, and Sam said—what?"

"Wal, Sam, he 'lowed he'd seen such a pair of cuff-buttons in a shirt belongin' to Mr. Bailey—Mr. Jack Bailey, sah."

"I'll keep this link, Thomas, for a while," the detective said. "That's all I wanted to know. Good night."

As Thomas shuffled out, Mr. Jamieson watched me sharply.

"You see, Miss Innes," he said, "Mr. Bailey insists on mixing himself with this thing. If Mr. Bailey came here that Friday night expecting to meet Arnold Armstrong, and missed him—if, as I say, he had done this, might he not, seeing him enter the following night, have struck him down, as he had intended before?"

"But the motive?" I gasped.

"There could be motive proved, I think. Arnold Armstrong and John Bailey have been enemies since the latter, as cashier of the Traders' Bank, brought Arnold almost into the clutches of the law. Also, you forget that both men have been paying attention to Miss Gertrude. Bailey's flight looks bad, too."

"And you think Halsey helped him to escape?"

"Undoubtedly. Why, what could it be but flight? Miss Innes, let me reconstruct that evening, as I see it. Bailey and Armstrong had quarreled at the club. I learned this to-day. Your nephew brought Bailey over. Prompted by jealous, insane fury, Armstrong followed, coming across by the path. He entered the billiard-room wing—perhaps rapping, and being admitted by your nephew. Just inside he was shot, by some one on the circular staircase. The shot fired, your nephew and Bailey left the house at once, going toward the automobile house. They left by the lower road, which prevented them being heard, and when you and Miss Gertrude got down-stairs everything was quiet."

"But—Gertrude's story," I stammered.

"Miss Gertrude only brought forward her explanation the following morning. I do not believe it, Miss Innes. It is the story of a loving and ingenious woman."

"And—this thing to-night?"

"May upset my whole view of the case. We must give the benefit of every doubt, after all. We may, for instance, come back to the figure on the porch: if it was a woman you saw that night through the window, we might start with other premises. Or Mr. Innes' explanation may turn us in a new direction. It is possible that he shot Arnold Armstrong as a burglar and then fled, frightened at what he had done. In any case, however, I feel confident that the body was here when he left. Mr. Armstrong left the club ostensibly for a moonlight saunter, about half after eleven o'clock. It was three when the shot was fired."

I leaned back bewildered. It seemed to me that the evening had been full of significant happenings, had I only held the key. Had Gertrude been the fugitive in the clothes chute? Who was the man on the drive near the lodge, and whose gold-mounted dressing-bag had I seen in the lodge sitting-room?

It was late when Mr. Jamieson finally got up to go. I went with him to the door, and together we stood looking out over the valley. Below lay the village of Casanova, with its Old World houses, its blossoming trees and its peace. Above on the hill across the valley were the lights of the Greenwood Club. It was even possible to see the curving row of parallel lights that marked the carriage road. Rumors that I had heard about the club came back—of drinking, of high play, and once, a year ago, of a suicide under those very lights.

Mr. Jamieson left, taking a short cut to the village, and I still stood there. It must have been after eleven, and the monotonous tick of the big clock on the stairs behind me was the only sound.

Then I was conscious that some one was running up the drive. In a minute a woman darted into the area of light made by the open door, and caught me by the arm. It was Rosie—Rosie in a state of collapse from terror, and, not the least important, clutching one of my Coalport plates and a silver spoon.

She stood staring into the darkness behind, still holding the plate. I got her into the house and secured the plate; then I stood and looked down at her where she crouched tremblingly against the doorway.

"Well," I asked, "didn't your young man enjoy his meal?"

She couldn't speak. She looked at the spoon she still held—I wasn't so anxious about it: thank Heaven, it wouldn't chip—and then she stared at me.

"I appreciate your desire to have everything nice for him," I went on, "but the next time, you might take the Limoges china It's more easily duplicated and less expensive."

"I haven't a young man—not here." She had got her breath now, as I had guessed she would. "I—I have been chased by a thief, Miss Innes."

"Did he chase you out of the house and back again?" I asked.

Then Rosie began to cry—not silently, but noisily, hysterically.

I stopped her by giving her a good shake.

"What in the world is the matter with you?" I snapped. "Has the day of good common sense gone by! Sit up and tell me the whole thing." Rosie sat up then, and sniffled.

"I was coming up the drive—" she began.

"You must start with when you went DOWN the drive, with my dishes and my silver," I interrupted, but, seeing more signs of hysteria, I gave in. "Very well. You were coming up the drive—"

"I had a basket of—of silver and dishes on my arm and I was carrying the plate, because—because I was afraid I'd break it. Part-way up the road a man stepped out of the bushes, and held his arm like this, spread out, so I couldn't get past. He said—he said—'Not so fast, young lady; I want you to let me see what's in that basket.'"

She got up in her excitement and took hold of my arm.

"It was like this, Miss Innes," she said, "and say you was the man. When he said that, I screamed and ducked under his arm like this. He caught at the basket and I dropped it. I ran as fast as I could, and he came after as far as the trees. Then he stopped. Oh, Miss Innes, it must have been the man that killed that Mr. Armstrong!"

"Don't be foolish," I said. "Whoever killed Mr. Armstrong would put as much space between himself and this house as he could. Go up to bed now; and mind, if I hear of this story being repeated to the other maids, I shall deduct from your wages for every broken dish I find in the drive."

I listened to Rosie as she went up-stairs, running past the shadowy places and slamming her door. Then I sat down and looked at the Coalport plate and the silver spoon. I had brought my own china and silver, and, from all appearances, I would have little enough to take back. But though I might jeer at Rosie as much as I wished, the fact remained that some one had been on the drive that night who had no business there. Although neither had Rosie, for that matter.

I could fancy Liddy's face when she missed the extra pieces of china—she had opposed Rosie from the start. If Liddy once finds a prophecy fulfilled, especially an unpleasant one, she never allows me to forget it. It seemed to me that it was absurd to leave that china dotted along the road for her to spy the next morning; so with a sudden resolution, I opened the door again and stepped out into the darkness. As the door closed behind me I half regretted my impulse; then I shut my teeth and went on.

I have never been a nervous woman, as I said before. Moreover, a minute or two in the darkness enabled me to see things fairly well. Beulah gave me rather a start by rubbing unexpectedly against my feet; then we two, side by side, went down the drive.

There were no fragments of china, but where the grove began I picked up a silver spoon. So far Rosie's story was borne out: I began to wonder if it were not indiscreet, to say the least, this midnight prowling in a neighborhood with such a deservedly bad reputation. Then I saw something gleaming, which proved to be the handle of a cup, and a step or two farther on I found a V-shaped bit of a plate. But the most surprising thing of all was to find the basket sitting comfortably beside the road, with the rest of the broken crockery piled neatly within, and a handful of small silver, spoon, forks, and the like, on top! I could only stand and stare. Then Rosie's story was true. But where had Rosie carried her basket? And why had the thief, if he were a thief, picked up the broken china out of the road and left it, with his booty?

It was with my nearest approach to a nervous collapse that I heard the familiar throbbing of an automobile engine. As it came closer I recognized the outline of the Dragon Fly, and knew that Halsey had come back.

Strange enough it must have seemed to Halsey, too, to come across me in the middle of the night, with the skirt of my gray silk gown over my shoulders to keep off the dew, holding a red and green basket under one arm and a black cat under the other. What with relief and joy, I began to cry, right there, and very nearly wiped my eyes on Beulah in the excitement.

CHAPTER IX
JUST LIKE A GIRL

"Aunt Ray!" Halsey said from the gloom behind the lamps. "What in the world are you doing here?"

"Taking a walk," I said, trying to be composed. I don't think the answer struck either of us as being ridiculous at the time. "Oh, Halsey, where have you been?"

"Let me take you up to the house." He was in the road, and had Beulah and the basket out of my arms in a moment. I could see the car plainly now, and Warner was at the wheel—Warner in an ulster and a pair of slippers, over Heaven knows what. Jack Bailey was not there. I got in, and we went slowly and painfully up to the house.

We did not talk. What we had to say was too important to commence there, and, besides, it took all kinds of coaxing from both men to get the Dragon Fly up the last grade. Only when we had closed the front door and stood facing each other in the hall, did Halsey say anything. He slipped his strong young arm around my shoulders and turned me so I faced the light.

"Poor Aunt Ray!" he said gently. And I nearly wept again. "I—I must see Gertrude, too; we will have a three-cornered talk."

And then Gertrude herself came down the stairs. She had not been to bed, evidently: she still wore the white negligee she had worn earlier in the evening, and she limped somewhat. During her slow progress down the stairs I had time to notice one thing: Mr. Jamieson had said the woman who escaped from the cellar had worn no shoe on her right foot. Gertrude's right ankle was the one she had sprained!

The meeting between brother and sister was tense, but without tears. Halsey kissed her tenderly, and I noticed evidences of strain and anxiety in both young faces.

"Is everything—right?" she asked.

"Right as can be," with forced cheerfulness.

I lighted the living-room and we went in there. Only a half-hour before I had sat with Mr. Jamieson in that very room, listening while he overtly accused both Gertrude and Halsey of at least a knowledge of the death of Arnold Armstrong. Now Halsey was here to speak for himself: I should learn everything that had puzzled me.

"I saw it in the paper to-night for the first time," he was saying. "It knocked me dumb. When I think of this houseful of women, and a thing like that occurring!"

Gertrude's face was still set and white. "That isn't all, Halsey," she said. "You and—and Jack left almost at the time it happened. The detective here thinks that you—that we—know something about it."

"The devil he does!" Halsey's eyes were fairly starting from his head. "I beg your pardon, Aunt Ray, but—the fellow's a lunatic."

"Tell me everything, won't you, Halsey?" I begged. "Tell me where you went that night, or rather morning, and why you went as you did. This has been a terrible forty-eight hours for all of us."

He stood staring at me, and I could see the horror of the situation dawning in his face.

"I can't tell you where I went, Aunt Ray," he said, after a moment. "As to why, you will learn that soon enough. But Gertrude knows that Jack and I left the house before this thing—this horrible murder—occurred."

"Mr. Jamieson does not believe me," Gertrude said drearily. "Halsey, if the worst comes, if they should arrest you, you must—tell."

"I shall tell nothing," he said with a new sternness in his voice. "Aunt Ray, it was necessary for Jack and me to leave that night. I can not tell you why—just yet. As to where we went, if I have to depend on that as an alibi, I shall not tell. The whole thing is an absurdity, a trumped-up charge that can not possibly be serious."

"Has Mr. Bailey gone back to the city," I demanded, "or to the club?"

"Neither," defiantly; "at the present moment I do not know where he is."

"Halsey," I asked gravely, leaning forward, "have you the slightest suspicion who killed Arnold Armstrong? The police think he was admitted from within, and that he was shot down from above, by someone on the circular staircase."

"I know nothing of it," he maintained; but I fancied I caught a sudden glance at Gertrude, a flash of something that died as it came.

As quietly, as calmly as I could, I went over the whole story, from the night Liddy and I had been alone up to the strange experience of Rosie and her pursuer. The basket still stood on the table, a mute witness to this last mystifying occurrence.

"There is something else," I said hesitatingly, at the last. "Halsey, I have never told this even to Gertrude, but the morning after the crime, I found, in a tulip bed, a revolver. It—it was yours, Halsey."

For an appreciable moment Halsey stared at me. Then he turned to Gertrude.

"My revolver, Trude!" he exclaimed. "Why, Jack took my revolver with him, didn't he?"

"Oh, for Heaven's sake don't say that," I implored. "The detective thinks possibly Jack Bailey came back, and—and the thing happened then."

"He didn't come back," Halsey said sternly. "Gertrude, when you brought down a revolver that night for Jack to take with him, what one did you bring? Mine?"

Gertrude was defiant now.

"No. Yours was loaded, and I was afraid of what Jack might do. I gave him one I have had for a year or two. It was empty."

Halsey threw up both hands despairingly.

"If that isn't like a girl!" he said. "Why didn't you do what I asked you to, Gertrude? You send Bailey off with an empty gun, and throw mine in a tulip bed, of all places on earth! Mine was a thirty-eight caliber. The inquest will show, of course, that the bullet that killed Armstrong was a thirty-eight. Then where shall I be?"

"You forget," I broke in, "that I have the revolver, and that no one knows about it."

But Gertrude had risen angrily.

"I can not stand it; it is always with me," she cried. "Halsey, I did not throw your revolver into the tulip bed. I—think—you—did it—yourself!"

They stared at each other across the big library table, with young eyes all at once hard, suspicious. And then Gertrude held out both hands to him appealingly.

"We must not," she said brokenly. "Just now, with so much at stake, it—is shameful. I know you are as ignorant as I am. Make me believe it, Halsey."

Halsey soothed her as best he could, and the breach seemed healed. But long after I went to bed he sat down-stairs in the living-room alone, and I knew he was going over the case as he had learned it. Some things were clear to him that were dark to me. He knew, and Gertrude, too, why Jack Bailey and he had gone away that night, as they did. He knew where they had been for the last forty-eight hours, and why Jack Bailey had not returned with him. It seemed to me that without fuller confidence from both the children—they are always children to me—I should never be able to learn anything.

As I was finally getting ready for bed, Halsey came up-stairs and knocked at my door. When I had got into a negligee—I used to say wrapper before Gertrude came back from school—I let him in. He stood in the doorway a moment, and then he went into agonies of silent mirth. I sat down on the side of the bed and waited in severe silence for him to stop, but he only seemed to grow worse.

When he had recovered he took me by the elbow and pulled me in front of the mirror.

"'How to be beautiful,'" he quoted. "'Advice to maids and matrons,' by Beatrice Fairfax!" And then I saw myself. I had neglected to remove my wrinkle eradicators, and I presume my appearance was odd. I believe that it is a woman's duty to care for her looks, but it is much like telling a necessary falsehood—one must not be found out. By the time I got them off Halsey was serious again, and I listened to his story.

"Aunt Ray," he began, extinguishing his cigarette on the back of my ivory hair-brush, "I would give a lot to tell you the whole thing. But—I can't, for a day or so, anyhow. But one thing I might have told you a long time ago. If you had known it, you would not have suspected me for a moment of—of having anything to do with the attack on Arnold Armstrong. Goodness knows what I might do to a fellow like that, if there was enough provocation, and I had a gun in my hand—under ordinary circumstances. But—I care a great deal about Louise Armstrong, Aunt Ray. I hope to marry her some day. Is it likely I would kill her brother?"

"Her stepbrother," I corrected. "No, of course, it isn't likely, or possible. Why didn't you tell me, Halsey?"

"Well, there were two reasons," he said slowly.

"One was that you had a girl already picked out for me—"

"Nonsense," I broke in, and felt myself growing red. I had, indeed, one of the—but no matter.

"And the second reason," he pursued, "was that the Armstrongs would have none of me."

I sat bolt upright at that and gasped.

"The Armstrongs!" I repeated. "With old Peter Armstrong driving a stage across the mountains while your grandfather was war governor—"

"Well, of course, the war governor's dead, and out of the matrimonial market," Halsey interrupted. "And the present Innes admits himself he isn't good enough for—for Louise."

"Exactly," I said despairingly, "and, of course, you are taken at your own valuation. The Inneses are not always so self-depreciatory."

"Not always, no," he said, looking at me with his boyish smile. "Fortunately, Louise doesn't agree with her family. She's willing to take me, war governor or no, provided her mother consents. She isn't overly-fond of her stepfather, but she adores her mother. And now, can't you see where this thing puts me? Down and out, with all of them."

"But the whole thing is absurd," I argued. "And besides, Gertrude's sworn statement that you left before Arnold Armstrong came would clear you at once."

Halsey got up and began to pace the room, and the air of cheerfulness dropped like a mask.

"She can't swear it," he said finally. "Gertrude's story was true as far as it went, but she didn't tell everything. Arnold Armstrong came here at two-thirty—came into the billiard-room and left in five minutes. He came to bring—something."

"Halsey," I cried, "you MUST tell me the whole truth. Every time I see a way for you to escape you block it yourself with this wall of mystery. What did he bring?"

"A telegram—for Bailey," he said. "It came by special messenger from town, and was—most important. Bailey had started for here, and the messenger had gone back to the city. The steward gave it to Arnold, who had been drinking all day and couldn't sleep, and was going for a stroll in the direction of Sunnyside."

"And he brought it?"

"Yes."

"What was in the telegram?"

"I can tell you—as soon as certain things are made public. It is only a matter of days now," gloomily.

"And Gertrude's story of a telephone message?"

"Poor Trude!" he half whispered. "Poor loyal little girl! Aunt Ray, there was no such message. No doubt your detective already knows that and discredits all Gertrude told him."

"And when she went back, it was to get—the telegram?"

"Probably," Halsey said slowly. "When you get to thinking about it, Aunt Ray, it looks bad for all three of us, doesn't it? And yet—I will take my oath none of us even inadvertently killed that poor devil."

I looked at the closed door into Gertrude's dressing-room, and lowered my voice.

"The same horrible thought keeps recurring to me," I whispered. "Halsey, Gertrude probably had your revolver: she must have examined it, anyhow, that night. After you—and Jack had gone, what if that ruffian came back, and she—and she—"

I couldn't finish. Halsey stood looking at me with shut lips.

"She might have heard him fumbling at the door he had no key, the police say—and thinking it was you, or Jack, she admitted him. When she saw her mistake she ran up the stairs, a step or two, and turning, like an animal at bay, she fired."

Halsey had his hand over my lips before I finished, and in that position we stared each at the other, our stricken glances crossing.

"The revolver—my revolver—thrown into the tulip bed!" he muttered to himself. "Thrown perhaps from an upper window: you say it was buried deep. Her prostration ever since, her— Aunt Ray, you don't think it was Gertrude who fell down the clothes chute?"

I could only nod my head in a hopeless affirmative.

CHAPTER X
THE TRADERS BANK

The morning after Halsey's return was Tuesday. Arnold Armstrong had been found dead at the foot of the circular staircase at three o'clock on Sunday morning. The funeral services were to be held on Tuesday, and the interment of the body was to be deferred until the Armstrongs arrived from California. No one, I think, was very sorry that Arnold Armstrong was dead, but the manner of his death aroused some sympathy and an enormous amount of curiosity. Mrs. Ogden Fitzhugh, a cousin, took charge of the arrangements, and everything, I believe, was as quiet as possible. I gave Thomas Johnson and Mrs. Watson permission to go into town to pay their last respects to the dead man, but for some reason they did not care to go.

Halsey spent part of the day with Mr. Jamieson, but he said nothing of what happened. He looked grave and anxious, and he had a long conversation with Gertrude late in the afternoon.

Tuesday evening found us quiet, with the quiet that precedes an explosion. Gertrude and Halsey were both gloomy and distraught, and as Liddy had already discovered that some of the china was broken—it is impossible to have any secrets from an old servant—I was not in a pleasant humor myself. Warner brought up the afternoon mail and the evening papers at seven—I was curious to know what the papers said of the murder. We had turned away at least a dozen reporters. But I read over the head-line that ran half-way across the top of the Gazette twice before I comprehended it. Halsey had opened the Chronicle and was staring at it fixedly.

"The Traders' Bank closes its doors!" was what I read, and then I put down the paper and looked across the table.

"Did you know of this?" I asked Halsey.

"I expected it. But not so soon," he replied.

"And you?" to Gertrude.

"Jack—told us—something," Gertrude said faintly. "Oh, Halsey, what can he do now?"

"Jack!" I said scornfully. "Your Jack's flight is easy enough to explain now. And you helped him, both of you, to get away! You get that from your mother; it isn't an Innes trait. Do you know that every dollar you have, both of you, is in that bank?"

Gertrude tried to speak, but Halsey stopped her.

"That isn't all, Gertrude," he said quietly; "Jack is—under arrest."

"Under arrest!" Gertrude screamed, and tore the paper out of his hand. She glanced at the heading, then she crumpled the newspaper into a ball and flung it to the floor. While Halsey, looking stricken and white, was trying to smooth it out and read it, Gertrude had dropped her head on the table and was sobbing stormily.

I have the clipping somewhere, but just now I can remember only the essentials.

On the afternoon before, Monday, while the Traders' Bank was in the rush of closing hour, between two and three, Mr. Jacob Trautman, President of the Pearl Brewing Company, came into the bank to lift a loan. As security for the loan he had deposited some three hundred International Steamship Company 5's, in total value three hundred thousand dollars. Mr.

Trautman went to the loan clerk and, after certain formalities had been gone through, the loan clerk went to the vault. Mr. Trautman, who was a large and genial German, waited for a time, whistling under his breath. The loan clerk did not come back. After an interval, Mr. Trautman saw the loan clerk emerge from the vault and go to the assistant cashier: the two went hurriedly to the vault. A lapse of another ten minutes, and the assistant cashier came out and approached Mr. Trautman. He was noticeably white and trembling. Mr. Trautman was told that through an oversight the bonds had been misplaced, and was asked to return the following morning, when everything would be made all right.

Mr. Trautman, however, was a shrewd business man, and he did not like the appearance of things. He left the bank apparently satisfied, and within thirty minutes he had called up three different members of the Traders' Board of Directors. At three-thirty there was a hastily convened board meeting, with some stormy scenes, and late in the afternoon a national bank examiner was in possession of the books. The bank had not opened for business on Tuesday.

At twelve-thirty o'clock the Saturday before, as soon as the business of the day was closed, Mr. John Bailey, the cashier of the defunct bank, had taken his hat and departed. During the afternoon he had called up Mr. Aronson, a member of the board, and said he was ill, and might not be at the bank for a day or two. As Bailey was highly thought of, Mr. Aronson merely expressed a regret. From that time until Monday night, when Mr. Bailey had surrendered to the police, little was known of his movements. Some time after one on Saturday he had entered the Western Union office at Cherry and White Streets and had sent two telegrams. He was at the Greenwood Country Club on Saturday night, and appeared unlike himself. It was reported that he would be released under enormous bond, some time that day, Tuesday.

The article closed by saying that while the officers of the bank refused to talk until the examiner had finished his work, it was known that securities aggregating a million and a quarter were missing. Then there was a diatribe on the possibility of such an occurrence; on the folly of a one-man bank, and of a Board of Directors that met only to lunch together and to listen to a brief report from the cashier, and on the poor policy of a government that arranges a three or four-day examination twice a year. The mystery, it insinuated, had not been cleared by the arrest of the cashier. Before now minor officials had been used to cloak the misdeeds of men higher up. Inseparable as the words "speculation" and "peculation" have grown to be, John Bailey was not known to be in the stock market. His only words, after his surrender, had been "Send for Mr. Armstrong at once." The telegraph message which had finally reached the President of the Traders' Bank, in an interior town in California, had been responded to by a telegram from Doctor Walker, the young physician who was traveling with the Armstrong family, saying that Paul Armstrong was very ill and unable to travel.

That was how things stood that Tuesday evening. The Traders' Bank had suspended payment, and John Bailey was under arrest, charged with wrecking it; Paul Armstrong lay very ill in California, and his only son had been murdered two days before. I sat dazed and bewildered. The children's money was gone: that was bad enough, though I had plenty, if they would let me share. But Gertrude's grief was beyond any power of mine to comfort; the man she had chosen stood accused of a colossal embezzlement—and even worse. For in the instant that I sat there I seemed to see the coils closing around John Bailey as the murderer of Arnold Armstrong.

Gertrude lifted her head at last and stared across the table at Halsey.

"Why did he do it?" she wailed. "Couldn't you stop him, Halsey? It was suicidal to go back!"

Halsey was looking steadily through the windows of the breakfast-room, but it was evident he saw nothing.

"It was the only thing he could do, Trude," he said at last. "Aunt Ray, when I found Jack at the Greenwood Club last Saturday night, he was frantic. I can not talk until Jack tells me I may, but—he is absolutely innocent of all this, believe me. I thought, Trude and I thought, we were helping him, but it was the wrong way. He came back. Isn't that the act of an innocent man?"

"Then why did he leave at all?" I asked, unconvinced. "What innocent man would run away from here at three o'clock in the morning? Doesn't it look rather as though he thought it impossible to escape?"

Gertrude rose angrily. "You are not even just!" she flamed. "You don't know anything about it, and you condemn him!"

"I know that we have all lost a great deal of money," I said. "I shall believe Mr. Bailey innocent the moment he is shown to be. You profess to know the truth, but you can not tell me! What am I to think?"

Halsey leaned over and patted my hand.

"You must take us on faith," he said. "Jack Bailey hasn't a penny that doesn't belong to him; the guilty man will be known in a day or so."

"I shall believe that when it is proved," I said grimly. "In the meantime, I take no one on faith. The Inneses never do."

Gertrude, who had been standing aloof at a window, turned suddenly. "But when the bonds are offered for sale, Halsey, won't the thief be detected at once?"

Halsey turned with a superior smile.

"It wouldn't be done that way," he said. "They would be taken out of the vault by some one who had access to it, and used as collateral for a loan in another bank. It would be possible to realize eighty per cent. of their face value."

"In cash?"

"In cash."

"But the man who did it—he would be known?"

"Yes. I tell you both, as sure as I stand here, I believe that Paul Armstrong looted his own bank. I believe he has a million at least, as the result, and that he will never come back. I'm worse than a pauper now. I can't ask Louise to share nothing a year with me and when I think of this disgrace for her, I'm crazy."

The most ordinary events of life seemed pregnant with possibilities that day, and when Halsey was called to the telephone, I ceased all pretense at eating. When he came back from the telephone his face showed that something had occurred. He waited, however, until Thomas left the dining-room: then he told us.

"Paul Armstrong is dead," he announced gravely. "He died this morning in California. Whatever he did, he is beyond the law now."

Gertrude turned pale.

"And the only man who could have cleared Jack can never do it!" she said despairingly.

"Also," I replied coldly, "Mr. Armstrong is for ever beyond the power of defending himself. When your Jack comes to me, with some two hundred thousand dollars in his hands, which is about what you have lost, I shall believe him innocent."

Halsey threw his cigarette away and turned on me.

"There you go!" he exclaimed. "If he was the thief, he could return the money, of course. If he is innocent, he probably hasn't a tenth of that amount in the world. In his hands! That's like a woman."

Gertrude, who had been pale and despairing during the early part of the conversation, had flushed an indignant red. She got up and drew herself to her slender height, looking down at me with the scorn of the young and positive.

"You are the only mother I ever had," she said tensely. "I have given you all I would have given my mother, had she lived—my love, my trust. And now, when I need you most, you fail me. I tell you, John Bailey is a good man, an honest man. If you say he is not, you—you—"

"Gertrude," Halsey broke in sharply. She dropped beside the table and, burying her face in her arms broke into a storm of tears.

"I love him—love him," she sobbed, in a surrender that was totally unlike her. "Oh, I never thought it would be like this. I can't bear it. I can't."

Halsey and I stood helpless before the storm. I would have tried to comfort her, but she had put me away, and there was something aloof in her grief, something new and strange. At last, when her sorrow had subsided to the dry shaking sobs of a tired child, without raising her head she put out one groping hand.

"Aunt Ray!" she whispered. In a moment I was on my knees beside her, her arm around my neck, her cheek against my hair.

"Where am I in this?" Halsey said suddenly and tried to put his arms around us both. It was a welcome distraction, and Gertrude was soon herself again. The little storm had cleared the air. Nevertheless, my opinion remained unchanged. There was much to be cleared up before I would consent to any renewal of my acquaintance with John Bailey. And Halsey and Gertrude knew it, knowing me.

CHAPTER XI
HALSEY MAKES A CAPTURE

It was about half-past eight when we left the dining-room and still engrossed with one subject, the failure of the bank and its attendant evils Halsey and I went out into the grounds for a stroll Gertrude followed us shortly. "The light was thickening," to appropriate Shakespeare's description of twilight, and once again the tree-toads and the crickets were making night throb with their tiny life. It was almost oppressively lonely, in spite of its beauty, and I felt a sickening pang of homesickness for my city at night—for the clatter of horses' feet on cemented paving, for the lights, the voices, the sound of children playing. The country after dark oppresses me. The stars, quite eclipsed in the city by the electric lights, here become insistent, assertive. Whether I want to or not, I find myself looking for the few I know by name, and feeling ridiculously new and small by contrast—always an unpleasant sensation.

After Gertrude joined us, we avoided any further mention of the murder. To Halsey, as to me, there was ever present, I am sure, the thought of our conversation of the night before. As we strolled back and forth along the drive, Mr. Jamieson emerged from the shadow of the trees.

"Good evening," he said, managing to include Gertrude in his bow.

Gertrude had never been even ordinarily courteous to him, and she nodded coldly. Halsey, however, was more cordial, although we were all constrained enough. He and Gertrude went on together, leaving the detective to walk with me. As soon as they were out of earshot, he turned to me.

"Do you know, Miss Innes," he said, "the deeper I go into this thing, the more strange it seems to me. I am very sorry for Miss Gertrude. It looks as if Bailey, whom she has tried so hard to save, is worse than a rascal; and after her plucky fight for him, it seems hard."

I looked through the dusk to where Gertrude's light dinner dress gleamed among the trees. She HAD made a plucky fight, poor child. Whatever she might have been driven to do, I could find nothing but a deep sympathy for her. If she had only come to me with the whole truth then!

"Miss Innes," Mr. Jamieson was saying, "in the last three days, have you seen a—any suspicious figures around the grounds? Any—woman?"

"No," I replied. "I have a houseful of maids that will bear watching, one and all. But there has been no strange woman near the house or Liddy would have seen her, you may be sure. She has a telescopic eye."

Mr. Jamieson looked thoughtful.

"It may not amount to anything," he said slowly. "It is difficult to get any perspective on things around here, because every one down in the village is sure he saw the murderer, either before or since the crime. And half of them will stretch a point or two as to facts, to be obliging. But the man who drives the hack down there tells a story that may possibly prove to be important."

"I have heard it, I think. Was it the one the parlor maid brought up yesterday, about a ghost wringing its hands on the roof? Or perhaps it's the one the milk-boy heard: a tramp washing a dirty shirt, presumably bloody, in the creek below the bridge?"

I could see the gleam of Mr. Jamieson's teeth, as he smiled.

"Neither," he said. "But Matthew Geist, which is our friend's name, claims that on Saturday night, at nine-thirty, a veiled lady—"

"I knew it would be a veiled lady," I broke in.

"A veiled lady," he persisted, "who was apparently young and beautiful, engaged his hack and asked to be driven to Sunnyside. Near the gate, however, she made him stop, in spite of his remonstrances, saying she preferred to walk to the house. She paid him, and he left her there. Now, Miss Innes, you had no such visitor, I believe?"

"None," I said decidedly.

"Geist thought it might be a maid, as you had got a supply that day. But he said her getting out near the gate puzzled him. Anyhow, we have now one veiled lady, who, with the ghostly intruder of Friday night, makes two assets that I hardly know what to do with."

"It is mystifying," I admitted, "although I can think of one possible explanation. The path from the Greenwood Club to the village enters the road near the lodge gate. A woman who wished to reach the Country Club, unperceived, might choose such a method. There are plenty of women there."

I think this gave him something to ponder, for in a short time he said good night and left. But I myself was far from satisfied. I was determined, however, on one thing. If my suspicions—for I had suspicions—were true, I would make my own investigations, and Mr. Jamieson should learn only what was good for him to know.

We went back to the house, and Gertrude, who was more like herself since her talk with Halsey, sat down at the mahogany desk in the living-room to write a letter. Halsey prowled up and down the entire east wing, now in the card-room, now in the billiard-room, and now and then blowing his clouds of tobacco smoke among the pink and gold hangings of the drawing-room. After a little I joined him in the billiard-room, and together we went over the details of the discovery of the body.

The card-room was quite dark. Where we sat, in the billiard-room, only one of the side brackets was lighted, and we spoke in subdued tones, as the hour and the subject seemed to demand. When I spoke of the figure Liddy and I had seen on the porch through the card-room window Friday night, Halsey sauntered into the darkened room, and together we stood there, much as Liddy and I had done that other night.

The window was the same grayish rectangle in the blackness as before. A few feet away in the hall was the spot where the body of Arnold Armstrong had been found. I was a bit nervous, and I put my hand on Halsey's sleeve. Suddenly, from the top of the staircase above us came the sound of a cautious footstep. At first I was not sure, but Halsey's attitude told me he had heard and was listening. The step, slow, measured, infinitely cautious, was nearer now. Halsey tried to loosen my fingers, but I was in a paralysis of fright.

The swish of a body against the curving rail, as if for guidance, was plain enough, and now whoever it was had reached the foot of the staircase and had caught a glimpse of our rigid silhouettes against the billiard-room doorway. Halsey threw me off then and strode forward.

"Who is it?" he called imperiously, and took a half dozen rapid strides toward the foot of the staircase. Then I heard him mutter something; there was the crash of a falling body, the slam of the outer door, and, for an instant, quiet. I screamed, I think. Then I remember turning on the lights and finding Halsey, white with fury, trying to untangle himself from something warm and fleecy. He had cut his forehead a little on the lowest step of the stairs, and he was rather a ghastly sight.

He flung the white object at me, and, jerking open the outer door, raced into the darkness.

Gertrude had come on hearing the noise, and now we stood, staring at each other over—of all things on earth—a white silk and wool blanket, exquisitely fine! It was the most unghostly thing in the world, with its lavender border and its faint scent. Gertrude was the first to speak.

"Somebody—had it?" she asked.

"Yes. Halsey tried to stop whoever it was and fell. Gertrude, that blanket is not mine. I have never seen before."

She held it up and looked at it: then she went to the door on to the veranda and threw it open. Perhaps a hundred feet from the house were two figures, that moved slowly toward us as we looked.

When they came within range of the light, I recognized Halsey, and with him Mrs. Watson, the housekeeper.

CHAPTER XII
ONE MYSTERY FOR ANOTHER

The most commonplace incident takes on a new appearance if the attendant circumstances are unusual. There was no reason on earth why Mrs. Watson should not have carried a blanket down the east wing staircase, if she so desired. But to take a blanket down at eleven o'clock at night, with every precaution as to noise, and, when discovered, to fling it at Halsey and bolt—Halsey's word, and a good one—into the grounds,—this made the incident more than significant.

They moved slowly across the lawn and up the steps. Halsey was talking quietly, and Mrs. Watson was looking down and listening. She was a woman of a certain amount of dignity, most efficient, so far as I could see, although Liddy would have found fault if she dared. But just now Mrs. Watson's face was an enigma. She was defiant, I think, under her mask of submission, and she still showed the effect of nervous shock.

"Mrs. Watson," I said severely, "will you be so good as to explain this rather unusual occurrence?"

"I don't think it so unusual, Miss Innes." Her voice was deep and very clear: just now it was somewhat tremulous. "I was taking a blanket down to Thomas, who is—not well to-night, and I used this staircase, as being nearer the path to the lodge. When—Mr. Innes called and then rushed at me, I—I was alarmed, and flung the blanket at him."

Halsey was examining the cut on his forehead in a small mirror on the wall. It was not much of an injury, but it had bled freely, and his appearance was rather terrifying.

"Thomas ill?" he said, over his shoulder. "Why, *I* thought I saw Thomas out there as you made that cyclonic break out of the door and over the porch."

I could see that under pretense of examining his injury he was watching her through the mirror.

"Is this one of the servants' blankets, Mrs. Watson?" I asked, holding up its luxurious folds to the light.

"Everything else is locked away," she replied. Which was true enough, no doubt. I had rented the house without bed furnishings.

"If Thomas is ill," Halsey said, "some member of the family ought to go down to see him. You needn't bother, Mrs. Watson. I will take the blanket."

She drew herself up quickly, as if in protest, but she found nothing to say. She stood smoothing the folds of her dead black dress, her face as white as chalk above it. Then she seemed to make up her mind.

"Very well, Mr. Innes," she said. "Perhaps you would better go. I have done all I could."

And then she turned and went up the circular staircase, moving slowly and with a certain dignity. Below, the three of us stared at one another across the intervening white blanket.

"Upon my word," Halsey broke out, "this place is a walking nightmare. I have the feeling that we three outsiders who have paid our money for the privilege of staying in this spook-factory, are living on the very top of things. We're on the lid, so to speak. Now and then we get a sight of the things inside, but we are not a part of them."

"Do you suppose," Gertrude asked doubtfully, "that she really meant that blanket for Thomas?"

"Thomas was standing beside that magnolia tree," Halsey replied, "when I ran after Mrs. Watson. It's down to this, Aunt Ray. Rosie's basket and Mrs. Watson's blanket can only mean one thing: there is somebody hiding or being hidden in the lodge. It wouldn't surprise me if we hold the key to the whole situation now. Anyhow, I'm going to the lodge to investigate."

Gertrude wanted to go, too, but she looked so shaken that I insisted she should not. I sent for Liddy to help her to bed, and then Halsey and I started for the lodge. The grass was heavy with dew, and, man-like, Halsey chose the shortest way across the lawn. Half-way, however, he stopped.

"We'd better go by the drive," he said. "This isn't a lawn; it's a field. Where's the gardener these days?"

"There isn't any," I said meekly. "We have been thankful enough, so far, to have our meals prepared and served and the beds aired. The gardener who belongs here is working at the club."

"Remind me to-morrow to send out a man from town," he said. "I know the very fellow."

I record this scrap of conversation, just as I have tried to put down anything and everything that had a bearing on what followed, because the gardener Halsey sent the next day played an important part in the events of the next few weeks—events that culminated, as you know, by stirring the country profoundly. At that time, however, I was busy trying to keep my skirts dry, and paid little or no attention to what seemed then a most trivial remark.

Along the drive I showed Halsey where I had found Rosie's basket with the bits of broken china piled inside. He was rather skeptical.

"Warner probably," he said when I had finished. "Began it as a joke on Rosie, and ended by picking up the broken china out of the road, knowing it would play hob with the tires of the car." Which shows how near one can come to the truth, and yet miss it altogether.

At the lodge everything was quiet. There was a light in the sitting-room down-stairs, and a faint gleam, as if from a shaded lamp, in one of the upper rooms. Halsey stopped and examined the lodge with calculating eyes.

"I don't know, Aunt Ray," he said dubiously; "this is hardly a woman's affair. If there's a scrap of any kind, you hike for the timber." Which was Halsey's solicitous care for me, put into vernacular.

"I shall stay right here," I said, and crossing the small veranda, now shaded and fragrant with honeysuckle, I hammered the knocker on the door.

Thomas opened the door himself—Thomas, fully dressed and in his customary health. I had the blanket over my arm.

"I brought the blanket, Thomas," I said; "I am sorry you are so ill."

The old man stood staring at me and then at the blanket. His confusion under other circumstances would have been ludicrous.

"What! Not ill?" Halsey said from the step. "Thomas, I'm afraid you've been malingering."

Thomas seemed to have been debating something with himself. Now he stepped out on the porch and closed the door gently behind him.

"I reckon you bettah come in, Mis' Innes," he said, speaking cautiously. "It's got so I dunno what to do, and it's boun' to come out some time er ruther."

He threw the door open then, and I stepped inside, Halsey close behind. In the sitting-room the old negro turned with quiet dignity to Halsey.

"You bettah sit down, sah," he said. "It's a place for a woman, sah."

Things were not turning out the way Halsey expected. He sat down on the center-table, with his hands thrust in his pockets, and watched me as I followed Thomas up the narrow stairs. At the top a woman was standing, and a second glance showed me it was Rosie.

She shrank back a little, but I said nothing. And then Thomas motioned to a partly open door, and I went in.

The lodge boasted three bedrooms up-stairs, all comfortably furnished. In this one, the largest and airiest, a night lamp was burning, and by its light I could make out a plain white metal bed. A girl was asleep there—or in a half stupor, for she muttered something now and then. Rosie had taken her courage in her hands, and coming in had turned up the light. It was only then that I knew. Fever-flushed, ill as she was, I recognized Louise Armstrong.

I stood gazing down at her in a stupor of amazement. Louise here, hiding at the lodge, ill and alone! Rosie came up to the bed and smoothed the white counterpane.

"I am afraid she is worse to-night," she ventured at last. I put my hand on the sick girl's forehead. It was burning with fever, and I turned to where Thomas lingered in the hallway.

"Will you tell me what you mean, Thomas Johnson, by not telling me this before?" I demanded indignantly.

Thomas quailed.

"Mis' Louise wouldn' let me," he said earnestly. "I wanted to. She ought to 'a' had a doctor the night she came, but she wouldn' hear to it. Is she—is she very bad, Mis' Innes?"

"Bad enough," I said coldly. "Send Mr. Innes up."

Halsey came up the stairs slowly, looking rather interested and inclined to be amused. For a moment he could not see anything distinctly in the darkened room; he stopped, glanced at Rosie and at me, and then his eyes fell on the restless head on the pillow.

I think he felt who it was before he really saw her; he crossed the room in a couple of strides and bent over the bed.

"Louise!" he said softly; but she did not reply, and her eyes showed no recognition. Halsey was young, and illness was new to him. He straightened himself slowly, still watching her, and caught my arm.

"She's dying, Aunt Ray!" he said huskily. "Dying! Why, she doesn't know me!"

"Fudge!" I snapped, being apt to grow irritable when my sympathies are aroused. "She's doing nothing of the sort,—and don't pinch my arm. If you want something to do, go and choke Thomas."

But at that moment Louise roused from her stupor to cough, and at the end of the paroxysm, as Rosie laid her back, exhausted, she knew us. That was all Halsey wanted; to him consciousness was recovery. He dropped on his knees beside the bed, and tried to tell her she was all right, and we would bring her around in a hurry, and how beautiful she looked—only to break down utterly and have to stop. And at that I came to my senses, and put him out.

"This instant!" I ordered, as he hesitated. "And send Rosie here."

He did not go far. He sat on the top step of the stairs, only leaving to telephone for a doctor, and getting in everybody's way in his eagerness to fetch and carry. I got him away finally, by sending him to fix up the car as a sort of ambulance, in case the doctor would allow the sick girl to be moved. He sent Gertrude down to the lodge loaded with all manner of impossible things, including an armful of Turkish towels and a box of mustard plasters, and as the two girls had known each other somewhat before, Louise brightened perceptibly when she saw her.

When the doctor from Englewood—the Casanova doctor, Doctor Walker, being away—had started for Sunnyside, and I had got Thomas to stop trying to explain what he did not understand himself, I had a long talk with the old man, and this is what I learned.

On Saturday evening before, about ten o'clock, he had been reading in the sitting-room down-stairs, when some one rapped at the door. The old man was alone, Warner not having arrived, and at first he was uncertain about opening the door. He did so finally, and was amazed at being confronted by Louise Armstrong. Thomas was an old family servant, having been with the present Mrs. Armstrong since she was a child, and he was overwhelmed at seeing Louise. He saw that she was excited and tired, and he drew her into the sitting-room and made her sit down. After a while he went to the house and brought Mrs. Watson, and they talked until late. The old man said Louise was in trouble, and seemed frightened. Mrs. Watson made some tea and took it to the lodge, but Louise made them both promise to keep her presence a secret. She had not known that Sunnyside was rented, and whatever her trouble was, this complicated things. She seemed puzzled. Her stepfather and her mother were still in California—that was all she would say about them. Why she had run away no one could imagine. Mr. Arnold Armstrong was at the Greenwood Club, and at last Thomas, not knowing what else to do, went over there along the path. It was almost midnight. Part-way over he met Armstrong himself and brought him to the lodge. Mrs. Watson had gone to the house for some bed-linen, it having been arranged that under the circumstances Louise would be better at the lodge until morning. Arnold Armstrong and Louise had a long conference, during which he was heard to storm and become very violent. When he left it was after two. He had gone up to the house—Thomas did not know why—and at three o'clock he was shot at the foot of the circular staircase.

The following morning Louise had been ill. She had asked for Arnold, and was told he had left town. Thomas had not the moral courage to tell her of the crime. She refused a doctor, and shrank morbidly from having her presence known. Mrs. Watson and Thomas had had their hands full, and at last Rosie had been enlisted to help them. She carried necessary provisions—little enough—to the lodge, and helped to keep the secret.

Thomas told me quite frankly that he had been anxious to keep Louise's presence hidden for this reason: they had all seen Arnold Armstrong that night, and he, himself, for one, was known to have had no very friendly feeling for the dead man. As to the reason for Louise's flight from California, or why she had not gone to the Fitzhughs', or to some of her people in town, he had no more information than I had. With the death of her stepfather and the prospect of the immediate return of the family, things had become more and more impossible. I gathered that Thomas was as relieved as I at the turn events had taken. No, she did not know of either of the deaths in the family.

Taken all around, I had only substituted one mystery for another.

If I knew now why Rosie had taken the basket of dishes, I did not know who had spoken to her and followed her along the drive. If I knew that Louise was in the lodge, I did not know why she was there. If I knew that Arnold Armstrong had spent some time in the lodge the night before he was murdered, I was no nearer the solution of the crime. Who was the midnight intruder who had so alarmed Liddy and myself? Who had fallen down the clothes chute? Was Gertrude's lover a villain or a victim? Time was to answer all these things.

CHAPTER XIII
LOUISE

The doctor from Englewood came very soon, and I went up to see the sick girl with him. Halsey had gone to supervise the fitting of the car with blankets and pillows, and Gertrude was opening and airing Louise's own rooms at the house. Her private sitting-room, bedroom and dressing-room were as they had been when we came. They occupied the end of the east wing, beyond the circular staircase, and we had not even opened them.

The girl herself was too ill to notice what was being done. When, with the help of the doctor, who was a fatherly man with a family of girls at home, we got her to the house and up the stairs into bed, she dropped into a feverish sleep, which lasted until morning. Doctor Stewart—that was the Englewood doctor—stayed almost all night, giving the medicine himself, and watching her closely. Afterward he told me that she had had a narrow escape from pneumonia, and that the cerebral symptoms had been rather alarming. I said I was glad it wasn't an "itis" of some kind, anyhow, and he smiled solemnly.

He left after breakfast, saying that he thought the worst of the danger was over, and that she must be kept very quiet.

"The shock of two deaths, I suppose, has done this," he remarked, picking up his case. "It has been very deplorable."

I hastened to set him right.

"She does not know of either, Doctor," I said. "Please do not mention them to her."

He looked as surprised as a medical man ever does.

"I do not know the family," he said, preparing to get into his top buggy. "Young Walker, down in Casanova, has been attending them. I understand he is going to marry this young lady."

"You have been misinformed," I said stiffly. "Miss Armstrong is going to marry my nephew."

The doctor smiled as he picked up the reins.

"Young ladies are changeable these days," he said. "We thought the wedding was to occur soon. Well, I will stop in this afternoon to see how my patient is getting along."

He drove away then, and I stood looking after him. He was a doctor of the old school, of the class of family practitioner that is fast dying out; a loyal and honorable gentleman who was at once physician and confidential adviser to his patients. When I was a girl we called in the doctor alike when we had measles, or when mother's sister died in the far West. He cut out redundant tonsils and brought the babies with the same air of inspiring self-confidence. Nowadays it requires a different specialist for each of these occurrences. When the babies cried, old Doctor Wainwright gave them peppermint and dropped warm sweet oil in their ears with sublime faith that if it was not colic it was earache. When, at the end of a year, father met him driving in his high side-bar buggy with the white mare ambling along, and asked for a bill, the doctor used to go home, estimate what his services were worth for that period, divide it in half—I don't think he kept any books—and send father a statement, in a cramped hand, on a sheet of ruled white paper. He was an honored guest at all the weddings, christenings, and funerals—yes, funerals—for every one knew he had done his best, and there was no gainsaying the ways of Providence.

Ah, well, Doctor Wainwright is gone, and I am an elderly woman with an increasing tendency to live in the past. The contrast between my old doctor at home and the Casanova doctor, Frank Walker, always rouses me to wrath and digression.

Some time about noon of that day, Wednesday, Mrs. Ogden Fitzhugh telephoned me. I have the barest acquaintance with her—she managed to be put on the governing board of the Old Ladies' Home and ruins their digestions by sending them ice-cream and cake on every holiday. Beyond that, and her reputation at bridge, which is insufferably bad—she is the worst player at the bridge club—I know little of her. It was she who had taken charge of Arnold Armstrong's funeral, however, and I went at once to the telephone.

"Yes," I said, "this is Miss Innes."

"Miss Innes," she said volubly, "I have just received a very strange telegram from my cousin, Mrs. Armstrong. Her husband died yesterday, in California and—wait, I will read you the message."

I knew what was coming, and I made up my mind at once. If Louise Armstrong had a good and sufficient reason for leaving her people and coming home, a reason, moreover, that kept her from going at once to Mrs. Ogden Fitzhugh, and that brought her to the lodge at Sunnyside instead, it was not my intention to betray her. Louise herself must notify her people. I do not justify myself now, but remember, I was in a peculiar position toward the Armstrong family. I was connected most unpleasantly with a cold-blooded crime, and my niece and nephew were practically beggared, either directly or indirectly, through the head of the family.

Mrs. Fitzhugh had found the message.

"'Paul died yesterday. Heart disease,'" she read. "'Wire at once if Louise is with you.' You see, Miss Innes, Louise must have started east, and Fanny is alarmed about her."

"Yes," I said.

"Louise is not here," Mrs. Fitzhugh went on, "and none of her friends—the few who are still in town—has seen her. I called you because Sunnyside was not rented when she went away, and Louise might have, gone there."

"I am sorry, Mrs. Fitzhugh, but I can not help you," I said, and was immediately filled with compunction. Suppose Louise grew worse? Who was I to play Providence in this case? The anxious mother certainly had a right to know that her daughter was in good hands. So I broke in on Mrs. Fitzhugh's voluble excuses for disturbing me.

"Mrs. Fitzhugh," I said. "I was going to let you think I knew nothing about Louise Armstrong, but I have changed my mind. Louise is here, with me." There was a clatter of ejaculations at the other end of the wire. "She is ill, and not able to be moved. Moreover, she is unable to see any one. I wish you would wire her mother that she is with me, and tell her not to worry. No, I do not know why she came east."

"But my dear Miss Innes!" Mrs. Fitzhugh began. I cut in ruthlessly.

"I will send for you as soon as she can see you," I said. "No, she is not in a critical state now, but the doctor says she must have absolute quiet."

When I had hung up the receiver, I sat down to think. So Louise had fled from her people in California, and had come east alone! It was not a new idea, but why had she done it? It occurred to me that Doctor Walker might be concerned in it, might possibly have bothered her with unwelcome attentions; but it seemed to me that Louise was hardly a girl to take refuge in flight under such circumstances. She had always been high-spirited, with the well-poised head and buoyant step of the outdoors girl. It must have been much more in keeping with Louise's character, as I knew it, to resent vigorously any unwelcome attentions from Doctor Walker. It was the suitor whom I should have expected to see in headlong flight, not the lady in the case.

The puzzle was no clearer at the end of the half-hour. I picked up the morning papers, which were still full of the looting of the Traders' Bank, the interest at fever height again, on account of Paul Armstrong's death. The bank examiners were working on the books, and said nothing for publication: John Bailey had been released on bond. The body of Paul Armstrong would arrive Sunday and would be buried from the Armstrong town house. There were rumors that the dead man's estate had been a comparatively small one. The last paragraph was the important one.

Walter P. Broadhurst, of the Marine Bank, had produced two hundred American Traction bonds, which had been placed as security with the Marine Bank for a loan of one hundred and sixty thousand dollars, made to Paul Armstrong, just before his California trip. The bonds were a part of the missing traction bonds from the Traders' Bank! While this involved the late president of the wrecked bank, to my mind it by no means cleared its cashier.

The gardener mentioned by Halsey came out about two o'clock in the afternoon, and walked up from the station. I was favorably impressed by him. His references were good—he had been employed by the Brays' until they went to Europe, and he looked young and vigorous. He asked for one assistant, and I was glad enough to get off so easily. He was a pleasant-faced young fellow, with black hair and blue eyes, and his name was Alexander Graham. I have been particular about Alex, because, as I said before, he played an important part later.

That afternoon I had a new insight into the character of the dead banker. I had my first conversation with Louise. She sent for me, and against my better judgment I went. There were so many things she could not be told, in her weakened condition, that I dreaded the interview. It was much easier than I expected, however, because she asked no questions.

Gertrude had gone to bed, having been up almost all night, and Halsey was absent on one of those mysterious absences of his that grew more and more frequent as time went on, until it culminated in the event of the night of June the tenth. Liddy was in attendance in the sick-room. There being little or nothing to do, she seemed to spend her time smoothing the wrinkles from the counterpane. Louise lay under a field of virgin white, folded back at an angle of geometrical exactness, and necessitating a readjustment every time the sick girl turned.

Liddy heard my approach and came out to meet me. She seemed to be in a perpetual state of goose-flesh, and she had got in the habit of looking past me when she talked, as if she saw things. It had the effect of making me look over my shoulder to see what she was staring at, and was intensely irritating.

"She's awake," Liddy said, looking uneasily down the circular staircase, which was beside me. "She was talkin' in her sleep something awful—about dead men and coffins."

"Liddy," I said sternly, "did you breathe a word about everything not being right here?"

Liddy's gaze had wandered to the door of the chute, now bolted securely.

"Not a word," she said, "beyond asking her a question or two, which there was no harm in. She says there never was a ghost known here."

I glared at her, speechless, and closing the door into Louise's boudoir, to Liddy's great disappointment, I went on to the bedroom beyond.

Whatever Paul Armstrong had been, he had been lavish with his stepdaughter. Gertrude's rooms at home were always beautiful apartments, but the three rooms in the east wing at Sunnyside, set apart for the daughter of the house, were much more splendid.

From the walls to the rugs on the floor, from the furniture to the appointments of the bath, with its pool sunk in the floor instead of the customary unlovely tub, everything was luxurious. In the bedroom Louise was watching for me. It was easy to see that she was much improved; the flush was going, and the peculiar gasping breathing of the night before was now a comfortable and easy respiration.

She held out her hand and I took it between both of mine.

"What can I say to you, Miss Innes?" she said slowly. "To have come like this—"

I thought she was going to break down, but she did not.

"You are not to think of anything but of getting well," I said, patting her hand. "When you are better, I am going to scold you for not coming here at once. This is your home, my dear, and of all people in the world, Halsey's old aunt ought to make you welcome."

She smiled a little, sadly, I thought.

"I ought not to see Halsey," she said. "Miss Innes, there are a great many things you will never understand, I am afraid. I am an impostor on your sympathy, because I—I stay here and let you lavish care on me, and all the time I know you are going to despise me."

"Nonsense!" I said briskly. "Why, what would Halsey do to me if I even ventured such a thing? He is so big and masterful that if I dared to be anything but rapturous over you, he would throw me out of a window. Indeed, he would be quite capable of it."

She seemed scarcely to hear my facetious tone. She had eloquent brown eyes—the Inneses are fair, and are prone to a grayish-green optic that is better for use than appearance—and they seemed now to be clouded with trouble.

"Poor Halsey!" she said softly. "Miss Innes, I can not marry him, and I am afraid to tell him. I am a coward—a coward!"

I sat beside the bed and stared at her. She was too ill to argue with, and, besides, sick people take queer fancies.

"We will talk about that when you are stronger," I said gently.

"But there are some things I must tell you," she insisted. "You must wonder how I came here, and why I stayed hidden at the lodge. Dear old Thomas has been almost crazy, Miss Innes. I did not know that Sunnyside was rented. I knew my mother wished to rent it, without telling my—stepfather, but the news must have reached her after I left. When I started east, I had only one idea—to be alone with my thoughts for a time, to bury myself here. Then, I—must have taken a cold on the train."

"You came east in clothing suitable for California," I said, "and, like all young girls nowadays, I don't suppose you wear flannels." But she was not listening.

"Miss Innes," she said, "has my stepbrother Arnold gone away?"

"What do you mean?" I asked, startled. But Louise was literal.

"He didn't come back that night," she said, "and it was so important that I should see him."

"I believe he has gone away," I replied uncertainly. "Isn't it something that we could attend to instead?"

But she shook her head. "I must do it myself," she said dully. "My mother must have rented Sunnyside without telling my stepfather, and—Miss Innes, did you ever hear of any one being wretchedly poor in the midst of luxury?

"Did you ever long, and long, for money—money to use without question, money that no one would take you to task about? My mother and I have been surrounded for years with every indulgence everything that would make a display. But we have never had any money, Miss Innes; that must have been why mother rented this house. My stepfather pays out bills. It's the most maddening, humiliating existence in the world. I would love honest poverty better."

"Never mind," I said; "when you and Halsey are married you can be as honest as you like, and you will certainly be poor."

Halsey came to the door at that moment and I could hear him coaxing Liddy for admission to the sick room.

"Shall I bring him in?" I asked Louise, uncertain what to do. The girl seemed to shrink back among her pillows at the sound of his voice. I was vaguely irritated with her; there are few young fellows like Halsey—straightforward, honest, and willing to sacrifice everything for the one woman. I knew one once, more than thirty years ago, who was like that: he died a long time ago. And sometimes I take out his picture, with its cane and its queer silk hat, and look at it. But of late years it has grown too painful: he is always a boy—and I am an old woman. I would not bring him back if I could.

Perhaps it was some such memory that made me call out sharply.

"Come in, Halsey." And then I took my sewing and went into the boudoir beyond, to play propriety. I did not try to hear what they said, but every word came through the open door with curious distinctness. Halsey had evidently gone over to the bed and I suppose he kissed her. There was silence for a moment, as if words were superfluous things.

"I have been almost wild, sweetheart,"—Halsey's voice. "Why didn't you trust me, and send for me before?"

"It was because I couldn't trust myself," she said in a low tone.

"I am too weak to struggle to-day; oh, Halsey, how I have wanted to see you!"

There was something I did not hear, then Halsey again.

"We could go away," he was saying. "What does it matter about any one in the world but just the two of us? To be always together, like this, hand in hand; Louise—don't tell me it isn't going to be. I won't believe you."

"You don't know; you don't know," Louise repeated dully. "Halsey, I care—you know that—but—not enough to marry you."

"That is not true, Louise," he said sternly. "You can not look at me with your honest eyes and say that."

"I can not marry you," she repeated miserably. "It's bad enough, isn't it? Don't make it worse. Some day, before long, you will be glad."

"Then it is because you have never loved me." There were depths of hurt pride in his voice. "You saw how much I loved you, and you let me think you cared—for a while. No—that isn't like you, Louise. There is something you haven't told me. Is it—because there is some one else?"

"Yes," almost inaudibly.

"Louise! Oh, I don't believe it."

"It is true," she said sadly. "Halsey, you must not try to see me again. As soon as I can, I am going away from here—where you are all so much kinder than I deserve. And whatever you hear about me, try to think as well of me as you can. I am going to marry—another man. How you must hate me—hate me!"

I could hear Halsey cross the room to the window. Then, after a pause, he went back to her again. I could hardly sit still; I wanted to go in and give her a good shaking.

"Then it's all over," he was saying with a long breath. "The plans we made together, the hopes, the—all of it—over! Well, I'll not be a baby, and I'll give you up the minute you say 'I don't love you and I do love—some one else'!"

"I can not say that," she breathed, "but, very soon, I shall marry—the other man."

I could hear Halsey's low triumphant laugh.

"I defy him," he said. "Sweetheart, as long as you care for me, I am not afraid."

The wind slammed the door between the two rooms just then, and I could hear nothing more, although I moved my chair quite close. After a discreet interval, I went into the other room, and found Louise alone. She was staring with sad eyes at the cherub painted on the ceiling over the bed, and because she looked tired I did not disturb her.

CHAPTER XIV
AN EGG-NOG AND A TELEGRAM

We had discovered Louise at the lodge Tuesday night. It was Wednesday I had my interview with her. Thursday and Friday were uneventful, save as they marked improvement in our patient. Gertrude spent almost all the time with her, and the two had grown to be great friends. But certain things hung over me constantly; the coroner's inquest on the death of Arnold Armstrong, to be held Saturday, and the arrival of Mrs. Armstrong and young Doctor Walker, bringing the body of the dead president of the Traders' Bank. We had not told Louise of either death.

Then, too, I was anxious about the children. With their mother's inheritance swept away in the wreck of the bank, and with their love affairs in a disastrous condition, things could scarcely be worse. Added to that, the cook and Liddy had a flare-up over the proper way to make beef-tea for Louise, and, of course, the cook left.

Mrs. Watson had been glad enough, I think, to turn Louise over to our care, and Thomas went upstairs night and morning to greet his young mistress from the doorway. Poor Thomas! He had the faculty—found still in some old negroes, who cling to the traditions of slavery days—of making his employer's interest his. It was always "we" with Thomas; I miss him sorely; pipe-smoking, obsequious, not over reliable, kindly old man!

On Thursday Mr. Harton, the Armstrongs' legal adviser, called up from town. He had been advised, he said, that Mrs. Armstrong was coming east with her husband's body and would arrive Monday. He came with some hesitation, he went on, to the fact that he had been further instructed to ask me to relinquish my lease on Sunnyside, as it was Mrs. Armstrong's desire to come directly there.

I was aghast.

"Here!" I said. "Surely you are mistaken, Mr. Harton. I should think, after—what happened here only a few days ago, she would never wish to come back."

"Nevertheless," he replied, "she is most anxious to come. This is what she says. 'Use every possible means to have Sunnyside vacated. Must go there at once.'"

"Mr. Harton," I said testily, "I am not going to do anything of the kind. I and mine have suffered enough at the hands of this family. I rented the house at an exorbitant figure and I have moved out here for the summer. My city home is dismantled and in the hands of decorators. I have been here one week, during which I have had not a single night of uninterrupted sleep, and I intend to stay until I have recuperated. Moreover, if Mr. Armstrong died insolvent, as I believe was the case, his widow ought to be glad to be rid of so expensive a piece of property."

The lawyer cleared his throat.

"I am very sorry you have made this decision," he said. "Miss Innes, Mrs. Fitzhugh tells me Louise Armstrong is with you."

"She is."

"Has she been informed of this—double bereavement?"

"Not yet," I said. "She has been very ill; perhaps to-night she can be told."

"It is very sad; very sad," he said. "I have a telegram for her, Mrs. Innes. Shall I send it out?"

"Better open it and read it to me," I suggested. "If it is important, that will save time."

There was a pause while Mr. Harton opened the telegram. Then he read it slowly, judicially.

"'Watch for Nina Carrington. Home Monday. Signed F. L. W.'"

"Hum!" I said. "'Watch for Nina Carrington. Home Monday.' Very well, Mr. Harton, I will tell her, but she is not in condition to watch for any one."

"Well, Miss Innes, if you decide to—er—relinquish the lease, let me know," the lawyer said.

"I shall not relinquish it," I replied, and I imagined his irritation from the way he hung up the receiver.

I wrote the telegram down word for word, afraid to trust my memory, and decided to ask Doctor Stewart how soon Louise might be told the truth. The closing of the Traders' Bank I considered unnecessary for her to know, but the death of her stepfather and stepbrother must be broken to her soon, or she might hear it in some unexpected and shocking manner.

Doctor Stewart came about four o'clock, bringing his leather satchel into the house with a great deal of care, and opening it at the foot of the stairs to show me a dozen big yellow eggs nesting among the bottles.

"Real eggs," he said proudly. "None of your anemic store eggs, but the real thing—some of them still warm. Feel them! Egg-nog for Miss Louise."

He was beaming with satisfaction, and before he left, he insisted on going back to the pantry and making an egg-nog with his own hands. Somehow, all the time he was doing it, I had a vision of Doctor Willoughby, my nerve specialist in the city, trying to make an egg-nog. I wondered if he ever prescribed anything so plebeian—and so delicious. And while Doctor Stewart whisked the eggs he talked.

"I said to Mrs. Stewart," he confided, a little red in the face from the exertion, "after I went home the other day, that you would think me an old gossip, for saying what I did about Walker and Miss Louise."

"Nothing of the sort," I protested.

"The fact is," he went on, evidently justifying himself, "I got that piece of information just as we get a lot of things, through the kitchen end of the house. Young Walker's chauffeur—Walker's more fashionable than I am, and he goes around the country in a Stanhope car—well, his chauffeur comes to see our servant girl, and he told her the whole thing. I thought it was probable, because Walker spent a lot of time up here last summer, when the family was here, and besides, Riggs, that's Walker's man, had a very pat little story about the doctor's building a house on this property, just at the foot of the hill. The sugar, please."

The egg-nog was finished. Drop by drop the liquor had cooked the egg, and now, with a final whisk, a last toss in the shaker, it was ready, a symphony in gold and white. The doctor sniffed it.

"Real eggs, real milk, and a touch of real Kentucky whisky," he said.

He insisted on carrying it up himself, but at the foot of the stairs he paused.

"Riggs said the plans were drawn for the house," he said, harking back to the old subject. "Drawn by Huston in town. So I naturally believed him."

When the doctor came down, I was ready with a question.

"Doctor," I asked, "is there any one in the neighborhood named Carrington? Nina Carrington?"

"Carrington?" He wrinkled his forehead. "Carrington? No, I don't remember any such family. There used to be Covingtons down the creek."

"The name was Carrington," I said, and the subject lapsed.

Gertrude and Halsey went for a long walk that afternoon, and Louise slept. Time hung heavy on my hands, and I did as I had fallen into a habit of doing lately—I sat down and thought things over. One result of my meditations was that I got up suddenly and went to the telephone. I had taken the most intense dislike to this Doctor Walker, whom I had never seen, and who was being talked of in the countryside as the fiance of Louise Armstrong.

I knew Sam Huston well. There had been a time, when Sam was a good deal younger than he is now, before he had married Anne Endicott, when I knew him even better. So now I felt no hesitation in calling him over the telephone. But when his office boy had given way to his confidential clerk, and that functionary had condescended to connect his employer's desk telephone, I was somewhat at a loss as to how to begin.

"Why, how are you, Rachel?" Sam said sonorously. "Going to build that house at Rock View?" It was a twenty-year-old joke of his.

"Sometime, perhaps," I said. "Just now I want to ask you a question about something which is none of my business."

"I see you haven't changed an iota in a quarter of a century, Rachel." This was intended to be another jest. "Ask ahead: everything but my domestic affairs is at your service."

"Try to be serious," I said. "And tell me this: has your firm made any plans for a house recently, for a Doctor Walker, at Casanova?"

"Yes, we have."

"Where was it to be built? I have a reason for asking."

"It was to be, I believe, on the Armstrong place. Mr. Armstrong himself consulted me, and the inference was—in fact, I am quite certain—the house was to be occupied by Mr. Armstrong's daughter, who was engaged to marry Doctor Walker."

When the architect had inquired for the different members of my family, and had finally rung off, I was certain of one thing. Louise Armstrong was in love with Halsey, and the man she was going to marry was Doctor Walker. Moreover, this decision was not new; marriage had been contemplated for some time. There must certainly be some explanation—but what was it?

That day I repeated to Louise the telegram Mr. Warton had opened.

She seemed to understand, but an unhappier face I have never seen. She looked like a criminal whose reprieve is over, and the day of execution approaching.

CHAPTER XV
LIDDY GIVES THE ALARM

The next day, Friday, Gertrude broke the news of her stepfather's death to Louise. She did it as gently as she could, telling her first that he was very ill, and finally that he was dead. Louise received the news in the most unexpected manner, and when Gertrude came out to tell me how she had stood it, I think she was almost shocked.

"She just lay and stared at me, Aunt Ray," she said. "Do you know, I believe she is glad, glad! And she is too honest to pretend anything else. What sort of man was Mr. Paul Armstrong, anyhow?"

"He was a bully as well as a rascal, Gertrude," I said. "But I am convinced of one thing; Louise will send for Halsey now, and they will make it all up."

For Louise had steadily refused to see Halsey all that day, and the boy was frantic.

We had a quiet hour, Halsey and I, that evening, and I told him several things; about the request that we give up the lease to Sunnyside, about the telegram to Louise, about the rumors of an approaching marriage between the girl and Doctor Walker, and, last of all, my own interview with her the day before.

He sat back in a big chair, with his face in the shadow, and my heart fairly ached for him. He was so big and so boyish! When I had finished he drew a long breath.

"Whatever Louise does," he said, "nothing will convince me, Aunt Ray, that she doesn't care for me. And up to two months ago, when she and her mother went west, I was the happiest fellow on earth. Then something made a difference: she wrote me that her people were opposed to the marriage; that her feeling for me was what it had always been, but that something had happened which had changed her ideas as to the future. I was not to write until she wrote me, and whatever occurred, I was to think the best I could of her. It sounded like a puzzle. When I saw her yesterday, it was the same thing, only, perhaps, worse."

"Halsey," I asked, "have you any idea of the nature of the interview between Louise Armstrong and Arnold the night he was murdered?"

"It was stormy. Thomas says once or twice he almost broke into the room, he was so alarmed for Louise."

"Another thing, Halsey," I said, "have you ever heard Louise mention a woman named Carrington, Nina Carrington?"

"Never," he said positively.

For try as we would, our thoughts always came back to that fatal Saturday night, and the murder. Every conversational path led to it, and we all felt that Jamieson was tightening the threads of evidence around John Bailey. The detective's absence was hardly reassuring; he must have had something to work on in town, or he would have returned.

The papers reported that the cashier of the Traders' Bank was ill in his apartments at the Knickerbocker—a condition not surprising, considering everything. The guilt of the defunct president was no longer in doubt; the missing bonds had been advertised and some of them discovered. In every instance they had been used as collateral for large loans, and the belief was current that not less than a million and a half dollars had been realized. Every one connected with the bank had been placed under arrest, and released on heavy bond.

Was he alone in his guilt, or was the cashier his accomplice? Where was the money? The estate of the dead man was comparatively small—a city house on a fashionable street, Sunnyside, a large estate largely mortgaged, an insurance of fifty thousand dollars, and some personal property—this was all.

The rest lost in speculation probably, the papers said. There was one thing which looked uncomfortable for Jack Bailey: he and Paul Armstrong together had promoted a railroad company in New Mexico, and it was rumored that together they had sunk large sums of money there. The business alliance between the two men added to the belief that Bailey knew something of the looting. His unexplained absence from the bank on Monday lent color to the suspicion against him. The strange thing seemed to be his surrendering himself on the point of departure. To me, it seemed the shrewd calculation of a clever rascal. I was not actively antagonistic to Gertrude's lover, but I meant to be convinced, one way or the other. I took no one on faith.

That night the Sunnyside ghost began to walk again. Liddy had been sleeping in Louise's dressing-room on a couch, and the approach of dusk was a signal for her to barricade the entire suite. Situated as its was, beyond the circular staircase, nothing but an extremity of excitement would have made her pass it after dark. I confess myself that the place seemed to me to have a sinister appearance, but we kept that wing well lighted, and until the lights went out at midnight it was really cheerful, if one did not know its history.

On Friday night, then, I had gone to bed, resolved to go at once to sleep. Thoughts that insisted on obtruding themselves I pushed resolutely to the back of my mind, and I systematically relaxed every muscle. I fell asleep soon, and was dreaming that Doctor Walker was building his new house immediately in front of my windows: I could hear the thump-thump of the hammers, and then I waked to a knowledge that somebody was pounding on my door.

I was up at once, and with the sound of my footstep on the floor the low knocking ceased, to be followed immediately by sibilant whispering through the keyhole.

"Miss Rachel! Miss Rachel!" somebody was saying, over and over.

"Is that you, Liddy?" I asked, my hand on the knob.

"For the love of mercy, let me in!" she said in a low tone.

She was leaning against the door, for when I opened it, she fell in. She was greenish-white, and she had a red and black barred flannel petticoat over her shoulders.

"Listen," she said, standing in the middle of the floor and holding on to me. "Oh, Miss Rachel, it's the ghost of that dead man hammering to get in!"

Sure enough, there was a dull thud—thud—thud from some place near. It was muffled: one rather felt than heard it, and it was impossible to locate. One moment it seemed to come, three taps and a pause, from the floor under us: the next, thud—thud—thud—it came apparently from the wall.

"It's not a ghost," I said decidedly. "If it was a ghost it wouldn't rap: it would come through the keyhole." Liddy looked at the keyhole. "But it sounds very much as though some one is trying to break into the house."

Liddy was shivering violently. I told her to get me my slippers and she brought me a pair of kid gloves, so I found my things myself, and prepared to call Halsey. As before, the night alarm had found the electric lights gone: the hall, save for its night lamp, was in darkness, as I went across to Halsey's room. I hardly know what I feared, but it was a relief to find him there, very sound asleep, and with his door unlocked.

"Wake up, Halsey," I said, shaking him.

He stirred a little. Liddy was half in and half out of the door, afraid as usual to be left alone, and not quite daring to enter. Her scruples seemed to fade, however, all at once. She gave a suppressed yell, bolted into the room, and stood tightly clutching the foot-board of the bed. Halsey was gradually waking.

"I've seen it," Liddy wailed. "A woman in white down the hall!"

I paid no attention.

"Halsey," I persevered, "some one is breaking into the house. Get up, won't you?"

"It isn't our house," he said sleepily. And then he roused to the exigency of the occasion. "All right, Aunt Ray," he said, still yawning. "If you'll let me get into something—"

It was all I could do to get Liddy out of the room. The demands of the occasion had no influence on her: she had seen the ghost, she persisted, and she wasn't going into the hall. But I got her over to my room at last, more dead than alive, and made her lie down on the bed.

The tappings, which seemed to have ceased for a while, had commenced again, but they were fainter. Halsey came over in a few minutes, and stood listening and trying to locate the sound.

"Give me my revolver, Aunt Ray," he said; and I got it—the one I had found in the tulip bed—and gave it to him. He saw Liddy there and divined at once that Louise was alone.

"You let me attend to this fellow, whoever it is, Aunt Ray, and go to Louise, will you? She may be awake and alarmed."

So in spite of her protests, I left Liddy alone and went back to the east wing. Perhaps I went a little faster past the yawning blackness of the circular staircase; and I could hear Halsey creaking cautiously down the main staircase. The rapping, or pounding, had ceased, and the silence was almost painful. And then suddenly, from apparently under my very feet, there rose a woman's scream, a cry of terror that broke off as suddenly as it came. I stood frozen and still. Every drop of blood in my body seemed to leave the surface and gather around my heart. In the dead silence that followed it throbbed as if it would burst. More dead than alive, I stumbled into Louise's bedroom. She was not there!

CHAPTER XVI
IN THE EARLY MORNING

I stood looking at the empty bed. The coverings had been thrown back, and Louise's pink silk dressing-gown was gone from the foot, where it had lain. The night lamp burned dimly, revealing the emptiness of the place. I picked it up, but my hand shook so that I put it down again, and got somehow to the door.

There were voices in the hall and Gertrude came running toward me.

"What is it?" she cried. "What was that sound? Where is Louise?"

"She is not in her room," I said stupidly. "I think—it was she—who screamed."

Liddy had joined us now, carrying a light. We stood huddled together at the head of the circular staircase, looking down into its shadows. There was nothing to be seen, and it was absolutely quiet down there. Then we heard Halsey running up the main staircase. He came quickly down the hall to where we were standing.

"There's no one trying to get in. I thought I heard some one shriek. Who was it?"

Our stricken faces told him the truth.

"Some one screamed down there," I said. "And—and Louise is not in her room."

With a jerk Halsey took the light from Liddy and ran down the circular staircase. I followed him, more slowly. My nerves seemed to be in a state of paralysis: I could scarcely step. At the foot of the stairs Halsey gave an exclamation and put down the light.

"Aunt Ray," he called sharply.

At the foot of the staircase, huddled in a heap, her head on the lower stair, was Louise Armstrong. She lay limp and white, her dressing-gown dragging loose from one sleeve of her night-dress, and the heavy braid of her dark hair stretching its length a couple of steps above her head, as if she had slipped down.

She was not dead: Halsey put her down on the floor, and began to rub her cold hands, while Gertrude and Liddy ran for stimulants. As for me, I sat there at the foot of that ghostly staircase—sat, because my knees wouldn't hold me—and wondered where it would all end. Louise was still unconscious, but she was breathing better, and I suggested that we get her back to bed before she came to. There was something grisly and horrible to me, seeing her there in almost the same attitude and in the same place where we had found her brother's body. And to add to the similarity, just then the hall clock, far off, struck faintly three o'clock.

It was four before Louise was able to talk, and the first rays of dawn were coming through her windows, which faced the east, before she could tell us coherently what had occurred. I give it as she told it. She lay propped in bed, and Halsey sat beside her, unrebuffed, and held her hand while she talked.

"I was not sleeping well," she began, "partly, I think, because I had slept during the afternoon. Liddy brought me some hot milk at ten o'clock and I slept until twelve. Then I wakened and—I got to thinking about things, and worrying, so I could not go to sleep.

"I was wondering why I had not heard from Arnold since the—since I saw him that night at the lodge. I was afraid he was ill, because—he was to have done something for me, and he had not come back. It must have been three when I heard some one rapping. I sat up and listened, to be quite sure, and the rapping kept up. It was cautious, and I was about to call Liddy.

"Then suddenly I thought I knew what it was. The east entrance and the circular staircase were always used by Arnold when he was out late, and sometimes, when he forgot his key, he would rap and I would go down and let him in. I thought he had come back to see me—I didn't think about the time, for his hours were always erratic. But I was afraid I was too weak to get down the stairs.

"The knocking kept up, and just as I was about to call Liddy, she ran through the room and out into the hall. I got up then, feeling weak and dizzy, and put on my dressing-gown. If it was Arnold, I knew I must see him.

"It was very dark everywhere, but, of course, I knew my way. I felt along for the stair-rail, and went down as quickly as I could. The knocking had stopped, and I was afraid I was too late. I got to the foot of the staircase and over to the door on to the east veranda. I had never thought of anything but that it was Arnold, until I reached the door. It was unlocked and opened about an inch. Everything was black: it was perfectly dark outside. I felt very queer and shaky. Then I thought perhaps Arnold had used his key; he did—strange things sometimes, and I turned around. Just as I reached the foot of the staircase I thought I heard some one coming. My nerves were going anyhow, there in the dark, and I could scarcely stand. I got up as far as the third or fourth step; then I felt that some one was coming toward me on the staircase. The next instant a hand met mine on the stair-rail. Some one brushed past me, and I screamed. Then I must have fainted."

That was Louise's story. There could be no doubt of its truth, and the thing that made it inexpressibly awful to me was that the poor girl had crept down to answer the summons of a brother who would never need her kindly offices again. Twice now, without apparent cause, some one had entered the house by means of the east entrance: had apparently gone his way unhindered through the house, and gone out again as he had entered. Had this unknown visitor been there a third time, the night Arnold Armstrong was murdered? Or a fourth, the time Mr. Jamieson had locked some one in the clothes chute?

Sleep was impossible, I think, for any of us. We dispersed finally to bathe and dress, leaving Louise little the worse for her experience. But I determined that before the day was over she must know the true state of affairs. Another decision I made, and I put it into execution immediately after breakfast. I had one of the unused bedrooms in the east wing, back along the small corridor, prepared for occupancy, and from that time on, Alex, the gardener, slept there. One man in that barn of a house was an absurdity, with things happening all the time, and I must say that Alex was as unobjectionable as any one could possibly have been.

The next morning, also, Halsey and I made an exhaustive examination of the circular staircase, the small entry at its foot, and the card-room opening from it. There was no evidence of anything unusual the night before, and had we not ourselves heard the rapping noises, I should have felt that Louise's imagination had run away with her. The outer door was closed and locked, and the staircase curved above us, for all the world like any other staircase.

Halsey, who had never taken seriously my account of the night Liddy and I were there alone, was grave enough now. He examined the paneling of the wainscoting above and below the stairs, evidently looking for a secret door, and suddenly there flashed into my mind the recollection of a scrap of paper that Mr. Jamieson had found among Arnold Armstrong's effects. As nearly as possible I repeated its contents to him, while Halsey took them down in a note-book.

"I wish you had told me that before," he said, as he put the memorandum carefully away. We found nothing at all in the house, and I expected little from any examination of the porch and grounds. But as we opened the outer door something fell into the entry with a clatter. It was a cue from the billiard-room.

Halsey picked it up with an exclamation.

"That's careless enough," he said. "Some of the servants have been amusing themselves."

I was far from convinced. Not one of the servants would go into that wing at night unless driven by dire necessity. And a billiard cue! As a weapon of either offense or defense it was an absurdity, unless one accepted Liddy's hypothesis of a ghost, and even then, as Halsey pointed out, a billiard-playing ghost would be a very modern evolution of an ancient institution.

That afternoon we, Gertrude, Halsey and I, attended the coroner's inquest in town. Doctor Stewart had been summoned also, it transpiring that in that early Sunday morning, when Gertrude and I had gone to our rooms, he had been called to view the body. We went, the four of us, in the machine, preferring the execrable roads to the matinee train, with half of Casanova staring at us. And on the way we decided to say nothing of Louise and her interview with her stepbrother the night he died. The girl was in trouble enough as it was.

CHAPTER XVII
A HINT OF SCANDAL

In giving the gist of what happened at the inquest, I have only one excuse—to recall to the reader the events of the night of Arnold Armstrong's murder. Many things had occurred which were not brought out at the inquest and some things were told there that were new to me. Altogether, it was a gloomy affair, and the six men in the corner, who constituted the coroner's jury, were evidently the merest puppets in the hands of that all-powerful gentleman, the coroner.

Gertrude and I sat well back, with our veils down. There were a number of people I knew: Barbara Fitzhugh, in extravagant mourning—she always went into black on the slightest provocation, because it was becoming—and Mr. Jarvis, the man who had come over from the Greenwood Club the night of the murder. Mr. Harton was there, too, looking impatient as the inquest dragged, but alive to every particle of evidence. From a corner Mr. Jamieson was watching the proceedings intently.

Doctor Stewart was called first. His evidence was told briefly, and amounted to this: on the Sunday morning previous, at a quarter before five, he had been called to the telephone. The message was from a Mr. Jarvis, who asked him to come at once to Sunnyside, as there had been an accident there, and Mr. Arnold Armstrong had been shot. He had dressed hastily, gathered up some instruments, and driven to Sunnyside.

He was met by Mr. Jarvis, who took him at once to the east wing. There, just as he had fallen, was the body of Arnold Armstrong. There was no need of the instruments: the man was dead. In answer to the coroner's question—no, the body had not been moved, save to turn it over. It lay at the foot of the circular staircase. Yes, he believed death had been instantaneous. The body was still somewhat warm and rigor mortis had not set in. It occurred late in cases of sudden death. No, he believed the probability of suicide might be eliminated; the wounds could have been self-inflicted, but with difficulty, and there had been no weapon found.

The doctor's examination was over, but he hesitated and cleared his throat.

"Mr. Coroner," he said, "at the risk of taking up valuable time, I would like to speak of an incident that may or may not throw some light on this matter."

The audience was alert at once.

"Kindly proceed, Doctor," the coroner said.

"My home is in Englewood, two miles from Casanova," the doctor began. "In the absence of Doctor Walker, a number of Casanova people have been consulting me. A month ago—five weeks, to be exact—a woman whom I had never seen came to my office. She was in deep mourning and kept her veil down, and she brought for examination a child, a boy of six. The little fellow was ill; it looked like typhoid, and the mother was frantic. She wanted a permit to admit the youngster to the Children's Hospital in town here, where I am a member of the staff, and I gave her one. The incident would have escaped me, but for a curious thing. Two days before Mr. Armstrong was shot, I was sent for to go to the Country Club: some one had been struck with a golf-ball that had gone wild. It was late when I left—I was on foot, and about a mile from the club, on the Claysburg road, I met two people. They were disputing violently, and I had no difficulty in recognizing Mr. Armstrong. The woman, beyond doubt, was the one who had consulted me about the child."

At this hint of scandal, Mrs. Ogden Fitzhugh sat up very straight. Jamieson was looking slightly skeptical, and the coroner made a note.

"The Children's Hospital, you say, Doctor?" he asked.

"Yes. But the child, who was entered as Lucien Wallace, was taken away by his mother two weeks ago. I have tried to trace them and failed."

All at once I remembered the telegram sent to Louise by some one signed F. L. W.—presumably Doctor Walker. Could this veiled woman be the Nina Carrington of the message? But it was only idle speculation. I had no way of finding out, and the inquest was proceeding.

The report of the coroner's physician came next. The post-mortem examination showed that the bullet had entered the chest in the fourth left intercostal space and had taken an oblique course downward and backward, piercing both the heart and lungs. The left lung was collapsed, and the exit point of the ball had been found in the muscles of the back to the left of the spinal column. It was improbable that such a wound had been self-inflicted, and its oblique downward course pointed to the fact that the shot had been fired from above. In other words, as the murdered man had been found dead at the foot of a staircase, it was probable that the shot had been fired by some one higher up on the stairs. There were no marks of powder. The bullet, a thirty-eight caliber, had been found in the dead man's clothing, and was shown to the jury.

Mr. Jarvis was called next, but his testimony amounted to little.

He had been summoned by telephone to Sunnyside, had come over at once with the steward and Mr. Winthrop, at present out of town. They had been admitted by the housekeeper, and had found the body lying at the foot of the staircase. He had made a search for a weapon, but there was none around. The outer entry door in the east wing had been unfastened and was open about an inch.

I had been growing more and more nervous. When the coroner called Mr. John Bailey, the room was filled with suppressed excitement. Mr. Jamieson went forward and spoke a few words to the coroner, who nodded. Then Halsey was called.

"Mr. Innes," the coroner said, "will you tell under what circumstances you saw Mr. Arnold Armstrong the night he died?"

"I saw him first at the Country Club," Halsey said quietly. He was rather pale, but very composed. "I stopped there with my automobile for gasolene. Mr. Armstrong had been playing cards. When I saw him there, he was coming out of the card-room, talking to Mr. John Bailey."

"The nature of the discussion—was it amicable?"

Halsey hesitated.

"They were having a dispute," he said. "I asked Mr. Bailey to leave the club with me and come to Sunnyside over Sunday."

"Isn't it a fact, Mr. Innes, that you took Mr. Bailey away from the club-house because you were afraid there would be blows?"

"The situation was unpleasant," Halsey said evasively.

"At that time had you any suspicion that the Traders' Bank had been wrecked?"

"No."

"What occurred next?"

"Mr. Bailey and I talked in the billiard-room until two-thirty."

"And Mr. Arnold Armstrong came there, while you were talking?"

"Yes. He came about half-past two. He rapped at the east door, and I admitted him."

The silence in the room was intense. Mr. Jamieson's eyes never left Halsey's face.

"Will you tell us the nature of his errand?"

"He brought a telegram that had come to the club for Mr. Bailey."

"He was sober?"

"Perfectly, at that time. Not earlier."

"Was not his apparent friendliness a change from his former attitude?"

"Yes. I did not understand it."

"How long did he stay?"

"About five minutes. Then he left, by the east entrance."

"What occurred then?"

"We talked for a few minutes, discussing a plan Mr. Bailey had in mind. Then I went to the stables, where I kept my car, and got it out."

"Leaving Mr. Bailey alone in the billiard-room?"

Halsey hesitated.

"My sister was there?"

Mrs. Ogden Fitzhugh had the courage to turn and eye Gertrude through her lorgnon.

"And then?"

"I took the car along the lower road, not to disturb the household. Mr. Bailey came down across the lawn, through the hedge, and got into the car on the road."

"Then you know nothing of Mr. Armstrong's movements after he left the house?"

"Nothing. I read of his death Monday evening for the first time."

"Mr. Bailey did not see him on his way across the lawn?"

"I think not. If he had seen him he would have spoken of it."

"Thank you. That is all. Miss Gertrude Innes."

Gertrude's replies were fully as concise as Halsey's. Mrs. Fitzhugh subjected her to a close inspection, commencing with her hat and ending with her shoes. I flatter myself she found nothing wrong with either her gown or her manner, but poor Gertrude's testimony was the reverse of comforting. She had been summoned, she said, by her brother, after Mr. Armstrong had gone.

She had waited in the billiard-room with Mr. Bailey, until the automobile had been ready. Then she had locked the door at the foot of the staircase, and, taking a lamp, had accompanied Mr. Bailey to the main entrance of the house, and had watched him cross the lawn. Instead of going at once to her room, she had gone back to the billiard-room for something which had been left there. The card-room and billiard-room were in darkness. She had groped around, found the article she was looking for, and was on the point of returning to her room, when she had heard some one fumbling at the lock at the east outer door. She had thought it was probably her brother, and had been about to go to the door, when she heard it open. Almost immediately there was a shot, and she had run panic-stricken through the drawing-room and had roused the house.

"You heard no other sound?" the coroner asked. "There was no one with Mr. Armstrong when he entered?"

"It was perfectly dark. There were no voices and I heard nothing. There was just the opening of the door, the shot, and the sound of somebody falling."

"Then, while you went through the drawing-room and up-stairs to alarm the household, the criminal, whoever it was, could have escaped by the east door?"

"Yes."

"Thank you. That will do."

I flatter myself that the coroner got little enough out of me. I saw Mr. Jamieson smiling to himself, and the coroner gave me up, after a time. I admitted I had found the body, said I had not known who it was until Mr. Jarvis told me, and ended by looking up at Barbara Fitzhugh and saying that in renting the house I had not expected to be involved in any family scandal. At which she turned purple.

The verdict was that Arnold Armstrong had met his death at the hands of a person or persons unknown, and we all prepared to leave. Barbara Fitzhugh flounced out without waiting to speak to me, but Mr. Harton came up, as I knew he would.

"You have decided to give up the house, I hope, Miss Innes," he said. "Mrs. Armstrong has wired me again."

"I am not going to give it up," I maintained, "until I understand some things that are puzzling me. The day that the murderer is discovered, I will leave."

"Then, judging by what I have heard, you will be back in the city very soon," he said. And I knew that he suspected the discredited cashier of the Traders' Bank.

Mr. Jamieson came up to me as I was about to leave the coroner's office.

"How is your patient?" he asked with his odd little smile.

"I have no patient," I replied, startled.

"I will put it in a different way, then. How is Miss Armstrong?"

"She—she is doing very well," I stammered.

"Good," cheerfully. "And our ghost? Is it laid?"

"Mr. Jamieson," I said suddenly, "I wish you would do one thing: I wish you would come to Sunnyside and spend a few days there. The ghost is not laid. I want you to spend one night at least watching the circular staircase. The murder of Arnold Armstrong was a beginning, not an end."

He looked serious.

"Perhaps I can do it," he said. "I have been doing something else, but—well, I will come out to-night."

We were very silent during the trip back to Sunnyside. I watched Gertrude closely and somewhat sadly. To me there was one glaring flaw in her story, and it seemed to stand out for every one to see. Arnold Armstrong had had no key, and yet she said she had locked the east door. He must have been admitted from within the house; over and over I repeated it to myself.

That night, as gently as I could, I told Louise the story of her stepbrother's death. She sat in her big, pillow-filled chair, and heard me through without interruption. It was clear that she was shocked beyond words: if I had hoped to learn anything from her expression, I had failed. She was as much in the dark as we were.

CHAPTER XVIII
A HOLE IN THE WALL

My taking the detective out to Sunnyside raised an unexpected storm of protest from Gertrude and Halsey. I was not prepared for it, and I scarcely knew how to account for it. To me Mr. Jamieson was far less formidable under my eyes where I knew what he was doing, than he was of in the city, twisting circumstances and motives to suit himself and learning what he wished to know, about events at Sunnyside, in some occult way. I was glad enough to have him there, when excitements began to come thick and fast.

A new element was about to enter into affairs: Monday, or Tuesday at the latest, would find Doctor Walker back in his green and white house in the village, and Louise's attitude to him in the immediate future would signify Halsey's happiness or wretchedness, as it might turn out. Then, too, the return of her mother would mean, of course, that she would have to leave us, and I had become greatly attached to her.

From the day Mr. Jamieson came to Sunnyside there was a subtle change in Gertrude's manner to me. It was elusive, difficult to analyze, but it was there. She was no longer frank with me, although I think her affection never wavered. At the time I laid the change to the fact that I had forbidden all communication with John Bailey, and had refused to acknowledge any engagement between the two. Gertrude spent much of her time wandering through the grounds, or taking long cross-country walks. Halsey played golf at the Country Club day after day, and after Louise left, as she did the following week, Mr. Jamieson and I were much together. He played a fair game of cribbage, but he cheated at solitaire.

The night the detective arrived, Saturday, I had a talk with him.

I told him of the experience Louise Armstrong had had the night before, on the circular staircase, and about the man who had so frightened Rosie on the drive. I saw that he thought the information was important, and to my suggestion that we put an additional lock on the east wing door he opposed a strong negative.

"I think it probable," he said, "that our visitor will be back again, and the thing to do is to leave things exactly as they are, to avoid rousing suspicion. Then I can watch for at least a part of each night and probably Mr. Innes will help us out. I would say as little to Thomas as possible. The old man knows more than he is willing to admit."

I suggested that Alex, the gardener, would probably be willing to help, and Mr. Jamieson undertook to make the arrangement. For one night, however, Mr. Jamieson preferred to watch alone. Apparently nothing occurred. The detective sat in absolute darkness on the lower step of the stairs, dozing, he said afterwards, now and then. Nothing could pass him in either direction, and the door in the morning remained as securely fastened as it had been the night before. And yet one of the most inexplicable occurrences of the whole affair took place that very night.

Liddy came to my room on Sunday morning with a face as long as the moral law. She laid out my things as usual, but I missed her customary garrulousness. I was not regaled with the new cook's extravagance as to eggs, and she even forbore to mention "that Jamieson," on whose arrival she had looked with silent disfavor.

"What's the matter, Liddy?" I asked at last. "Didn't you sleep last night?"

"No, ma'm," she said stiffly.

"Did you have two cups of coffee at your dinner?" I inquired.

"No, ma'm," indignantly.

I sat up and almost upset my hot water—I always take a cup of hot water with a pinch of salt, before I get up. It tones the stomach.

"Liddy Allen," I said, "stop combing that switch and tell me what is wrong with you."

Liddy heaved a sigh.

"Girl and woman," she said, "I've been with you twenty-five years, Miss Rachel, through good temper and bad—" the idea! and what I have taken from her in the way of sulks!—"but I guess I can't stand it any longer. My trunk's packed."

"Who packed it?" I asked, expecting from her tone to be told she had wakened to find it done by some ghostly hand.

"I did; Miss Rachel, you won't believe me when I tell you this house is haunted. Who was it fell down the clothes chute? Who was it scared Miss Louise almost into her grave?"

"I'm doing my best to find out," I said. "What in the world are you driving at?" She drew a long breath.

"There is a hole in the trunk-room wall, dug out since last night. It's big enough to put your head in, and the plaster's all over the place."

"Nonsense!" I said. "Plaster is always falling."

But Liddy clenched that.

"Just ask Alex," she said. "When he put the new cook's trunk there last night the wall was as smooth as this. This morning it's dug out, and there's plaster on the cook's trunk. Miss Rachel, you can get a dozen detectives and put one on every stair in the house, and you'll never catch anything. There's some things you can't handcuff."

Liddy was right. As soon as I could, I went up to the trunk-room, which was directly over my bedroom. The plan of the upper story of the house was like that of the second floor, in the main. One end, however, over the east wing, had been left only roughly finished, the intention having been to convert it into a ball-room at some future time. The maids' rooms, trunk-room, and various store-rooms, including a large airy linen-room, opened from a long corridor, like that on the second floor. And in the trunk-room, as Liddy had said, was a fresh break in the plaster.

Not only in the plaster, but through the lathing, the aperture extended. I reached into the opening, and three feet away, perhaps, I could touch the bricks of the partition wall. For some reason, the architect, in building the house, had left a space there that struck me, even in the surprise of the discovery, as an excellent place for a conflagration to gain headway.

"You are sure the hole was not here yesterday?" I asked Liddy, whose expression was a mixture of satisfaction and alarm. In answer she pointed to the new cook's trunk—that necessary adjunct of the migratory domestic. The top was covered with fine white plaster, as was the floor. But there were no large pieces of mortar lying around—no bits of lathing. When I mentioned this to Liddy she merely raised her eyebrows. Being quite confident that the gap was of unholy origin, she did not concern herself with such trifles as a bit of mortar and lath. No doubt they were even then heaped neatly on a gravestone in the Casanova churchyard!

I brought Mr. Jamieson up to see the hole in the wall, directly after breakfast. His expression was very odd when he looked at it, and the first thing he did was to try to discover what object, if any, such a hole could have. He got a piece of candle, and by enlarging the aperture a little was able to examine what lay beyond. The result was nil. The trunk-room, although heated by steam heat, like the rest of the house, boasted of a fireplace and mantel as well. The opening had been made between the flue and the outer wall of the house. There was revealed, however, on inspection, only the brick of the chimney on one side and the outer wall of the house on the other; in depth the space extended only to the flooring. The breach had been made about four feet from the floor, and inside were all the missing bits of plaster. It had been a methodical ghost.

It was very much of a disappointment. I had expected a secret room, at the very least, and I think even Mr. Jamieson had fancied he might at last have a clue to the mystery. There was evidently nothing more to be discovered: Liddy reported that everything was serene among the servants, and that none of them had been disturbed by the noise. The maddening thing, however, was that the nightly visitor had evidently more than one way of gaining access to the house, and we made arrangements to redouble our vigilance as to windows and doors that night.

Halsey was inclined to pooh-pooh the whole affair. He said a break in the plaster might have occurred months ago and gone unnoticed, and that the dust had probably been stirred up the day before. After all, we had to let it go at that, but we put in an uncomfortable Sunday. Gertrude went to church, and Halsey took a long walk in the morning. Louise was able to sit up, and she allowed Halsey and Liddy to assist her down-stairs late in the afternoon. The east veranda was shady, green with vines and palms, cheerful with cushions and lounging chairs. We put Louise in a steamer chair, and she sat there passively enough, her hands clasped in her lap.

We were very silent. Halsey sat on the rail with a pipe, openly watching Louise, as she looked broodingly across the valley to the hills. There was something baffling in the girl's eyes; and gradually Halsey's boyish features lost their glow at seeing her about again, and settled into grim lines. He was like his father just then.

We sat until late afternoon, Halsey growing more and more moody. Shortly before six, he got up and went into the house, and in a few minutes he came out and called me to the telephone. It was Anna Whitcomb, in town, and she kept me for twenty minutes, telling me the children had had the measles, and how Madame Sweeny had botched her new gown.

When I finished, Liddy was behind me, her mouth a thin line.

"I wish you would try to look cheerful, Liddy," I groaned, "your face would sour milk." But Liddy seldom replied to my gibes. She folded her lips a little tighter.

"He called her up," she said oracularly, "he called her up, and asked her to keep you at the telephone, so he could talk to Miss Louise. A THANKLESS CHILD IS SHARPER THAN A SERPENT'S TOOTH."

"Nonsense!" I said bruskly. "I might have known enough to leave them. It's a long time since you and I were in love, Liddy, and—we forget."

Liddy sniffed.

"No man ever made a fool of me," she replied virtuously.

"Well, something did," I retorted.

CHAPTER XIX
CONCERNING THOMAS

"Mr. Jamieson," I said, when we found ourselves alone after dinner that night, "the inquest yesterday seemed to me the merest recapitulation of things that were already known. It developed nothing new beyond the story of Doctor Stewart's, and that was volunteered."

"An inquest is only a necessary formality, Miss Innes," he replied. "Unless a crime is committed in the open, the inquest does nothing beyond getting evidence from witnesses while events are still in their minds. The police step in later. You and I both know how many important things never transpired. For instance: the dead man had no key, and yet Miss Gertrude testified to a fumbling at the lock, and then the opening of the door. The piece of evidence you mention, Doctor Stewart's story, is one of those things we have to take cautiously: the doctor has a patient who wears black and does not raise her veil. Why, it is the typical mysterious lady! Then the good doctor comes across Arnold Armstrong, who was a graceless scamp—de mortuis—what's the rest of it?—and he is quarreling with a lady in black. Behold, says the doctor, they are one and the same."

"Why was Mr. Bailey not present at the inquest?"

The detective's expression was peculiar.

"Because his physician testified that he is ill, and unable to leave his bed."

"Ill!" I exclaimed. "Why, neither Halsey nor Gertrude has told me that."

"There are more things than that, Miss Innes, that are puzzling. Bailey gives the impression that he knew nothing of the crash at the bank until he read it in the paper Monday night, and that he went back and surrendered himself immediately. I do not believe it. Jonas, the watchman at the Traders' Bank, tells a different story. He says that on the Thursday night before, about eight-thirty, Bailey went back to the bank. Jonas admitted him, and he says the cashier was in a state almost of collapse. Bailey worked until midnight, then he closed the vault and went away. The occurrence was so unusual that the watchman pondered over it an the rest of the night. What did Bailey do when he went back to the Knickerbocker apartments that night? He packed a suit-case ready for instant departure. But he held off too long; he waited for something. My personal opinion is that he waited to see Miss Gertrude before flying from the country. Then, when he had shot down Arnold Armstrong that night, he had to choose between two evils. He did the thing that would immediately turn public opinion in his favor, and surrendered himself, as an innocent man. The strongest thing against him is his preparation for flight, and his deciding to come back after the murder of Arnold Armstrong. He was shrewd enough to disarm suspicion as to the graver charge?"

The evening dragged along slowly. Mrs. Watson came to my bedroom before I went to bed and asked if I had any arnica. She showed me a badly swollen hand, with reddish streaks running toward the elbow; she said it was the hand she had hurt the night of the murder a week before, and that she had not slept well since. It looked to me as if it might be serious, and I told her to let Doctor Stewart see it.

The next morning Mrs. Watson went up to town on the eleven train, and was admitted to the Charity Hospital. She was suffering from blood-poisoning. I fully meant to go up and see her there, but other things drove her entirely from my mind. I telephoned to the hospital that day, however, and ordered a private room for her, and whatever comforts she might be allowed.

Mrs. Armstrong arrived Monday evening with her husband's body, and the services were set for the next day. The house on Chestnut Street, in town, had been opened, and Tuesday morning Louise left us to go home. She sent for me before she went, and I saw she had been crying.

"How can I thank you, Miss Innes?" she said. "You have taken me on faith, and—you have not asked me any questions. Some time, perhaps, I can tell you; and when that time comes, you will all despise me,—Halsey, too."

I tried to tell her how glad I was to have had her but there was something else she wanted to say. She said it finally, when she had bade a constrained good-by to Halsey and the car was waiting at the door.

"Miss Innes," she said in a low tone, "if they—if there is any attempt made to—to have you give up the house, do it, if you possibly can. I am afraid—to have you stay."

That was all. Gertrude went into town with her and saw her safely home. She reported a decided coolness in the greeting between Louise and her mother, and that Doctor Walker was there, apparently in charge of the arrangements for the funeral. Halsey disappeared shortly after Louise left and came home about nine that night, muddy and tired. As for Thomas, he went around dejected and sad, and I saw the detective watching him closely at dinner. Even now I wonder—what did Thomas know? What did he suspect?

At ten o'clock the household had settled down for the night. Liddy, who was taking Mrs. Watson's place, had finished examining the tea-towels and the corners of the shelves in the cooling-room, and had gone to bed. Alex, the gardener, had gone heavily up the circular staircase to his room, and Mr. Jamieson was examining the locks of the windows. Halsey dropped into a chair in the living-room, and stared moodily ahead. Once he roused.

"What sort of a looking chap is that Walker, Gertrude?" he asked!

"Rather tall, very dark, smooth-shaven. Not bad looking," Gertrude said, putting down the book she had been pretending to read. Halsey kicked a taboret viciously.

"Lovely place this village must be in the winter," he said irrelevantly. "A girl would be buried alive here."

It was then some one rapped at the knocker on the heavy front door. Halsey got up leisurely and opened it, admitting Warner. He was out of breath from running, and he looked half abashed.

"I am sorry to disturb you," he said. "But I didn't know what else to do. It's about Thomas."

"What about Thomas?" I asked. Mr. Jamieson had come into the hall and we all stared at Warner.

"He's acting queer," Warner explained. "He's sitting down there on the edge of the porch, and he says he has seen a ghost. The old man looks bad, too; he can scarcely speak."

"He's as full of superstition as an egg is of meat," I said. "Halsey, bring some whisky and we will all go down."

No one moved to get the whisky, from which I judged there were three pocket flasks ready for emergency. Gertrude threw a shawl around my shoulders, and we all started down over the hill: I had made so many nocturnal excursions around the place that I knew my way perfectly. But Thomas was not on the veranda, nor was he inside the house. The men exchanged significant glances, and Warner got a lantern.

"He can't have gone far," he said. "He was trembling so that he couldn't stand, when I left."

Jamieson and Halsey together made the round of the lodge, occasionally calling the old man by name. But there was no response. No Thomas came, bowing and showing his white teeth through the darkness. I began to be vaguely uneasy, for the first time. Gertrude, who was never nervous in the dark, went alone down the drive to the gate, and stood there, looking along the yellowish line of the road, while I waited on the tiny veranda.

Warner was puzzled. He came around to the edge of the veranda and stood looking at it as if it ought to know and explain.

"He might have stumbled into the house," he said, "but he could not have climbed the stairs. Anyhow, he's not inside or outside, that I can see." The other members of the party had come back now, and no one had found any trace of the old man. His pipe, still warm, rested on the edge of the rail, and inside on the table his old gray hat showed that its owner had not gone far.

He was not far, after all. From the table my eyes traveled around the room, and stopped at the door of a closet. I hardly know what impulse moved me, but I went in and turned the knob. It burst open with the impetus of a weight behind it, and something fell partly forward in a heap on the floor. It was Thomas—Thomas without a mark of injury on him, and dead.

CHAPTER XX
DOCTOR WALKER'S WARNING

Warner was on his knees in a moment, fumbling at the old man's collar to loosen it, but Halsey caught his hand.

"Let him alone?" he said. "You can't help him; he is dead."

We stood there, each avoiding the other's eyes; we spoke low and reverently in the presence of death, and we tacitly avoided any mention of the suspicion that was in every mind. When Mr. Jamieson had finished his cursory examination, he got up and dusted the knees of his trousers.

"There is no sign of injury," he said, and I know I, for one, drew a long breath of relief. "From what Warner says and from his hiding in the closet, I should say he was scared to death. Fright and a weak heart, together."

"But what could have done it?" Gertrude asked. "He was all right this evening at dinner. Warner, what did he say when you found him on the porch?"

Warner looked shaken: his honest, boyish face was colorless.

"Just what I told you, Miss Innes. He'd been reading the paper down-stairs; I had put up the car, and, feeling sleepy, I came down to the lodge to go to bed. As I went up-stairs, Thomas put down the paper and, taking his pipe, went out on the porch. Then I heard an exclamation from him."

"What did he say?" demanded Jamieson.

"I couldn't hear, but his voice was strange; it sounded startled. I waited for him to call out again, but he did not, so I went down-stairs. He was sitting on the porch step, looking straight ahead, as if he saw something among the trees across the road. And he kept mumbling about having seen a ghost. He looked queer, and I tried to get him inside, but he wouldn't move. Then I thought I'd better go up to the house."

"Didn't he say anything else you could understand?" I asked.

"He said something about the grave giving up its dead."

Mr. Jamieson was going through the old man's pockets, and Gertrude was composing his arms, folding them across his white shirt-bosom, always so spotless.

Mr. Jamieson looked up at me.

"What was that you said to me, Miss Innes, about the murder at the house being a beginning and not an end? By jove, I believe you were right!"

In the course of his investigations the detective had come to the inner pocket of the dead butler's black coat. Here he found some things that interested him. One was a small flat key, with a red cord tied to it, and the other was a bit of white paper, on which was written something in Thomas' cramped hand. Mr. Jamieson read it: then he gave it to me. It was an address in fresh ink—

LUCIEN WALLACE, 14 Elm Street, Richfield.

As the card went around, I think both the detective and I watched for any possible effect it might have, but, beyond perplexity, there seemed to be none.

"Richfield!" Gertrude exclaimed. "Why, Elm Street is the main street; don't you remember, Halsey?"

"Lucien Wallace!" Halsey said. "That is the child Stewart spoke of at the inquest."

Warner, with his mechanic's instinct, had reached for the key. What he said was not a surprise.

"Yale lock," he said. "Probably a key to the east entry."

There was no reason why Thomas, an old and trusted servant, should not have had a key to that particular door, although the servants' entry was in the west wing. But I had not known of

87

this key, and it opened up a new field of conjecture. Just now, however, there were many things to be attended to, and, leaving Warner with the body, we all went back to the house. Mr. Jamieson walked with me, while Halsey and Gertrude followed.

"I suppose I shall have to notify the Armstrongs," I said. "They will know if Thomas had any people and how to reach them. Of course, I expect to defray the expenses of the funeral, but his relatives must be found. What do you think frightened him, Mr. Jamieson?"

"It is hard to say," he replied slowly, "but I think we may be certain it was fright, and that he was hiding from something. I am sorry in more than one way: I have always believed that Thomas knew something, or suspected something, that he would not tell. Do you know hour much money there was in that worn-out wallet of his? Nearly a hundred dollars! Almost two months' wages—and yet those darkies seldom have a penny. Well—what Thomas knew will be buried with him."

Halsey suggested that the grounds be searched, but Mr. Jamieson vetoed the suggestion.

"You would find nothing," he said. "A person clever enough to get into Sunnyside and tear a hole in the wall, while I watched down-stairs, is not to be found by going around the shrubbery with a lantern."

With the death of Thomas, I felt that a climax had come in affairs at Sunnyside. The night that followed was quiet enough. Halsey watched at the foot of the staircase, and a complicated system of bolts on the other doors seemed to be effectual.

Once in the night I wakened and thought I heard the tapping again. But all was quiet, and I had reached the stage where I refused to be disturbed for minor occurrences.

The Armstrongs were notified of Thomas' death, and I had my first interview with Doctor Walker as a result. He came up early the next morning, just as we finished breakfast, in a professional looking car with a black hood. I found him striding up and down the living-room, and, in spite of my preconceived dislike, I had to admit that the man was presentable. A big fellow he was, tall and dark, as Gertrude had said, smooth-shaven and erect, with prominent features and a square jaw. He was painfully spruce in his appearance, and his manner was almost obtrusively polite.

"I must make a double excuse for this early visit, Miss Innes," he said as he sat down. The chair was lower than he expected, and his dignity required collecting before he went on. "My professional duties are urgent and long neglected, and"—a fall to the every-day manner—"something must be done about that body."

"Yes," I said, sitting on the edge of my chair. "I merely wished the address of Thomas' people. You might have telephoned, if you were busy."

He smiled.

"I wished to see you about something else," he said. "As for Thomas, it is Mrs. Armstrong's wish that you would allow her to attend to the expense. About his relatives, I have already notified his brother, in the village. It was heart disease, I think. Thomas always had a bad heart."

"Heart disease and fright," I said, still on the edge of my chair. But the doctor had no intention of leaving.

"I understand you have a ghost up here, and that you have the house filled with detectives to exorcise it," he said.

For some reason I felt I was being "pumped," as Halsey says. "You have been misinformed," I replied.

"What, no ghost, no detectives!" he said, still with his smile. "What a disappointment to the village!"

I resented his attempt at playfulness. It had been anything but a joke to us.

"Doctor Walker," I said tartly, "I fail to see any humor in the situation. Since I came here, one man has been shot, and another one has died from shock. There have been intruders in the house, and strange noises. If that is funny, there is something wrong with my sense of humor."

"You miss the point," he said, still good-naturedly. "The thing that is funny, to me, is that you insist on remaining here, under the circumstances. I should think nothing would keep you."

"You are mistaken. Everything that occurs only confirms my resolution to stay until the mystery is cleared."

"I have a message for you, Miss Innes," he said, rising at last. "Mrs. Armstrong asked me to thank you for your kindness to Louise, whose whim, occurring at the time it did, put her to great inconvenience. Also—and this is a delicate matter—she asked me to appeal to your natural sympathy for her, at this time, and to ask you if you will not reconsider your decision about the house. Sunnyside is her home; she loves it dearly, and just now she wishes to retire here for quiet and peace."

"She must have had a change of heart," I said, ungraciously enough. "Louise told me her mother despised the place. Besides, this is no place for quiet and peace just now. Anyhow, doctor, while I don't care to force an issue, I shall certainly remain here, for a time at least."

"For how long?" he asked.

"My lease is for six months. I shall stay until some explanation is found for certain things. My own family is implicated now, and I shall do everything to clear the mystery of Arnold Armstrong's murder."

The doctor stood looking down, slapping his gloves thoughtfully against the palm of a well-looked-after hand.

"You say there have been intruders in the house?" he asked. "You are sure of that, Miss Innes?"

"Certain."

"In what part?"

"In the east wing."

"Can you tell me when these intrusions occurred, and what the purpose seemed to be? Was it robbery?"

"No," I said decidedly. "As to time, once on Friday night a week ago, again the following night, when Arnold Armstrong was murdered, and again last Friday night."

The doctor looked serious. He seemed to be debating some question in his mind, and to reach a decision.

"Miss Innes," he said, "I am in a peculiar position; I understand your attitude, of course; but—do you think you are wise? Ever since you have come here there have been hostile demonstrations against you and your family. I'm not a croaker, but—take a warning. Leave before anything occurs that will cause you a lifelong regret."

"I am willing to take the responsibility," I said coldly.

I think he gave me up then as a poor proposition. He asked to be shown where Arnold Armstrong's body had been found, and I took him there. He scrutinized the whole place carefully, examining the stairs and the lock. When he had taken a formal farewell I was confident of one thing. Doctor Walker would do anything he could to get me away from Sunnyside.

CHAPTER XXI
FOURTEEN ELM STREET

It was Monday evening when we found the body of poor old Thomas. Monday night had been uneventful; things were quiet at the house and the peculiar circumstances of the old man's death had been carefully kept from the servants. Rosie took charge of the dining-room and pantry, in the absence of a butler, and, except for the warning of the Casanova doctor, everything breathed of peace.

Affairs at the Traders' Bank were progressing slowly. The failure had hit small stock-holders very hard, the minister of the little Methodist chapel in Casanova among them. He had received as a legacy from an uncle a few shares of stock in the Traders' Bank, and now his joy was turned to bitterness: he had to sacrifice everything he had in the world, and his feeling against Paul Armstrong, dead, as he was, must have been bitter in the extreme. He was asked to officiate at the simple services when the dead banker's body was interred in Casanova churchyard, but the good man providentially took cold, and a substitute was called in.

A few days after the services he called to see me, a kind-faced little man, in a very bad frock-coat and laundered tie. I think he was uncertain as to my connection with the Armstrong family, and dubious whether I considered Mr. Armstrong's taking away a matter for condolence or congratulation. He was not long in doubt.

I liked the little man. He had known Thomas well, and had promised to officiate at the services in the rickety African Zion Church. He told me more of himself than he knew, and before he left, I astonished him—and myself, I admit—by promising a new carpet for his church. He was much affected, and I gathered that he had yearned over his ragged chapel as a mother over a half-clothed child.

"You are laying up treasure, Miss Innes," he said brokenly, "where neither moth nor rust corrupt, nor thieves break through and steal."

"It is certainly a safer place than Sunnyside," I admitted. And the thought of the carpet permitted him to smile. He stood just inside the doorway, looking from the luxury of the house to the beauty of the view.

"The rich ought to be good," he said wistfully. "They have so much that is beautiful, and beauty is ennobling. And yet—while I ought to say nothing but good of the dead—Mr. Armstrong saw nothing of this fair prospect. To him these trees and lawns were not the work of God. They were property, at so much an acre. He loved money, Miss Innes. He offered up everything to his golden calf. Not power, not ambition, was his fetish: it was money." Then he dropped his pulpit manner, and, turning to me with his engaging smile: "In spite of all this luxury," he said, "the country people here have a saying that Mr. Paul Armstrong could sit on a dollar and see all around it. Unlike the summer people, he gave neither to the poor nor to the church. He loved money for its own sake."

"And there are no pockets in shrouds!" I said cynically.

I sent him home in the car, with a bunch of hot-house roses for his wife, and he was quite overwhelmed. As for me, I had a generous glow that was cheap at the price of a church carpet. I received less gratification—and less gratitude—when I presented the new silver communion set to St. Barnabas.

I had a great many things to think about in those days. I made out a list of questions and possible answers, but I seemed only to be working around in a circle. I always ended where I began. The list was something like this:

Who had entered the house the night before the murder?

Thomas claimed it was Mr. Bailey, whom he had seen on the foot-path, and who owned the pearl cuff-link.

Why did Arnold Armstrong come back after he had left the house the night he was killed?

No answer. Was it on the mission Louise had mentioned?

Who admitted him?

Gertrude said she had locked the east entry. There was no key on the dead man or in the door. He must have been admitted from within.

Who had been locked in the clothes chute?

Some one unfamiliar with the house, evidently. Only two people missing from the household, Rosie and Gertrude. Rosie had been at the lodge. Therefore—but was it Gertrude? Might it not have been the mysterious intruder again?

Who had accosted Rosie on the drive?

Again—perhaps the nightly visitor. It seemed more likely some one who suspected a secret at the lodge. Was Louise under surveillance?

Who had passed Louise on the circular staircase?

Could it have been Thomas? The key to the east entry made this a possibility. But why was he there, if it were indeed he?

Who had made the hole in the trunk-room wall?

It was not vandalism. It had been done quietly, and with deliberate purpose. If I had only known how to read the purpose of that gaping aperture what I might have saved in anxiety and mental strain!

Why had Louise left her people and come home to hide at the lodge?

There was no answer, as yet, to this, or to the next questions.

Why did both she and Doctor Walker warn us away from the house?

Who was Lucien Wallace?

What did Thomas see in the shadows the night he died?

What was the meaning of the subtle change in Gertrude?

Was Jack Bailey an accomplice or a victim in the looting of the Traders' Bank?

What all-powerful reason made Louise determine to marry Doctor Walker?

The examiners were still working on the books of the Traders' Bank, and it was probable that several weeks would elapse before everything was cleared up. The firm of expert accountants who had examined the books some two months before testified that every bond, every piece of valuable paper, was there at that time. It had been shortly after their examination that the president, who had been in bad health, had gone to California. Mr. Bailey was still ill at the Knickerbocker, and in this, as in other ways, Gertrude's conduct puzzled me. She seemed indifferent, refused to discuss matters pertaining to the bank, and never, to my knowledge, either wrote to him or went to see him.

Gradually I came to the conclusion that Gertrude, with the rest of the world, believed her lover guilty, and—although I believed it myself, for that matter—I was irritated by her indifference. Girls in my day did not meekly accept the public's verdict as to the man they loved.

But presently something occurred that made me think that under Gertrude's surface calm there was a seething flood of emotions.

Tuesday morning the detective made a careful search of the grounds, but he found nothing. In the afternoon he disappeared, and it was late that night when he came home. He said he would have to go back to the city the following day, and arranged with Halsey and Alex to guard the house.

Liddy came to me on Wednesday morning with her black silk apron held up like a bag, and her eyes big with virtuous wrath. It was the day of Thomas' funeral in the village, and Alex and I were in the conservatory cutting flowers for the old man's casket. Liddy is never so happy as when she is making herself wretched, and now her mouth drooped while her eyes were triumphant.

"I always said there were plenty of things going on here, right under our noses, that we couldn't see," she said, holding out her apron.

"I don't see with my nose," I remarked. "What have you got there?"

Liddy pushed aside a half-dozen geranium pots, and in the space thus cleared she dumped the contents of her apron—a handful of tiny bits of paper. Alex had stepped back, but I saw him watching her curiously.

"Wait a moment, Liddy," I said. "You have been going through the library paper-basket again!"

Liddy was arranging her bits of paper with the skill of long practice and paid no attention.

"Did it ever occur to you," I went on, putting my hand over the scraps, "that when people tear up their correspondence, it is for the express purpose of keeping it from being read?"

"If they wasn't ashamed of it they wouldn't take so much trouble, Miss Rachel," Liddy said oracularly. "More than that, with things happening every day, I consider it my duty. If you don't read and act on this, I shall give it to that Jamieson, and I'll venture he'll not go back to the city to-day."

That decided me. If the scraps had anything to do with the mystery ordinary conventions had no value. So Liddy arranged the scraps, like working out one of the puzzle-pictures children play with, and she did it with much the same eagerness. When it was finished she stepped aside while I read it.

"Wednesday night, nine o'clock. Bridge," I real aloud. Then, aware of Alex's stare, I turned on Liddy.

"Some one is to play bridge to-night at nine o'clock," I said. "Is that your business, or mine?"

Liddy was aggrieved. She was about to reply when I scooped up the pieces and left the conservatory.

"Now then," I said, when we got outside, "will you tell me why you choose to take Alex into your confidence? He's no fool. Do you suppose he thinks any one in this house is going to play bridge to-night at nine o'clock, by appointment! I suppose you have shown it in the kitchen, and instead of my being able to slip down to the bridge to-night quietly, and see who is there, the whole household will be going in a procession."

"Nobody knows it," Liddy said humbly. "I found it in the basket in Miss Gertrude's dressing-room. Look at the back of the sheet." I turned over some of the scraps, and, sure enough, it was a blank deposit slip from the Traders' Bank. So Gertrude was going to meet Jack Bailey that night by the bridge! And I had thought he was ill! It hardly seemed like the action of an innocent man—this avoidance of daylight, and of his fiancee's people. I decided to make certain, however, by going to the bridge that night.

After luncheon Mr. Jamieson suggested that I go with him to Richfield, and I consented.

"I am inclined to place more faith in Doctor Stewart's story," he said, "since I found that scrap in old Thomas' pocket. It bears out the statement that the woman with the child, and the woman who quarreled with Armstrong, are the same. It looks as if Thomas had stumbled on to some affair which was more or less discreditable to the dead man, and, with a certain loyalty to the family, had kept it to himself. Then, you see, your story about the woman at the card-room window begins to mean something. It is the nearest approach to anything tangible that we have had yet."

Warner took us to Richfield in the car. It was about twenty-five miles by railroad, but by taking a series of atrociously rough short cuts we got there very quickly. It was a pretty little town, on the river, and back on the hill I could see the Mortons' big country house, where Halsey and Gertrude had been staying until the night of the murder.

Elm Street was almost the only street, and number fourteen was easily found. It was a small white house, dilapidated without having gained anything picturesque, with a low window and a porch only a foot or so above the bit of a lawn. There was a baby-carriage in the path, and from a swing at the side came the sound of conflict. Three small children were disputing vociferously, and a faded young woman with a kindly face was trying to hush the clamor. When she saw us she untied her gingham apron and came around to the porch.

"Good afternoon," I said. Jamieson lifted his hat, without speaking. "I came to inquire about a child named Lucien Wallace."

"I am glad you have come," she said. "In spite of the other children, I think the little fellow is lonely. We thought perhaps his mother would be here to-day."

Mr. Jamieson stepped forward.

"You are Mrs. Tate?" I wondered how the detective knew.

"Yes, sir."

"Mrs. Tate, we want to make some inquiries. Perhaps in the house—"

"Come right in," she said hospitably. And soon we were in the little shabby parlor, exactly like a thousand of its prototypes. Mrs. Tate sat uneasily, her hands folded in her lap.

"How long has Lucien been here?" Mr. Jamieson asked.

"Since a week ago last Friday. His mother paid one week's board in advance; the other has not been paid."

"Was he ill when he came?"

"No, sir, not what you'd call sick. He was getting better of typhoid, she said, and he's picking up fine."

"Will you tell me his mother's name and address?"

"That's the trouble," the young woman said, knitting her brows. "She gave her name as Mrs. Wallace, and said she had no address. She was looking for a boarding-house in town. She said she worked in a department store, and couldn't take care of the child properly, and he needed fresh air and milk. I had three children of my own, and one more didn't make much difference in the work, but—I wish she would pay this week's board."

"Did she say what store it was?"

"No, sir, but all the boy's clothes came from King's. He has far too fine clothes for the country."

There was a chorus of shouts and shrill yells from the front door, followed by the loud stamping of children's feet and a throaty "whoa, whoa!" Into the room came a tandem team of two chubby youngsters, a boy and a girl, harnessed with a clothes-line, and driven by a laughing boy of about seven, in tan overalls and brass buttons. The small driver caught my attention at once: he was a beautiful child, and, although he showed traces of recent severe illness, his skin had now the clear transparency of health.

"Whoa, Flinders," he shouted. "You're goin' to smash the trap."

Mr. Jamieson coaxed him over by holding out a lead-pencil, striped blue and yellow.

"Now, then," he said, when the boy had taken the lead-pencil and was testing its usefulness on the detective's cuff, "now then, I'll bet you don't know what your name is!"

"I do," said the boy. "Lucien Wallace."

"Great! And what's your mother's name?"

"Mother, of course. What's your mother's name?" And he pointed to me! I am going to stop wearing black: it doubles a woman's age.

"And where did you live before you came here?" The detective was polite enough not to smile.

"Grossmutter," he said. And I saw Mr. Jamieson's eyebrows go up.

"German," he commented. "Well, young man, you don't seem to know much about yourself."

"I've tried it all week," Mrs. Tate broke in. "The boy knows a word or two of German, but he doesn't know where he lived, or anything about himself."

Mr. Jamieson wrote something on a card and gave it to her.

"Mrs. Tate," he said, "I want you to do something. Here is some money for the telephone call. The instant the boy's mother appears here, call up that number and ask for the person whose name is there. You can run across to the drug-store on an errand and do it quietly. Just say, 'The lady has come.'"

"'The lady has come,'" repeated Mrs. Tate. "Very well, sir, and I hope it will be soon. The milk-bill alone is almost double what it was."

"How much is the child's board?" I asked.

"Three dollars a week, including his washing."

"Very well," I said. "Now, Mrs. Tate, I am going to pay last week's board and a week in advance. If the mother comes, she is to know nothing of this visit—absolutely not a word, and, in return for your silence, you may use this money for—something for your own children."

Her tired, faded face lighted up, and I saw her glance at the little Tates' small feet. Shoes, I divined—the feet of the genteel poor being almost as expensive as their stomachs.

As we went back Mr. Jamieson made only one remark: I think he was laboring under the weight of a great disappointment.

"Is King's a children's outfitting place?" he asked.

"Not especially. It is a general department store."

He was silent after that, but he went to the telephone as soon as we got home, and called up King and Company, in the city.

After a time he got the general manager, and they talked for some time. When Mr. Jamieson hung up the receiver he turned to me.

"The plot thickens," he said with his ready smile. "There are four women named Wallace at King's none of them married, and none over twenty. I think I shall go up to the city to-night. I want to go to the Children's Hospital. But before I go, Miss Innes, I wish you would be more frank with me than you have been yet. I want you to show me the revolver you picked up in the tulip bed."

So he had known all along!

"It WAS a revolver, Mr. Jamieson," I admitted, cornered at last, "but I can not show it to you. It is not in my possession."

CHAPTER XXII
A LADDER OUT OF PLACE

At dinner Mr. Jamieson suggested sending a man out in his place for a couple of days, but Halsey was certain there would be nothing more, and felt that he and Alex could manage the situation. The detective went back to town early in the evening, and by nine o'clock Halsey, who had been playing golf—as a man does anything to take his mind away from trouble—was sleeping soundly on the big leather davenport in the living-room.

I sat and knitted, pretending not to notice when Gertrude got up and wandered out into the starlight. As soon as I was satisfied that she had gone, however, I went out cautiously. I had no intention of eavesdropping, but I wanted to be certain that it was Jack Bailey she was meeting. Too many things had occurred in which Gertrude was, or appeared to be, involved, to allow anything to be left in question.

I went slowly across the lawn, skirted the hedge to a break not far from the lodge, and found myself on the open road. Perhaps a hundred feet to the left the path led across the valley to the Country Club, and only a little way off was the foot-bridge over Casanova Creek. But just as I was about to turn down the path I heard steps coming toward me, and I shrank into the bushes. It was Gertrude, going back quickly toward the house.

I was surprised. I waited until she had had time to get almost to the house before I started. And then I stepped back again into the shadows. The reason why Gertrude had not kept her tryst was evident. Leaning on the parapet of the bridge in the moonlight, and smoking a pipe, was Alex, the gardener. I could have throttled Liddy for her carelessness in reading the torn note where he could hear. And I could cheerfully have choked Alex to death for his audacity.

But there was no help for it: I turned and followed Gertrude slowly back to the house.

The frequent invasions of the house had effectually prevented any relaxation after dusk. We had redoubled our vigilance as to bolts and window-locks but, as Mr. Jamieson had suggested, we allowed the door at the east entry to remain as before, locked by the Yale lock only. To provide only one possible entrance for the invader, and to keep a constant guard in the dark at the foot of the circular staircase, seemed to be the only method.

In the absence of the detective, Alex and Halsey arranged to change off, Halsey to be on duty from ten to two, and Alex from two until six. Each man was armed, and, as an additional precaution, the one off duty slept in a room near the head of the circular staircase and kept his door open, to be ready for emergency.

These arrangements were carefully kept from the servants, who were only commencing to sleep at night, and who retired, one and all, with barred doors and lamps that burned full until morning.

The house was quiet again Wednesday night. It was almost a week since Louise had encountered some one on the stairs, and it was four days since the discovery of the hole in the trunk-room wall.

Arnold Armstrong and his father rested side by side in the Casanova churchyard, and at the Zion African Church, on the hill, a new mound marked the last resting-place of poor Thomas.

Louise was with her mother in town, and, beyond a polite note of thanks to me, we had heard nothing from her. Doctor Walker had taken up his practice again, and we saw him now and then flying past along the road, always at top speed. The murder of Arnold Armstrong was still unavenged, and I remained firm in the position I had taken—to stay at Sunnyside until the thing was at least partly cleared.

And yet, for all its quiet, it was on Wednesday night that perhaps the boldest attempt was made to enter the house. On Thursday afternoon the laundress sent word she would like to speak to me, and I saw her in my private sitting-room, a small room beyond the dressing-room.

Mary Anne was embarrassed. She had rolled down her sleeves and tied a white apron around her waist, and she stood making folds in it with fingers that were red and shiny from her soap-suds.

"Well, Mary," I said encouragingly, "what's the matter? Don't dare to tell me the soap is out."

"No, ma'm, Miss Innes." She had a nervous habit of looking first at my one eye and then at the other, her own optics shifting ceaselessly, right eye, left eye, right eye, until I found myself doing the same thing. "No, ma'm. I was askin' did you want the ladder left up the clothes chute?"

"The what?" I screeched, and was sorry the next minute. Seeing her suspicions were verified, Mary Anne had gone white, and stood with her eyes shifting more wildly than ever.

"There's a ladder up the clothes chute, Miss Innes," she said. "It's up that tight I can't move it, and I didn't like to ask for help until I spoke to you."

It was useless to dissemble; Mary Anne knew now as well as I did that the ladder had no business to be there. I did the best I could, however. I put her on the defensive at once.

"Then you didn't lock the laundry last night?"

"I locked it tight, and put the key in the kitchen on its nail."

"Very well, then you forgot a window."

Mary Anne hesitated.

"Yes'm," she said at last. "I thought I locked them all, but there was one open this morning."

I went out of the room and down the hall, followed by Mary Anne. The door into the clothes chute was securely bolted, and when I opened it I saw the evidence of the woman's story. A pruning-ladder had been brought from where it had lain against the stable and now stood upright in the clothes shaft, its end resting against the wall between the first and second floors.

I turned to Mary.

"This is due to your carelessness," I said. "If we had all been murdered in our beds it would have been your fault." She shivered. "Now, not a word of this through the house, and send Alex to me."

The effect on Alex was to make him apoplectic with rage, and with it all I fancied there was an element of satisfaction. As I look back, so many things are plain to me that I wonder I could not see at the time. It is all known now, and yet the whole thing was so remarkable that perhaps my stupidity was excusable.

Alex leaned down the chute and examined the ladder carefully.

"It is caught," he said with a grim smile. "The fools, to have left a warning like that! The only trouble is, Miss Innes, they won't be apt to come back for a while."

"I shouldn't regard that in the light of a calamity," I replied.

Until late that evening Halsey and Alex worked at the chute. They forced down the ladder at last, and put a new bolt on the door. As for myself, I sat and wondered if I had a deadly enemy, intent on my destruction.

I was growing more and more nervous. Liddy had given up all pretense at bravery, and slept regularly in my dressing-room on the couch, with a prayer-book and a game knife from the kitchen under her pillow, thus preparing for both the natural and the supernatural. That was the way things stood that Thursday night, when I myself took a hand in the struggle.

CHAPTER XXIII
WHILE THE STABLES BURNED

About nine o'clock that night Liddy came into the living-room and reported that one of the housemaids declared she had seen two men slip around the corner of the stable. Gertrude had been sitting staring in front of her, jumping at every sound. Now she turned on Liddy pettishly.

"I declare, Liddy," she said, "you are a bundle of nerves. What if Eliza did see some men around the stable? It may have been Warner and Alex."

"Warner is in the kitchen, miss," Liddy said with dignity. "And if you had come through what I have, you would be a bundle of nerves, too. Miss Rachel, I'd be thankful if you'd give me my month's wages to-morrow. I'll be going to my sister's."

"Very well," I said, to her evident amazement. "I will make out the check. Warner can take you down to the noon train."

Liddy's face was really funny.

"You'll have a nice time at your sister's," I went on. "Five children, hasn't she?"

"That's it," Liddy said, suddenly bursting into tears. "Send me away, after all these years, and your new shawl only half done, and nobody knowin' how to fix the water for your bath."

"It's time I learned to prepare my own bath." I was knitting complacently. But Gertrude got up and put her arms around Liddy's shaking shoulders.

"You are two big babies," she said soothingly. "Neither one of you could get along for an hour without the other. So stop quarreling and be good. Liddy, go right up and lay out Aunty's night things. She is going to bed early."

After Liddy had gone I began to think about the men at the stable, and I grew more and more anxious. Halsey was aimlessly knocking the billiard-balls around in the billiard-room, and I called to him.

"Halsey," I said when he sauntered in, "is there a policeman in Casanova?"

"Constable," he said laconically. "Veteran of the war, one arm; in office to conciliate the G. A. R. element. Why?"

"Because I am uneasy to-night." And I told him what Liddy had said. "Is there any one you can think of who could be relied on to watch the outside of the house to-night?"

"We might get Sam Bohannon from the club," he said thoughtfully. "It wouldn't be a bad scheme. He's a smart darky, and with his mouth shut and his shirt-front covered, you couldn't see him a yard off in the dark."

Halsey conferred with Alex, and the result, in an hour, was Sam. His instructions were simple. There had been numerous attempts to break into the house; it was the intention, not to drive intruders away, but to capture them. If Sam saw anything suspicious outside, he was to tap at the east entry, where Alex and Halsey were to alternate in keeping watch through the night.

It was with a comfortable feeling of security that I went to bed that night. The door between Gertrude's rooms and mine had been opened, and, with the doors into the hall bolted, we were safe enough. Although Liddy persisted in her belief that doors would prove no obstacles to our disturbers.

As before, Halsey watched the east entry from ten until two. He had an eye to comfort, and he kept vigil in a heavy oak chair, very large and deep. We went up-stairs rather early, and through the open door Gertrude and I kept up a running fire of conversation. Liddy was brushing my hair, and Gertrude was doing her own, with a long free sweep of her strong round arms.

"Did you know Mrs. Armstrong and Louise are in the village?" she called.

"No," I replied, startled. "How did you hear it?"

"I met the oldest Stewart girl to-day, the doctor's daughter, and she told me they had not gone back to town after the funeral. They went directly to that little yellow house next to Doctor Walker's, and are apparently settled there. They took the house furnished for the summer."

"Why, it's a bandbox," I said. "I can't imagine Fanny Armstrong in such a place."

"It's true, nevertheless. Ella Stewart says Mrs. Armstrong has aged terribly, and looks as if she is hardly able to walk."

I lay and thought over some of these things until midnight. The electric lights went out then, fading slowly until there was only a red-hot loop to be seen in the bulb, and then even that died away and we were embarked on the darkness of another night.

Apparently only a few minutes elapsed, during which my eyes were becoming accustomed to the darkness. Then I noticed that the windows were reflecting a faint pinkish light, Liddy noticed it at the same time, and I heard her jump up. At that moment Sam's deep voice boomed from somewhere just below.

"Fire!" he yelled. "The stable's on fire!"

I could see him in the glare dancing up and down on the drive, and a moment later Halsey joined him. Alex was awake and running down the stairs, and in five minutes from the time the fire was discovered, three of the maids were sitting on their trunks in the drive, although, excepting a few sparks, there was no fire nearer than a hundred yards.

Gertrude seldom loses her presence of mind, and she ran to the telephone. But by the time the Casanova volunteer fire department came toiling up the hill the stable was a furnace, with the Dragon Fly safe but blistered, in the road. Some gasolene exploded just as the volunteer department got to work, which shook their nerves as well as the burning building. The stable, being on a hill, was a torch to attract the population from every direction. Rumor had it that Sunnyside was burning, and it was amazing how many people threw something over their night-clothes and flew to the conflagration.

I take it Casanova has few fires, and Sunnyside was furnishing the people, in one way and another, the greatest excitement they had had for years.

The stable was off the west wing. I hardly know how I came to think of the circular staircase and the unguarded door at its foot. Liddy was putting my clothes into sheets, preparatory to tossing them out the window, when I found her, and I could hardly persuade her to stop.

"I want you to come with me, Liddy," I said. "Bring a candle and a couple of blankets."

She lagged behind considerably when she saw me making for the east wing, and at the top of the staircase she balked.

"I am not going down there," she said firmly.

"There is no one guarding the door down there," I explained. "Who knows?—this may be a scheme to draw everybody away from this end of the house, and let some one in here."

The instant I had said it I was convinced I had hit on the explanation, and that perhaps it was already too late. It seemed to me as I listened that I heard stealthy footsteps on the east porch, but there was so much shouting outside that it was impossible to tell. Liddy was on the point of retreat.

"Very well," I said, "then I shall go down alone. Run back to Mr. Halsey's room and get his revolver. Don't shoot down the stairs if you hear a noise: remember—I shall be down there. And hurry."

I put the candle on the floor at the top of the staircase and took off my bedroom slippers. Then I crept down the stairs, going very slowly, and listening with all my ears. I was keyed to such a pitch that I felt no fear: like the condemned who sleep and eat the night before execution, I was no longer able to suffer apprehension. I was past that. Just at the foot of the stairs I stubbed my toe against Halsey's big chair, and had to stand on one foot in a soundless agony until the pain subsided to a dull ache. And then—I knew I was right. Some one had put a key into the lock, and was turning it. For some reason it refused to work, and the key was withdrawn. There was a muttering of voices outside: I had only a second. Another trial, and the door would open. The candle above made a faint gleam down the well-like staircase, and at that moment, with a second, no more, to spare, I thought of a plan.

The heavy oak chair almost filled the space between the newel post and the door. With a crash I had turned it on its side, wedging it against the door, its legs against the stairs. I could hear a faint scream from Liddy, at the crash, and then she came down the stairs on a run, with the revolver held straight out in front of her.

"Thank God," she said, in a shaking voice. "I thought it was you."

I pointed to the door, and she understood.

"Call out the windows at the other end of the house," I whispered. "Run. Tell them not to wait for anything."

She went up the stairs at that, two at a time. Evidently she collided with the candle, for it went out, and I was left in darkness.

I was really astonishingly cool. I remember stepping over the chair and gluing my ear to the door, and I shall never forget feeling it give an inch or two there in the darkness, under a steady pressure from without. But the chair held, although I could hear an ominous cracking of one of the legs. And then, without the slightest warning, the card-room window broke with a crash. I had my finger on the trigger of the revolver, and as I jumped it went off, right through the door. Some one outside swore roundly, and for the first time I could hear what was said.

"Only a scratch. . . . Men are at the other end of the house. . . . Have the whole rat's nest on us." And a lot of profanity which I won't write down. The voices were at the broken window now, and although I was trembling violently, I was determined that I would hold them until help came. I moved up the stairs until I could see into the card-room, or rather through it, to the window. As I looked a small man put his leg over the sill and stepped into the room. The curtain confused him for a moment; then he turned, not toward me, but toward the billiard-room door. I fired again, and something that was glass or china crashed to the ground. Then I ran up the stairs and along the corridor to the main staircase. Gertrude was standing there, trying to locate the shots, and I must have been a peculiar figure, with my hair in crimps, my dressing-gown flying, no slippers, and a revolver clutched in my hands I had no time to talk. There was the sound of footsteps in the lower hall, and some one bounded up the stairs.

I had gone Berserk, I think. I leaned over the stair-rail and fired again. Halsey, below, yelled at me.

"What are you doing up there?" he yelled. "You missed me by an inch."

And then I collapsed and fainted. When I came around Liddy was rubbing my temples with eau de quinine, and the search was in full blast.

Well, the man was gone. The stable burned to the ground, while the crowd cheered at every falling rafter, and the volunteer fire department sprayed it with a garden hose. And in the house Alex and Halsey searched every corner of the lower floor, finding no one.

The truth of my story was shown by the broken window and the overturned chair. That the unknown had got up-stairs was almost impossible. He had not used the main staircase, there was no way to the upper floor in the east wing, and Liddy had been at the window, in the west wing, where the servants' stair went up. But we did not go to bed at all. Sam Bohannon and Warner helped in the search, and not a closet escaped scrutiny. Even the cellars were given a thorough overhauling, without result. The door in the east entry had a hole through it where my bullet had gone.

The hole slanted downward, and the bullet was embedded in the porch. Some reddish stains showed it had done execution.

"Somebody will walk lame," Halsey said, when he had marked the course of the bullet. "It's too low to have hit anything but a leg or foot."

From that time on I watched every person I met for a limp, and to this day the man who halts in his walk is an object of suspicion to me. But Casanova had no lame men: the nearest approach to it was an old fellow who tended the safety gates at the railroad, and he, I learned on inquiry, had two artificial legs. Our man had gone, and the large and expensive stable at Sunnyside was a heap of smoking rafters and charred boards. Warner swore the fire was incendiary, and in view of the attempt to enter the house, there seemed to be no doubt of it.

CHAPTER XXIV
FLINDERS

If Halsey had only taken me fully into his confidence, through the whole affair, it would have been much simpler. If he had been altogether frank about Jack Bailey, and if the day after the fire he had told me what he suspected, there would have been no harrowing period for all of us, with the boy in danger. But young people refuse to profit by the experience of their elders, and sometimes the elders are the ones to suffer.

I was much used up the day after the fire, and Gertrude insisted on my going out. The machine was temporarily out of commission, and the carriage horses had been sent to a farm for the summer. Gertrude finally got a trap from the Casanova liveryman, and we went out. Just as we turned from the drive into the road we passed a woman. She had put down a small valise, and stood inspecting the house and grounds minutely. I should hardly have noticed her, had it not been for the fact that she had been horribly disfigured by smallpox.

"Ugh!" Gertrude said, when we had passed, "what a face! I shall dream of it to-night. Get up, Flinders."

"Flinders?" I asked. "Is that the horse's name?"

"It is." She flicked the horse's stubby mane with the whip. "He didn't look like a livery horse, and the liveryman said he had bought him from the Armstrongs when they purchased a couple of motors and cut down the stable. Nice Flinders—good old boy!"

Flinders was certainly not a common name for a horse, and yet the youngster at Richfield had named his prancing, curly-haired little horse Flinders! It set me to thinking.

At my request Halsey had already sent word of the fire to the agent from whom we had secured the house. Also, he had called Mr. Jamieson by telephone, and somewhat guardedly had told him of the previous night's events. Mr. Jamieson promised to come out that night, and to bring another man with him. I did not consider it necessary to notify Mrs. Armstrong, in the village. No doubt she knew of the fire, and in view of my refusal to give up the house, an interview would probably have been unpleasant enough. But as we passed Doctor Walker's white and green house I thought of something.

"Stop here, Gertrude," I said. "I am going to get out."

"To see Louise?" she asked.

"No, I want to ask this young Walker something."

She was curious, I knew, but I did not wait to explain. I went up the walk to the house, where a brass sign at the side announced the office, and went in. The reception-room was empty, but from the consulting-room beyond came the sound of two voices, not very amicable.

"It is an outrageous figure," some one was storming. Then the doctor's quiet tone, evidently not arguing, merely stating something. But I had not time to listen to some person probably disputing his bill, so I coughed. The voices ceased at once: a door closed somewhere, and the doctor entered from the hall of the house. He looked sufficiently surprised at seeing me.

"Good afternoon, Doctor," I said formally. "I shall not keep you from your patient. I wish merely to ask you a question."

"Won't you sit down?"

"It will not be necessary. Doctor, has any one come to you, either early this morning or to-day, to have you treat a bullet wound?"

"Nothing so startling has happened to me," he said. "A bullet wound! Things must be lively at Sunnyside."

"I didn't say it was at Sunnyside. But as it happens, it was. If any such case comes to you, will it be too much trouble for you to let me know?"

"I shall be only too happy," he said. "I understand you have had a fire up there, too. A fire and shooting in one night is rather lively for a quiet place like that."

"It is as quiet as a boiler-shop," I replied, as I turned to go.

"And you are still going to stay?"

"Until I am burned out," I responded. And then on my way down the steps, I turned around suddenly.

"Doctor," I asked at a venture, "have you ever heard of a child named Lucien Wallace?"

Clever as he was, his face changed and stiffened. He was on his guard again in a moment.

"Lucien Wallace?" he repeated. "No, I think not. There are plenty of Wallaces around, but I don't know any Lucien."

I was as certain as possible that he did. People do not lie readily to me, and this man lied beyond a doubt. But there was nothing to be gained now; his defenses were up, and I left, half irritated and wholly baffled.

Our reception was entirely different at Doctor Stewart's. Taken into the bosom of the family at once, Flinders tied outside and nibbling the grass at the roadside, Gertrude and I drank some home-made elderberry wine and told briefly of the fire. Of the more serious part of the night's experience, of course, we said nothing. But when at last we had left the family on the porch and the good doctor was untying our steed, I asked him the same question I had put to Doctor Walker.

"Shot!" he said. "Bless my soul, no. Why, what have you been doing up at the big house, Miss Innes?"

"Some one tried to enter the house during the fire, and was shot and slightly injured," I said hastily. "Please don't mention it; we wish to make as little of it as possible."

There was one other possibility, and we tried that. At Casanova station I saw the station master, and asked him if any trains left Casanova between one o'clock and daylight. There was none until six A.M. The next question required more diplomacy.

"Did you notice on the six-o'clock train any person—any man—who limped a little?" I asked. "Please try to remember: we are trying to trace a man who was seen loitering around Sunnyside last night before the fire."

He was all attention in a moment.

"I was up there myself at the fire," he said volubly. "I'm a member of the volunteer company. First big fire we've had since the summer house burned over to the club golf links. My wife was sayin' the other day, 'Dave, you might as well 'a' saved the money in that there helmet and shirt.' And here last night they came in handy. Rang that bell so hard I hadn't time scarcely to get 'em on."

"And—did you see a man who limped?" Gertrude put in, as he stopped for breath.

"Not at the train, ma'm," he said. "No such person got on here to-day. But I'll tell you where I did see a man that limped. I didn't wait till the fire company left; there's a fast freight goes through at four forty-five, and I had to get down to the station. I seen there wasn't much more to do anyhow at the fire—we'd got the flames under control"—Gertrude looked at me and smiled—"so I started down the hill. There was folks here and there goin' home, and along by the path to the Country Club I seen two men. One was a short fellow. He was sitting on a big rock, his back to me, and he had something white in his hand, as if he was tying up his foot. After I'd gone on a piece I looked back, and he was hobbling on and—excuse me, miss—he was swearing something sickening."

"Did they go toward the club?" Gertrude asked suddenly, leaning forward.

"No, miss. I think they came into the village. I didn't get a look at their faces, but I know every chick and child in the place, and everybody knows me. When they didn't shout at me—in my uniform, you know—I took it they were strangers."

So all we had for our afternoon's work was this: some one had been shot by the bullet that went through the door; he had not left the village, and he had not called in a physician. Also, Doctor Walker knew who Lucien Wallace was, and his very denial made me confident that, in that one direction at least, we were on the right track.

The thought that the detective would be there that night was the most cheering thing of all, and I think even Gertrude was glad of it. Driving home that afternoon, I saw her in the clear sunlight for the first time in several days, and I was startled to see how ill she looked. She was thin and colorless, and all her bright animation was gone.

"Gertrude," I said, "I have been a very selfish old woman. You are going to leave this miserable house to-night. Annie Morton is going to Scotland next week, and you shall go right with her."

To my surprise, she flushed painfully.

"I don't want to go, Aunt Ray," she said. "Don't make me leave now."

"You are losing your health and your good looks," I said decidedly. "You should have a change."

"I shan't stir a foot." She was equally decided. Then, more lightly: "Why, you and Liddy need me to arbitrate between you every day in the week."

Perhaps I was growing suspicious of every one, but it seemed to me that Gertrude's gaiety was forced and artificial. I watched her covertly during the rest of the drive, and I did not like the two spots of crimson in her pale cheeks. But I said nothing more about sending her to Scotland: I knew she would not go.

CHAPTER XXV
A VISIT FROM LOUISE

That day was destined to be an eventful one, for when I entered the house and found Eliza ensconced in the upper hall on a chair, with Mary Anne doing her best to stifle her with household ammonia, and Liddy rubbing her wrists—whatever good that is supposed to do—I knew that the ghost had been walking again, and this time in daylight.

Eliza was in a frenzy of fear. She clutched at my sleeve when I went close to her, and refused to let go until she had told her story. Coming just after the fire, the household was demoralized, and it was no surprise to me to find Alex and the under-gardener struggling downstairs with a heavy trunk between them.

"I didn't want to do it, Miss Innes," Alex said. "But she was so excited, I was afraid she would do as she said—drag it down herself, and scratch the staircase."

I was trying to get my bonnet off and to keep the maids quiet at the same time. "Now, Eliza, when you have washed your face and stopped bawling," I said, "come into my sitting-room and tell me what has happened."

Liddy put away my things without speaking. The very set of her shoulders expressed disapproval.

"Well," I said, when the silence became uncomfortable, "things seem to be warming up."

Silence from Liddy, and a long sigh.

"If Eliza goes, I don't know where to look for another cook." More silence.

"Rosie is probably a good cook." Sniff.

"Liddy," I said at last, "don't dare to deny that you are having the time of your life. You positively gloat in this excitement. You never looked better. It's my opinion all this running around, and getting jolted out of a rut, has stirred up that torpid liver of yours."

"It's not myself I'm thinking about," she said, goaded into speech. "Maybe my liver was torpid, and maybe it wasn't; but I know this: I've got some feelings left, and to see you standing at the foot of that staircase shootin' through the door—I'll never be the same woman again."

"Well, I'm glad of that—anything for a change," I said. And in came Eliza, flanked by Rosie and Mary Anne.

Her story, broken with sobs and corrections from the other two, was this: At two o'clock (two-fifteen, Rosie insisted) she had gone up-stairs to get a picture from her room to show Mary Anne. (A picture of a LADY, Mary Anne interposed.) She went up the servants' staircase and along the corridor to her room, which lay between the trunk-room and the unfinished ball-room. She heard a sound as she went down the corridor, like some one moving furniture, but she was not nervous. She thought it might be men examining the house after the fire the night before, but she looked in the trunk-room and saw nobody.

She went into her room quietly. The noise had ceased, and everything was quiet. Then she sat down on the side of her bed, and, feeling faint—she was subject to spells—("I told you that when I came, didn't I, Rosie?" "Yes'm, indeed she did!")—she put her head down on her pillow and—

"Took a nap. All right!" I said. "Go on."

"When I came to, Miss Innes, sure as I'm sittin' here, I thought I'd die. Somethin' hit me on the face, and I set up, sudden. And then I seen the plaster drop, droppin' from a little hole in the wall. And the first thing I knew, an iron bar that long" (fully two yards by her measure) "shot through that hole and tumbled on the bed. If I'd been still sleeping" ("Fainting," corrected Rosie) "I'd 'a' been hit on the head and killed!"

"I wisht you'd heard her scream," put in Mary Anne. "And her face as white as a pillow-slip when she tumbled down the stairs."

"No doubt there is some natural explanation for it, Eliza," I said. "You may have dreamed it, in your 'fainting' attack. But if it is true, the metal rod and the hole in the wall will show it."

Eliza looked a little bit sheepish.

"The hole's there all right, Miss Innes," she said. "But the bar was gone when Mary Anne and Rosie went up to pack my trunk."

"That wasn't all," Liddy's voice came funereally from a corner. "Eliza said that from the hole in the wall a burning eye looked down at her!"

"The wall must be at least six inches thick," I said with asperity. "Unless the person who drilled the hole carried his eyes on the ends of a stick, Eliza couldn't possibly have seen them."

But the fact remained, and a visit to Eliza's room proved it. I might jeer all I wished: some one had drilled a hole in the unfinished wall of the ball-room, passing between the bricks of the partition, and shooting through the unresisting plaster of Eliza's room with such force as to send the rod flying on to her bed. I had gone up-stairs alone, and I confess the thing puzzled me: in two or three places in the wall small apertures had been made, none of them of any depth. Not the least mysterious thing was the disappearance of the iron implement that had been used.

I remembered a story I read once about an impish dwarf that lived in the spaces between the double walls of an ancient castle. I wondered vaguely if my original idea of a secret entrance to a hidden chamber could be right, after all, and if we were housing some erratic guest, who played pranks on us in the dark, and destroyed the walls that he might listen, hidden safely away, to our amazed investigations.

Mary Anne and Eliza left that afternoon, but Rosie decided to stay. It was about five o'clock when the hack came from the station to get them, and, to my amazement, it had an occupant. Matthew Geist, the driver, asked for me, and explained his errand with pride.

"I've brought you a cook, Miss Innes," he said. "When the message came to come up for two girls and their trunks, I supposed there was something doing, and as this here woman had been looking for work in the village, I thought I'd bring her along."

Already I had acquired the true suburbanite ability to take servants on faith; I no longer demanded written and unimpeachable references. I, Rachel Innes, have learned not to mind if the cook sits down comfortably in my sitting-room when she is taking the orders for the day, and I am grateful if the silver is not cleaned with scouring soap. And so that day I merely told Liddy to send the new applicant in. When she came, however, I could hardly restrain a gasp of surprise. It was the woman with the pitted face.

She stood somewhat awkwardly just inside the door, and she had an air of self-confidence that was inspiring. Yes, she could cook; was not a fancy cook, but could make good soups and desserts if there was any one to take charge of the salads. And so, in the end, I took her. As Halsey said, when we told him, it didn't matter much about the cook's face, if it was clean.

I have spoken of Halsey's restlessness. On that day it seemed to be more than ever a resistless impulse that kept him out until after luncheon. I think he hoped constantly that he might meet Louise driving over the hills in her runabout: possibly he did meet her occasionally, but from his continued gloom I felt sure the situation between them was unchanged.

Part of the afternoon I believe he read—Gertrude and I were out, as I have said, and at dinner we both noticed that something had occurred to distract him. He was disagreeable, which is unlike him, nervous, looking at his watch every few minutes, and he ate almost nothing. He asked twice during the meal on what train Mr. Jamieson and the other detective were coming, and had long periods of abstraction during which he dug his fork into my damask cloth and did not hear when he was spoken to. He refused dessert, and left the table early, excusing himself on the ground that he wanted to see Alex.

Alex, however, was not to be found. It was after eight when Halsey ordered the car, and started down the hill at a pace that, even for him, was unusually reckless. Shortly after, Alex reported that he was ready to go over the house, preparatory to closing it for the night. Sam Bohannon came at a quarter before nine, and began his patrol of the grounds, and with the arrival of the two detectives to look forward to, I was not especially apprehensive.

At half-past nine I heard the sound of a horse driven furiously up the drive. It came to a stop in front of the house, and immediately after there were hurried steps on the veranda. Our nerves were not what they should have been, and Gertrude, always apprehensive lately, was at the door almost instantly. A moment later Louise had burst into the room and stood there bareheaded and breathing hard!

"Where is Halsey?" she demanded. Above her plain black gown her eyes looked big and somber, and the rapid drive had brought no color to her face. I got up and drew forward a chair.

"He has not come back," I said quietly. "Sit down, child; you are not strong enough for this kind of thing."

I don't think she even heard me.

"He has not come back?" she asked, looking from me to Gertrude. "Do you know where he went? Where can I find him?"

"For Heaven's sake, Louise," Gertrude burst out, "tell us what is wrong. Halsey is not here. He has gone to the station for Mr. Jamieson. What has happened?"

"To the station, Gertrude? You are sure?"

"Yes," I said. "Listen. There is the whistle of the train now."

She relaxed a little at our matter-of-fact tone, and allowed herself to sink into a chair.

"Perhaps I was wrong," she said heavily. "He—will be here in a few moments if—everything is right."

We sat there, the three of us, without attempt at conversation. Both Gertrude and I recognized the futility of asking Louise any questions: her reticence was a part of a role she had assumed. Our ears were strained for the first throb of the motor as it turned into the drive and commenced the climb to the house. Ten minutes passed, fifteen, twenty. I saw Louise's hands grow rigid as they clutched the arms of her chair. I watched Gertrude's bright color slowly ebbing away, and around my own heart I seemed to feel the grasp of a giant hand.

Twenty-five minutes, and then a sound. But it was not the chug of the motor: it was the unmistakable rumble of the Casanova hack. Gertrude drew aside the curtain and peered into the darkness.

"It's the hack, I am sure," she said, evidently relieved. "Something has gone wrong with the car, and no wonder—the way Halsey went down the hill."

It seemed a long time before the creaking vehicle came to a stop at the door. Louise rose and stood watching, her hand to her throat. And then Gertrude opened the door, admitting Mr. Jamieson and a stocky, middle-aged man. Halsey was not with them. When the door had closed and Louise realized that Halsey had not come, her expression changed. From tense watchfulness to relief, and now again to absolute despair, her face was an open page.

"Halsey?" I asked unceremoniously, ignoring the stranger. "Did he not meet you?"

"No." Mr. Jamieson looked slightly surprised. "I rather expected the car, but we got up all right."

"You didn't see him at all?" Louise demanded breathlessly.

Mr. Jamieson knew her at once, although he had not seen her before. She had kept to her rooms until the morning she left.

"No, Miss Armstrong," he said. "I saw nothing of him. What is wrong?"

"Then we shall have to find him," she asserted. "Every instant is precious. Mr. Jamieson, I have reason for believing that he is in danger, but I don't know what it is. Only—he must be found."

The stocky man had said nothing. Now, however, he went quickly toward the door.

"I'll catch the hack down the road and hold it," he said. "Is the gentleman down in the town?"

"Mr. Jamieson," Louise said impulsively, "I can use the hack. Take my horse and trap outside and drive like mad. Try to find the Dragon Fly—it ought to be easy to trace. I can think of no other way. Only, don't lose a moment."

The new detective had gone, and a moment later Jamieson went rapidly down the drive, the cob's feet striking fire at every step. Louise stood looking after them. When she turned around she faced Gertrude, who stood indignant, almost tragic, in the hall.

"You KNOW what threatens Halsey, Louise," she said accusingly. "I believe you know this whole horrible thing, this mystery that we are struggling with. If anything happens to Halsey, I shall never forgive you."

Louise only raised her hands despairingly and dropped them again.

"He is as dear to me as he is to you," she said sadly. "I tried to warn him."

"Nonsense!" I said, as briskly as I could. "We are making a lot of trouble out of something perhaps very small. Halsey was probably late—he is always late. Any moment we may hear the car coming up the road."

But it did not come. After a half-hour of suspense, Louise went out quietly, and did not come back. I hardly knew she was gone until I heard the station hack moving off. At eleven o'clock the telephone rang. It was Mr. Jamieson.

"I have found the Dragon Fly, Miss Innes," he said. "It has collided with a freight car on the siding above the station. No, Mr. Innes was not there, but we shall probably find him. Send Warner for the car."

But they did not find him. At four o'clock the next morning we were still waiting for news, while Alex watched the house and Sam the grounds. At daylight I dropped into exhausted sleep. Halsey had not come back, and there was no word from the detective.

CHAPTER XXVI
HALSEY'S DISAPPEARANCE

Nothing that had gone before had been as bad as this. The murder and Thomas' sudden death we had been able to view in a detached sort of way. But with Halsey's disappearance everything was altered. Our little circle, intact until now, was broken. We were no longer onlookers who saw a battle passing around them. We were the center of action. Of course, there was no time then to voice such an idea. My mind seemed able to hold only one thought: that Halsey had been foully dealt with, and that every minute lost might be fatal.

Mr. Jamieson came back about eight o'clock the next morning: he was covered with mud, and his hat was gone. Altogether, we were a sad-looking trio that gathered around a breakfast that no one could eat. Over a cup of black coffee the detective told us what he had learned of Halsey's movements the night before. Up to a certain point the car had made it easy enough to follow him. And I gathered that Mr. Burns, the other detective, had followed a similar car for miles at dawn, only to find it was a touring car on an endurance run.

"He left here about ten minutes after eight," Mr. Jamieson said. "He went alone, and at eight twenty he stopped at Doctor Walker's. I went to the doctor's about midnight, but he had been called out on a case, and had not come back at four o'clock. From the doctor's it seems Mr. Innes walked across the lawn to the cottage Mrs. Armstrong and her daughter have taken. Mrs. Armstrong had retired, and he said perhaps a dozen words to Miss Louise. She will not say what they were, but the girl evidently suspects what has occurred. That is, she suspects foul play, but she doesn't know of what nature. Then, apparently, he started directly for the station. He was going very fast—the flagman at the Carol Street crossing says he saw the car pass. He knew the siren. Along somewhere in the dark stretch between Carol Street and the depot he evidently swerved suddenly—perhaps some one in the road—and went full into the side of a freight. We found it there last night."

"He might have been thrown under the train by the force of the shock," I said tremulously. Gertrude shuddered.

"We examined every inch of track. There was—no sign."

"But surely—he can't be—gone!" I cried. "Aren't there traces in the mud—anything?"

"There is no mud—only dust. There has been no rain. And the footpath there is of cinders. Miss Innes, I am inclined to think that he has met with bad treatment, in the light of what has gone before. I do not think he has been murdered." I shrank from the word. "Burns is back in the country, on a clue we got from the night clerk at the drug-store. There will be two more men here by noon, and the city office is on the lookout."

"The creek?" Gertrude asked.

"The creek is shallow now. If it were swollen with rain, it would be different. There is hardly any water in it. Now, Miss Innes," he said, turning to me, "I must ask you some questions. Had Mr. Halsey any possible reason for going away like this, without warning?"

"None whatever."

"He went away once before," he persisted. "And you were as sure then."

"He did not leave the Dragon Fly jammed into the side of a freight car before."

"No, but he left it for repairs in a blacksmith shop, a long distance from here. Do you know if he had any enemies? Any one who might wish him out of the way?"

"Not that I know of, unless—no, I can not think of any."

"Was he in the habit of carrying money?"

"He never carried it far. No, he never had more than enough for current expenses."

Mr. Jamieson got up then and began to pace the room. It was an unwonted concession to the occasion.

"Then I think we get at it by elimination. The chances are against flight. If he was hurt, we find no trace of him. It looks almost like an abduction. This young Doctor Walker—have you any idea why Mr. Innes should have gone there last night?"

"I can not understand it," Gertrude said thoughtfully. "I don't think he knew Doctor Walker at all, and—their relations could hardly have been cordial, under the circumstances."

Jamieson pricked up his ears, and little by little he drew from us the unfortunate story of Halsey's love affair, and the fact that Louise was going to marry Doctor Walker.

Mr. Jamieson listened attentively.

"There are some interesting developments here," he said thoughtfully. "The woman who claims to be the mother of Lucien Wallace has not come back. Your nephew has apparently been spirited away. There is an organized attempt being made to enter this house; in fact, it has been entered. Witness the incident with the cook yesterday. And I have a new piece of information."

He looked carefully away from Gertrude. "Mr. John Bailey is not at his Knickerbocker apartments, and I don't know where he is. It's a hash, that's what it is. It's a Chinese puzzle. They won't fit together, unless—unless Mr. Bailey and your nephew have again—"

And once again Gertrude surprised me. "They are not together," she said hotly. "I—know where Mr. Bailey is, and my brother is not with him."

The detective turned and looked at her keenly.

"Miss Gertrude," he said, "if you and Miss Louise would only tell me everything you know and surmise about this business, I should be able to do a great many things. I believe I could find your brother, and I might be able to—well, to do some other things." But Gertrude's glance did not falter.

"Nothing that I know could help you to find Halsey," she said stubbornly. "I know absolutely as little of his disappearance as you do, and I can only say this: I do not trust Doctor Walker. I think he hated Halsey, and he would get rid of him if he could."

"Perhaps you are right. In fact, I had some such theory myself. But Doctor Walker went out late last night to a serious case in Summitville, and is still there. Burns traced him there. We have made guarded inquiry at the Greenwood Club, and through the village. There is absolutely nothing to go on but this. On the embankment above the railroad, at the point where we found the machine, is a small house. An old woman and a daughter, who is very lame, live there. They say that they distinctly heard the shock when the Dragon Fly hit the car, and they went to the bottom of their garden and looked over. The automobile was there; they could see the lights, and they thought someone had been injured. It was very dark, but they could make out two figures, standing together. The women were curious, and, leaving the fence, they went back and by a roundabout path down to the road. When they got there the car was still standing, the headlight broken and the bonnet crushed, but there was no one to be seen."

The detective went away immediately, and to Gertrude and me was left the woman's part, to watch and wait. By luncheon nothing had been found, and I was frantic. I went up-stairs to Halsey's room finally, from sheer inability to sit across from Gertrude any longer, and meet her terror-filled eyes.

Liddy was in my dressing-room, suspiciously red-eyed, and trying to put a right sleeve in a left armhole of a new waist for me. I was too much shaken to scold.

"What name did that woman in the kitchen give?" she demanded, viciously ripping out the offending sleeve.

"Bliss. Mattie Bliss," I replied.

"Bliss. M. B. Well, that's not what she has on he suitcase. It is marked N. F. C."

The new cook and her initials troubled me not at all. I put on my bonnet and sent for what the Casanova liveryman called a "stylish turnout." Having once made up my mind to a course of action, I am not one to turn back. Warner drove me; he was plainly disgusted, and he steered the livery horse as he would the Dragon Fly, feeling uneasily with his left foot for the clutch, and working his right elbow at an imaginary horn every time a dog got in the way.

Warner had something on his mind, and after we had turned into the road, he voiced it.

"Miss Innes," he said. "I overheard a part of a conversation yesterday that I didn't understand. It wasn't my business to understand it, for that matter. But I've been thinking all day that I'd better tell you. Yesterday afternoon, while you and Miss Gertrude were out driving, I had got the car in some sort of shape again after the fire, and I went to the library to call Mr. Innes to see it. I went into the living-room, where Miss Liddy said he was, and half-way across to the library I heard him talking to some one. He seemed to be walking up and down, and he was in a rage, I can tell you."

"What did he say?"

"The first thing I heard was—excuse me, Miss Innes, but it's what he said, 'The damned rascal,' he said, 'I'll see him in'—well, in hell was what he said, 'in hell first.' Then somebody else spoke up; it was a woman. She said, 'I warned them, but they thought I would be afraid.'"

"A woman! Did you wait to see who it was?"

"I wasn't spying, Miss Innes," Warner said with dignity. "But the next thing caught my attention. She said, 'I knew there was something wrong from the start. A man isn't well one day, and dead the next, without some reason.' I thought she was speaking of Thomas."

"And you don't know who it was!" I exclaimed. "Warner, you had the key to this whole occurrence in your hands, and did not use it!"

However, there was nothing to be done. I resolved to make inquiry when I got home, and in the meantime, my present errand absorbed me. This was nothing less than to see Louise Armstrong, and to attempt to drag from her what she knew, or suspected, of Halsey's disappearance. But here, as in every direction I turned, I was baffled.

A neat maid answered the bell, but she stood squarely in the doorway, and it was impossible to preserve one's dignity and pass her.

"Miss Armstrong is very ill, and unable to see any one," she said. I did not believe her.

"And Mrs. Armstrong—is she also ill?"

"She is with Miss Louise and can not be disturbed."

"Tell her it is Miss Innes, and that it is a matter of the greatest importance."

"It would be of no use, Miss Innes. My orders are positive."

At that moment a heavy step sounded on the stairs. Past the maid's white-strapped shoulder I could see a familiar thatch of gray hair, and in a moment I was face to face with Doctor Stewart. He was very grave, and his customary geniality was tinged with restraint.

"You are the very woman I want to see," he said promptly. "Send away your trap, and let me drive you home. What is this about your nephew?"

"He has disappeared, doctor. Not only that, but there is every evidence that he has been either abducted, or—" I could not finish. The doctor helped me into his capacious buggy in silence. Until we had got a little distance he did not speak; then he turned and looked at me.

"Now tell me about it," he said. He heard me through without speaking.

"And you think Louise knows something?" he said when I had finished. "I don't—in fact, I am sure of it. The best evidence of it is this: she asked me if he had been heard from, or if anything had been learned. She won't allow Walker in the room, and she made me promise to see you and tell you this: don't give up the search for him. Find him, and find him soon. He is living."

"Well," I said, "if she knows that, she knows more. She is a very cruel and ungrateful girl."

"She is a very sick girl," he said gravely. "Neither you nor I can judge her until we know everything. Both she and her mother are ghosts of their former selves. Under all this, these two sudden deaths, this bank robbery, the invasions at Sunnyside and Halsey's disappearance, there is some mystery that, mark my words, will come out some day. And when it does, we shall find Louise Armstrong a victim."

I had not noticed where we were going, but now I saw we were beside the railroad, and from a knot of men standing beside the track I divined that it was here the car had been found. The siding, however, was empty. Except a few bits of splintered wood on the ground, there was no sign of the accident.

"Where is the freight car that was rammed?" the doctor asked a bystander.

"It was taken away at daylight, when the train was moved."

There was nothing to be gained. He pointed out the house on the embankment where the old lady and her daughter had heard the crash and seen two figures beside the car. Then we drove slowly home. I had the doctor put me down at the gate, and I walked to the house—past the lodge where we had found Louise, and, later, poor Thomas; up the drive where I had seen a man watching the lodge and where, later, Rosie had been frightened; past the east entrance, where so short a time before the most obstinate effort had been made to enter the house, and where, that night two weeks ago, Liddy and I had seen the strange woman. Not far from the west wing lay the blackened ruins of the stables. I felt like a ruin myself, as I paused on the broad veranda before I entered the house.

Two private detectives had arrived in my absence, and it was a relief to turn over to them the responsibility of the house and grounds. Mr. Jamieson, they said, had arranged for more to assist in the search for the missing man, and at that time the country was being scoured in all directions.

The household staff was again depleted that afternoon. Liddy was waiting to tell me that the new cook had gone, bag and baggage, without waiting to be paid. No one had admitted the visitor whom Warner had heard in the library, unless, possibly, the missing cook. Again I was working in a circle.

CHAPTER XXVII
WHO IS NINA CARRINGTON?

The four days, from Saturday to the following Tuesday, we lived, or existed, in a state of the most dreadful suspense. We ate only when Liddy brought in a tray, and then very little. The papers, of course, had got hold of the story, and we were besieged by newspaper men. From all over the country false clues came pouring in and raised hopes that crumbled again to nothing. Every morgue within a hundred miles, every hospital, had been visited, without result.

Mr. Jamieson, personally, took charge of the organized search, and every evening, no matter where he happened to be, he called us by long distance telephone. It was the same formula. "Nothing to-day. A new clue to work on. Better luck to-morrow."

And heartsick we would put up the receiver and sit down again to our vigil.

The inaction was deadly. Liddy cried all day, and, because she knew I objected to tears, sniffled audibly around the corner.

"For Heaven's sake, smile!" I snapped at her. And her ghastly attempt at a grin, with her swollen nose and red eyes, made me hysterical. I laughed and cried together, and pretty soon, like the two old fools we were, we were sitting together weeping into the same handkerchief.

Things were happening, of course, all the time, but they made little or no impression. The Charity Hospital called up Doctor Stewart and reported that Mrs. Watson was in a critical condition. I understood also that legal steps were being taken to terminate my lease at Sunnyside. Louise was out of danger, but very ill, and a trained nurse guarded her like a gorgon. There was a rumor in the village, brought up by Liddy from the butcher's, that a wedding had already taken place between Louise and Doctor Walkers and this roused me for the first time to action.

On Tuesday, then, I sent for the car, and prepared to go out. As I waited at the porte-cochere I saw the under-gardener, an inoffensive, grayish-haired man, trimming borders near the house.

The day detective was watching him, sitting on the carriage block. When he saw me, he got up.

"Miss Innes," he said, taking of his hat, "do you know where Alex, the gardener, is?"

"Why, no. Isn't he here?" I asked.

"He has been gone since yesterday afternoon. Have you employed him long?"

"Only a couple of weeks."

"Is he efficient? A capable man?"

"I hardly know," I said vaguely. "The place looks all right, and I know very little about such things. I know much more about boxes of roses than bushes of them."

"This man," pointing to the assistant, "says Alex isn't a gardener. That he doesn't know anything about plants."

"That's very strange," I said, thinking hard. "Why, he came to me from the Brays, who are in Europe."

"Exactly." The detective smiled. "Every man who cuts grass isn't a gardener, Miss Innes, and just now it is our policy to believe every person around here a rascal until he proves to be the other thing."

Warner came up with the car then, and the conversation stopped. As he helped me in, however, the detective said something further.

"Not a word or sign to Alex, if he comes back," he said cautiously.

I went first to Doctor Walker's. I was tired of beating about the bush, and I felt that the key to Halsey's disappearance was here at Casanova, in spite of Mr. Jamieson's theories.

The doctor was in. He came at once to the door of his consulting-room, and there was no mask of cordiality in his manner.

"Please come in," he said curtly.

"I shall stay here, I think, doctor." I did not like his face or his manner; there was a subtle change in both. He had thrown of the air of friendliness, and I thought, too, that he looked anxious and haggard.

"Doctor Walker," I said, "I have come to you to ask some questions. I hope you will answer them. As you know, my nephew has not yet been found."

"So I understand," stiffly.

"I believe, if you would, you could help us, and that leads to one of my questions. Will you tell me what was the nature of the conversation you held with him the night he was attacked and carried off?"

"Attacked! Carried off!" he said, with pretended surprise. "Really, Miss Innes, don't you think you exaggerate? I understand it is not the first time Mr. Innes has—disappeared."

"You are quibbling, doctor. This is a matter of life and death. Will you answer my question?"

"Certainly. He said his nerves were bad, and I gave him a prescription for them. I am violating professional ethics when I tell you even as much as that."

I could not tell him he lied. I think I looked it. But I hazarded a random shot.

"I thought perhaps," I said, watching him narrowly, "that it might be about—Nina Carrington."

For a moment I thought he was going to strike me. He grew livid, and a small crooked blood-vessel in his temple swelled and throbbed curiously. Then he forced a short laugh.

"Who is Nina Carrington?" he asked.

"I am about to discover that," I replied, and he was quiet at once. It was not difficult to divine that he feared Nina Carrington a good deal more than he did the devil. Our leave-taking was brief; in fact, we merely stared at each other over the waiting-room table, with its litter of year-old magazines. Then I turned and went out.

"To Richfield," I told Warner, and on the way I thought, and thought hard.

"Nina Carrington, Nina Carrington," the roar and rush of the wheels seemed to sing the words. "Nina Carrington, N. C." And I then knew, knew as surely as if I had seen the whole thing. There had been an N. C. on the suit-case belonging to the woman with the pitted face. How simple it all seemed. Mattie Bliss had been Nina Carrington. It was she Warner had heard in the library. It was something she had told Halsey that had taken him frantically to Doctor

Walker's office, and from there perhaps to his death. If we could find the woman, we might find what had become of Halsey.

We were almost at Richfield now, so I kept on. My mind was not on my errand there now. It was back with Halsey on that memorable night. What was it he had said to Louise, that had sent her up to Sunnyside, half wild with fear for him? I made up my mind, as the car drew up before the Tate cottage, that I would see Louise if I had to break into the house at night.

Almost exactly the same scene as before greeted my eyes at the cottage. Mrs. Tate, the baby-carriage in the path, the children at the swing—all were the same.

She came forward to meet me, and I noticed that some of the anxious lines had gone out of her face. She looked young, almost pretty.

"I am glad you have come back," she said. "I think I will have to be honest and give you back your money."

"Why?" I asked. "Has the mother come?"

"No, but some one came and paid the boy's board for a month. She talked to him for a long time, but when I asked him afterward he didn't know her name."

"A young woman?"

"Not very young. About forty, I suppose. She was small and fair-haired, just a little bit gray, and very sad. She was in deep mourning, and, I think, when she came, she expected to go at once. But the child, Lucien, interested her. She talked to him for a long time, and, indeed, she looked much happier when she left."

"You are sure this was not the real mother?"

"O mercy, no! Why, she didn't know which of the three was Lucien. I thought perhaps she was a friend of yours, but, of course, I didn't ask."

"She was not—pock-marked?" I asked at a venture. "No, indeed. A skin like a baby's. But perhaps you will know the initials. She gave Lucien a handkerchief and forgot it. It was very fine, black-bordered, and it had three hand-worked letters in the corner—F. B. A."

"No," I said with truth enough, "she is not a friend of mine." F. B. A. was Fanny Armstrong, without a chance of doubt!

With another warning to Mrs. Tate as to silence, we started back to Sunnyside. So Fanny Armstrong knew of Lucien Wallace, and was sufficiently interested to visit him and pay for his support. Who was the child's mother and where was she? Who was Nina Carrington? Did either of them know where Halsey was or what had happened to him?

On the way home we passed the little cemetery where Thomas had been laid to rest. I wondered if Thomas could have helped us to find Halsey, had he lived. Farther along was the more imposing burial-ground, where Arnold Armstrong and his father lay in the shadow of a tall granite shaft. Of the three, I think Thomas was the only one sincerely mourned.

CHAPTER XXVIII
A TRAMP AND THE TOOTHACHE

The bitterness toward the dead president of the Traders' Bank seemed to grow with time. Never popular, his memory was execrated by people who had lost nothing, but who were filled with disgust by constantly hearing new stories of the man's grasping avarice. The Traders' had been a favorite bank for small tradespeople, and in its savings department it had solicited the smallest deposits. People who had thought to be self-supporting to the last found themselves confronting the poorhouse, their two or three hundred dollar savings wiped away. All bank failures have this element, however, and the directors were trying to promise twenty per cent. on deposits.

But, like everything else those days, the bank failure was almost forgotten by Gertrude and myself. We did not mention Jack Bailey: I had found nothing to change my impression of his guilt, and Gertrude knew how I felt. As for the murder of the bank president's son, I was of two minds. One day I thought Gertrude knew or at least suspected that Jack had done it; the next I feared that it had been Gertrude herself, that night alone on the circular staircase. And then the mother of Lucien Wallace would obtrude herself, and an almost equally good case might be made against her. There were times, of course, when I was disposed to throw all those suspicions aside, and fix definitely on the unknown, whoever that might be.

I had my greatest disappointment when it came to tracing Nina Carrington. The woman had gone without leaving a trace. Marked as she was, it should have been easy to follow her, but she was not to be found. A description to one of the detectives, on my arrival at home, had started the ball rolling. But by night she had not been found. I told Gertrude, then, about the telegram to Louise when she had been ill before; about my visit to Doctor Walker, and my suspicions that Mattie Bliss and Nina Carrington were the same. She thought, as I did, that there was little doubt of it.

I said nothing to her, however, of the detective's suspicions about Alex. Little things that I had not noticed at the time now came back to me. I had an uncomfortable feeling that perhaps Alex was a spy, and that by taking him into the house I had played into the enemy's hand. But at eight o'clock that night Alex himself appeared, and with him a strange and repulsive individual. They made a queer pair, for Alex was almost as disreputable as the tramp, and he had a badly swollen eye.

Gertrude had been sitting listlessly waiting for the evening message from Mr. Jamieson, but when the singular pair came in, as they did, without ceremony, she jumped up and stood staring. Winters, the detective who watched the house at night, followed them, and kept his eyes sharply on Alex's prisoner. For that was the situation as it developed.

He was a tall lanky individual, ragged and dirty, and just now he looked both terrified and embarrassed. Alex was too much engrossed to be either, and to this day I don't think I ever asked him why he went off without permission the day before.

"Miss Innes," Alex began abruptly, "this man can tell us something very important about the disappearance of Mr. Innes. I found him trying to sell this watch."

He took a watch from his pocket and put it on the table. It was Halsey's watch. I had given it to him on his twenty-first birthday: I was dumb with apprehension.

"He says he had a pair of cuff-links also, but he sold them—"

"Fer a dollar'n half," put in the disreputable individual hoarsely, with an eye on the detective.

"He is not—dead?" I implored. The tramp cleared his throat.

"No'm," he said huskily. "He was used up pretty bad, but he weren't dead. He was comin' to hisself when I"—he stopped and looked at the detective. "I didn't steal it, Mr. Winters," he whined. "I found it in the road, honest to God, I did."

Mr. Winters paid no attention to him. He was watching Alex.

"I'd better tell what he told me," Alex broke in. "It will be quicker. When Jamieson—when Mr. Jamieson calls up we can start him right. Mr. Winters, I found this man trying to sell that watch on Fifth Street. He offered it to me for three dollars."

"How did you know the watch?" Winters snapped at him.

"I had seen it before, many times. I used it at night when I was watching at the foot of the staircase." The detective was satisfied. "When he offered the watch to me, I knew it, and I pretended I was going to buy it. We went into an alley and I got the watch." The tramp shivered. It was plain how Alex had secured the watch. "Then—I got the story from this fellow. He claims to have seen the whole affair. He says he was in an empty car—in the car the automobile struck."

The tramp broke in here, and told his story, with frequent interpretations by Alex and Mr. Winters. He used a strange medley, in which familiar words took unfamiliar meanings, but it was gradually made clear to us.

On the night in question the tramp had been "pounding his ear"—this stuck to me as being graphic—in an empty box-car along the siding at Casanova. The train was going west, and due to leave at dawn. The tramp and the "brakey" were friendly, and things going well. About ten o'clock, perhaps earlier, a terrific crash against the side of the car roused him. He tried to open the door, but could not move it. He got out of the other side, and just as he did so, he heard some one groan.

The habits of a lifetime made him cautious. He slipped on to the bumper of a car and peered through. An automobile had struck the car, and stood there on two wheels. The tail lights were burning, but the headlights were out. Two men were stooping over some one who lay on the ground. Then the taller of the two started on a dog-trot along the train looking for an empty. He found one four cars away and ran back again. The two lifted the unconscious man into the empty box-car, and, getting in themselves, stayed for three or four minutes. When they came out, after closing the sliding door, they cut up over the railroad embankment toward the town. One, the short one, seemed to limp.

The tramp was wary. He waited for ten minutes or so. Some women came down a path to the road and inspected the automobile. When they had gone, he crawled into the box-car and closed the door again. Then he lighted a match. The figure of a man, unconscious, gagged, and with his hands tied, lay far at the end.

The tramp lost no time; he went through his pockets, found a little money and the cuff-links, and took them. Then he loosened the gag—it had been cruelly tight—and went his way, again closing the door of the box-car. Outside on the road he found the watch. He got on the fast freight east, some time after, and rode into the city. He had sold the cuff-links, but on offering the watch to Alex he had been "copped."

The story, with its cold recital of villainy, was done. I hardly knew if I were more anxious, or less. That it was Halsey, there could be no doubt. How badly he was hurt, how far he had been carried, were the questions that demanded immediate answer. But it was the first real information we had had; my boy had not been murdered outright. But instead of vague terrors there was now the real fear that he might be lying in some strange hospital receiving the casual attention commonly given to the charity cases. Even this, had we known it, would have been paradise to the terrible truth. I wake yet and feel myself cold and trembling with the horror of Halsey's situation for three days after his disappearance.

Mr. Winters and Alex disposed of the tramp with a warning. It was evident he had told us all he knew. We had occasion, within a day or two, to be doubly thankful that we had given him his freedom. When Mr. Jamieson telephoned that night we had news for him; he told me what I had not realized before—that it would not be possible to find Halsey at once, even with this clue. The cars by this time, three days, might be scattered over the Union.

But he said to keep on hoping, that it was the best news we had had. And in the meantime, consumed with anxiety as we were, things were happening at the house in rapid succession.

We had one peaceful day—then Liddy took sick in the night. I went in when I heard her groaning, and found her with a hot-water bottle to her face, and her right cheek swollen until it was glassy.

"Toothache?" I asked, not too gently. "You deserve it. A woman of your age, who would rather go around with an exposed nerve in her head than have the tooth pulled! It would be over in a moment."

"So would hanging," Liddy protested, from behind the hot-water bottle.

I was hunting around for cotton and laudanum.

"You have a tooth just like it yourself, Miss Rachel," she whimpered. "And I'm sure Doctor Boyle's been trying to take it out for years."

There was no laudanum, and Liddy made a terrible fuss when I proposed carbolic acid, just because I had put too much on the cotton once and burned her mouth. I'm sure it never did her any permanent harm; indeed, the doctor said afterward that living on liquid diet had been a splendid rest for her stomach. But she would have none of the acid, and she kept me awake groaning, so at last I got up and went to Gertrude's door. To my surprise, it was locked.

I went around by the hall and into her bedroom that way. The bed was turned down, and her dressing-gown and night-dress lay ready in the little room next, but Gertrude was not there. She had not undressed.

I don't know what terrible thoughts came to me in the minute I stood there. Through the door I could hear Liddy grumbling, with a squeal now and then when the pain stabbed harder. Then, automatically, I got the laudanum and went back to her.

It was fully a half-hour before Liddy's groans subsided. At intervals I went to the door into the hall and looked out, but I saw and heard nothing suspicious. Finally, when Liddy had dropped into a doze, I even ventured as far as the head of the circular staircase, but there floated up to me only the even breathing of Winters, the night detective, sleeping just inside the entry. And then, far off, I heard the rapping noise that had lured Louise down the staircase that other night, two weeks before. It was over my head, and very faint—three or four short muffled taps, a pause, and then again, stealthily repeated.

The sound of Mr. Winters' breathing was comforting; with the thought that there was help within call, something kept me from waking him. I did not move for a moment; ridiculous things Liddy had said about a ghost—I am not at all superstitious, except, perhaps, in the middle of the night, with everything dark—things like that came back to me. Almost beside me was the clothes chute. I could feel it, but I could see nothing. As I stood, listening intently, I heard a sound near me. It was vague, indefinite. Then it ceased; there was an uneasy movement and a grunt from the foot of the circular staircase, and silence again.

I stood perfectly still, hardly daring to breathe.

Then I knew I had been right. Some one was stealthily-passing the head of the staircase and coming toward me in the dark. I leaned against the wall for support—my knees were giving way. The steps were close now, and suddenly I thought of Gertrude. Of course it was Gertrude. I put out one hand in front of me, but I touched nothing. My voice almost refused me, but I managed to gasp out, "Gertrude!"

"Good Lord!" a man's voice exclaimed, just beside me. And then I collapsed. I felt myself going, felt some one catch me, a horrible nausea—that was all I remembered.

When I came to it was dawn. I was lying on the bed in Louise's room, with the cherub on the ceiling staring down at me, and there was a blanket from my own bed thrown over me. I felt weak and dizzy, but I managed to get up and totter to the door. At the foot of the circular staircase Mr. Winters was still asleep. Hardly able to stand, I crept back to my room. The door into Gertrude's room was no longer locked: she was sleeping like a tired child. And in my dressing-room Liddy hugged a cold hot-water bottle, and mumbled in her sleep.

"There's some things you can't hold with hand cuffs," she was muttering thickly.

For the first time in twenty years, I kept my bed that day. Liddy was alarmed to the point of hysteria, and sent for Doctor Stewart just after breakfast. Gertrude spent the morning with me, reading something—I forget what. I was too busy with my thoughts to listen. I had said nothing to the two detectives. If Mr. Jamieson had been there, I should have told him everything, but I could not go to these strange men and tell them my niece had been missing in the middle of the night; that she had not gone to bed at all; that while I was searching for her through the house, I had met a stranger who, when I fainted, had carried me into a room and left me there, to get better or not, as it might happen.

The whole situation was terrible: had the issues been less vital, it would have been absurd. Here we were, guarded day and night by private detectives, with an extra man to watch the grounds, and yet we might as well have lived in a Japanese paper house, for all the protection we had.

And there was something else: the man I had met in the darkness had been even more startled than I, and about his voice, when he muttered his muffled exclamation, there was something vaguely familiar. All that morning, while Gertrude read aloud, and Liddy watched for the doctor, I was puzzling over that voice, without result.

And there were other things, too. I wondered what Gertrude's absence from her room had to do with it all, or if it had any connection. I tried to think that she had heard the rapping noises before I did and gone to investigate, but I'm afraid I was a moral coward that day. I could not ask her.

Perhaps the diversion was good for me. It took my mind from Halsey, and the story we had heard the night before. The day, however, was a long vigil, with every ring of the telephone full of possibilities. Doctor Walker came up, some time just after luncheon, and asked for me.

"Go down and see him," I instructed Gertrude. "Tell him I am out—for mercy's sake don't say I'm sick. Find out what he wants, and from this time on, instruct the servants that he is not to be admitted. I loathe that man."

Gertrude came back very soon, her face rather flushed.

"He came to ask us to get out," she said, picking up her book with a jerk. "He says Louise Armstrong wants to come here, now that she is recovering."

"And what did you say?"

"I said we were very sorry we could not leave, but we would be delighted to have Louise come up here with us. He looked daggers at me. And he wanted to know if we would recommend Eliza as a cook. He has brought a patient, a man, out from town, and is increasing his establishment—that's the way he put it."

"I wish him joy of Eliza," I said tartly. "Did he ask for Halsey?"

"Yes. I told him that we were on the track last night, and that it was only a question of time. He said he was glad, although he didn't appear to be, but he said not to be too sanguine."

"Do you know what I believe?" I asked. "I believe, as firmly as I believe anything, that Doctor Walker knows something about Halsey, and that he could put his finger on him, if he wanted to."

There were several things that day that bewildered me. About three o'clock Mr. Jamieson telephoned from the Casanova station and Warner went down to meet him. I got up and dressed hastily, and the detective was shown up to my sitting-room.

"No news?" I asked, as he entered. He tried to look encouraging, without success. I noticed that he looked tired and dusty, and, although he was ordinarily impeccable in his appearance, it was clear that he was at least two days from a razor.

"It won't be long now, Miss Innes," he said. "I have come out here on a peculiar errand, which I will tell you about later. First, I want to ask some questions. Did any one come out here yesterday to repair the telephone, and examine the wires on the roof?"

"Yes," I said promptly; "but it was not the telephone. He said the wiring might have caused the fire at the stable. I went up with him myself, but he only looked around."

Mr. Jamieson smiled.

"Good for you!" he applauded. "Don't allow any one in the house that you don't trust, and don't trust anybody. All are not electricians who wear rubber gloves."

He refused to explain further, but he got a slip of paper out of his pocketbook and opened it carefully.

"Listen," he said. "You heard this before and scoffed. In the light of recent developments I want you to read it again. You are a clever woman, Miss Innes. Just as surely as I sit here, there is something in this house that is wanted very anxiously by a number of people. The lines are closing up, Miss Innes."

The paper was the one he had found among Arnold Armstrong's effects, and I read it again:

"——by altering the plans for——rooms, may be possible. The best way, in my opinion, would be to——the plan for——in one of the——rooms——chimney."

"I think I understand," I said slowly. "Some one is searching for the secret room, and the invaders—"

"And the holes in the plaster—"

"Have been in the progress of his—"

"Or her—investigations."

"Her?" I asked.

"Miss Innes," the detective said, getting up, "I believe that somewhere in the walls of this house is hidden some of the money, at least, from the Traders' Bank. I believe, just as surely, that young Walker brought home from California the knowledge of something of the sort and, failing in his effort to reinstall Mrs. Armstrong and her daughter here, he, or a confederate, has tried to break into the house. On two occasions I think he succeeded."

"On three, at least," I corrected. And then I told him about the night before. "I have been thinking hard," I concluded, "and I do not believe the man at the head of the circular staircase was Doctor Walker. I don't think he could have got in, and the voice was not his."

Mr. Jamieson got up and paced the floor, his hands behind him.

"There is something else that puzzles me," he said, stepping before me. "Who and what is the woman Nina Carrington? If it was she who came here as Mattie Bliss, what did she tell Halsey that sent him racing to Doctor Walker's, and then to Miss Armstrong? If we could find that woman we would have the whole thing."

"Mr. Jamieson, did you ever think that Paul Armstrong might not have died a natural death?"

"That is the thing we are going to try to find out," he replied. And then Gertrude came in, announcing a man below to see Mr. Jamieson.

"I want you present at this interview, Miss Innes," he said. "May Riggs come up? He has left Doctor Walker and he has something he wants to tell us."

Riggs came into the room diffidently, but Mr. Jamieson put him at his ease. He kept a careful eye on me, however, and slid into a chair by the door when he was asked to sit down.

"Now, Riggs," began Mr. Jamieson kindly. "You are to say what you have to say before this lady."

"You promised you'd keep it quiet, Mr. Jamieson." Riggs plainly did not trust me. There was nothing friendly in the glance he turned on me.

"Yes, yes. You will be protected. But, first of all, did you bring what you promised?"

Riggs produced a roll of papers from under his coat, and handed them over. Mr. Jamieson examined them with lively satisfaction, and passed them to me. "The blue-prints of Sunnyside," he said. "What did I tell you? Now, Riggs, we are ready."

"I'd never have come to you, Mr. Jamieson," he began, "if it hadn't been for Miss Armstrong. When Mr. Innes was spirited away, like, and Miss Louise got sick because of it, I thought things had gone far enough. I'd done some things for the doctor before that wouldn't just bear looking into, but I turned a bit squeamish."

"Did you help with that?" I asked, leaning forward.

"No, ma'm. I didn't even know of it until the next day, when it came out in the Casanova Weekly Ledger. But I know who did it, all right. I'd better start at the beginning.

"When Doctor Walker went away to California with the Armstrong family, there was talk in the town that when he came back he would be married to Miss Armstrong, and we all expected it. First thing I knew, I got a letter from him, in the west. He seemed to be excited, and he said Miss Armstrong had taken a sudden notion to go home and he sent me some money. I was to watch for her, to see if she went to Sunnyside, and wherever she was, not to lose sight of her until he got home. I traced her to the lodge, and I guess I scared you on the drive one night, Miss Innes."

"And Rosie!" I ejaculated.

Riggs grinned sheepishly.

"I only wanted to make sure Miss Louise was there. Rosie started to run, and I tried to stop her and tell her some sort of a story to account for my being there. But she wouldn't wait."

"And the broken china—in the basket?"

"Well, broken china's death to rubber tires," he said. "I hadn't any complaint against you people here, and the Dragon Fly was a good car."

So Rosie's highwayman was explained.

"Well, I telegraphed the doctor where Miss Louise was and I kept an eye on her. Just a day or so before they came home with the body, I got another letter, telling me to watch for a woman who had been pitted with smallpox. Her name was Carrington, and the doctor made things pretty strong. If I found any such woman loafing around, I was not to lose sight of her for a minute until the doctor got back.

"Well, I would have had my hands full, but the other woman didn't show up for a good while, and when she did the doctor was home."

"Riggs," I asked suddenly, "did you get into this house a day or two after I took it, at night?"

"I did not, Miss Innes. I have never been in the house before. Well, the Carrington woman didn't show up until the night Mr. Halsey disappeared. She came to the office late, and the doctor was out. She waited around, walking the floor and working herself into a passion. When the doctor didn't come back, she was in an awful way. She wanted me to hunt him, and when he didn't appear, she called him names; said he couldn't fool her. There was murder being done, and she would see him swing for it.

"She struck me as being an ugly customer, and when she left, about eleven o'clock, and went across to the Armstrong place, I was not far behind her. She walked all around the house first, looking up at the windows. Then she rang the bell, and the minute the door was opened she was through it, and into the hall."

"How long did she stay?"

"That's the queer part of it," Riggs said eagerly. "She didn't come out that night at all. I went to bed at daylight, and that was the last I heard of her until the next day, when I saw her on a truck at the station, covered with a sheet. She'd been struck by the express and you would hardly have known her—dead, of course. I think she stayed all night in the Armstrong house, and the agent said she was crossing the track to take the up-train to town when the express struck her."

"Another circle!" I exclaimed. "Then we are just where we started."

"Not so bad as that, Miss Innes," Riggs said eagerly. "Nina Carrington came from the town in California where Mr. Armstrong died. Why was the doctor so afraid of her? The Carrington woman knew something. I lived with Doctor Walker seven years, and I know him well. There are few things he is afraid of. I think he killed Mr. Armstrong out in the west somewhere, that's what I think. What else he did I don't know—but he dismissed me and pretty nearly throttled me—for telling Mr. Jamieson here about Mr. Innes' having been at his office the night he disappeared, and about my hearing them quarreling."

"What was it Warner overheard the woman say to Mr. Innes, in the library?" the detective asked me.

"She said 'I knew there was something wrong from the start. A man isn't well one day and dead the next without some reason.'"

How perfectly it all seemed to fit!

CHAPTER XXX
WHEN CHURCHYARDS YAWN

It was on Wednesday Riggs told us the story of his connection with some incidents that had been previously unexplained. Halsey had been gone since the Friday night before, and with the passage of each day I felt that his chances were lessening. I knew well enough that he might be carried thousands of miles in the box-car, locked in, perhaps, without water or food. I had read of cases where bodies had been found locked in cars on isolated sidings in the west, and my spirits went down with every hour.

His recovery was destined to be almost as sudden as his disappearance, and was due directly to the tramp Alex had brought to Sunnyside. It seems the man was grateful for his release, and when he learned some thing of Halsey's whereabouts from another member of his fraternity—for it is a fraternity—he was prompt in letting us know.

On Wednesday evening Mr. Jamieson, who had been down at the Armstrong house trying to see Louise—and failing—was met near the gate at Sunnyside by an individual precisely as repulsive and unkempt as the one Alex had captured. The man knew the detective, and he gave him a piece of dirty paper, on which was scrawled the words—"He's at City Hospital, Johnsville." The tramp who brought the paper pretended to know nothing, except this: the paper had been passed along from a "hobo" in Johnsville, who seemed to know the information would be valuable to us.

Again the long distance telephone came into requisition. Mr. Jamieson called the hospital, while we crowded around him. And when there was no longer any doubt that it was Halsey, and that he would probably recover, we all laughed and cried together. I am sure I kissed Liddy, and I have had terrible moments since when I seem to remember kissing Mr. Jamieson, too, in the excitement.

Anyhow, by eleven o'clock that night Gertrude was on her way to Johnsville, three hundred and eighty miles away, accompanied by Rosie. The domestic force was now down to Mary Anne and Liddy, with the under-gardener's wife coming every day to help out. Fortunately, Warner and the detectives were keeping bachelor hall in the lodge. Out of deference to Liddy they washed their dishes once a day, and they concocted queer messes, according to their several abilities. They had one triumph that they ate regularly for breakfast, and that clung to their clothes and their hair the rest of the day. It was bacon, hardtack and onions, fried together. They were almost pathetically grateful, however, I noticed, for an occasional broiled tenderloin.

It was not until Gertrude and Rosie had gone and Sunnyside had settled down for the night, with Winters at the foot of the staircase, that Mr. Jamieson broached a subject he had evidently planned before he came.

"Miss Innes," he said, stopping me as I was about to go to my room up-stairs, "how are your nerves tonight?"

"I have none," I said happily. "With Halsey found, my troubles have gone."

"I mean," he persisted, "do you feel as though you could go through with something rather unusual?"

"The most unusual thing I can think of would be a peaceful night. But if anything is going to occur, don't dare to let me miss it."

"Something is going to occur," he said. "And you're the only woman I can think of that I can take along." He looked at his watch. "Don't ask me any questions, Miss Innes. Put on heavy shoes, and some old dark clothes, and make up your mind not to be surprised at anything."

Liddy was sleeping the sleep of the just when I went up-stairs, and I hunted out my things cautiously. The detective was waiting in the hall, and I was astonished to see Doctor Stewart with him.

They were talking confidentially together, but when I came down they ceased. There were a few preparations to be made: the locks to be gone over, Winters to be instructed as to renewed vigilance, and then, after extinguishing the hall light, we crept, in the darkness, through the front door, and into the night.

I asked no questions. I felt that they were doing me honor in making me one of the party, and I would show them I could be as silent as they. We went across the fields, passing through the woods that reached almost to the ruins of the stable, going over stiles now and then, and sometimes stepping over low fences. Once only somebody spoke, and then it was an emphatic bit of profanity from Doctor Stewart when he ran into a wire fence.

We were joined at the end of five minutes by another man, who fell into step with the doctor silently. He carried something over his shoulder which I could not make out. In this way we walked for perhaps twenty minutes. I had lost all sense of direction: I merely stumbled along in silence, allowing Mr. Jamieson to guide me this way or that as the path demanded. I hardly know what I expected. Once, when through a miscalculation I jumped a little short over a ditch and landed above my shoe-tops in the water and ooze, I remember wondering if this were really I, and if I had ever tasted life until that summer. I walked along with the water sloshing in my boots, and I was actually cheerful. I remember whispering to Mr. Jamieson that I had never seen the stars so lovely, and that it was a mistake, when the Lord had made the night so beautiful, to sleep through it!

The doctor was puffing somewhat when we finally came to a halt. I confess that just at that minute even Sunnyside seemed a cheerful spot. We had paused at the edge of a level cleared place, bordered all around with primly trimmed evergreen trees. Between them I caught a glimpse of starlight shining down on rows of white headstones and an occasional more imposing monument, or towering shaft. In spite of myself, I drew my breath in sharply. We were on the edge of the Casanova churchyard.

I saw now both the man who had joined the party and the implements he carried. It was Alex, armed with two long-handled spades. After the first shock of surprise, I flatter myself I was both cool and quiet. We went in single file between the rows of headstones, and although, when I found myself last, I had an instinctive desire to keep looking back over my shoulder, I found that, the first uneasiness past, a cemetery at night is much the same as any other country place, filled with vague shadows and unexpected noises. Once, indeed—but Mr. Jamieson said it was an owl, and I tried to believe him.

In the shadow of the Armstrong granite shaft we stopped. I think the doctor wanted to send me back.

"It's no place for a woman," I heard him protesting angrily. But the detective said something about witnesses, and the doctor only came over and felt my pulse.

"Anyhow, I don't believe you're any worse off here than you would be in that nightmare of a house," he said finally, and put his coat on the steps of the shaft for me to sit on.

There is an air of finality about a grave: one watches the earth thrown in, with the feeling that this is the end. Whatever has gone before, whatever is to come in eternity, that particular temple of the soul has been given back to the elements from which it came. Thus, there is a sense of desecration, of a reversal of the everlasting fitness of things, in resurrecting a body from its mother clay. And yet that night, in the Casanova churchyard, I sat quietly by, and watched Alex and Mr. Jamieson steaming over their work, without a single qualm, except the fear of detection.

The doctor kept a keen lookout, but no one appeared. Once in a while he came over to me, and gave me a reassuring pat on the shoulder.

"I never expected to come to this," he said once. "There's one thing sure—I'll not be suspected of complicity. A doctor is generally supposed to be handier at burying folks than at digging them up."

The uncanny moment came when Alex and Jamieson tossed the spades on the grass, and I confess I hid my face. There was a period of stress, I think, while the heavy coffin was being raised. I felt that my composure was going, and, for fear I would shriek, I tried to think of something else—what time Gertrude would reach Halsey—anything but the grisly reality that lay just beyond me on the grass.

And then I heard a low exclamation from the detective and I felt the pressure of the doctor's fingers on my arm.

"Now, Miss Innes," he said gently. "If you will come over—"

I held on to him frantically, and somehow I got there and looked down. The lid of the casket had been raised and a silver plate on it proved we had made no mistake. But the face that showed in the light of the lantern was a face I had never seen before. The man who lay before us was not Paul Armstrong!

CHAPTER XXXI
BETWEEN TWO FIREPLACES

What with the excitement of the discovery, the walk home under the stars in wet shoes and draggled skirts, and getting up-stairs and undressed without rousing Liddy, I was completely used up. What to do with my boots was the greatest puzzle of all, there being no place in the house safe from Liddy, until I decided to slip upstairs the next morning and drop them into the hole the "ghost" had made in the trunk-room wall.

I went asleep as soon as I reached this decision, and in my dreams I lived over again the events of the night. Again I saw the group around the silent figure on the grass, and again, as had happened at the grave, I heard Alex's voice, tense and triumphant:

"Then we've got them," he said. Only, in my dreams, he said it over and over until he seemed to shriek it in my ears.

I wakened early, in spite of my fatigue, and lay there thinking. Who was Alex? I no longer believed that he was a gardener. Who was the man whose body we had resurrected? And where was Paul Armstrong? Probably living safely in some extraditionless country on the fortune he had stolen. Did Louise and her mother know of the shameful and wicked deception? What had Thomas known, and Mrs. Watson? Who was Nina Carrington?

This last question, it seemed to me, was answered. In some way the woman had learned of the substitution, and had tried to use her knowledge for blackmail. Nina Carrington's own story died with her, but, however it happened, it was clear that she had carried her knowledge to Halsey the afternoon Gertrude and I were looking for clues to the man I had shot on the east veranda. Halsey had been half crazed by what he heard; it was evident that Louise was marrying Doctor Walker to keep the shameful secret, for her mother's sake. Halsey, always reckless, had gone at once to Doctor Walker and denounced him. There had been a scene, and he left on his way to the station to meet and notify Mr. Jamieson of what he had learned. The doctor was active mentally and physically. Accompanied perhaps by Riggs, who had shown himself not overscrupulous until he quarreled with his employer, he had gone across to the railroad embankment, and, by jumping in front of the car, had caused Halsey to swerve. The rest of the story we knew.

That was my reconstructed theory of that afternoon and evening: it was almost correct— not quite.

There was a telegram that morning from Gertrude.

"Halsey conscious and improving. Probably home in day or so.
GERTRUDE."

With Halsey found and improving in health, and with at last something to work on, I began that day, Thursday, with fresh courage. As Mr. Jamieson had said, the lines were closing up. That I was to be caught and almost finished in the closing was happily unknown to us all.

It was late when I got up. I lay in my bed, looking around the four walls of the room, and trying to imagine behind what one of them a secret chamber might lie. Certainly, in daylight, Sunnyside deserved its name: never was a house more cheery and open, less sinister in general appearance. There was not a corner apparently that was not open and above-board, and yet, somewhere behind its handsomely papered walls I believed firmly that there lay a hidden room, with all the possibilities it would involve.

I made a mental note to have the house measured during the day, to discover any discrepancy between the outer and inner walls, and I tried to recall again the exact wording of the paper Jamieson had found.

The slip had said "chimney." It was the only clue, and a house as large as Sunnyside was full of them. There was an open fireplace in my dressing-room, but none in the bedroom, and as I lay there, looking around, I thought of something that made me sit up suddenly. The trunk-room, just over my head, had an open fireplace and a brick chimney, and yet, there was nothing of the kind in my room. I got out of bed and examined the opposite wall closely. There was apparently no flue, and I knew there was none in the hall just beneath. The house was heated by steam, as I have said before. In the living-room was a huge open fireplace, but it was on the other side.

Why did the trunk-room have both a radiator and an open fireplace? Architects were not usually erratic! It was not fifteen minutes before I was up-stairs, armed with a tape-measure in lieu of a foot-rule, eager to justify Mr. Jamieson's opinion of my intelligence, and firmly resolved not to tell him of my suspicion until I had more than theory to go on. The hole in the trunk-room wall still yawned there, between the chimney and the outer wall. I examined it again, with no new result. The space between the brick wall and the plaster and lath one, however, had a new significance. The hole showed only one side of the chimney, and I determined to investigate what lay in the space on the other side of the mantel.

I worked feverishly. Liddy had gone to the village to market, it being her firm belief that the store people sent short measure unless she watched the scales, and that, since the failure of the Traders' Bank, we must watch the corners; and I knew that what I wanted to do must be done before she came back. I had no tools, but after rummaging around I found a pair of garden scissors and a hatchet, and thus armed, I set to work. The plaster came out easily: the lathing was more obstinate. It gave under the blows, only to spring back into place again, and the necessity for caution made it doubly hard.

I had a blister on my palm when at last the hatchet went through and fell with what sounded like the report of a gun to my overstrained nerves. I sat on a trunk, waiting to hear Liddy fly up the stairs, with the household behind her, like the tail of a comet. But nothing happened, and with a growing feeling of uncanniness I set to work enlarging the opening.

The result was absolutely nil. When I could hold a lighted candle in the opening, I saw precisely what I had seen on the other side of the chimney—a space between the true wall and the false one, possibly seven feet long and about three feet wide. It was in no sense of the word a secret chamber, and it was evident it had not been disturbed since the house was built. It was a supreme disappointment.

It had been Mr. Jamieson's idea that the hidden room, if there was one, would be found somewhere near the circular staircase. In fact, I knew that he had once investigated the entire length of the clothes chute, hanging to a rope, with this in view. I was reluctantly about to concede that he had been right, when my eyes fell on the mantel and fireplace. The latter had evidently never been used: it was closed with a metal fire front, and only when the front refused to move, and investigation showed that it was not intended to be moved, did my spirits revive.

I hurried into the next room. Yes, sure enough, there was a similar mantel and fireplace there, similarly closed. In both rooms the chimney flue extended well out from the wall. I measured with the tape-line, my hands trembling so that I could scarcely hold it. They extended two feet and a half into each room, which, with the three feet of space between the two partitions, made eight feet to be accounted for. Eight feet in one direction and almost seven in the other—what a chimney it was!

But I had only located the hidden room. I was not in it, and no amount of pressing on the carving of the wooden mantels, no search of the floors for loose boards, none of the customary methods availed at all. That there was a means of entrance, and probably a simple one, I could be certain. But what? What would I find if I did get in? Was the detective right, and were the bonds and money from the Traders' Bank there? Or was our whole theory wrong? Would not Paul Armstrong have taken his booty with him? If he had not, and if Doctor Walker was in the secret, he would have known how to enter the chimney room. Then—who had dug the other hole in the false partition?

Liddy discovered the fresh break in the trunk-room wall while we were at luncheon, and ran shrieking down the stairs. She maintained that, as she entered, unseen hands had been digging at the plaster; that they had stopped when she went in, and she had felt a gust of cold damp air. In support of her story she carried in my wet and muddy boots, that I had unluckily forgotten to hide, and held them out to the detective and myself.

"What did I tell you?" she said dramatically. "Look at 'em. They're yours, Miss Rachel— and covered with mud and soaked to the tops. I tell you, you can scoff all you like; something has been wearing your shoes. As sure as you sit there, there's the smell of the graveyard on them. How do we know they weren't tramping through the Casanova churchyard last night, and sitting on the graves!"

Mr. Jamieson almost choked to death. "I wouldn't be at all surprised if they were doing that very thing, Liddy," he said, when he got his breath. "They certainly look like it."

I think the detective had a plan, on which he was working, and which was meant to be a coup. But things went so fast there was no time to carry it into effect. The first thing that occurred was a message from the Charity Hospital that Mrs. Watson was dying, and had asked for me. I did not care much about going. There is a sort of melancholy pleasure to be had out of a funeral, with its pomp and ceremony, but I shrank from a death-bed. However, Liddy got out the black things and the crape veil I keep for such occasions, and I went. I left Mr. Jamieson and the day detective going over every inch of the circular staircase, pounding, probing and measuring. I was inwardly elated to think of the surprise I was going to give them that night; as it turned out, I DID surprise them almost into spasms.

I drove from the train to the Charity Hospital, and was at once taken to a ward. There, in a gray-walled room in a high iron bed, lay Mrs. Watson. She was very weak, and she only opened her eyes and looked at me when I sat down beside her. I was conscience-stricken. We had been so engrossed that I had left this poor creature to die without even a word of sympathy.

The nurse gave her a stimulant, and in a little while she was able to talk. So broken and half-coherent, however, was her story that I shall tell it in my own way. In an hour from the time I entered the Charity Hospital, I had heard a sad and pitiful narrative, and had seen a woman slip into the unconsciousness that is only a step from death.

Briefly, then, the housekeeper's story was this:

She was almost forty years old, and had been the sister-mother of a large family of children. One by one they had died, and been buried beside their parents in a little town in the Middle West. There was only one sister left, the baby, Lucy. On her the older girl had lavished all the love of an impulsive and emotional nature. When Anne, the elder, was thirty-two and Lucy was nineteen, a young man had come to the town. He was going east, after spending the summer at a celebrated ranch in Wyoming—one of those places where wealthy men send worthless and dissipated sons, for a season of temperance, fresh air and hunting. The sisters, of course, knew nothing of this, and the young man's ardor rather carried them away. In a word, seven years before, Lucy Haswell had married a young man whose name was given as Aubrey Wallace.

Anne Haswell had married a carpenter in her native town, and was a widow. For three months everything went fairly well. Aubrey took his bride to Chicago, where they lived at a hotel. Perhaps the very unsophistication that had charmed him in Valley Mill jarred on him in the city. He had been far from a model husband, even for the three months, and when he disappeared Anne was almost thankful. It was different with the young wife, however. She drooped and fretted, and on the birth of her baby boy, she had died. Anne took the child, and named him Lucien.

Anne had had no children of her own, and on Lucien she had lavished all her aborted maternal instinct. On one thing she was determined, however: that was that Aubrey Wallace should educate his boy. It was a part of her devotion to the child that she should be ambitious for him: he must have every opportunity. And so she came east. She drifted around, doing plain sewing and keeping a home somewhere always for the boy. Finally, however, she realized that her only training had been domestic, and she put the boy in an Episcopalian home, and secured the position of housekeeper to the Armstrongs. There she found Lucien's father, this time under his own name. It was Arnold Armstrong.

I gathered that there was no particular enmity at that time in Anne's mind. She told him of the boy, and threatened exposure if he did not provide for him. Indeed, for a time, he did so. Then he realized that Lucien was the ruling passion in this lonely woman's life. He found out where the child was hidden, and threatened to take him away. Anne was frantic. The positions became reversed. Where Arnold had given money for Lucien's support, as the years went on he forced money from Anne Watson instead until she was always penniless. The lower Arnold sank in the scale, the heavier his demands became. With the rupture between him and his family, things were worse. Anne took the child from the home and hid him in a farmhouse near Casanova, on the Claysburg road. There she went sometimes to see the boy, and there he had taken fever. The people were Germans, and he called the farmer's wife Grossmutter. He had grown into a beautiful boy, and he was all Anne had to live for.

The Armstrongs left for California, and Arnold's persecutions began anew. He was furious over the child's disappearance and she was afraid he would do her some hurt. She left the big house and went down to the lodge. When I had rented Sunnyside, however, she had thought the persecutions would stop. She had applied for the position of housekeeper, and secured it.

That had been on Saturday. That night Louise arrived unexpectedly. Thomas sent for Mrs. Watson and then went for Arnold Armstrong at the Greenwood Club. Anne had been fond of Louise—she reminded her of Lucy. She did not know what the trouble was, but Louise had been in a state of terrible excitement. Mrs. Watson tried to hide from Arnold, but he was ugly. He left the lodge and went up to the house about two-thirty, was admitted at the east entrance and came out again very soon. Something had occurred, she didn't know what; but very soon Mr. Innes and another gentleman left, using the car.

Thomas and she had got Louise quiet, and a little before three, Mrs. Watson started up to the house. Thomas had a key to the east entry, and gave it to her.

On the way across the lawn she was confronted by Arnold, who for some reason was determined to get into the house. He had a golf-stick in his hand, that he had picked up somewhere, and on her refusal he had struck her with it. One hand had been badly cut, and it was that, poisoning having set in, which was killing her. She broke away in a frenzy of rage and fear, and got into the house while Gertrude and Jack Bailey were at the front door. She went up-stairs, hardly knowing what she was doing. Gertrude's door was open, and Halsey's revolver lay there on the bed. She picked it up and turning, ran part way down the circular staircase. She could hear Arnold fumbling at the lock outside. She slipped down quietly and opened the door: he was inside before she had got back to the stairs. It was quite dark, but she could see his white shirt-bosom. From the fourth step she fired. As he fell, somebody in the billiard-room screamed and ran. When the alarm was raised, she had had no time to get up-stairs: she hid in the west wing until every one was down on the lower floor. Then she slipped upstairs, and threw the revolver out of an upper window, going down again in time to admit the men from the Greenwood Club.

If Thomas had suspected, he had never told. When she found the hand Arnold had injured was growing worse, she gave the address of Lucien at Richfield to the old man, and almost a hundred dollars. The money was for Lucien's board until she recovered. She had sent for me to ask me if I would try to interest the Armstrongs in the child. When she found herself growing worse, she had written to Mrs. Armstrong, telling her nothing but that Arnold's legitimate child was at Richfield, and imploring her to recognize him. She was dying: the boy was an Armstrong, and entitled to his father's share of the estate. The papers were in her trunk at Sunnyside, with letters from the dead man that would prove what she said. She was going; she would not be judged by earthly laws; and somewhere else perhaps Lucy would plead for her. It was she who had crept down the circular staircase, drawn by a magnet, that night Mr. Jamieson had heard some one there. Pursued, she had fled madly, anywhere—through the first door she came to. She had fallen down the clothes chute, and been saved by the basket beneath. I could have cried with relief; then it had not been Gertrude, after all!

That was the story. Sad and tragic though it was, the very telling of it seemed to relieve the dying woman. She did not know that Thomas was dead, and I did not tell her. I promised to look after little Lucien, and sat with her until the intervals of consciousness grew shorter and finally ceased altogether. She died that night.

CHAPTER XXXIII
AT THE FOOT OF THE STAIRS

As I drove rapidly up to the house from Casanova Station in the hack, I saw the detective Burns loitering across the street from the Walker place. So Jamieson was putting the screws on—lightly now, but ready to give them a twist or two, I felt certain, very soon.

The house was quiet. Two steps of the circular staircase had been pried off, without result, and beyond a second message from Gertrude, that Halsey insisted on coming home and they would arrive that night, there was nothing new. Mr. Jamieson, having failed to locate the secret room, had gone to the village. I learned afterwards that he called at Doctor Walker's, under pretense of an attack of acute indigestion, and before he left, had inquired about the evening trains to the city. He said he had wasted a lot of time on the case, and a good bit of the mystery was in my imagination! The doctor was under the impression that the house was guarded day and night. Well, give a place a reputation like that, and you don't need a guard at all,—thus Jamieson. And sure enough, late in the afternoon, the two private detectives, accompanied by Mr. Jamieson, walked down the main street of Casanova and took a city-bound train.

That they got off at the next station and walked back again to Sunnyside at dusk, was not known at the time. Personally, I knew nothing of either move; I had other things to absorb me at that time.

Liddy brought me some tea while I rested after my trip, and on the tray was a small book from the Casanova library. It was called The Unseen World and had a cheerful cover on which a half-dozen sheeted figures linked hands around a headstone.

At this point in my story, Halsey always says: "Trust a woman to add two and two together, and make six." To which I retort that if two and two plus X make six, then to discover the unknown quantity is the simplest thing in the world. That a houseful of detectives missed it entirely was because they were busy trying to prove that two and two make four.

The depression due to my visit to the hospital left me at the prospect of seeing Halsey again that night. It was about five o'clock when Liddy left me for a nap before dinner, having put me into a gray silk dressing-gown and a pair of slippers. I listened to her retreating footsteps, and as soon as she was safely below stairs, I went up to the trunk-room. The place had not been disturbed, and I proceeded at once to try to discover the entrance to the hidden room. The openings on either side, as I have said, showed nothing but perhaps three feet of brick wall.

There was no sign of an entrance—no levers, no hinges, to give a hint. Either the mantel or the roof, I decided, and after a half-hour at the mantel, productive of absolutely no result, I decided to try the roof.

I am not fond of a height. The few occasions on which I have climbed a step-ladder have always left me dizzy and weak in the knees. The top of the Washington monument is as impossible to me as the elevation of the presidential chair. And yet—I climbed out on to the Sunnyside roof without a second's hesitation. Like a dog on a scent, like my bearskin progenitor, with his spear and his wild boar, to me now there was the lust of the chase, the frenzy of pursuit, the dust of battle. I got quite a little of the latter on me as I climbed from the unfinished ball-room out through a window to the roof of the east wing of the building, which was only two stories in height.

Once out there, access to the top of the main building was rendered easy—at least it looked easy—by a small vertical iron ladder, fastened to the wall outside of the ball-room, and perhaps twelve feet high. The twelve feet looked short from below, but they were difficult to climb. I gathered my silk gown around me, and succeeded finally in making the top of the ladder.

Once there, however, I was completely out of breath. I sat down, my feet on the top rung, and put my hair pins in more securely, while the wind bellowed my dressing-gown out like a sail. I had torn a great strip of the silk loose, and now I ruthlessly finished the destruction of my gown by jerking it free and tying it around my head.

From far below the smallest sounds came up with peculiar distinctness. I could hear the paper boy whistling down the drive, and I heard something else. I heard the thud of a stone, and a spit, followed by a long and startled meiou from Beulah. I forgot my fear of a height, and advanced boldly almost to the edge of the roof.

It was half-past six by that time, and growing dusk.

"You boy, down there!" I called.

The paper boy turned and looked around. Then, seeing nobody, he raised his eyes. It was a moment before he located me: when he did, he stood for one moment as if paralyzed, then he gave a horrible yell, and dropping his papers, bolted across the lawn to the road without stopping to look around. Once he fell, and his impetus was so great that he turned an involuntary somersault. He was up and off again without any perceptible pause, and he leaped the hedge—which I am sure under ordinary stress would have been a feat for a man.

I am glad in this way to settle the Gray Lady story, which is still a choice morsel in Casanova. I believe the moral deduced by the village was that it is always unlucky to throw a stone at a black cat.

With Johnny Sweeny a cloud of dust down the road, and the dinner-hour approaching, I hurried on with my investigations. Luckily, the roof was flat, and I was able to go over every inch of it. But the result was disappointing; no trap-door revealed itself, no glass window; nothing but a couple of pipes two inches across, and standing perhaps eighteen inches high and three feet apart, with a cap to prevent rain from entering and raised to permit the passage of air. I picked up a pebble from the roof and dropped it down, listening with my ear at one of the pipes. I could hear it strike on something with a sharp, metallic sound, but it was impossible for me to tell how far it had gone.

I gave up finally and went down the ladder again, getting in through the ball-room window without being observed. I went back at once to the trunk-room, and, sitting down on a box, I gave my mind, as consistently as I could, to the problem before me. If the pipes in the roof were ventilators to the secret room, and there was no trap-door above, the entrance was probably in one of the two rooms between which it lay—unless, indeed, the room had been built, and the opening then closed with a brick and mortar wall.

The mantel fascinated me. Made of wood and carved, the more I looked the more I wondered that I had not noticed before the absurdity of such a mantel in such a place. It was covered with scrolls and panels, and finally, by the merest accident, I pushed one of the panels to the side. It moved easily, revealing a small brass knob.

It is not necessary to detail the fluctuations of hope and despair, and not a little fear of what lay beyond, with which I twisted and turned the knob. It moved, but nothing seemed to happen, and then I discovered the trouble. I pushed the knob vigorously to one side, and the whole mantel swung loose from the wall almost a foot, revealing a cavernous space beyond.

I took a long breath, closed the door from the trunk-room into the hall—thank Heaven, I did not lock it—and pulling the mantel-door wide open, I stepped into the chimney-room. I had time to get a hazy view of a small portable safe, a common wooden table and a chair—then the mantel door swung to, and clicked behind me. I stood quite still for a moment, in the darkness, unable to comprehend what had happened. Then I turned and beat furiously at the door with my fists. It was closed and locked again, and my fingers in the darkness slid over a smooth wooden surface without a sign of a knob.

I was furiously angry—at myself, at the mantel door, at everything. I did not fear suffocation; before the thought had come to me I had already seen a gleam of light from the two small ventilating pipes in the roof. They supplied air, but nothing else. The room itself was shrouded in blackness.

I sat down in the stiff-backed chair and tried to remember how many days one could live without food and water. When that grew monotonous and rather painful, I got up and, according to the time-honored rule for people shut in unknown and ink-black prisons, I felt my way around—it was small enough, goodness knows. I felt nothing but a splintery surface of boards, and in endeavoring to get back to the chair, something struck me full in the face, and fell with the noise of a thousand explosions to the ground. When I had gathered up my nerves again, I found it had been the bulb of a swinging electric light, and that had it not been for the accident, I might have starved to death in an illuminated sepulcher.

I must have dozed off. I am sure I did not faint. I was never more composed in my life. I remember planning, if I were not discovered, who would have my things. I knew Liddy would want my heliotrope poplin, and she's a fright in lavender. Once or twice I heard mice in the partitions, and so I sat on the table, with my feet on the chair. I imagined I could hear the search going on through the house, and once some one came into the trunk-room; I could distinctly hear footsteps.

"In the chimney! In the chimney!" I called with all my might, and was rewarded by a piercing shriek from Liddy and the slam of the trunk-room door.

I felt easier after that, although the room was oppressively hot and enervating. I had no doubt the search for me would now come in the right direction, and after a little, I dropped into a doze. How long I slept I do not know.

It must have been several hours, for I had been tired from a busy day, and I wakened stiff from my awkward position. I could not remember where I was for a few minutes, and my head felt heavy and congested. Gradually I roused to my surroundings, and to the fact that in spite of the ventilators, the air was bad and growing worse. I was breathing long, gasping respirations, and my face was damp and clammy. I must have been there a long time, and the searchers were probably hunting outside the house, dredging the creek, or beating the woodland. I knew that another hour or two would find me unconscious, and with my inability to cry out would go my only chance of rescue. It was the combination of bad air and heat, probably, for some inadequate ventilation was coming through the pipes. I tried to retain my consciousness by walking the length of the room and back, over and over, but I had not the strength to keep it up, so I sat down on the table again, my back against the wall.

The house was very still. Once my straining ears seemed to catch a footfall beneath me, possibly in my own room. I groped for the chair from the table, and pounded with it frantically on the floor. But nothing happened: I realized bitterly that if the sound was heard at all, no doubt it was classed with the other rappings that had so alarmed us recently.

It was impossible to judge the flight of time. I measured five minutes by counting my pulse, allowing seventy-two beats to the minute. But it took eternities, and toward the last I found it hard to count; my head was confused.

And then—I heard sounds from below me, in the house. There was a peculiar throbbing, vibrating noise that I felt rather than heard, much like the pulsing beat of fire engines in the city. For one awful moment I thought the house was on fire, and every drop of blood in my body gathered around my heart; then I knew. It was the engine of the automobile, and Halsey had come back. Hope sprang up afresh. Halsey's clear head and Gertrude's intuition might do what Liddy's hysteria and three detectives had failed in.

After a time I thought I had been right. There was certainly something going on down below; doors were slamming, people were hurrying through the halls, and certain high notes of excited voices penetrated to me shrilly. I hoped they were coming closer, but after a time the sounds died away below, and I was left to the silence and heat, to the weight of the darkness, to the oppression of walls that seemed to close in on me and stifle me.

The first warning I had was a stealthy fumbling at the lock of the mantel-door. With my mouth open to scream, I stopped. Perhaps the situation had rendered me acute, perhaps it was instinctive. Whatever it was, I sat without moving, and some one outside, in absolute stillness, ran his fingers over the carving of the mantel and—found the panel.

Now the sounds below redoubled: from the clatter and jarring I knew that several people were running up the stairs, and as the sounds approached, I could even hear what they said.

"Watch the end staircases!" Jamieson was shouting. "Damnation—there's no light here!" And then a second later. "All together now. One—two—three—"

The door into the trunk-room had been locked from the inside. At the second that it gave, opening against the wall with a crash and evidently tumbling somebody into the room, the stealthy fingers beyond the mantel-door gave the knob the proper impetus, and—the door swung open, and closed again. Only—and Liddy always screams and puts her fingers in her ears at this point—only now I was not alone in the chimney room. There was some one else in the darkness, some one who breathed hard, and who was so close I could have touched him with my hand.

I was in a paralysis of terror. Outside there were excited voices and incredulous oaths. The trunks were being jerked around in a frantic search, the windows were thrown open, only to show a sheer drop of forty feet. And the man in the room with me leaned against the mantel-door and listened. His pursuers were plainly baffled: I heard him draw a long breath, and turn to grope his way through the blackness. Then—he touched my hand, cold, clammy, death-like.

A hand in an empty room! He drew in his breath, the sharp intaking of horror that fills lungs suddenly collapsed. Beyond jerking his hand away instantly, he made no movement. I think absolute terror had him by the throat. Then he stepped back, without turning, retreating foot by foot from The Dread in the corner, and I do not think he breathed.

Then, with the relief of space between us, I screamed, ear-splittingly, madly, and they heard me outside.

"In the chimney!" I shrieked. "Behind the mantel! The mantel!"

With an oath the figure hurled itself across the room at me, and I screamed again. In his blind fury he had missed me; I heard him strike the wall. That one time I eluded him; I was across the room, and I had got the chair. He stood for a second, listening, then—he made another rush, and I struck out with my weapon. I think it stunned him, for I had a second's respite when I could hear him breathing, and some one shouted outside:

"We—Can't—get—in. How—does—it—open?"

128

But the man in the room had changed his tactics. I knew he was creeping on me, inch by inch, and I could not tell from where. And then—he caught me. He held his hand over my mouth, and I bit him. I was helpless, strangling,—and some one was trying to break in the mantel from outside. It began to yield somewhere, for a thin wedge of yellowish light was reflected on the opposite wall. When he saw that, my assailant dropped me with a curse; then— the opposite wall swung open noiselessly, closed again without a sound, and I was alone. The intruder was gone.

"In the next room!" I called wildly. "The next room!" But the sound of blows on the mantel drowned my voice. By the time I had made them understand, a couple of minutes had elapsed. The pursuit was taken up then, by all except Alex, who was determined to liberate me. When I stepped out into the trunk-room, a free woman again, I could hear the chase far below.

I must say, for all Alex's anxiety to set me free, he paid little enough attention to my plight. He jumped through the opening into the secret room, and picked up the portable safe.

"I am going to put this in Mr. Halsey's room, Miss Innes," he said, "and I shall send one of the detectives to guard it."

I hardly heard him. I wanted to laugh and cry in the same breath—to crawl into bed and have a cup of tea, and scold Liddy, and do any of the thousand natural things that I had never expected to do again. And the air! The touch of the cool night air on my face!

As Alex and I reached the second floor, Mr. Jamieson met us. He was grave and quiet, and he nodded comprehendingly when he saw the safe.

"Will you come with me for a moment, Miss Innes?" he asked soberly, and on my assenting, he led the way to the east wing. There were lights moving around below, and some of the maids were standing gaping down. They screamed when they saw me, and drew back to let me pass. There was a sort of hush over the scene; Alex, behind me, muttered something I could not hear, and brushed past me without ceremony. Then I realized that a man was lying doubled up at the foot of the staircase, and that Alex was stooping over him.

As I came slowly down, Winters stepped back, and Alex straightened himself, looking at me across the body with impenetrable eyes. In his hand he held a shaggy gray wig, and before me on the floor lay the man whose headstone stood in Casanova churchyard—Paul Armstrong.

Winters told the story in a dozen words. In his headlong flight down the circular staircase, with Winters just behind, Paul Armstrong had pitched forward violently, struck his head against the door to the east veranda, and probably broken his neck. He had died as Winters reached him.

As the detective finished, I saw Halsey, pale and shaken, in the card-room doorway, and for the first time that night I lost my self-control. I put my arms around my boy, and for a moment he had to support me. A second later, over Halsey's shoulder, I saw something that turned my emotion into other channels, for, behind him, in the shadowy card-room, were Gertrude and Alex, the gardener, and—there is no use mincing matters—he was kissing her!

I was unable to speak. Twice I opened my mouth: then I turned Halsey around and pointed. They were quite unconscious of us; her head was on his shoulder, his face against her hair. As it happened, it was Mr. Jamieson who broke up the tableau.

He stepped over to Alex and touched him on the arm.

"And now," he said quietly, "how long are you and I to play OUR little comedy, Mr. Bailey?"

CHAPTER XXXIV
THE ODDS AND ENDS

Of Doctor Walker's sensational escape that night to South America, of the recovery of over a million dollars in cash and securities in the safe from the chimney room—the papers have kept the public well informed. Of my share in discovering the secret chamber they have been singularly silent. The inner history has never been told. Mr. Jamieson got all kinds of credit, and some of it he deserved, but if Jack Bailey, as Alex, had not traced Halsey and insisted on the disinterring of Paul Armstrong's casket, if he had not suspected the truth from the start, where would the detective have been?

When Halsey learned the truth, he insisted on going the next morning, weak as he was, to Louise, and by night she was at Sunnyside, under Gertrude's particular care, while her mother had gone to Barbara Fitzhugh's.

What Halsey said to Mrs. Armstrong I never knew, but that he was considerate and chivalrous I feel confident. It was Halsey's way always with women.

He and Louise had no conversation together until that night. Gertrude and Alex—I mean Jack—had gone for a walk, although it was nine o'clock, and anybody but a pair of young geese would have known that dew was falling, and that it is next to impossible to get rid of a summer cold.

At half after nine, growing weary of my own company, I went downstairs to find the young people. At the door of the living-room I paused. Gertrude and Jack had returned and were there, sitting together on a divan, with only one lamp lighted. They did not see or hear me, and I beat a hasty retreat to the library. But here again I was driven back. Louise was sitting in a deep chair, looking the happiest I had ever seen her, with Halsey on the arm of the chair, holding her close.

It was no place for an elderly spinster. I retired to my upstairs sitting-room and got out Eliza Klinefelter's lavender slippers. Ah, well, the foster motherhood would soon have to be put away in camphor again.

The next day, by degrees, I got the whole story.

Paul Armstrong had a besetting evil—the love of money. Common enough, but he loved money, not for what it would buy, but for its own sake. An examination of the books showed no irregularities in the past year since John had been cashier, but before that, in the time of Anderson, the old cashier, who had died, much strange juggling had been done with the records. The railroad in New Mexico had apparently drained the banker's private fortune, and he determined to retrieve it by one stroke. This was nothing less than the looting of the bank's securities, turning them into money, and making his escape.

But the law has long arms. Paul Armstrong evidently studied the situation carefully. Just as the only good Indian is a dead Indian, so the only safe defaulter is a dead defaulter. He decided to die, to all appearances, and when the hue and cry subsided, he would be able to enjoy his money almost anywhere he wished.

The first necessity was an accomplice. The connivance of Doctor Walker was suggested by his love for Louise. The man was unscrupulous, and with the girl as a bait, Paul Armstrong soon had him fast. The plan was apparently the acme of simplicity: a small town in the west, an attack of heart disease, a body from a medical college dissecting-room shipped in a trunk to Doctor Walker by a colleague in San Francisco, and palmed off for the supposed dead banker. What was simpler?

The woman, Nina Carrington, was the cog that slipped. What she only suspected, what she really knew, we never learned. She was a chambermaid in the hotel at C—, and it was evidently her intention to blackmail Doctor Walker. His position at that time was uncomfortable: to pay the woman to keep quiet would be confession. He denied the whole thing, and she went to Halsey.

It was this that had taken Halsey to the doctor the night he disappeared. He accused the doctor of the deception, and, crossing the lawn, had said something cruel to Louise. Then, furious at her apparent connivance, he had started for the station. Doctor Walker and Paul Armstrong—the latter still lame where I had shot him—hurried across to the embankment, certain only of one thing. Halsey must not tell the detective what he suspected until the money had been removed from the chimney-room. They stepped into the road in front of the car to stop it, and fate played into their hands. The car struck the train, and they had only to dispose of the unconscious figure in the road. This they did as I have told. For three days Halsey lay in the box car, tied hand and foot, suffering tortures of thirst, delirious at times, and discovered by a tramp at Johnsville only in time to save his life.

To go back to Paul Armstrong. At the last moment his plans had been frustrated. Sunnyside, with its hoard in the chimney-room, had been rented without his knowledge! Attempts to dislodge me having failed, he was driven to breaking into his own house. The ladder in the chute, the burning of the stable and the entrance through the card-room window—all were in the course of a desperate attempt to get into the chimney-room.

Louise and her mother had, from the first, been the great stumbling-blocks. The plan had been to send Louise away until it was too late for her to interfere, but she came back to the hotel at C— just at the wrong time. There was a terrible scene. The girl was told that something of the kind was necessary, that the bank was about to close and her stepfather would either avoid arrest and disgrace in this way, or kill himself. Fanny Armstrong was a weakling, but Louise was more difficult to manage. She had no love for her stepfather, but her devotion to her mother was entire, self-sacrificing. Forced into acquiescence by her mother's appeals, overwhelmed by the situation, the girl consented and fled.

From somewhere in Colorado she sent an anonymous telegram to Jack Bailey at the Traders' Bank. Trapped as she was, she did not want to see an innocent man arrested. The telegram, received on Thursday, had sent the cashier to the bank that night in a frenzy.

Louise arrived at Sunnyside and found the house rented. Not knowing what to do, she sent for Arnold at the Greenwood Club, and told him a little, not all. She told him that there was something wrong, and that the bank was about to close. That his father was responsible. Of the conspiracy she said nothing. To her surprise, Arnold already knew, through Bailey that night, that things were not right. Moreover, he suspected what Louise did not, that the money was hidden at Sunnyside. He had a scrap of paper that indicated a concealed room somewhere.

His inherited cupidity was aroused. Eager to get Halsey and Jack Bailey out of the house, he went up to the east entry, and in the billiard-room gave the cashier what he had refused earlier in the evening—the address of Paul Armstrong in California and a telegram which had been forwarded to the club for Bailey, from Doctor Walker. It was in response to one Bailey had sent, and it said that Paul Armstrong was very ill.

Bailey was almost desperate. He decided to go west and find Paul Armstrong, and to force him to disgorge. But the catastrophe at the bank occurred sooner than he had expected. On the moment of starting west, at Andrews Station, where Mr. Jamieson had located the car, he read that the bank had closed, and, going back, surrendered himself.

John Bailey had known Paul Armstrong intimately. He did not believe that the money was gone; in fact, it was hardly possible in the interval since the securities had been taken. Where was it? And from some chance remark let fall some months earlier by Arnold Armstrong at a dinner, Bailey felt sure there was a hidden room at Sunnyside. He tried to see the architect of the building, but, like the contractor, if he knew of the such a room he refused any information. It was Halsey's idea that John Bailey come to the house as a gardener, and pursue his investigations as he could. His smooth upper lip had been sufficient disguise, with his change of clothes, and a hair-cut by a country barber.

So it was Alex, Jack Bailey, who had been our ghost. Not only had he alarmed—Louise and himself, he admitted—on the circular staircase, but he had dug the hole in the trunk-room wall, and later sent Eliza into hysteria. The note Liddy had found in Gertrude's scrap-basket was from him, and it was he who had startled me into unconsciousness by the clothes chute, and, with Gertrude's help, had carried me to Louise's room. Gertrude, I learned, had watched all night beside me, in an extremity of anxiety about me.

That old Thomas had seen his master, and thought he had seen the Sunnyside ghost, there could be no doubt. Of that story of Thomas', about seeing Jack Bailey in the footpath between the club and Sunnyside, the night Liddy and I heard the noise on the circular staircase—that, too, was right. On the night before Arnold Armstrong was murdered, Jack Bailey had made his first attempt to search for the secret room. He secured Arnold's keys from his room at the club and got into the house, armed with a golf-stick for sounding the walls. He ran against the hamper at the head of the stairs, caught his cuff-link in it, and dropped the golf-stick with a crash. He was glad enough to get away without an alarm being raised, and he took the "owl" train to town.

The oddest thing to me was that Mr. Jamieson had known for some time that Alex was Jack Bailey. But the face of the pseudo-gardener was very queer indeed, when that night, in the card-room, the detective turned to him and said:

"How long are you and I going to play our little comedy, MR. BAILEY?"

Well, it is all over now. Paul Armstrong rests in Casanova churchyard, and this time there is no mistake. I went to the funeral, because I wanted to be sure he was really buried, and I looked at the step of the shaft where I had sat that night, and wondered if it was all real. Sunnyside is for sale—no, I shall not buy it. Little Lucien Armstrong is living with his step-grandmother, and she is recovering gradually from troubles that had extended over the entire period of her second marriage. Anne Watson lies not far from the man she killed, and who as surely caused her death. Thomas, the fourth victim of the conspiracy, is buried on the hill. With Nina Carrington, five lives were sacrificed in the course of this grim conspiracy.

There will be two weddings before long, and Liddy has asked for my heliotrope poplin to wear to the church. I knew she would. She has wanted it for three years, and she was quite ugly the time I spilled coffee on it. We are very quiet, just the two of us. Liddy still clings to her ghost theory, and points to my wet and muddy boots in the trunk-room as proof. I am gray, I admit, but I haven't felt as well in a dozen years. Sometimes, when I am bored, I ring for Liddy, and we talk things over. When Warner married Rosie, Liddy sniffed and said what I took for faithfulness in Rosie had been nothing but mawkishness. I have not yet outlived Liddy's contempt because I gave them silver knives and forks as a wedding gift.

So we sit and talk, and sometimes Liddy threatens to leave, and often I discharge her, but we stay together somehow. I am talking of renting a house next year, and Liddy says to be sure there is no ghost. To be perfectly frank, I never really lived until that summer. Time has passed since I began this story. My neighbors are packing up for another summer. Liddy is having the awnings put up, and the window boxes filled. Liddy or no Liddy, I shall advertise to-morrow for a house in the country, and I don't care if it has a Circular Staircase.

The Breaking Point

"Heaven and earth," sang the tenor, Mr. Henry Wallace, owner of the Wallace garage. His larynx, which gave him somewhat the effect of having swallowed a crab-apple and got it only part way down, protruded above his low collar.

"Heaven and earth," sang the bass, Mr. Edwin Goodno, of the meat market and the Boy Scouts. "Heaven and earth, are full—" His chin, large and fleshy, buried itself deep; his eyes were glued on the music sheet in his hand.

"Are full, are full, are full," sang the soprano, Clare Rossiter, of the yellow colonial house on the Ridgely Road. She sang with her eyes turned up, and as she reached G flat she lifted herself on her toes. "Of the majesty, of Thy glory."

"Ready," barked the choir master. "Full now, and all together."

The choir room in the parish house resounded to the twenty voices of the choir. The choir master at the piano kept time with his head. Earnest and intent, they filled the building with the Festival Te Deum of Dudley Buck, Opus 63, No. 1.

Elizabeth Wheeler liked choir practice. She liked the way in which, after the different parts had been run through, the voices finally blended into harmony and beauty. She liked the small sense of achievement it gave her, and of being a part, on Sundays, of the service. She liked the feeling, when she put on the black cassock and white surplice and the small round velvet cap of having placed in her locker the things of this world, such as a rose-colored hat and a blue georgette frock, and of being stripped, as it were, for aspirations.

At such times she had vague dreams of renunciation. She saw herself cloistered in some quiet spot, withdrawn from the world; a place where there were long vistas of pillars and Gothic arches, after a photograph in the living room at home, and a great organ somewhere, playing.

She would go home from church, however, clad in the rose-colored hat and the blue georgette frock, and eat a healthy Sunday luncheon; and by two o'clock in the afternoon, when the family slept and Jim had gone to the country club, her dreams were quite likely to be entirely different. Generally speaking, they had to do with love. Romantic, unclouded young love dramatic only because it was love, and very happy.

Sometime, perhaps, some one would come and say he loved her. That was all. That was at once the beginning and the end. Her dreams led up to that and stopped. Not by so much as a hand clasp did they pass that wall.

So she sat in the choir room and awaited her turn.

"Altos a little stronger, please."

"Of the majesty, of the majesty, of the majesty, of Thy gl-o-o-ry," sang Elizabeth. And was at once a nun and a principal in a sentimental dream of two.

What appeared to the eye was a small and rather ethereal figure with sleek brown hair and wistful eyes; nice eyes, of no particular color. Pretty with the beauty of youth, sensitive and thoughtful, infinitely loyal and capable of suffering and not otherwise extraordinary was Elizabeth Wheeler in her plain wooden chair. A figure suggestive of no drama and certainly of no tragedy, its attitude expectant and waiting, with that alternate hope and fear which is youth at twenty, when all of life lies ahead and every to-morrow may hold some great adventure.

Clare Rossiter walked home that night with Elizabeth. She was a tall blonde girl, lithe and graceful, and with a calculated coquetry in her clothes.

"Do you mind going around the block?" she asked. "By Station Street?" There was something furtive and yet candid in her voice, and Elizabeth glanced at her.

"All right. But it's out of your way, isn't it?"

"Yes. I—You're so funny, Elizabeth. It's hard to talk to you. But I've got to talk to somebody. I go around by Station Street every chance I get."

"By Station Street? Why?"

"I should think you could guess why."

She saw that Clare desired to be questioned, and at the same time she felt a great distaste for the threatened confidence. She loathed arm-in-arm confidences, the indecency of dragging up and exposing, in whispers, things that should have been buried deep in reticence. She hesitated, and Clare slipped an arm through hers.

"You don't know, then, do you? Sometimes I think every one must know. And I don't care. I've reached that point."

Her confession, naive and shameless, and yet somehow not without a certain dignity, flowed on. She was mad about Doctor Dick Livingstone. Goodness knew why, for he never looked at her. She might be the dirt under his feet for all he knew. She trembled when she met him in the street, and sometimes he looked past her and never saw her. She didn't sleep well any more.

Elizabeth listened in great discomfort. She did not see in Clare's hopeless passion the joy of the flagellant, or the self-dramatization of a neurotic girl. She saw herself unwillingly forced to peer into the sentimental windows of Clare's soul, and there to see Doctor Dick Livingstone, an unconscious occupant. But she had a certain fugitive sense of guilt, also. Formless as her dreams had been, vague and shy, they had nevertheless centered about some one who should be tall, like Dick Livingstone, and alternately grave, which was his professional manner, and gay, which was his manner when it turned out to be only a cold, and he could take a few minutes to be himself. Generally speaking, they centered about some one who resembled Dick Livingstone, but who did not, as did Doctor Livingstone, assume at times an air of frightful maturity and pretend that in years gone by he had dandled her on his knee.

"Sometimes I think he positively avoids me," Clare wailed. "There's the house, Elizabeth. Do you mind stopping a moment? He must be in his office now. The light's burning."

"I wish you wouldn't, Clare. He'd hate it if he knew."

She moved on and Clare slowly followed her. The Rossiter girl's flow of talk had suddenly stopped. She was thoughtful and impulsively suspicious.

"Look here, Elizabeth, I believe you care for him yourself."

"I? What is the matter with you to-night, Clare?"

"I'm just thinking. Your voice was so queer."

They walked on in silence. The flow of Clare's confidences had ceased, and her eyes were calculating and a trifle hard.

"There's a good bit of talk about him," she jerked out finally. "I suppose you've heard it."

"What sort of talk?"

"Oh, gossip. You'll hear it. Everybody's talking about it. It's doing him a lot of harm."

"I don't believe it," Elizabeth flared. "This town hasn't anything else to do, and so it talks. It makes me sick."

She did not attempt to analyze the twisted motives that made Clare belittle what she professed to love. And she did not ask what the gossip was. Half way up Palmer Lane she turned in at the cement path between borders of early perennials which led to the white Wheeler house. She was flushed and angry, hating Clare for her unsolicited confidence and her malice, hating even Haverly, that smiling, tree-shaded suburb which "talked."

She opened the door quietly and went in. Micky, the Irish terrier, lay asleep at the foot of the stairs, and her father's voice, reading aloud, came pleasantly from the living room. Suddenly her sense of resentment died. With the closing of the front door the peace of the house enveloped her. What did it matter if, beyond that door, there were unrequited love and petty gossip, and even tragedy? Not that she put all that into conscious thought; she had merely a sensation of sanctuary and peace. Here, within these four walls, were all that one should need, love and security and quiet happiness. Walter Wheeler, pausing to turn a page, heard her singing as she went up the stairs. In the moment of the turning he too had a flash of content. Twenty-five years of married life and all well; Nina married, Jim out of college, Elizabeth singing her way up the stairs, and here by the lamp his wife quietly knitting while he read to her. He was reading Paradise Lost: "The mind is its own place, and in itself can make a Heaven of Hell, a Hell of Heaven."

He did a certain amount of serious reading every year.

On Sunday mornings, during the service, Elizabeth earnestly tried to banish all worldly thoughts. In spite of this resolve, however, she was always conscious of a certain regret that the choir seats necessitated turning her profile to the congregation. At the age of twelve she had decided that her nose was too short, and nothing had happened since to change her conviction. She seldom so much as glanced at the congregation. During her slow progress up and down the main aisle behind the Courtney boy, who was still a soprano and who carried the great gold cross, she always looked straight ahead. Or rather, although she was unconscious of this, slightly up. She always looked up when she sang, for she had commenced to take singing lessons when the piano music rack was high above her head.

So she still lifted her eyes as she went up the aisle, and was extremely serious over the whole thing. Because it is a solemn matter to take a number of people who have been up to that moment engrossed in thoughts of food or golf or servants or business, and in the twinkling of an eye, as the prayer book said about death, turn their minds to worship.

Nevertheless, although she never looked at the pews, she was always conscious of two of them. The one near the pulpit was the Sayres' and it was the social calendar of the town. When Mrs. Sayre was in it, it was the social season. One never knew when Mrs. Sayre's butler would call up and say:

"I am speaking for Mrs. Sayre. Mrs. Sayre would like to have the pleasure of Miss Wheeler's company on Thursday to luncheon, at one-thirty."

When the Sayre pew was empty, the town knew, if it happened to be winter, that the Florida or Santa Barbara season was on; or in summer the Maine coast.

The other pew was at the back of the church. Always it had one occupant; sometimes it had three. But the behavior of this pew was very erratic. Sometimes an elderly and portly gentleman with white hair and fierce eyebrows would come in when the sermon was almost over. Again, a hand would reach through the grill behind it, and a tall young man who had had his eyes fixed in the proper direction, but not always on the rector, would reach for his hat, get up and slip out. On these occasions, however, he would first identify the owner of the hand and then bend over the one permanent occupant of the pew, a little old lady. His speech was as Yea, yea, or Nay, nay, for he either said, "I'll be back for dinner," or "Don't look for me until you see me."

And Mrs. Crosby, without taking her eyes from the sermon, would nod.

Of late years, Doctor David Livingstone had been taking less and less of the "Don't-look-for-me-until-you-see-me" cases, and Doctor Dick had acquired a car, which would not freeze when left outside all night like a forgotten dog, and a sense of philosophy about sleep. That is, that eleven o'clock P.M. was bed-time to some people, but was just eleven o'clock for him.

When he went to church he listened to the sermon, but rather often he looked at Elizabeth Wheeler. When his eyes wandered, as the most faithful eyes will now and then, they were apt to rest on the flag that had hung, ever since the war, beside the altar. He had fought for his country in a sea of mud, never nearer than two hundred miles to the battle line, fought with a surgical kit instead of a gun, but he was content. Not to all the high adventure.

Had he been asked, suddenly, the name of the tall blonde girl who sang among the sopranos, he could not have told it.

The Sunday morning following Clare Rossiter's sentimental confession, Elizabeth tried very hard to banish all worldly thoughts, as usual, and to see the kneeling, rising and sitting congregation as there for worship. But for the first time she wondered. Some of the faces were blank, as though behind the steady gaze the mind had wandered far afield, or slept. Some were intent, some even devout. But for the first time she began to feel that people in the mass might be cruel, too. How many of them, for instance, would sometime during the day pass on, behind their hands, the gossip Clare had mentioned?

She changed her position, and glanced quickly over the church. The Livingstone pew was fully occupied, and well up toward the front, Wallie Sayre was steadfastly regarding her. She looked away quickly.

Came the end of the service. Came down the aisle the Courtney boy, clean and shining and carrying high his glowing symbol. Came the choir, two by two, the women first, sopranos, altos and Elizabeth. Came the men, bass and tenor, neatly shaved for Sunday morning. Came the rector, Mr. Oglethorpe, a trifle wistful, because always he fell so far below the mark he had set. Came the benediction. Came the slow rising from its knees of the congregation and its cheerful bustle of dispersal.

Doctor Dick Livingstone stood up and helped Doctor David into his new spring overcoat. He was very content. It was May, and the sun was shining. It was Sunday, and he would have an hour or two of leisure. And he had made a resolution about a matter that had been in his mind for some time. He was very content.

He looked around the church with what was almost a possessive eye. These people were his friends. He knew them all, and they knew him. They had, against his protest, put his name on the bronze tablet set in the wall on the roll of honor. Small as it was, this was his world.

Half smiling, he glanced about. He did not realize that behind their bows and greetings there was something new that day, something not so much unkind as questioning.

Outside in the street he tucked his aunt, Mrs. Crosby, against the spring wind, and waited at the wheel of the car while David entered with the deliberation of a man accustomed to the sagging of his old side-bar buggy under his weight. Long ago Dick had dropped the titular "uncle," and as David he now addressed him.

"You're going to play some golf this afternoon, David," he said firmly. "Mike had me out this morning to look at your buggy springs."

David chuckled. He still stuck to his old horse, and to the ancient vehicle which had been the signal of distress before so many doors for forty years. "I can trust old Nettie," he would say. "She doesn't freeze her radiator on cold nights, she doesn't skid, and if I drop asleep she'll take me home and into my own barn, which is more than any automobile would do."

"I'm going to sleep," he said comfortably. "Get Wallie Sayre—I see he's back from some place again—or ask a nice girl. Ask Elizabeth Wheeler. I don't think Lucy here expects to be the only woman in your life."

Dick stared into the windshield.

"I've been wondering about that, David," he said, "just how much right—"

"Balderdash!" David snorted. "Don't get any fool notion in your head."

Followed a short silence with Dick driving automatically and thinking. Finally he drew a long breath.

"All right," he said, "how about that golf—you need exercise. You're putting on weight, and you know it. And you smoke too much. It's either less tobacco or more walking, and you ought to know it."

David grunted, but he turned to Lucy Crosby, in the rear seat:

"Lucy, d'you know where my clubs are?"

"You loaned them to Jim Wheeler last fall. If you get three of them back you're lucky." Mrs. Crosby's voice was faintly tart. Long ago she had learned that her brother's belongings were his only by right of purchase, and were by way of being community property. When, early in her widowhood and her return to his home, she had found that her protests resulted only in a sort of clandestine giving or lending, she had exacted a promise from him. "I ask only one thing, David," she had said. "Tell me where the things go. There wasn't a blanket for the guest-room bed at the time of the Diocesan Convention."

"I'll run around to the Wheelers' and get them," Dick observed, in a carefully casual voice. "I'll see the Carter baby, too, David, and that clears the afternoon. Any message?"

Lucy glanced at him, but David moved toward the house.

"Give Elizabeth a kiss for me," he called over his shoulder, and went chuckling up the path.

II

Mrs. Crosby stood on the pavement, gazing after the car as it moved off. She had not her brother's simplicity nor his optimism. Her married years had taken her away from the environment which had enabled him to live his busy, uncomplicated life; where, the only medical man in a growing community, he had learned to form his own sturdy decisions and then to abide by them.

Black and white, right and wrong, the proper course and the improper course—he lived in a sort of two-dimensional ethical world. But to Lucy Crosby, between black and white there was a gray no-man's land of doubt and indecision; a half-way house of compromise, and sometimes David frightened her. He was so sure.

She passed the open door into the waiting-room, where sat two or three patient and silent figures, and went back to the kitchen. Minnie, the elderly servant, sat by the table reading, amid the odor of roasting chicken; outside the door on the kitchen porch was the freezer containing the dinner ice-cream. An orderly Sunday peace was in the air, a gesture of homely comfort, order and security.

Minnie got up.

"I'll unpin your veil for you," she offered, obligingly. "You've got time to lie down about ten minutes. Mrs. Morgan said she's got to have her ears treated."

"I hope she doesn't sit and talk for an hour."

"She'll talk, all right," Minnie observed, her mouth full of pins. "She'd be talking to me yet if I'd stood there. She's got her nerve, too, that woman."

"I don't like to hear you speak so of the patients who come to the house, Minnie."

"Well, I don't like their asking me questions about the family either," said Minnie, truculently. "She wanted to know who was Doctor Dick's mother. Said she had had a woman here from Wyoming, and she thought she'd known his people."

Mrs. Crosby stood very still.

"I think she should bring her questions to the family," she said, after a silence. "Thank you, Minnie."

Bonnet in hand, she moved toward the stairs, climbed them and went into her room. Recently life had been growing increasingly calm and less beset with doubts. For the first time, with Dick's coming to live with them ten years before, a boy of twenty-two, she had found a vicarious maternity and gloried in it. Recently she had been very happy. The war was over and he was safely back; again she could sew on his buttons and darn his socks, and turn down his bed at night. He filled the old house with cheer and with vitality. And, as David gave up more and more of the work, he took it on his broad shoulders, efficient, tireless, and increasingly popular.

She put her bonnet away in its box, and suddenly there rose in her frail old body a fierce and unexpected resentment against David. He had chosen a course and abided by it. He had even now no doubt or falterings. Just as in the first anxious days there had been no doubt in him as to the essential rightness of what he was doing. And now—This was what came of taking a life and moulding it in accordance with a predetermined plan. That was for God to do, not man.

She sat down near her window and rocked slowly, to calm herself. Outside the Sunday movement of the little suburban town went by: the older Wheeler girl, Nina, who had recently married Leslie Ward, in her smart little car; Harrison Miller, the cynical bachelor who lived next door, on his way to the station news stand for the New York papers; young couples taking small babies for the air in a perambulator; younger couples, their eyes on each other and on the future.

That, too, she reflected bitterly! Dick was in love. She had not watched him for that very thing for so long without being fairly sure now. She had caught, as simple David with his celibate heart could never have caught, the tone in Dick's voice when he mentioned the Wheelers. She had watched him for the past few months in church on Sunday mornings, and she knew that as she watched him, so he looked at Elizabeth.

And David was so sure! So sure.

The office door closed and Mrs. Morgan went out, a knitted scarf wrapping her ears against the wind, and following her exit came the slow ascent of David as he climbed the stairs to wash for dinner.

She stopped rocking.

"David!" she called sharply.

He opened the door and came in, a bulky figure, still faintly aromatic of drugs, cheerful and serene.

"D'you call me?" he inquired.

"Yes. Shut the door and come in. I want to talk to you." He closed the door and went to the hearth-rug. There was a photograph of Dick on the mantel, taken in his uniform, and he looked at it for a moment. Then he turned. "All right, my dear. Let's have it."

"Did Mrs. Morgan have anything to say?" He stared at her.

"She usually has," he said. "I never knew you considered it worth repeating. No. Nothing in particular."

The very fact that Mrs. Morgan had limited her inquiry to Minnie confirmed her suspicions. But somehow, face to face with David, she could not see his contentment turned to anxiety.

"I want to talk to you about Dick."

"Yes?"

"I think he's in love, David."

David's heavy body straightened, but his face remained serene.

"We had to expect that, Lucy. Is it Elizabeth Wheeler, do you think?"

"Yes."

For a moment there was silence. The canary in its cage hopped about, a beady inquisitive eye now on one, now on the other of them.

"She's a good girl, Lucy."

"That's not the point, is it?"

"Do you think she cares for him?"

"I don't know. There's some talk of Wallie Sayre. He's there a good bit."

"Wallie Sayre!" snorted David. "He's never done a day's work in his life and never will." He reflected on that with growing indignation. "He doesn't hold a candle to Dick. Of course, if the girl's a fool—"

Hands thrust deep into his pockets David took a turn about the room. Lucy watched him. At last:

"You're evading the real issue, David, aren't you?"

"Perhaps I am," he admitted. "I'd better talk to him. I think he's got an idea he shouldn't marry. That's nonsense."

"I don't mean that, exactly," Lucy persisted. "I mean, won't he want a good many things cleared up before he marries? Isn't he likely to want to go back to Norada?"

Some of the ruddy color left David's face. He stood still, staring at her and silent.

"You know he meant to go three years ago, but the war came, and—"

Her voice trailed off. She could not even now easily recall those days when Dick was drilling on the golf links, and that later period of separation.

138

"If he does go back—"

"Donaldson is dead," David broke in, almost roughly.

"Maggie Donaldson is still living."

"What if she is? She's loyal to the core, in the first place. In the second, she's criminally liable. As liable as I am."

"There is one thing, David, I ought to know. What has become of the Carlysle girl?"

"She left the stage. There was a sort of general conviction she was implicated and—I don't know, Lucy. Sometimes I think she was." He sighed. "I read something about her coming back, some months ago, in 'The Valley.' That was the thing she was playing the spring before it happened." He turned on her. "Don't get that in your head with the rest."

"I wonder, sometimes."

"I know it."

Outside the slamming of an automobile door announced Dick's return, and almost immediately Minnie rang the old fashioned gong which hung in the lower hall. Mrs. Crosby got up and placed a leaf of lettuce between the bars of the bird cage.

"Dinner time, Caruso," she said absently. Caruso was the name Dick had given the bird. And to David: "She must be in her thirties now."

"Probably." Then his anger and anxiety burst out. "What difference can it make about her? About Donaldson's wife? About any hang-over from that rotten time? They're gone, all of them. He's here. He's safe and happy. He's strong and fine. That's gone."

In the lower hall Dick was taking off his overcoat.

"Smell's like chicken, Minnie," he said, into the dining room.

"Chicken and biscuits, Mr. Dick."

"Hi, up there!" he called lustily. "Come and feed a starving man. I'm going to muffle the door-bell!"

He stood smiling up at them, very tidy in his Sunday suit, very boyish, for all his thirty-two years. His face, smilingly tender as he watched them, was strong rather than handsome, quietly dependable and faintly humorous.

"In the language of our great ally," he said, "Madame et Monsieur, le diner est servi."

In his eyes there was not only tenderness but a somewhat emphasized affection, as though he meant to demonstrate, not only to them but to himself, that this new thing that had come to him did not touch their old relationship. For the new thing had come. He was still slightly dazed with the knowledge of it, and considerably anxious. Because he had just taken a glance at himself in the mirror of the walnut hat-rack, and had seen nothing there particularly to inspire—well, to inspire what he wanted to inspire.

At the foot of the stairs he drew Lucy's arm through his, and held her hand. She seemed very small and frail beside him.

"Some day," he said, "a strong wind will come along and carry off Mrs. Lucy Crosby, and the Doctors Livingstone will be obliged hurriedly to rent aeroplanes, and to search for her at various elevations!"

David sat down and picked up the old fashioned carving knife.

"Get the clubs?" he inquired.

Dick looked almost stricken.

"I forgot them, David," he said guiltily. "Jim Wheeler went out to look them up, and I—I'll go back after dinner."

It was sometime later in the meal that Dick looked up from his plate and said:

"I'd like to cut office hours on Wednesday night, David. I've asked Elizabeth Wheeler to go into town to the theater."

"What about the baby at the Homer place?"

"Not due until Sunday. I'll leave my seat number at the box office, anyhow."

"What are you going to see, Dick?" Mrs. Crosby asked. "Will you have some dumplings?"

"I will, but David shouldn't. Too much starch. Why, it's 'The Valley,' I think. An actress named Carlysle, Beverly Carlysle, is starring in it."

He ate on, his mind not on his food, but back in the white house on Palmer Lane, and a girl. Lucy Crosby, fork in air, stared at him, and then glanced at David.

But David did not look up from his plate.

III

The Wheeler house was good, modern and commonplace. Walter Wheeler and his wife were like the house. Just as here and there among the furniture there was a fine thing, an antique highboy, a Sheraton sideboard or some old cut glass, so they had, with a certain mediocrity their own outstanding virtues. They liked music, believed in the home as the unit of the nation, put happiness before undue ambition, and had devoted their lives to their children.

For many years their lives had centered about the children. For years they had held anxious conclave about whooping cough, about small early disobediences, later about Sunday tennis. They stood united to protect the children against disease, trouble and eternity.

Now that the children were no longer children, they were sometimes lonely and still apprehensive. They feared motor car accidents, and Walter Wheeler had withstood the appeals of Jim for a half dozen years. They feared trains for them, and journeys, and unhappy marriages, and hid their fears from each other. Their nightly prayers were "to keep them safe and happy."

But they saw life reaching out and taking them, one by one. They saw them still as children, but as children determined to bear their own burdens. Jim stayed out late sometimes, and considered his manhood in question if interrogated. Nina was married and out of the home, but there loomed before them the possibility of maternity and its dangers for her. There remained only Elizabeth, and on her they lavished the care formerly divided among the three.

It was their intention and determination that she should never know trouble. She was tenderer than the others, more docile and gentle. They saw her, not as a healthy, normal girl, but as something fragile and very precious.

Nina was different. They had always worried a little about Nina, although they had never put their anxiety to each other. Nina had always overrun her dress allowance, although she had never failed to be sweetly penitent about it, and Nina had always placed an undue emphasis on things. Her bedroom before her marriage was cluttered with odds and ends, cotillion favors and photographs, college pennants and small unwise purchases—trophies of the gayety and conquest which were her life.

And Nina had "come out." It had cost a great deal, and it was not so much to introduce her to society as to put a family recognition on a fact already accomplished, for Nina had brought herself out unofficially at sixteen. There had been the club ballroom, and a great many flowers which withered before they could be got to the hospital; and new clothing for all the family, and a caterer and orchestra. After that, for a cold and tumultuous winter Mrs. Wheeler had sat up with the dowagers night after night until all hours, and the next morning had let Nina sleep, while she went about her household duties. She had aged, rather, and her determined smile had grown a little fixed.

She was a good woman, and she wanted her children's happiness more than anything in the world, but she had a faint and sternly repressed feeling of relief when Nina announced her engagement. Nina did it with characteristic sangfroid, at dinner one night.

"Don't ring for Annie for a minute, mother," she said. "I want to tell you all something. I'm going to marry Leslie Ward."

There had been a momentary pause. Then her father said:

"Just a minute. Is that Will Ward's boy?"

140

"Yes. He's not a boy."

"Well, he'll come around to see me before there's any engagement. Has that occurred to either of you?"

"Oh, he'll be around. He'd have come to-night, but Howard Moore is having his bachelor dinner. I hope he doesn't look shot to pieces to-morrow. These bachelor things—! We'd better have a dinner or something, mother, and announce it."

There had been the dinner, with a silver loving cup bought for the occasion, and thereafter to sit out its useless days on the Sheraton sideboard. And there had been a trousseau and a wedding so expensive that a small frown of anxiety had developed between Walter Wheeler's eyebrows and stayed there.

For Nina's passion for things was inherent, persisting after her marriage. She discounted her birthday and Christmases in advance, coming around to his office a couple of months before the winter holidays and needing something badly.

"It's like this, daddy," she would say. "You're going to give me a check for Christmas anyhow, aren't you? And it would do me more good now. I simply can't go to another ball."

"Where's your trousseau?"

"It's worn out-danced to rags. And out of date, too."

"I don't understand it, Nina. You and Leslie have a good income. Your mother and I—"

"You didn't have any social demands. And wedding presents! If one more friend of mine is married—"

He would get out his checkbook and write a check slowly and thoughtfully. And tearing it off would say:

"Now remember, Nina, this is for Christmas. Don't feel aggrieved when the time comes and you have no gift from us."

But he knew that when the time came Margaret, his wife, would hold out almost to the end, and then slip into a jeweler's and buy Nina something she simply couldn't do without.

It wasn't quite fair, he felt. It wasn't fair to Jim or to Elizabeth. Particularly to Elizabeth.

Sometimes he looked at Elizabeth with a little prayer in his heart, never articulate, that life would be good to her; that she might keep her illusions and her dreams; that the soundness and wholesomeness of her might keep her from unhappiness. Sometimes, as she sat reading or sewing, with the light behind her shining through her soft hair, he saw in her a purity that was almost radiant.

He was in arms at once a night or two before Dick had invited Elizabeth to go to the theater when Margaret Wheeler said:

"The house was gayer when Nina was at home."

"Yes. And you were pretty sick of it. Full of roistering young idiots. Piano and phonograph going at once, pairs of gigglers in the pantry at the refrigerator, pairs on the stairs and on the verandah, cigar-ashes—my cigars—and cigarettes over everything, and more infernal spooning going on than I've ever seen in my life."

He had resumed his newspaper, to put it down almost at once.

"What's that Sayre boy hanging around for?"

"I think he's in love with her, Walter."

"Love? Any of the Sayre tribe? Jim Sayre drank himself to death, and this boy is like him. And Jim Sayre wasn't faithful to his wife. This boy is—well, he's an heir. That's why he was begotten."

Margaret Wheeler stared at him.

"Why, Walter!" she said. "He's a nice boy, and he's a gentleman."

"Why? Because he gets up when you come into the room? Why in heaven's name don't you encourage real men to come here? There's Dick Livingstone. He's a man."

Margaret hesitated.

141

"Walter, have you ever thought there was anything queer about Dick Livingstone's coming here?"

"Darned good for the town that he did come."

"But—nobody ever dreamed that David and Lucy had a nephew. Then he turns up, and they send him to medical college, and all that."

"I've got some relations I haven't notified the town I possess," he said grimly.

"Well, there's something odd. I don't believe Henry Livingstone, the Wyoming brother, ever had a son."

"What possible foundation have you for a statement like that?"

"Mrs. Cook Morgan's sister-in-law has been visiting her lately. She says she knew Henry Livingstone well years ago in the West, and she never heard he was married. She says positively he was not married."

"And trust the Morgan woman to spread the good news," he said with angry sarcasm. "Well, suppose that's true? Suppose Dick is an illegitimate child? That's the worst that's implied, I daresay. That's nothing against Dick himself. I'll tell the world there's good blood on the Livingstone side, anyhow."

"You were very particular about Wallie Sayre's heredity, Walter."

"That's different," he retorted, and retired into gloomy silence behind his newspaper. Drat these women anyhow. It was like some fool female to come there and rake up some old and defunct scandal. He'd stand up for Dick, if it ever came to a show-down. He liked Dick. What the devil did his mother matter, anyhow? If this town hadn't had enough evidence of Dick Livingstone's quality the last few years he'd better go elsewhere. He—

He got up and whistled for the dog.

"I'm going to take a walk," he said briefly, and went out. He always took a walk when things disturbed him.

On the Sunday afternoon after Dick had gone Elizabeth was alone in her room upstairs. On the bed lay the sort of gown Nina would have called a dinner dress, and to which Elizabeth referred as her dark blue. Seen thus, in the room which was her own expression, there was a certain nobility about her very simplicity, a steadiness about her eyes that was almost disconcerting.

"She's the saintly-looking sort that would go on the rocks for some man," Nina had said once, rather flippantly, "and never know she was shipwrecked. No man in the world could do that to me."

But just then Elizabeth looked totally unlike shipwreck. Nothing seemed more like a safe harbor than the Wheeler house that afternoon, or all the afternoons. Life went on, the comfortable life of an upper middle-class household. Candles and flowers on the table and a neat waitress to serve; little carefully planned shopping expeditions; fine hand-sewing on dainty undergarments for rainy days; small tributes of books and candy; invitations and consultations as to what to wear; choir practice, a class in the Sunday school, a little work among the poor; the volcano which had been Nina overflowing elsewhere in a smart little house with a butler out on the Ridgely Road.

She looked what she was, faithful and quietly loyal, steady—and serene; not asking greatly but hoping much; full of small unvisualized dreams and little inarticulate prayers; waiting, without knowing that she was waiting.

Sometimes she worried. She thought she ought to "do something." A good many of the girls she knew wanted to do something, but they were vague as to what. She felt at those times that she was not being very useful, and she had gone so far as to lay the matter before her father a couple of years before, when she was just eighteen.

"Just what do you think of doing?" he had inquired.

"That's it," she had said despondently. "I don't know. I haven't any particular talent, you know. But I don't think I ought to go on having you support me in idleness all my life."

"Well, I don't think it likely that I'll have to," he had observed, dryly. "But here's the point, and I think it's important. I don't intend to work without some compensation, and my family is my compensation. You just hang around and make me happy, as you do, and you're fulfilling your economic place in the nation. Don't you forget it, either."

That had comforted her. She had determined then never to marry but to hang around, as he suggested, for the rest of her life. She was quite earnest about it, and resolved.

She picked up the blue dress and standing before her mirror, held it up before her. It looked rather shabby, she thought, but the theater was not like a dance, and anyhow it would look better at night. She had been thinking about next Wednesday evening ever since Dick Livingstone had gone. It seemed, better somehow, frightfully important. It was frightfully important. For the first time she acknowledged to herself that she had been fond of him, as she put it, for a long time. She had an odd sense, too, of being young and immature, and as though he had stooped to her from some height: such as thirty-two years and being in the war, and having to decide about life and death, and so on.

She hoped he did not think she was only a child.

She heard Nina coming up the stairs. At the click of her high heels on the hard wood she placed the dress on the bed again, and went to the window. Her father was on the path below, clearly headed for a walk. She knew then that Nina had been asking for something.

Nina came in and closed the door. She was smaller than Elizabeth and very pretty. Her eyebrows had been drawn to a tidy line, and from the top of her shining head to her brown suede pumps she was exquisite with the hours of careful tending and careful dressing she gave her young body. Exquisitely pretty, too.

She sat down on Elizabeth's bed with a sigh.

"I really don't know what to do with father," she said. "He flies off at a tangent over the smallest things. Elizabeth dear, can you lend me twenty dollars? I'll get my allowance on Tuesday."

"I can give you ten."

"Well, ask mother for the rest, won't you? You needn't say it's for me. I'll give it to you Tuesday."

"I'm not going to mother, Nina. She has had a lot of expenses this month."

"Then I'll borrow it from Wallie Sayre," Nina said, accepting her defeat cheerfully. "If it was an ordinary bill it could wait, but I lost it at bridge last night and it's got to be paid."

"You oughtn't to play bridge for money," Elizabeth said, a bit primly. "And if Leslie knew you borrowed from Wallace Sayre—"

"I forgot! Wallie's downstairs, Elizabeth. Really, if he wasn't so funny, he'd be tragic."

"Why tragic? He has everything in the world."

"If you use a little bit of sense, you can have it too."

"I don't want

"Pooh! That's what you think now. Wallie's a nice person. Lots of girls are mad about him. And he has about all the money there is." Getting no response from Elizabeth, she went on: "I was thinking it over last night. You'll have to marry sometime, and it isn't as though Wallie was dissipated, or anything like that. I suppose he knows his way about, but then they all do."

She got up.

"Be nice to him, anyhow," she said. "He's crazy about you, and when I think of you in that house! It's a wonderful house, Elizabeth. She's got a suite waiting for Wallie to be married before she furnishes it."

Elizabeth looked around her virginal little room, with its painted dressing table, its chintz, and its white bed with the blue dress on it.

"I'm very well satisfied as I am," she said.

While she smoothed her hair before the mirror Nina surveyed the room and her eyes lighted on the frock.

"Are you still wearing that shabby old thing?" she demanded. "I do wish you'd get some proper clothes. Are you going somewhere?"

"I'm going to the theater on Wednesday night."

"Who with?" Nina in her family was highly colloquial.

"With Doctor Livingstone."

"Are you joking?" Nina demanded.

"Joking? Of course not."

Nina sat down again on the bed, her eyes on her sister, curious and not a little apprehensive.

"It's the first time it's ever happened, to my knowledge," she declared. "I know he's avoided me like poison. I thought he hated women. You know Clare Rossiter is—"

Elizabeth turned suddenly.

"Clare is ridiculous," she said. "She hasn't any reserve, or dignity, or anything else. And I don't see what my going to the theater with Dick Livingstone has to do with her anyhow."

Nina raised her carefully plucked eyebrows.

"Really!" she said. "You needn't jump down my throat, you know." She considered, her eyes on her sister. "Don't go and throw yourself away on Dick Livingstone, Sis. You're too good-looking, and he hasn't a cent. A suburban practice, out all night, that tumble-down old house and two old people hung around your necks, for Doctor David is letting go pretty fast. It just won't do. Besides, there's a story going the rounds about him, that—"

"I don't want to hear it, if you don't mind."

She went to the door and opened it.

"I've hardly spoken a dozen words to him in my life. But just remember this. When I do find the man I want to marry, I shall make up my own mind. As you did," she added as a parting shot.

She was rather sorry as she went down the stairs. She had begun to suspect what the family had never guessed, that Nina was not very happy. More and more she saw in Nina's passion for clothes and gaiety, for small possessions, an attempt to substitute them for real things. She even suspected that sometimes Nina was a little lonely.

Wallie Sayre rose from a deep chair as she entered the living-room.

"Hello," he said, "I was on the point of asking Central to give me this number so I could get you on the upstairs telephone."

"Nina and I were talking. I'm sorry."

Wallie, in spite of Walter Wheeler's opinion of him, was an engaging youth with a wide smile, an air of careless well-being, and an obstinate jaw. What he wanted he went after and generally secured, and Elizabeth, enlightened by Nina, began to have a small anxious feeling that afternoon that what he wanted just now happened to be herself.

"Nina coming down?" he asked.

"I suppose so. Why?"

"You couldn't pass the word along that you are going to be engaged for the next half hour?"

"I might, but I certainly don't intend to."

"You are as hard to isolate as a—as a germ," he complained. "I gave up a perfectly good golf game to see you, and as your father generally calls the dog the moment I appear and goes for a walk, I thought I might see you alone."

"You're seeing me alone now, you know."

Suddenly he leaned over and catching up her hand, kissed it.

"You're so cool and sweet," he said. "I—I wish you liked me a little." He smiled up at her, rather wistfully. "I never knew any one quite like you."

She drew her hand away. Something Nina had said, that he knew his way about, came into her mind, and made her uncomfortable. Back of him, suddenly, was that strange and mysterious region where men of his sort lived their furtive man-life, where they knew their way about. She had no curiosity and no interest, but the mere fact of its existence as revealed by Nina repelled her.

"There are plenty like me," she said. "Don't be silly, Wallie. I hate having my hand kissed."

"I wonder," he observed shrewdly, "whether that's really true, or whether you just hate having me do it?"

When Nina came in he was drawing a rough sketch of his new power boat, being built in Florida.

Nina's delay was explained by the appearance, a few minutes later, of a rather sullen Annie with a tea tray. Afternoon tea was not a Wheeler institution, but was notoriously a Sayre one. And Nina believed in putting one's best foot foremost, even when that resulted in a state of unstable domestic equilibrium.

"Put in a word for me, Nina," Wallie begged. "I intend to ask Elizabeth to go to the theater this week, and I think she is going to refuse."

"What's the play?" Nina inquired negligently. She was privately determining that her mother needed a tea cart and a new tea service. There were some in old Georgian silver—

"'The Valley.' Not that the play matters. It's Beverly Carlysle."

"I thought she was dead, or something."

"Or something is right. She retired years ago, at the top of her success. She was a howling beauty, I'm told. I never saw her. There was some queer story. I've forgotten it. I was a kid then. How about it, Elizabeth?"

"I'm sorry. I'm going Wednesday night."

He looked downcast over that, and he was curious, too. But he made no comment save:

"Well, better luck next time."

"Just imagine," said Nina. "She's going with Dick Livingstone. Can you imagine it?"

But Wallace Sayre could and did. He had rather a stricken moment, too. Of course, there might be nothing to it; but on the other hand, there very well might. And Livingstone was the sort to attract the feminine woman; he had gravity and responsibility. He was older too, and that flattered a girl.

"He's not a bit attractive," Nina was saying. "Quiet, and—well, I don't suppose he knows what he's got on."

Wallie was watching Elizabeth.

"Oh, I don't know," he said, with masculine fairness. "He's a good sort, and he's pretty much of a man."

He was quite sure that the look Elizabeth gave him was grateful.

He went soon after that, keeping up an appearance of gaiety to the end, and very careful to hope that Elizabeth would enjoy the play.

"She's a wonder, they say," he said from the doorway. "Take two hankies along, for it's got more tears than 'East Lynne' and 'The Old Homestead' put together."

He went out, holding himself very erect and looking very cheerful until he reached the corner. There however he slumped, and it was a rather despondent young man who stood sometime later, on the center of the deserted bridge over the small river, and surveyed the water with moody eyes.

In the dusky living-room Nina was speaking her mind.

"You treat him like a dog," she said. "Oh, I know you're civil to him, but if any man looked at me the way Wallie looks at you—I don't know, though," she added, thoughtfully. "It may be that that is why he is so keen. It may be good tactics. Most girls fall for him with a crash."

But when she glanced at Elizabeth she saw that she had not heard. Her eyes were fixed on something on the street beyond the window. Nina looked out. With a considerable rattle of loose joints and four extraordinarily worn tires the Livingstone car was going by.

IV

David did not sleep well that night. He had not had his golf after all, for the Homer baby had sent out his advance notice early in the afternoon, and had himself arrived on Sunday evening, at the hour when Minnie was winding her clock and preparing to retire early for the Monday washing, and the Sayre butler was announcing dinner. Dick had come in at ten o'clock weary and triumphant, to announce that Richard Livingstone Homer, sex male, color white, weight nine pounds, had been safely delivered into this vale of tears.

David lay in the great walnut bed which had been his mother's, and read his prayer book by the light of his evening lamp. He read the Evening Prayer and the Litany, and then at last he resorted to the thirty-nine articles, which usually had a soporific effect on him. But it was no good.

He got up and took to pacing his room, a portly, solid old figure in striped pajamas and the pair of knitted bedroom slippers which were always Mrs. Morgan's Christmas offering. "To Doctor David, with love and a merry Xmas, from Angeline Morgan."

At last he got his keys from his trousers pocket and padded softly down the stairs and into his office, where he drew the shade and turned on the lights. Around him was the accumulated professional impedimenta of many years; the old-fashioned surgical chair; the corner closet which had been designed for china, and which held his instruments; the bookcase; his framed diplomas on the wall, their signatures faded, their seals a little dingy; his desk, from which Dick had removed the old ledger which had held those erratic records from which, when he needed money, he had been wont—and reluctant—to make out his bills.

Through an open door was Dick's office, a neat place of shining linoleum and small glass stands, highly modern and business-like. Beyond the office and opening from it was his laboratory, which had been the fruit closet once, and into which Dick on occasion retired to fuss with slides and tubes and stains and a microscope.

Sometimes he called David in, and talked at length and with enthusiasm about such human interest things as the Staphylococcus pyogenes aureus, and the Friedlander bacillus. The older man would listen, but his eyes were oftener on Dick than on the microscope or the slide.

David went to the bookcase and got down a large book, much worn, and carried it to his desk.

An hour or so later he heard footsteps in the hall and closed the book hastily. It was Lucy, a wadded dressing gown over her nightdress and a glass of hot milk in her hand.

"You drink this and come to bed, David," she said peremptorily. "I've been lying upstairs waiting for you to come up, and I need some sleep."

He had no sort of hope that she would not notice the book.

"I just got to thinking things over, Lucy," he explained, his tone apologetic. "There's no use pretending I'm not worried. I am."

"Well, it's in God's hands," she said, quite simply. "Take this up and drink it slowly. If you gulp it down it makes a lump in your stomach."

She stood by while he replaced the book in the bookcase and put out the lights. Then in the darkness she preceded him up the stairs.

"You'd better take the milk yourself, Lucy," he said. "You're not sleeping either."

"I've had some. Good-night."

He went in and sitting on the side of his bed sipped at his milk. Lucy was right. It was not in their hands. He had the feeling all at once of having relinquished a great burden. He crawled into bed and was almost instantly asleep.

So sometime after midnight found David sleeping, and Lucy on her knees. It found Elizabeth dreamlessly unconscious in her white bed, and Dick Livingstone asleep also, but in his clothing, and in a chair by the window. In the light from a street lamp his face showed lines of fatigue and nervous stress, lines only revealed when during sleep a man casts off the mask with which he protects his soul against even friendly eyes.

But midnight found others awake. It found Nina, for instance, in her draped French bed, consulting her jeweled watch and listening for Leslie's return from the country club. An angry and rather heart-sick Nina. And it found the night editor of one of the morning papers drinking a cup of coffee that a boy had brought in, and running through a mass of copy on his desk. He picked up several sheets of paper, with a photograph clamped to them, and ran through them quickly. A man in a soft hat, sitting on the desk, watched him idly.

"Beverly Carlysle," commented the night editor. "Back with bells on!" He took up the photograph. "Doesn't look much older, does she? It's a queer world."

Louis Bassett, star reporter and feature writer of the Times-Republican, smiled reminiscently.

"She was a wonder," he said. "I interviewed her once, and I was crazy about her. She had the stage set for me, all right. The papers had been full of the incident of Jud Clark and the night he lined up fifteen Johnnies in the lobby, each with a bouquet as big as a tub, all of them in top hats and Inverness coats, and standing in a row. So she played up the heavy domestic for me; knitting or sewing, I forget."

"Fell for her, did you?"

"Did I? That was ten years ago, and I'm not sure I'm over it yet."

"Probably that's the reason," said the city editor, drily. "Go and see her, and get over it. Get her views on the flapper and bobbed hair, for next Sunday. Smith would be crazy about it."

He finished his coffee.

"You might ask, too, what she thinks has become of Judson Clark," he added. "I have an idea she knows, if any one does." Bassett stared at him.

"You're joking, aren't you?"

"Yes. But it would make a darned good story."

V

When he finished medical college Dick Livingstone had found, like other men, that the two paths of ambition and duty were parallel and did not meet. Along one lay his desire to focus all his energy in one direction, to follow disease into the laboratory instead of the sick room, and there to fight its unsung battles. And win. He felt that he would win.

Along the other lay David.

It was not until he had completed his course and had come home that he had realized that David was growing old. Even then he might have felt that, by the time David was compelled to relinquish his hold on his practice, he himself would be sufficiently established in his specialty to take over the support of the household. But here there was interposed a new element, one he had not counted on. David was fiercely jealous of his practice; the thought that it might pass into new and alien hands was bitter to him. To hand it down to his adopted son was one thing; to pass it over to "some young whipper-snapper" was another.

Nor were David's motives selfish or unworthy. His patients were his friends. He had a sense of responsibility to them, and very little faith in the new modern methods. He thought there was a great deal of tomfoolery about them, and he viewed the gradual loss of faith in drugs with alarm. When Dick wore rubber gloves during their first obstetric case together he snorted.

"I've delivered about half the population of this town," he said, "and slapped 'em to make 'em breathe with my own bare hands. And I'm still here and so are they."

147

For by that time Dick had made his decision. He could not abandon David. For him then and hereafter the routine of a general practice in a suburban town, the long hours, the varied responsibilities, the feeling he had sometimes that by doing many things passably he was doing none of them well. But for compensation he had old David's content and greater leisure, and Lucy Crosby's gratitude and love.

Now and then he chafed a little when he read some article in a medical journal by one of his fellow enthusiasts, or when, in France, he saw men younger than himself obtaining an experience in their several specialties that would enable them to reach wide fields at home. But mostly he was content, or at least resigned. He was building up the Livingstone practice, and his one anxiety was lest the time should come when more patients asked for Doctor Dick than for Doctor David. He did not want David hurt.

After ten years the strangeness of his situation had ceased to be strange. Always he meant some time to go back to Norada, and there to clear up certain things, but it was a long journey, and he had very little time. And, as the years went on, the past seemed unimportant compared with the present. He gave little thought to the future.

Then, suddenly, his entire attention became focused on the future.

Just when he had fallen in love with Elizabeth Wheeler he did not know. He had gone away to the war, leaving her a little girl, apparently, and he had come back to find her, a woman. He did not even know he was in love, at first. It was when, one day, he found himself driving past the Wheeler house without occasion that he began to grow uneasy.

The future at once became extraordinarily important and so also, but somewhat less vitally, the past. Had he the right to marry, if he could make her care for him?

He sat in his chair by the window the night after the Homer baby's arrival, and faced his situation. Marriage meant many things. It meant love and companionship, but it also meant, should mean, children. Had he the right to go ahead and live his life fully and happily? Was there any chance that, out of the years behind him, there would come some forgotten thing, some taint or incident, to spoil the carefully woven fabric of his life?

Not his life. Hers.

On the Monday night after he had asked Elizabeth to go to the theater he went into David's office and closed the door. Lucy, alive to every movement in the old house, heard him go in and, rocking in her chair overhead, her hands idle in her lap, waited in tense anxiety for the interview to end. She thought she knew what Dick would ask, and what David would answer. And, in a way, David would be right. Dick, fine, lovable, upstanding Dick, had a right to the things other men had, to love and a home of his own, to children, to his own full life.

But suppose Dick insisted on clearing everything up before he married? For to Lucy it was unthinkable that any girl in her senses would refuse him. Suppose he went back to Norada? He had not changed greatly in ten years. He had been well known there, a conspicuous figure.

Her mind began to turn on the possibility of keeping him away from Norada.

Some time later she heard the office door open and then close with Dick's characteristic slam. He came up the stairs, two at a time as was his custom, and knocked at her door. When he came in she saw what David's answer had been, and she closed her eyes for an instant.

"Put on your things," he said gayly, "and we'll take a ride on the hill-tops. I've arranged for a moon."

And when she hesitated:

"It makes you sleep, you know. I'm going, if I have to ride alone and talk to an imaginary lady beside me."

She rather imagined that that had been his first idea, modified by his thought of her. She went over and put a wrinkled hand on his arm.

"You look happy, Dick," she said wistfully.

"I am happy, Aunt Lucy," he replied, and bending over, kissed her.

On Wednesday he was in a state of alternating high spirits and periods of silence. Even Minnie noticed it.

"Mr. Dick's that queer I hardly know how to take him." she said to Lucy. "He came back and asked for noodle soup, and he put about all the hardware in the kitchen on him and said he was a knight in armor. And when I took the soup in he didn't eat it."

It was when he was ready to go out that Lucy's fears were realized. He came in, as always when anything unusual was afoot, to let her look him over. He knew that she waited for him, to give his tie a final pat, to inspect the laundering of his shirt bosom, to pick imaginary threads off his dinner coat.

"Well?" he said, standing before her, "how's this? Art can do no more, Mrs. Crosby."

"I'll brush your back," she said, and brought the brush. He stooped to her, according to the little ceremony she had established, and she made little dabs at his speckless back. "There, that's better."

He straightened.

"How do you think Uncle David is?" he asked, unexpectedly.

"Better than he has been in years. Why?"

"Because I'm thinking of taking a little trip. Only ten days," he added, seeing her face. "You could house-clean my office while I'm away. You know you've been wanting to."

She dropped the brush, and he stooped to pick it up. That gave her a moment.

"'Where?" she managed.

"To Dry River, by way of Norada."

"Why should you go back there?" she asked, in a carefully suppressed voice. "Why don't you go East? You've wanted to go back to Johns Hopkins for months?"

"On the other hand, why shouldn't I go back to Norada?" he asked, with an affectation of lightness. Then he put his hand on her shoulders. "Why shouldn't I go back and clear things up in my own mind? Why shouldn't I find out, for instance, that I am a free man?"

"You are free."

"I've got to know," he said, almost doggedly. "I can't take a chance. I believe I am. I believe David, of course. But anyhow I'd like to see the ranch. I want to see Maggie Donaldson."

"She's not at the ranch. Her husband died, you know."

"I have an idea I can find her," he said. "I'll make a good try, anyhow."

When he had gone she got her salts bottle and lay down on her bed. Her heart was hammering wildly.

Elizabeth was waiting for him in the living-room, in the midst of her family. She looked absurdly young and very pretty, and he had a momentary misgiving that he was old to her, and that—Heaven save the mark!—that she looked up to him. He considered the blue dress the height of fashion and the mold of form, and having taken off his overcoat in the hall, tried to put on Mr. Wheeler's instead in his excitement. Also, becoming very dignified after the overcoat incident, and making an exit which should conceal his wild exultation and show only polite pleasure, he stumbled over Micky, so that they finally departed to a series of staccato yelps.

He felt very hot and slightly ridiculous as he tucked Elizabeth into the little car, being very particular about her feet, and starting with extreme care, so as not to jar her. He had the feeling of being entrusted temporarily with something infinitely precious, and very, very dear. Something that must never suffer or be hurt.

VI

On Wednesday morning David was in an office in the city. He sat forward on the edge of his chair, and from time to time he took out his handkerchief and wiped his face or polished his glasses, quite unconscious of either action. He was in his best suit, with the tie Lucy had given him for Christmas.

Across from him, barricaded behind a great mahogany desk, sat a small man with keen eyes and a neat brown beard. On the desk were a spotless blotter, an inkstand of silver and a pen. Nothing else. The terrible order of the place had at first rather oppressed David.

The small man was answering a question.

"Rather on the contrary, I should say. The stronger the character the greater the smash."

David pondered this.

"I've read all you've written on the subject," he said finally. "Especially since the war."

The psycho-analyst put his finger tips together, judicially. "Yes. The war bore me out," he observed with a certain complacence. "It added a great deal to our literature, too, although some of the positions are not well taken. Van Alston, for instance—"

"You have said, I think, that every man has a breaking point."

"Absolutely. All of us. We can go just so far. Where the mind is strong and very sound we can go further than when it is not. Some men, for instance, lead lives that would break you or me. Was there—was there such a history in this case?"

"Yes." Doctor David's voice was reluctant.

"The mind is a strange thing," went on the little man, musingly. "It has its censors, that go off duty during sleep. Our sternest and often unconscious repressions pass them then, and emerge in the form of dreams. But of course you know all that. Dream symbolism. Does the person in this case dream? That would be interesting, perhaps important."

"I don't know," David said unhappily.

"The walling off, you say, followed a shock?"

"Shock and serious illness."

"Was there fear with the shock?"

David hesitated. "Yes," he said finally. "Very great fear, I believe."

Doctor Lauler glanced quickly at David and then looked away.

"I see," he nodded. "Of course the walling off of a part of the past—you said a part—?"

"Practically all of it. I'll tell you about that later. What about the walling off?"

"It is generally the result of what we call the protective mechanism of fear. Back of most of these cases lies fear. Not cowardice, but perhaps we might say the limit of endurance. Fear is a complex, of course. Dislike, in a small way, has the same reaction. We are apt to forget the names of persons we dislike. But if you have been reading on the subject—"

"I've been studying it for ten years."

"Ten years! Do you mean that this condition has persisted for ten years?"

David moistened his dry lips. "Yes," he admitted. "It might not have done so, but the—the person who made this experiment used suggestion. The patient was very ill, and weak. It was desirable that he should not identify himself with his past. The loss of memory of the period immediately preceding was complete, but of course, gradually, the cloud began to lift over the earlier periods. It was there that suggestion was used, so that such memories as came back were,—well, the patient adapted them to fit what he was told."

Again Doctor Lauler shot a swift glance at David, and looked away.

"An interesting experiment," he commented. "It must have taken courage."

"A justifiable experiment," David affirmed stoutly. "And it took courage. Yes."

David got up and reached for his hat. Then he braced himself for the real purpose of his visit.

"What I have been wondering about," he said, very carefully, "is this: this mechanism of fear, this wall—how strong is it?"

"Strong?"

"It's like a dam, I take it. It holds back certain memories, like a floodgate. Is anything likely to break it down?"

"Possibly something intimately connected with the forgotten period might do it. I don't know, Livingstone. We've only commenced to dig into the mind, and we have many theories and a few established facts. For instance, the primal instincts—"

He talked on, with David nodding now and then in apparent understanding, but with his thoughts far away. He knew the theories; a good many of them he considered poppycock. Dreams might come from the subconscious mind, but a good many of them came from the stomach. They might be safety valves for the mind, but also they might be rarebit. He didn't want dreams; what he wanted was facts. Facts and hope.

The office attendant came in. She was as tidy as the desk, as obsessed by order, as wooden. She placed a pad before the small man and withdrew. He rose.

"Let me know if I can be of any further assistance, Doctor," he said. "And I'll be glad to see your patient at any time. I'd like the record for my files."

"Thank you," David said. He stood fingering his hat.

"I suppose there's nothing to do? The dam will either break, or it won't."

"That's about it. Of course since the conditions that produced the setting up of the defensive machinery were unhappy, I'd say that happiness will play a large part in the situation. That happiness and a normal occupation will do a great deal to maintain the status quo. Of course I would advise no return to the unhappy environment, and no shocks. Nothing, in other words, to break down the wall."

Outside, in the corridor, David remembered to put on his hat. Happiness and a normal occupation, yes. But no shock.

Nevertheless, he felt vaguely comforted, and as though it had helped to bring the situation out into the open and discuss it. He had carried his burden alone for ten years, or with only the additional weight of Lucy's apprehensions. He wandered out into the city streets, and found himself, some time later, at the railway station, without remembering how he got there.

Across from the station was a large billboard, and on it the name of Beverly Carlysle and her play, "The Valley." He stood for some time and looked at it, before he went in to buy his ticket. Not until he was in the train did he realize that he had forgotten to get his lunch.

He attended to his work that evening as usual, but he felt very tired, and Lucy, going in at nine o'clock, found him dozing in his chair, his collar half choking him and his face deeply suffused. She wakened him and then, sitting down across from him, joined him in the vigil that was to last until they heard the car outside.

She had brought in her sewing, and David pretended to read. Now and then he looked at his watch.

At midnight they heard the car go in, and the slamming of the stable door, followed by Dick's footsteps on the walk outside. Lucy was very pale, and the hands that held her sewing twitched nervously. Suddenly she stood up and put a hand on David's shoulder.

Dick was whistling on the kitchen porch.

VII

Louis Bassett was standing at the back of the theater, talking to the publicity man of The Valley company, Fred Gregory. Bassett was calm and only slightly interested. By the end of the first act he had realized that the star was giving a fine performance, that she had even grown in power, and that his sentimental memory of her was considerably dearer than the reality.

"Going like a house afire," he said, as the curtain fell.

Beside his robust physique, Gregory, the publicity man, sank into insignificance. Even his pale spats, at which Bassett had shot a contemptuous glance, his highly expensive tailoring, failed to make him appear more than he was, a little, dapper man, with a pale cold eye and a rather too frequent smile. "She's the best there is," was his comment. He hesitated, then added: "She's my sister, you know. Naturally, for business reasons, I don't publish the relationship."

Bassett glanced at him.

"That so? Well, I'm glad she decided to come back. She's too good to bury."

But if he expected Gregory to follow the lead he was disappointed. His eyes, blank and expressionless, were wandering over the house as the lights flashed up.

"This whole tour has been a triumph. She's the best there is," Gregory repeated, "and they know it."

"Does she know it?" Bassett inquired.

"She doesn't throw any temperament, if that's what you mean. She—"

He checked himself suddenly, and stood, clutching the railing, bent forward and staring into the audience. Bassett watched him, considerably surprised. It took a great deal to startle a theatrical publicity man, yet here was one who looked as though he had seen a ghost.

After a time Gregory straightened and moistened his dry lips.

"There's a man sitting down there—see here, the sixth row, next the aisle; there's a girl in a blue dress beside him. See him? Do you know who he is?"

"Never saw him before."

For perhaps two minutes Gregory continued to stare. Then he moved over to the side of the house and braced against the wall continued his close and anxious inspection. After a time he turned away and, passing behind the boxes, made his way into the wings. Bassett's curiosity was aroused, especially when, shortly after, Gregory reappeared, bringing with him a small man in an untidy suit who was probably, Bassett surmised, the stage manager.

He saw the small man stare, nod, stand watching, and finally disappear, and Gregory resume his former position and attitude against the side wall. Throughout the last act Gregory did not once look at the stage. He continued his steady, unwavering study of the man in the sixth row seat next the aisle, and Bassett continued his study of the little man.

His long training made him quick to scent a story. He was not sure, of course, but the situation appeared to him at least suggestive. With the end of the play he wandered out with the crowd, edging his way close to the man and girl who had focused Gregory's attention, and following them into the street. He saw only a tall man with a certain quiet distinction of bearing, and a young and pretty girl, still flushed and excited, who went up the street a short distance and got into a small and shabby car. Bassett noted, carefully, the license number of the car.

Then, still curious and extremely interested, he walked briskly around to the stage entrance, nodded to the doorkeeper, and went in.

Gregory was not in sight, but the stage manager was there, directing the striking of the last set.

"I'm waiting for Gregory," Bassett said. "Hasn't fainted, has he?"

"What d'you mean, fainted?" inquired the stage manager, with a touch of hostility.

"I was with him when he thought he recognized somebody. You know who. You can tell him I got his automobile number."

The stage manager's hostility faded, and he fell into the trap. "You know about it, then?"

"I was with him when he saw him. Unfortunately I couldn't help him out."

"It's just possible it's a chance resemblance. I'm darned if I know. Look at the facts! He's supposed to be dead. Ten years dead. His money's been split up a dozen ways from the ace. Then—I knew him, you know—I don't think even he would have the courage to come here and sit through a performance. Although," he added reflectively, "Jud Clark had the nerve for anything."

Bassett gave him a cigar and went out into the alley way that led to the street. Once there, he stood still and softly whistled. Jud Clark! If that was Judson Clark, he had the story of a lifetime.

152

For some time he walked the deserted streets of the city, thinking and puzzling over the possibility of Gregory's being right. Sometime after midnight he went back to the office and to the filing room. There, for two hours, he sat reading closely old files of the paper, going through them methodically and making occasional brief notes in a memorandum. Then, at two o'clock he put away the files, and sitting back, lighted a cigar.

It was all there; the enormous Clark fortune inherited by a boy who had gone mad about this same Beverly Carlysle; her marriage to her leading man, Howard Lucas; the subsequent killing of Lucas by Clark at his Wyoming ranch, and Clark's escape into the mountains. The sensational details of Clark's infatuation, the drama of a crime and Clark's subsequent escape, and the later certainty of his death in a mountain storm had filled the newspapers of the time for weeks. Judson Clark had been famous, notorious, infamous and dead, all in less than two years. A shameful and somehow a pitiful story.

But if Judson Clark had died, the story still lived. Every so often it came up again. Three years before he had been declared legally dead, and his vast estates, as provided by the will of old Elihu Clark, had gone to universities and hospitals. But now and then came a rumor. Jud Clark was living in India; he had a cattle ranch in Venezuela; he had been seen on the streets of New Orleans.

Bassett ran over the situation in his mind.

First then, grant that Clark was still living and had been in the theater that night. It became necessary to grant other things. To grant, for instance, that Clark was capable of sitting, with a girl beside him, through a performance by the woman for whom he had wrecked his life, of a play he had once known from the opening line to the tag. To grant that he could laugh and applaud, and at the drop of the curtain go calmly away, with such memories behind him as must be his. To grant, too, that he had survived miraculously his sensational disappearance, found a new identity and a new place for himself; even, witness the girl, possible new ties.

At half past two Bassett closed his memorandum book, stuffed it into his pocket, and started for home. As he passed the Ardmore Hotel he looked up at its windows. Gregory would have told her, probably. He wondered, half amused, whether the stage manager had told him of his inquiries, and whether in that case they might not fear him more than Clark himself. After all, they had nothing to fear from Clark, if this were Clark.

No. What they might see and dread, knowing he had had a hint of a possible situation, was the revival of the old story she had tried so hard to live down. She was ambitious, and a new and rigid morality was sweeping the country. What once might have been an asset stood now to be a bitter liability.

He slowed down, absorbed in deep thought. It was a queer story. It might be even more queer than it seemed. Gregory had been frightened rather than startled. The man had even gone pale.

Motive, motive, that was the word. What motive lay behind action. Conscious and unconscious, every volitional act was the result of motive.

He wondered what she had done when Gregory had told her.

As a matter of fact, Beverly Carlysle had shown less anxiety than her brother. Still pale and shocked, he had gone directly to her dressing-room when the curtain was rung down, had tapped and gone in. She was sitting wearily in a chair, a cigarette between her fingers. Around was the usual litter of a stage dressing-room after the play, the long shelf beneath the mirror crowded with powders, rouge and pencils, a bunch of roses in the corner washstand basin, a wardrobe trunk, and a maid covering with cheese-cloth bags the evening's costumes.

"It went all right, I think, Fred."

"Yes," he said absently. "Go on out, Alice. I'll let you come back in a few minutes."

He waited until the door closed.

"What's the matter?" she asked rather indifferently. "If it's more quarreling in the company I don't want to hear it. I'm tired." Then she took a full look at him, and sat up.

"Fred! What is it?"

He gave her the truth, brutally and at once.

"I think Judson Clark was in the house to-night."

"I don't believe it."

"Neither would I, if somebody told me," he agreed sullenly. "I saw him. Don't you suppose I know him? And if you don't believe me, call Saunders. I got him out front. He knows."

"You called Saunders!"

"Why not? I tell you, Bev, I was nearly crazy. I'm nearly crazy now."

"What did Saunders say?"

"If he didn't know Clark was dead, he'd say it was Clark."

She was worried by that time, but far more collected than he was. She sat, absently tapping the shelf with a nail file, and reflecting.

"All right," she said. "Suppose he was? What then? He has been in hiding for ten years. Why shouldn't he continue to hide? What would bring him out now? Unless he needed money. Was he shabby?"

"No," he said sulkily. "He was with a girl. He was dressed all right."

"You didn't say anything, except to Saunders?"

"No I'm not crazy."

"I'd better see Joe," she reflected. "Go and get him, Fred. And tell Alice she needn't wait."

She got up and moved about the room, putting things away and finding relief in movement, a still beautiful woman, with rather accentuated features and an easy carriage. Without her make-up the stage illusion of her youth was gone, and she showed past suffering and present strain. Just then she was uneasy and resentful, startled but not particularly alarmed. Her reason told her that Judson Clark, even if he still lived and had been there that night, meant to leave the dead past to care for itself, and wished no more than she to revive it. She was surprised to find, as she moved about, that she was trembling.

Her brother came back, and she turned to meet him. To her surprise he was standing inside the door, white to the lips and staring at her with wild eyes.

"Saunders!" he said chokingly, "Saunders, the damned fool! He's given it away."

He staggered to a chair, and ran a handkerchief across his shaking lips.

"He told Bassett, of the Times-Republican," he managed to say. "Do you—do you know what that means? And Bassett got Clark's automobile number. He said so."

He looked up at her, his face twitching. "They're hound dogs on a scent, Bev. They'll get the story, and blow it wide open."

"You know I'm prepared for that. I have been for ten years."

"I know." He was suddenly emotional. He reached out and took her hand. "Poor old Bev!" he said. "After the way you've come back, too. It's a damned shame."

She was calmer than he was, less convinced for one thing, and better balanced always. She let him stroke her hand, standing near him with her eyes absent and a little hard.

"I'd better make sure that was Jud first," he offered, after a time, "and then warn him."

"Why?"

"Bassett will be after him."

"No!" she commanded sharply. "No, Fred. You let the thing alone. You've built up an imaginary situation, and you're not thinking straight. Plenty of things might happen. What probably has happened is that this Bassett is at home and in bed."

She sent him out for a taxi soon after, and they went back to the hotel. But, alone later on in her suite in the Ardmore she did not immediately go to bed. She put on a dressing gown and stood for a long time by her window, looking out. Instead of the city lights, however, she saw a range of snow-capped mountains, and sheltered at their foot the Clark ranch house, built by the old millionaire as a place of occasional refuge from the pressure of his life. There he had raised his fine horses, and trained them for the track. There, when late in life he married, he had taken his wife for their honeymoon and two years later, for the birth of their son. And there, when she died, he had returned with the child, himself broken and prematurely aged, to be killed by one of his own stallions when the boy was fifteen.

Six years his own master, Judson had been twenty-one to her twenty, when she first met him. Going the usual pace, too, and throwing money right and left. He had financed her as a star, ransacking Europe for her stage properties, and then he fell in love with her. She shivered as she remembered it. It had been desperate and terrible, because she had cared for some one else.

Standing by the window, she wondered as she had done over and over again for ten years, what would have happened if, instead of marrying Howard, she had married Judson Clark? Would he have settled down? She had felt sometimes that in his wildest moments he was only playing a game that amused him; that the hard-headed part of him inherited from his father sometimes stood off and watched, with a sort of interested detachment, the follies of the other. That he played his wild game with his tongue in his cheek.

She left the window, turned out the lights and got into her bed. She was depressed and lonely, and she cried a little. After a time she remembered that she had not put any cream on her face. She crawled out again and went through the familiar motions in the dark.

VIII

Dick rose the next morning with a sense of lightness and content that sent him singing into his shower. In the old stable which now housed both Nettie and the little car Mike was washing them both with indiscriminate wavings of the hose nozzle, his old pipe clutched in his teeth. From below there came up the odors of frying sausages and of strong hot coffee.

The world was a good place. A fine old place. It had work and play and love. It had office hours and visits and the golf links, and it had soft feminine eyes and small tender figures to be always cared for and looked after.

She liked him. She did not think he was old. She thought his profession was the finest in the world. She had wondered if he would have time to come and see her, some day. Time! He considered very seriously, as he shaved before the slightly distorted mirror in the bathroom, whether it would be too soon to run in that afternoon, just to see if she was tired, or had caught cold or anything? Perhaps to-morrow would look better. No, hang it all, to-day was to-day.

On his way from the bathroom to his bedroom he leaned over the staircase.

"Aunt Lucy!" he called.

"Yes, Dick?"

"The top of the morning to you. D'you think Minnie would have time to press my blue trousers this morning?"

There was the sound of her chair being pushed back in the dining-room, of a colloquy in the kitchen, and Minnie herself appeared below him.

"Just throw them down, Doctor Dick," she said. "I've got an iron hot now."

"Some day, Minnie," he announced, "you will wear a halo and with the angels sing."

This mood of unreasoning happiness continued all morning. He went from house to house, properly grave and responsible but with a small song in his heart, and about eleven o'clock he found time to stop at the village haberdasher's and to select a new tie, which he had wrapped and stuffed in his pocket. And which, inspected in broad day later on a country road, gave him uneasy qualms as to its brilliance.

At the luncheon table he was almost hilarious, and David played up to him, albeit rather heavily. But Lucy was thoughtful and quiet. She had a sense of things somehow closing down on them, of hands reaching out from the past, and clutching; Mrs. Morgan, Beverly Carlysle, Dick in love and possibly going back to Norada. Unlike David, who was content that one emergency had passed, she looked ahead and saw their common life a series of such chances, with their anxieties and their dangers.

She could not eat.

Nevertheless when she herself admitted a new patient for Dick that afternoon, she had no premonition of trouble. She sent him into the waiting-room, a tall, robust and youngish man, perhaps in his late thirties, and went quietly on her way to her sitting-room, and to her weekly mending.

On the other hand, Louis Bassett was feeling more or less uncomfortable. There was an air of peace and quiet respectability about the old house, a domestic odor of baking cake, a quietness and stability that somehow made his errand appear absurd. To connect it with Judson Clark and his tumultuous past seemed ridiculous.

His errand, on the surface, was a neuralgic headache.

When, hat in hand, he walked into Dick's consulting room, he had made up his mind that he would pay the price of an overactive imagination for a prescription, walk out again, and try to forget that he had let a chance resemblance carry him off his feet.

But, as he watched the man who sat across from him, tilted back in his swivel chair, he was not so sure. Here was the same tall figure, the heavy brown hair, the features and boyish smile of the photograph he had seen the night before. As Judson Clark might have looked at thirty-two this man looked.

He made his explanation easily. Was in town for the day. Subject to these headaches. Worse over the right eye. No, he didn't wear glasses; perhaps he should.

It wasn't Clark. It couldn't be. Jud Clark sitting there tilted back in an old chair and asking questions as to the nature of his fictitious pain! Impossible. Nevertheless he was of a mind to clear the slate and get some sleep that night, and having taken his prescription and paid for it, he sat back and commenced an apparently casual interrogation.

"Two names on your sign, I see. Father and son, I suppose?"

"Doctor David Livingstone is my uncle."

"I should think you'd be in the city. Limitations to this sort of thing, aren't there?"

"I like it," said Dick, with an eye on the office clock.

"Patients are your friends, of course. Born and raised here, I suppose?"

"Not exactly. I was raised on a ranch in Wyoming. My father had a ranch out there."

Bassett shot a glance at him, but Dick was calm and faintly smiling.

"Wyoming!" the reporter commented. "That's a long way from here. Anywhere near the new oil fields?"

"Not far from Norada. That's the oil center," Dick offered, good-naturedly. He rose, and glanced again at the clock. "If those headaches continue you'd better have your eyes examined."

Bassett was puzzled. It seemed to him that there had been a shade of evasion in the other man's manner, slightly less frankness in his eyes. But he showed no excitement, nothing furtive or alarmed. And the open and unsolicited statement as to Norada baffled him. He had to admit to himself either that a man strongly resembling Judson Clark had come from the same neighborhood, or—

"Norada?" he said. "That's where the big Clark ranch was located, wasn't it? Ever happen to meet Judson Clark?"

"Our place was very isolated."

Bassett found himself being politely ushered out, considerably more at sea than when he went in and slightly irritated. His annoyance was not decreased by the calm voice behind him which said:

"Better drink considerable water when you take that stuff. Some stomachs don't tolerate it very well."

The door closed. The reporter stood in the waiting-room for a moment. Then he clapped on his hat.

156

"Well, I'm a damned fool," he muttered, and went out into the street.

He was disappointed and a trifle sheepish. Life was full of queer chances, that was all. No resemblance on earth, no coincidence of birthplace, could make him believe that Judson Clark, waster, profligate and fugitive from the law was now sitting up at night with sick children, or delivering babies.

After a time he remembered the prescription in his hand, and was about to destroy it. He stopped and examined it, and then carefully placed it in his pocket-book. After all, there were things that looked queer. The fellow had certainly evaded that last question of his.

He made his way, head bent, toward the station.

He had ten minutes to wait, and he wandered to the newsstand. He made a casual inspection of its display, bought a newspaper and was turning away, when he stopped and gazed after a man who had just passed him from an out-bound train.

The reporter looked after him with amused interest. Gregory, too! The Livingstone chap had certainly started something. But it was odd, too. How had Gregory traced him? Wasn't there something more in Gregory's presence there than met the eye? Gregory's visit might be, like his own, the desire to satisfy himself that the man was or was not Clark. Or it might be the result of a conviction that it was Clark, and a warning against himself. But if he had traced him, didn't that indicate that Clark himself had got into communication with him? In other words, that the chap was Clark, after all? Gregory, having made an inquiry of a hackman, had started along the street, and, after a moment's thought, Bassett fell into line behind him. He was extremely interested and increasingly cheerful. He remained well behind, and with his newspaper rolled in his hand assumed the easy yet brisk walk of the commuters around him, bound for home and their early suburban dinners.

Half way along Station Street Gregory stopped before the Livingstone house, read the sign, and rang the doorbell. The reporter slowed down, to give him time for admission, and then slowly passed. In front of Harrison Miller's house, however, he stopped and waited. He lighted a cigarette and made a careful survey of the old place. Strange, if this were to prove the haven where Judson Clark had taken refuge, this old brick two-story dwelling, with its ramshackle stable in the rear, its small vegetable garden, its casual beds of simple garden flowers set in a half acre or so of ground.

A doctor. A pill shooter. Jud Clark!

IX

Elizabeth had gone about all day with a smile on her lips and a sort of exaltation in her eyes. She had, girl fashion, gone over and over the totally uneventful evening they had spent together, remembering small speeches and gestures; what he had said and she had answered.

She had, for instance, mentioned Clare Rossiter, very casually. Oh very, very casually. And he had said: "Clare Rossiter? Oh, yes, the tall blonde girl, isn't she?"

She was very happy. He had not seemed to find her too young or particularly immature. He had asked her opinion on quite important things, and listened carefully when she replied. She felt, though, that she knew about one-tenth as much as he did, and she determined to read very seriously from that time on. Her mother, missing her that afternoon, found her curled up in the library, beginning the first volume of Gibbon's "Rome" with an air of determined concentration, and wearing her best summer frock.

She did not intend to depend purely on Gibbon's "Rome," evidently.

"Are you expecting any one, Elizabeth?" she asked, with the frank directness characteristic of mothers, and Elizabeth, fixing a date in her mind with terrible firmness, looked up absently and said:

"No one in particular."

At three o'clock, with a slight headache from concentration, she went upstairs and put up her hair again; rather high this time to make her feel taller. Of course, it was not likely he would come. He was very busy. So many people depended on him. It must be wonderful to be like that, to have people needing one, and looking out of the door and saying: "I think I see him coming now."

Nevertheless when the postman rang her heart gave a small leap and then stood quite still. When Annie slowly mounted the stairs she was already on her feet, but it was only a card announcing: "Mrs. Sayre, Wednesday, May fifteenth, luncheon at one-thirty."

However, at half past four the bell rang again, and a masculine voice informed Annie, a moment later, that it would put its overcoat here, because lately a dog had eaten a piece out of it and got most awful indigestion.

The time it took Annie to get up the stairs again gave her a moment so that she could breathe more naturally, and she went down very deliberately and so dreadfully poised that at first he thought she was not glad to see him.

"I came, you see," he said. "I intended to wait until to-morrow, but I had a little time. But if you're doing anything—"

"I was reading Gibbon's 'Rome,'" she informed him. "I think every one should know it. Don't you?"

"Good heavens, what for?" he inquired.

"I don't know." They looked at each other, and suddenly they laughed.

"I wanted to improve my mind," she explained. "I felt, last night, that you-that you know so many things, and that I was frightfully stupid."

"Do you mean to say," he asked, aghast, "that I—! Great Scott!"

Settled in the living-room, they got back rather quickly to their status of the night before, and he was moved to confession.

"I didn't really intend to wait until to-morrow," he said. "I got up with the full intention of coming here to-day, if I did it over the wreck of my practice. At eleven o'clock this morning I held up a consultation ten minutes to go to Yardsleys and buy a tie, for this express purpose. Perhaps you have noticed it already."

"I have indeed. It's a wonderful tie."

"Neat but not gaudy, eh?" He grinned at her, happily. "You know, you might steer me a bit about my ties. I have the taste of an African savage. I nearly bought a purple one, with red stripes. And Aunt Lucy thinks I should wear white lawn, like David!"

They talked, those small, highly significant nothings which are only the barrier behind which go on the eager questionings and unspoken answers of youth and love. They had known each other for years, had exchanged the same give and take of neighborhood talk when they met as now. To-day nothing was changed, and everything.

Then, out of a clear sky, he said:

"I may be going away before long, Elizabeth."

He was watching her intently. She had a singular feeling that behind this, as behind everything that afternoon, was something not spoken. Something that related to her. Perhaps it was because of his tone.

"You don't mean-not to stay?"

"No. I want to go back to Wyoming. Where I was born. Only for a few weeks."

And in that "only for a few weeks" there lay some of the unspoken things. That he would miss her and come back quickly to her. That she would miss him, and that subconsciously he knew it. And behind that, too, a promise. He would come back to her.

"Only for a few weeks," he repeated. "I thought perhaps, if you wouldn't mind my writing to you, now and then—I write a rotten hand, you know. Most medical men do."

"I should like it very much," she said, primly.

She felt suddenly very lonely, as though he had already gone, and slightly resentful, not at him but at the way things happened. And then, too, everyone knew that once a Westerner always a Westerner. The West always called its children. Not that she put it that way. But she had a sort of vision, gained from the moving pictures, of a country of wide spaces and tall mountains, where men wore quaint clothing and the women rode wild horses and had the dash she knew she lacked. She was stirred by vague jealousy.

"You may never come back," she said, casually. "After all, you were born there, and we must seem very quiet to you."

"Quiet!" he exclaimed. "You are heavenly restful and comforting. You—" he checked himself and got up. "Then I'm to write, and you are to make out as much of my scrawl as you can and answer. Is that right?"

"I'll write you all the town gossip."

"If you do—!" he threatened her. "You're to write me what you're doing, and all about yourself. Remember, I'll be counting on you."

And, if their voices were light, there was in both of them the sense of a pact made, of a bond that was to hold them, like clasped hands, against their coming separation. It was rather anti-climacteric after that to have him acknowledge that he didn't know exactly when he could get away!

She went with him to the door and stood there, her soft hair blowing, as he got into the car. When he looked back, as he turned the corner, she was still there. He felt very happy affable, and he picked up an elderly village woman with her and went considerably out of his way to take her home.

He got back to the office at half past six to find a red-eyed Minnie in the hall.

X

AT half past five that afternoon David had let himself into the house with his latch key, hung up his overcoat on the old walnut hat rack, and went into his office. The strain of the days before had told on him, and he felt weary and not entirely well. He had fallen asleep in his buggy, and had wakened to find old Nettie drawing him slowly down the main street of the town, pursuing an erratic but homeward course, while the people on the pavements watched and smiled.

He went into his office, closed the door, and then, on the old leather couch with its sagging springs he stretched himself out to finish his nap.

Almost immediately, however, the doorbell rang, and a moment later Minnie opened his door.

"Gentleman to see you, Doctor David."

He got up clumsily and settled his collar. Then he opened the door into his waiting-room.

"Come in," he said resignedly.

A small, dapper man, in precisely the type of clothes David most abominated, and wearing light-colored spats, rose from his chair and looked at him with evident surprise.

"I'm afraid I've made a mistake. A Doctor Livingstone left his seat number for calls at the box office of the Annex Theater last night—the Happy Valley company—but he was a younger man. I—"

David stiffened, but he surveyed his visitor impassively from under his shaggy white eyebrows.

"I haven't been in a theater for a dozen years, sir."

Gregory was convinced that he had made a mistake. Like Louis Bassett, the very unlikeliness of Jud Clark being connected with the domestic atmosphere and quiet respectability of the old

159

house made him feel intrusive and absurd. He was about to apologize and turn away, when he thought of something.

"There are two names on your sign. The other one, was he by any chance at the theater last night?"

"I think I shall have to have a reason for these inquiries," David said slowly.

He was trying to place Gregory, to fit him into the situation; straining back over ten years of security, racking his memory, without result.

"Just what have you come to find out?" he asked, as Gregory turned and looked around the room.

"The other Doctor Livingstone is your brother?"

"My nephew."

Gregory shot a sharp glance at him, but all he saw was an elderly man, with heavy white hair and fierce shaggy eyebrows, a portly and dignified elderly gentleman, rather resentfully courteous.

"Sorry to trouble you," he said. "I suppose I've made a mistake. I—is your nephew at home?"

"No."

"May I see a picture of him, if you have one?"

David's wild impulse was to smash Gregory to the earth, to annihilate him. His collar felt tight, and he pulled it away from his throat.

"Not unless I know why you want to see it."

"He is tall, rather spare? And he took a young lady to the theater last night?" Gregory persisted.

"He answers that description. What of it?"

"And he is your nephew?"

"My brother's son," David said steadily.

Somehow it began to dawn on him that there was nothing inimical in this strange visitor, that he was anxious and ill at ease. There was, indeed, something almost beseeching in Gregory's eyes, as though he stood ready to give confidence for confidence. And, more than that, a sort of not unfriendly stubbornness, as though he had come to do something he meant to do.

"Sit down," he said, relaxing somewhat. "Certainly my nephew is making no secret of the fact that he went to the theater last night. If you'll tell me who you are—"

But Gregory did not sit down. He stood where he was, and continued to eye David intently.

"I don't know just what it conveys to you, Doctor, but I am Beverly Carlysle's brother."

David lowered himself into his chair. His knees were suddenly weak under him. But he was able to control his voice.

"I see," he said. And waited.

"Something happened last night at the theater. It may be important. I'd have to see your nephew, in order to find out if it is. I can't afford to make a mistake."

David's ruddy color had faded. He opened a drawer of his desk and produced a copy of the photograph of Dick in his uniform. "Maybe this will help you."

Gregory studied it carefully, carrying it to the window to do so. When he confronted David again he was certain of himself and his errand for the first time, and his manner had changed.

"Yes," he said, significantly. "It does."

He placed the photograph on the desk, and sitting down, drew his chair close to David's. "I'll not use any names, Doctor. I think you know what I'm talking about. I was sure enough last night. I'm certain now."

David nodded. "Go on."

"We'll start like this. God knows I don't want to make any trouble. But I'll put a hypothetical case. Suppose that a man when drunk commits a crime and then disappears; suppose he leaves behind him a bad record and an enormous fortune; suppose then he reforms and becomes a useful citizen, and everything is buried."

Doctor David listened stonily. Gregory lowered his voice.

"Suppose there's a woman mixed up in that situation. Not guiltily, but there's a lot of talk. And suppose she lives it down, for ten years, and then goes back to her profession, in a play the families take the children to see, and makes good. It isn't hard to suppose that neither of those two people wants the thing revived, is it?"

David cleared his throat.

"You mean, then, that there is danger of such a revival?"

"I think there is," Gregory said bitterly. "I recognized this man last night, and called a fellow who knew him in the old days, Saunders, our stage manager. And a newspaper man named Bassett wormed it out of Saunders. You know what that means."

David heard him clearly, but as though from a great distance.

"You can see how it appears to Bassett. If he's found it, it's the big story of a lifetime. I thought he'd better be warned."

When David said nothing, but sat holding tight to the arms of his old chair, Gregory reached for his hat and got up.

"The thing for him to do," he said, "is to leave town for a while. This Bassett is a hound-hog on a scent. They all are. He is Bassett of the Times-Republican. And he took Jud—he took your nephew's automobile license number."

Still David sat silent, and Gregory moved to the door.

"Get him away, to-night if you can."

"Thank you," David said. His voice was thick. "I appreciate your coming."

He got up dizzily, as Gregory said, "Good-evening" and went out. The room seemed very dark and unsteady, and not familiar. So this was what had happened, after all the safe years! A man could work and build and pray, but if his house was built on the sand—

As the outer door closed David fell to the floor with a crash.

XI

Bassett lounged outside the neat privet hedge which it was Harrison Miller's custom to clip with his own bachelor hands, and waited. And as he waited he tried to imagine what was going on inside, behind the neatly curtained windows of the old brick house.

He was tempted to ring the bell again, pretend to have forgotten something, and perhaps happen in on what might be drama of a rather high order; what, supposing the man was Clark after all, was fairly sure to be drama. He discarded the idea, however, and began again his interested survey of the premises. Whoever conceived this sort of haven for Clark, if it were Clark, had shown considerable shrewdness. The town fairly smelt of respectability; the tree-shaded streets, the children in socks and small crisp-laundered garments, the houses set back, each in its square of shaved lawn, all peaceful, middle class and unexciting. The last town in the world for Judson Clark, the last profession, the last house, this shabby old brick before him.

He smiled rather grimly as he reflected that if Gregory had been right in his identification, he was, beyond those windows at that moment, very possibly warning Clark against himself. Gregory would know his type, that he never let go. He drew himself up a little.

The house door opened, and Gregory came out, turning toward the station. Bassett caught up with him and put a hand on his arm.

"Well?" he said cheerfully. "It was, wasn't it?"

Gregory stopped dead and stared at him. Then:

"Old dog Tray!" he said sneeringly. "If your brain was as good as your nose, Bassett, you'd be a whale of a newspaper man."

"Don't bother about my brain. It's working fine to-day, anyhow. Well, what had he to say for himself?"

Gregory's mind was busy, and he had had a moment to pull himself together.

"We both get off together," he said, more amiably. "That fellow isn't Jud Clark and never was. He's a doctor, and the nephew of the old doctor there. They're in practice together."

"Did you see them both?"

"Yes."

Bassett eyed him. Either Gregory was a good actor, or the whole trail ended there after all. He himself had felt, after his interview, with Dick, that the scent was false. And there was this to be said: Gregory had been in the house scarcely ten minutes. Long enough to acknowledge a mistake, but hardly long enough for any dramatic identification. He was keenly disappointed, but he had had long experience of disappointment, and after a moment he only said:

"Well, that's that. He certainly looked like Clark to me."

"I'll say he did."

"Rather surprised him, didn't you?"

"Oh, he was all right," Gregory said. "I didn't tell him anything, of course."

Bassett looked at his watch.

"I was after you, all right," he said, cheerfully. "But if I was barking up the wrong tree, I'm done. I don't have to be hit on the head to make me stop. Come and have a soda-water on me," he finished amiably. "There's no train until seven."

But Gregory refused.

"No, thanks. I'll wander on down to the station and get a paper."

The reporter smiled. Gregory was holding a grudge against him, for a bad night and a bad day.

"All right," he said affably. "I'll see you at the train. I'll walk about a bit."

He turned and started back up the street again, walking idly. His chagrin was very real. He hated to be fooled, and fooled he had been. Gregory was not the only one who had lost a night's sleep. Then, unexpectedly, he was hailed from the curbstone, and he saw with amazement that it was Dick Livingstone.

"Take you anywhere?" Dick asked. "How's the headache?"

"Better, thanks." Bassett stared at him. "No, I'm just walking around until train-time. Are you starting out or going home, at this hour?"

"Going home. Well, glad the head's better."

He drove on, leaving the reporter gazing after him. So Gregory had been lying. He hadn't seen this chap at all. Then why—? He walked on, turning this new phase of the situation over in his mind. Why this elaborate fiction, if Gregory had merely gone in, waited for ten minutes, and come out again?

It wasn't reasonable. It wasn't logical. Something had happened inside the house to convince Gregory that he was right. He had seen somebody, or something. He hadn't needed to lie. He could have said frankly that he had seen no one. But no, he had built up a fabric carefully calculated to throw Bassett off the scent.

He saw Dick stop in front of the house, get out and enter. And coming to a decision, he followed him and rang the doorbell. For a long time no one answered. Then the maid of the afternoon opened the door, her eyes red with crying, and looked at him with hostility.

"Doctor Richard Livingstone?"

"You can't see him."

"It's important."

"Well, you can't see him. Doctor David has just had a stroke. He's in the office now, on the floor."

She closed the door on him, and he turned and went away. It was all clear to him; Gregory had seen, not Clark, but the older man; had told him and gone away. And under the shock the older man had collapsed. That was sad. It was very sad. But it was also extremely convincing.

He sat up late that night again, running over the entries in his notebook. The old story, as he pieced it out, ran like this:

It had been twelve years ago, when, according to the old files, Clark had financed Beverly Carlysle's first starring venture. He had, apparently, started out in the beginning only to give her the publicity she needed. In devising it, however, he had shown a sort of boyish recklessness and ingenuity that had caught the interest of the press, and set newspaper men to chuckling wherever they got together.

He had got together a dozen or so of young men like himself, wealthy, idle and reckless with youth, and, headed by him, they had made the exploitation of the young star an occupation. The newspapers referred to the star and her constellation as Beverly Carlysle and her Broadway Beauties. It had been unvicious, young, and highly entertaining, and it had cost Judson Clark his membership in his father's conservative old clubs.

For a time it livened the theatrical world with escapades that were harmless enough, if sensational. Then, after a time, newspaper row began to whisper that young Clark was in love with the girl. The Broadway Beauties broke up, after a wild farewell dinner. The audiences ceased to expect a row of a dozen youths, all dressed alike with gardenias in their buttonholes and perhaps red neckties with their evening suits, to rise in their boxes on the star's appearance and solemnly bow. And the star herself lost a little of the anxious look she frequently wore.

The story went, after a while, that Judson Clark had been refused, and was taking his refusal badly. Reporters saw him, carelessly dressed, outside the stage door waiting, and the story went that the girl had thrown him over, money and all, for her leading man. One thing was clear; Clark, not a drinker before, had taken to drinking hard, and after a time, and some unpleasant scenes probably, she refused to see him any more.

When the play closed, in June, 1911, she married Howard Lucas, her leading man; his third wife. Lucas had been not a bad chap, a good-looking, rather negligible man, given to all-day Sunday poker, carefully valeted, not very keen mentally, but amiable. They had bought a house on East Fifty-sixth Street, and were looking for a new play with Lucas as co-star, when he unaccountably went to pieces nervously, stopped sleeping, and developed a slight twitching of his handsome, rather vacuous face.

Judson Clark had taken his yacht and gone to Europe, and was reported from here and there not too favorably. But when he came back, in early September, he had apparently recovered from his infatuation, was his old, carefully dressed self again, and when interviewed declared his intention of spending the winter on his Wyoming ranch.

Of course he must have heard of Lucas's breakdown, and equally, of course, he must have seen them both. What happened at that interview, by what casual attitude he allayed Lucas's probable jealousy and the girl's own nervousness, Bassett had no way of discovering. It was clear that he convinced them both of his good faith, for the next note in the reporter's book was simply a date, September 12, 1911.

That was the day they had all started West together, traveling in Clark's private car, with Lucas, twitching slightly, smiling and waving farewell from a window.

The big smash did not come until the middle of October.

Bassett sat back and considered. He had a fairly clear idea of the conditions at the ranch; daily riding, some little reading, and a great deal too much of each other. A sick man, too, unhappy in his exile, chafing against his restrictions, lonely and irritable. The girl, early seeing her mistake, and Clark's jealousy of her husband. The door into their apartment closing, the thousand and one unconscious intimacies between man and wife, the breakfast for two going up the stairs, and below that hot-eyed boy, agonized and passionately jealous, yet meeting them and looking after them, their host and a gentleman.

Lucas took to drinking, after a time, to allay his sheer boredom. And Jud Clark drank with him. At the end of three weeks they were both drinking heavily, and were politely quarrelsome. Bassett could fill that in also. He could see the girl protesting, watching, increasingly anxious as she saw that Clark's jealousy was matched by her husband's.

A queer picture, he reflected, the three of them shut away on the great ranch, and every day some new tension, some new strain.

Then, one night at dinner, they quarreled, and Beverly left the table. She was going to pack her things and go back to New York. She had felt, probably, that something was bound to snap. And while she was upstairs Clark had shot and killed Howard Lucas, and himself disappeared.

He had run, testimony at the inquest revealed, to the corral, and saddled a horse. Although it was only October, it was snowing hard, but in spite of that he had turned his horse toward the mountains. By midnight a posse from Norada had started out, and another up the Dry River Canyon, but the storm turned into a blizzard in the mountains, and they were obliged to turn back. A few inches more snow, and they could not have got their horses out. A week or so later, with a crust of ice over it, a few of them began again, with no expectation, however, of finding Clark alive. They came across his horse on the second day, but they did not find him, and there were some among them who felt that, after all, old Elihu Clark's boy had chosen the better way.

Bassett closed his notebook and lighted a cigar.

There was a big story to be had for the seeking, a whale of a story. He could go to the office, give them a hint, draw expense money and start for Norada the next night. He knew well enough that he would have to begin there, and that it would not be easy. Witnesses of the affair at the ranch would be missing now, or when found the first accuracy of their statements would either be dulled by time or have been added to with the passing years. The ranch itself might have passed into other hands. To reconstruct the events of ten years ago might be impossible, or nearly so. But that was not his problem. He would have to connect Norada with Haverly, Clark with Livingstone. One thing only was simple. If he found Livingstone's story was correct, that he had lived on a ranch near Norada before the crime and as Livingstone, then he would acknowledge that two men could look precisely alike and come from the same place, and yet not be the same. If not—

But, after he had turned out his light and got into bed, he began to feel a certain distaste for his self-appointed task. If Livingstone were Clark, if after years of effort he had pulled himself up by his own boot-straps, had made himself a man out of the reckless boy he had been, a decent and useful citizen, why pull him down? After all, the world hadn't lost much in Lucas; a sleek, not over-intelligent big animal, that had been Howard Lucas.

He decided to sleep over it, and by morning he found himself not only disinclined to the business, but firmly resolved to let it drop. Things were well enough as they were. The woman in the case was making good. Jud was making good. And nothing would restore Howard Lucas to that small theatrical world of his which had waved him good-bye at the station so long ago.

He shaved and dressed, his resolution still holding. He had indeed almost a conscious glow of virtue, for he was making one of those inglorious and unsung sacrifices which ought to bring a man credit in the next world, because they certainly got him nowhere in this. He was quite affable to the colored waiter who served his breakfasts in the bachelor apartment house, and increased his weekly tip to a dollar and a half. Then he sat down and opened the Times-Republican, skimming over it after his habit for his own space, and frowning over a row of exclamation and interrogation points unwittingly set behind the name of the mayor.

On the second page, however, he stopped, coffee cup in air. "Is Judson Clark alive? Wife of former ranch manager makes confession."

A woman named Margaret Donaldson, it appeared, fatally injured by an automobile near the town of Norada, Wyoming, had made a confession on her deathbed. In it she stated that, afraid to die without shriving her soul, she had sent for the sheriff of Dallas County and had made the following confession:

That following the tragedy at the Clark ranch her husband, John Donaldson, since dead, had immediately following the inquest, where he testified, started out into the mountains in the hope of finding Clark alive, as he knew of a deserted ranger's cabin where Clark sometimes camped when hunting. It was his intention to search for Clark at this cabin and effect his escape. He carried with him food and brandy.

That, owing to the blizzard, he was very nearly frozen; that he was obliged to abandon his horse, shooting it before he did so, and that, close to death himself, he finally reached the cabin and there found Judson Clark, the fugitive, who was very ill.

She further testified that her husband cared for Clark for four days, Clark being delirious at the time, and that on the fifth day he started back on foot for the Clark ranch, having left Clark locked in the cabin, and that on the following night he took three horses, two saddled, and one packed with food and supplies. That accompanied by herself they went back to the cabin in the mountains and that she remained there to care for Clark, while her husband returned to the ranch, to prevent suspicion.

That, a day or so later, looking out of her window, she had perceived a man outside in the snow coming toward the cabin, and that she had thought it one of the searching party. That her first instinct had been to lock him outside, but that she had finally admitted him, and that thereafter he had remained and had helped her to care for the sick man.

Unfortunately for the rest of the narrative it appeared that the injured woman had here lapsed into a coma, and had subsequently died, carrying her further knowledge with her.

But, the article went on, the story opened a field of infinite surmise. In all probability Judson Clark was still alive, living under some assumed identity, free of punishment, outwardly respectable. Three years before he had been adjudged legally dead, and the estate divided, under bond of the legatees.

Close to a hundred million dollars had gone to charities, and Judson Clark, wherever he was, would be dependent on his own efforts for existence. He could have summoned all the legal talent in the country to his defense, but instead he had chosen to disappear.

The whole situation turned on the deposition of Mrs. Donaldson, now dead. The local authorities at Norada maintained that the woman had not been sane for several years. On the other hand, the cabin to which she referred was well known, and no search of it had been made at the time. Clark's horse had been found not ten miles from the town, and the cabin was buried in snow twenty miles further away. If Clark had made that journey on foot he had accomplished the impossible.

Certain facts, according to the local correspondent, bore out Margaret Donaldson's confession. Inquiry showed that she was supposed to have spent the winter following Judson Clark's crime with relatives in Omaha. She had returned to the ranch the following spring.

A detailed description of Judson Clark, and a photograph of him accompanied the story. Bassett re-read the article carefully, and swore a little, under his breath. If he had needed confirmation of his suspicions, it lay to his hand. But the situation had changed over night. There would be a search for Clark now, as wide as the knowledge of his disappearance. Local police authorities would turn him up in every city from Maine to the Pacific coast. Even Europe would be on the lookout and South America.

But it was not the police he feared so much as the press. Not all of the papers, but some of them, would go after that story, and send their best men on it. It offered not so much a chance of solution as an opportunity to revive the old dramatic story. He could see, when he closed his eyes, the local photographers climbing to that cabin and later sending its pictures broadcast, and divers gentlemen of the press, eager to pit their wits against ten years of time and the ability of a once conspicuous man to hide from the law, packing their suitcases for Norada.

No, he couldn't stop now. He would go on, like the others, and with this advantage, that he was morally certain he could lay his hands on Clark at any time. But he would have to prove his case, connect it. Who, for instance, was the other man in the cabin? He must have known who the boy was who lay in that rough bunk, delirious. Must have suspected anyhow. That made him, like the Donaldsons, accessory after the fact, and criminally liable. Small chance of him coming out with any confession. Yet he was the connecting link. Must be.

On his third reading the reporter began to visualize the human elements of the fight to save the boy; he saw moving before him the whole pitiful struggle; the indomitable ranch manager, his heart-breaking struggle with the blizzard, the shooting of his horse, the careful disarming of suspicion, and later the intrepid woman, daring that night ride through snow that had sent the posse back to its firesides to the boy, locked in the cabin and raving.

His mind was busy as he packed his suitcase. Already he had forgotten his compunctions of the early morning; he moved about methodically, calculating roughly what expense money he would need, and the line of attack, if any, required at the office. Between Norada and that old brick house at Haverly lay his story. Ten years of it. He was closing his bag when he remembered the little girl in the blue dress, at the theater. He straightened and scowled. After a moment he snapped the bag shut. Damn it all, if Clark had chosen to tie up with a girl, that was on Clark's conscience, not his.

But he was vaguely uncomfortable.

"It's a queer world, Joe," he observed to the waiter, who had come in for the breakfast dishes.

"Yes, sir. It is that," said Joe.

XII

DURING all the long night Dick sat by David's bedside. Earlier in the evening there had been a consultation; David had suffered a light stroke, but there was no paralysis, and the prognosis was good. For this time, at least, David had escaped, but there must be no other time. He was to be kept quiet and free from worry, his diet was to be carefully regulated, and with care he still had long years before him.

David slept, his breathing heavy and slow. In the morning there would be a nurse, but that night Dick, having sent Lucy to bed, himself kept watch. On the walnut bed lay Doctor David's portly figure, dimly outlined by the shaded lamp, and on a chair drawn close sat Dick.

He was wide-awake and very anxious, but as time went on and no untoward symptoms appeared, as David's sleep seemed to grow easier and more natural, Dick's thoughts wandered. They went to Elizabeth first, and then on and on from that starting point, through the years ahead. He saw the old house with Elizabeth waiting in it for his return; he saw both their lives united and flowing on together, with children, with small cares, with the routine of daily living, and behind it all the two of them, hand in hand.

Then his mind turned on himself. How often in the past ten years it had done that! He had sat off, with a sort of professional detachment, and studied his own case. With the entrance into his world of the new science of psycho-analysis he had made now and then small, not very sincere, attempts to penetrate the veil of his own unconscious devising. Not very sincere, for with the increase of his own knowledge of the mind he had learned that behind such conditions as his lay generally, deeply hidden, the desire to forget. And that behind that there lay, acknowledged or not, fear.

"But to forget what?" he used to say to David, when the first text-books on the new science appeared, and he and David were learning the new terminology, Dick eagerly and David with contemptuous snorts of derision. "To forget what?"

"You had plenty to forget," David would say, stolidly. "I think this man's a fool, but at that— you'd had your father's death, for one thing. And you'd gone pretty close to the edge of eternity yourself. You'd fought single-handed the worst storm of ten years, you came out of it with double pneumonia, and you lay alone in that cabin about fifty-six hours. Forget! You had plenty to forget."

It had never occurred to Dick to doubt David's story. It did not, even now. He had accepted it unquestioningly from the first, supplemented the shadowy childish memories that remained to him with it, and gradually co-ordinating the two had built out of them his house of the past.

Thus, the elderly man whom he dimly remembered was not only his father; he was David's brother. And he had died. It was the shock of that death, according to David, that had sent him into the mountains, where David had followed and nursed him back to health.

It was quite simple, and even explicable by the new psychology. Not that he had worried about the new psychology in those early days. He had been profoundly lethargic, passive and incurious. It had been too much trouble even to think.

True, he had brought over from those lost years certain instincts and a few mental pictures. He had had a certain impatience at first over the restrictions of comparative poverty; he had had to learn the value of money. And the pictures he retained had had a certain opulence which the facts appeared to contradict. Thus he remembered a large ranch house, and innumerable horses, grazing in meadows or milling in a corral. But David had warned him early that there was no estate; that his future depended entirely on his own efforts.

Then the new life had caught and held him. For the first time he had mothering and love. Lucy was his mother, and David the pattern to which he meant to conform. He was happy and contented.

Now and then, in the early days, he had been conscious of a desire to go back and try to reconstruct his past again. Later on he knew that if he were ever to fill up the gap in his life, it would be easier in that environment of once familiar things. But in the first days he had been totally dependent on David, and money was none too plentiful. Later on, as the new life took hold, as he went to medical college and worked at odd clerical jobs in vacations to help pay his way, there had been no chance. Then the war came, and on his return there had been the practice, and his knowledge that David's health was not what it should have been.

But as time went on he was more and more aware that there was in him a peculiar shrinking from going back, an almost apprehension. He knew more of the mind than he had before, and he knew that not physical hardship, but mental stress, caused such lapses as his. But what mental stress had been great enough for such a smash? His father's death?

Strain and fear, said the new psychology. Fear? He had never found himself lacking in courage. Certainly he would have fought a man who called him a coward. But there was cowardice behind all such conditions as his; a refusal of the mind to face reality. It was weak. Weak. He hated himself for that past failure of his to face reality.

But that night, sitting by David's bed, he faced reality with a vengeance. He was in love, and he wanted the things that love should bring to a normal man. He felt normal. He felt, strengthened by love, that he could face whatever life had to bring, so long as also it brought Elizabeth.

Painfully he went back over his talk with David the preceding Sunday night.

"Don't be a fool," David had said. "Go ahead and take her, if she'll have you. And don't be too long about it. I'm not as young as I used to be."

"What I feel," he had replied, "is this: I don't know, of course, if she cares." David had grunted. "I do know I'm going to try to make her care, if it—if it's humanly possible. But I'd like to go back to the ranch again, David, before things go any further."

"Why?"

"I'd like to fill the gap. Attempt it anyhow."

What he was thinking about, as he sat by David's bedside, was David's attitude toward that threatened return of his. For David had opposed it, offering a dozen trivial, almost puerile reasons. Had shown indeed, a dogged obstinacy and an irritability that were somehow oddly

167

like fear. David afraid! David, whose life and heart were open books! David, whose eyes never wavered, nor his courage!

"You let well enough alone, Dick," he had finished. "You've got everything you want. And a medical man can't afford to go gadding about. When people want him they want him."

But he had noticed that David had been different, since. He had taken to following him with his faded old eyes, had even spoken once of retiring and turning all the work over to him. Was it possible that David did not want him to go back to Norada?

He bent over and felt the sick man's pulse. It was stronger, not so rapid. The mechanical act took him back to his first memory of David.

He had been lying in a rough bunk in the mountain cabin, and David, beside him on a wooden box, had been bending forward and feeling his pulse. He had felt weak and utterly inert, and he knew now that he had been very ill. The cabin had been a small and lonely one, with snow-peaks not far above it, and it had been very cold. During the day a woman kept up the fire. Her name was Maggie, and she moved about the cabin like a thin ghost. At night she slept in a lean-to shed and David kept the fire going. A man who seemed to know him well—John Donaldson, he learned, was his name—was Maggie's husband, and every so often he came, about dawn, and brought food and supplies.

After a long time, as he grew stronger, Maggie had gone away, and David had fried the bacon and heated the canned tomatoes or the beans. Before she left she had written out a recipe for biscuits, and David would study over it painstakingly, and then produce a panfull of burned and blackened lumps, over which he would groan and agonize.

He himself had been totally incurious. He had lived a sort of animal life of food and sleep, and later on of small tentative excursions around the room on legs that shook when he walked. The snows came and almost covered the cabin, and David had read a great deal, and talked at intervals. David had tried to fill up the gap in his mind. That was how he learned that David was his father's brother, and that his father had recently died.

Going over it all now, it had certain elements that were not clear. They had, for instance, never gone back to the ranch at all. With the first clearing of the snow in the spring John Donaldson had appeared again, leading two saddled horses and driving a pack animal, and they had started off, leaving him standing in the clearing and gazing after them. But they had not followed Donaldson's trail. They had started West, over the mountains, and David did not know the country. Once they were lost for three days.

He looked at the figure on the bed. Only ten years, and yet at that time David had been vigorous, seemed almost young. He had aged in that ten years. On the bed he was an old man, a tired old man at that. On that long ride he had been tireless. He had taken the burden of the nightly camps, and had hacked a trail with his hatchet across snow fields while Dick, still weak but furiously protesting, had been compelled to stand and watch.

Now, with the perspective of time behind him, and with the clearly defined issue of David's protest against his return to the West, he went again over the details of that winter and spring. Why had they not taken Donaldson's trail? Or gone back to the ranch? Why, since Donaldson could make it, had not other visitors come? Another doctor, the night he almost died, and David sat under the lamp behind the close-screened windows, and read the very pocket prayer-book that now lay on the stand beside the bed? Why had they burned his clothes, and Donaldson brought a new outfit? Why did Donaldson, for all his requests, never bring a razor, so that when they struck the railroad, miles from anywhere, they were both full bearded?

He brought himself up sharply. He had allowed his imagination to run away with him. He had been depicting a flight and no one who knew David could imagine him in flight.

Nevertheless he was conscious of a new uneasiness and anxiety. When David recovered sufficiently he would go to Norada, as he had told Elizabeth, and there he would find the Donaldsons, and clear up the things that bothered him. After that—

He thought of Elizabeth, of her sweetness and sanity. He remembered her at the theater the evening before, lost in its fictitious emotions, its counterfeit drama. He had felt moved to comfort her, when he found her on the verge of tears.

"Just remember, they're only acting," he had said.

"Yes. But life does do things like that to people."

"Not often. The theater deals in the dramatic exceptions to life. You and I, plain bread and butter people, come to see these things because we get a sort of vicarious thrill out of them."

"Doesn't anything ever happen to the plain bread and butter people?"

"A little jam, sometimes. Or perhaps they drop it, butter side down, on the carpet."

"But that is tragedy, isn't it?"

He had had to acknowledge that it might be. But he had been quite emphatic over the fact that most people didn't drop it.

After a long time he slept in his chair. The spring wind came in through the opened window, and fluttered the leaves of the old prayer-book on the stand.

XIII

The week that followed was an anxious one. David's physical condition slowly improved. The slight thickness was gone from his speech, and he sipped resignedly at the broths Lucy or the nurse brought at regular intervals. Over the entire house there hung all day the odor of stewing chicken or of beef tea in the making, and above the doorbell was a white card which said: "Don't ring. Walk in."

As it happened, no one in the old house had seen Maggie Donaldson's confession in the newspaper. Lucy was saved that anxiety, at least. Appearing, as it did, the morning after David's stroke, it came in with the morning milk, lay about unnoticed, and passed out again, to start a fire or line a pantry shelf. Harrison Miller, next door, read it over his coffee. Walter Wheeler in the eight-thirty train glanced at it and glanced away. Nina Ward read it in bed. And that was all.

There came to the house a steady procession of inquirers and bearers of small tribute, flowers and jellies mostly, but other things also. A table in David's room held a steadily growing number of bedroom slippers, and Mrs. Morgan had been seen buying soles for still others. David, propped up in his bed, would cheer a little at these votive offerings, and then relapse again into the heavy troubled silence that worried Dick and frightened Lucy Crosby. Something had happened, she was sure. Something connected with Dick. She watched David when Dick was in the room, and she saw that his eyes followed the younger man with something very like terror.

And for the first time since he had walked into the house that night so long ago, followed by the tall young man for whose coming a letter had prepared her, she felt that David had withdrawn himself from her. She went about her daily tasks a little hurt, and waited for him to choose his own time. But, as the days went on, she saw that whatever this new thing might be, he meant to fight it out alone, and that the fighting it out alone was bad for him. He improved very slowly.

She wondered, sometimes, if it was after all because of Dick's growing interest in Elizabeth Wheeler. She knew that he was seeing her daily, although he was too busy now for more than a hasty call. She felt that she could even tell when he had seen her; he would come in, glowing and almost exalted, and, as if to make up for the moments stolen from David, would leap up the stairs two at a time and burst into the invalid's room like a cheerful cyclone. Wasn't it possible that David had begun to feel as she did, that the girl was entitled to a clean slate before she pledged herself to Dick? And the slate—poor Dick!—could never be cleaned.

Then, one day, David astonished them both. He was propped up in his bed, and he had demanded a cigar, and been very gently but firmly refused. He had been rather sulky about it, and Dick had been attempting to rally him into better humor when he said suddenly:

"I've had time to think things over, Dick. I haven't been fair to you. You're thrown away here. Besides—" he hesitated. Then: "We might as well face it. The day of the general practitioner has gone."

"I don't believe it," Dick said stoutly. "Maybe we are only signposts to point the way to the other fellows, but the world will always need signposts."

"What I've been thinking of," David pursued his own train of thought, "is this: I want you to go to Johns Hopkins and take up the special work you've been wanting to do. I'll be up soon and—"

"Call the nurse, Aunt Lucy," said Dick. "He's raving."

"Not at all," David retorted testily. "I've told you. This whole town only comes here now to be told what specialist to go to, and you know it."

"I don't know anything of the sort."

"If you don't, it's because you won't face the facts." Dick chuckled, and threw an arm over David's shoulder, "You old hypocrite!" he said. "You're trying to get rid of me, for some reason. Don't tell me you're going to get married!"

But David did not smile. Lucy, watching him from her post by the window, saw his face and felt a spasm of fear. At the most, she had feared a mental conflict in David. Now she saw that it might be something infinitely worse, something impending and immediate. She could hardly reply when Dick appealed to her.

"Are you going to let him get rid of me like this, Aunt Lucy?" he demanded. "Sentenced to Johns Hopkins, like Napoleon to St. Helena! Are you with me, or forninst me?"

"I don't know, Dick," she said, with her eyes on David. "If it's for your good—"

She went out after a time, leaving them at it hammer and tongs. David was vanquished in the end, but Dick, going down to the office later on, was puzzled. Somehow it was borne in on him that behind David's insistence was a reason, unspoken but urgent, and the only reason that occurred to him as possible was that David did not, after all, want him to marry Elizabeth Wheeler. He put the matter to the test that night, wandering in in dressing-gown and slippers, as was his custom before going to bed, for a brief chat. The nurse was downstairs, and Dick moved about the room restlessly. Then he stopped and stood by the bed, looking down.

"A few nights ago, David, I asked you if you thought it would be right for me to marry; if my situation justified it, and if to your knowledge there was any other reason why I could not or should not. You said there was not."

"There is no reason, of course. If she'll have you."

"I don't know that. I know that whether she will or not is a pretty vital matter to me, David."

David nodded, silently.

"But now you want me to go away. To leave her. You're rather urgent about it. And I feel-well I begin to think you have a reason for it."

David clenched his hands under the bed-clothing, but he returned Dick's gaze steadily.

"She's a good girl," he said. "But she's entitled to more than you can give her, the way things are."

"That is presupposing that she cares for me. I haven't an idea that she does. That she may, in time—Then, that's the reason for this Johns Hopkins thing, is it?"

"That's the reason," David said stoutly. "She would wait for you. She's that sort. I've known her all her life. She's as steady as a rock. But she's been brought up to have a lot of things. Walter Wheeler is well off. You do as I want you to; pack your things and go to Baltimore. Bring Reynolds down here to look after the work until I'm around again."

But Dick evaded the direct issue thus opened and followed another line of thought.

"Of course you understand," he observed, after a renewal of his restless pacing, "that I've got to tell her my situation first. I don't need to tell you that I funk doing it, but it's got to be done."

"Don't be a fool," David said querulously. "You'll set a lot of women cackling, and what they don't know they'll invent. I know 'em."

"Only herself and her family."

"Why?"

"Because they have a right to know it."

But when he saw David formulating a further protest he dropped the subject.

"I'll not do it until we've gone into it together," he promised. "There's plenty of time. You settle down now and get ready for sleep."

When the nurse came in at eleven o'clock she found Dick gone and David, very still, with his face to the wall.

It was the end of May before David began to move about his upper room. The trees along the shaded streets had burst into full leaf by that time, and Mike was enjoying that gardener's interval of paradise when flowers grow faster than the weeds among them. Harrison Miller, having rolled his lawn through all of April, was heard abroad in the early mornings with the lawn mower or hoe in hand was to be seen behind his house in his vegetable patch.

Cars rolled through the streets, the rear seats laden with blossoming loot from the country lanes, and the Wheeler dog was again burying bones in the soft warm ground under the hedge.

Elizabeth Wheeler was very happy. Her look of expectant waiting, once vague, had crystallized now into definite form. She was waiting, timidly and shyly but with infinite content. In time, everything would come. And in the meantime there was to-day, and some time to-day a shabby car would stop at the door, and there would be five minutes, or ten. And then Dick would have to hurry to work, or back to David. After that, of course, to-day was over, but there would always be to-morrow.

Now and then, at choir practice or at service, she saw Clare Rossiter. But Clare was very cool to her, and never on any account sought her, or spoke to her alone. She was rather unhappy about Clare, when she remembered her. Because it must be so terrible to care for a man who only said, when one spoke of Clare, "Oh, the tall blonde girl?"

Once or twice, too, she had found Clare's eyes on her, and they were hostile eyes. It was almost as though they said: "I hate you because you know. But don't dare to pity me."

Yet, somehow, Elizabeth found herself not entirely believing that Clare's passion was real. Because the real thing you hid with all your might, at least until you were sure it was wanted. After that, of course, you could be so proud of it that you might become utterly shameless. She was afraid sometimes that she was the sort to be utterly shameless. Yet, for all her halcyon hours, there were little things that worried her. Wallie Sayre, for instance, always having to be kept from saying things she didn't want to hear. And Nina. She wasn't sure that Nina was entirely happy. And, of course, there was Jim.

Jim was difficult. Sometimes he was a man, and then again he was a boy, and one never knew just which he was going to be. He was too old for discipline and too young to manage himself. He was spending almost all his evenings away from home now, and her mother always drew an inaudible sigh when he was spoken of.

Elizabeth had waited up for him one night, only a short time before, and beckoning him into her room, had talked to him severely.

"You ought to be ashamed, Jim," she said. "You're simply worrying mother sick."

"Well, why?" he demanded defiantly. "I'm old enough to take care of myself."

"You ought to be taking care of her, too."

He had looked rather crestfallen at that, and before he went out he offered a half-sheepish explanation.

"I'd tell them where I go," he said, "but you'd think a pool room was on the direct road to hell. Take to-night, now. I can't tell them about it, but it was all right. I met Wallie Sayre and Leslie at the club before dinner, and we got a fourth and played bridge. Only half a cent a point. I swear we were going on playing, but somebody brought in a chap named Gregory for a cocktail. He turned out to be a brother of Beverly Carlysle, the actress, and he took us around to the theater and gave us a box. Not a thing wrong with it, was there?"

"Where did you go from there?" she persisted inexorably. "It's half past one."

"Went around and met her. She's wonderful, Elizabeth. But do you know what would happen if I told them? They'd have a fit."

She felt rather helpless, because she knew he was right from his own standpoint.

"I know. I'm surprised at Les, Jim."

"Oh, Les! He just trailed along. He's all right."

She kissed him and he went out, leaving her to lie awake for a long time. She would have had all her world happy those days, and all her world good. She didn't want anybody's bread and butter spilled on the carpet.

So the days went on, and the web slowly wove itself into its complicated pattern: Bassett speeding West, and David in his quiet room; Jim and Leslie Ward seeking amusement, and finding it in the littered dressing-room of a woman star at a local theater; Clare Rossiter brooding, and the little question being whispered behind hands, figuratively, of course—the village was entirely well-bred; Gregory calling round to see Bassett, and turning away with the information that he had gone away for an indefinite time; and Maggie Donaldson, lying in the cemetery at the foot of the mountains outside Norada, having shriven her soul to the limit of her strength so that she might face her Maker.

Out of all of them it was Clare Rossiter who made the first conscious move of the shuttle; Clare, affronted and not a little malicious, but perhaps still dramatizing herself, this time as the friend who feels forced to carry bad tidings. Behind even that, however, was an unconscious desire to see Dick again, and this time so to impress herself on him that never again could he pass her in the street unnoticed.

On the day, then, that David first sat up in bed Clare went to the house and took her place in the waiting-room. She was dressed with extreme care, and she carried a parasol. With it, while she waited, she drilled small nervous indentations in the old office carpet, and formulated her line of action.

Nevertheless she found it hard to begin.

"I don't want to keep you, if you're busy," she said, avoiding his eyes. "If you are in a hurry—"

"This is my business," he said patiently. And waited.

"I wonder if you are going to understand me, when I do begin?"

"You sound alarmingly ominous." He smiled at her, and she had a moment of panic. "You don't look like a young lady with anything eating at her damask cheek, or however it goes."

"Doctor Livingstone," she said suddenly, "people are saying something about you that you ought to know."

He stared at her, amazed and incredulous.

"About me? What can they say? That's absurd."

"I felt you ought to know. Of course I don't believe it. Not for a moment. But you know what this town is."

"I know it's a very good town," he said steadily. "However, let's have it. I daresay it is not very serious."

She was uneasy enough by that time, and rather frightened when she had finished. For he sat, quiet and rather pale, not looking at her at all, but gazing fixedly at an old daguerreotype of David that stood on his desk. One that Lucy had shown him one day and which he had preempted; David at the age of eight, in a small black velvet suit and with very thin legs.

"I thought you ought to know," she justified herself, nervously.

Dick got up.

"Yes," he said. "I ought to know, of course. Thank you."

When she had gone he went back and stood before the picture again. From Clare's first words he had had a stricken conviction that the thing was true; that, as Mrs. Cook Morgan's visitor from Wyoming had insisted, Henry Livingstone had never married, never had a son. He stood and gazed at the picture. His world had collapsed about him, but he was steady and very erect.

"David, David!" he thought. "Why did you do it? And what am I? And who?"

Characteristically his first thought after that was of David himself. Whatever David had done, his motive had been right. He would have to start with that. If David had built for him a false identity it was because there was a necessity for it. Something shameful, something he was to be taken away from. Wasn't it probable that David had heard the gossip, and had then collapsed? Wasn't the fear that he himself would hear it behind David's insistence that he go to Baltimore?

His thoughts flew to Elizabeth. Everything was changed now, as to Elizabeth. He would have to be very certain of that past of his before he could tell her that he loved her, and he had a sense of immediate helplessness. He could not go to David, as things were. To Lucy?

Probably he would have gone to Lucy at once, but the telephone rang. He answered it, got his hat and bag and went out to the car. Years with David had made automatic the subordination of self to the demands of the practice.

At half past six Lucy heard him come in and go into his office. When he did not immediately reappear and take his flying run up the stairs to David's room, she stood outside the office door and listened. She had a premonition of something wrong, something of the truth, perhaps. Anyhow, she tapped at the door and opened it, to find him sitting very quietly at his desk with his head in his hands.

"Dick!" she exclaimed. "Is anything wrong?"

"I have a headache," he said. He looked at his watch and got up. "I'll take a look at David, and then we'll have dinner. I didn't know it was so late."

But when she had gone out he did not immediately move. He had been going over again, painfully and carefully, the things that puzzled him, that he had accepted before without dispute. David and Lucy's reluctance to discuss his father; the long days in the cabin, with David helping him to reconstruct his past; the spring, and that slow progress which now he felt, somehow, had been an escape.

He ate very little dinner, and Lucy's sense of dread increased. When, after the meal, she took refuge in her sitting-room on the lower floor and picked up her knitting, it was with a conviction that it was only a temporary reprieve. She did not know from what.

She heard him, some time later, coming down from David's room. But he did not turn into his office. Instead, he came on to her door, stood for a moment like a man undecided, then came in. She did not look up, even when very gently he took her knitting from her and laid it on the table.

"Aunt Lucy."

"Yes, Dick."

"Don't you think we'd better have a talk?"

"What about?" she asked, with her heart hammering.

"About me." He stood above her, and looked down, still with the tenderness with which he always regarded her, but with resolution in his very attitude. "First of all, I'll tell you something. Then I'll ask you to tell me all you can."

She yearned over him as he told her, for all her terror. His voice, for all its steadiness, was strained.

"I have felt for some time," he finished, "that you and David were keeping something from me. I think, now, that this is what it was. Of course, you realize that I shall have to know."

"Dick! Dick!" was all she could say.

"I was about," he went on, with his almost terrible steadiness, "to ask a girl to take my name. I want to know if I have a name to offer her. I have, you see, only two alternatives to believe about myself. Either I am Henry Livingstone's illegitimate son, and in that case I have no right to my name, or to offer it to any one, or I am—"

He made a despairing gesture.

"—or I am some one else, some one who was smuggled out of the mountains and given an identity that makes him a living lie."

Always she had known that this might come some time, but always too she had seen David bearing the brunt of it. He should bear it. It was not of her doing or of her approving. For years the danger of discovery had hung over her like a cloud.

"Do you know which?" he persisted.

"Yes, Dick."

"Would you have the unbelievable cruelty not to tell me?"

She got up, a taut little figure with a dignity born of her fear and of her love for him.

"I shall not betray David's confidence," she said. "Long ago I warned him that this time would come. I was never in favor of keeping you in ignorance. But it is David's problem, and I cannot take the responsibility of telling you."

He knew her determination and her obstinate loyalty. But he was fairly desperate.

"You know that if you don't tell me, I shall go to David?"

"If you go now you will kill him."

"It's as bad as that, is it?" he asked grimly. "Then there is something shameful behind it, is there?"

"No, no, Dick. Not that. And I want you, always, to remember this. What David did was out of love for you. He has made many sacrifices for you. First he saved your life, and then he made you what you are. And he has had a great pride in it. Don't destroy his work of years."

Her voice broke and she turned to go out, her chin quivering, but half way to the door he called to her.

"Aunt Lucy—" he said gently.

She heard him behind her, felt his strong arms as he turned her about. He drew her to him and stooping, kissed her cheek.

"You're right," he said. "Always right. I'll not worry him with it. My word of honor. When the time comes he'll tell me, and until it comes, I'll wait. And I love you both. Don't ever forget that."

He kissed her again and let her go.

But long after David had put down his prayer-book that night, and after the nurse had rustled down the stairs to the night supper on the dining-room table, Lucy lay awake and listened to Dick's slow pacing of his bedroom floor.

He was very gentle with David from that time on, and tried to return to his old light-hearted ways. On the day David was to have his first broiled sweetbread he caught the nurse outside, borrowed her cap and apron and carried in the tray himself.

"I hope your food is to your taste, Doctor David," he said, in a high falsetto which set the nurse giggling in the hall. "I may not be much of a nurse, but I can cook."

Even Lucy was deceived at times. He went his customary round, sent out the monthly bills, opened and answered David's mail, bore the double burden of David's work and his own ungrudgingly, but off guard he was grave and abstracted. He began to look very thin, too, and Lucy often heard him pacing the floor at night. She thought that he seldom or never went to the Wheelers'.

And so passed the tenth day of David's illness, with the smile on Elizabeth's face growing a trifle fixed as three days went by without the shabby car rattling to the door; with "The Valley" playing its second and final week before going into New York; and with Leslie Ward unconsciously taking up the shuttle Clare had dropped, and carrying the pattern one degree further toward completion.

XIV

JUST how Leslie Ward had drifted into his innocuous affair with the star of "The Valley" he was not certain himself. Innocuous it certainly was. Afterwards, looking back, he was to wonder sometimes if it had not been precisely for the purpose it served. But that was long months after. Not until the pattern was completed and he was able to recognize his own work in it.

The truth was that he was not too happy at home. Nina's smart little house on the Ridgely Road had at first kept her busy. She had spent unlimited time with decorators, had studied and rejected innumerable water-color sketches of interiors, had haunted auction rooms and bid recklessly on things she felt at the moment she could not do without, later on to have to wheedle Leslie into straightening her bank balance. Thought, too, and considerable energy had gone into training and outfitting her servants, and still more into inducing them to wear the expensive uniforms and livery she provided.

But what she made, so successfully, was a house rather than a home. There were times, indeed, when Leslie began to feel that it was not even a house, but a small hotel. They almost never dined alone, and when they did Nina would explain that everybody was tied up. Then, after dinner, restlessness would seize her, and she would want to run in to the theater, or to make a call. If he refused, she nursed a grievance all evening.

And he did not like her friends. Things came to a point where, when he knew one of the gay evenings was on, he would stay in town, playing billiards at his club, or occasionally wandering into a theater, where he stood or sat at the back of the house and watched the play with cynical, discontented eyes.

The casual meeting with Gregory and the introduction to his sister brought a new interest. Perhaps the very novelty was what first attracted him, the oddity of feeling that he was on terms of friendship, for it amounted to that with surprising quickness, with a famous woman, whose face smiled out at him from his morning paper or, huge and shockingly colored, from the sheets on the bill boards.

He formed the habit of calling on her in the afternoons at her hotel, and he saw that she liked it. It was often lonely, she explained. He sent her flowers and cigarettes, and he found her poised and restful, and sometimes, when she was off guard, with the lines of old suffering in her face.

She sat still. She didn't fidget, as Nina did. She listened, too. She was not as beautiful as she appeared on the stage, but she was attractive, and he stilled his conscience with the knowledge that she placed no undue emphasis on his visits. In her world men came and went, brought or sent small tribute, and she was pleased and grateful. No more. The next week, or the week after, and other men in other places would be doing the same things.

But he wondered about her, sometimes. Did she ever think of Judson Clark, and the wreck he had made of her life? What of resentment and sorrow lay behind her quiet face, or the voice with its careful intonations which was so unlike Nina's?

Now and then he saw her brother. He neither liked nor disliked Gregory, but he suspected him of rather bullying Beverly. On the rare occasions when he saw them together there was a sort of nervous tension in the air, and although Leslie was not subtle he sensed some hidden difference between them. A small incident one day almost brought this concealed dissension to a head. He said to Gregory:

"By the way, I saw you in Haverly yesterday afternoon."

"Must have seen somebody else. Haverly? Where's Haverly?"

Leslie Ward had been rather annoyed. There had been no mistake about the recognition. But he passed it off with that curious sense of sex loyalty that will actuate a man even toward his enemies.

"Funny," he said. "Chap looked like you. Maybe a little heavier."

Nevertheless he had a conviction that he had said something better left unsaid, and that Beverly Carlysle's glance at her brother was almost hostile. He had that instantaneous picture of the two of them, the man defiant and somehow frightened, and the woman's eyes anxious and yet slightly contemptuous. Then, in a flash, it was gone.

He had meant to go home that evening, would have, probably, for he was not ignorant of where he was drifting. But when he went back to the office Nina was on the wire, with the news that they were to go with a party to a country inn.

"For chicken and waffles, Les," she said. "It will be oceans of fun. And I've promised the cocktails."

"I'm tired," he replied, sulkily. "And why don't you let some of the other fellows come over with the drinks? It seems to me I'm always the goat."

"Oh, if that's the way you feel!" Nina said, and hung up the receiver.

He did not go home. He went to the theater and stood at the back, with his sense of guilt deadened by the knowledge that Nina was having what she would call a heavenly time. After all, it would soon be over. He counted the days. "The Valley" had only four more before it moved on.

He had already played his small part in the drama that involved Dick Livingstone, but he was unaware of it. He went home that night, to find Nina settled in bed and very sulky, and he retired himself in no pleasant frame of mind. But he took a firmer hold of himself that night before he slept. He didn't want a smash, and yet they might be headed that way. He wouldn't see Beverly Carlysle again.

He lived up to his resolve the next day, bought his flowers as usual, but this time for Nina and took them with him. And went home with the orchids which were really an offering to his own conscience.

But Nina was not at home. The butler reported that she was dining at the Wheelers', and he thought the man eyed him with restrained commiseration.

"Did she say I am expected there?" he asked.

"She ordered dinner for you here, sir."

Even for Nina that sounded odd. He took his coat and went out again to the car; after a moment's hesitation he went back and got the orchids.

Dick Livingstone's machine was at the curb before the Wheeler house, and in the living-room he found Walter Wheeler, pacing the floor. Mr. Wheeler glanced at him and looked away.

"Anybody sick?" Leslie asked, his feeling of apprehension growing.

"Nina is having hysterics upstairs," Mr. Wheeler said, and continued his pacing.

"Nina! Hysterics?"

"That's what I said," replied Mr. Wheeler, suddenly savage. "You've made a nice mess of things, haven't you?"

Leslie placed the box of orchids on the table and drew off his gloves. His mind was running over many possibilities.

"You'd better tell me about it, hadn't you?"

"Oh, I will. Don't worry. I've seen this coming for months. I'm not taking her part. God knows I know her, and she has as much idea of making a home as—as"—he looked about—"as that poker has. But that's the worst you can say of her. As to you—"

"Well?"

Mr. Wheeler's anxiety was greater than his anger. He lowered his voice.

"She got a bill to-day for two or three boxes of flowers, sent to some actress." And when Leslie said nothing, "I'm not condoning it, mind you. You'd no business to do it. But," he added fretfully, "why the devil, if you've got to act the fool, don't you have your bills sent to your office?"

"I suppose I don't need to tell you that's all there was to it? Flowers, I mean."

"I'm taking that for granted. But she says she won't go back."

Leslie was aghast and frightened. Not at the threat; she would go back, of course. But she would always hold it against him. She cherished small grudges faithfully. And he knew she would never understand, never see her own contribution to his mild defection, nor comprehend the actual innocence of those afternoons of tea and talk.

There was no sound from upstairs. Mr. Wheeler got his hat and went out, calling to the dog. Jim came in whistling, looked in and said: "Hello, Les," and disappeared. He sat in the growing twilight and cursed himself for a fool. After all, where had he been heading? A man couldn't eat his cake and have it. But he was resentful, too; he stressed rather hard his own innocence, and chose to ignore the less innocent impulse that lay behind it.

After a half hour or so he heard some one descending and Dick Livingstone appeared in the hall. He called to him, and Dick entered the room. Before he sat down he lighted a cigarette and in the flare of the match Leslie got an impression of fatigue and of something new, of trouble. But his own anxieties obsessed him.

"She's told you about it, I suppose?"

"I was a fool, of course. But it was only a matter of a few flowers and some afternoon calls. She's a fine woman, Livingstone, and she is lonely. The women have given her a pretty cold deal since the Clark story. They copy her clothes and her walk, but they don't ask her into their homes."

"Isn't the trouble more fundamental than that, Ward? I was thinking about it upstairs. Nina was pretty frank. She says you've had your good time and want to settle down, and that she is young and now is her only chance. Later on there may be children, you know. She blames herself, too, but she has a fairly clear idea of how it happened."

"Do you think she'll go back home?"

"She promised she would."

They sat smoking in silence. In the dining-room Annie was laying the table for dinner, and a most untragic odor of new garden peas began to steal along the hall. Dick suddenly stirred and threw away his cigarette.

"I was going to talk to you about something else," he said, "but this is hardly the time. I'll get on home." He rose. "She'll be all right. Only I'd advise very tactful handling and—the fullest explanation you can make."

"What is it? I'd be glad to have something to keep my mind occupied. It's eating itself up just now."

"It's a personal matter."

Ward glanced up at him quickly.

"Yes?"

"Have you happened to hear a story that I believe is going round? One that concerns me?"

"Well, I have," Leslie admitted. "I didn't pay much attention. Nobody is taking it very seriously."

"That's not the point," Dick persisted. "I don't mind idle gossip. I don't give a damn about it. It's the statement itself."

"I should say that you are the only person who knows anything about it."

Dick made a restless, impatient gesture.

"I want to know one thing more," he said. "Nina told you, I suppose. Does—I suppose Elizabeth knows it, too?"

"I rather think she does."

Dick turned abruptly and went out of the room, and a moment later Leslie heard the front door slam. Elizabeth, standing at the head of the stairs, heard it also, and turned away, with a new droop to her usually valiant shoulders. Her world, too, had gone awry, that safe world of protection and cheer and kindliness. First had come Nina, white-lipped and shaken, and Elizabeth had had to face the fact that there were such things as treachery and the queer hidden things that men did, and that came to light and brought horrible suffering.

And that afternoon she had had to acknowledge that there was something wrong with Dick. No. Between Dick and herself. There was a formality in his speech to her, an aloofness that seemed to ignore utterly their new intimacy. He was there, but he was miles away from her. She tried hard to feel indignant, but she was only hurt.

Peace seemed definitely to have abandoned the Wheeler house. Then late in the evening a measure of it was restored when Nina and Leslie effected a reconciliation. It followed several bad hours when Nina had locked her door against them all, but at ten o'clock she sent for Leslie and faced him with desperate calmness.

To Elizabeth, putting cold cloths on her mother's head as she lay on the bed, there came a growing conviction that the relation between men and women was a complicated and baffling thing, and that love and hate were sometimes close together.

Love, and habit perhaps, triumphed in Nina's case, however, for at eleven o'clock they heard Leslie going down the stairs and later on moving about the kitchen and pantry while whistling softly. The servants had gone, and the air was filled with the odor of burning bread. Some time later Mrs. Wheeler, waiting uneasily in the upper hall, beheld her son-in-law coming up and carrying proudly a tray on which was toast of an incredible blackness, and a pot which smelled feebly of tea.

"The next time you're out of a cook just send for me," he said cheerfully.

Mrs. Wheeler, full and overflowing with indignation and the piece of her mind she had meant to deliver, retired vanquished to her bedroom.

Late that night when Nina had finally forgiven him and had settled down for sleep, Leslie went downstairs for a cigar, to find Elizabeth sitting there alone, a book on her knee, face down, and her eyes wistful and with a question in them.

"Sitting and thinking, or just sitting?" he inquired.

"I was thinking."

"Air-castles, eh? Well, be sure you put the right man into them!" He felt more or less a fool for having said that, for it was extremely likely that Nina's family was feeling some doubt about Nina's choice.

"What I mean is," he added hastily, "don't be a fool and take Wallie Sayre. Take a man, while you're about it."

"I would, if I could do the taking."

"That's piffle, Elizabeth." He sat down on the arm of a chair and looked at her. "Look here, what about this story the Rossiter girl and a few others are handing around about Dick Livingstone? You're not worrying about it, are you?"

"I don't believe it's true, and it wouldn't matter to me, anyhow."

"Good for you," he said heartily, and got up. "You'd better go to bed, young lady. It's almost midnight."

But although she rose she made no further move to go.

"What I am worrying about is this, Leslie. He may hear it."

"He has heard it, honey."

He had expected her to look alarmed, but instead she showed relief.

"I'll tell you the truth, Les," she said. "I was worrying. I'm terribly fond of him. It just came all at once, and I couldn't help it. And I thought he liked me, too, that way." She stopped and looked up at him to see if he understood, and he nodded gravely. "Then to-day, when he came to see Nina, he avoided me. He—I was waiting in the hall upstairs, and he just said a word or two and went on down."

"Poor devil!" Leslie said. "You see, he's in an unpleasant position, to say the least. But here's a thought to go to sleep on. If you ask me, he's keeping out of your way, not because he cares too little, but because he cares too much."

Long after a repentant and chastened Leslie had gone to sleep, his arm over Nina's unconscious shoulder, Elizabeth stood wide-eyed on the tiny balcony outside her room. From it in daylight she could see the Livingstone house. Now it was invisible, but an upper window was outlined in the light. Very shyly she kissed her finger tips to it.

"Good-night, dear," she whispered.

XV

Louis Bassett had left for Norada the day after David's sudden illness, but ten days later found him only as far as Chicago, and laid up in his hotel with a sprained knee. It was not until the day Nina went back to the little house in the Ridgely Road, having learned the first lesson of married life, that men must not only be captured but also held, that he was able to resume his journey.

He had chafed wretchedly under the delay. It was true that nothing in the way of a story had broken yet. The Tribune had carried a photograph of the cabin where Clark had according to the Donaldson woman spent the winter following the murder, and there were the usual reports that he had been seen recently in spots as diverse as Seattle and New Orleans. But when the following Sunday brought nothing further he surmised that the pack, having lost the scent, had been called off.

He confirmed this before starting West by visiting some of the offices of the leading papers and looking up old friends. The Clark story was dead for the time. They had run a lot of pictures of him, however, and some one might turn him up eventually, but a scent was pretty cold in ten years. The place had changed, too. Oil had been discovered five years ago, and the old settlers had, a good many of them, cashed in and moved away. The town had grown like all oil towns.

Bassett was fairly content. He took the night train out of Chicago and spent the next day crossing Nebraska, fertile, rich and interesting. On the afternoon of the second day he left the train and took a branch line toward the mountains and Norada, and from that time on he became an urbane, interested and generally cigar-smoking interrogation point.

"Railroad been here long?" he asked the conductor.

"Four years."

"Norada must have been pretty isolated before that."

"Thirty miles in a coach or a Ford car."

"I was reading the other day," said Bassett, "about the Judson Clark case. Have a cigar? Got time to sit down?"

"You a newspaper man?"

"Oil well supplies," said Bassett easily. "Well, in this article it seemed some woman or other had made a confession. It sounded fishy to me."

"Well, I'll tell you about that." The conductor sat down and bit off the end of his cigar. "I knew the Donaldsons well, and Maggie Donaldson was an honest woman. But I'll tell you how I explain the thing. Donaldson died, and that left her pretty much alone. The executors of the Clark estate kept her on the ranch, but when the estate was settled three years ago she had to move. That broke her all up. She's always said he wasn't dead. She kept the house just as it was, and my wife says she had his clothes all ready and everything."

"That rather sounds as though the story is true, doesn't it?"

"Not necessarily. It's my idea she got from hoping to moping, so to speak. She went in to town regular for letters for ten years, and the postmaster says she never got any. She was hurt in front of the post office. The talk around here is that she's been off her head for the last year or two."

"But they found the cabin."

"Sure they did," said the conductor equably. "The cabin was no secret. It was an old fire station before they put the new one on Goat Mountain. I spent a month in it myself, once, with a dude who wanted to take pictures of bear. We found a bear, but it charged the camera and I'd be running yet if I hadn't come to civilization."

When he had gone Bassett fell into deep thought. So Maggie Donaldson had gone to the post office for ten years. He tried to visualize those faithful, wearisome journeys, through spring mud and winter snow, always futile and always hopeful. He did not for a moment believe that she had "gone off her head." She had been faithful to the end, as some women were, and in the end, too, as had happened before, her faith had killed her.

And again he wondered at the curious ability of some men to secure loyalty. They might go through life, tearing down ideals and destroying illusions to the last, but always there was some faithful hand to rebuild, some faithful soul to worship.

He was somewhat daunted at the size and bustling activity of Norada. Its streets were paved and well-lighted, there were a park and a public library, and the clerk at the Commercial Hotel asked him if he wished a private bath! But the development was helpful in one way. In the old Norada a newcomer might have been subjected to a friendly but inquisitive interest. In this grown-up and self-centered community a man might come and go unnoticed.

And he had other advantages. The pack, as he cynically thought of them, would have started at the Clark ranch and the cabin. He would get to them, of course, but he meant to start on the outside of the circle and work in.

"Been here long?" he asked the clerk at the desk, after a leisurely meal.

The clerk grinned.

"I came here two years ago. I never saw Jud Clark. To get to the Clark place take the road north out of the town and keep straight about eight miles. The road's good now. You fellows have worn it smooth."

"Must have written that down and learned it off," Bassett said admiringly. "What the devil's the Clark place? And why should I go there? Unless," he added, "they serve a decent meal."

"Sorry." The clerk looked at him sharply, was satisfied, and picked up a pen. "You'll hear the story if you stay around here any time. Anything I can do for you?"

"Yes. Fire the cook," Bassett said, and moved away.

He spent the evening in going over his notes and outlining a campaign, and the next day he stumbled on a bit of luck. His elderly chambermaid had lived in and around the town for years.

"Ever hear of any Livingstones in these parts?" he asked.

"Why, yes. There used to be a Livingstone ranch at Dry River," she said, pausing with her carpet sweeper, and looking at him. "It wasn't much of a place. Although you can't tell these days. I sold sixty acres eight years ago for two thousand dollars, and the folks that bought it are getting a thousand a day out of it."

She sighed. She had touched the hem of fortune's garment and passed on; for some opportunity knocked but faintly, and for others it burst open the door and forced its way in.

"I'd be a millionaire now if I'd held on," she said somberly. That day Bassett engaged a car by the day, he to drive it himself and return it in good condition, the garage to furnish tires.

"I'd just like to say one thing," the owner said, as he tried the gears. "I don't know where you're going, and it's not exactly my business. Here in the oil country, where they're cutting each other's throats for new leases, we let a man alone. But if you've any idea of taking that car by the back road to the old fire station where Jud Clark's supposed to have spent the winter, I'll just say this: we've had two stuck up there for a week, and the only way I see to get them back is a cyclone."

"I'm going to Dry River," Bassett said shortly.

"Dry River's right, if you're looking for oil! Go easy on the brakes, old man. We need 'em in our business."

Dry River was a small settlement away from the railroad. It consisted of two intersecting unpaved streets, a dozen or so houses, a closed and empty saloon and two general stores. He chose one at random and found that the old Livingstone place had been sold ten years ago, on the death of its owner, Henry Livingstone.

"His brother from the East inherited it," said the storekeeper. "He came and sold out, lock, stock and barrel. Not that there was much. A few cattle and horses, and the stuff in the ranch house, which wasn't valuable. There were a lot of books, and the brother gave them for a library, but we haven't any building. The railroad isn't built this far yet, and unless we get oil here it won't be."

"The brother inherited it, eh? Do you know the brother's name?"

"David, I think. He was a doctor back East somewhere."

"Then this Henry Livingstone wasn't married? Or at least had no children?"

"He wasn't married. He was a sort of hermit. He'd been dead two days before any one knew it. My wife went out when they found him and got him ready for the funeral. He was buried before the brother got here." He glanced at Bassett shrewdly. "The place has been prospected for oil, and there's a dry hole on the next ranch. I tell my wife nature's like the railroad. It quit before it got this far."

Bassett's last scruple had fled. The story was there, ready for the gathering. So ready, indeed, that he was almost suspicious of his luck.

And that conviction, that things were coming too easy, persisted through his interview with the storekeeper's wife, in the small house behind the store. She was a talkative woman, eager to discuss the one drama in a drab life, and she showed no curiosity as to the reason for his question.

"Henry Livingstone!" she said. "Well, I should say so. I went out right away when we got the word he was dead, and there I stayed until it was all over. I guess I know as much about him as any one around here does, for I had to go over his papers to find out who his people were."

The papers, it seemed, had not been very interesting; canceled checks and receipted bills, and a large bundle of letters, all of them from a brother named David and a sister who signed herself Lucy. There had been a sealed one, too, addressed to David Livingstone, and to be opened after his death. She had had her husband wire to "David" and he had come out, too late for the funeral.

"Do you remember when that was?"

"Let me see. Henry Livingstone died about a month before the murder at the Clark ranch. We date most things around here from that time."

"How long did 'David' stay?" Bassett had tried to keep his tone carefully conversational, but he saw that it was not necessary. She was glad of a chance to talk.

"Well, I'd say about three or four weeks. He hadn't seen his brother for years, and I guess there was no love lost. He sold everything as quick as he could, and went back East." She glanced at the clock. "My husband will be in soon for dinner. I'd be glad to have you stay and take a meal with us."

The reporter thanked her and declined.

"It's an interesting story," he said. "I didn't tell your husband, for I wasn't sure I was on the right trail. But the David and Lucy business eliminates this man. There's a piece of property waiting in the East for a Henry Livingstone who came to this state in the 80's, or for his heirs. You can say positively that this man was not married?"

"No. He didn't like women. Never had one on the place. Two ranch hands that are still at the Wassons' and himself, that was all. The Wassons are the folks who bought the ranch."

No housekeeper then, and no son born out of wedlock, so far as any evidence went. All that glib lying in the doctor's office, all that apparent openness and frankness, gone by the board!

The man in the cabin, reported by Maggie Donaldson, had been David Livingstone. Somehow, some way, he had got Judson Clark out of the country and spirited him East. Not that the how mattered just yet. The essential fact was there, that David Livingstone had been in this part of the country at the time Maggie Donaldson had been nursing Judson Clark in the mountains.

Bassett sat back and chewed the end of his cigar thoughtfully. The sheer boldness of the scheme which had saved Judson Clark compelled his admiration, but the failure to cover the trail, the ease with which he had picked it up, made him suspicious.

He rose and threw away his cigar.

"You say this David went East, when he had sold out the place. Do you remember where he lived?"

"Some town in eastern Pennsylvania. I've forgotten the name."

"I've got to be sure I'm wrong, and then go ahead," he said, as he got his hat. "I'll see those men at the ranch, I guess, and then be on my way. How far is it?"

It was about ten miles, along a bad road which kept him too much occupied for any connected thought. But his sense of exultation persisted. He had found Judson Clark.

XVI

Dick's decision to cut himself off from Elizabeth was born of his certainty that he could not see her and keep his head. He was resolutely determined to keep his head, until he knew what he had to offer her. But he was very unhappy. He worked sturdily all day and slept at night out of sheer fatigue, only to rouse in the early morning to a conviction of something wrong before he was fully awake. Then would come the uncertainty and pain of full consciousness, and he would lie with his arms under his head, gazing unblinkingly at the ceiling and preparing to face another day.

There was no prospect of early relief, although David had not again referred to his going away. David was very feeble. The look of him sometimes sent an almost physical pain through Dick's heart. But there were times when he roused to something like his old spirit, shouted for tobacco, frowned over his diet tray, and fought Harrison Miller when he came in to play cribbage in much his old tumultuous manner.

Then, one afternoon late in May, when for four days Dick had not seen Elizabeth, suddenly he found the decision as to their relation taken out of his hands, and by Elizabeth herself.

He opened the door one afternoon to find her sitting alone in the waiting-room, clearly very frightened and almost inarticulate. He could not speak at all at first, and when he did his voice, to his dismay, was distinctly husky.

"Is anything wrong?" he asked, in a tone which was fairly sepulchral.

"That's what I want to know, Dick."

Suddenly he found himself violently angry. Not at her, of course. At everything.

"Wrong?" he said, savagely. "Yes. Everything is wrong!"

Then he was angry! She went rather pale.

"What have I done, Dick?"

As suddenly as he had been fierce he was abject and ashamed. Startled, too.

"You?" he said. "What have you done? You're the only thing that's right in a wrong world. You—"

He checked himself, put down his bag—he had just come in—and closed the door into the hall. Then he stood at a safe distance from her, and folded his arms in order to be able to keep his head-which shows how strange the English language is.

"Elizabeth," he said gravely. "I've been a self-centered fool. I stayed away because I've been in trouble. I'm still in trouble, for that matter. But it hasn't anything to do with you. Not directly, anyhow."

"Don't you think it's possible that I know what it is?"

"You do know."

He was too absorbed to notice the new maturity in her face, the brooding maternity born of a profound passion. To Elizabeth just then he was not a man, her man, daily deciding matters of life and death, but a worried boy, magnifying a trifle into importance.

"There is always gossip," she said, "and the only thing one can do is to forget it at once. You ought to be too big for that sort of thing."

"But—suppose it is true?"

"What difference would it make?"

He made a quick movement toward her.

"There may be more than that. I don't know, Elizabeth," he said, his eyes on hers. "I have always thought—I can't go to David now."

He was moved to go on. To tell her of his lost youth, of that strange trick by which his mind had shut off those hidden years. But he could not. He had a perfectly human fear of being abnormal in her eyes, precisely but greatly magnified the same instinct which had made him inspect his new tie in daylight for fear it was too brilliant. But greater than that was his new fear that something neither happy nor right lay behind him under lock and key in his memory.

"I want you to know this, Dick," she said. "That nothing, no gossip or anything, can make any difference to me. And I've been terribly hurt. We've been such friends. You—I've been lying awake at night, worrying."

That went to his heart first, and then to his head. This might be all, all he was ever to have. This hour, and this precious and tender child, so brave in her declaration, so simple and direct; all his world in that imitation mahogany chair.

"You're all I've got," he said. "The one real thing in a world that's going to smash. I think I love you more than God."

The same mood, of accepting what he had without question and of refusing to look ahead, actuated him for the next few days. He was incredibly happy.

He went about his work with his customary care and thoroughness, for long practice had made it possible for him to go on as though nothing had happened, to listen to querulous complaints and long lists of symptoms, and to write without error those scrawled prescriptions which were, so hopefully, to cure. Not that Dick himself believed greatly in those empirical doses, but he considered that the expectation of relief was half the battle. But that was the mind of him, which went about clothed in flesh, of course, and did its daily and nightly work, and put up a very fair imitation of Doctor Richard Livingstone. But hidden away was a heart that behaved in a highly unprofessional manner, and sang and dreamed, and jumped at the sight of a certain small figure on the street, and generally played hob with systole and diastole, and the vagus and accelerator nerves. Which are all any doctor really knows about the heart, until he falls in love.

He even began to wonder if he had read into the situation something that was not there, and in this his consciousness of David's essential rectitude helped him. David could not do a wrong thing, or an unworthy one. He wished he were more like David.

The new humility extended to his love for Elizabeth. Sometimes, in his room or shaving before the bathroom mirror, he wondered what she could see in him to care about. He shaved twice a day now, and his face was so sore that he had to put cream on it at night, to his secret humiliation. When he was dressed in the morning he found himself once or twice taking a final survey of the ensemble, and at those times he wished very earnestly that he had some outstanding quality of appearance that she might admire.

He refused to think. He was content for a time simply to feel, to be supremely happy, to live each day as it came and not to look ahead. And the old house seemed to brighten with him. Never had Lucy's window boxes been so bright, or Minnie's bread so light; the sun poured into David's sick room and turned the nurse so dazzling white in her uniform that David declared he was suffering from snow-blindness.

And David himself was improving rapidly. With the passage of each day he felt more secure. The reporter from the Times-Republican—if he were really on the trail of Dick he would have come to see him, would have told him the story. No. That bridge was safely crossed. And Dick was happy. David, lying in his bed, would listen and smile faintly when Dick came whistling into the house or leaped up the stairs two at a time; when he sang in his shower, or tormented the nurse with high-spirited nonsense. The boy was very happy. He would marry Elizabeth Wheeler, and things would be as they should be; there would be the fullness of life, young voices in the house, toys on the lawn. He himself would pass on, in the fullness of time, but Dick—

On Decoration Day they got him out of bed, making a great ceremony of it, and when he was settled by the window in his big chair with a blanket over his knees, Dick came in with a great box. Unwrapping it he disclosed a mass of paper and a small box, and within that still another.

"What fol-de-rol is all this?" David demanded fiercely, with a childish look of expectation in his eyes. "Give me that box. Some more slippers, probably!"

He worked eagerly, and at last he came to the small core of the mass. It was a cigar!

It was somewhat later, when the peace of good tobacco had relaxed him into a sort of benignant drowsiness, and when Dick had started for his late afternoon calls, that Lucy came into the room.

"Elizabeth Wheeler's downstairs," she said. "I told her you wanted to see her. She's brought some chicken jelly, too."

She gathered up the tissue paper that surrounded him, and gave the room a critical survey. She often felt that the nurse was not as tidy as she might be. Then she went over to him and put a hand on his shoulder.

"I don't want to worry you, David. Not now. But if he's going to marry her—"

"Well, why shouldn't he?" he demanded truculently. "A good woman would be one more anchor to windward."

She found that she could not go on. David was always incomprehensible to her when it came to Dick. Had been incomprehensible from the first. But she could not proceed without telling him that the village knew something, and what that something was; that already she felt a change in the local attitude toward Dick. He was, for one thing, not quite so busy as he had been.

She went out of the room, and sent Elizabeth to David.

In her love for Dick, Elizabeth now included everything that pertained to him, his shabby coats, his rattling car, and his people. She had an inarticulate desire for their endorsement, to be liked by them and wanted by them. Not that there could be any words, because both she and Dick were content just then with love, and were holding it very secret between them.

"Well, well!" said David. "And here we are reversed and I'm the patient and you're the doctor! And good medicine you are, my dear."

He looked her over with approval, and with speculation, too. She was a small and fragile vessel on which to embark all the hopes that, out of his own celibate and unfulfilled life, he had dreamed for Dick. She was even more than that. If Lucy was right, from now on she was a part of that experiment in a human soul which he had begun with only a professional interest, but which had ended by becoming a vital part of his own life.

She was a little shy with him, he saw; rather fluttered and nervous, yet radiantly happy. The combination of these mixed emotions, plus her best sick-room manner, made her slightly prim at first. But soon she was telling him the small news of the village, although David rather suspected her of listening for Dick's car all the while. When she got up to go and held out her hand he kept it, between both of his.

"I haven't been studying symptoms for all these years for nothing, my dear," he said. "And it seems to me somebody is very happy."

"I am, Doctor David."

He patted her hand.

"Mind you," he said, "I don't know anything and I'm not asking any questions. But if the Board of Trade, or the Chief of Police, had come to me and said, 'Who is the best wife for— well, for a young man who is an important part of this community?' I'd have said in reply, 'Gentlemen, there is a Miss Elizabeth Wheeler who—'"

Suddenly she bent down and kissed him.

"Oh, do you think so?" she asked, breathlessly. "I love him so much, Doctor David. And I feel so unworthy."

"So you are," he said. "So's he. So are all of us, when it comes to a great love, child. That is, we are never quite what the other fellow thinks we are. It's when we don't allow for what the scientist folk call a margin of error that we come our croppers. I wonder"—he watched her closely—"if you young people ever allow for a margin of error?"

"I only know this," she said steadily. "I can't imagine ever caring any less. I've never thought about myself very much, but I do know that. You see, I think I've cared for a long time."

When she had gone he sat in his chair staring ahead of him and thinking. Yes. She would stick. She had loyalty, loyalty and patience and a rare humility. It was up to Dick then. And again he faced the possibility of an opening door into the past, of crowding memories, of confusion and despair and even actual danger. And out of that, what?

Habit. That was all he had to depend on. The brain was a thing of habits, like the body; right could be a habit, and so could evil. As a man thought, so he was. For all of his childhood, and for the last ten years, Dick's mental habits had been right; his environment had been love, his teaching responsibility. Even if the door opened, then, there was only the evil thinking of two or three reckless years to combat, and the door might never open. Happiness, Lauler had said, would keep it closed, and Dick was happy.

When at five o'clock the nurse came in with a thermometer he was asleep in his chair, his mouth slightly open, and snoring valiantly. Hearing Dick in the lower hall, she went to the head of the stairs, her finger to her lips.

Dick nodded and went into the office. The afternoon mail was lying there, and he began mechanically to open it. His thoughts were elsewhere.

Now that he had taken the step he had so firmly determined not to take, certain things, such as Clare Rossiter's story, David's uneasiness, his own doubts, no longer involved himself alone, nor even Elizabeth and himself. They had become of vital importance to her family.

There was no evading the issue. What had once been only his own misfortune, mischance, whatever it was, had now become of vital importance to an entire group of hitherto disinterested people. He would have to put his situation clearly before them and let them judge. And he would have to clarify that situation for them and for himself.

He had had a weak moment or two. He knew that some men, many men, went to marriage with certain reticences, meaning to wipe the slate clean and begin again. He had a man's understanding of such concealments. But he did not for a moment compare his situation with theirs, even when the temptation to seize his happiness was strongest. No mere misconduct, but something hidden and perhaps terrible lay behind David's strange new attitude. Lay, too, behind the break in his memory which he tried to analyze with professional detachment. The mind in such cases set up its defensive machinery of forgetfulness, not against the trivial but against the unbearable.

For the last day or two he had faced the fact that, not only must he use every endeavor to revive his past, but that such revival threatened with cruelty and finality to separate him from the present.

With an open and unread letter in his hand he stared about the office. This place was his; he had fought for it, worked for it. He had an almost physical sense of unseen hands reaching out to drag him away from it; from David and Lucy, and from Elizabeth. And of himself holding desperately to them all, and to the believed commonplaceness of his surroundings.

He shook himself and began to read the letter.

"Dear Doctor: I have tried to see you, but understand you are laid up. Burn this as soon as you've read it. Louis Bassett has started for Norada, and I advise your getting the person we discussed out of town as soon as possible. Bassett is up to mischief. I'm not signing this fully, for obvious reasons. G."

XVII

The Sayre house stood on the hill behind the town, a long, rather low white house on Italian lines. In summer, until the family exodus to the Maine Coast, the brilliant canopy which extended out over the terrace indicated, as Harrison Miller put it, that the family was "in residence." Originally designed as a summer home, Mrs. Sayre now used it the year round. There was nothing there, as there was in the town house, to remind her of the bitter days before her widowhood.

She was a short, heavy woman, of fine taste in her house and of no taste whatever in her clothing.

"I never know," said Harrison Miller, "when I look up at the Sayre place, whether I'm seeing Ann Sayre or an awning."

She was not a shrewd woman, nor a clever one, but she was kindly in the main, tolerant and maternal. She liked young people, gave gay little parties to which she wore her outlandish clothes of all colors and all cuts, lavished gifts on the girls she liked, and was anxious to see Wallie married to a good steady girl and settled down. Between her son and herself was a quiet but undemonstrative affection. She viewed him through eyes that had lost their illusion about all men years ago, and she had no delusions about him. She had no idea that she knew all that he did with his time, and no desire to penetrate the veil of his private life.

"He spends a great deal of money," she said one day to her lawyer. "I suppose in the usual ways. But he is not quite like his father. He has real affections, which his father hadn't. If he marries the right girl she can make him almost anything."

She had her first inkling that he was interested in Elizabeth Wheeler one day when the head gardener reported that Mr. Wallace had ordered certain roses cut and sent to the Wheeler house. She was angry at first, for the roses were being saved for a dinner party. Then she considered.

"Very well, Phelps," she said. "Do it. And I'll select a plant also, to go to Mrs. Wheeler."

After all, why not the Wheeler girl? She had been carefully reared, if the Wheeler house was rather awful in spots, and she was a gentle little thing; very attractive, too, especially in church. And certainly Wallie had been seeing a great deal of her.

She went to the greenhouses, and from there upstairs and into the rooms that she had planned for Wallie and his bride, when the time came. She was more content than she had been for a long time. She was a lonely woman, isolated by her very grandeur from the neighborliness she craved; when she wanted society she had to ask for it, by invitation. Standing inside the door of the boudoir, her thoughts already at work on draperies and furniture, she had a vague dream of new young life stirring in the big house, of no more lonely evenings, of the bustle and activity of a family again.

She wanted Wallie to settle down. She was tired of paying his bills at his clubs and at various hotels, tired and weary of the days he lay in bed all morning while his valet concocted various things to enable him to pull himself together. He had been four years sowing his wild oats, and now at twenty-five she felt he should be through with them.

The south room could be the nursery.

On Decoration Day, as usual, she did her dutiful best by the community, sent flowers to the cemetery and even stood through a chilly hour there while services were read and taps sounded over the graves of those who had died in three wars. She felt very grateful that Wallie had come back safely, and that if only now he would marry and settle down all would be well.

The service left her emotionally untouched. She was one of those women who saw in war, politics, even religion, only their reaction on herself and her affairs. She had taken the German deluge as a personal affliction. And she stood only stoically enduring while the village soprano sang "The Star Spangled Banner." By the end of the service she had decided that Elizabeth Wheeler was the answer to her problem.

Rather under pressure, Wallie lunched with her at the country club, but she found him evasive and not particularly happy.

"You're twenty-five, you know," she said, toward the end of a discussion. "By thirty you'll be too set in your habits, too hard to please."

"I'm not going to marry for the sake of getting married, mother."

"Of course not. But you have a good bit of money. You'll have much more when I'm gone. And money carries responsibility with it."

He glanced at her, looked away, rapped a fork on the table cloth.

"It takes two to make a marriage, mother."

He closed up after that, but she had learned what she wanted.

At three o'clock that afternoon the Sayre limousine stopped in front of Nina's house, and Mrs. Sayre, in brilliant pink and a purple hat, got out. Leslie, lounging in a window, made the announcement.

"Here's the Queen of Sheba," he said. "I'll go upstairs and have a headache, if you don't mind."

He kissed Nina and departed hastily. He was feeling extremely gentle toward Nina those days and rather smugly virtuous. He considered that his conscience had brought him back and not a very bad fright, which was the fact, and he fairly exuded righteousness.

It was the great lady's first call, and Nina was considerably uplifted. It was for such moments as this one trained servants and put Irish lace on their aprons, and had decorators who stood off with their heads a little awry and devised backgrounds for one's personality.

"What a delightful room!" said Mrs. Sayre. "And how do you keep a maid as trim as that?"

"I must have service," Nina replied. "The butler's marching in a parade or something. How nice of you to come and see our little place. It's a band-box, of course."

Mrs. Sayre sat down, a gross disharmony in the room, but a solid and not unkindly woman for all that.

"My dear," she said, "I am not paying a call. Or not only that. I came to talk to you about something. About Wallace and your sister."

Nina was gratified and not a little triumphant.

"I see," she said. "Do you mean that they are fond of one another?"

"Wallace is. Of course, this talk is between ourselves, but—I'm going to be frank, Nina. I want Wallie to marry, and I want him to marry soon. You and I know that the life of an unattached man about town is full of temptations. I want him to settle down. I'm lonely, too, but that's not so important."

Nina hesitated.

"I don't know about Elizabeth. She's fond of Wallie, as who isn't? But lately—"

"Yes?"

"Well, for the last few days I have been wondering. She doesn't talk, you know. But she has been seeing something of Dick Livingstone."

"Doctor Livingstone! She'd be throwing herself away!"

"Yes, but she's like that. I mean, she isn't ambitious. We've always expected her to throw herself away; at least I have."

A half hour later Leslie, upstairs, leaned over the railing to see if there were any indications of departure. The door was open, and Mrs. Sayre evidently about to take her leave. She was saying:

"It's very close to my heart, Nina dear, and I know you will be tactful. I haven't stressed the material advantages, but you might point them out to her."

A few moments later Leslie came downstairs. Nina was sitting alone, thinking, with a not entirely pleasant look of calculation on her face.

"Well?" he said. "What were you two plotting?"

"Plotting? Nothing, of course."

He looked down at her. "Now see here, old girl," he said, "you keep your hands off Elizabeth's affairs. If I know anything she's making a damn good choice, and don't you forget it."

XVIII

Dick stood with the letter in his hand, staring at it. Who was Bassett? Who was "G"? What had the departure of whoever Bassett might be for Norada to do with David? And who was the person who was to be got out of town?

He did not go upstairs. He took the letter into his private office, closed the door, and sitting down at his desk turned his reading lamp on it, as though that physical act might bring some mental light.

Reread, the cryptic sentences began to take on meaning. An unknown named Bassett, whoever he might be, was going to Norada bent on "mischief," and another unknown who signed himself "G" was warning David of that fact. But the mischief was designed, not against David, but against a third unknown, some one who was to be got out of town.

David had been trying to get him out of town.—The warning referred to himself.

His first impulse was to go to David, and months later he was to wonder what would have happened had he done so. How far could Bassett have gone? What would have been his own decision when he learned the truth?

For a little while, then, the shuttle was in Dick's own hand. He went up to David's room, and with his hand on the letter in his pocket, carried on behind his casual talk the debate that was so vital. But David had a headache and a slightly faster pulse, and that portion of the pattern was never woven.

The association between anxiety and David's illness had always been apparent in Dick's mind, but now he began to surmise a concrete shock, a person, a telegram, or a telephone call. And after dinner that night he went back to the kitchen.

"Minnie," he inquired, "do you remember the afternoon Doctor David was taken sick?"

"I'll never forget it."

"Did he receive a telegram that day?"

"Not that I know of. He often answers the bell himself."

"Do you know whether he had a visitor, just before you heard him fall?"

"He had a patient, yes. A man."

"Who was it?"

"I don't know. He was a stranger to me."

"Do you remember what he looked like?"

Minnie reflected.

"He was a smallish man, maybe thirty-five or so," she said. "I think he had gaiters over his shoes, or maybe light tops. He was a nice appearing person."

"How soon after that did you hear Doctor David fall?"

"Right away. First the door slammed, and then he dropped."

Poor old David! Dick had not the slightest doubt now that David had received some unfortunate news, and that up there in his bedroom ever since, alone and helpless, he had been struggling with some secret dread he could not share with any one. Not even with Lucy, probably.

Nevertheless, Dick made a try with Lucy that evening.

"Aunt Lucy," he said, "do you know of anything that could have caused David's collapse?"

"What sort of thing?" she asked guardedly.

"A letter, we'll say, or a visitor?"

When he saw that she was only puzzled and thinking back, he knew she could not help him.

"Never mind," he said. "I was feeling about for some cause. That's all."

He was satisfied that Lucy knew no more than he did of David's visitor, and that David had kept his own counsel ever since. But the sense of impending disaster that had come with the letter did not leave him. He went through his evening office hours almost mechanically, with a part of his mind busy on the puzzle. How did it affect the course of action he had marked out? Wasn't it even more necessary than ever now to go to Walter Wheeler and tell him how things stood? He hated mystery. He liked to walk in the middle of the road in the sunlight. But even stronger than that was a growing feeling that he needed a sane and normal judgment on his situation; a fresh viewpoint and some unprejudiced advice.

He visited David before he left, and he was very gentle with him. In view of this new development he saw David from a different angle, facing and dreading something imminent, and it came to him with a shock that he might have to clear things up to save David. The burden, whatever it was, was breaking him.

He had telephoned, and Mr. Wheeler was waiting for him. Walter Wheeler thought he knew what was coming, and he had well in mind what he was going to say. He had thought it over, pacing the floor alone, with the dog at his heels. He would say:

"I like and respect you, Livingstone. If you're worrying about what these damned gossips say, let's call it a day and forget it. I know a man when I see one, and if it's all right with Elizabeth it's all right with me."

Things, however, did not turn out just that way. Dick came in, grave and clearly preoccupied, and the first thing he said was:

"I have a story to tell you, Mr. Wheeler. After you've heard it, and given me your opinion on it, I'll come to a matter that—well, that I can't talk about now."

"If it's the silly talk that I daresay you've heard—"

"No. I don't give a damn for talk. But there is something else. Something I haven't told Elizabeth, and that I'll have to tell you."

Walter Wheeler drew himself up rather stiffly. Leslie's defection was still in his mind.

"Don't tell me you're tangled up with another woman."

"No. At least I think not. I don't know."

It is doubtful if Walter Wheeler grasped many of the technicalities that followed. Dick talked and he listened, nodding now and then, and endeavoring very hard to get the gist of the matter. It seemed to him curious rather than serious. Certainly the mind was a strange thing. He must read up on it. Now and then he stopped Dick with a question, and Dick would break in on his narrative to reply. Thus, once:

"You've said nothing to Elizabeth at all? About the walling off, as you call it?"

"No. At first I was simply ashamed of it. I didn't want her to get the idea that I wasn't normal."

"I see."

"Now, as I tell you, I begin to think—I've told you that this walling off is an unconscious desire to forget something too painful to remember. It's practically always that. I can't go to her with just that, can I? I've got to know first what it is."

"I'd begun to think there was an understanding between you."

Dick faced him squarely.

"There is. I didn't intend it. In fact, I was trying to keep away from her. I didn't mean to speak to her until I'd cleared things up. But it happened anyhow; I suppose the way those things always happen."

It was Walter Wheeler's own decision, finally, that he go to Norada with Dick as soon as David could be safely left. It was the letter which influenced him. Up to that he had viewed the situation with a certain detachment; now he saw that it threatened the peace of two households.

"It's a warning, all right."

"Yes. Undoubtedly."

"You don't recognize the name Bassett?"

"No. I've tried, of course."

The result of some indecision was finally that Elizabeth should not be told anything until they were ready to tell it all. And in the end a certain resentment that she had become involved in an unhappy situation died in Walter Wheeler before Dick's white face and sunken eyes.

At ten o'clock the house-door opened and closed, and Walter Wheeler got up and went out into the hall.

"Go on upstairs, Margaret," he said to his wife. "I've got a visitor." He did not look at Elizabeth. "You settle down and be comfortable," he added, "and I'll be up before long. Where's Jim?"

"I don't know. He didn't go to Nina's."

"He started with you, didn't he?"

"Yes. But he left us at the corner."

They exchanged glances. Jim had been worrying them lately. Strange how a man could go along for years, his only worries those of business, his track a single one through comfortable fields where he reaped only what he sowed. And then his family grew up, and involved him without warning in new perplexities and new troubles. Nina first, then Jim, and now this strange story which so inevitably involved Elizabeth.

He put his arm around his wife and held her to him.

"Don't worry about Jim, mother," he said. "He's all right fundamentally. He's going through the bad time between being a boy and being a man. He's a good boy."

He watched her moving up the stairs, his eyes tender and solicitous. To him she was just "mother." He had never thought of another woman in all their twenty-four years together.

Elizabeth waited near him, her eyes on his face.

"Is it Dick?" she asked in a low tone.

"Yes."

"You don't mind, daddy, do you?"

"I only want you to be happy," he said rather hoarsely. "You know that, don't you?"

She nodded, and turned up her face to be kissed. He knew that she had no doubt whatever that this interview was to seal her to Dick Livingstone for ever and ever. She fairly radiated happiness and confidence. He left her standing there going back to the living-room closed the door.

XIX

Louis Bassett, when he started to the old Livingstone ranch, now the Wasson place, was carefully turning over in his mind David's participation in the escape of Judson Clark. Certain phases of it were quite clear, provided one accepted the fact that, following a heavy snowfall, an Easterner and a tenderfoot had gone into the mountains alone, under conditions which had caused the posse after Judson Clark to turn back and give him up for dead.

Had Donaldson sent him there, knowing he was a medical man? If he had, would Maggie Donaldson not have said so? She had said "a man outside that she had at first thought was a member of the searching party." Evidently, then, Donaldson had not prepared her to expect medical assistance.

Take the other angle. Say David Livingstone had not been sent for. Say he knew nothing of the cabin or its occupants until he stumbled on them. He had sold the ranch, distributed his brother's books, and apparently the townspeople at Dry River believed that he had gone back home. Then what had taken him, clearly alone and having certainly given the impression of a departure for the East, into the mountains? To hunt? To hunt what, that he went about it secretly and alone?

Bassett was inclined to the Donaldson theory, finally. John Donaldson would have been wanting a doctor, and not wanting one from Norada. He might have heard of this Eastern medical man at Dry River, have gone to him with his story, even have taken him part of the way. The situation was one that would have a certain appeal. It was possible, anyhow:

But instead of clarifying the situation Bassett's visit at the Wasson place brought forward new elements which fitted neither of the hypotheses in his mind.

To Wasson himself, whom he met on horseback on the road into the ranch, he gave the same explanation he had given to the store-keeper's wife. Wasson was a tall man in chaps and a Stetson, and he was courteously interested.

"Bill and Jake are still here," he said. "They're probably in for dinner now, and I'll see you get a chance to talk to them. I took them over with the ranch. Property, you say? Well, I hope it's better land than he had here."

He turned his horse and rode beside the car to the house.

"Comes a little late to do Henry Livingstone much good," he said. "He's been lying in the Dry River graveyard for about ten years. Not much mourned either. He was about as close-mouthed and uncompanionable as they make them."

The description Wasson had applied to Henry Livingstone, Bassett himself applied to the two ranch hands later on, during their interview. It could hardly have been called an interview at all, indeed, and after a time Bassett realized that behind their taciturnity was suspicion. They were watching him, undoubtedly; he rather thought, when he looked away, that once or twice they exchanged glances. He was certain, too, that Wasson himself was puzzled.

"Speak up, Jake," he said once, irritably. "This gentleman has come a long way. It's a matter of some property."

"What sort of property?" Jake demanded. Jake was the spokesman of the two.

"That's not important," Bassett observed, easily. "What we want to know is if Henry Livingstone had any family."

"He had a brother."

"No one else?"

"Then it's up to me to trail the brother," Bassett observed. "Either of you remember where he lived?"

"Somewhere in the East."

Bassett laughed.

"That's a trifle vague," he commented good-humoredly. "Didn't you boys ever mail any letters for him?"

191

He was certain again that they exchanged glances, but they continued to present an unbroken front of ignorance. Wasson was divided between irritation and amusement.

"What'd I tell you?" he asked. "Like master like man. I've been here ten years, and I've never got a word about the Livingstones out of either of them."

"I'm a patient man." Bassett grinned. "I suppose you'll admit that one of you drove David Livingstone to the train, and that you had a fair idea then of where he was going?"

He looked directly at Jake, but Jake's face was a solid mask. He made no reply whatever.

From that moment on Bassett was certain that David had not been driven away from the ranch at all. What he did not know, and was in no way to find out, was whether the two ranch hands knew that he had gone into the mountains, or why. He surmised back of their taciturnity a small mystery of their own, and perhaps a fear. Possibly David's going was as much a puzzle to them as to him. Conceivably, during the hours together on the range, or during the winter snows, for ten years they had wrangled and argued over a disappearance as mysterious in its way as Judson Clark's.

He gave up at last, having learned certain unimportant facts: that the recluse had led a lonely life; that he had never tried to make the place more than carry itself; that he was a student, and that he had no other peculiarities.

"Did he ever say anything that would lead you to believe that he had any family, outside of his brother and sister? That is, any direct heir?" Bassett asked.

"He never talked about himself," said Jake. "If that's all, Mr. Wasson, I've got a steer bogged down in the north pasture and I'll be going."

On the Wassons' invitation he remained to lunch, and when the ranch owner excused himself and rode away after the meal he sat for some time on the verandah, with Mrs. Wasson sewing and his own eyes fixed speculatively on the mountain range, close, bleak and mysterious.

"Strange thing," he commented. "Here's a man, a book-lover and student, who comes out here, not to make living and be a useful member of the community, but apparently to bury himself alive. I wonder, why."

"A great many come out here to get away from something, Mr. Bassett."

"Yes, to start again. But this man never started again. He apparently just quit."

Mrs. Wasson put down her sewing and looked at him thoughtfully.

"Did the boys tell you anything about the young man who visited Henry Livingstone now and then?"

"No. They were not very communicative."

"I suppose they wouldn't tell. Yet I don't see, unless—" She stopped, lost in some field of speculation where he could not follow her. "You know, we haven't much excitement here, and when this boy was first seen around the place—he was here mostly in the summer—we decided that he was a relative. I don't know why we considered him mysterious, unless it was because he was hardly ever seen. I don't even know that that was deliberate. For that matter Mr. Livingstone wasn't much more than a name to us."

"You mean, a son?"

"Nobody knew. He was here only now and then."

Bassett moved in his chair and looked at her.

"How old do you suppose this boy was?" he asked.

"He was here at different times. When Mr. Livingstone died I suppose he was in his twenties. The thing that makes it seem odd to me is that the men didn't mention him to you."

"I didn't ask about him, of course."

She went on with her sewing, apparently intending to drop the matter; but the reporter felt that now and then she was subjecting him to a sharp scrutiny, and that, in some shrewd woman-fashion, she was trying to place him.

"You said it was a matter of some property?"

"Yes."

"But it's rather late, isn't it? Ten years?"

"That's what makes it difficult."

There was another silence, during which she evidently made her decision.

"I have never said this before, except to Mr. Wasson. But I believe he was here when Henry Livingstone died."

Her tone was mysterious, and Bassett stared at her.

"You don't think Livingstone was murdered!"

"No. He died of heart failure. There was an autopsy. But he had a bad cut on his head. Of course, he may have fallen—Bill and Jake were away. They'd driven some cattle out on the range. It was two days before he was found, and it would have been longer if Mr. Wasson hadn't ridden out to talk to him about buying. He found him dead in his bed, but there was blood on the floor in the next room. I washed it up myself."

"Of course," she added, when Bassett maintained a puzzled silence, "I may be all wrong. He might have fallen in the next room and dragged himself to bed. But he was very neatly covered up."

"It's your idea, then, that this boy put him into the bed?"

"I don't know. He wasn't seen about the place. He's never been here since. But the posse found a horse with the Livingstone brand, saddled, dead in Dry River Canyon when it was looking for Judson Clark. Of course, that was a month later. The men here, Bill and Jake, claimed it had wandered off, but I've often wondered."

After a time Bassett got up and took his leave. He was confused and irritated. Here, whether creditably or not, was Dick Livingstone accounted for. There was a story there, probably, but not the story he was after. This unknown had been at the ranch when Henry Livingstone died, had perhaps been indirectly responsible for his death. He had, witness the horse, fled after the thing happened. Later on, then, David Livingstone had taken him into his family. That was all.

Except for that identification of Gregory's, and for the photograph of Judson Clark.... For a moment he wondered if the two, Jud Clark and the unknown, could be the same. But Dry River would have known Clark. That couldn't be.

He almost ditched the car on his way back to Norada, so deeply was he engrossed in thought.

XX

On the seventh of June David and Lucy went to the seashore, went by the order of various professional gentlemen who had differed violently during the course of David's illness, but who now suddenly agreed with an almost startling unanimity. Which unanimity was the result of careful coaching by Dick.

He saw in David's absence his only possible chance to go back to Norada without worry to the sick man, and he felt, too, that a change, getting away from the surcharged atmosphere of the old house, would be good for both David and Lucy.

For days before they started Lucy went about in a frenzy of nervous energy, writing out menus for Minnie for a month ahead, counting and recounting David's collars and handkerchiefs, cleaning and pressing his neckties. In the harness room in the stable Mike polished boots until his arms ached, and at the last moment with trunks already bulging, came three gift dressing-gowns for David, none of which he would leave behind.

"I declare," Lucy protested to Dick, "I don't know what's come over him. Every present he's had since he was sick he's taking along. You'd think he was going to be shut up on a desert island."

But Dick thought he understood. In David's life his friends had had to take the place of wife and children; he clung to them now, in his age and weakness, and Dick knew that he had a sense of deserting them, of abandoning them after many faithful years.

So David carried with him the calendars and slippers, dressing-gowns and bed-socks which were at once the tangible evidence of their friendliness and Lucy's despair.

Watching him, Dick was certain nothing further had come to threaten his recovery. Dick carefully inspected the mail, but no suspicious letter had arrived, and as the days went on David's peace seemed finally re-established. He made no more references to Johns Hopkins, slept like a child, and railed almost pettishly at his restricted diet.

"When we get away from Dick, Lucy," he would say, "we'll have beef again, and roast pork and sausage."

Lucy would smile absently and shake her head.

"You'll stick to your diet, David," she would say. "David, it's the strangest thing about your winter underwear. I'm sure you had five suits, and now there are only three."

Or it was socks she missed, or night-clothing. And David, inwardly chuckling, would wonder with her, knowing all the while that they had clothed some needy body.

On the night before the departure David went out for his first short walk alone, and brought Elizabeth back with him.

"I found a rose walking up the street, Lucy," he bellowed up the stairs, "and I brought it home for the dinner table."

Lucy came down, flushed from her final effort over the trunks, but gently hospitable.

"It's fish night, Elizabeth," she said. "You know Minnie's a Catholic, so we always have fish on Friday. I hope you eat it." She put her hand on Elizabeth's arm and gently patted it, and thus was Elizabeth taken into the old brick house as one of its own.

Elizabeth was finding this period of her tacit engagement rather puzzling. Her people puzzled her. Even Dick did, at times. And nobody seemed anxious to make plans for the future, or even to discuss the wedding. She was a little hurt about that, remembering the excitement over Nina's.

But what chiefly bewildered her was the seeming necessity for secrecy. Even Nina had not been told, nor Jim. She did not resent that, although it bewildered her. Her own inclination was to shout it from the house-tops. Her father had simply said: "I've told your mother, honey, and we'd better let it go at that, for a while. There's no hurry. And I don't want to lose you yet."

But there were other things. Dick himself varied. He was always gentle and very tender, but there were times when he seemed to hold himself away from her, would seem aloof and remote, but all the time watching her almost fiercely. But after that, as though he had tried an experiment in separation and failed with it, he would catch her to him savagely and hold her there. She tried, very meekly, to meet his mood; was submissive to his passion and acquiescent to those intervals when he withdrew himself and sat or stood near her, not touching her but watching her intently.

She thought men in love were very queer and quite incomprehensible. Because he varied in other ways, too. He was boyish and gay sometimes, and again silent and almost brooding. She thought at those times that perhaps he was tired, what with David's work and his own, and sometimes she wondered if he were still worrying about that silly story. But once or twice, after he had gone, she went upstairs and looked carefully into her mirror. Perhaps she had not looked her best that day. Girl-like, she set great value on looks in love. She wanted frightfully to be beautiful to him. She wished she could look like Beverly Carlysle, for instance.

Two days before David and Lucy's departure he had brought her her engagement ring, a square-cut diamond set in platinum. He kissed it first and then her finger, and slipped it into place. It became a rite, done as he did it, and she had a sense of something done that could never be undone. When she looked up at him he was very pale.

"Forsaking all others, so long as we both shall live," he said, unsteadily.

"So long as we both shall live," she repeated.

However she had to take it off later, for Mrs. Wheeler, it developed, had very pronounced ideas of engagement rings. They were put on the day the notices were sent to the newspapers, and not before. So Elizabeth wore her ring around her neck on a white ribbon, inside her camisole, until such time as her father would consent to announce that he was about to lose her.

Thus Elizabeth found her engagement full of unexpected turns and twists, and nothing precisely as she had expected. But she accepted things as they came, being of the type around which the dramas of life are enacted, while remaining totally undramatic herself. She lived her quiet days, worried about Jim on occasion, hemmed table napkins for her linen chest, and slept at night with her ring on her finger and a sense of being wrapped in protecting love that was no longer limited to the white Wheeler house, but now extended two blocks away and around the corner to a shabby old brick building in a more or less shabby yard.

They were very gay in the old brick house that night before the departure, very noisy over the fish and David's broiled lamb chop. Dick demanded a bottle of Lucy's home-made wine, and even David got a little of it. They toasted the seashore, and the departed nurse, and David quoted Robert Burns at some length and in a horrible Scotch accent. Then Dick had a trick by which one read the date on one of three pennies while he was not looking, and he could tell without failing which one it was. It was most mysterious. And after dinner Dick took her into his laboratory, and while she squinted one eye and looked into the finder of his microscope he kissed the white nape of her neck.

When they left the laboratory there were patients in the waiting-room, but he held her in his arms in the office for a moment or two, very quietly, and because the door was thin they made a sort of game of it, and pretended she was a patient.

"How did you sleep last night?" he said, in a highly professional and very distinct voice. Then he kissed her.

"Very badly, doctor," she said, also very clearly, and whispered, "I lay awake and thought about you, dear."

"I'd better give you this sleeping powder." Oh, frightfully professional, but the powder turned out to be another kiss. It was a wonderful game.

When she slipped out into the hall she had to stop and smooth her hair, before she went to Lucy's tidy sitting-room.

XXI

It was Jim Wheeler's turn to take up the shuttle. A girl met in some casual fashion; his own youth and the urge of it, perhaps the unconscious family indulgence of an only son—and Jim wove his bit and passed on.

There had been mild contention in the Wheeler family during all the spring. Looking out from his quiet windows Walter Wheeler saw the young world going by a-wheel, and going fast. Much that legitimately belonged to it, and much that did not in the laxness of the new code, he laid to the automobile. And doggedly he refused to buy one.

"We can always get a taxicab," was his imperturbable answer to Jim. "I pay pretty good-sized taxi bills without unpleasant discussion. I know you pretty well too, Jim. Better than you know yourself. And if you had a car, you'd try your best to break your neck in it."

Now and then Jim got a car, however. Sometimes he rented one, sometimes he cajoled Nina into lending him hers.

"A fellow looks a fool without one," he would say to her. "Girls expect to be taken out. It's part of the game."

And Nina, always reached by that argument of how things looked, now and then reluctantly acquiesced. But a night or two after David and Lucy had started for the seashore Nina came in like a whirlwind, and routed the family peace immediately.

"Father," she said, "you just must speak to Jim. He's taken our car twice at night without asking for it, and last night he broke a spring. Les is simply crazy."

"Taken your car!" Mrs. Wheeler exclaimed.

"Yes. I hate telling on him, but I spoke to him after the first time, and he did it anyhow."

Mrs. Wheeler glanced at her husband uneasily. She often felt he was too severe with Jim.

"Don't worry," he said grimly. "He'll not do it again."

"If we only had a car of our own—" Mrs. Wheeler protested.

"You know what I think about that, mother. I'm not going to have him joy-riding over the country, breaking his neck and getting into trouble. I've seen him driving Wallace Sayre's car, and he drives like a fool or a madman."

It was an old dispute and a bitter one. Mr. Wheeler got up, whistled for the dog, and went out. His wife turned on Nina.

"I wish you wouldn't bring these things to your father, Nina," she said. "He's been very nervous lately, and he isn't always fair to Jim."

"Well, it's time Jim was fair to Leslie," Nina said, with family frankness. "I'll tell you something, mother. Jim has a girl somewhere, in town probably. He takes her driving. I found a glove in the car. And he must be crazy about her, or he'd never do what he's done."

"Do you know who it is?"

"No. Somebody's he's ashamed of, probably, or he wouldn't be so clandestine about it."

"Nina!"

"Well, it looks like it. Jim's a man, mother. He's not a little boy. He'll go through his shady period, like the rest."

That night it was Mrs. Wheeler's turn to lie awake. Again and again she went over Nina's words, and her troubled mind found a basis in fact for them. Jim had been getting money from her, to supplement his small salary; he had been going out a great deal at night, and returning very late; once or twice, in the morning, he had looked ill and his eyes had been bloodshot, as though he had been drinking.

Anxiety gripped her. There were so many temptations for young men, so many who waited to waylay them. A girl. Not a good girl, perhaps.

She raised herself on her elbow and looked at her sleeping husband. Men were like that; they begot children and then forgot them. They never looked ahead or worried. They were taken up with business, and always they forgot that once they too had been young and liable to temptation.

She got up, some time later, and tiptoed to the door of Jim's room. Inside she could hear his heavy, regular breathing. Her boy. Her only son.

She went back and crawled carefully into the bed.

There was an acrimonious argument between Jim and his father the next morning, and Jim slammed out of the house, leaving chaos behind him. It was then that Elizabeth learned that her father was going away. He said:

"Maybe I'm wrong, mother. I don't know. Perhaps, when I come back, I'll look around for a car. I don't want him driven to doing underhand things."

"Are you going away?" Elizabeth asked, surprised.

It appeared that he was. More than that, that he was going West with Dick. It was all arranged and nobody had told her anything about it.

She was hurt and a trifle offended, and she cried a little about it. Yet, as Dick explained to her later that day, it was simple enough. Her father needed a rest, and besides, it was right that he should know all about Dick's life before he came to Haverly.

"He's going to make me a present of something highly valuable, you know."

"But it looks as though he didn't trust you!"

"He's being very polite about it; but, of course, in his eyes I'm a common thief, stealing—"

She would not let him go on.

A certain immaturity, the blind confidence of youth in those it loves, explains Elizabeth's docility at that time. But underneath her submission that day was a growing uneasiness, fiercely suppressed. Buried deep, the battle between absolute trust and fear was beginning, a battle which was so rapidly to mature her.

Nina, shrewd and suspicious, sensed something of nervous strain in her when she came in, later that day, to borrow a hat.

"Look here, Elizabeth," she began, "I want to talk to you. Are you going to live in this—this hole all your life?"

"Hole nothing," Elizabeth said, hotly. "Really, Nina, I do think you might be more careful of what you say."

"Oh, it's a dear old hole," Nina said negligently. "But hole it is, nevertheless. Why in the world mother don't manage her servants—but no matter about that now. Elizabeth, there's a lot of talk about you and Dick Livingstone, and it makes me furious. When I think that you can have Wallie Sayre by lifting your finger—"

"And that I don't intend to lift my finger," Elizabeth interrupted.

"Then you're a fool. And it is Dick Livingstone!"

"It is, Nina."

Nina's ambitious soul was harrowed.

"That stodgy old house," she said, "and two old people! A general house-work girl, and you cooking on her Thursdays out! I wish you joy of it."

"I wonder," Elizabeth said calmly, "whether it ever occurs to you that I may put love above houses and servants? Or that my life is my own, to live exactly as I please? Because that is what I intend to do."

Nina rose angrily.

"Thanks," she said. "I wish you joy of it." And went out, slamming the door behind her.

Then, with only a day or so remaining before Dick's departure, and Jim's hand already reaching for the shuttle, Elizabeth found herself the object of certain unmistakable advances from Mrs. Sayre herself, and that at a rose luncheon at the house on the hill.

The talk about Dick and Elizabeth had been slow in reaching the house on the hill. When it came, via a little group on the terrace after the luncheon, Mrs. Sayre was upset and angry and inclined to blame Wallie. Everything that he wanted had come to him, all his life, and he did not know how to go after things. He had sat by, and let this shabby-genteel doctor, years older than the girl, walk away with her.

Not that she gave up entirely. She knew the town, and its tendency toward over-statement. And so she made a desperate attempt, that afternoon, to tempt Elizabeth. She took her through the greenhouses, and then through the upper floors of the house. She showed her pictures of their boat at Miami, and of the house at Marblehead. Elizabeth was politely interested and completely unresponsive.

"When you think," Mrs. Sayre said at last, "that Wallie will have to assume a great many burdens one of these days, you can understand how anxious I am to have him marry the right sort of girl."

She thought Elizabeth flushed slightly.

"I am sure he will, Mrs. Sayre."

Mrs. Sayre tried a new direction.

"He will have all I have, my dear, and it is a great responsibility. Used properly, money can be an agent of great good. Wallie's wife can be a power, if she so chooses. She can look after the poor. I have a long list of pensioners, but I am too old to add personal service."

"That would be wonderful," Elizabeth said gravely. For a moment she wished Dick were rich. There was so much to be done with money, and how well he would know how to do it. She was thoughtful on the way downstairs, and Mrs. Sayre felt some small satisfaction. Now if Wallie would only do his part—

It was that night that Jim brought the tragedy on the Wheeler house that was to lie heavy on it for many a day.

There had been a little dinner, one of those small informal affairs where Mrs. Wheeler, having found in the market the first of the broiling chickens and some fine green peas, bought them first and then sat down to the telephone to invite her friends. Mr. Oglethorpe, the clergyman, and his wife accepted cheerfully; Harrison Miller, resignedly. Then Mrs. Wheeler drew a long, resolute breath and invited Mrs. Sayre. When that lady accepted with alacrity Mrs. Wheeler hastily revised her menu, telephoned the florist for flowers, and spent a long half-hour with Annie over plates and finger bowls.

Jim was not coming home, and Elizabeth was dining with Nina. Mrs. Wheeler bustled about the house contentedly. Everything was going well, after all. Before long there would be a car, and Jim would spend more time at home. Nina and Leslie were happy again. And Elizabeth— not a good match, perhaps, but a marriage for love, if ever there was one.

She sat at the foot of her table that night, rather too watchful of Annie, but supremely content. She had herself scoured the loving cup to the last degree of brightness and it stood, full of flowers, in the center of the cloth.

At Nina's was a smaller but similar group. All over the village at that time in the evening were similar groups, gathered around flowers and candles; neatly served, cheerful and undramatic groups, with the house doors closed and dogs waiting patiently outside in the long spring twilight.

Elizabeth was watching Nina. Just so, she was deciding, would she some day preside at her own board. Perhaps before so very long, too. A little separation, letters to watch for and answer, and then—

The telephone rang, and Leslie answered it. He did not come back; instead they heard the house door close, and soon after the rumble of the car as it left the garage. It stopped at the door, and Leslie came in.

"I'm sorry," he said, "but I guess Elizabeth will have to go home. You'd better come along, Nina."

"What is it? Is somebody sick?" Elizabeth gasped.

"Jim's been in an automobile accident. Steady now, Elizabeth! He's hurt, but he's going to be all right."

The Wheeler house, when they got there, was brightly lighted. Annie was crying in the hall, and in the living-room Mrs. Sayre stood alone, a strange figure in a gaudy dress, but with her face strong and calm.

"They've gone to the hospital in my car," she said. "They'll be there now any minute, and Mr. Oglethorpe will telephone at once. You are to wait before starting in."

They all knew what that meant. It might be too late to start in. Nina was crying hysterically, but Elizabeth could not cry. She stood dry-eyed by the telephone, listening to Mrs. Sayre and Leslie, but hardly hearing them. They had got Dick Livingstone and he had gone on in. Mrs. Sayre was afraid it had been one of Wallie's cars. She had begged Wallie to tell Jim to be careful in it. It had too much speed.

The telephone rang and Leslie took the receiver and pushed Elizabeth gently aside. He listened for a moment.

"Very well," he said. Then he hung up and stood still before he turned around:

"It isn't very good news," he said. "I wish I could—Elizabeth!"

Elizabeth had crumpled up in a small heap on the floor.

All through the long night that followed, with the movement of feet through the halls, with her mother's door closing and the ghastly silence that followed it, with the dawn that came through the windows, the dawn that to Jim meant not a new day, but a new life beyond their living touch, all through the night Elizabeth was aware of two figures that came and went. One was Dick, quiet, tender and watchful. And one was of a heavy woman in a gaudy dress, her face old and weary in the morning light, who tended her with gentle hands.

She fell asleep as the light was brightening in the East, with Dick holding her hands and kneeling on the floor beside her bed.

It was not until the next day that they knew that Jim had not been alone. A girl who was with him had been pinned under the car and had died instantly.

Jim had woven his bit in the pattern and passed on. The girl was negligible; she was, she had been. That was all. But Jim's death added the last element to the impending catastrophe. It sent Dick West alone.

XXII

For several days after his visit to the Livingstone ranch Louis Bassett made no move to go to the cabin. He wandered around the town, made promiscuous acquaintances and led up, in careful conversations with such older residents as he could find, to the Clark and Livingstone families. Of the latter he learned nothing; of the former not much that he had not known before.

One day he happened on a short, heavy-set man, the sheriff, who had lost his office on the strength of Jud Clark's escape, and had now recovered it. Bassett had brought some whisky with him, and on the promise of a drink lured Wilkins to his room. Over his glass the sheriff talked.

"All this newspaper stuff lately about Jud Clark being alive is dead wrong," he declared, irritably. "Maggie Donaldson was crazy. You can ask the people here about her. They all know it. Those newspaper fellows descended on us here with a tooth-brush apiece and a suitcase full of liquor, and thought they'd get something. Seemed to think we'd hold out on them unless we got our skins full. But there isn't anything to hold out. Jud Clark's dead. That's all."

"Sure he's dead," Bassett agreed, amiably. "You found his horse, didn't you?"

"Yes. Dead. And when you find a man's horse dead in the mountains in a blizzard, you don't need any more evidence. It was five months before you could see a trail up the Goat that winter."

Bassett nodded, rose and poured out another drink.

"I suppose," he observed casually, "that even if Clark turned up now, it would be hard to convict him, wouldn't it?"

The sheriff considered that, holding up his glass.

"Well, yes and no," he said. "It was circumstantial evidence, mostly. Nobody saw it done. The worst thing against him was his running off."

"How about witnesses?"

"Nobody actually saw it done. John Donaldson came the nearest, and he's dead. Lucas's wife was still alive, the last I heard, and I reckon the valet is floating around somewhere."

"I suppose if he did turn up you'd make a try for it." Bassett stared at the end of his cigar.

"We'd make a try for it, all right," Wilkins said somberly. "There are some folks in this county still giving me the laugh over that case."

The next day Bassett hired a quiet horse, rolled in his raincoat two days' supply of food, strapped it to the cantle of his saddle, and rode into the mountains. He had not ridden for years, and at the end of the first hour he began to realize that he was in for a bad time. By noon he was so sore that he could hardly get out of the saddle, and so stiff that once out, he could barely get back again. All morning the horse had climbed, twisting back and forth on a narrow canyon trail, grunting occasionally, as is the way of a horse on a steep grade. All morning they had followed a roaring mountain stream, descending in small cataracts from the ice fields far above. And all morning Bassett had been mentally following that trail as it had been ridden ten years ago by a boy maddened with fear and drink, who drove his horse forward through the night and the blizzard, with no objective and no hope.

He found it practically impossible to connect this frenzied fugitive with the quiet man in his office chair at Haverly, the man who was or was not Judson Clark. He lay on a bank at noon and faced the situation squarely, while his horse, hobbled, grazed with grotesque little forward jumps in an upland meadow. Either Dick Livingstone was Clark, or he was the unknown occasional visitor at the Livingstone Ranch. If he were Clark, and if that could be proved, there were two courses open to Bassett. He could denounce him to the authorities and then spring the big story of his career. Or he could let things stand. From a professional standpoint the first course attracted him, as a man he began to hate it. The last few days had shed a new light on Judson Clark. He had been immensely popular; there were men in the town who told about trying to save him from himself. He had been extravagant, but he had also been generous. He had been "a good kid," until liberty and money got hold of him. There had been more than one man in the sheriff's posse who hadn't wanted to find him.

He was tempted to turn back. The mountains surrounded him, somber and majestically still. They made him feel infinitely small and rather impertinent, as though he had come to penetrate the secrets they never yielded. He had almost to fight a conviction that they were hostile.

After an hour or so he determined to go on. Let them throw him over a gorge if they so determined. He got up, grunting, and leading the horse beside a boulder, climbed painfully into the saddle. To relieve his depression he addressed the horse:

"It would be easier on both of us if you were two feet narrower in the beam, old dear," he said.

Nevertheless, he made good time. By six o'clock he knew that he must have made thirty odd miles, and that he must be near the cabin. Also that it was going to be bitterly cold that night, under the snow fields, and that he had brought no wood axe. The deep valley was purple with twilight by seven, and he could scarcely see the rough-drawn trail map he had been following. And the trail grew increasingly bad. For the last mile or two the horse took its own way.

It wandered on, through fords and out of them, under the low-growing branches of scrub pine, brushing his bruised legs against rocks. He had definitely decided that he had missed the cabin when the horse turned off the trail, and he saw it.

It was built of rough logs, the chinks once closed with mud which had fallen away. The door stood open, and his entrance into its darkness was followed by the scurrying of many little feet. Bassett unstrapped his raincoat from the saddle with fingers numb with cold, and flung it to the ground. He uncinched and removed the heavy saddle, hobbled his horse and removed the bridle, and turned him loose with a slap on the flank.

"For the love of Mike, don't go far, old man," he besought him. And was startled by the sound of his own voice.

By the light of his candle lantern the prospects were extremely poor. The fir branches in the double-berthed bunk were dry and useless, the floor was crumbling under his feet, and the roof of the lean-to had fallen in and crushed the rusty stove. In the cabin itself some one had recently placed a large flat stone in a corner for a fireplace, with two slabs to back it, and above it had broken out a corner of the roof as a chimney. Bassett thought he saw the handwork of some enterprising journalist, and smiled grimly.

He set to work with the resource of a man who had learned to take what came, threw the dry bedding onto the slab and set a match to it, brought in portions of the lean-to roof for further supply for the fire, opened a can of tomatoes and set it on the edge of the hearth to heat, and sliced bacon into his diminutive frying-pan.

It was too late for any examination that night. He ate his supper from the rough table, drawing up to it a broken chair, and afterwards brought in more wood for his fire. Then, with a lighted cigar, and with his boots steaming on the hearth, he sat in front of the blaze and fell into deep study.

He was aching in every muscle when he finally stretched out on the bare boards of the lower bunk. While he slept small furry noses appeared in the openings in the broken floor, to be followed by little bodies that moved cautiously out into the open. He roused once and peered over the edge of the bunk. Several field mice were basking in front of the dying embers of the fire, and two were sitting on his boots. He grinned at them and lay back again, but he found himself fully awake and very uncomfortable. He lay there, contemplating his own folly, and demanding of himself almost fiercely what he had expected to get out of all this effort and misery. For ten years or so men had come here. Wilkins had come, for one, and there had been others. And had found nothing, and had gone away. And now he was there, the end of the procession, to look for God knows what.

He pulled the raincoat up around his shoulders, and lay back stiffly. Then—he was not an imaginative man—he began to feel that eyes were staring at him, furtive, hidden eyes, intently watching him.

Without moving he began to rake the cabin with his eyes, wall to wall, corner to corner. He turned, cautiously, and glanced at the door into the lean-to. It gaped, cavernous and empty. But the sense of being watched persisted, and when he looked at the floor the field mice had disappeared.

He began gradually to see more clearly as his eyes grew accustomed to the semi-darkness, and he felt, too, that he could almost locate the direction of the menace. For as a menace he found himself considering it. It was the broken, windowless East wall, opposite the bunk.

After a time the thing became intolerable. He reached for his revolver, and getting quickly out of the bunk, ran to the doorway and threw open the door, to find himself peering into a blackness like a wall, and to hear a hasty crunching of the underbrush that sounded like some animal in full flight.

With the sounds, and his own movement, the terror died. The cold night air on his face, the feel of the pine needles under his stockinged feet, brought him back to sense and normality. Some creature of the wilderness, a deer or a bear, perhaps, had been moving stealthily outside the cabin, and it was sound he had heard, not a gaze he had felt. He was rather cynically amused at himself. He went back into the cabin, closed the door, and stooped to turn his boots over before the fire.

It was while he was stooping that he heard a horse galloping off along the trail.

He did not go to sleep again. Now and then he considered the possibility of its having been his own animal, somehow freed of the rope and frightened by the same thing that had frightened him. But when with the first light he went outside, his horse, securely hobbled, was grazing on the scant pasture not far away.

Before he cooked his breakfast he made a minute examination of the ground beneath the East wall, but the earth was hard, and a broken branch or two might have been caused by his horse. He had no skill in woodcraft, and in the broad day his alarm seemed almost absurd. Some free horse on the range had probably wandered into the vicinity of the cabin, and had made off again on a trot. Nevertheless, he made up his mind not to remain over another night, but to look about after breakfast, and then to start down again.

He worked on his boots, dry and hard after yesterday's wetting, fried his bacon and dropped some crackers into the sizzling fat, and ate quickly. After that he went out to the trail and inspected it. He had an idea that range horses were mostly unshod, and that perhaps the trail would reveal something. But it was unused and overgrown. Not until he had gone some distance did he find anything. Then in a small bare spot he found in the dust the imprints of a horse's shoes, turned down the trail up which he had come.

Even then he was slow to read into the incident anything that related to himself or to his errand. He went over the various contingencies of the trail: a ranger, on his way to town; a forest fire somewhere; a belated hound from the newspaper pack. He was convinced now that human eyes had watched him for some time through the log wall the night before, but he could not connect them with the business in hand.

He set resolutely about his business, which was to turn up, somehow, some way, a proof of the truth of Maggie Donaldson's dying statement. To begin with then he accepted that statement, to find where it would lead him, and it led him, eventually, to the broken-down stove under the fallen roof of the lean-to.

He deliberately set himself to work, at first, to reconstruct the life in the cabin. Jud would have had the lower bunk, David the upper. The skeleton of a cot bed in the lean-to would have been Maggie's. But none of them yielded anything.

Very well. Having accepted that they lived here, it was from here that the escape was made. They would have started the moment the snow was melted enough to let them get out, and they would have taken, not the trail toward the town, but some other and circuitous route toward the railroad. But there had been things to do before they left. They would have cleared the cabin of every trace of occupancy; the tin cans, Clark's clothing, such bedding as they could not carry. The cans must have been a problem; the clothes, of course, could have been burned. But there were things, like buttons, that did not burn easily. Clark's watch, if he wore one, his cuff links. Buried?

It occurred to him that they might have disposed of some of the unburnable articles under the floor, and he lifted a rough board or two. But to pursue the search systematically he would have needed a pickaxe, and reluctantly he gave it up and turned his attention to the lean-to and the buried stove.

The stove lay in a shallow pit, filled with ancient ashes and crumbled bits of wood from the roof. It lay on its side, its sheet-iron sides collapsed, its long chimney disintegrated. He was in a heavy sweat before he had uncovered it and was able to remove it from its bed of ashes and pine needles. This done, he brought his candle-lantern and settled himself cross-legged on the ground.

His first casual inspection of the ashes revealed nothing. He set to work more carefully then, picking them up by handfuls, examining and discarding. Within ten minutes he had in a pile beside him some burned and blackened metal buttons, the eyelets and a piece of leather from a shoe, and the almost unrecognizable nib of a fountain pen.

He sat with them in the palm of his hand. Taken alone, each one was insignificant, proved nothing whatever. Taken all together, they assumed vast proportions, became convincing, became evidence.

Late that night he descended stiffly at the livery stable, and turned his weary horse over to a stableman.

"Looks dead beat," said the stableman, eyeing the animal.

"He's got nothing on me," Bassett responded cheerfully. "Better give him a hot bath and put him to bed. That's what I'm going to do."

He walked back to the hotel, glad to stretch his aching muscles. The lobby was empty, and behind the desk the night clerk was waiting for the midnight train. Bassett was wide awake by that time, and he went back to the desk and lounged against it.

"You look as though you'd struck oil," said the night clerk.

"Oil! I'll tell you what I have struck. I've struck a livery stable saddle two million times in the last two days."

The clerk grinned, and Bassett idly pulled the register toward him.

"J. Smith, Minneapolis," he read. Then he stopped and stared. Richard Livingstone was registered on the next line above.

XXIII

Dick had found it hard to leave Elizabeth, for she clung to him in her grief with childish wistfulness. He found, too, that her family depended on him rather than on Leslie Ward for moral support. It was to him that Walter Wheeler looked for assurance that the father had had no indirect responsibility for the son's death; it was to him that Jim's mother, lying gray-faced and listless in her bed or on her couch, brought her anxious questionings. Had Jim suffered? Could they have avoided it? And an insistent demand to know who and what had been the girl who was with him.

In spite of his own feeling that he would have to go to Norada quickly, before David became impatient over his exile, Dick took a few hours to find the answer to that question. But when he found it he could not tell them. The girl had been a dweller in the shady byways of life, had played her small unmoral part and gone on, perhaps to some place where men were kinder and less urgent. Dick did not judge her. He saw her, as her kind had been through all time, storm centers of the social world, passively and unconsciously blighting, at once the hunters and the prey.

He secured her former address from the police, a three-story brick rooming-house in the local tenderloin, and waited rather uncomfortably for the mistress of the place to see him. She came at last, a big woman, vast and shapeless and with an amiable loose smile, and she came in with the light step of the overfleshed, only to pause in the doorway and to stare at him.

"My God!" she said. "I thought you were dead!"

"I'm afraid you're mistaking me for some one else, aren't you?"

She looked at him carefully.

"I'd have sworn—" she muttered, and turning to the button inside the door she switched on the light. Then she surveyed him again.

"What's your name?"

"Livingstone. Doctor Livingstone. I called—"

"Is that for me, or for the police?"

"Now see here," he said pleasantly. "I don't know who you are mistaking me for, and I'm not hiding from the police. Here's my card, and I have come from the family of a young man named Wheeler, who was killed recently in an automobile accident."

She took the card and read it, and then resumed her intent scrutiny of him.

"Well, you fooled me all right," she said at last. "I thought you were—well, never mind that. What about this Wheeler family? Are they going to settle with the undertaker? Because I tell you flat, I can't and won't. She owed me a month's rent, and her clothes won't bring over seventy-five or a hundred dollars."

As he left he was aware that she stood in the doorway looking after him. He drove home slowly in the car, and on the way he made up a kindly story to tell the family. He could not let them know that Jim had been seeking love in the byways of life. And that night he mailed a check in payment of the undertaker's bill, carefully leaving the stub empty.

On the third day after Jim's funeral he started for Norada. An interne from a local hospital, having newly finished his service there, had agreed to take over his work for a time. But Dick was faintly jealous when he installed Doctor Reynolds in his office, and turned him over to a mystified Minnie to look after.

"Is he going to sleep in your bed?" she demanded belligerently.

She was only partially mollified when she found Doctor Reynolds was to have the spare room. She did not like the way things were going, she confided to Mike. Why wasn't she to let on to Mrs. Crosby that Doctor Dick had gone away? Or to the old doctor? Both of them away, and that little upstart in the office ready to steal their patients and hang out his own sign the moment they got back!

Unused to duplicity as he was, Dick found himself floundering along an extremely crooked path. He wrote a half dozen pleasant, non-committal letters to David and Lucy, spending an inordinate time on them, and gave them to Walter Wheeler to mail at stated intervals. But his chief difficulty was with Elizabeth. Perhaps he would have told her; there were times when he had to fight his desire to have her share his anxiety as well as know the truth about him. But she was already carrying the burden of Jim's tragedy, and her father, too, was insistent that she be kept in ignorance.

"Until she can have the whole thing," he said, with the new heaviness which had crept into his voice.

Beside that real trouble Dick's looked dim and nebulous. Other things could be set right; there was always a fighting chance. It was only death that was final.

Elizabeth went to the station to see him off, a small slim thing in a black frock, with eyes that persistently sought his face, and a determined smile. He pulled her arm through his, so he might hold her hand, and when he found that she was wearing her ring he drew her even closer, with a wave of passionate possession.

"You are mine. My little girl."

"I am yours. For ever and ever."

But they assumed a certain lightness after that, each to cheer the other. As when she asserted that she was sure she would always know the moment he stopped thinking about her, and he stopped, with any number of people about, and said:

"That's simply terrible! Suppose, when we are married, my mind turns on such a mundane thing as beefsteak and onions? Will you simply walk out on me?"

He stood on the lowest step of the train until her figure was lost in the darkness, and the porter expostulated. He was, that night, a little drunk with love, and he did not read the note she had thrust into his hand at the last moment until he was safely in his berth, his long figure stretched diagonally to find the length it needed.

"Darling, darling Dick," she had written. "I wonder so often how you can care for me, or what I have done to deserve you. And I cannot write how I feel, just as I cannot say it. But, Dick dear, I have such a terrible fear of losing you, and you are my life now. You will be careful and not run any risks, won't you? And just remember this always. Wherever you are and wherever I am, I am thinking of you and waiting for you."

He read it three times, until he knew it by heart, and he slept with it in the pocket of his pajama coat.

Three days later he reached Norada, and registered at the Commercial Hotel. The town itself conveyed nothing to him. He found it totally unfamiliar, and for its part the town passed him by without a glance. A new field had come in, twenty miles from the old one, and had brought with it a fresh influx of prospectors, riggers, and lease buyers. The hotel was crowded.

That was his first disappointment. He had been nursing the hope that surroundings which he must once have known well would assist him in finding himself. That was the theory, he knew. He stood at the window of his hotel room, with its angular furniture and the Gideon Bible, and for the first time he realized the difficulty of what he had set out to do. Had he been able to take David into his confidence he would have had the names of one or two men to go to, but as things were he had nothing.

The almost morbid shrinking he felt from exposing his condition was increased, rather than diminished, in the new surroundings. He would, of course, go to the ranch at Dry River, and begin his inquiries from there, but not until now had he realized what that would mean; his recognition by people he could not remember, the questions he could not answer.

He knew the letter to David from beginning to end, but he got it out and read it again. Who was this Bassett, and what mischief was he up to? Why should he himself be got out of town

204

quickly and the warning burned? Who was "G"? And why wouldn't the simplest thing be to locate this Bassett himself?

The more he considered that the more obvious it seemed as a solution, provided of course he could locate the man. Whether Bassett were friendly or inimical, he was convinced that he knew or was finding out something concerning himself which David was keeping from him.

He was relieved when he went down to the desk to find that his man was registered there, although the clerk reported him out of town. But the very fact that only a few hours or days separated him from a solution of the mystery heartened him.

He ate his dinner alone, unnoticed, and after dinner, in the writing room, with its mission furniture and its traveling men copying orders, he wrote a letter to Elizabeth. Into it he put some of the things that lay too deep for speech when he was with her, and because he had so much to say and therefore wrote extremely fast, a considerable portion of it was practically illegible. Then, as though he could hurry the trains East, he put a special delivery stamp on it.

With that off his mind, and the need of exercise after the trip insistent, he took his hat and wandered out into the town. The main street was crowded; moving picture theaters were summoning their evening audiences with bright lights and colored posters, and automobiles lined the curb. But here and there an Indian with braids and a Stetson hat, or a cowpuncher from a ranch in boots and spurs reminded him that after all this was the West, the horse and cattle country. It was still twilight, and when he had left the main street behind him he began to have a sense of the familiar. Surely he had stood here before, had seen the court-house on its low hill, the row of frame houses in small gardens just across the street. It seemed infinitely long ago, but very real. He even remembered dimly an open place at the other side of the building where the ranchmen tied their horses. To test himself he walked around. Yes, it was there, but no horses stood there now, heads drooping, bridle reins thrown loosely over the rail. Only a muddy automobile, without lights, and a dog on guard beside it.

He spoke to the dog, and it came and sniffed at him. Then it squatted in front of him, looking up into his face.

"Lonely, old chap, aren't you?" he said. "Well, you've got nothing on me."

He felt a little cheered as he turned back toward the hotel. A few encounters with the things of his youth, and perhaps the cloud would clear away. Already the court-house had stirred some memories. And on turning back down the hill he had another swift vision, photographically distinct but unrelated to anything that had preceded or followed it. It was like a few feet cut from a moving picture film.

He was riding down that street at night on a small horse, and his father was beside him on a tall one. He looked up at his father, and he seemed very large. The largest man in the world. And the most important.

It began and stopped there, and his endeavor to follow it further resulted in its ultimately leaving him. It faded, became less real, until he wondered if he had not himself conjured it. But that experience taught him something. Things out of the past would come or they would not come, but they could not be forced. One could not will to revive them.

He stood at a window facing north that night, under the impression it was east, and sent his love and an inarticulate sort of prayer to Elizabeth, for her safety and happiness, in the general direction of the Arctic Circle.

Bassett had not returned in the morning, and he found himself with a day on his hands. He decided to try the experiment of visiting the Livingstone ranch, or at least of viewing it from a safe distance, with the hope of a repetition of last night's experience. Of all his childish memories the ranch house, next to his father, was most distinct. When he had at various times tried to analyze what things he recalled he had found that what they lacked of normal memory was connection. They stood out, like the one the night before, each complete in itself, brief, and having no apparent relation to what had gone before or what came after.

But the ranch house had been different. The pictures were mostly superimposed on it; it was their background. Himself standing on the mountain looking down at it, and his father pointing to it; the tutor who was afraid of horses, sitting at a big table in a great wood-ceiled and wood-paneled room; a long gallery or porch along one side of the building and rooms added on to the house so that one had to go along the gallery to reach them; a gun-room full of guns.

When, much later, Dick was able calmly to review that day, he found his recollection of it confused by the events that followed, but one thing stood out as clearly as his later knowledge of the almost incredible fact that for one entire day and for the evening of another, he had openly appeared in Norada and had not been recognized. That fact was his discovery that the Livingstone ranch house had no place in his memory whatever.

He had hired a car and a driver, a driver who asserted that this was the old Livingstone ranch house. And it bore no resemblance, not the faintest, to the building he remembered. It did not lie where it should have lain. The mountains were too far behind it. It was not the house. The fields were not the proper fields. It was wrong, all wrong.

He went no closer than the highway, because it was not necessary. He ordered the car to turn and go back, and for the first and only time he was filled with bitter resentment against David. David had fooled him. He sat beside the driver, his face glowering and his eyes hot, and let his indignation burn in him like a flame.

Hours afterwards he had, of course, found excuses for David. Accepted them, rather, as a part of the mystery which wrapped him about. But they had no effect on the decision he made during that miserable ride back to Norada, when he determined to see the man Bassett and get the truth out of him if he had to choke it out.

XXIV

Bassett was astounded when he saw Dick's signature on the hotel register. It destroyed, in one line, every theory he held. That Judson Clark should return to Norada after his flight was incredible. Ten years was only ten years after all. It was not a lifetime. There were men in the town who had known Clark well.

Nevertheless for a time he held to his earlier conviction, even fought for it. He went so far as to wonder if Clark had come back for a tardy surrender. Men had done that before this, had carried a burden for years, had reached the breaking point, had broken. But he dismissed that. There had been no evidence of breaking in the young man in the office chair. He found himself thrown back, finally, on the story of the Wasson woman, and wondering if he would have to accept it after all.

The reaction from his certainty in the cabin to uncertainty again made him fretful and sleepless. It was almost morning before he relaxed on his hard hotel bed enough to sleep.

He wakened late, and telephoned down for breakfast. His confusion had not decreased with the night, and while he got painfully out of bed and prepared to shave and dress, his thoughts were busy. There was no doubt in his mind that, in spite of the growth of the town, the newcomer would be under arrest almost as soon as he made his appearance. A resemblance that could deceive Beverly Carlysle's brother could deceive others, and would. That he had escaped so long amazed him.

By the time he had bathed he had developed a sort of philosophic acceptance of the new situation. There would be no exclusive story now, no scoop. The events of the next few hours were for every man to read. He shrugged his shoulders as, partially dressed, he carried his shaving materials into the better light of his bedroom.

With his face partially lathered he heard a knock at the door, and sang out a not uncheerful "Come in." It happened, then, that it was in his mirror that he learned that his visitor was not the waiter, but Livingstone himself. He had an instant of stunned amazement before he turned.

"I beg your pardon," Dick said. "I was afraid you'd get out before I saw you. My name's Livingstone, and I want to talk to you, if you don't mind. If you like I'll come back later."

Bassett perceived two things simultaneously; that owing probably to the lather on his face he had not been recognized, and that the face of the man inside the door was haggard and strained.

"That's all right. Come in and sit down. I'll get this stuff off my face and be with you in a jiffy."

But he was very deliberate in the bathroom. His astonishment grew, rather than decreased. Clearly Livingstone had not known him. How, then, had he known that he was in Norada? And when he recognized him, as he would in a moment, what then? He put on his collar and tied his tie slowly. Gregory might be the key. Gregory might have found out that he had started for Norada and warned him. Then, if that were true, this man was Clark after all. But if he were Clark he wouldn't be there. It was like a kitten after its tail. It whirled in a circle and got nowhere.

The waiter had laid his breakfast and gone when he emerged from the bathroom, and Dick was standing by the window looking out. He turned.

"I'm here, Mr. Bassett, on rather a peculiar—" He stopped and looked at Bassett. "I see. You were in my office about a month ago, weren't you?"

"For a headache, yes." Bassett was very wary and watchful, but there was no particular unfriendliness in his visitor's eyes.

"It never occurred to me that you might be Bassett," Dick said gravely. "Never mind about that. Eat your breakfast. Do you mind if I talk while you do it?"

"Will you have some coffee? I can get a glass from the bathroom. It takes a week to get a waiter here."

"Thanks. Yes."

The feeling of unreality grew in the reporter's mind. It increased still further when they sat opposite each other, the small table with its Bible on the lower shelf between them, while he made a pretense at breakfasting.

"First of all," Dick said, at last, "I was not sure I had found the right man. You are the only Bassett in the place, however, and you're registered from my town. So I took a chance. I suppose that headache was not genuine."

Bassett hesitated.

"No" he said at last.

"What you really wanted to do was to see me, then?"

"In a way, yes."

"I'll ask you one more question. It may clear the air. Does this mean anything to you? I'll tell you now that it doesn't, to me."

From his pocketbook he took the note addressed to David, and passed it over the table. Bassett looked at him quickly and took it.

"Before you read it, I'll explain something. It was not sent to me. It was sent to my—to Doctor David Livingstone. It happened to fall into my hands. I've come a long way to find out what it means."

He paused, and looked the reporter straight in the eyes. "I am laying my cards on the table, Bassett. This 'G,' whoever he is, is clearly warning my uncle against you. I want to know what he is warning him about."

Bassett read the note carefully, and looked up.

"I suppose you know who 'G' is?"

"I do not. Do you?"

"I'll give you another name, and maybe you'll get it. A name that I think will mean something to you. Beverly Carlysle."

"The actress?"

Bassett had an extraordinary feeling of unreality, followed by one of doubt. Either the fellow was a very good actor, or—

"Sorry," Dick said slowly. "I don't seem to get it. I don't know that 'G' is as important as his warning. That note's a warning."

"Yes. It's a warning. And I don't think you need me to tell you what about."

"Concerning my uncle, or myself?"

"Are you trying to put it over on me that you don't know?"

"That's what I'm trying to do," Dick said, with a sort of grave patience.

The reporter liked courage when he saw it, and he was compelled to a sort of reluctant admiration.

"You've got your courage with you," he observed. "How long do you suppose it will be after you set foot on the streets of this town before you're arrested? How do you know I won't send for the police myself?"

"I know damned well you won't," Dick said grimly. "Not before I'm through with you. You've chosen to interest yourself in me. I suppose you don't deny the imputation in that letter. You'll grant that I have a right to know who and what you are, and just what you are interested in."

"Right-o," the reporter said cheerfully, glad to get to grips; and to stop a fencing that was getting nowhere. "I'm connected with the Times-Republican, in your own fair city. I was in the theater the night Gregory recognized you. Verbum sap."

"This Gregory is the 'G'?"

"Oh, quit it, Clark," Bassett said, suddenly impatient. "That letter's the last proof I needed. Gregory wrote it after he'd seen David Livingstone. He wouldn't have written it if he and the old man hadn't come to an understanding. I've been to the cabin. My God, man, I've even got the parts of your clothing that wouldn't burn! You can thank Maggie Donaldson for that."

"Donaldson," Dick repeated. "That was it. I couldn't remember her name. The woman in the cabin. Maggie. And Jack. Jack Donaldson."

He got up, and was apparently dizzy, for he caught at the table.

"Look here," Bassett said, "let me give you a drink. You look all in."

But Dick shook his head.

"No, thanks just the same. I'll ask you to be plain with me, Bassett. I am—I have become engaged to a girl, and—well, I want the story. That's all."

And, when Bassett only continued to stare at him:

"I suppose I've begun wrong end first. I forgot about how it must seem to you. I dropped a block out of my life about ten years ago. Can't remember it. I'm not proud of it, but it's the fact. What I'm trying to do now is to fill in the gap. But I've got to, somehow. I owe it to the girl."

When Bassett could apparently find nothing to say he went on:

"You say I may be arrested if I go out on the street. And you rather more than intimate that a woman named Beverly Carlysle is mixed up in it somehow. I take it that I knew her."

"Yes. You knew her," Bassett said slowly. At the intimation in his tone Dick surveyed him for a moment without speaking. His face, pale before, took on a grayish tinge.

"I wasn't—married to her?"

"No. You didn't marry her. See here, Clark, this is straight goods, is it? You're not trying to put something over on me? Because if you are, you needn't. I'd about made up my mind to follow the story through for my own satisfaction, and then quit cold on it. When a man's pulled himself out of the mud as you have it's not my business to pull him down. But I don't want you to pull any bunk."

Dick winced.

"Out of the mud!" he said. "No. I'm telling you the truth, Bassett. I have some fragmentary memories, places and people, but no names, and all of them, I imagine from my childhood. I pick up at a cabin in the mountains, with snow around, and David Livingstone feeding me soup with a tin spoon." He tried to smile and failed. His face twitched. "I could stand it for myself," he said, "but I've tied another life to mine, like a cursed fool, and now you speak of a woman, and of arrest. Arrest! For what?"

"Suppose," Bassett said after a moment, "suppose you let that go just now, and tell me more about this—this gap. You're a medical man. You've probably gone into your own case pretty thoroughly. I'm accepting your statement, you see. As a matter of fact it must be true, or you wouldn't be here. But I've got to know what I'm doing before I lay my cards on the table. Make it simple, if you can. I don't know your medical jargon."

Dick did his best. The mind closed down now and then, mainly from a shock. No, there was no injury required. He didn't think he had had an injury. A mental shock would do it, if it were strong enough. And fear. It was generally fear. He had never considered himself braver than the other fellow, but no man liked to think that he had a cowardly mind. Even if things hadn't broken as they had, he'd have come back before he went to the length of marriage, to find out what it was he had been afraid of. He paused then, to give Bassett a chance to tell him, but the reporter only said: "Go on, you put your cards on the table, and then I'll lay mine out."

Dick went on. He didn't blame Bassett. If there was something that was in his line of work, he understood. At the same time he wanted to save David anything unpleasant. (The word "unpleasant" startled Bassett, by its very inadequacy.) He knew now that David had built up for him an identity that probably did not exist, but he wanted Bassett to know that there could never be doubt of David's high purpose and his essential fineness.

"Whatever I was before." he finished simply, "and I'll get that from you now, if I am any sort of a man at all it is his work."

He stood up and braced himself. It had been clear to Bassett for ten minutes that Dick was talking against time, against the period of revelation. He would have it, but he was mentally bracing himself against it.

"I think," he said, "I'll have that whisky now."

Bassett poured him a small drink, and took a turn about the room while he drank it. He was perplexed and apprehensive. Strange as the story was, he was convinced that he had heard the truth. He had, now and then, run across men who came back after a brief disappearance, with a cock and bull story of forgetting who they were, and because nearly always these men vanished at the peak of some crisis they had always been open to suspicion. Perhaps, poor devils, they had been telling the truth after all. So the mind shut down, eh? Closed like a grave over the unbearable!

His own part in the threatening catastrophe began to obsess him. Without the warning from Gregory there would have been no return to Norada, no arrest. It had all been dead and buried, until he himself had revived it. And a girl, too! The girl in the blue dress at the theater, of course.

Dick put down the glass.

"I'm ready, if you are."

"Does the name of Clark recall anything to you?"

"Nothing."

"Judson Clark? Jud Clark?"

Dick passed his hand over his forehead wearily.

"I'm not sure," he said. "It sounds familiar, and then it doesn't. It doesn't mean anything to me, if you get that. If it's a key, it doesn't unlock. That's all. Am I Judson Clark?"

Oddly enough, Bassett found himself now seeking for hope of escape in the very situation that had previously irritated him, in the story he had heard at Wasson's. He considered, and said, almost violently:

"Look here, I may have made a mistake. I came out here pretty well convinced I'd found the solution to an old mystery, and for that matter I think I have. But there's a twist in it that isn't clear, and until it is clear I'm not going to saddle you with an identity that may not belong to you. You are one of two men. One of them is Judson Clark, and I'll be honest with you; I'm pretty sure you're Clark. The other I don't know, but I have reason to believe that he spent part of his time with Henry Livingstone at Dry River."

"I went to the Livingstone ranch yesterday. I remember my early home. That wasn't it. Which one of these two men will be arrested if he is recognized?"

"Clark."

"For what?"

"I'm coming to that. I suppose you'll have to know. Another drink? No? All right. About ten years ago, or a little less, a young chap called Judson Clark got into trouble here, and headed into the mountains in a blizzard. He was supposed to have frozen to death. But recently a woman named Donaldson made a confession on her deathbed. She said that she had helped to nurse Clark in a mountain cabin, and that with the aid of some one unnamed he had got away."

"Then I'm Clark. I remember her, and the cabin."

There was a short silence following that admission. To Dick, it was filled with the thought of Elizabeth, and of her relation to what he was about to hear. Again he braced himself for what was coming.

"I suppose," he said at last, "that if I ran away I was in pretty serious trouble. What was it?"

"We've got no absolute proof that you are Clark, remember. You don't know, and Maggie Donaldson was considered not quite sane before she died. I've told you there's a chance you are the other man."

"All right. What had Clark done?"

"He had shot a man."

The reporter was instantly alarmed. If Dick had been haggard before, he was ghastly now. He got up slowly and held to the back of his chair.

"Not—murder?" he asked, with stiff lips.

"No," Bassett said quickly. "Not at all. See here, you've had about all you can stand. Remember, we don't even know you are Clark. All I said was—"

"I understand that. It was murder, wasn't it?"

"Well, there had been a quarrel, I understand. The law allows for that, I think."

Dick went slowly to the window, and stood with his back to Bassett. For a long time the room was quiet. In the street below long lines of cars in front of the hotel denoted the luncheon hour. An Indian woman with a child in the shawl on her back stopped in the street, looked up at Dick and extended a beaded belt. With it still extended she continued to stare at his white face.

"The man died, of course?" he asked at last, without turning.

"Yes. I knew him. He wasn't any great loss. It was at the Clark ranch. I don't believe a conviction would be possible, although they would try for one. It was circumstantial evidence."

"And I ran away?"

"Clark ran away," Bassett corrected him. "As I've told you, the authorities here believe he is dead."

After an even longer silence Dick turned.

"I told you there was a girl. I'd like to think out some way to keep the thing from her, before I surrender myself. If I can protect her, and David—"

"I tell you, you don't even know you are Clark."

"All right. If I'm not, they'll know. If I am—I tell you I'm not going through the rest of my life with a thing like that hanging over me. Maggie Donaldson was sane enough. Why, when I look back, I know our leaving the cabin was a flight. I'm not Henry Livingstone's son, because he never had a son. I can tell you what the Clark ranch house looks like." And after a pause:

"Can you imagine the reverse of a dream when you've dreamed you are guilty of something and wake up to find you are innocent? Who was the man?"

Bassett watched him narrowly.

"His name was Lucas. Howard Lucas."

"All right. Now we have that, where does Beverly Carlysle come in?"

"Clark was infatuated with her. The man he shot was the man she had married."

XXV

Shortly after that Dick said he would go to his room. He was still pale, but his eyes looked bright and feverish, and Bassett went with him, uneasily conscious that something was not quite right. Dick spoke only once on the way.

"My head aches like the mischief," he said, and his voice was dull and lifeless.

He did not want Bassett to go with him, but Bassett went, nevertheless. Dick's statement, that he meant to surrender himself, had filled him with uneasiness. He determined, following him along the hall, to keep a close guard on him for the next few hours, but beyond that, just then, he did not try to go. If it were humanly possible he meant to smuggle him out of the town and take him East. But he had an uneasy conviction that Dick was going to be ill. The mind did strange things with the body.

Dick sat down on the edge of the bed.

"My head aches like the mischief," he repeated. "Look in that grip and find me some tablets, will you? I'm dizzy."

He made an effort and stretched out on the bed. "Good Lord," he muttered, "I haven't had such a headache since—"

His voice trailed off. Bassett, bending over the army kit bag in the corner, straightened and looked around. Dick was suddenly asleep and breathing heavily.

For a long time the reporter sat by the side of the bed, watching him and trying to plan some course of action. He was overcome by his own responsibility, and by the prospect of tragedy that threatened. That Livingstone was Clark, and that he would insist on surrendering himself when he wakened, he could no longer doubt. His mind wandered back to that day when he had visited the old house as a patient, and from that along the strange road they had both come since then. He reflected, not exactly in those terms, that life, any man's life, was only one thread in a pattern woven of an infinite number of threads, and that to tangle the one thread was to interfere with all the others. David Livingstone, the girl in the blue dress, the man twitching uneasily on the bed, Wilkins the sheriff, himself, who could tell how many others, all threads.

He swore in a whisper.

The maid tapped at the door. He opened it an inch or so and sent her off. In view of his new determination even the maid had become a danger. She was the same elderly woman who looked after his own bedroom, and she might have known Clark. Just what Providence had kept him from recognition before this he did not know, but it could not go on indefinitely.

After an hour or so Bassett locked the door behind him and went down to lunch. He was not hungry, but he wanted to get out of the room, to think without that quiet figure before him. Over the pretence of food he faced the situation. Lying ready to his hand was the biggest story of his career, but he could not carry it through. It was characteristic of him that, before abandoning it, he should follow through to the end the result of its publication. He did not believe, for instance, that either Dick's voluntary surrender or his own disclosure of the situation necessarily meant a conviction for murder. To convict a man of a crime he did not know he had committed would be difficult. But, with his customary thoroughness he followed that through also. Livingstone acquitted was once again Clark, would be known to the world as Clark. The new place he had so painfully made for himself would be gone. The story would follow him, never to be lived down. And in his particular profession confidence and respect were half the game. All that would be gone.

Thus by gradual stages he got back to David, and he struggled for the motive which lay behind every decisive human act. A man who followed a course by which he had nothing to gain and everything to lose was either a fool or was actuated by some profound unselfishness. To save a life? But with all the resources Clark could have commanded, added to his personal popularity, a first degree sentence would have been unlikely. Not a life, then, but perhaps something greater than a life. A man's soul.

It came to him, then, in a great light of comprehension, the thing David had tried to do; to take this waster and fugitive, the slate of his mind wiped clean by shock and illness, only his childish memories remaining, and on it to lead him to write a new record. To take the body he had found, and the always untouched soul, and from them to make a man.

And with that comprehension came the conviction, too, that David had succeeded. He had indeed made a man.

He ate absently, consulting his railroad schedule and formulating the arguments he meant to use against Dick's determination to give himself up. He foresaw a struggle there, but he himself held one or two strong cards—the ruthless undoing of David's work, the involving of David for conspiring against the law. And Dick's own obligation to the girl at home.

He was more at ease in the practical arrangements. An express went through on the main line at midnight, and there was a local on the branch line at eight. But the local train, the railway station, too, were full of possible dangers. After some thought he decided to get a car, drive down to the main line with Dick, and then send the car back.

He went out at once and made an arrangement for a car, and on returning notified the clerk that he was going to leave, and asked to have his bill made out. After some hesitation he said: "I'll pay three-twenty too, while I'm at it. Friend of mine there, going with me. Yes, up to to-night."

As he turned away he saw the short, heavy figure of Wilkins coming in. He stood back and watched. The sheriff went to the desk, pulled the register toward him and ran over several pages of it. Then he shoved it away, turned and saw him.

"Been away, haven't you?" he asked.

"Yes. I took a little horseback trip into the mountains. My knees are still not on speaking terms."

The sheriff chuckled. Then he sobered.

"Come and sit down," he said. "I'm going to watch who goes in and out of here for a while."

Bassett followed him unwillingly to two chairs that faced the desk and the lobby. He had the key of Dick's room in his pocket, but he knew that if he wakened he could easily telephone and have his door unlocked. But that was not his only anxiety. He had a sudden conviction that the sheriff's watch was connected with Dick himself. Wilkins, from a friendly and gregarious fellow-being, had suddenly grown to sinister proportions in his mind.

And, as the minutes went by, with the sheriff sitting forward and watching the lobby and staircase with intent, unblinking eyes, Bassett's anxiety turned to fear. He found his heart leaping when the room bells rang, and the clerk, with a glance at the annunciator, sent boys hurrying off. His hands shook, and he felt them cold and moist. And all the time Wilkins was holding him with a flow of unimportant chatter.

"Watching for any one in particular?" he managed, after five minutes or so.

"Yes. I'll tell you about it as soon as—Bill! Is Alex outside?"

Bill stopped in front of them, and nodded.

"All right. Now get this—I want everything decent and in order. No excitement. I'll come out behind him, and you and Bill stand by. Outside I'll speak to him, and when we walk off, just fall in behind. But keep close."

Bill wandered off, to take up a stand of extreme nonchalance inside the entrance. When Wilkins turned to him again Bassett had had a moment to adjust himself, and more or less to plan his own campaign.

"Somebody's out of luck," he commented. "And speaking of being out of luck, I've got a sick man on my hands. Friend of mine from home. We've got to catch the midnight, too."

"Too bad," Wilkins commented rather absently. Then, perhaps feeling that he had not shown proper interest, "Tell you what I'll do. I've got some business on hand now, but it'll be cleared up one way or another pretty soon. I'll bring my car around and take him to the station. These hacks are the limit to ride in."

The disaster to his plans thus threatened steadied the reporter, and he managed to keep his face impassive.

"Thanks," he said. "I'll let you know if he's able to travel. Is this—is this business you're on confidential?"

"Well, it is and it isn't. I've talked some to you, and as you're leaving anyhow—it's the Jud Clark case again."

"Sort of hysteria, I suppose. He'll be seen all over the country for the next six months."

"Yes. But I never saw a hysterical Indian. Well, a little while ago an Indian woman named Lizzie Lazarus blew into my office. She's a smart woman. Her husband was a breed, dairy hand on the Clark ranch for years. Lizzie was the first Indian woman in these parts to go to school, and besides being smart, she's got Indian sight. You know these Indians. When they aren't blind with trachoma they can see further and better than a telescope."

Bassett made an effort.

"What's that got to do with Jud Clark?" he asked.

"Well, she blew in. You know there was a reward out for him, and I guess it still stands. I'll have to look it up, for if Maggie Donaldson wasn't crazy some one will turn him up some day, probably. Well, Lizzie blew in, and she said she'd seen Jud Clark. Saw him standing at a second story window of this hotel. Can you beat that?"

"Not for pure invention. Hardly."

"That's what I said at first. But I don't know. In some ways it would be like him. He wouldn't mind coming back and giving us the laugh, if he thought he could get away with it. He didn't know fear. Only time he ever showed funk was when he beat it after the shooting, and then he was full of hootch, and on the edge of D.T.'s."

"A man doesn't play jokes with the hangman's rope," Bassett commented, dryly. He looked at his watch and rose. "It's a good story, but I wouldn't wear out any trouser-seats sitting here watching for him. If he's living he's taken pretty good care for ten years not to put his head in the noose; and I'd remember this, too. Wherever he is, if he is anywhere, he's probably so changed his appearance that Telescope Lizzie wouldn't know him. Or you either."

"Probably," the sheriff said, comfortably. "Still I'm not taking any chances. I'm up for reelection this fall, and that Donaldson woman's story nearly queered me. I've got a fellow at the railroad station, just for luck."

Bassett went up the stairs and along the corridor, deep in dejected thought. The trap of his own making was closing, and his active mind was busy with schemes for getting Dick away before it shut entirely.

It might be better, in one way, to keep Livingstone there in his room until the alarm blew over. On the other hand, Livingstone himself had to be dealt with, and that he would remain quiescent under the circumstances was unlikely. The motor to the main line seemed to be the best thing. True, he would have first to get Livingstone to agree to go. That done, and he did not underestimate its difficulty, there was the question of getting him out of the hotel, now that the alarm had been given.

When he found Dick still sleeping he made a careful survey of the second floor. There was a second staircase, but investigation showed that it led into the kitchens. He decided finally on a

213

fire-escape from a rear hall window, which led into a courtyard littered with the untidy rubbish of an overcrowded and undermanned hotel, and where now two or three saddled horses waited while their riders ate within.

When he had made certain that he was not observed he unlocked and opened the window, and removed the wire screen. There was a red fire-exit lamp in the ceiling nearby, but he could not reach it, nor could he find any wall switch. Nevertheless he knew by that time that through the window lay Dick's only chance of escape. He cleared the grating of a broken box and an empty flower pot, stood the screen outside the wall, and then, still unobserved, made his way back to his own bedroom and packed his belongings.

Dick was still sleeping, stretched on his bed, when he returned to three-twenty. And here Bassett's careful plans began to go awry, for Dick's body was twitching, and his face was pale and covered with a cold sweat. From wondering how they could get away, Bassett began to wonder whether they would get away at all. The sleep was more like a stupor than sleep. He sat down by the bed, closer to sheer fright than he had ever been before, and wretched with the miserable knowledge of his own responsibility.

As the afternoon wore on, it became increasingly evident that somehow or other he must get a doctor. He turned the subject over in his mind, pro and con. If he could get a new man, one who did not remember Jud Clark, it might do. But he hesitated until, at seven, Dick opened his eyes and clearly did not know him. Then he knew that the matter was out of his hands, and that from now on whatever it was that controlled the affairs of men, David's God or his own vague Providence, was in charge.

He got his hat and went out, and down the stairs again. Wilkins had disappeared, but Bill still stood by the entrance, watching the crowd that drifted in and out. In his state of tension he felt that the hotel clerk's eyes were suspicious as he retained the two rooms for another day, and that Bill watched him out with more than casual interest. Even the matter of cancelling the order for the car loomed large and suspicion-breeding before him, but he accomplished it, and then set out to find medical assistance.

There, however, chance favored him. The first doctor's sign led him to a young man, new to the town, and obviously at leisure. Not that he found that out at once. He invented a condition for himself, as he had done once before, got a prescription and paid for it, learned what he wanted, and then mentioned Dick. He was careful to emphasize his name and profession, and his standing "back home."

"I'll admit he's got me worried," he finished. "He saw me registered and came to my room this morning to see me, and got sick there. That is, he said he had a violent headache and was dizzy. I got him to his room and on the bed, and he's been sleeping ever since. He looks pretty sick to me."

He was conscious of Bill's eyes on him as they went through the lobby again, but he realized now that they were unsuspicious. Bassett himself was in a hot sweat. He stopped outside the room and mopped his face.

"Look kind of shot up yourself," the doctor commented. "Watch this sun out here. Because it's dry here you Eastern people don't notice the heat until it plays the deuce with you."

He made a careful examination of the sleeping man, while Bassett watched his face.

"Been a drinking man? Or do you know?"

"No. But I think not. I gave him a small drink this morning, when he seemed to need it."

"Been like this all day?"

"Since noon. Yes."

Once more the medical man stooped. When he straightened it was to deliver Bassett a body blow.

"I don't like his condition, or that twitching. If these were the good old days in Wyoming I'd say he is on the verge of delirium tremens. But that's only snap judgment. He might be on the verge of a good many things. Anyhow, he'd better be moved to the hospital. This is no place for him."

And against this common-sense suggestion Bassett had nothing to offer. If the doctor had been looking he would have seen him make a gesture of despair.

"I suppose so," he said, dully. "Is it near? I'll go myself and get a room."

"That's my advice. I'll look in later, and if the stupor continues I'll have in a consultant." He picked up his bag and stood looking down at the bed. "Big fine-looking chap, isn't he?" he commented. "Married?"

"No."

"Well, we'll get the ambulance, and later on we'll go over him properly. I'd call a maid to sit with him, if I were you." In the grip of a situation that was too much for him, Bassett rang the bell. It was answered by the elderly maid who took care of his own bedroom.

Months later, puzzling over the situation, Bassett was to wonder, and not to know, whether chance or design brought the Thorwald woman to the door that night. At the time, and for weeks, he laid it to tragic chance, the same chance which had placed in Dick's hand the warning letter that had brought him West. But as months went on, the part played in the tragedy by that faded woman with her tired dispirited voice and her ash colored hair streaked with gray, assumed other proportions, loomed large and mysterious.

There were times when he wished that some prescience of danger had made him throttle her then and there, so she could not have raised her shrill, alarming voice! But he had no warning. All he saw was a woman in a washed-out blue calico dress and a fresh white apron, raising incurious eyes to his.

"I suppose it's all right if she sits in the hall?" Bassett inquired, still fighting his losing fight. "She can go in if he stirs."

"Right-o," said the doctor, who had been to France and had brought home some British phrases.

Bassett walked back from the hospital alone. The game was up and he knew it. Sooner or later—In a way he tried to defend himself to himself. He had done his best. Two or three days ago he would have been exultant over the developments. After all, mince things as one would, Clark was a murderer. Other men killed and paid the penalty. And the game was not up entirely, at that. The providence which had watched over him for so long might continue to. The hospital was new. (It was, ironically enough, the Clark Memorial hospital.) There was still a chance.

He was conscious of something strange as he entered the lobby. The constable was gone, and there was no clerk behind the desk. At the foot of the stairs stood a group of guests and loungers, looking up, while a bell-boy barred the way.

Even then Bassett's first thought was of fire. He elbowed his way to the foot of the stairs, and demanded to be allowed to go up, but he was refused.

"In a few minutes," said the boy. "No need of excitement."

"Is it a fire?"

"I don't know myself. I've got my orders. That's all." Wilkins came hurrying in. The crowd, silent and respectful before the law, opened to let him through and closed behind him.

Bassett stood at the foot of the stairs, looking up.

XXVI

To Elizabeth the first days of Dick's absence were unbelievably dreary. She seemed to live only from one visit of the postman to the next. She felt sometimes that only part of her was at home in the Wheeler house, slept at night in her white bed, donned its black frocks and took them off, and made those sad daily pilgrimages to the cemetery above the town, where her mother tidied with tender hands the long narrow mound, so fearfully remindful of Jim's tall slim body.

That part of her grieved sorely, and spent itself in small comforting actions and little caressing touches on bowed heads and grief-stooped shoulders. It put away Jim's clothing, and kept immaculate the room where now her mother spent most of her waking hours. It sent her on her knees at night to pray for Jim's happiness in some young-man heaven which would please him. But the other part of her was not there at all. It was off with Dick in some mysterious place of mountains and vast distance called Wyoming.

And because of this division in herself, because she felt that her loyalty to her people had wavered, because she knew that already she had forsaken her father and her mother and would follow her love through the rest of her life, she was touchingly anxious to comfort and to please them.

"She's taking Dick's absence very hard," Mrs. Wheeler said one night, when she had kissed them and gone upstairs to bed. "She worries me sometimes."

Mr. Wheeler sighed. Why was it that a man could not tell his children what he had learned,— that nothing was so great as one expected; that love was worth living for, but not dying for. The impatience of youth for life! It had killed Jim. It was hurting Nina. It would all come, all come, in God's good time. The young did not live to-day, but always to-morrow. There seemed no time to live to-day, for any one. First one looked ahead and said, "I will be so happy." And before one knew it one was looking back and saying: "I was so happy."

"She'll be all right," he said aloud.

He got up and whistled for the dog.

"I'll take him around the block before I lock up," he said heavily. He bent over and kissed his wife. She was a sad figure to him in her black dress. He did not say to her what he thought sometimes; that Jim had been saved a great deal. That to live on, and to lose the things one loved, one by one, was harder than to go quickly, from a joyous youth.

He had not told her what he knew about Jim's companion that night. She would never have understood. In her simple and child-like faith she knew that her boy sat that day among the blessed company of heaven. He himself believed that Jim had gone forgiven into whatever lay behind the veil we call death, had gone shriven and clean before the Judge who knew the urge of youth and life. He did not fear for Jim. He only missed him.

He walked around the block that night, a stooped commonplace figure, the dog at his heels. Now and then he spoke to him, for companionship. At the corner he stopped and looked along the side street toward the Livingstone house. And as he looked he sighed. Jim and Nina, and now Elizabeth. Jim and Nina were beyond his care now. He could do no more. But what could he do for Elizabeth? That, too, wasn't that beyond him? He stood still, facing the tragedy of his helplessness, beset by vague apprehensions. Then he went on doggedly, his hands clasped behind him, his head sunk on his breast.

He lay awake for a long time that night, wondering whether he and Dick had been quite fair to Elizabeth. She should, he thought, have been told. Then, if Dick's apprehensions were justified, she would have had some preparation. As it was—Suppose something turned up out there, something that would break her heart?

He had thought Margaret was sleeping, but after a time she moved and slipped her hand into his. It comforted him. That, too, was life. Very soon now they would be alone together again, as in the early days before the children came. All the years and the struggle, and then back where they started. But still, thank God, hand in hand.

Ever since the night of Jim's death Mrs. Sayre had been a constant visitor to the house. She came in, solid, practical, and with an everyday manner neither forcedly cheerful nor too decorously mournful, which made her very welcome. After the three first days, when she had practically lived at the house, there was no necessity for small pretensions with her. She knew the china closet and the pantry, and the kitchen. She had even penetrated to Mr. Wheeler's shabby old den on the second floor, and had slept a part of the first night there on the leather couch with broken springs which he kept because it fitted his body.

She was a kindly woman, and she had ached with pity. And, because of her usual detachment from the town and its affairs, the feeling that she was being of service gave her a little glow of content. She liked the family, too, and particularly she liked Elizabeth. But after she had seen Dick and Elizabeth together once or twice she felt that no plan she might make for Wallace could possibly succeed. Lying on the old leather couch that first night, between her frequent excursions among the waking family, she had thought that out and abandoned it.

But, during the days that followed the funeral, she was increasingly anxious about Wallace. She knew that rumors of the engagement had reached him, for he was restless and irritable. He did not care to go out, but wandered about the house or until late at night sat smoking alone on the terrace, looking down at the town with sunken, unhappy eyes. Once or twice in the evening he had taken his car and started out, and lying awake in her French bed she would hear him coming hours later. In the mornings his eyes were suffused and his color bad, and she knew that he was drinking in order to get to sleep.

On the third day after Dick's departure for the West she got up when she heard him coming in, and putting on her dressing gown and slippers, knocked at his door.

"Come in," he called ungraciously.

She found him with his coat off, standing half defiantly with a glass of whisky and soda in his hand. She went up to him and took it from him.

"We've had enough of that in the family, Wallie," she said. "And it's a pretty poor resource in time of trouble."

"I'll have that back, if you don't mind."

"Nonsense," she said briskly, and flung it, glass and all, out of the window. She was rather impressive when she turned.

"I've been a fairly indulgent mother," she said. "I've let you alone, because it's a Sayre trait to run away when they feel a pull on the bit. But there's a limit to my patience, and it is reached when my son drinks to forget a girl."

He flushed and glowered at her in somber silence, but she moved about the room calmly, giving it a housekeeper's critical inspection, and apparently unconscious of his anger.

"I don't believe you ever cared for any one in all your life," he said roughly. "If you had, you would know."

She was straightening a picture over the mantel, and she completed her work before she turned.

"I care for you."

"That's different."

"Very well, then. I cared for your father. I cared terribly. And he killed my love."

She padded out of the room, her heavy square body in its blazing kimono a trifle rigid, but her face still and calm. He remained staring at the door when she had closed it, and for some time after. He knew what message for him had lain behind that emotionless speech of hers, not only understanding, but a warning. She had cared terribly, and his father had killed that love. He had drunk and played through his gay young life, and then he had died, and no one had greatly mourned him.

She had left the decanter on its stand, and he made a movement toward it. Then, with a half smile, he picked it up and walked to the window with it. He was still smiling, half boyishly, as he put out his light and got into bed. It had occurred to him that the milkman's flivver, driving in at the break of dawn, would encounter considerable glass.

By morning, after a bad night, he had made a sort of double-headed resolution, that he was through with booze, as he termed it, and that he would find out how he stood with Elizabeth. But for a day or two no opportunity presented itself. When he called there was always present some grave-faced sympathizing visitor, dark clad and low of voice, and over the drawing-room

217

would hang the indescribable hush of a house in mourning. It seemed to touch Elizabeth, too, making her remote and beyond earthly things. He would go in, burning with impatience, hungry for the mere sight of her, fairly overcharged with emotion, only to face that strange new spirituality that made him ashamed of the fleshly urge in him.

Once he found Clare Rossiter there, and was aware of something electric in the air. After a time he identified it. Behind the Rossiter girl's soft voice and sympathetic words, there was a veiled hostility. She was watching Elizabeth, was overconscious of her. And she was, for some reason, playing up to himself. He thought he saw a faint look of relief on Elizabeth's face when Clare at last rose to go.

"I'm on my way to see the man Dick Livingstone left in his place," Clare said, adjusting her veil at the mirror. "I've got a cold. Isn't it queer, the way the whole Livingstone connection is broken up?"

"Hardly queer. And it's only temporary."

"Possibly. But if you ask me, I don't believe Dick will come back. Mind, I don't defend the town, but it doesn't like to be fooled. And he's fooled it for years. I know a lot of people who'd quit going to him." She turned to Wallie.

"He isn't David's nephew, you know. The question is, who is he? Of course I don't say it, but a good many are saying that when a man takes a false identity he has something to hide."

She gave them no chance to reply, but sauntered out with her sex-conscious, half-sensuous walk. Outside the door her smile faded, and her face was hard and bitter. She might forget Dick Livingstone, but never would she forgive herself for her confession to Elizabeth, nor Elizabeth for having heard it.

Wallie turned to Elizabeth when she had gone, slightly bewildered.

"What's got into her?" he inquired. And then, seeing Elizabeth's white face, rather shrewdly: "That was one for him and two for you, was it?"

"I don't know. Probably."

"I wonder if you would look like that if any one attacked me!"

"No one attacks you, Wallie."

"That's not an answer. You wouldn't, would you? It's different, isn't it?"

"Yes. A little."

He straightened, and looked past her, unseeing, at the wall. "I guess I've known it for quite a while," he said at last. "I didn't want to believe it, so I wouldn't. Are you engaged to him?"

"Yes. It's not to be known just yet, Wallie."

"He's a good fellow," he said, after rather a long silence. "Not that that makes it easier," he added with a twisted smile. Then, boyishly and unexpectedly he said, "Oh, my God!"

He sat down, and when the dog came and placed a head on his knee he patted it absently. He wanted to go, but he had a queer feeling that when he went he went for good.

"I've cared for you for years," he said. "I've been a poor lot, but I'd have been a good bit worse, except for you."

And again:

"Only last night I made up my mind that if you'd have me, I'd make something out of myself. I suppose a man's pretty weak when he puts a responsibility like that on a girl."

She yearned over him, rather. She made little tentative overtures of friendship and affection. But he scarcely seemed to hear them, wrapped as he was in the selfish absorption of his disappointment. When she heard the postman outside and went to the door for the mail, she thought he had not noticed her going. But when she returned he was watching her with jealous, almost tragic eyes.

"I suppose you hear from him by every mail."

"There has been nothing to-day."

Something in her voice or her face made him look at her closely.

"Has he written at all?"

"The first day he got there. Not since."

He went away soon, and not after all with the feeling of going for good. In his sceptical young mind, fed by Clare's malice, was growing a comforting doubt of Dick's good faith.

XXVII

When Wilkins had disappeared around the angle of the staircase Bassett went to a chair and sat down. He felt sick, and his knees were trembling. Something had happened, a search for Clark room by room perhaps, and the discovery had been made.

He was totally unable to think or to plan. With Dick well they could perhaps have made a run for it. The fire-escape stood ready. But as things were—The murmuring among the crowd at the foot of the stairs ceased, and he looked up. Wilkins was on the staircase, searching the lobby with his eyes. When he saw Bassett he came quickly down and confronted him, his face angry and suspicious.

"You're mixed up in this somehow," he said sharply. "You might as well come over with the story. We'll get him. He can't get out of this town."

With the words, and the knowledge that in some incredible fashion Dick had made his escape, Bassett's mind reacted instantly.

"What's eating you, Wilkins?" he demanded. "Who got away? I couldn't get that tongue-tied bell-hop to tell me. Thought it was a fire."

"Don't stall, Bassett. You've had Jud Clark hidden upstairs in three-twenty all day."

Bassett got up and towered angrily over the sheriff. The crowd had turned and was watching.

"In three-twenty?" he said. "You're crazy. Jud Clark! Let me tell you something. I don't know what you've got in your head, but three-twenty is a Doctor Livingstone from near my home town. Well known and highly respected, too. What's more, he's a sick man, and if he's got away, as you say, it's because he is delirious. I had a doctor in to see him an hour ago. I've just arranged for a room at the hospital for him. Does that look as though I've been hiding him?"

The positiveness of his identification and his indignation resulted in a change in Wilkins' manner.

"I'll ask you to stay here until I come back." His tone was official, but less suspicious. "We'll have him in a half hour. It's Clark all right. I'm not saying you knew it was Clark, but I want to ask you some questions."

He went out, and Bassett heard him shouting an order in the street. He went to the street door, and realized that a search was going on, both by the police and by unofficial volunteers. Men on horseback clattered by to guard the borders of the town, and in the vicinity of the hotel searchers were investigating yards and alleyways.

Bassett himself was helpless. He stood by, watching the fire of his own igniting, conscious of the curious scrutiny of the few hotel loungers who remained, and expecting momentarily to hear of Dick's capture. It must come eventually, he felt sure. As to how Dick had been identified, or by what means he had escaped, he was in complete ignorance; and an endeavor to learn by establishing the former entente cordiale between the room clerk and himself was met by a suspicious glance and what amounted to a snub. He went back to his chair against the wall and sat there, waiting for the end.

It was an hour before the sheriff returned, and he came in scowling.

"I'll see you now," he said briefly, and led the way back to the hotel office behind the desk. Bassett's last hope died when he saw sitting there, pale but composed, the elderly maid. The sheriff lost no time.

"Now I'll tell you what we know about your connection with this case, Bassett," he said. "You engaged a car to take you both to the main line to-night. You paid off Clark's room as well as your own this afternoon. When you found he was sick you canceled your going. That's true, isn't it?"

"It is. I've told you I knew him at home, but not as Clark."

"I'll let that go. You intended to take the midnight on the main line, but you ordered a car instead of using the branch road."

"Livingstone was sick. I thought it would be easier. That's all." His voice sharpened. "You can't drag me into this, Sheriff. In the first place I don't believe it was Clark, or he wouldn't have come here, of all places on the earth. I didn't even know he was here, until he came into my room this morning."

"Why did he come into your room?"

"He had seen that I was registered. He said he felt sick. I took him back and put him to bed. To-night I got a doctor."

The sheriff felt in his pocket and produced a piece of paper. Bassett's morale was almost destroyed when he saw that it was Gregory's letter to David.

"I'll ask you to explain this. It was on Clark's bed."

Bassett took it and read it slowly. He was thinking hard.

"I see," he said. "Well, that explains why he came here. He was too sick to talk when I saw him. You see, this is not addressed to him, but to his uncle, David Livingstone. David Livingstone is a brother of Henry Livingstone, who died some years ago at Dry River. This refers to a personal matter connected with the Livingstone estate."

The sheriff took the letter and reread it. He was puzzled.

"You're a good talker," he acknowledged grudgingly. He turned to the maid.

"All right, Hattie," he said. "We'll have that story again. But just a minute." He turned to the reporter. "Mrs. Thorwald here hasn't seen Lizzie Lazarus, the squaw. Lizzie has been sitting in my office ever since noon. Now, Hattie."

Hattie moistened her dry lips.

"It was Jud Clark, all right," she said. "I knew him all his life, off and on. But I wish I hadn't screamed. I don't believe he killed Lucas, and I never will. I hope he gets away."

She eyed the sheriff vindictively, but he only smiled grimly.

"What did I tell you?" he said to Bassett. "Hell with the women—that was Jud Clark. And we'll get him, Hattie. Don't worry. Go on."

She looked at Bassett.

"When you left me, I sat outside the door, as you said. Then I heard him moving, and I went in. The room was not very light, and I didn't know him at first. He sat up in bed and looked at me, and he said, 'Why, hello, Hattie Thorwald.' That's my name. I married a Swede. Then he looked again, and he said, 'Excuse me, I thought you were a Mrs. Thorwald, but I see now you're older.' I recognized him then, and I thought I was going to faint. I knew he'd be arrested the moment it was known he was here. I said, 'Lie down, Mr. Jud. You're not very well.' And I closed the door and locked it. I was scared."

Her voice broke; she fumbled for a handkerchief. The sheriff glanced at Bassett.

"Now where's your Livingstone story?" he demanded. "All right, Hattie. Let's have it."

"I said, 'For God's sake, Mr. Jud, lie still, until I think what to do. The sheriff's likely downstairs this very minute.' And then he went queer and wild. He jumped off the bed and stood listening and staring, and shaking all over. 'I've got to get away,' he said, very loud. 'I won't let them take me. I'll kill myself first!' When I put my hand on his arm he threw it off, and he made for the door. I saw then that he was delirious with fever, and I stood in front of the door and begged him not to go out. But he threw me away so hard that that I fell, and I screamed."

"And then what?"

"That's all. If I hadn't been almost out of my mind I'd never have told that it was Jud Clark. That'll hang on me dying day."

An hour or so later Bassett went back to his room in a state of mental and nervous exhaustion. He knew that from that time on he would be under suspicion and probably under espionage, and he proceeded methodically, his door locked, to go over his papers. His notebook and the cuttings from old files relative to the Clark case he burned in his wash basin and then carefully washed the basin. That done, his attendance on a sick man, and the letter found on the bed was all the positive evidence they had to connect him with the case. He had had some thought of slipping out by the fire-escape and making a search for Dick on his own account, but his lack of familiarity with his surroundings made that practically useless.

At midnight he stretched out on his bed without undressing, and went over the situation carefully. He knew nothing of the various neuroses which affect the human mind, but he had a vague impression that memory when lost did eventually return, and Dick's recognition of the chambermaid pointed to such a return. He wondered what a man would feel under such conditions, what he would think. He could not do it. He abandoned the effort finally, and lay frowning at the ceiling while he considered his own part in the catastrophe. He saw himself, following his training and his instinct, leading the inevitable march toward this night's tragedy, planning, scheming, searching, and now that it had come, lying helpless on his bed while the procession of events went on past him and beyond his control.

When an automobile engine back-fired in the street below he went sick with fear.

He made the resolution then that was to be the guiding motive for his life for the next few months, to fight the thing of his own creating to a finish. But with the resolution newly made he saw the futility of it. He might fight, would fight, but nothing could restore to Dick Livingstone the place he had made for himself in the world. He might be saved from his past, but he could not be given a future.

All at once he was aware that some one was working stealthily at the lock of the door which communicated with a room beyond. He slid cautiously off the bed and went to the light switch, standing with a hand on it, and waited. The wild thought that it might be Livingstone was uppermost in his mind, and when the door creaked open and closed again, that was the word he breathed into the darkness.

"No," said a woman's voice in a whisper. "It's the maid, Hattie. Be careful. There's a guard at the top of the stairs."

He heard her moving to his outer door, and he knew that she stood there, listening, her head against the panel. When she was satisfied she slipped, with the swiftness of familiarity with her surroundings, to the stand beside his bed, and turned on the lamp. In the shaded light he saw that she wore a dark cape, with its hood drawn over her head. In some strange fashion the maid, even the woman, was lost, and she stood, strange, mysterious, and dramatic in the little room.

"If you found Jud Clark, what would you do with him?" she demanded. From beneath the hood her eyes searched his face. "Turn him over to Wilkins and his outfit?"

"I think you know better than that."

"Have you got any plan?"

"Plan? No. They've got every outlet closed, haven't they? Do you know where he is?"

"I know where he isn't, or they'd have him by now. And I know Jud Clark. He'd take to the mountains, same as he did before. He's got a good horse."

"A horse!"

"Listen. I haven't told this, and I don't mean to. They'll learn it in a couple of hours, anyhow. He got out by a back fire-escape—they know that. But they don't know he took Ed Rickett's black mare. They think he's on foot. I've been down there now, and she's gone. Ed's shut up in a room on the top floor, playing poker. They won't break up until about three o'clock and he'll miss his horse then. That's two hours yet."

Bassett tried to see her face in the shadow of the hood. He was puzzled and suspicious at her change of front, more than half afraid of a trap.

"How do I know you are not working with Wilkins?" he demanded. "You could have saved the situation to-night by saying you weren't sure."

"I was upset. I've had time to think since."

He was forced to trust her, eventually, although the sense of some hidden motive, some urge greater than compassion, persisted in him.

"You've got some sort of plan for me, then? I can't follow him haphazard into the mountains at night, and expect to find him."

"Yes. He was delirious when he left. That thing about the sheriff being after him—he wasn't after him then. Not until I gave the alarm. He's delirious, and he thinks he's back to the night he—you know. Wouldn't he do the same thing again, and make for the mountains and the cabin? He went to the cabin before."

Bassett looked at his watch. It was half past twelve.

"Even if I could get a horse I couldn't get out of the town."

"You might, on foot. They'll be trailing Rickett's horse by dawn. And if you can get out of town I can get you a horse. I can get you out, too, I think. I know every foot of the place."

A feeling of theatrical unreality was Bassett's chief emotion during the trying time that followed. The cloaked and shrouded figure of the woman ahead, the passage through two dark and empty rooms by pass key to an unguarded corridor in the rear, the descent of the fire-escape, where they stood flattened against the wall while a man, possibly one of the posse, rode in, tied his horse and stamped in high heeled boots into the building, and always just ahead the sure movement and silent tread of the woman, kept his nerves taut and increased his feeling of the unreal.

At the foot of the fire-escape the woman slid out of sight noiselessly, but under Bassett's feet a tin can rolled and clattered. Then a horse snorted close to his shoulder, and he was frozen with fright. After that she gave him her hand, and led him through an empty outbuilding and another yard into a street.

At two o'clock that morning Bassett, waiting in a lonely road near what he judged to be the camp of a drilling crew, heard a horse coming toward him and snorting nervously as it came and drew back into the shadows until he recognized the shrouded silhouette leading him.

"It belongs to my son," she said. "I'll fix it with him to-morrow. But if you're caught you'll have to say you came out and took him, or you'll get us all in trouble."

She gave him careful instructions as to how to find the trail, and urged him to haste.

"If you get him," she advised, "better keep right on over the range."

He paused, with his foot in the stirrup.

"You seem pretty certain he's taken to the mountains."

"It's your only chance. They'll get him anywhere else."

He mounted and prepared to ride off. He would have shaken hands with her, but the horse was still terrified at her shrouded figure and veered and snorted when she approached. "However it turns out," he said, "you've done your best, and I'm grateful."

The horse moved off and left her standing there, her cowl drawn forward and her hands crossed on her breast. She stood for a moment, facing toward the mountains, oddly monkish in outline and posture. Then she turned back toward the town.

XXVIII

Dick had picked up life again where he had left it off so long before. Gone was David's house built on the sands of forgetfulness. Gone was David himself, and Lucy. Gone not even born into his consciousness was Elizabeth. The war, his work, his new place in the world, were all obliterated, drowned in the flood of memories revived by the shock of Bassett's revelations.

Not that the breaking point had revealed itself as such at once. There was confusion first, then stupor and unconsciousness, and out of that, sharply and clearly, came memory. It was not ten years ago, but an hour ago, a minute ago, that he had stood staring at Howard Lucas on the floor of the billiard room, and had seen Beverly run in through the door.

"Bev!" he was saying. "Bev! Don't look like that!"

He moved and found he was in bed. It had been a dream. He drew a long breath, looked about the room, saw the woman and greeted her. But already he knew he had not been dreaming. Things were sharpening in his mind. He shuddered and looked at the floor, but nobody lay there. Only the horror in his mind, and the instinct to get away from it. He was not thinking at all, but rising in him was not only the need for flight, but the sense of pursuit. They were after him. They would get him. They must never get him alive.

Instinct and will took the place of thought, and whatever closed chamber in his brain had opened, it clearly influenced his physical condition. He bore all the stigmata of prolonged and heavy drinking; his nerves were gone; he twitched and shook. When he got down the fire-escape his legs would scarcely hold him.

The discovery of Ed Rickett's horse in the courtyard, saddled and ready, fitted in with the brain pattern of the past.

Like one who enters a room for the first time, to find it already familiar, for a moment he felt that this thing that he was doing he had done before. Only for a moment. Then partial memory ceased, and he climbed into the saddle, rode out and turned toward the mountains and the cabin. By that strange quality of the brain which is called habit, although the habit be of only one emphatic precedent, he followed the route he had taken ten years before. How closely will never be known. Did he stop at this turn to look back, as he had once before? Did he let his horse breathe there? Not the latter, probably, for as, following the blind course that he had followed ten years before, he left the town and went up the canyon trail, he was riding as though all the devils of hell were behind him.

One thing is certain. The reproduction of the conditions of the earlier flight, the familiar associations of the trail, must have helped rather than hindered his fixation in the past. Again he was Judson Clark, who had killed a man, and was flying from himself and from pursuit.

Before long his horse was in acute distress, but he did not notice it. At the top of the long climb the animal stopped, but he kicked him on recklessly. He was as unaware of his own fatigue, or that he was swaying in the saddle, until galloping across a meadow the horse stumbled and threw him.

He lay still for some time; not hurt but apparently lacking the initiative to get up again. He had at that period the alternating lucidity and mental torpor of the half drunken man. But struggling up through layers of blackness at last there came again the instinct for flight, and he got on the horse and set off.

The torpor again overcame him and he slept in the saddle. When the horse stopped he roused and kicked it on. Once he came up through the blackness to the accompaniment of a great roaring, and found that the animal was saddle deep in a ford, and floundering badly among the rocks. He turned its head upstream, and got it out safely.

Toward dawn some of the confusion was gone, but he firmly fixed in the past. The horse wandered on, head down, occasionally stopping to seize a leaf as it passed, and once to drink deeply at a spring. Dick was still not thinking—there was something that forbade him to think-but he was weak and emotional. He muttered:

"Poor Bev! Poor old Bev!"

A great wave of tenderness and memory swept over him. Poor Bev! He had made life hell for her, all right. He had an almost uncontrollable impulse to turn the horse around, go back and see her once more. He was gone anyhow. They would get him. And he wanted her to know that he would have died rather than do what he had done.

The flight impulse died; he felt sick and very cold, and now and then he shook violently. He began to watch the trail behind him for the pursuit, but without fear. He seemed to have been wandering for a thousand black nights through deep gorges and over peaks as high as the stars, and now he wanted to rest, to stop somewhere and sleep, to be warm again. Let them come and take him, anywhere out of this nightmare.

With the dawn still gray he heard a horse behind and below him on the trail up the cliff face. He stopped and sat waiting, twisted about in his saddle, his expression ugly and defiant, and yet touchingly helpless, the look of a boy in trouble and at bay. The horseman came into sight on the trail below, riding hard, a middle-aged man in a dark sack suit and a straw hat, an oddly incongruous figure and manifestly weary. He rode bent forward, and now and again he raised his eyes from the trail and searched the wall above with bloodshot, anxious eyes.

On the turn below Dick, Bassett saw him for the first time, and spoke to him in a quiet voice.

"Hello, old man," he said. "I began to think I was going to miss you after all."

His scrutiny of Dick's face had rather reassured him. The delirium had passed, apparently. Dishevelled although he was, covered with dust and with sweat from the horse, Livingstone's eyes were steady enough. As he rode up to him, however, he was not so certain. He found himself surveyed with a sort of cool malignity that startled him.

"Miss me!" Livingstone sneered bitterly. "With every damned hill covered by this time with your outfit! I'll tell you this. If I'd had a gun you'd never have got me alive."

Bassett was puzzled and slightly ruffled.

"My outfit! I'll tell you this, son, I've risked my neck half the night to get you out of this mess."

"God Almighty couldn't get me out of this mess," Dick said somberly.

It was then that Bassett saw something not quite normal in his face, and he rode closer.

"See here, Livingstone," he said, in a soothing tone, "nobody's going to get you. I'm here to keep them from getting you. We've got a good start, but we'll have to keep moving."

Dick sat obstinately still, his horse turned across the trail, and his eyes still suspicious and unfriendly.

"I don't know you," he said doggedly. "And I've done all the running away I'm going to do. You go back and tell Wilkins I'm here and to come and get me. The sooner the better." The sneer faded, and he turned on Bassett with a depth of tragedy in his eyes that frightened the reporter. "My God," he said, "I killed a man last night! I can't go through life with that on me. I'm done, I tell you."

"Last night!" Some faint comprehension began to dawn in Bassett's mind, a suspicion of the truth. But there was no time to verify it. He turned and carefully inspected the trail to where it came into sight at the opposite rim of the valley. When he was satisfied that the pursuit was still well behind them he spoke again.

"Pull yourself together, Livingstone," he said, rather sharply. "Think a bit. You didn't kill anybody last night. Now listen," he added impressively. "You are Livingstone, Doctor Richard Livingstone. You stick to that, and think about it."

But Dick was not listening, save to some bitter inner voice, for suddenly he turned his horse around on the trail. "Get out of the way," he said, "I'm going back to give myself up."

He would have done it, probably, would have crowded past Bassett on the narrow trail and headed back toward capture, but for his horse. It balked and whirled on the ledge, but it would not pass Bassett. Dick swore and kicked it, his face ugly and determined, but it refused sullenly. He slid out of the saddle then and tried to drag it on, but he was suddenly weak and sick. He staggered. Bassett was off his horse in a moment and caught him. He eased him onto a boulder, and he sat there, his shoulders sagging and his whole body twitching.

"Been drinking my head off," he said at last. "If I had a drink now I'd straighten out." He tried to sit up. "That's what's the matter with me. I'm funking, of course, but that's not all. I'd give my soul for some whisky.'"

"I can get you a drink, if you'll come on about a mile," Bassett coaxed. "At the cabin you and I talked about yesterday."

"Now you're talking." Dick made an effort and got to his feet, shaking off Bassett's assisting arm. "For God's sake keep your hands off me," he said irritably. "I've got a hangover, that's all."

He got into his saddle without assistance and started off up the trail. Bassett once more searched the valley, but it was empty save for a deer drinking at the stream far below. He turned and followed.

He was fairly hopeless by that time, what with Dick's unexpected resistance and the change in the man himself. He was dealing with something he did not understand, and the hypothesis of delirium did not hold. There was a sort of desperate sanity in Dick's eyes. That statement, now, about drinking his head off—he hadn't looked yesterday like a drinking man. But now he did. He was twitching, his hands shook. On the rock his face had been covered with a cold sweat. What was that the doctor yesterday had said about delirium tremens? Suppose he collapsed? That meant capture.

He did not need to guide Dick to the cabin. He turned off the trail himself, and Bassett, following, saw him dismount and survey the ruin with a puzzled face. But he said nothing. Bassett waiting outside to tie the horses came in to find him sitting on one of the dilapidated chairs, staring around, but all he said was:

"Get me that drink, won't you? I'm going to pieces." Bassett found his tin cup where he had left it on a shelf and poured out a small amount of whisky from his flask.

"This is all we have," he explained. "We'll have to go slow with it."

It had an almost immediate effect. The twitching grew less, and a faint color came into Dick's face. He stood up and stretched himself. "That's better," he said. "I was all in. I must have been riding that infernal horse for years."

He wandered about while the reporter made a fire and set the coffee pot to boil. Bassett, glancing up once, saw him surveying the ruined lean-to from the doorway, with an expression he could not understand. But he did not say anything, nor did he speak again until Bassett called him to get some food. Even then he was laconic, and he seemed to be listening and waiting.

Once something startled the horses outside, and he sat up and listened.

"They're here!" he said.

"I don't think so," Bassett replied, and went to the doorway. "No," he called back over his shoulder, "you go on and finish. I'll watch."

"Come back and eat," Dick said surlily.

He ate very little, but drank of the coffee. Bassett too ate almost nothing. He was pulling himself together for the struggle that was to come, marshaling his arguments for flight, and trying to fathom the extent of the change in the man across the small table.

Dick put down his tin cup and got up. He was strong again, and the nightmare confusion of the night had passed away. Instead of it there was a desperate lucidity and a courage born of desperation. He remembered it all distinctly; he had killed Howard Lucas the night before. Before long Wilkins or some of his outfit would ride up to the door, and take him back to Norada. He was not afraid of that. They would always think he had run away because he was afraid of capture, but it was not that. He had run away from Bev's face. Only he had not got away from it. It had been with him all night, and it was with him now.

But he would have to go back. He couldn't be caught like a rat in a trap. The Clarks didn't run away. They were fighters. Only the Clarks didn't kill. They fought, but they didn't murder.

He picked up his hat and went to the door.

"Well, you've been mighty kind, old man," he said. "But I've got to go back. I ran last night like a scared kid, but I'm through with that sort of foolishness."

"I'd give a good bit," Bassett said, watching him, "to know what made you run last night. You were safe where you were."

225

"I don't know what you are talking about," Dick said drearily. "I didn't run from them. I ran to get away from something." He turned away irritably. "You wouldn't understand. Say I was drunk. I was, for that matter. I'm not over it yet."

Bassett watched him.

"I see," he said quietly. "It was last night, was it, that this thing happened?"

"You know it, don't you?"

"And, after it happened, do you remember what followed?"

"I've been riding all night. I didn't care what happened. I knew I'd run into a whale of a blizzard, but I—"

He stopped and stared outside, to where the horses grazed in the upland meadow, knee deep in mountain flowers. Bassett, watching him, saw the incredulity in his eyes, and spoke very gently.

"My dear fellow," he said, "you are right. Try to understand what I am saying, and take it easy. You rode into a blizzard, right enough. But that was not last night. It was ten years ago."

XXIX

Had Bassett had some wider knowledge of Dick's condition he might have succeeded better during that bad hour that followed. Certainly, if he had hoped that the mere statement of fact and its proof would bring results, he failed. And the need for haste, the fear of the pursuit behind them, made him nervous and incoherent.

He had first to accept the incredible, himself—that Dick Livingstone no longer existed, that he had died and was buried deep in some chamber of an unconscious mind. He made every effort to revive him, to restore him into the field of consciousness, but without result. And his struggle was increased in difficulty by the fact that he knew so little of Dick's life. David's name meant nothing, apparently, and it was the only name he knew. He described the Livingstone house; he described Elizabeth as he had seen her that night at the theater. Even Minnie. But Dick only shook his head. And until he had aroused some instinct, some desire to live, he could not combat Dick's intention to return and surrender.

"I understand what you are saying," Dick would say. "I'm trying to get it. But it doesn't mean anything to me."

He even tried the war.

"War? What war?" Dick asked. And when he heard about it he groaned.

"A war!" he said. "And I've missed it!"

But soon after that he got up, and moved to the door.

"I'm going back," he said.

"Why?"

"They're after me, aren't they?"

"You're forgetting again. Why should they be after you now, after ten years?"

"I see. I can't get it, you know. I keep listening for them."

Bassett too was listening, but he kept his fears to himself.

"Why did you do it?" he asked finally.

"I was drunk, and I hated him. He married a girl I was crazy about."

Bassett tried new tactics. He stressed the absurdity of surrendering for a crime committed ten years before and forgotten.

"They won't convict you anyhow," he urged. "It was a quarrel, wasn't it? I mean, you didn't deliberately shoot him?"

"I don't remember. We quarreled. Yes. I don't remember shooting him."

"What do you remember?"

226

Dick made an effort, although he was white to the lips.

"I saw him on the floor," he said slowly, and staggered a little.

"Then you don't even know you did it."

"I hated him."

But Bassett saw that his determination to surrender himself was weakening. Bassett fought it with every argument he could summon, and at last he brought forward the one he felt might be conclusive.

"You see, you've not only made a man's place in the world, Clark, as I've told you. You've formed associations you can't get away from. You've got to think of the Livingstones, and you told me yesterday a shock would kill the old man. But it's more than that. There's a girl back in your town. I think you were engaged to her."

But if he had hoped to pierce the veil with that statement he failed. Dick's face flushed, and he went to the door of the cabin, much as he had gone to the window the day before. He did not look around when he spoke.

"Then I'm an unconscionable cad," he said. "I've only cared for one woman in my life. And I've shipwrecked her for good."

"You mean—"

"You know who I mean."

Sometime later Bassett got on his horse and rode out to a ledge which commanded a long stretch of trail in the valley below. Far away horsemen were riding along it, one behind the other, small dots that moved on slowly but steadily. He turned and went back to the cabin.

"We'd better be moving," he said, "and it's up to you to say where. You've got two choices. You can go back to Norada and run the chance of arrest. You know what that means. Without much chance of a conviction you will stand trial and bring wretchedness to the people who stood by you before and who care for you now. Or you can go on over the mountains with me and strike the railroad somewhere to the West. You'll have time to think things over, anyhow. They've waited ten years. They can wait longer."

To his relief Dick acquiesced. He had become oddly passive; he seemed indeed not greatly interested. He did not even notice the haste with which Bassett removed the evidences of their meal, or extinguished the dying fire and scattered the ashes. Nor, when they were mounted, the care with which they avoided the trail. He gave, when asked, information as to the direction of the railroad at the foot of the western slope of the range, and at the same instigation found a trail for them some miles beyond their starting point. But mostly he merely followed, in a dead silence.

They made slow progress. Both horses were weary and hungry, and the going was often rough and even dangerous. But for Dick's knowledge of the country they would have been hopelessly lost. Bassett, however, although tortured with muscular soreness, felt his spirits rising as the miles were covered, and there was no sign of the pursuit.

By mid-afternoon they were obliged to rest their horses and let them graze, and the necessity of food for themselves became insistent. Dick stretched out and was immediately asleep, but the reporter could not rest. The magnitude of his undertaking obsessed him. They had covered perhaps twenty miles since leaving the cabin, and the railroad was still sixty miles away. With fresh horses they could have made it by dawn of the next morning, but he did not believe their jaded animals could go much farther. The country grew worse instead of better. A pass ahead, which they must cross, was full of snow.

He was anxious, too, as to Dick's physical condition. The twitching was gone, but he was very pale and he slept like a man exhausted and at his physical limit. But the necessity of crossing the pass before nightfall or of waiting until dawn to do it drove Bassett back from an anxious reconnoitering of the trail at five o'clock, to rouse the sleeping man and start on again.

Near the pass, however, Dick roused himself and took the lead.

"Let me ahead, Bassett," he said peremptorily. "And give your horse his head. He'll take care of you if you give him a chance."

Bassett was glad to fall back. He was exhausted and nervous. The trail frightened him. It clung to the side of a rocky wall, twisting and turning on itself; it ran under milky waterfalls of glacial water, and higher up it led over an ice field which was a glassy bridge over a rushing stream beneath. To add to their wretchedness mosquitoes hung about them in voracious clouds, and tiny black gnats which got into their eyes and their nostrils and set the horses frantic.

Once across the ice field Dick's horse fell and for a time could not get up again. He lay, making ineffectual efforts to rise, his sides heaving, his eyes rolling in distress. They gave up then, and prepared to make such camp as they could.

With the setting of the sun it had grown bitterly cold, and Bassett was forced to light a fire. He did it under the protection of the mountain wall, and Dick, after unsaddling his fallen horse, built a rough shelter of rocks against the wind. After a time the exhausted horse got up, but there was no forage, and the two animals stood disconsolate, or made small hopeless excursions, noses to the ground, among the moss and scrub pines.

Before turning in Bassett divided the remaining contents of the flask between them, and his last cigarettes. Dick did not talk. He sat, his back to the shelter, facing the fire, his mind busy with what Bassett knew were bitter and conflicting thoughts. Once, however, as the reporter was dozing off, Dick spoke.

"You said I told you there was a girl," he said. "Did I tell you her name?"

"No."

"All right. Go to sleep. I thought if I heard it it might help."

Bassett lay back and watched him.

"Better get some sleep, old man," he said.

He dozed, to waken again cold and shivering. The fire had burned low, and Dick was sitting near it, unheeding, and in a deep study. He looked up, and Bassett was shocked at the quiet tragedy in his face.

"Where is Beverly Carlysle now?" he asked. "Or do you know?"

"Yes. I saw her not long ago."

"Is she married again?"

"No. She's revived 'The Valley,' and she's in New York with it."

Dick slept for only an hour or so that night, but as he slept he dreamed. In his dream he was at peace and happy, and there was a girl in a black frock who seemed to be a part of that peace. When he roused, however, still with the warmth of his dream on him, he could not summon her. She had slipped away among the shadows of the night.

He sat by the fire in the grip of a great despair. He had lost ten years out of his life, his best years. And he could not go back to where he had left off. There was nothing to go back to but shame and remorse. He looked at Bassett, lying by the fire, and tried to fit him into the situation. Who was he, and why was he here? Why had he ridden out at night alone, into unknown mountains, to find him?

As though his intent gaze had roused the sleeper, Bassett opened his eyes, at first drowsily, then wide awake. He raised himself on his elbow and listened, as though for some far-off sound, and his face was strained and anxious. But the night was silent, and he relaxed and slept again.

Something that had been forming itself in Dick's mind suddenly crystallized into conviction. He rose and walked to the edge of the mountain wall and stood there listening. When he went back to the fire he felt in his pockets, found a small pad and pencil, and bending forward to catch the light, commenced to write... At dawn Bassett wakened. He was stiff and wretched, and he grunted as he moved. He turned over and surveyed the small plateau. It was empty, except for his horse, making its continuous, hopeless search for grass.

XXX

David was enjoying his holiday. He lay in bed most of the morning, making the most of his one after-breakfast cigar and surrounded by newspaper and magazines. He had made friends of the waiter who brought his breakfast, and of the little chambermaid who looked after his room, and such conversations as this would follow:

"Well, Nellie," he would say, "and did you go to the dance on the pier last night?"

"Oh, yes, doctor."

"Your gentleman friend showed up all right, then?"

"Oh, yes. He didn't telephone because he was on a job out of town."

Here perhaps David would lower his voice, for Lucy was never far away.

"Did you wear the flowers?"

"Yes, violets. I put one away to remember you by. It was funny at first. I wouldn't tell him who gave them to me."

David would chuckle delightedly.

"That's right," he would say. "Keep him guessing, the young rascal. We men are kittle cattle, Nellie, kittle cattle!"

Even the valet unbent to him, and inquired if the doctor needed a man at home to look after him and his clothes. David was enormously tickled.

"Well," he said, with a twinkle in his eye. "I'll tell you how I manage now, and then you'll see. When I want my trousers pressed I send them downstairs and then I wait in my bathrobe until they come back. I'm a trifle better off for boots, but you'd have to knock Mike, my hired man, unconscious before he'd let you touch them."

The valet grinned understandingly.

"Of course, there's my nephew," David went on, a little note of pride in his voice. "He's become engaged recently, and I notice he's bought some clothes. But still I don't think even he will want anybody to hold his trousers while he gets into them."

David chuckled over that for a long time after the valet had gone.

He was quite happy and contented. He spent all afternoon in a roller chair, conversing affably with the man who pushed him, and now and then when Lucy was out of sight getting out and stretching his legs. He picked up lost children and lonely dogs, and tried his eye in a shooting gallery, and had hard work keeping off the roller coasters and out of the sea.

Then, one day, when he had been gone some time, he was astonished on entering his hotel to find Harrison Miller sitting in the lobby. David beamed with surprise and pleasure.

"You old humbug!" he said. "Off on a jaunt after all! And the contempt of you when I was shipped here!"

Harrison Miller was constrained and uncomfortable. He had meant to see Lucy first. She was a sensible woman, and she would know just what David could stand, or could not. But David did not notice his constraint; took him to his room, made him admire the ocean view, gave him a cigar, and then sat down across from him, beaming and hospitable.

"Suffering Crimus, Miller," he said. "I didn't know I was homesick until I saw you. Well, how's everything? Dick's letters haven't been much, and we haven't had any for several days."

Harrison Miller cleared his throat. He knew that David had not been told of Jim Wheeler's death, but that Lucy knew. He knew too from Walter Wheeler that David did not know that Dick had gone west. Did Lucy know that, or not? Probably yes. But he considered the entire benevolent conspiracy an absurdity and a mistake. It was making him uncomfortable, and most of his life had been devoted to being comfortable.

He decided to temporize.

"Things are about the same," he said. "They're going to pave Chisholm Street. And your Mike knocked down the night watchman last week. I got him off with a fine."

"I hope he hasn't been in my cellar. He's got a weakness, but then—How's Dick? Not overworking?"

"No. He's all right."

But David was no man's fool. He began to see something strange in Harrison's manner, and he bent forward in his chair.

"Look here, Harrison," he said, "there's something the matter with you. You've got something on your mind."

"Well, I have and I haven't. I'd like to see Lucy, David, if she's about."

"Lucy's gadding. You can tell me if you can her. What is it? Is it about Dick?"

"In a way, yes."

"He's not sick?"

"No. He's all right, as far as I know. I guess I'd better tell you, David. Walter Wheeler has got some sort of bee in his bonnet, and he got me to come on. Dick was pretty tired and—well, one or two things happened to worry him. One was that Jim Wheeler—you'll get this sooner or later—was in an automobile accident, and it did for him."

David had lost some of his ruddy color. It was a moment before he spoke.

"Poor Jim," he said hoarsely. "He was a good boy, only full of life. It will be hard on the family."

"Yes," Harrison Miller said simply.

But David was resentful, too. When his friends were in trouble he wanted to know about it. He was somewhat indignant and not a little hurt. But he soon reverted to Dick.

"I'll go back and send him off for a rest," he said. "I'm as good as I'll ever be, and the boy's tired. What's the bee in Wheeler's bonnet?"

"Look here, David, you know your own business best, and Wheeler didn't feel at liberty to tell me very much. But he seemed to think you were the only one who could tell us certain things. He'd have come himself, but it's not easy for him to leave the family just now. Dick went away just after Jim's funeral. He left a young chap named Reynolds in his place, and, I believe, in order not to worry you, some letters to be mailed at intervals."

"Went where?" David asked, in a terrible voice.

"To a town called Norada, in Wyoming. Near his old home somewhere. And the Wheelers haven't heard anything from him since the day he got there. That's three weeks ago. He wrote Elizabeth the night he got there, and wired her at the same time. There's been nothing since."

David was gripping the arms of his chair with both hands, but he forced himself to calmness.

"I'll go to Norada at once," he said. "Get a time-table, Harrison, and ring for the valet."

"Not on your life you won't. I'm here to do that, when I've got something to go on. Wheeler thought you might have heard from him. If you hadn't, I was to get all the information I could and then start. Elizabeth's almost crazy. We wired the chief of police of Norada yesterday."

"Yes!" David said thickly. "Trust your friends to make every damned mistake possible! You've set the whole pack on his trail." And then he fell back in his chair, and gasped, "Open the window!"

When Lucy came in, a half hour later, she found David on his bed with the hotel doctor beside him, and Harrison Miller in the room. David was fighting for breath, but he was conscious and very calm. He looked up at her and spoke slowly and distinctly.

"They've got Dick, Lucy," he said.

He looked aged and pinched, and entirely hopeless. Even after his heart had quieted down and he lay still among his pillows, he gave no evidence of his old fighting spirit. He lay with his eyes shut, relaxed and passive. He had done his best, and he had failed. It was out of his hands now, and in the hands of God. Once, as he lay there, he prayed. He said that he had failed, and that now he was too old and weak to fight. That God would have to take it on, and do the best

He could. But he added that if God did not save Dick and bring him back to happiness, that he, David, was through.

Toward morning he wakened from a light sleep. The door into Lucy's room was open and a dim light was burning beyond it. David called her, and by her immediate response he knew she had not been sleeping.

"Yes, David," she said, and came padding in in her bedroom slippers and wadded dressing-gown, a tragic figure of apprehension, determinedly smiling. "What do you want?"

"Sit down, Lucy."

When she had done so he put out his hand, fumbling for hers. She was touched and alarmed, for it was a long while since there had been any open demonstration of affection between them. David was silent for a time, absorbed in thought. Then:

"I'm not in very good shape, Lucy. I suppose you know that. This old pump of mine has sprung a leak or something. I don't want you to worry if anything happens. I've come to the time when I've got a good many over there, and it will be like going home."

Lucy nodded. Her chin quivered. She smoothed his hand, with its high twisted veins.

"I know, David," she said. "Mother and father, and Henry, and a good many friends. But I need you, too. You're all I have, now that Dick—"

"That's why I called you. If I can get out there, I'll go. And I'll put up a fight that will make them wish they'd never started anything. But if I can't, if I—" She felt his fingers tighten on her hand. "If Hattie Thorwald is still living, we'll put her on the stand. If I can't go, for any reason, I want you to see that she is called. And you know where Henry's statement is?"

"In your box, isn't it?"

"Yes. Have the statement read first, and then have her called to corroborate it. Tell the story I have told you—or no, I'll dictate it to you in the morning, and sign it before witnesses. Jake and Bill will testify too."

He felt easier in his mind after that. He had marshalled his forces and begun his preparations for battle. He felt less apprehension now in case he fell asleep, to waken among those he had loved long since and lost awhile. After a few moments his eyes closed, and Lucy went back to her bed and crawled into it.

It was, however, Harrison Miller who took the statement that morning. Lucy's cramped old hand wrote too slowly for David's impatience. Harrison Miller took it, on hotel stationery, covering the carefully numbered pages with his neat, copper-plate writing. He wrote with an impassive face, but with intense interest, for by that time he knew Dick's story.

Never, in his orderly bachelor life, of daily papers and a flower garden and political economy at night, had he been so close to the passions of men to love and hate and the disorder they brought with them.

XXXI

"My brother, Henry Livingstone, was not a strong man," David dictated. "He had the same heart condition I have, but it developed earlier. After he left college he went to Arizona and bought a ranch, and there he met and chummed with Elihu Clark, who had bought an old mine and was reworking it. Henry loaned him a small amount of money at that time, and a number of years later in return for that, when Henry's health failed, Clark, who had grown wealthy, bought him a ranch in Wyoming at Dry River, not far from Clark's own property.

"Henry had been teaching in an Eastern university, and then taken up tutoring. We saw little of him. He was a student, and he became almost a recluse. I saw less of him than ever after Clark gave him the ranch.

"In the spring of 1910 Henry wrote me that he was not well, and I went out to see him. He seemed worried and was in bad shape physically. Elihu Clark had died five years before, and left him a fair sum of money, fifty thousand dollars, but he was living in a way which made me think he was not using it. The ranch buildings were dilapidated, and there was nothing but the barest necessities in the house.

"I taxed Henry with miserliness, and he then told me that the money was not his, but left to him to be used for an illegitimate son of Clark's, born before his marriage, the child of a small rancher's daughter named Hattie Burgess. The Burgess girl had gone to Omaha for its birth, and the story was not known. In early years Clark had paid the child's board through his lawyer to an Omaha woman named Hines, and had later sent him to college. The Burgess girl married a Swede named Thorwald. The boy was eight years older than Judson, Clark's legitimate son.

"After the death of his wife Elihu Clark began to think about the child, especially after Judson became a fair-sized boy. He had the older boy, who went by the name of Hines, sent to college, and in summer he stayed at Henry's tutoring school. Henry said the boy was like the Burgess family, blonde and excitable and rather commonplace. He did not get on well at college, and did not graduate. So far as he knew, Clark never saw him.

"The boy himself believed that he was an orphan, and that the Hines woman had adopted him as a foundling. But on the death of the woman he found that she had no estate, and that a firm of New York attorneys had been paying his college bills.

"He had spent considerable time with Henry, one way and another, and he began to think that Henry knew who he was. He thought at first that Henry was his father, and there was some trouble. In order to end it Henry finally acknowledged that he knew who the father was, and after that he had no peace. Clifton—his name was Clifton Hines—attacked Henry once, and if it had not been for the two men on the place he would have hurt him.

"Henry began to give him money. Clark had left the fifty thousand for the boy with the idea that Henry should start him in business with it. But he only turned up wild-cat schemes that Henry would not listen to. He did not know how Henry got the money, or from where. He thought for a long time that Henry had saved it.

"I'd better say here that Henry was fond of Clifton, although he didn't approve of him. He'd never married, and the boy was like a son to him for a good many years. He didn't have him at the ranch much, however, for he was a Burgess through and through and looked like them. And he was always afraid that somehow the story would get out.

"Then Clifton learned, somehow or other, of Clark's legacy to Henry, and he put two and two together. There was a bad time, but Henry denied it and they went upstairs to bed. That night Clifton broke into Henry's desk and found some letters from Elihu Clark that told the story.

"He almost went crazy. He took the papers up to Henry's and wakened him, standing over Henry with them in hand, and shaking all over. I think they had a struggle, too. All Henry told me was that he took them from him and threw them in the fire.

"That was a year before Henry died, and at the time young Jud Clark's name was in all the newspapers. He had left college after a wild career there, and although Elihu had tied up the property until Jud was twenty-one, Jud had his mother's estate and a big allowance. Then, too, he borrowed on his prospects, and he lost a hundred thousand dollars at Monte Carlo within six weeks after he graduated.

"One way and another he was always in the newspapers, and when he saw how Jud was throwing money away Clifton went wild.

"As Henry had burned the letters he had no proofs. He didn't know who his mother was, but he set to work to find out. He ferreted into Elihu's past life, and he learned something about Hattie Burgess, or Thorwald. She was married by that time, and lived on a little ranch near Norada. He went to see her, and he accused her downright of being his mother. It must have been a bad time for her, for after all he was her son, and she had to disclaim him. She had a husband and a boy by that husband, however, by that time, and she was desperate. She threw

232

him off the track somehow, lied and talked him down, and then went to bed in collapse. She sent for Henry later and told him.

"The queer thing was that as soon as she saw him she wanted him. He was her son. She went to Henry one night, and said she had perjured her soul, and that she wanted him back. She wasn't in love with Thorwald. I think she'd always cared for Clark. She went away finally, however, after promising Henry she would keep Clark's secret. But I have a suspicion that later on she acknowledged the truth to the boy.

"What he wanted, of course, was a share of the Clark estate. Of course he hadn't a chance in law, but he saw a chance to blackmail young Jud Clark and he tried it. Not personally, for he hadn't any real courage, but by mail. Clark's attorneys wrote back saying they would jail him if he tried it again, and he went back to Dry River and after Henry again.

"That was in the spring of 1911. Henry was uneasy, for Clifton was not like himself. He had spells of brooding, and he took to making long trips on his horse into the mountains, and coming in with the animal run to death. Henry thought, too, that he was seeing the Thorwald woman, the mother. Thorwald had died, and she was living with the son on their ranch and trying to sell it. He thought Hines was trying to have her make a confession which would give him a hold on Jud Clark.

"Henry was not well, and in the early fall he knew he hadn't long to live. He wrote out the story and left it in his desk for me to read after he had gone, and as he added to it from time to time, when I got it it was almost up to date.

"Judson came back to the Clark ranch in September, bringing along an actress named Beverly Carlysle, and her husband, Howard Lucas. There was considerable talk, because it was known Jud had been infatuated with the woman. But no one saw much of the party, outside of the ranch. The Carlysle woman seemed to be a lady, but the story was that both men were drinking a good bit, especially Jud.

"Henry wrote that Hines had been in the East for some months at that time, and that he had not heard from him. But he felt that it was only a truce, and that he would turn up again, hell bent for trouble. He made a will and left the money to me, with instructions to turn it over to Hines. It is still in the bank, and amounts to about thirty-five thousand dollars. It is not mine, and I will not touch it. But I have never located Clifton Hines.

"In the last entry in his record I call attention to my brother's statement that he did not regard Clifton Hines as entirely sane on this one matter, and to his conviction that the hatred Hines then bore him, amounting to a delusion of persecution, might on his death turn against Judson Clark. He instructed me to go to Clark, tell him the story, and put him on his guard.

"Clark and his party had been at the ranch only a day or two when one night Hines turned up at Dry River. He wanted the fifty thousand, or what was left of it, and when he failed to move Henry he attacked him. The two men on the place heard the noise and ran in, but Hines got away. Henry swore them to secrecy, and told them the story. He felt he might need help.

"From what the two men at the ranch told me when I got there, I think Hines stayed somewhere in the mountains for the next day or two, and that he came down for food the night Henry died.

"Just what he contributed to Henry's death I do not know. Henry fell in one room, and was found in bed in another when the hands had been taking the cattle to the winter range, and he'd been alone in the house.

"When I got there the funeral was over. I read the letter he had left, and then I talked to the two hands, Bill Ardary and Jake Mazetti. They would not talk at first, but I showed them Henry's record and then they were free enough. The autopsy had shown that Henry died from heart disease, but he had a cut on his head also, and they believed that Hines had come back, had quarreled with him again, and had knocked him down.

"As Henry had in a way handed over to me his responsibility for the boy, and as I wanted to transfer the money, I waited for three weeks at the ranch, hoping he would turn up again. I saw the Thorwald woman, but she protested that she did not know where he was. And I made two attempts to see and warn Jud Clark, but failed both times. Then one night the Thorwald woman came in, looking like a ghost, and admitted that Hines had been hiding in the mountains since Henry's death, that he insisted he had killed him, and that he blamed Jud Clark for that, and for all the rest of his troubles. She was afraid he would kill Clark. The three of us, the two men at the ranch and myself, prepared to go into the mountains and hunt for him, before he got snowed in.

"Then came the shooting at the Clark place, and I rode over that night in a howling storm and helped the coroner and a Norada doctor in the examination. All the evidence was against Clark, especially his running away. But I happened on Hattie Thorwald outside on a verandah—she'd been working at the house—and I didn't need any conversation to tell me what she thought. All she said was:

"He didn't do it, doctor. He's still in the mountains."

"He's been here to-night, Hattie, and you know it. He shot the wrong man."

"But she swore he hadn't been, and at the end I didn't know. I'll say right now that I don't know. But I'll say, too, that I believe that is what happened, and that Hines probably stayed hidden that night on Hattie Thorwald's place. I went there the next day, but she denied it all, and said he was still in the mountains. She carried on about the blizzard and his being frozen to death, until I began to think she was telling the truth.

"The next day I did what only a tenderfoot would do, started into the mountains alone. Bill and Jake were out with a posse after Clark, and I packed up some food and started. I'll not go into the details of that trip. I went in from the Dry River Canyon, and I guess I faced death a dozen times the first day. I had a map, but I lost myself in six hours. I had food and blankets and an axe along, and I built a shelter and stayed there overnight. I had to cut up one of my blankets the next morning and tie up the horse's feet, so he wouldn't sink too deep in the snow. But it stayed cold and the snow hardened, and we got along better after that.

"I'd have turned back more than once, but I thought I'd meet up with some of the sheriff's party. I didn't do that, but I stumbled on a trail on the third day, toward evening. It was the trail made by John Donaldson, as I learned later. I followed it, but I concluded after a while that whoever made it was lost, too. It seemed to be going in a circle. I was in bad shape and had frozen a part of my right hand, when I saw a cabin, and there was smoke coming out of the chimney."

From that time on David's statement dealt with the situation in the cabin; with Jud Clark and the Donaldsons, and with the snow storm, which began again and lasted for days. He spoke at length of his discovery of Clark's identity, and of the fact that the boy had lost all memory of what had happened, and even of who he was. He went into that in detail; the peculiar effect of fear and mental shock on a high-strung nature, especially where the physical condition was lowered by excess and wrong-living; his early attempts, as the boy improved, to pierce the veil, and then his slow-growing conviction that it were an act of mercy not to do so. The Donaldsons' faithfulness, the cessation of the search under the conviction that Clark was dead, both were there, and also David's growing liking for Judson himself. But David's own psychology was interesting and clearly put.

"First of all," he dictated, in his careful old voice, "it must be remembered that I was not certain that the boy had committed the crime. I believed, and I still believe, that Lucas was shot by Clifton Hines, probably through an open window. There were no powder marks on the body. I believed, too, and still believe, that Hines had fled after the crime, either to Hattie Thorwald's house or to the mountains. In one case he had escaped and could not be brought to justice, and in the other he was dead, and beyond conviction.

"But there is another element which I urge, not in defense but in explanation. The boy Judson Clark was a new slate to write on. He had never had a chance. He had had too much money, too much liberty, too little responsibility. His errors had been wiped away by the loss of his memory, and he had, I felt, a chance for a new and useful life.

"I did not come to my decision quickly. It was a long fight for his life, for he had contracted pneumonia, and he had the drinker's heart. But in the long days of his convalescence while Maggie worked in the lean-to, I had time to see what might be done. If in making an experiment with a man's soul I usurped the authority of my Lord and Master, I am sorry. But he knows that I did it for the best.

"I deliberately built up for Judson Clark a new identity. He was my nephew, my brother Henry's son. He had the traditions of an honorable family to carry on, and those traditions were honor, integrity, clean living and work. I did not stress love, for that I felt must be experienced, not talked about. But love was to be the foundation on which I built. The boy had had no love in his life.

"It has worked out. I may not live to see it at its fullest, but I defy the world to produce today a finer or more honorable gentleman, a more useful member of the community. And it will last. The time may come when Judson Clark will again be Judson Clark. I have expected it for many years. But he will never again be the Judson Clark of ten years ago. He may even will to return to the old reckless ways, but as I lie here, perhaps never to see him, I say this: he cannot go back. His character and habits of thought are established.

"To convict Judson Clark of the murder of Howard Lucas is to convict a probably or at least possibly innocent man. To convict Richard Livingstone of that crime is to convict a different man, innocent of the crime, innocent of its memory, innocent of any single impulse to lift his hand against a law of God or the state."

XXXII

For a month Haverly had buzzed with whispered conjectures. It knew nothing, and yet somehow it knew everything. Doctor David was ill at the seashore, and Dick was not with him. Harrison Miller, who was never known to depart farther from his comfortable hearth than the railway station in one direction and the Sayre house in the other, had made a trip East and was now in the far West. Doctor Reynolds, who might or might not know something, had joined the country club and sent for his golf bag.

And Elizabeth Wheeler was going around with a drawn white face and a determined smile that faded the moment one looked away.

The village was hurt and suspicious. It resented its lack of knowledge, and turned cynical where, had it been taken into confidence, it would have been solicitous. It believed that Elizabeth had been jilted, for it knew, via Annie and the Oglethorpe's laundress, that no letters came from Dick. And against Dick its indignation was directed, in a hot flame of mainly feminine anger.

But it sensed a mystery, too, and if it hated a jilt it loved a mystery.

Nina had taken to going about with her small pointed chin held high, and angrily she demanded that Elizabeth do the same.

"You know what they are saying, and yet you go about looking crushed."

"I can't act, Nina. I do go about."

And Nina had a softened moment.

"Don't think about him," she said. "He isn't sick, or he would have had some one wire or write, and he isn't dead, or they'd have found his papers and let us know."

"Then he's in some sort of trouble. I want to go out there. I want to go out there!"

That, indeed, had been her constant cry for the last two weeks. She would have done it probably, packed her bag and slipped away, but she had no money of her own, and even Leslie, to whom she appealed, had refused her when he knew her purpose.

"We're following him up, little sister," he said. "Harrison Miller has gone out, and there's enough talk as it is."

She thought, lying in her bed at night, that they were all too afraid of what people might say. It seemed so unimportant to her. And she could not understand the conspiracy of silence. Other men went away and were not heard from, and the police were notified and the papers told. It seemed to her, too, that every one, her father and Nina and Leslie and even Harrison Miller, knew more than she did.

There had been that long conference behind closed doors, when Harrison Miller came back from seeing David, and before he went west. Leslie had been there, and even Doctor Reynolds, but they had shut her out. And her father had not been the same since.

He seemed, sometimes, to be burning with a sort of inner anger. Not at her, however. He was very gentle with her.

And here was a curious thing. She had always felt that she knew when Dick was thinking of her. All at once, and without any warning, there would come a glow of happiness and warmth, and a sort of surrounding and encircling sense of protection. Rather like what she had felt as a little girl when she had run home through the terrors of twilight, and closed the house door behind her. She was in the warm and lighted house, safe and cared for.

That was completely gone. It was as though the warm and lighted house of her love had turned her out and locked the door, and she was alone outside, cold and frightened.

She avoided the village, and from a sense of delicacy it left her alone. The small gaieties of the summer were on, dinners, dances and picnics, but her mourning made her absence inconspicuous. She could not, however, avoid Mrs. Sayre. She tried to, at first, but that lady's insistence and her own apathy made it easier to accept than to refuse. Then, after a time, she found the house rather a refuge. She seldom saw Wallie, and she found her hostess tactful, kindly and uninquisitive.

"Take the scissors and a basket, child, and cut your mother some roses," she would say. Or they would loot the green houses and, going in the car to the cemetery, make of Jim's grave a thing of beauty and remembrance.

Now and then, of course, she saw Wallie, but he never reverted to the day she had told him of her engagement. Mother and son, she began to feel that only with them could she be herself. For the village, her chin high as Nina had said. At home, assumed cheerfulness. Only at the house on the hill could she drop her pose.

She waited with a sort of desperate courage for word from Harrison Miller. What she wanted that word to be she did not know. There were, of course, times when she had to face the possibility that Dick had deliberately cut himself off from her. After all, there had never been any real reason why he should care for her. She was not clever and not beautiful. Perhaps he had been disappointed in her, and this was the thing they were concealing. Perhaps he had gone back to Wyoming and had there found some one more worthy of im, some one who understood when he talked about the things he did in his laboratory, and did not just sit and listen with loving, rather bewildered eyes.

Then, one night at dinner, a telegram was brought in, and she knew it was the expected word. She felt her mother's eyes on her, and she sat very still with her hands clenched in her lap. But her father did not read it at the table; he got up and went out, and some time later he came to the door. The telegram was not in sight.

"That was from Harrison Miller," he said. "He has traced Dick to a hotel at Norada, but he had left the hotel, and he hasn't got in touch with him yet."

He went away then, and they heard the house door close.

Then, some days later, she learned that Harrison Miller was coming home, and that David was being brought back. She saw that telegram from Mr. Miller, and read into it failure and discouragement, and something more ominous than either.

"Reach home Tuesday night. Nothing definite. Think safe."

"Think safe?" she asked, breathlessly. "Then he has been in danger? What are you keeping from me?" And when no one spoke: "Oh, don't you see how cruel it is? You are all trying to protect me, and you are killing me instead."

"Not danger," her father said, slowly. "So far as we know, he is well. Is all right." And seeing her face: "It is nothing that affects his feeling for you, dear. He is thinking of you and loving you, wherever he is. Only, we don't know where he is."

But when he came back on Tuesday, after seeing Harrison Miller, he was discouraged and sick at heart. He went directly upstairs to his wife, and shut the bedroom door.

"Not a trace," he said, in reply to the question in her eyes. "The situation is as he outlined it in the letter. He elaborated, of course. The fact is, and David will have to see it, that that statement of his doesn't help at all, unless he can prove there is a Clifton Hines. And even then it's all supposition. There's a strong sentiment out there that Dick either killed himself or met with an accident and died in the mountains. The horse wandered into town last week. I'll have to tell her."

Over this possibility they faced each other, a tragic middle-aged pair, helpless as is the way of middle-age before the attacks of life on their young.

"It will kill her, Walter."

"She's young," he said sturdily. "She'll get over it."

But he did not think so, and she knew it.

"There is a rather queer element in it," he observed, after a time. "Another man, named Bassett, disappeared the same night. His stuff is at the hotel, but no papers to identify him. He had looked after Dick that day when he was sick, and he simply vanished. He didn't take the train. He was under suspicion for being with Dick, and the station was being watched." But she was not interested in Bassett. The name meant nothing to her. She harked back to the question that had been in both their minds since they had read, in stupefied amazement, David's statement.

"In a way, Walter, it would be better, if he..."

"Why?"

"My little girl, and—Judson Clark!"

But he fought that sturdily. They had ten years of knowledge and respect to build on. The past was past. All he prayed for was Dick's return, an end to this long waiting. There would be no reservations in his welcome, if only—

Some time later he went downstairs, to where Elizabeth sat waiting in the library. He went like a man to his execution, and his resolution nearly gave way when he saw her, small in her big chair and pathetically patient. He told her the story as guardedly as he could. He began with Dick's story to him, about his forgotten youth, and went on carefully to Dick's own feeling that he must clear up that past before he married. She followed him carefully, bewildered a little and very tense.

"But why didn't he tell me?"

"He saw it as a sort of weakness. He meant to when he came back."

He fought Dick's fight for him valiantly, stressing certain points that were to prepare her for others to come. He plunged, indeed, rather recklessly into the psychology of the situation, and only got out of the unconscious mind with an effort. But behind it all was his overwhelming desire to save her pain.

"You must remember," he said, "that Dick's life before this happened, and since, are two different things. Whatever he did then should not count against him now."

"Of course not," she said. "Then he—had done something?"

"Yes. Something that brought him into conflict with the authorities."

She did not shrink from that, and he was encouraged to go on.

"He was young then, remember. Only twenty-one or so. And there was a quarrel with another man. The other man was shot."

"You mean Dick shot him?"

"Yes. You understand, don't you," he added anxiously, "that he doesn't remember doing it?"

In spite of his anxiety he was forced to marvel at the sublime faith with which she made her comment, through lips that had gone white.

"Then it was either an accident, or he deserved shooting," she said. But she inquired, he thought with difficulty, "Did he die?"

He could not lie to her. "Yes," he said.

She closed her eyes, but a moment later she was fighting her valiant fight again for Dick.

"But they let him go," she protested. "Men do shoot in the West, don't they? There must have been a reason for it. You know Dick as well as I do. He couldn't do a wrong thing."

He let that pass. "Nothing was done about it at the time," he said. "And Dick came here and lived his useful life among us. He wouldn't have known the man's name if he heard it. But do you see, sweetheart, where this is taking us? He went back, and they tried to get him, for a thing he didn't remember doing."

"Father!" she said, and went very white. "Is that where he is? In prison?"

He tried to steady his voice.

"No, dear. He escaped into the mountains. But you can understand his silence. You can understand, too, that he may feel he cannot come back to us, with this thing hanging over him. What we have to do now is to find him, and to tell him that it makes no difference. That he has his place in the world waiting for him, and that we are waiting too."

When it was all over, her questions and his sometimes stumbling replies, he saw that out of it all the one thing that mattered vitally to her was that Dick was only a fugitive, and not dead. But she said, just before they went, arm in arm, up the stairs:

"It is queer in one way, father. It isn't like him to run away."

He told Margaret, later, and she listened carefully.

"Then you didn't tell her about the woman in the case?"

"Certainly not. Why should I?"

Mrs. Wheeler looked at him, with the eternal surprise of woman at the lack of masculine understanding.

"Because, whether you think it or not, she will resent and hate that as she hates nothing else. Murder will be nothing, to that. And she will have to know it some time."

He pondered her flat statement unhappily, standing by the window and looking out into the shaded street, and a man who had been standing, cigar in mouth, on a pavement across withdrew into the shadow of a tree box.

"It's all a puzzle to me," he said, at last. "God alone knows how it will turn out. Harrison Miller seems to think this Bassett, whoever he is, could tell us something. I don't know."

He drew the shade and wound his watch. "I don't know," he repeated.

Outside, on the street, the man with the cigar struck a match and looked at his watch. Then he walked briskly toward the railway station. A half hour later he walked into the offices of the Times-Republican and to the night editor's desk.

"Hello, Bassett," said that gentleman. "We thought you were dead. Well, how about the sister in California? It was the Clark story, wasn't it?"

"Yes," said Bassett, noncommittally.

"And it blew up on you! Well, there were others who were fooled, too. You had a holiday, anyhow."

"Yes, I had a holiday," said Bassett, and going over to his own desk began to sort his vast accumulation of mail. Sometime later he found the night editor at his elbow.

"Did you get anything on the Clark business at all?" he asked. "Williams thinks there's a page in it for Sunday, anyhow. You've been on the ground, and there's a human interest element in it. The last man who talked to Clark; the ranch to-day. That sort of thing."

Bassett went on doggedly sorting his mail.

"You take it from me," he said, "the story's dead, and so is Clark. The Donaldson woman was crazy. That's all."

XXXIII

David was brought home the next day, a shrivelled and aged David, but with a fighting fire in his eyes and a careful smile at the station for the group of friends who met him.

David had decided on a course and meant to follow it. That course was to protect Dick's name, and to keep the place he had made in the world open for him. Not even to Lucy had he yet breathed the terror that was with him day and night, that Dick had reached the breaking point and had gone back. But he knew it was possible. Lauler had warned him against shocks and trouble, and looking back David could see the gradually accumulating pressure against that mental wall of Dick's subconscious building; overwork and David's illness, his love affair and Jim Wheeler's tragedy, and coming on top of that, in some way he had not yet learned, the knowledge that he was Judson Clark and a fugitive from the law. The work of ten years perhaps undone.

Both David and Lucy found the home-coming painful. Harrison Miller rode up with them from the station, and between him and Doctor Reynolds David walked into his house and was assisted up the stairs. At the door of Dick's room he stopped and looked in, and then went on, his face set and rigid. He would not go to bed, but sat in his chair while about him went on the bustle of the return, the bringing up of trunks and bags; but the careful smile was gone, and his throat, now so much too thin for his collar, worked convulsively.

He had got Harrison Miller's narrative from him on the way from the station, and it had only confirmed his suspicions.

"He had been in a stupor all day," Miller related, "and was being cared for by a man named Bassett. I daresay that's the man Gregory had referred to. He may have become suspicious of Bassett. I don't know. But a chambermaid recognized him as he was making his escape, and raised an alarm. He got a horse out of the courtyard of the hotel, and not a sign of him has been found since."

"It wasn't Bassett who raised the alarm?"

"No, apparently not. The odd thing is that this Bassett disappeared, too, the same night. I called up his paper yesterday, but he hasn't shown up."

And with some small amplifications, that is all there was to it.

Before Harrison Miller and Doctor Reynolds left him to rest, David called Lucy in, and put his plea to all of them.

"It is my hope," he said, "to carry on exactly as though Dick might walk in to-morrow and take his place again. As I hold to my belief in God, so I hold to my conviction that he will come back, and that before I—before long. But our friends will be asking where he is and what he is doing, and we would better agree on that beforehand. What we'd better say is simply that Dick was called away on business connected with some property in the West. They may not believe it, but they'll hardly disprove it."

So the benevolent conspiracy to protect Dick Livingstone's name was arranged, and from that time on the four of them who were a party to it turned to the outside world an unbroken front of loyalty and courage. Even to Minnie, anxious and red-eyed in her kitchen, Lucy gave the same explanation while she arranged David's tray.

"He has been detained in the West on business," Lucy said.

"He might have sent me a postcard. And he hasn't written Doctor Reynolds at all."

"He has been very busy. Get the sugar bowl, Minnie. He'll be back soon, I'm sure."

But Minnie did not immediately move.

"He'd better come soon if he wants to see Doctor David," she said, with twitching lips. "And I'll just say this, Mrs. Crosby. The talk that's going on in this town is something awful."

"I don't want to hear it," Lucy said firmly.

She ate alone, painfully remembering that last gay little feast before they started away. But before she sat down she did a touching thing. She rang the bell and called Minnie.

"After this, Minnie," she said, "we will always set Doctor Richard's place. Then, when he comes—"

Her voice broke and Minnie, scenting a tragedy but ignorant of it, went back to her kitchen to cry into the roller towel. Her world was gone to pieces. By years of service to the one family she had no other world, no home, no ties. She was with the Livingstones, but not one of them. Alone in her kitchen she felt lonely and cut off. She thought that David, had he not been ill, would have told her.

Lucy found David moving about upstairs some time later, and when she went up she found him sitting in Dick's room, on a stiff chair inside the door. She stood beside him and put her hand on his shoulder, but he did not say anything, and she went away.

That night David had a caller. All evening the bell had been ringing, and the little card tray on the hatrack was filled with visiting cards. There were gifts, too, flowers and jellies and some squab from Mrs. Sayre. Lucy had seen no one, excusing herself on the ground of fatigue, but the man who came at nine o'clock was not inclined to be turned away.

"You take this card up to Doctor Livingstone, anyhow," he said. "I'll wait."

He wrote in pencil on the card, placing it against the door post to do so, and passed it to Minnie. She calmly read it, and rather defiantly carried it off. But she came down quickly, touched by some contagion of expectation from the room upstairs.

"Hang your hat on the rack and go on up."

So it was that David and the reporter met, for the first time, in David's old fashioned chamber, with its walnut bed and the dresser with the marble top, and Dick's picture in his uniform on the mantle.

Bassett was shocked at the sight of David, shocked and alarmed. He was uncertain at first as to the wisdom of telling his startling story to an obviously sick man, but David's first words reassured him.

"Come in," he said. "You are the Bassett who was with Doctor Livingstone at Norada?"

"Yes. I see you know about it."

"We know something, not everything." Suddenly David's pose deserted him. He got up and stood very straight, searching eyes on his visitor. "Is he living?" he asked, in a low voice.

"I think so. I'm not certain."

"Then you don't know where he is?"

"No. He got away—but you know that. Sit down, doctor. I've got a long story to tell."

"I'll get you to call my sister first," David said. "And tell her to get Harrison Miller. Mr. Miller is our neighbor, and he very kindly went west when my health did not permit me to go."

While they waited David asked only one question.

"The report we have had is that he was in a stupor in the hotel, and the doctor who saw him—you got him, I think—said he appeared to have been drinking heavily. Is that true? He was not a drinking man."

"I am quite sure he had not."

There was another question in David's mind, but he did not put it. He sat, with the patience of his age and his new infirmity, waiting for Lucy to bring Harrison Miller, and had it not been for the trembling of his hands Bassett would have thought him calm and even placid.

During the recital that followed somewhat later David did not move. He sat silent, his eyes closed, his face set.

"That's about all," Bassett finished. "He had been perfectly clear in his head all day, and it took headwork to get over the pass. But, as I say, he had simply dropped ten years, and was back to the Lucas trouble. I tried everything I knew, used your name and would have used the young lady's, because sometimes that sort of thing strikes pretty deep, but I didn't know it. He was convinced after a while, but he was dazed, of course. He knew it, that is, but he couldn't comprehend it.

"I was done up, and I've cursed myself for it since, but I must have slept like the dead. I wakened once, early in the night, and he was still sitting by the fire, staring at it. I've forgotten to say that he had been determined all day to go back and give himself up, and the only way I prevented it was by telling him what a blow it would be to you and to the girl. I wakened once and said to him, 'Better get some sleep, old man.' He did not answer at once, and then he said, 'All right.' I was dozing off when he spoke again. He said, 'Where is Beverly Carlysle now? Has she married again?' 'She's revived "The Valley," and she's in New York with it,' I told him.

"When I wakened in the morning he was gone, but he'd left a piece of paper in a cleft stick beside me, with directions for reaching the railroad, and—well, here it is."

Bassett took from his pocket-book a note, and passed it over to David, who got out his spectacles with shaking hands and read it. It was on Dick's prescription paper, with his name at the top and the familiar Rx below it. David read it aloud, his voice husky.

"Many thanks for everything, Bassett," he read. "I don't like to leave you, but you'll get out all right if you follow the map on the back of this. I've had all night to think things out, and I'm leaving you because you are safer without me. I realize now what you've known all day and kept from me. That woman at the hotel recognized me, and they are after me.

"I can't make up my mind what to do. Ultimately I think I'll go back and give myself up. I am a dead man, anyhow, to all who might have cared, but I've got to do one or two things first, and I want to think things over. One thing you've got a right to know. I hated Lucas, but it never entered my head to kill him. How it happened God only knows. I don't."

It was signed "J. C."

Bassett broke the silence that followed the reading.

"I made every effort to find him. I had to work alone, you understand, and from the west side of the range, not to arouse suspicion. They were after me, too, you know. His horse, I heard, worked its way back a few days ago. It's a forsaken country, and if he lost his horse he was in it on foot and without food. Of course there's a chance—"

His voice trailed off. In the stillness David sat, touching with tender tremulous fingers what might be Dick's last message, and gazing at the picture of Dick in his uniform. He knew what they all thought, that Dick was dead and that he held his final words in his hands, but his militant old spirit refused to accept that silent verdict. Dick might be dead to them, but he was living. He looked around the room defiantly, resentfully. Of all of them he was the only one to have faith, and he was bound to a chair. He knew them. They would sit down supinely and grieve, while time passed and Dick fought his battle alone.

No, by God, he would not be bound to a chair. He raised himself and stood, swaying on his shaking legs.

"You've given up," he said scornfully. "You make a few days' search, and then you quit. It's easy to say he's dead, and so you say he's dead. I'm going out there myself, and I'll make a search—"

He collapsed into the chair again, and looked at them with shamed, appealing eyes. Bassett was the first to break the silence, speaking in a carefully emotionless tone.

"I haven't given up for a minute. I've given up the search, because he's beyond finding just now. Either he's got away, or he is—well, beyond help. We have to go on the hypothesis that he got away, and in that case sooner or later you'll hear from him. He's bound to remember you in time. The worst thing is this charge against him."

"He never killed Howard Lucas," David said, in a tone of conviction. "Harrison, read Mr. Bassett my statement to you."

Bassett took the statement home with him that night, and studied it carefully. It explained a great deal that had puzzled him before; Mrs. Wasson's story and David's arrival at the mountain cabin. But most of all it explained why the Thorwald woman had sent him after Dick. She knew then, in spite of her protests to David, that Jud Clark had not killed Lucas.

He paced the floor for an hour or two, sunk in thought, and then unlocked a desk drawer and took out his bankbook. He had saved a little money. Not much, but it would carry him over if he couldn't get another leave of absence. He thought, as he put the book away and prepared for bed, that it was a small price to pay for finding Clifton Hines and saving his own soul.

XXXIV

Dick had written his note, and placed it where Bassett would be certain to see it. Then he found his horse and led him for the first half mile or so of level ground before the trail began to descend. He mounted there, for he knew the animal could find its way in the darkness where he could not.

He felt no weariness and no hunger, although he had neither slept nor eaten for thirty-odd hours, and as contrasted with the night before his head was clear. He was able to start a train of thought and to follow it through consecutively for the first time in hours. Thought, however, was easier than realization, and to add to his perplexity, he struggled to place Bassett and failed entirely. He remained a mysterious and incomprehensible figure, beginning and ending with the trail.

Then he had an odd thought, that brought him up standing. He had only Bassett's word for the story. Perhaps Bassett was lying to him, or mad. He rode on after a moment, considering that, but there was something, not in Bassett's circumstantial narrative but in himself, that refused to accept that loophole of escape. He could not have told what it was.

And, with his increasing clarity, he began to make out the case for Bassett and against himself; the unfamiliar clothing he wore, the pad with the name of Livingstone on it and the sign Rx, the other contents of his pockets.

He tried to orient himself in Bassett's story. A doctor. The devil's irony of it! Some poor hack, losing sleep and bringing babies. Peddling pills. Leading what Bassett had called a life of usefulness! That was a career for you, a pill peddler. God!

But underlying all his surface thinking was still the need of flight, and he was continually confusing it with the earlier one. One moment he was looking about for the snow of that earlier escape, and the next he would remember, and the sense of panic would leave him. After all he meant to surrender eventually. It did not matter if they caught him.

But, like the sense of flight, there was something else in his mind, something that he fought down and would not face. When it came up he thrust it back fiercely. That something was the figure of Beverly Carlysle, stooping over her husband's body. He would have died to save her pain, and yet last night—no, it wasn't last night. It was years and years ago, and all this time she had hated him.

It was unbearable that she had gone on hating him, all this time.

He was very thirsty, and water did not satisfy him. He wanted a real drink. He wanted alcohol. Suddenly he wanted all the liquor in the world. The craving came on at dawn, and after that he kicked his weary horse on recklessly, so that it rocked and stumbled down the trail. He had only one thought after the frenzy seized him, and that was to get to civilization and whisky.

242

It was as though he saw in drunkenness his only escape from the unbearable. In all probability he would have killed both his horse and himself in the grip of that sudden madness, but deliverance came in the shape of a casual rider, a stranger who for a moment took up the shuttle, wove his bit of the pattern and passed on, to use his blow-pipe, his spirit lamp and his chemicals in some prospector's paradise among the mountains.

When Dick heard somewhere ahead the creaking of saddle leather and the rattle of harness he drew aside on the trail and waited. He had lost all caution in the grip of his craving, and all fear. A line of loaded burros rounded a point ahead and came toward him, picking their way delicately with small deliberate feet and walking on the outer edge of the trail, after the way of pack animals the world over. Behind them was a horseman, rifle in the scabbard on his saddle and spurs jingling. Dick watched him with thirsty, feverish eyes as he drew near. He could hardly wait to put his question.

"Happen to have a drink about you, partner?" he called.

The man stopped his horse and grinned.

"Pretty early in the morning for a drink, isn't it?" he inquired. Then he saw Dick's eyes, and reached reluctantly into his saddle bag. "I've got a quart here," he said. "I've traveled forty miles and spent nine dollars to get it, but I guess you need some."

"You wouldn't care to sell it, I suppose?"

"The bottle? Not on your life."

He untied a tin cup from his saddle and carefully poured a fair amount into it, steadying the horse the while.

"Here," he said, and passed it over. "But you'd better cut it out after this. It's bad medicine. You've got two good drinks there. Be careful."

Dick took the cup and looked at the liquor. The odor assailed him, and for a queer moment he felt a sudden distaste for it. He had a revulsion that almost shook him. But he drank it down and passed the cup back.

"You've traveled a long way for it," he said, "and I needed it, I guess. If you'll let me pay for it—"

"Forget it," said the man amiably, and started his horse. "But better cut it out, first chance you get. It's bad medicine."

He rode on after his vanishing pack, and Dick took up the trail again. But before long he began to feel sick and dizzy. The aftertaste of the liquor in his mouth nauseated him. The craving had been mental habit, not physical need, and his body fought the poison rebelliously. After a time the sickness passed, and he slept in the saddle. He roused once, enough to know that the horse had left the trail and was grazing in a green meadow. Still overcome with his first real sleep he tumbled out of the saddle and stretched himself out on the ground. He slept all day, lying out in the burning sun, his face upturned to the sky.

When he wakened it was twilight, and the horse had disappeared. His face burned from the sun, and his head ached violently. He was weak, too, from hunger, and the morning's dizziness persisted. Connected thought was impossible, beyond the fact that if he did not get out soon, he would be too weak to travel. Exhausted and on the verge of sunstroke, he set out on foot to find the trail.

He traveled all night, and the dawn found him still moving, a mere automaton of a man, haggard and shambling, no longer willing his progress, but somehow incredibly advancing. He found water and drank it, fell, got up, and still, right foot, left foot, he went on. Some time during that advance he had found a trail, and he kept to it automatically. He felt no surprise and no relief when he saw a cabin in a clearing and a woman in the doorway, watching him with curious eyes. He pulled himself together and made a final effort, but without much interest in the result.

"I wonder if you could give me some food?" he said. "I have lost my horse and I've been wandering all night."

243

"I guess I can," she replied, not unamiably. "You look as though you need it, and a wash, too. There's a basin and a pail of water on that bench."

But when she came out later to call him to breakfast she found him sitting on the bench and the pail overturned on the ground.

"I'm sorry," he said, dully, "I tried to lift it, but I'm about all in."

"You'd better come in. I've made some coffee."

He could not rise. He could not even raise his hands.

She called her husband from where he was chopping wood off in the trees, and together they got him into the house. It was days before he so much as spoke again.

So it happened that the search went on. Wilkins from the east of the range, and Bassett from the west, hunted at first with furious energy, then spasmodically, then not at all, while Dick lay in a mountain cabin, on the bed made of young trees, and for the second time in his life watched a woman moving in a lean-to kitchen, and was fed by a woman's hand.

He forced himself to think of this small panorama of life that moved before him, rather than of himself. The woman was young, and pretty in a slovenly way. The man was much older, and silent. He was of better class than the woman, and underlying his assumption of crudity there were occasional outcroppings of some cultural background. Not then, nor at any subsequent time, did he learn the story, if story there was. He began to see them, however, not so much pioneers as refugees. The cabin was, he thought, a haven to the man and a prison to the woman.

But they were uniformly kind to him, and for weeks he stayed there, slowly readjusting. In his early convalescence he would sit paring potatoes or watching a cooking pot for her. As he gained in strength he cut a little firewood. Always he sought something to keep him from thinking.

Two incidents always stood out afterwards in his memory of the cabin. One was the first time he saw himself in a mirror. He knew by that time that Bassett's story had been true, and that he was ten years older than he remembered himself to be. He thought he was in a measure prepared. But he saw in the glass a man whose face was lined and whose hair was streaked with gray. The fact that his beard had grown added to the terrible maturity of the reflection he saw, and he sent the mirror clattering to the ground.

The other incident was later, and when he was fairly strong again. The man was caught under a tree he was felling, and badly hurt. During the hour or so that followed, getting the tree cut away, and moving the injured man to the cabin on a wood sledge, Dick had the feeling of helplessness of any layman in an accident. He was solicitous but clumsy. But when they had got the patient into his bed, quite automatically he found himself making an investigation and pronouncing a verdict.

Later he was to realize that this was the first peak of submerged memory, rising above the flood. At the time all he felt was a great certainty. He must act quickly or the man would not live. And that night, with such instruments as he could extemporize, he operated. There was no time to send to a town.

All night, after the operation, Dick watched by the bedside, the woman moving back and forth restlessly. He got his only knowledge of the story, such as it was, then when she said once:

"I deserved this, but he didn't. I took him away from his wife."

He had to stay on after that, for the woman could not be left alone. And he was glad of the respite, willing to drift until he got his bearings. Certain things had come back, more as pictures than realities. Thus he saw David clearly, Lucy dimly, Elizabeth not at all. But David came first; David in the buggy with the sagging springs, David's loud voice and portly figure, David, steady and upright and gentle as a woman. But there was something wrong about David. He puzzled over that, but he was learning not to try to force things, to let them come to the surface themselves.

It was two or three days later that he remembered that David was ill, and was filled with a sickening remorse and anxiety. For the first time he made plans to get away, for whatever happened after that he knew he must see David again. But all his thought led him to an impasse at that time, and that impasse was the feeling that he was a criminal and a fugitive, and that he had no right to tie up innocent lives with his. Even a letter to David might incriminate him.

Coupled with his determination to surrender, the idea of atonement was strong in him. An eye for an eye, and a tooth for a tooth. That had been his father's belief, and well he remembered it. But during the drifting period he thrust it back, into that painful niche where he held Beverly, and the thing he would not face.

That phase of his readjustment, then, when he reached it, was painful and confused. There was the necessity for atonement, which involved surrender, and there was the call of David, and the insistent desire to see Beverly again, which was the thing he would not face. Of the three, the last, mixed up as it was with the murder and its expiation, was the strongest. For by the very freshness of his released memories, it was the days before his flight from the ranch that seemed most recent, and his life with David that was long ago, and blurred in its details as by the passing of infinite time.

When Elizabeth finally came back to him it was as something very gentle and remote, out of the long-forgotten past. Even his image of her was blurred and shadowy. He could not hear the tones of her voice, or remember anything she had said. He could never bring her at will, as he could David, for instance. She only came clearly at night, while he slept. Then the guard was down, and there crept into his dreams a small figure, infinitely loving and tender; but as he roused from sleep she changed gradually into Beverly. It was Beverly's arms he felt around his neck. Nevertheless he held to Elizabeth more completely than he knew, for the one thing that emerged from his misty recollection of her was that she cared for him. In a world of hate and bitterness she cared.

But she was never real to him, as the other woman was real. And he knew that she was lost to him, as David was lost. He could never go back to either of them.

As time went on he reached the point of making practical plans. He had lost his pocketbook somewhere, probably during his wanderings afoot, and he had no money. He knew that the obvious course was to go to the nearest settlement and surrender himself and he played with the thought, but even as he did so he knew that he would not do it. Surrender he would, eventually, but before he did that he would satisfy a craving that was in some ways like his desire for liquor that morning on the trail. A reckless, mad, and irresistible impulse to see Beverly Lucas again.

In August he started for the railroad, going on foot and without money, his immediate destination the harvest fields of some distant ranch, his object to earn his train fare to New York.

XXXV

The summer passed slowly. To David and Elizabeth it was a long waiting, but with this difference, that David was kept alive by hope, and that Elizabeth felt sometimes that hope was killing her. To David each day was a new day, and might hold Dick. To Elizabeth, after a time, each day was but one more of separation.

Doctor Reynolds had become a fixture in the old house, but he was not like Dick. He was a heavy, silent young man, shy of intruding into the family life and already engrossed in a budding affair with the Rossiter girl. David tolerated him, but with a sort of smouldering jealousy increased by the fact that he had introduced innovations David resented; had for instance moved Dick's desk nearer the window, and instead of doing his own laboratory work had what David considered a damnably lazy fashion of sending his little tubes, carefully closed with cotton, to a hospital in town.

David found the days very long and infinitely sad. He wakened each morning to renewed hope, watched for the postman from his upper window, and for Lucy's step on the stairs with the mail. His first glimpse of her always told him the story. At the beginning he had insisted on talking about Dick, but he saw that it hurt her, and of late they had fallen into the habit of long silences.

The determination to live on until that return which he never ceased to expect only carried him so far, however. He felt no incentive to activity. There were times when he tried Lucy sorely, when she felt that if he would only move about, go downstairs and attend to his office practice, get out into the sun and air, he would grow stronger. But there were times, too, when she felt that only the will to live was carrying him on.

Nothing further had developed, so far as they knew. The search had been abandoned. Lucy was no longer so sure as she had been that the house was under surveillance, against Dick's possible return. Often she lay in her bed and faced the conviction that Dick was dead. She had never understood the talk that at first had gone on about her, when Bassett and Harrison Miller, and once or twice the psycho-analyst David had consulted in town, had got together in David's bedroom. The mind was the mind, and Dick was Dick. This thing about habit, over which David pored at night when he should have been sleeping, or brought her in to listen to, with an air of triumphant vindication, meant nothing to her.

A man properly trained in right habits of thinking and of action could not think wrong and go wrong, David argued. He even went further. He said that love was a habit, and that love would bring Dick back to him. That he could not forget them.

She believed that, of course, if he still lived. But hadn't Mr. Bassett, who seemed so curiously mixed in the affair, been out again to Norada without result? No, it was all over, and she felt that it would be a comfort to know where he lay, and to bring him back to some well-loved and tended grave.

Elizabeth came often to see them. She looked much the same as ever, although she was very slender and her smile rather strained, and she and David would have long talks together. She always felt rather like an empty vessel when she went in, but David filled her with hope and sent her away cheered and visibly brighter to her long waiting. She rather avoided Lucy, for Lucy's fears lay in her face and were like a shadow over her spirit. She came across her one day putting Dick's clothing away in camphor, and the act took on an air of finality that almost crushed her.

So far they had kept from her Dick's real identity, but certain things they had told her. She knew that he had gone back, in some strange way, to the years before he came to Haverly, and that he had temporarily forgotten everything since. But they had told her too, and seemed to believe themselves, that it was only temporary.

At first the thought had been more than she could bear. But she had to live her life, and in such a way as to hide her fears. Perhaps it was good for her, the necessity of putting up a bold front, to join the conspiracy that was to hold Dick's place in the world against the hope of his return. And she still went to the Sayre house, sure that there at least there would be no curious glances, no too casual questions. She could not be sure of that even at home, for Nina was constantly conjecturing.

"I sometimes wonder-" Nina began one day, and stopped.

"Wonder what?"

"Oh, well, I suppose I might as well go on. Do you ever think that if Dick had gone back, as they say he has, that there might be somebody else?"

"Another girl, you mean?"

"Yes. Some one he knew before."

Nina was watching her. Sometimes she almost burst with the drama she was suppressing. She had been a small girl when Judson Clark had disappeared, but even at twelve she had known something of the story. She wanted frantically to go about the village and say to them: "Do you know who has been living here, whom you used to patronize? Judson Clark, one of the richest men in the world!" She built day dreams on that foundation. He would come back, for of course he would be found and acquitted, and buy the Sayre place perhaps, or build a much larger one, and they would all go to Europe in his yacht. But she knew now that the woman Leslie had sent his flowers to had loomed large in Dick's past, and she both hated and feared her. Not content with having given her, Nina, some bad hours, she saw the woman now possibly blocking her ambitions for Elizabeth.

"What I'm getting at is this," she said, examining her polished nails critically. "If it does turn out that there was somebody, you'd have to remember that it was all years and years ago, and be sensible."

"I only want him back," Elizabeth said. "I don't care how he comes, so he comes."

Louis Bassett had become a familiar figure in the village life by that time. David depended on him with a sort of wistful confidence that set him to grinding his teeth occasionally in a fury at his own helplessness. And, as the extent of the disaster developed, as he saw David failing and Lucy ageing, and when in time he met Elizabeth, the feeling of his own guilt was intensified.

He spent hours studying the case, and he was chiefly instrumental in sending Harrison Miller back to Norada in September. He had struck up a friendship with Miller over their common cause, and the night he was to depart that small inner group which was fighting David's battle for him formed a board of strategy in Harrison's tidy living-room; Walter Wheeler and Bassett, Miller and, tardily taken into their confidence, Doctor Reynolds.

The same group met him on his return, sat around with expectant faces while he got out his tobacco and laid a sheaf of papers on the table, and waited while their envoy, laying Bassett's map on the table, proceeded carefully to draw in a continuation of the trail beyond the pass, some sketchy mountains, and a small square.

"I've got something," he said at last. "Not much, but enough to work on. Here's where you lost him, Bassett." He pointed with his pencil. "He went on for a while on the horse. Then somehow he must have lost the horse, for he turned up on foot, date unknown, in a state of exhaustion at a cabin that lies here. I got lost myself, or I'd never have found the place. He was sick there for weeks, and he seems to have stayed on quite a while after he recovered, as though he couldn't decide what to do next."

Walter Wheeler stirred and looked up.

"What sort of condition was he in when he left?"

"Very good, they said."

"You're sure it was Livingstone?"

"The man there had a tree fall on him. He operated. I guess that's the answer."

He considered the situation.

"It's the answer to more than that," Reynolds said slowly. "It shows he had come back to himself. If he hadn't he couldn't have done it."

"And after that?" some one asked.

"I lost him. He left to hike to the railroad, and he said nothing of his plans. If I'd been able to make open inquiries I might have turned up something, but I couldn't. It's a hard proposition. I had trouble finding Hattie Thorwald, too. She'd left the hotel, and is living with her son. She swears she doesn't know where Clifton Hines is, and hasn't seen him for years."

Bassett had been listening intently, his head dropped forward.

"I suppose the son doesn't know about Hines?"

"No. She warned me. He was surly and suspicious. The sheriff had sent for him and questioned him about how you got his horse, and I gathered that he thought I was a detective. When I told him I was a friend of yours, he sent you a message. You may be able to make something out of it. I can't. He said: `You can tell him I didn't say anything about the other time.'"

Bassett sat forward.

"The other time?"

"He is under the impression that his mother got the horse for you once before, about ten days before Clark escaped. At night, also."

"Not for me," Bassett said decisively. "Ten days before that I was—" he got out his notebook and consulted it. "I was on my way to the cabin in the mountains, where the Donaldsons had hidden Jud Clark. I hired a horse at a livery stable."

"Could the Thorwald woman have followed you?"

"Why the devil should she do that?" he asked irritably. "She didn't know who I was. She hadn't a chance at my papers, for I kept them on me. If she did suspect I was on the case, a dozen fellows had preceded me, and half of them had gone to the cabin."

"Nevertheless," he finished, "I believe she did. She or Hines himself. There was some one on a horse outside the cabin that night."

There was silence in the room, Harrison Miller thoughtfully drawing at random on the map before him. Each man was seeing the situation from his own angle; to Reynolds, its medical interest, and the possibility of his permanency in the town; to Walter Wheeler, Elizabeth's spoiled young life; to Harrison Miller, David; and to the reporter a conviction that the clues he now held should lead him somewhere, and did not.

Before the meeting broke up Miller took a folded manuscript from the table and passed it to Bassett.

"Copy of the Coroner's inquiry, after the murder," he said. "Thought it might interest you..."

Then, for a time, that was all. Bassett, poring at home over the inquest records, and finding them of engrossing interest, saw the futility of saving a man who could not be found. And even Nina's faith, that the fabulously rich could not die obscurely, began to fade as the summer waned. She restored some of her favor to Wallie Sayre, and even listened again to his alternating hopes and fears.

And by the end of September he felt that he had gained real headway with Elizabeth. He had come to a point where she needed him more than she realized, where the call in her of youth for youth, even in trouble, was insistent. In return he felt his responsibility and responded to it. In the vernacular of the town he had "settled down," and the general trend of opinion, which had previously disapproved him, was now that Elizabeth might do worse.

On a crisp night early in October he had brought her home from Nina's, and because the moon was full they sat for a time on the steps of the veranda, Wallie below her, stirring the dead leaves on the walk with his stick, and looking up at her with boyish adoring eyes when she spoke. He was never very articulate with her, and her trouble had given her a strange new aloofness that almost frightened him. But that night, when she shivered a little, he reached up and touched her hand.

"You're cold," he said almost roughly. He was sometimes rather savage, for fear he might be tender.

"I'm not cold. I think it's the dead leaves."

"Dead leaves?" he repeated, puzzled. "You're a queer girl, Elizabeth. Why dead leaves?"

"I hate the fall. It's the death of the year."

"Nonsense. It's going to bed for a long winter's nap. That's all. I'll bring you a wrap."

He went in, and came out in a moment with her father's overcoat.

"Here," he said peremptorily, "put this on. I'm not going to be called on the carpet for giving you a sniffle."

She stood up obediently and he put the big coat around her. Then, obeying an irresistible impulse, he caught her to him. He released her immediately, however, and stepped back.

"I love you so," he stammered. "I'm sorry. I'll not do it again."

She was startled, but not angry.

248

"I don't like it," was all she said. And because she did not want him to think she was angry, she sat down again. But the boy was shaken. He got out a cigarette and lighted it, his hands trembling. He could not think of anything to say. It was as though by that one act he had cut a bridge behind him and on the other side lay all the platitudes, the small give and take of their hours together. What to her was a regrettable incident was to him a great dramatic climax. Boylike, he refused to recognize its unimportance to her. He wanted to talk about it.

"When you said just now that you didn't like what I did just then, do you mean you didn't like me to do it? Or that you don't care for that sort of thing? Of course I know," he added hastily, "you're not that kind of girl. I—"

He turned and looked at her.

"You know I'm still in love with you, don't you, Elizabeth?"

She returned his gaze frankly.

"I don't see how you can be when you know what you do know."

"I know how you feel now. But I know that people don't go on loving hopelessly all their lives. You're young. You've got"—he figured quickly—"you've got about fifty-odd years to live yet, and some of these days you'll be—not forgetting," he changed, when he saw her quick movement. "I know you'll not forget him. But remembering and loving are different."

"I wonder," she said, her eyes on the moon, and full of young tragedy. "If they are, if one can remember without loving, then couldn't one love without remembering?"

He stared at her.

"You're too deep for me sometimes," he said. "I'm not subtle, Elizabeth. I daresay I'm stupid in lots of things. But I'm not stupid about this. I'm not trying to get a promise, you know. I only want you to know how things are. I don't want to know why he went away, or why he doesn't come back. I only want you to face the facts. I'd be good to you," he finished, in a low tone. "I'd spend my life thinking of ways to make you happy."

She was touched. She reached down and put her hand on his shoulder.

"You deserve the best, Wallie. And you're asking for a second best. Even that—I'm just not made that way, I suppose. Fifty years or a hundred, it would be all the same."

"You'd always care for him, you mean?"

"Yes. I'm afraid so."

When he looked at her her eyes had again that faraway and yet flaming look which he had come to associate with her thoughts of Dick. She seemed infinitely removed from him, traveling her lonely road past loving outstretched hands and facing ahead toward—well, toward fifty years of spinsterhood. The sheer waste of it made him shudder.

"You're cold, too, Wallie," she said gently. "You'd better go home."

He was about to repudiate the idea scornfully, when he sneezed! She got up at once and held out her hand.

"You are very dear to feel about me the way you do" she said, rather rapidly. "I appreciate your telling me. And if you're chilly when you get home, you'd better take some camphor."

He saw her in, hat in hand, and then turned and stalked up the street. Camphor, indeed! But so stubborn was hope in his young heart that before he had climbed the hill he was finding comfort in her thought for him.

Mrs. Sayre had been away for a week, visiting in Michigan, and he had not expected her for a day or so. To his surprise he found her on the terrace, wrapped in furs, and evidently waiting for him.

"I wasn't enjoying it," she explained, when he had kissed her. "It's a summer place, not heated to amount to anything, and when it turned cold—where have you been to-night?"

"Dined at the Wards', and then took Elizabeth home."

"How is she?"

"She's all right."

"And there's no news?"

He knew her very well, and he saw then that she was laboring under suppressed excitement.

"What's the matter, mother? You're worried about something, aren't you?"

"I have something to tell you. We'd better go inside." He followed her in, unexcited and half smiling. Her world was a small one, of minor domestic difficulties, of not unfriendly gossip, of occasional money problems, investments and what not. He had seen her hands tremble over a matter of a poorly served dinner. So he went into the house, closed the terrace window and followed her to the library. When she closed the door he recognized her old tactics when the servants were in question.

"Well?" he inquired. "I suppose—" Then he saw her face. "Sorry, mother. What's the trouble?"

"Wallie, I saw Dick Livingstone in Chicago."

XXXVI

During August Dick had labored in the alfalfa fields of Central Washington, a harvest hand or "working stiff" among other migratory agricultural workers. Among them, but not entirely of them. Recruited from the lowest levels as men grade, gathered in at a slave market on the coast, herded in bunk houses alive with vermin, fully but badly fed, overflowing with blasphemy and filled with sullen hate for those above them in the social scale, the "stiffs" regarded him with distrust from the start.

In the beginning he accepted their sneers with a degree of philosophy. His physical condition was poor. At night he ached intolerably, collapsing into his wooden bunk to sleep the dreamless sleep of utter exhaustion. There were times when he felt that it would be better to return at once to Norada and surrender, for that he must do so eventually he never doubted. It was as well perhaps that he had no time for brooding, but he gained sleep at the cost of superhuman exertion all day.

A feeling of unreality began to obsess him, so that at times he felt like a ghost walking among sweating men, like a resurrection into life, but without life. And more than once he tried to sink down to the level of the others, to unite himself again with the crowd, to feel again the touch of elbows, the sensation of fellowship. The primal instinct of the herd asserted itself, the need of human companionship of any sort.

But he failed miserably, as Jud Clark could never have failed. He could not drink with them. He could not sink to their level of degradation. Their oaths and obscenity sickened and disgusted him, and their talk of women drove him into the fresh air.

The fact that he could no longer drink himself into a stupor puzzled him. Bad whiskey circulated freely among the hay stacks and bunk houses where the harvest hands were quartered, and at ruinous prices. The men clubbed together to buy it, and he put in his share, only to find that it not only sickened him, but that he had a mental inhibition against it.

They called him the "Dude," and put into it gradually all the class hatred of their wretched sullen lives. He had to fight them, more than once, and had they united against him he might have been killed. But they never united. Their own personal animosities and angers kept them apart, as their misery held them together. And as time went on and his muscles hardened he was able to give a better account of himself. The time came when they let him alone, and when one day a big shocker fell off a stack and broke his leg and Dick set it, he gained their respect. They asked no questions, for their law was that the past was the past. They did not like him, but in the queer twisted ethics of the camp they judged the secret behind him by the height from which he had fallen, and began slowly to accept him as of the brotherhood of derelicts.

With his improvement in his physical condition there came, toward the end of the summer, a more rapid subsidence of the flood of the long past. He had slept out one night in the fields, where the uncut alfalfa was belled with purple flowers and yellow buttercups rose and nodded above him. With the first touch of dawn on the mountains he wakened to a clarity of mind like that of the morning. He felt almost an exaltation. He stood up and threw out his arms.

It was all his again, never to lose, the old house, and David and Lucy; the little laboratory; the church on Sunday mornings. Mike, whistling in the stable. A wave of love warmed him, a great surging tenderness. He would go back to them. They were his and he was theirs. It was at first only a great emotion; a tingling joyousness, a vast relief, as of one who sees, from a far distance, the lights in the windows of home. Save for the gap between the drunken revel at the ranch and his awakening to David's face bending over him in the cabin, everything was clear. Still by an effort, but successfully, he could unite now the two portions of his life with only a scar between them.

Not that he formulated it. It was rather a mood, an impulse of unreasoning happiness. The last cloud had gone, the last bit of mist from the valley. He saw Haverly, and the children who played in its shaded streets; Mike washing the old car, and the ice cream freezer on Sundays, wrapped in sacking on the kitchen porch. Jim Wheeler came back to him, the weight of his coffin dragging at his right hand as he helped to carry it; he was kneeling beside Elizabeth's bed, and putting his hand over her staring eyes so she would go to sleep.

The glow died away, and he began to suffer intensely. They were all lost to him, along with the life they represented. And already he began to look back on his period of forgetfulness with regret. At least then he had not known what he had lost.

He wondered again what they knew. What did they think? If they believed him dead, was that not kinder than the truth? Outside of David and Lucy, and of course Bassett, the sole foundation on which any search for him had rested had been the semi-hysterical recognition of Hattie Thorwald. But he wondered how far that search had gone.

Had it extended far enough to involve David? Had the hue and cry died away, or were the police still searching for him? Could he even write to David, without involving him in his own trouble? For David, fine, wonderful old David—David had deliberately obstructed the course of justice, and was an accessory after the fact.

Up to that time he had drifted, unable to set a course in the fog, but now he could see the way, and it led him back to Norada. He would not communicate with David. He would go out of the lives at the old house as he had gone in, under a lie. When he surrendered it would be as Judson Clark, with his lips shut tight on the years since his escape. Let them think, if they would, that the curtain that had closed down over his memory had not lifted, and that he had picked up life again where he had laid it down. The police would get nothing from him to incriminate David.

But he had a moment, too, when surrender seemed to him not strength but weakness; where its sheer supineness, its easy solution to his problem revolted him, where he clenched his fist and looked at it, and longed for the right to fight his way out.

When smoke began to issue from the cook-house chimney he stirred, rose and went back. He ate no breakfast, and the men, seeing his squared jaw and set face, let him alone. He worked with the strength of three men that day, but that night, when the foreman offered him a job as pacer, with double wages, he refused it.

"Give it to somebody else, Joe," he said. "I'm quitting."

"The hell you are! When?"

"I'd like to check out to-night."

His going was without comment. They had never fully accepted him, and comings and goings without notice in the camp were common. He rolled up his bedding, his change of undergarments inside it, and took the road that night.

The railroad was ten miles away, and he made the distance easily. He walked between wire fences, behind which horses moved restlessly as he passed and cattle slept around a water hole, and as he walked he faced a situation which all day he had labored like three men to evade.

He was going out of life. It did not much matter whether it was to be behind bars or to pay the ultimate price. The shadow that lay over him was that he was leaving forever David and all that he stood for, and a woman. And the woman was not Elizabeth.

He cursed himself in the dark for a fool and a madman; he cursed the infatuation which rose like a demoniac possession from his early life. When that failed he tried to kill it by remembering the passage of time, the loathing she must have nursed all these years. He summoned the image of Elizabeth to his aid, to find it eclipsed by something infinitely more real and vital. Beverly in her dressing-room, grotesque and yet lovely in her make-up; Beverly on the mountain-trail, in her boyish riding clothes. Beverly.

Probably at that stage of his recovery his mind had reacted more quickly than his emotions. And by that strange faculty by which an idea often becomes stronger in memory than in its original production he found himself in the grip of a passion infinitely more terrible than his earlier one for her. It wiped out the memory, even the thought, of Elizabeth, and left him a victim of its associated emotions. Bitter jealousy racked him, remorse and profound grief. The ten miles of road to the railroad became ten miles of torture, of increasing domination of the impulse to go to her, and of final surrender.

In Spokane he outfitted himself, for his clothes were ragged, and with the remainder of his money bought a ticket to Chicago. Beyond Chicago he had no thought save one. Some way, somehow, he must get to New York. Yet all the time he was fighting. He tried again and again to break away from the emotional associations from which his memory of her was erected; when that failed he struggled to face reality; the lapse of time, the certainty of his disappointment, at the best the inevitable parting when he went back to Norada. But always in the end he found his face turned toward the East, and her.

He had no fear of starving. If he had learned the cost of a dollar in blood and muscle, he had the blood and the muscle. There was a time, in Chicago, when the necessity of thinking about money irritated him, for the memory of his old opulent days was very clear. Times when his temper was uncertain, and he turned surly. Times when his helplessness brought to his lips the old familiar blasphemies of his youth, which sounded strange and revolting to his ears.

He had no fear, then, but a great impatience, as though, having lost so much time, he must advance with every minute. And Chicago drove him frantic. There came a time there when he made a deliberate attempt to sink to the very depths, to seek forgetfulness by burying one wretchedness under another. He attempted to find work and failed, and he tried to let go and sink. The total result of the experiment was that he wakened one morning in his lodging-house ill and with his money gone, save for some small silver. He thought ironically, lying on his untidy bed, that even the resources of the depths were closed to him.

He never tried that experiment again. He hated himself for it.

For days he haunted the West Madison Street employment agencies. But the agencies and sidewalks were filled with men who wandered aimlessly with the objectless shuffle of the unemployed. Beds had gone up in the lodging-houses to thirty-five cents a night, and the food in the cheap restaurants was almost uneatable. There came a day when the free morning coffee at a Bible Rescue Home, and its soup and potatoes and carrots at night was all he ate.

For the first time his courage began to fail him. He went to the lakeside that night and stood looking at the water. He meant to fight that impulse of cowardice at the source.

Up to that time he had given no thought whatever to his estate, beyond the fact that he had been undoubtedly adjudged legally dead and his property divided. But that day as he turned away from the lake front, he began to wonder about it. After all, since he meant to surrender himself before long, why not telegraph collect to the old offices of the estate in New York and have them wire him money? But even granting that they were still in existence, he knew with what lengthy caution, following stunned surprise, they would go about investigating the message. And there were leaks in the telegraph. He would have a pack of newspaper hounds at his heels within a few hours. The police, too. No, it wouldn't do.

The next day he got a job as a taxicab driver, and that night and every night thereafter he went back to West Madison Street and picked up one or more of the derelicts there and bought them food. He developed quite a system about it. He waited until he saw a man stop outside an eating-house look in and then pass on. But one night he got rather a shock. For the young fellow he accosted looked at him first with suspicion, which was not unusual, and later with amazement.

"Captain Livingstone!" he said, and checked his hand as it was about to rise to the salute. His face broke into a smile, and he whipped off his cap. "You've forgotten me, sir," he said. "But I've got your visiting card on the top of my head all right. Can you see it?"

He bent his head and waited, but on no immediate reply being forthcoming, for Dick was hastily determining on a course of action, he looked up. It was then that he saw Dick's cheap and shabby clothes, and his grin faded.

"I say," he said. "You are Livingstone, aren't you? I'd have known—"

"I think you've made a mistake, old man," Dick said, feeling for his words carefully. "That's not my name, anyhow. I thought, when I saw you staring in at that window—How about it?"

The boy looked at him again, and then glanced away.

"I was looking, all right," he said. "I've been having a run of hard luck."

It had been Dick's custom to eat with his finds, and thus remove from the meal the quality of detached charity. Men who would not take money would join him in a meal. But he could not face the lights with this keen-eyed youngster. He offered him money instead.

"Just a lift," he said, awkwardly, when the boy hesitated. "I've been there myself, lately."

But when at last he had prevailed and turned away he was conscious that the doughboy was staring after him, puzzled and unconvinced.

He had a bad night after that. The encounter had brought back his hard-working, care-free days in the army. It had brought back, too, the things he had put behind him, his profession and his joy in it, the struggles and the aspirations that constitute a man's life. With them there came, too, a more real Elizabeth, and a wave of tenderness for her, and of regret. He turned on his sagging bed, and deliberately put her away from him. Even if this other ghost were laid, he had no right to her.

Then, one day, he met Mrs. Sayre, and saw that she knew him.

XXXVII

Wallie stared at his mother. His mind was at once protesting the fact and accepting it, with its consequences to himself. There was a perceptible pause before he spoke. He stood, if anything, somewhat straighter, but that was all.

"Are you sure it was Livingstone?"

"Positive. I talked to him. I wasn't sure myself, at first. He looked shabby and thin, as though he'd been ill, and he had the audacity to pretend at first he didn't know me. He closed the door on me and—"

"Wait a minute, mother. What door?"

"He was driving a taxicab."

He looked at her incredulously.

"I don't believe it," he said slowly. "I think you've made a mistake, that's all."

"Nonsense. I know him as well as I know you."

"Did he acknowledge his identity?"

"Not in so many words," she admitted. "He said I had made a mistake, and he stuck to it. Then he shut the door and drove me to the station. The only other chance I had was at the station, and there was a line of cabs behind us, so I had only a second. I saw he didn't intend to admit anything, so I said: 'I can see you don't mean to recognize me, Doctor Livingstone, but I must know whether I am to say at home that I've seen you.' He was making change for me at the time—I'd have known his hands, I think, if I hadn't seen anything else-and when he looked up his face was shocking. He said, 'Are they all right?' 'David is very ill,' I said. The cars behind were waiting and making a terrific din, and a traffic man ran up then and made him move on. He gave me the strangest look as he went. I stood and waited, thinking he would turn and come back again at the end of the line, but he didn't. I almost missed my train."

Wallie's first reaction to the news was one of burning anger and condemnation.

"The blackguard!" he said. "The insufferable cad! To have run away as he did, and then to let them believe him dead! For that's what they do believe. It is killing David Livingstone, and as for Elizabeth—She'll have to be told, mother. He's alive. He's well. And he has deliberately deserted them all. He ought to be shot."

"You didn't see him, Wallie. I did. He's been through something, I don't know what. I didn't sleep last night for thinking of his face. It had despair in it."

"All right," he said, angrily pausing before her. "What do you intend to do? Let them go on as they are, hoping and waiting; lauding him to the skies as a sort of superman? The thing to do is to tell the truth."

"But we don't know the truth, Wallie. There's something behind it all."

"Nothing very creditable, be sure of that," he pronounced. "Do you think it is fair to Elizabeth to let her waste her life on the memory of a man who's deserted her?"

"It would be cruel to tell her."

"You've got to be cruel to be kind, sometimes," he said oracularly. "Why, the man may be married. May be anything. A taxi driver! Doesn't that in itself show that he's hiding from something?"

She sat, a small obese figure made larger by her furs, and stared at him with troubled eyes.

"I don't know, Wallie," she said helplessly. "In a way, it might be better to tell her. She could put him out of her mind, then. But I hate to do it. It's like stabbing a baby."

He understood her, and nodded. When, after taking a turn or two about the room he again stopped in front of her his angry flush had subsided.

"It's the devil of a mess," he commented. "I suppose the square thing to do is to tell Doctor David, and let him decide. I've got too much at stake to be a judge of what to do."

He went upstairs soon after that, leaving her still in her chair, swathed in furs, her round anxious face bent forward in thought. He had rarely seen her so troubled, so uncertain of her next move, and he surmised, knowing her, that her emotions were a complex of anxiety for himself with Elizabeth, of pity for David, and of the memory of Dick Livingstone's haggard face.

She sat alone for some time and then went reluctantly up the stairs to her bedroom. She felt, like Wallie, that she had too much at stake to decide easily what to do.

In the end she decided to ask Doctor Reynolds' advice, and in the morning she proceeded to do it. Reynolds was interested, even a little excited, she thought, but he thought it better not to tell David. He would himself go to Harrison Miller with it.

"You say he knew you?" he inquired, watching her. "I suppose there is no doubt of that?"

"Certainly not. He's known me for years. And he asked about David."

"I see." He fell into profound thought, while she sat in her chair a trifle annoyed with him. He was wondering how all this would affect him and his prospects, and through them his right to marry. He had walked into a good thing, and into a very considerable content.

"I see," he repeated, and got up. "I'll tell Miller, and we'll get to work. We are all very grateful to you, Mrs. Sayre—"

As a result of that visit Harrison Miller and Bassett went that night to Chicago. They left it to Doctor Reynolds' medical judgment whether David should be told or not, and Reynolds himself did not know. In the end he passed the shuttle the next evening to Clare Rossiter.

"Something's troubling you," she said. "You're not a bit like yourself, old dear."

He looked at her. To him she was all that was fine and good and sane of judgment.

"I've got something to settle," he said. "I was wondering while you were singing, dear, whether you could help me out."

"When I sing you're supposed to listen. Well? What is it?" She perched herself on the arm of his chair, and ran her fingers over his hair. She was very fond of him, and she meant to be a good wife. If she ever thought of Dick Livingstone now it was in connection with her own reckless confession to Elizabeth. She had hated Elizabeth ever since.

"I'll take a hypothetical case. If you guess, you needn't say. Of course it's a great secret."

She listened, nodding now and then. He used no names, and he said nothing of any crime.

"The point is this," he finished. "Is it better to believe the man is dead, or to know that he is alive, but has cut himself off?"

"There's no mistake about the recognition?"

"Somebody from the village saw him in Chicago within day or two, and talked to him."

She had the whole picture in a moment. She knew that Mrs. Sayre had been in Chicago, that she had seen Dick there and talked to him. She turned the matter over in her mind, shrewdly calculating, planning her small revenge on Elizabeth even as she talked.

"I'd wait," she advised him. "He may come back with them, and in that case David will know soon enough. Or he may refuse to, and that would kill him. He'd rather think him dead than that."

She slept quietly that night, and spent rather more time than usual in dressing that morning. Then she took her way to the Wheeler house. She saw in what she was doing no particularly culpable thing. She had no great revenge in mind; all that she intended was an evening of the score between them. "He preferred you to me, when you knew I cared. But he has deserted you." And perhaps, too, a small present jealousy, for she was to live in the old brick Livingstone house, or in one like it, while all the village expected ultimately to see Elizabeth installed in the house on the hill.

She kept her message to the end of her visit, and delivered her blow standing.

"I have something I ought to tell you, Elizabeth. But I don't know how you'll take it."

"Maybe it's something I won't want to hear."

"I'll tell you, if you won't say where you heard it."

But Elizabeth made a small, impatient gesture. "I don't like secrets, Clare. I can't keep them, for one thing. You'd better not tell me."

Clare was nearly balked of her revenge, but not entirely.

"All right," she said, and prepared to depart. "I won't. But you might just find out from your friend Mrs. Sayre who it was she saw in Chicago this week."

It was in this manner, bit by bit and each bit trivial, that the case against Dick was built up for Elizabeth. Mrs. Sayre, helpless before her quiet questioning, had to acknowledge one damning thing after another. He had known her; he had not asked for Elizabeth, but only for David; he looked tired and thin, but well. She stood at the window watching Elizabeth go down the hill, with a feeling that she had just seen something die before her.

XXXVIII

On the night Bassett and Harrison Miller were to return from Chicago Lucy sat downstairs in her sitting-room waiting for news.

At ten o'clock, according to her custom, she went up to see that David was comfortable for the night, and to read him that prayer for the absent with which he always closed his day of waiting. But before she went she stopped before the old mirror in the hall, to see if she wore any visible sign of tension.

The door into Dick's office was open, and on his once neat desk there lay a litter of papers and letters. She sighed and went up the stairs.

David lay propped up in his walnut bed. An incredibly wasted and old David; the hands on the log-cabin quilt which their mother had made were old hands, and tired. Sometimes Lucy, with a frightened gasp, would fear that David's waiting now was not all for Dick. That he was waiting for peace.

There had been something new in David lately. She thought it was fear. Always he had been so sure of himself; he had made his experiment in a man's soul, and whatever the result he had been ready to face his Creator with it. But he had lost courage. He had tampered with the things that were to be and not he, but Dick, was paying for that awful audacity.

Once, picking up his prayer-book to read evening prayer as was her custom now, it had opened at a verse marked with an uneven line:

"I will arise and go to my Father, and will say unto Him, Father, I have sinned against Heaven and before Thee, and am no more worthy to be called Thy son."

That had frightened her

David's eyes followed her about the room.

"I've got an idea you're keeping something from me, Lucy."

"I? Why should I do that?"

"Then where's Harrison?" he demanded, querulously.

She told him one of the few white lies of her life when she said: "He hasn't been well. He'll be over to-morrow." She sat down and picked up the prayer-book, only to find him lifting himself in the bed and listening.

"Somebody closed the hall door, Lucy. If it's Reynolds, I want to see him."

She got up and went to the head of the stairs. The light was low in the hall beneath, and she saw a man standing there. But she still wore her reading glasses, and she saw at first hardly more than a figure.

"Is that you, Doctor Reynolds?" she asked, in her high old voice.

Then she put her hand to her throat and stood rigid, staring down. For the man had whipped off his cap and stood with his arms wide, looking up.

Holding to the stair-rail, her knees trembling under her, Lucy went down, and not until Dick's arms were around her was she sure that it was Dick, and not his shabby, weary ghost. She clung to him, tears streaming down her face, still in that cautious silence which governed them both; she held him off and looked at him, and then strained herself to him again, as though the sense of unreality were too strong, and only the contact of his rough clothing made him real to her.

It was not until they were in her sitting-room with the door closed that either of them dared to speak. Or perhaps, could speak. Even then she kept hold of him.

"Dick!" she said. "Dick!"

And that, over and over.

"How is he?" he was able to ask finally.

"He has been very ill. I began to think—Dick, I'm afraid to tell him. I'm afraid he'll die of joy."

He winced at that. There could not be much joy in the farewell that was coming. Winced, and almost staggered. He had walked all the way from the city, and he had had no food that day.

"We'll have to break it to him very gently," he said. "And he mustn't see me like this. If you can find some of my clothes and Reynolds' razor, I'll—" He caught suddenly to the back of a chair and held on to it. "I haven't taken time to eat much to-day," he said, smiling at her. "I guess I need food, Aunt Lucy."

For the first time then she saw his clothes, his shabbiness and his pallor, and perhaps she guessed the truth. She got up, her face twitching, and pushed him into a chair.

"You sit here," she said, "and leave the door closed. The nurse is out for a walk, and she'll be in soon. I'll bring some milk and cookies now, and start the fire. I've got some chops in the house."

When she came back almost immediately, with the familiar tray and the familiar food, he was sitting where she had left him. He had spent the entire time, had she known it, in impressing on his mind the familiar details of the room, to carry away with him.

She stood beside him, a hand on his shoulder, to see that he drank the milk slowly.

"I've got the fire going," she said. "And I'll run up now and get your clothes. I—had put them away." Her voice broke a little. "You see, we—You can change in your laboratory. Richard, can't you? If you go upstairs he'll hear you."

He reached up and caught her hand. That touch, too, of the nearest to a mother's hand that he had known, he meant to carry away with him. He could not speak.

She bustled away, into her bright kitchen first, and then with happy stealth to the store-room. Her very heart was singing within her. She neither thought nor reasoned. Dick was back, and all would be well. If she had any subconscious anxieties they were quieted, also subconsciously, by confidence in the men who were fighting his battle for him, by Walter Wheeler and Bassett and Harrison Miller. That Dick himself would present any difficulty lay beyond her worst fears.

She had been out of the room only twenty minutes when she returned to David and prepared to break her great news. At first she thought he was asleep. He was lying back with his eyes closed and his hands crossed on the prayer-book. But he looked up at her, and was instantly roused to full attention by her face.

"You've had some news," he said.

"Yes, David. There's a little news. Don't count too much on it. Don't sit up. David, I have heard something that makes me think he is alive. Alive and well."

He made a desperate effort and controlled himself.

"Where is he?"

She sat down beside him and took his hand between hers.

"David," she said slowly, "God has been very good to us. I want to tell you something, and I want you to prepare yourself. We have heard from Dick. He is all right. He loves us, as he always did. And—he is downstairs, David."

He lay very still and without speaking. She was frightened at first, afraid to go on with her further news. But suddenly David sat up in bed and in a full, firm voice began the Te Deum Laudamus. "We praise thee, O God: we acknowledge thee to be the Lord. All the earth doth worship thee, the Father everlasting."

He repeated it in its entirety. At the end, however, his voice broke.

"O Lord, in thee have I trusted—I doubted Him, Lucy," he said.

Dick, waiting at the foot of the stairs, heard that triumphant paean of thanksgiving and praise and closed his eyes.

It was a few minutes later that Lucy came down the stairs again.

"You heard him?" she asked. "Oh, Dick, he had frightened me. It was more than a question of himself and you. He was making it one of himself and God."

She let him go up alone and waited below, straining her ears, but she heard nothing beyond David's first hoarse cry, and after a little she went into her sitting-room and shut the door.

Whatever lay underneath, there was no surface drama in the meeting. The determination to ignore any tragedy in the situation was strong in them both, and if David's eyes were blurred and his hands trembling, if Dick's first words were rather choked, they hid their emotion carefully.

"Well, here I am, like a bad penny!" said Dick huskily from the doorway.

"And a long time you've been about it," grumbled David. "You young rascal!"

He held out his hand, and Dick crushed it between both of his. He was startled at the change in David. For a moment he could only stand there, holding his hand, and trying to keep his apprehension out of his face.

"Sit down," David said awkwardly, and blew his nose with a terrific blast. "I've been laid up for a while, but I'm all right now. I'll fool them all yet," he boasted, out of his happiness and content. "Business has been going to the dogs, Dick. Reynolds is a fool."

"Of course you'll fool them." There was still a band around Dick's throat. It hurt him to look at David, so thin and feeble, so sunken from his former portliness. And David saw his eyes, and knew.

"I've dropped a little flesh, eh, Dick?" he inquired. "Old bulge is gone, you see. The nurse makes up the bed when I'm in it, flat as when I'm out."

Suddenly his composure broke. He was a feeble and apprehensive old man, shaken with the tearless sobbing of weakness and age. Dick put an arm across his shoulders, and they sat without speech until David was quiet again.

"I'm a crying old woman, Dick," David said at last. "That's what comes of never feeling a pair of pants on your legs and being coddled like a baby." He sat up and stared around him ferociously. "They sprinkle violet water on my pillows, Dick! Can you beat that?"

Warned by Lucy, the nurse went to her room and did not disturb them. But she sat for a time in her rocking-chair, before she changed into the nightgown and kimono in which she slept on the couch in David's room. She knew the story, and her kindly heart ached within her. What good would it do after all, this home-coming? Dick could not stay. It was even dangerous. Reynolds had confided to her that he suspected a watch on the house by the police, and that the mail was being opened. What good was it?

Across the hall she could hear Lucy moving briskly about in Dick's room, changing the bedding, throwing up the windows, opening and closing bureau drawers. After a time Lucy tapped at her door and she opened it.

"I put a cake of scented soap among your handkerchiefs," she said, rather breathlessly. "Will you let me have it for Doctor Dick's room?"

She got the soap and gave it to her.

"He is going to stay, then?"

"Certainly he is going to stay," Lucy said, surprised. "This is his home. Where else should he go?"

But David knew. He lay, listening with avid interest to Dick's story, asking a question now and then, nodding over Dick's halting attempt to reconstruct the period of his confusion, but all the time one part of him, a keen and relentless inner voice, was saying: "Look at him well. Hold him close. Listen to his voice. Because this hour is yours, and perhaps only this hour."

"Then the Sayre woman doesn't know about your coming?" he asked, when Dick had finished.

"Still, she mustn't talk about having seen you. I'll send Reynolds up in the morning."

He was eager to hear of what had occurred in the long interval between them, and good, bad and indifferent Dick told him. But he limited himself to events, and did not touch on his mental battles, and David saw and noted it. The real story, he knew, lay there, but it was not time for it. After a while he raised himself in his bed.

"Call Lucy, Dick."

When she had come, a strangely younger Lucy, her withered cheeks flushed with exercise and excitement, he said:

"Bring me the copy of the statement I made to Harrison Miller, Lucy."

She brought it, patted Dick's shoulder, and went away. David held out the paper.

"Read it slowly, boy," he said. "It is my justification, and God willing, it may help you. The letter is from my brother, Henry. Read that, too."

Lucy, having got Dick's room in readiness, sat down in it to await his coming. Downstairs, in the warming oven, was his supper. His bed, with the best blankets, was turned down and ready. His dressing-gown and slippers were in their old accustomed place. She drew a long breath.

Below, Doctor Reynolds came in quietly and stood listening. The house was very still, and he decided that his news, which was after all no news, could wait. He went into the office and got out a sheet of note-paper, with his name at the top, and began his nightly letter to Clare Rossiter.

"My darling," it commenced.

Above, David lay in his bed and Dick read the papers in his hand. And as he read them David watched him. Not once, since Dick's entrance, had he mentioned Elizabeth. David lay still and pondered that. There was something wrong about it. This was Dick, their own Dick; no shadowy ghost of the past, but Dick himself. True, an older Dick, strangely haggard and with gray running in the brown of his hair, but still Dick; the Dick whose eyes had lighted at the sight of a girl, who had shamelessly persisted in holding her hand at that last dinner, who had almost idolatrously loved her.

And he had not mentioned her name.

When he had finished the reading Dick sat for a moment with the papers in his hand, thinking.

"I see," he said finally. "Of course, it's possible. Good God, if I could only think it."

"It's the answer," David said stubbornly. "He was prowling around, and fired through the window. Donaldson made the statement at the inquest that some one had been seen on the place, and that he notified you that night after dinner. He'd put guards around the place."

"It gives me a fighting chance, anyhow." Dick got up and threw back his shoulders. "That's all I want. A chance to fight. I know this. I hated Lucas—he was a poor thing and you know what he did to me. But I never thought of killing him. That wouldn't have helped matters. It was too late."

"What about—that?" David asked, not looking at him. When Dick did not immediately reply David glanced at him, to find his face set and pained.

"Perhaps we'd better not go into that now," David said hastily. "It's natural that the readjustments will take time."

"We'll have to go into it. It's the hardest thing I have to face."

"It's not dead, then?"

"No," Dick said slowly. "It's not dead, David. And I'd better bring it into the open. I've fought it to the limit by myself. It's the one thing that seems to have survived the shipwreck. I can't argue it down or think it down."

"Maybe, if you see Elizabeth—"

"I'd break her heart, that's all."

He tried to make David understand. He told in its sordid details his failure to kill it, his attempts to sink memory and conscience in Chicago and their failure, the continued remoteness of Elizabeth and what seemed to him the flesh and blood reality of the other woman. That she was yesterday, and Elizabeth was long ago.

"I can't argue it down," he finished. "I've tried to, desperately. It's a—I think it's a wicked thing, in a way. And God knows all she ever got out of it was suffering. She must loathe the thought of me."

David was compelled to let it rest there. He found that Dick was doggedly determined to see Beverly Carlysle. After that, he didn't know. No man wanted to surrender himself for trial, unless he was sure himself of whether he was innocent or guilty. If there was a reasonable doubt—but what did it matter one way or the other? His place was gone, as he'd made it, gone if he was cleared, gone if he was convicted.

"I can't come back, David. They wouldn't have me."

After a silence he asked:

"How much is known here? What does Elizabeth know?"

"The town knows nothing. She knows a part of it. She cares a great deal, Dick. It's a tragedy for her."

"Shall you tell her I have been here?"

"Not unless you intend to see her."

But Dick shook his head.

"Even if other things were the same I haven't a right to see her, until I've got a clean slate."

"That's sheer evasion," David said, almost with irritation.

"Yes," Dick acknowledged gravely. "It is sheer evasion."

"What about the police?" he inquired after a silence. "I was registered at Norada. I suppose they traced me?"

"Yes. The house was watched for a while; I understand they've given it up now."

In response to questions about his own condition David was almost querulous. He was all right. He would get well if they'd let him, and stop coddling him. He would get up now, in spite of them. He was good for one more fight before he died, and he intended to make it, in a court if necessary.

"They can't prove it, Dick," he said triumphantly. "I've been over it every day for months. There is no case. There never was a case, for that matter. They're a lot of pin-headed fools, and we'll show them up, boy. We'll show them up."

But for all his excitement fatigue was telling on him. Lucy tapped at the door and came in.

"You'd better have your supper before it spoils," she said. "And David needs a rest. Doctor Reynolds is in the office. I haven't told him yet."

The two men exchanged glances.

"Time for that later," David said. "I can't keep him out of my office, but I can out of my family affairs for an hour or so."

So it happened that Dick followed Lucy down the back stairs and ate his meal stealthily in the kitchen.

"I don't like you to eat here," she protested.

"I've eaten in worse places," he said, smiling at her. "And sometimes not at all." He was immediately sorry for that, for the tears came to her eyes.

He broke as gently as he could the news that he could not stay, but it was a great blow to her. Her sagging chin quivered piteously, and it took all the cheerfulness he could summon and all the promises of return he could make to soften the shock.

"You haven't even seen Elizabeth," she said at last.

"That will have to wait until things are cleared up, Aunt Lucy."

"Won't you write her something then, Richard? She looks like a ghost these days."

Her eyes were on him, puzzled and wistful. He met them gravely.

"I haven't the right to see her, or to write to her."

And the finality in his tone closed the discussion, that and something very close to despair in his face.

For all his earlier hunger he ate very little, and soon after he tiptoed up the stairs again to David's room. When he came down to the kitchen later on he found her still there, at the table where he had left her, her arms across it and her face buried in them. On a chair was the suitcase she had hastily packed for him, and a roll of bills lay on the table.

"You must take it," she insisted. "It breaks my heart to think—Dick, I have the feeling that I am seeing you for the last time." Then for fear she had hurt him she forced a determined smile. "Don't pay any attention to me. David will tell you that I have said, over and over, that I'd never see you again. And here you are!"

He was going. He had said good-bye to David and was going at once. She accepted it with a stoicism born of many years of hail and farewell, kissed him tenderly, let her hand linger for a moment on the rough sleeve of his coat, and then let him out by the kitchen door into the yard. But long after he had gone she stood in the doorway, staring out...

In the office Doctor Reynolds was finishing a long and carefully written letter.

"I am not good at putting myself on paper, as you know, dear heart. But this I do know. I do not believe that real love dies. We may bury it, so deep that it seems to be entirely dead, but some day it sends up a shoot, and it either lives, or the business of killing it has to be begun all over again. So when we quarrel, I always know—"

XXXIX

The evening had shaken Dick profoundly. David's appearance and Lucy's grief and premonition, most of all the talk of Elizabeth, had depressed and unnerved him. Even the possibility of his own innocence was subordinated to an overwhelming yearning for the old house and the old life.

Through a side window as he went toward the street he could see Reynolds at his desk in the office, and he was possessed by a fierce jealousy and resentment at his presence there. The laboratory window was dark, and he stood outside and looked at it. He would have given his hope of immortality just then to have been inside it once more, working over his tubes and his cultures, his slides and microscope. Even the memory of certain dearly-bought extravagances in apparatus revived in him, and sent the blood to his head in a wave of unreasoning anger and bitterness.

He had a wild desire to go in at the front door, confront Reynolds in his smug complacency and drive him out; to demand his place in the world and take it. He could hardly tear himself away.

Under a street lamp he looked at his watch. It was eleven o'clock, and he had a half hour to spare before train-time. Following an impulse he did not analyze he turned toward the Wheeler house. Just so months ago had he turned in that direction, but with this difference, that then he went with a sort of hurried expectancy, and that now he loitered on the way. Yet that it somehow drew him he knew. Not with the yearning he had felt toward the old brick house, but with the poignancy of a long past happiness. He did not love, but he remembered.

Yet, for a man who did not love, he was oddly angry at the sight of two young figures on the doorstep. Their clear voices came to him across the quiet street, vibrant and full of youth. It was the Sayre boy and Elizabeth.

He half stopped, and looked across. They were quite oblivious of him, intent and self-absorbed. As he had viewed Reynolds' unconscious figure with jealous dislike, so he viewed Wallace Sayre. Here, everywhere, his place was filled. He was angry with an unreasoning, inexplicable anger, angry at Elizabeth, angry at the boy, and at himself.

He had but to cross the street and take his place there. He could drive that beardless youngster away with a word. The furious possessive jealousy of the male animal, which had nothing to do with love, made him stop and draw himself up as he stared across.

Then he smiled wryly and went on. He could do it, but he did not want to. He would never do it. Let them live their lives, and let him live his. But he knew that there, across the street, so near that he might have raised his voice and summoned her, he was leaving the best thing that had come into his life; the one fine and good thing, outside of David and Lucy. That against its loss he had nothing but an infatuation that had ruined three lives already, and was not yet finished.

He stopped and, turning, looked back. He saw the girl bend down and put a hand on Wallie Sayre's shoulder, and the boy's face upturned and looking into hers. He shook himself and went on. After all, that was best. He felt no anger now. She deserved better than to be used to help a man work out his salvation. She deserved youth, and joyousness, and the forgetfulness that comes with time. She was already forgetting.

He smiled again as he went on up the street, but his hands as he buttoned his overcoat were shaking.

It was shortly after that that he met the rector, Mr. Oglethorpe. He passed him quickly, but he was conscious that the clergyman had stopped and was staring after him. Half an hour later, sitting in the empty smoker of the train, he wondered if he had not missed something there. Perhaps the church could have helped him, a good man's simple belief in right and wrong. He was wandering in a gray no-man's land, without faith or compass.

David had given him the location of Bassett's apartment house, and he found it quickly. He was in a state of nervous irritability by that time, for the sense of being a fugitive was constantly stressed in the familiar streets by the danger of recognition. It was in vain that he argued with himself that only the police were interested in his movements, and the casual roundsman not at all. He found himself shying away from them like a nervous horse.

But if he expected any surprise from Bassett he was disappointed. He greeted him as if he had seen him yesterday, and explained his lack of amazement in his first words.

"Doctor Livingstone telephoned me. Sit down, man, and let me look at you. You've given me more trouble than any human being on earth."

"Sorry," Dick said awkwardly, "I seem to have a faculty of involving other people in my difficulties."

"Want a drink?"

"No, thanks. I'll smoke, if you have any tobacco. I've been afraid to risk a shop."

Bassett talked cheerfully as he found cigarettes and matches. "The old boy had a different ring to his voice to-night. He was going down pretty fast, Livingstone; was giving up the fight. But I fancy you've given him a new grip on the earth." When they were seated, however, a sort of awkwardness developed. To Dick, Bassett had been a more or less shadowy memory, clouded over with the details and miseries of the flight. And Bassett found Dick greatly altered. He was older than he remembered him. The sort of boyishness which had come with the resurrection of his early identity had gone, and the man who sat before him was grave, weary, and much older. But his gaze was clear and direct.

"Well, a good bit of water has gone over the dam since we met," Bassett said. "I nearly broke a leg going down that infernal mountain again. And I don't mind telling you that I came within an ace of landing in the Norada jail. They knew I'd helped you get away. But they couldn't prove it."

"I got out, because I didn't see any need of dragging you down with me. I was a good bit of a mess just then, but I could reason that out, anyhow. It wasn't entirely unselfish, either. I had a better chance without you. Or thought I did."

Bassett was watching him intently.

"Has it all come back?" he inquired.

"Practically all. Not much between the thing that happened at the ranch and David Livingstone's picking me up at the cabin."

"Did it ever occur to you to wonder just how I got in on your secret?"

"I suppose you read Maggie Donaldson's confession."

"I came to see you before that came out."

"Then I don't know, I'm afraid."

"I suppose you would stake your life on the fact that Beverly Carlysle knows nothing of what happened that night at the ranch?"

Dick's face twitched, but he returned Bassett's gaze steadily.

"She has no criminal knowledge, if that is what you mean."

"I am not so sure of it."

"I think you'd better explain that."

At the cold anger in Dick's voice Bassett stared at him. So that was how the wind lay. Poor devil! And out of the smug complacence of his bachelor peace Bassett thanked his stars for no women in his life.

"I'm afraid you misunderstand me, Livingstone," he said easily. "I don't think that she shot Lucas. But I don't think she has ever told all she knows. I've got the coroner's inquest here, and we'll go over it later. I'll tell you how I got onto your trail. Do you remember taking Elizabeth Wheeler to see 'The Valley?'"

"I had forgotten it. I remember now."

"Well, Gregory, the brother, saw you and recognized you. I was with him. He tried to deny you later, but I was on. Of course he told her, and I think she sent him to warn David Livingstone. They knew I was on the trail of a big story. Then I think Gregory stayed here to watch me when the company made its next jump. He knew I'd started, for he sent David Livingstone the letter you got. By the way, that letter nearly got me jailed in Norada."

"I'm not hiding behind her skirts," Dick said shortly. "And there's nothing incriminating in what you say. She saw me as a fugitive, and she sent me a warning. That's all."

"Easy, easy, old man. I'm not pinning anything on her. But I want, if you don't mind, to carry this through. I have every reason to believe that, some time before you got to Norada, the Thorwald woman was on my trail. I know that I was followed to the cabin the night I stayed there, and that she got a saddle horse from her son that night, her son by Thorwald, either for herself or some one else."

"All right. I accept that, tentatively."

"That means that she knew I was coming to Norada. Think a minute; I'd kept my movements quiet, but Beverly Carlysle knew, and her brother. When they warned David they warned her."

"I don't believe it."

"If you had killed Lucas," Bassett asserted positively, "the Thorwald woman would have let the sheriff get you, and be damned to you. She had no reason to love you. You'd kept her son out of what she felt was his birthright."

He got up and opened a table drawer.

"I've got a copy of the coroner's inquest here. It will bear going over. And it may help you to remember, too. We needn't read it all. There's a lot that isn't pertinent."

He got out a long envelope, and took from it a number of typed pages, backed with a base of heavy paper.

"'Inquest in the Coroner's office on the body of Howard Lucas,'" he read. "'October 10th, 1911.' That was the second day after. 'Examination of witnesses by Coroner Samuel J. Burkhardt. Mrs. Lucas called and sworn.'" He glanced at Dick and hesitated. "I don't know about this to-night, Livingstone. You look pretty well shot to pieces."

"I didn't sleep last night. I'm all right. Go on."

During the reading that followed he sat back in his deep chair, his eyes closed. Except that once or twice he clenched his hands he made no movement whatever.

Q. "What is your name?"

A. "Anne Elizabeth Lucas. My stage name is Beverly Carlysle."

Q. "Where do you live, Mrs. Lucas?"

A. "At 26 East 56th Street, New York City."

Q. "I shall have to ask you some questions that are necessarily painful at this time. I shall be as brief as possible. Perhaps it will be easier for you to tell so much as you know of what happened the night before last at the Clark ranch."

A. "I cannot tell very much. I am confused, too. I was given a sleeping powder last night. I can only say that I heard a shot, and thought at first that it was fired from outside. I ran down the stairs, and back to the billiard room. As I entered the room Mr. Donaldson came in through a window. My husband was lying on the floor. That is all."

Q. "Where was Judson Clark?"

A. "He was leaning on the roulette table, staring at the—at my husband."

Q. "Did you see him leave the room?"

A. "No. I was on my knees beside Mr. Lucas. I think when I got up he was gone. I didn't notice."

Q. "Did you see a revolver?"

A. "No. I didn't look for one."

Q. "Now I shall ask you one more question, and that is all. Had there been any quarrel between Mr. Lucas and Mr. Clark that evening in your presence?"

A. "No. But I had quarreled with them both. They were drinking too much. I had gone to my room to pack and go home. I was packing when I heard the shot."

Witness excused and Mr. John Donaldson called.

Q. "What is your name?"

A. "John Donaldson."

Q. "Where do you live?"

A. "At the Clark ranch."

Q. "What is your business?"

A. "You know all about me. I'm foreman of the ranch."

Q. "I want you to tell what you know, Jack, about last night. Begin with where you were when you heard the shot."

A. "I was on the side porch. The billiard room opens on to it. I'd been told by the corral boss earlier in the evening that he'd seen a man skulking around the house. There'd been a report like that once or twice before, and I set a watch. I put Ben Haggerty at the kitchen wing with a gun, and I took up a stand on the porch. Before I did that I told Judson, but I don't think he took it in. He'd been lit up like a house afire all evening. I asked for his gun, but he said he didn't know where it was, and I went back to my house and got my own. Along about eight o'clock I thought I saw some one in the shrubbery, and I went out as quietly as I could. But it was a woman, Hattie Thorwald, who was working at the ranch.

"When I left the men were playing roulette. I looked in as I went back, and Judson had a gun in his hand. He said; 'I found it, Jack.' I saw he was very drunk, and I told him to put it up, I'd got mine. It had occurred to me that I'd better warn Haggerty to be careful, and I started along the verandah to tell him not to shoot except to scare. I had only gone a few steps when I heard a shot, and ran back. Mr. Lucas was on the floor dead, and Judson was as the lady said. He must have gone out while I was bending over the body."

Q. "Did you see the revolver in his hand?"

A. "No."

Q. "How long between your warning Mr. Clark and the shot?"

A. "I suppose I'd gone a dozen yards."

Q. "Were you present when the revolver was found?"

A. "No, sir."

Q. "Did you see Judson Clark again?"

A. "No, sir. From what I gather he went straight to the corral and got his horse."

Q. "You entered the room as Mrs. Lucas came in the door?"

A. "Well, she's wrong about that. She was there a little ahead of me. She'd reached the body before I got in. She was stooping over it."

Bassett looked up from his reading.

"I want you to get this, Livingstone," he said. "How did she reach the billiard room? Where was it in the house?"

"Off the end of the living-room."

"A large living-room?"

"Forty or forty-five feet, about."

"Will you draw it for me, roughly?"

He passed over a pad and pencil, and Dick made a hasty outline. Bassett watched with growing satisfaction.

"Here's the point," he said, when Dick had finished. "She was there before Donaldson, or at the same time," as Dick made an impatient movement. "But he had only a dozen yards to go. She was in her room, upstairs. To get down in that time she had to leave her room, descend a staircase, cross a hall and run the length of the living-room, forty-five feet. If the case had ever gone to trial she'd have had to do some explaining."

"She or Donaldson," Dick said obstinately.

Bassett read on:

Jean Melis called and sworn.

Q. "Your name?"

A. "Jean Melis."

Q. "Have you an American residence, Mr. Melis?"

A. "Only where I am employed. I am now living at the Clark ranch."

Q. "What is your business?"

A. "I am Mr. Clark's valet."

Q. "It was you who found Mr. Clark's revolver?"

A. "Yes."

Q. "Tell about how and where you found it."

A. "I made a search early in the evening. I will not hide from you that I meant to conceal it if I discovered it. A man who is drunk is not guilty of what he does. I did not find it. I went back that night, when the people had gone, and found it beneath the carved woodbox, by the fireplace. I did not know that the sheriff had placed a man outside the window."

"Get that, too," Bassett said, putting down the paper. "The Frenchman was fond of you, and he was doing his blundering best. But the sheriff expected you back and had had the place watched, so they caught him. But that's not the point. A billiard room is a hard place to hide things in. I take it yours was like the average."

Dick nodded.

"All right. This poor boob of a valet made a search and didn't find it. Later he found it. Why did he search? Wasn't it the likely thing that you'd carried it away with you? Do you suppose for a moment that with Donaldson and the woman in the room you hid it there, and then went back and stood behind the roulette table, leaning on it with both hands, and staring? Not at all. Listen to this:

Q. "You recognize this revolver as the one you found?"

A. "Yes."

Q. "You are familiar with it?"

A. "Yes. It is Mr. Clark's."

Q. "You made the second search because you had not examined the woodbox earlier?"

A. "No. I had examined the woodbox. I had a theory that—"

Q. "The Jury cannot listen to any theories. This is an inquiry into facts."

"I'm going to find Melis," the reporter said thoughtfully, as he folded up the papers. "The fact is, I mailed an advertisement to the New York papers to-day. I want to get that theory of his. It's the servants in the house who know what is going on. I've got an idea that he'd stumbled onto something. He'd searched for the revolver, and it wasn't there. He went back and it was. All that conflicting evidence, and against it, what? That you'd run away!"

But he saw that Dick was very tired, and even a little indifferent. He would be glad to know that his hands were clean, but against the intimation that Beverly Carlysle had known more than she had disclosed he presented a dogged front of opposition. After a time Bassett put the papers away and essayed more general conversation, and there he found himself met half way and more. He began to get Dick as a man, for the first time, and as a strong man. He watched his quiet, lined face, and surmised behind it depths of tenderness and gentleness. No wonder the little Wheeler girl had worshipped him.

It was settled that Dick was to spend the night there, and such plans as he had Bassett left until morning. But while he was unfolding the bed-lounge on which Dick was to sleep, Dick opened a line of discussion that cost the reporter an hour or two's sleep before he could suppress his irritation.

"I must have caused you considerable outlay, one way and another," he said. "I want to defray that, Bassett, as soon as I've figured out some way to get at my bank account."

Bassett jerked out a pillow and thumped it.

"Forget it." Then he grinned. "You can fix that when you get your estate, old man. Buy a newspaper and let me run it!"

He bent over the davenport and put the pillow in place. "All you'll have to do is to establish your identity. The institutions that got it had to give bond. I hope you're not too long for this bed."

But he looked up at Dick's silence, to see him looking at him with a faint air of amusement over his pipe.

"They're going to keep the money, Bassett."

Bassett straightened and stared at him.

"Don't be a damned fool," he protested. "It's your money. Don't tell me you're going to give it to suffering humanity. That sort of drivel makes me sick. Take it, give it away if you like, but for God's sake don't shirk your job."

Dick got up and took a turn or two around the room. Then, after an old habit, he went to the window and stood looking out, but seeing nothing.

"It's not that, Bassett. I'm afraid of the accursed thing. I might talk a lot of rot about wanting to work with my hands. I wouldn't if I didn't have to, any more than the next fellow. I might fool myself, too, with thinking I could work better without any money worries. But I've got to remember this. It took work to make a man of me before, and it will take work to keep me going the way I intend to go, if I get my freedom."

Sometime during the night Bassett saw that the light was still burning by the davenport, and went in. Dick was asleep with a volume of Whitman open on his chest, and Bassett saw what he had been reading.

"You broken resolutions, you racking angers, you short-lived ennuis; Ah, think not you shall finally triumph, my real self has yet to come forth. It shall march forth over-mastering, till all lie beneath me, It shall stand up, the soldier of unquestioned victory."

Bassett took the book away and stood rereading the paragraph. For the first time he sensed the struggle going on at that time behind Dick's quiet face, and he wondered. Unquestioned victory, eh? That was a pretty large order.

XL

Leslie Ward had found the autumn extremely tedious. His old passion for Nina now and then flamed up in him, but her occasional coquetries no longer deceived him. They had their source only in her vanity. She exacted his embraces only as tribute to her own charm, her youth, her fresh young body.

And Nina out of her setting of gaiety, of a thumping piano, of chattering, giggling crowds, of dancing and bridge and theater boxes, was a queen dethroned. She did not read or think. She spent the leisure of her mourning period in long hours before her mirror fussing with her hair, in trimming and retrimming hats, or in the fastidious care of her hands and body.

He was ashamed sometimes of his pitilessly clear analysis of her. She was not discontented, save at the enforced somberness of their lives. She had found in marriage what she wanted; a good house, daintily served; a man to respond to her attractions as a woman, and to provide for her needs as a wife; dignity and an established place in the world; liberty and privilege.

But she was restless. She chafed at the quiet evenings they spent at home, and resented the reading in which he took refuge from her uneasy fidgeting.

"For Heaven's sake, Nina, sit down and read or sew, or do something. You've been at that window a dozen times."

"I'm not bothering you. Go on and read."

When nobody dropped in she would go upstairs and spend the hour or so before bedtime in the rites of cold cream, massage, and in placing the little combs of what Leslie had learned was called a water-wave.

But her judgment was as clear as his, and even more pitiless; the difference between them lay in the fact that while he rebelled, she accepted the situation. She was cleverer than he was; her mind worked more quickly, and she had the adaptability he lacked. If there were times when she wearied him, there were others when she sickened him. Across from her at the table he ate slowly and enormously. He splashed her dainty bathroom with his loud, gasping cold baths. He flung his soiled clothing anywhere. He drank whisky at night and crawled into the lavender-scented sheets redolent of it, to drop into a heavy sleep and snore until she wanted to scream. But she played the game to the limit of her ability.

Then, seeing that they might go on the rocks, he made a valiant effort, and since she recognized it as an effort, she tried to meet him half way. They played two-handed card games. He read aloud to her, poetry which she loathed, and she to him, short stories he hated. He suggested country walks and she agreed, to limp back after a half mile or so in her high-heeled pumps.

He concealed his boredom from her, but there were nights when he lay awake long after she was asleep and looked ahead into a future of unnumbered blank evenings. He had formerly taken an occasional evening at his club, but on his suggesting it now Nina's eyes would fill with suspicion, and he knew that although she never mentioned Beverly Carlysle, she would neither forget nor entirely trust him again. And in his inner secret soul he knew that she was right.

He had thought that he had buried that brief madness, but there were times when he knew he lied to himself. One fiction, however, he persisted in; he had not been infatuated with Beverly. It was only that she gave him during those few days something he had not found at home, companionship and quiet intelligent talk. She had been restful. Nina was never restful.

He bought a New York paper daily, and read it in the train. "The Valley" had opened to success in New York, and had settled for a long run. The reviews of her work had been extraordinary, and when now and then she gave an interview he studied the photographs accompanying it. But he never carried the paper home.

He began, however, to play with the thought of going to New York. He would not go to see her at her house, but he would like to see her before a metropolitan audience, to add his mite to her triumph. There were times when he fully determined to go, when he sat at his desk with his hand on the telephone, prepared to lay the foundations of the excursion by some manipulation of business interests. For months, however, he never went further than the preliminary movement.

But by October he began to delude himself with a real excuse for going, and this was the knowledge that by a strange chain of circumstance this woman who so dominated his secret thoughts was connected with Elizabeth's life through Judson Clark. The discovery, communicated to him by Walter Wheeler, that Dick was Clark had roused in him a totally different feeling from Nina's. He saw no glamour of great wealth. On the contrary, he saw in Clark the author of a great unhappiness to a woman who had not deserved it. And Nina, judging him with deadly accuracy, surmised even that.

That he was jealous of Judson Clark, and of his part in the past, he denied to himself absolutely. But his resentment took the form of violent protest to the family, against even allowing Elizabeth to have anything to do with Dick if he turned up.

"He'll buy his freedom, if he isn't dead," he said to Nina, "and he'll come snivelling back here, with that lost memory bunk, and they're just fool enough to fall for it."

"I've fallen for it, and I'm at least as intelligent as you are."

Before her appraising eyes his own fell.

"Suppose I did something I shouldn't and turned up here with such a story, would you believe it?"

"No. When you want to do something you shouldn't you don't appear to need any excuse."

But, on the whole, they managed to live together comfortably enough. They each had their reservations, but especially after Jim's death they tacitly agreed to stop bickering and to make their mutual concessions. What Nina never suspected was that he corresponded with Beverly Carlysle. Not that the correspondence amounted to much. He had sent her flowers the night of the New York opening, with the name of his club on his card, and she wrote there in acknowledgment. Then, later, twice he sent her books, one a biography, which was a compromise with his conscience, and later a volume of exotic love verse, which was not. As he replied to her notes of thanks a desultory correspondence had sprung up, letters which the world might have read, and yet which had to him the savor and interest of the clandestine.

He did not know that that, and not infatuation, was behind his desire to see Beverly again; never reasoned that he was demonstrating to himself that his adventurous love life was not necessarily ended; never acknowledged that the instinct of the hunter was as alive in him as in the days before his marriage. Partly, then, a desire for adventure, partly a hope that romance was not over but might still be waiting around the next corner, was behind his desire to see her again.

Probably Nina knew that, as she knew so many things; why he had taken to reading poetry, for instance. Certain it is that when he began, early in October, to throw out small tentative remarks about the necessity of a business trip before long to New York, she narrowed her eyes. She was determined to go with him, if he went at all, and he was equally determined that she should not.

It became, in a way, a sort of watchful waiting on both sides. Then there came a time when some slight excuse offered, and Leslie took up the shuttle for forty-eight hours, and wove his bit in the pattern. It happened to be on the same evening as Dick's return to the old house.

He was a little too confident, a trifle too easy to Nina.

"Has the handle of my suitcase been repaired yet?" he asked. He was lighting a cigarette at the time.

"Yes. Why?"

"I'll have to run over to New York to-morrow. I wanted Joe to go alone, but he thinks he needs me." Joe was his partner. "Oh. So Joe's going?"

"That's what I said."

She was silent. Joe's going was clever of him. It gave authenticity to his business, and it kept her at home.

"How long shall you be gone?"

"Only a day or two." He could not entirely keep the relief out of his voice. It had been easy, incredibly easy. He might have done it a month ago. And he had told the truth; Joe was going.

"I'll pack to-night, and take my suitcase in with me in the morning."

"If you'll get your things out I'll pack them." She was still thinking, but her tone was indifferent. "You won't want your dress clothes, of course."

"I'd better have a dinner suit."

She looked at him then, with a half contemptuous smile. "Yes," she said slowly. "I suppose you will. You'll be going to the theater."

He glanced away.

"Possibly. But we'll be rushing to get through. There's a lot to do. Amazing how business piles up when you find you're going anywhere. There won't be much time to play."

She sat before the mirror in her small dressing-room that night, ostensibly preparing for bed but actually taking stock of her situation. She had done all she could, had been faithful and loyal, had made his home attractive, had catered to his tastes and tried to like his friends, had met his needs and responded to them. And now, this. She was bewildered and frightened. How did women hold their husbands?

She found him in bed and unmistakably asleep when she went into the bedroom. Man-like, having got his way, he was not troubled by doubts or introspection. It was done.

He was lying on his back, with his mouth open. She felt a sudden and violent repugnance to getting into the bed beside him. Sometime in the night he would turn over and throwing his arm about her, hold her close in his sleep; and it would be purely automatic, the mechanical result of habit.

She lay on the edge of the bed and thought things over.

He had his good qualities. He was kind and affectionate to her family. He had been wonderful when Jim died, and he loved Elizabeth dearly. He was generous and open-handed. He was handsome, too, in a big, heavy way.

She began to find excuses for him. Men were always a child-like prey to some women. They were vain, and especially they were sex-vain; good looking men were a target for every sort of advance. She transferred her loathing of him to the woman she suspected of luring him away from her, and lay for hours hating her.

She saw Leslie off in the morning with a perfunctory good-bye while cold anger and suspicion seethed in her. And later she put on her hat and went home to lay the situation before her mother. Mrs. Wheeler was out, however, and she found only Elizabeth sewing by her window.

Nina threw her hat on the bed and sat down dispiritedly.

"I suppose there's no news?" she asked.

Nina watched her. She was out of patience with Elizabeth, exasperated with the world.

"Are you going to go on like this all your life?" she demanded. "Sitting by a window, waiting? For a man who ran away from you?"

"That's not true, and you know it."

"They're all alike," Nina declared recklessly. "They go along well enough, and they are all for virtue and for the home and fireside stuff, until some woman comes their way. I ought to know."

Elizabeth looked up quickly.

"Why, Nina!" she said. "You don't mean—"

"He went to New York this morning. He pretended to be going on business, but he's actually gone to see that actress. He's been mad about her for months."

"I don't believe it."

"Oh, wake up," Nina said impatiently. "The world isn't made up of good, kind, virtuous people. It's rotten. And men are all alike. Dick Livingstone and Les and all the rest—tarred with the same stick. As long as there are women like this Carlysle creature they'll fall for them. And you and I can sit at home and chew our nails and plan to keep them by us. And we can't do it."

In spite of herself a little question of doubt crept that day into Elizabeth's mind. She had always known that they had not told her all the truth; that the benevolent conspiracy to protect Dick extended even to her. But she had never thought that it might include a woman. Once there, the very humility of her love for Dick was an element in favor of the idea. She had never been good enough, or wise or clever enough, for him. She was too small and unimportant to be really vital.

Dismissing the thought did no good. It came back. But because she was a healthy-minded and practical person she took the one course she could think of, and put the question that night to her father, when he came back from seeing David.

David had sent for him early in the evening. All day he had thought over the situation between Dick and Elizabeth, with growing pain and uneasiness. He had not spoken of it to Lucy, or to Harrison Miller; he knew that they would not understand, and that Lucy would suffer. She was bewildered enough by Dick's departure.

At noon he had insisted on getting up and being helped into his trousers. So clad he felt more of a man and better able to cope with things, although his satisfaction in them was somewhat modified by the knowledge of two safety-pins at the sides, to take up their superfluous girth at the waistband.

But even the sense of being clothed as a man again did not make it easier to say to Walter Wheeler what must be said.

Walter took the news of Dick's return with a visible brightening. It was as though, out of the wreckage of his middle years, he saw that there was now some salvage, but he was grave and inarticulate over it, wrung David's hand and only said:

"Thank God for it, David." And after a pause: "Was he all right? He remembered everything?"

But something strange in the situation began to obtrude itself into his mind. Dick had come back twenty-four hours ago. Last night. And all this time—

"Where is he now?"

"He's not here, Walter."

"He has gone away again, without seeing Elizabeth?"

David cleared his throat.

"He is still a fugitive. He doesn't himself know he isn't guilty. I think he feels that he ought not to see her until—"

"Come, come," Walter Wheeler said impatiently. "Don't try to find excuses for him. Let's have the truth, David. I guess I can stand it."

Poor David, divided between his love for Dick and his native honesty, threw out his hands.

"I don't understand it, Wheeler," he said. "You and I wouldn't, I suppose. We are not the sort to lose the world for a woman. The plain truth is that there is not a trace of Judson Clark in him to-day, save one. That's the woman."

When Wheeler said nothing, but sat twisting his hat in his hands, David went on. It might be only a phase. As its impression on Dick's youth had been deeper than others, so its effect was more lasting. It might gradually disappear. He was confident, indeed, that it would. He had been reading on the subject all day.

Walter Wheeler hardly heard him. He was facing the incredible fact, and struggling with his own problem. After a time he got up, shook hands with David and went home, the dog at his heels.

During the evening that followed he made his resolution, not to tell her, never to let her suspect the truth. But he began to wonder if she had heard something, for he found her eyes on him more than once, and when Margaret had gone up to bed she came over and sat on the arm of his chair. She said an odd thing then, and one that made it impossible to lie to her later.

"I come to you, a good bit as I would go to God, if he were a person," she said. "I have got to know something, and you can tell me."

He put his arm around her and held her close.

"Go ahead, honey."

"Daddy, do you realize that I am a woman now?"

"I try to. But it seems about six months since I was feeding you hot water for colic."

She sat still for a moment, stroking his hair and being very careful not to spoil his neat parting.

"You have never told me all about Dick, daddy. You have always kept something back. That's true, isn't it?"

"There were details," he said uncomfortably. "It wasn't necessary—"

"Here's what I want to know. If he has gone back to the time—you know, wouldn't he go back to caring for the people he loved then?" Then, suddenly, her childish appeal ceased, and she slid from the chair and stood before him. "I must know, father. I can bear it. The thing you have been keeping from me was another woman, wasn't it?"

"It was so long ago," he temporized. "Think of it, Elizabeth. A boy of twenty-one or so."

"Then there was?"

"I believe so, at one time. But I know positively that he hadn't seen or heard from her in ten years."

"What sort of woman?"

"I wouldn't think about it, honey. It's all so long ago."

"Did she live in Wyoming?"

"She was an actress," he said, hard driven by her persistence.

"Do you know her name?"

"Only her stage name, honey."

"But you know she was an actress!"

He sighed.

"All right, dear," he said. "I'll tell you all I know. She was an actress, and she married another man. That's all there is to it. She's not young now. She must be thirty now—if she's living," he added, as an afterthought.

It was some time before she spoke again.

"I suppose she was beautiful," she said slowly.

"I don't know. Most of them aren't, off the stage. Anyhow, what does it matter now?"

"Only that I know he has gone back to her. And you know it too."

He heard her going quietly out of the room.

Long after, he closed the house and went cautiously upstairs. She was waiting for him in the doorway of her room, in her nightgown.

"I know it all now," she said steadily. "It was because of her he shot the other man, wasn't it?"

She saw her answer in his startled face, and closed her door quickly. He stood outside, and then he tapped lightly.

"Let me in, honey," he said. "I want to finish it. You've got a wrong idea about it."

When she did not answer he tried the door, but it was locked. He turned and went downstairs again...

When he came home the next afternoon Margaret met him in the hall.

"She knows it, Walter."

"Knows what?"

"Knows he was back here and didn't see her. Annie blurted it out; she'd got it from the Oglethorpe's laundress. Mr. Oglethorpe saw him on the street."

It took him some time to drag a coherent story from her. Annie had told Elizabeth in her room, and then had told Margaret. She had gone to Elizabeth at once, to see what she could do, but Elizabeth had been in her closet, digging among her clothes. She had got out her best frock and put it on, while her mother sat on the bed not even daring to broach the matter in her mind, and had gone out. There was a sort of cold determination in her that frightened Margaret. She had laughed a good bit, for one thing.

"She's terribly proud," she finished. "She'll do something reckless, I'm sure. It wouldn't surprise me to see her come back engaged to Wallie Sayre. I think that's where she went."

But apparently she had not, or if she had she said nothing about it. From that time on they saw a change in her; she was as loving as ever, but she affected a sort of painful brightness that was a little hard. As though she had clad herself in armor against further suffering.

XLI

For months Beverly Carlysle had remained a remote and semi-mysterious figure. She had been in some hearts and in many minds, but to most of them she was a name only. She had been the motive behind events she never heard of, the quiet center in a tornado of emotions that circled about without touching her.

On the whole she found her life, with the settling down of the piece to a successful, run, one of prosperous monotony. She had re-opened and was living in the 56th Street house, keeping a simple establishment of cook, butler and maid, and in the early fall she added a town car and a driver. After that she drove out every afternoon except on matinee days, almost always alone, but sometimes with a young girl from the company.

She was very lonely. The kaleidoscope that is theatrical New York had altered since she left it. Only one or two of her former friends remained, and she found them uninteresting and narrow with the narrowness of their own absorbing world. She had forgotten that the theater was like an island, cut off from the rest of the world, having its own politics, its own society divided by caste, almost its own religion. Out of its insularity it made occasional excursions to dinners and week-ends; even into marriage, now and then with an outlander. But almost always it went back, eager for its home of dressing-room and footlights, of stage entrances up dirty alleys, of door-keepers and managers and parts and costumes.

Occasionally she had callers, men she had met or who were brought to see her. She saw them over a tea-table, judged them remorselessly, and eliminated gradually all but one or two. She watched her dignity and her reputation with the care of an ambitious woman trying to live down the past, and she succeeded measurably well. Now and then a critic spoke of her as a second Maude Adams, and those notices she kept and treasured.

But she was always uneasy. Never since the night he had seen Judson Clark in the theater had they rung up without her brother having carefully combed the house with his eyes. She knew her limitations; they would have to ring down if she ever saw him over the footlights. And the season had brought its incidents, to connect her with the past. One night Gregory had come back and told her Jean Melis was in the balcony.

The valet was older and heavier, but he had recognized him.

"Did he see you?" was her first question.

"Yes. What about it? He never saw me but once, and that was at night and out of doors."

"Sometimes I think I can't stand it, Fred. The eternal suspense, the waiting for something to happen."

"If anything was going to happen it would have happened months ago. Bassett has given it up. And Jud's dead. Even Wilkins knows that."

She turned on him angrily.

"You haven't a heart, have you? You're glad he's dead."

"Not at all. As long as he kept under cover he was all right. But if he is, I don't see why you should fool yourself into thinking you're sorry. It's the best solution to a number of things."

"What do you suppose brought Jean Melis here?"

"What? To see the best play in New York. Besides, why not allow the man a healthy curiosity? He was pretty closely connected with a hectic part of your life, my dear. Now buck up, and for the Lord's sake forget the Frenchman. He's got nothing."

"He saw me that night, on the stairs. He never took his eyes off me at the inquest."

272

She gave, however, an excellent performance that night, and nothing more was heard of the valet.

There were other alarms, all of them without foundation. She went on her way, rejected an offer or two of marriage, spent her mornings in bed and her afternoons driving or in the hands of her hair-dresser and manicure, cared for the flowers that came in long casket-like boxes, and began to feel a sense of security again. She did not intend to marry, or to become interested in any one man.

She had hardly given a thought to Leslie Ward. He had come and gone, one of that steady procession of men, mostly married, who battered their heads now and then like night beetles outside a window, against the hard glass of her ambition. Because her business was to charm, she had been charming to him. And could not always remember his name!

As the months went by she began to accept Fred's verdict that nothing was going to happen. Bassett was back and at work. Either dead or a fugitive somewhere was Judson Clark, but that thought she had to keep out of her mind. Sometimes, as the play went on, and she was able to make her solid investments out of it, she wondered if her ten years of retirement had been all the price she was to pay for his ruin; but she put that thought away too, although she never minimized her responsibility when she faced it.

But her price had been heavy at that. She was childless and alone, lavishing her aborted maternity on a brother who was living his prosperous, cheerful and not too moral life at her expense. Fred was, she knew, slightly drunk with success; he attended to his minimum of labor with the least possible effort, had an expensive apartment on the Drive, and neglected her except, when he needed money. She began to see, as other women had seen before her, that her success had, by taking away the necessity for initiative, been extremely bad for him.

That was the situation when, one night late in October, the trap of Bassett's devising began to close in. It had been raining, but in spite of that they had sold standing room to the fire limit. Having got the treasurer's report on the night's business and sent it to Beverly's dressing-room, Gregory wandered into his small, low-ceiled office under the balcony staircase, and closing the door sat down. It was the interval after the second act, and above the hum of voices outside the sound of the orchestra penetrated faintly.

He was entirely serene. He had a supper engagement after the show, he had a neat car waiting outside to take him to it, and the night's business had been extraordinary. He consulted his watch and then picked up an evening paper. A few moments later he found himself reading over and over a small notice inserted among the personals.

"Personal: Jean Melis, who was in Norada, Wyoming, during the early fall of 1911 please communicate with L 22, this office."

The orchestra was still playing outside; the silly, giggling crowds were moving back to their seats, and somewhere Jean Melis, or the friends of Jean Melis, who would tell him of it, were reading that message.

He got his hat and went out, forgetful of the neat car at the curb, of the supper engagement, of the night's business, and wandered down the street through the rain. But his first uneasiness passed quickly. He saw Bassett in the affair, and probably Clark himself, still living and tardily determined to clear his name. But if the worst came to the worst, what could they do? They could go only so far, and then they would have to quit.

It would be better, however, if they did not see Melis. Much better; there was no use involving a simple situation. And Bev could be kept out of it altogether, until it was over. Ashamed of his panic he went back to the theater, got a railway schedule and looked up trains. He should have done it long before, he recognized, have gone to Bassett in the spring. But how could he have known then that Bassett was going to make a life-work of the case?

He had only one uncertainty. Suppose that Bassett had learned about Clifton Hines?

By the time the curtain rang down on the last act he was his dapper, debonair self again, made his supper engagement, danced half the night, and even dozed a little on the way home.

But he slept badly and was up early, struggling with the necessity for keeping Jean Melis out of the way.

He wondered through what formalities L 22, for instance, would have to go in order to secure a letter addressed to him? Whether he had to present a card or whether he walked in demanded his mail and went away. That thought brought another with it. Wasn't it probable that Bassett was in New York, and would call for his mail himself?

He determined finally to take the chance, claim to be L 22, and if Melis had seen the advertisement and replied, get the letter. It would be easy to square it with the valet, by saying that he had recognized him in the theater and that Miss Carlysle wished to send him a box.

He had small hope of a letter at his first call, unless the Frenchman had himself seen the notice, but his anxiety drove him early to the office. There was nothing there, but he learned one thing. He had to go through with no formalities. The clerk merely looked in a box, said "Nothing here," and went on about his business. At eleven o'clock he went back again, and after a careful scrutiny of the crowd presented himself once more.

"L 22? Here you are."

He had the letter in his hand. He had glanced at it and had thrust it deep in his pocket, when he felt a hand on his shoulder. He wheeled and faced Bassett.

"I thought I recognized that back," said the reporter, cheerfully. "Come over here, old man. I want to talk to you."

But he held to Gregory's shoulder. In a corner Bassett dropped the friendliness he had assumed for the clerk's benefit, and faced him with cold anger.

"I'll have that letter now, Gregory," he said. "And I've got a damned good notion to lodge an information against you."

"I don't know what you're talking about."

"Forget it. I was behind you when you asked for that letter. Give it here. I want to show you something."

Suddenly, with the letter in his hand, Bassett laughed and then tore it open. There was only a sheet of blank paper inside.

"I wasn't sure you'd see it, and I didn't think you'd fall for it if you did," he observed. "But I was pretty sure you didn't want me to see Melis. Now I know it."

"Well, I didn't," Gregory said sullenly.

"Just the same, I expect to see him. The day's early yet, and that's not a common name. But I'll take darned good care you don't get any more letters from here."

"What do you think Melis can tell you, that you don't know?"

"I'll explain that to you some day," Bassett said cheerfully. "Some day when you are in a more receptive mood than you are now. The point at this moment seems to me to be, what does Melis know that you don't want me to know? I suppose you don't intend to tell me."

"Not here. You may believe it or not, Bassett, but I was going to your town to-night to see you."

"Well," Bassett said sceptically, "I've got your word for it. And I've got nothing to do all day but to listen to you."

To his proposition that they go to his hotel Gregory assented sullenly, and they moved out to find a taxicab. On the pavement, however, he held back.

"I've got a right to know something," he said, "considering what he's done to me and mine. Clark's alive, I suppose?"

"He's alive all right."

"Then I'll trade you, Bassett. I'll come over with what I know, if you'll tell me one thing. What sent him into hiding for ten years, and makes him turn up now, yelling for help?"

Bassett reflected. The offer of a statement from Gregory was valuable, but, on the other hand, he was anxious not to influence his narrative. And Gregory saw his uncertainty. He planted himself firmly on the pavement.

"How about it?" he demanded.

"I'll tell you this much, Gregory. He never meant to bring the thing up again. In a way, it's me you're up against. Not Clark. And you can be pretty sure I know what I'm doing. I've got Clark, and I've got the report of the coroner's inquest, and I'll get Melis. I'm going to get to the bottom of this if I have to dig a hole that buries me."

In a taxicab Gregory sat tense and erect, gnawing at his blond mustache. After a time he said:

"What are you after, in all this? The story, I suppose. And the money. I daresay you're not doing it for love."

Bassett surveyed him appraisingly.

"You wouldn't understand my motives if I told you. As a matter of fact, he doesn't want the money."

Gregory sneered.

"Don't kid yourself," he said. "However, as a matter of fact I don't think he'll take it. It might cost too much. Where is he? Shooting pills again?"

"You'll see him in about five minutes."

If the news was a surprise Gregory gave no evidence of it, except to comment:

"You're a capable person, aren't you? I'll bet you could tune a piano if you were put to it."

He carried the situation well, the reporter had to admit; the only evidence he gave of strain was that the hands with which he lighted a cigarette were unsteady. He surveyed the obscure hotel at which the cab stopped with a sneering smile, and settled his collar as he looked it over.

"Not advertising to the world that you're in town, I see."

"We'll do that, just as soon as we're ready. Don't worry."

The laugh he gave at that struck unpleasantly on Bassett's ears. But inside the building he lost some of his jauntiness. "Queer place to find Judson Clark," he said once.

And again:

"You'd better watch him when I go in. He may bite me."

To which Bassett grimly returned: "He's probably rather particular what he bites."

He was uneasily conscious that Gregory, while nervous and tense, was carrying the situation with a certain assurance. If he was acting it was very good acting. And that opinion was strengthened when he threw open the door and Gregory advanced into the room.

"Well, Clark," he said, coolly. "I guess you didn't expect to see me, did you?"

He made no offer to shake hands as Dick turned from the window, nor did Dick make any overtures. But there was no enmity at first in either face; Gregory was easy and assured, Dick grave, and, Bassett thought, slightly impatient. From that night in his apartment the reporter had realized that he was constantly fighting a sort of passive resistance in Dick, a determination not at any cost to involve Beverly. Behind that, too, he felt that still another battle was going on, one at which he could only guess, but which made Dick somber at times and grimly quiet always.

"I meant to look you up," was his reply to Gregory's nonchalant greeting.

"Well, your friend here did that for you," Gregory said, and smiled across at Bassett. "He has his own methods, and I'll say they're effectual."

He took off his overcoat and flung it on the bed, and threw a swift, appraising glance at Dick. It was on Dick that he was banking, not on Bassett. He hated and feared Bassett. He hated Dick, but he was not afraid of him. He lighted a cigarette and faced Dick with a malicious smile.

"So here we are, again, Jud!" he said. "But with this change, that now it's you who are the respectable member of the community, and I'm the—well, we'll call it the butterfly."

There was unmistakable insult in his tone, and Dick caught it.

"Then I take it you're still living off your sister?"

The contempt in Dick's voice whipped the color to Gregory's face and clenched his fist. But he relaxed in a moment and laughed.

"Don't worry, Bassett," he said, his eyes on Dick. "We haven't any reason to like each other, but he's bigger than I am. I won't hit him." Then he hardened his voice. "But I'll remind you, Clark, that personally I don't give a God-damn whether you swing or not. Also that I can keep my mouth shut, walk out of here, and have you in quod in the next hour, if I decide to."

"But you won't," Bassett said smoothly. "You won't, any more than you did it last spring, when you sent that little letter of yours to David Livingstone."

"No. You're right. I won't. But if I tell you what I came here to say, Bassett, get this straight. It's not because I'm afraid of you, or of him. Donaldson's dead. What value would Melis's testimony have after ten years, if you put him on the stand? It's not that. It's because you'll put your blundering foot into it and ruin Bev's career, unless I tell you the truth."

It was to Bassett then that he told his story, he and Bassett sitting, Dick standing with his elbow on the mantelpiece, tall and weary and almost detached.

"I've got to make my own position plain in this," he said. "I didn't like Clark, and I kept her from marrying him. There was one time, before she met Lucas, when she almost did it. I was away when she decided on that fool trip to the Clark ranch. We couldn't get a New York theater until November, and she had some time, so they went. I've got her story of what happened there. You can check it up with what you know."

He turned to Dick for a moment.

"You were drinking pretty hard that night, but you may remember this: She had quarreled with Lucas at dinner that night and with you. That's true, isn't it?"

"Yes."

"She went to her room and began to pack her things. Then she thought it over, and she decided to try to persuade Lucas to go too. Things had begun all right, but they were getting strained and unpleasant. She went down the stairs, and Melis saw her, the valet. The living-room was dark, but there was a light coming through the billiard room door, and against it she saw the figure of a man in the doorway. He had his back to her, and he had a revolver in his hand. She ran across the room when he heard her and when he turned she saw it was Lucas. Do you remember, Jud, having a revolver and Lucas taking it from you?"

"No. Donaldson testified I'd had a revolver."

"Well, that's how we figure he'd got the gun. She thought at once that Lucas and you had quarreled, and that he was going to shoot. She tried to take it from him, but he was drunk and stubborn. It went off and killed him."

Bassett leaned forward.

"That's straight, is it?"

"I'm telling you."

"Then why in God's name didn't she say that at the inquest?"

"She was afraid it wouldn't be believed. Look at the facts. She'd quarreled with Lucas. There had been a notorious situation with regard to Clark. And remember this. She had done it. I know her well enough, however, to say that she would have confessed, eventually, but Clark had beaten it. It was reasonably sure that he was lost in the blizzard. You've got to allow for that."

Bassett said nothing. After a silence Dick spoke:

"What about the revolver?"

"She had it in her hand. She dropped it and stood still, too stunned to scream. Lucas, she says, took a step or two forward, and fell through the doorway. Donaldson came running in, and you know the rest."

Bassett was the first to break the silence.

"She will be willing to testify to that now, of course?"

"And stand trial?"

"Not necessarily. Clark would be on trial. He's been indicted. He has to be tried."

"Why does he have to be tried? He's free now. He's been free for ten years. And I tell you as an honest opinion that the thing would kill her. Accident and all, she did it. And there would be some who'd never believe she hadn't tired of Lucas, and wanted the Clark money."

"That's a chance she'll have to take," Bassett said doggedly. "The only living witness who could be called would be the valet. And remember this: for ten years he has believed that she did it. He'll have built up a story by this time, perhaps unconsciously, that might damn her."

Dick moved.

"There's only one thing to do. You're right, Gregory. I'll never expose her to that."

"You're crazy," Bassett said angrily.

"Not at all. I told you I wouldn't hide behind a woman. As a matter of fact, I've learned what I wanted. Lucas wasn't murdered. I didn't shoot him. That's what really matters. I'm no worse off than I was before; considerably better, in fact. And I don't see what's to be gained by going any further."

In spite of his protests, Bassett was compelled finally to agree. He was sulky and dispirited. He saw the profound anticlimax to all his effort of Dick wandering out again, legally dead and legally guilty, and he swore roundly under his breath.

"All right," he grunted at last. "I guess that's the last word, Gregory. But you tell her from me that if she doesn't reopen the matter of her own accord, she'll have a man's life on her conscience."

"I'll not tell her anything about it. I'm not only her brother; I'm her manager now. And I'm not kicking any hole in the boat that floats me."

He was self-confident and slightly insolent; the hands with which he lighted a fresh cigarette no longer trembled, and the glance he threw at Dick was triumphant and hostile.

"As a man sows, Clark!" he said. "You sowed hell for a number of people once."

Bassett had to restrain an impulse to kick him out of the door. When he had gone Bassett turned to Dick with assumed lightness.

"Well," he said, "here we are, all dressed up and nowhere to go!"

He wandered around the room, restless and disappointed. He knew, and Dick knew, that they had come to the end of the road, and that nothing lay beyond. In his own unpleasant way Fred Gregory had made a case for his sister that tied their hands, and the crux of the matter had lain in his final gibe: "As a man sows, Clark, so shall he reap." The moral issue was there.

"I suppose the Hines story goes by the board, eh?" he commented after a pause.

"Yes. Except that I wish I'd known about him when I could have done something. He's my half-brother, any way you look at it, and he had a rotten deal. Sometimes a man sows," he added, with a wry smile, "and the other fellow reaps."

Bassett went out after that, going to the office on the chance of a letter from Melis, but there was none. When he came back he found Dick standing over a partially packed suitcase, and knew that they had come to the end of the road indeed.

"What's the next step?" he asked bluntly.

"I'll have to leave here. It's too expensive."

"And after that, what?"

"I'll get a job. I suppose a man is as well hidden here as anywhere. I can grow a beard-that's the usual thing, isn't it?"

Bassett made an impatient gesture, and fell to pacing the floor. "It's incredible," he said. "It's monstrous. It's a joke. Here you are, without a thing against you, and hung like Mahomet's coffin between heaven and earth. It makes me sick."

He went home that night, leaving word to have any letters for L 22 forwarded, but without much hope. His last clutch of Dick's hand had a sort of desperate finality in it, and he carried with him most of the way home the tall, worn and rather shabby figure that saw him off with a smile.

By the next afternoon's mail he received a note from New York, with a few words of comment penciled on it in Dick's writing. "This came this evening. I sent back the money. D." The note was from Gregory and had evidently enclosed a one-hundred dollar bill. It began without superscription: "Enclosed find a hundred dollars, as I imagine funds may be short. If I were you I'd get out of here. There has been considerable excitement, and you know too many people in this burg."

Bassett sat back in his chair and studied the note.

"Now why the devil did he do that?" he reflected. He sat for some time, thinking deeply, and he came to one important conclusion. The story Gregory had told was the one which was absolutely calculated to shut off all further inquiry. They had had ten years; ten years to plan, eliminate and construct; ten years to prepare their defense, in case Clark turned up. Wasn't that why Gregory had been so assured? But he had not been content to let well enough alone; he had perhaps overreached himself.

Then what was the answer? She had killed Lucas, but was it an accident? And there must have been a witness, or they would have had nothing to fear. He wrote out on a bit of paper three names, and sat looking at them:

Hattie Thorwald Jean Melis Clifton Hines.

XLII

Elizabeth had quite definitely put Dick out of her heart. On the evening of the day she learned he had come back and had not seen her, she deliberately killed her love and decently interred it. She burned her notes and his one letter and put away her ring, performing the rites not as rites but as a shameful business to be done with quickly. She tore his photograph into bits and threw them into her waste basket, and having thus housecleaned her room set to work to houseclean her heart.

She found very little to do. She was numb and totally without feeling. The little painful constriction in her chest which had so often come lately with her thoughts of him was gone. She felt extraordinarily empty, but not light, and her feet dragged about the room.

She felt no sense of Dick's unworthiness, but simply that she was up against something she could not fight, and no longer wanted to fight. She was beaten, but the strange thing was that she did not care. Only, she would not be pitied. As the days went on she resented the pity that had kept her in ignorance for so long, and had let her wear her heart on her sleeve; and she even wondered sometimes whether the story of Dick's loss of memory had not been false, evolved out of that pity and the desire to save her pain.

David sent for her, but she wrote him a little note, formal and restrained. She would come in a day or two, but now she must get her bearings. He was, to know that she was not angry, and felt it all for the best, and she was very lovingly his, Elizabeth.

She knew now that she would eventually marry Wallie Sayre if only to get away from pity. He would have to know the truth about her, that she did not love any one; not even her father and her mother. She pretended to care for fear of hurting them, but she was actually frozen quite hard. She did not believe in love. It was a terrible thing, to be avoided by any one who wanted to get along, and this avoiding was really quite simple. One simply stopped feeling.

On the Sunday after she had come to this comfortable knowledge she sat in the church as usual, in the choir stalls, and suddenly she hated the church. She hated the way the larynx of Henry Wallace, the tenor, stuck out like a crabapple over his low collar. She hated the fat double chin of the bass. She hated the talk about love and the certain rewards of virtue, and the faces of the congregation, smug and sure of salvation.

She went to the choir master after the service to hand in her resignation. And did not, because it had occurred to her that it might look, to use Nina's word, as though she were crushed. Crushed! That was funny.

Wallie Sayre was waiting for her outside, and she went up with him to lunch, and afterwards they played golf. They had rather an amusing game, and once she had to sit down on a bunker and laugh until she was weak, while he fought his way out of a pit. Crushed, indeed!

So the weaving went on, almost completed now. With Wallie Sayre biding his time, but fairly sure of the result. With Jean Melis happening on a two-days' old paper, and reading over and over a notice addressed to him. With Leslie Ward, neither better nor worse than his kind, seeking adventure in a bypath, which was East 56th Street. And with Dick wandering the streets of New York after twilight, and standing once with his coat collar turned up against the rain outside of the Metropolitan Club, where the great painting of his father hung over a mantelpiece.

Now that he was near Beverly, Dick hesitated to see her. He felt no resentment at her long silence, nor at his exile which had resulted from it. He made excuses for her, recognized his own contribution to the catastrophe, knew, too, that nothing was to be gained by seeing her again. But he determined finally to see her once more, and then to go away, leaving her to peace and to success.

She would know now that she had nothing to fear from him. All he wanted was to satisfy the hunger that was in him by seeing her, and then to go away.

Curiously, that hunger to see her had been in abeyance while Bassett was with him. It was only when he was alone again that it came up; and although he knew that, he was unconscious of another fact, that every word, every picture of her on the great boardings which walled in every empty lot, everything, indeed, which brought her into the reality of the present, loosened by so much her hold on him out of the past.

When he finally went to the 56th Street house it was on impulse. He had meant to pass it, but he found himself stopping, and half angrily made his determination. He would follow the cursed thing through now and get it over. Perhaps he had discounted it too much in advance, waited too long, hoped too much. Perhaps it was simply that that last phase was already passing. But he felt no thrill, no expectancy, as he rang the bell and was admitted to the familiar hall.

It was peopled with ghosts, for him. Upstairs, in the drawing-room that extended across the front of the house, she had told him of her engagement to Howard Lucas. Later on, coming back from Europe, he had gone back there to find Lucas installed in the house, his cigars on the table, his photographs on the piano, his books scattered about. And Lucas himself, smiling, handsome and triumphant on the hearth rug, dressed for dinner except for a brocaded dressing-gown, putting his hand familiarly on Beverly's shoulder, and calling her "old girl."

He wandered into the small room to the right of the hall, where in other days he had waited to be taken upstairs, and stood looking out of the window. He heard some one, a caller, come down, get into his overcoat in the hall and go out, but he was not interested. He did not know that Leslie Ward had stood outside the door for a minute, had seen and recognized him, and had then slammed out.

He was quite steady as the butler preceded him up the stairs. He even noticed certain changes in the house, the door at the landing converted into an arch, leaded glass in the dining-room windows beyond it. But he caught a glimpse of himself in a mirror, and saw himself a shabby contrast to the former days.

He faced her, still with that unexpected composure, and he saw her very little changed. Even the movement with which she came toward him with both hands out was familiar.

"Jud!" she said. "Oh, my dear!"

He saw that she was profoundly moved, and suddenly he was sorry for her. Sorry for the years behind them both, for the burden she had carried, for the tears in her eyes.

"Dear old Bev!" he said.

279

She put her head against his shoulder, and cried unrestrainedly; and he held her there, saying small, gentle, soothing things, smoothing her hair. But all the time he knew that life had been playing him another trick; he felt a great tenderness for her and profound pity, but he did not love her, or want her. He saw that after all the suffering and waiting, the death and exile, he was left at the end with nothing. Nothing at all.

When she was restored to a sort of tense composure he found to his discomfort that woman-like she intended to abase herself thoroughly and completely. She implored his forgiveness for his long exile, gazing at him humbly, and when he said in a matter-of-fact tone that he had been happy, giving him a look which showed that she thought he was lying to save her unhappiness.

"You are trying to make it easier for me. But I know, Jud."

"I'm telling you the truth," he said, patiently. "There's one point I didn't think necessary to tell your brother. For a good while I didn't remember anything about it. If it hadn't been for that-well, I don't know. Anyhow, don't look at me as though I willfully saved you. I didn't."

She sat still, pondering that, and twisting a ring on her finger.

"What do you mean to do?" she asked, after a pause.

"I don't know. I'll find something."

"You won't go back to your work?"

"I don't see how I can. I'm in hiding, in a sort of casual fashion."

To his intense discomfiture she began to cry again. She couldn't go through with it. She would go back to Norada and tell the whole thing. She had let Fred influence her, but she saw now she couldn't do it. But for the first time he felt that in this one thing she was not sincere. Her grief and abasement had been real enough, but now he felt she was acting.

"Suppose we don't go into that now," he said gently. "You've had about all you can stand." He got up awkwardly. "I suppose you are playing to-night?"

She nodded, looking up at him dumbly.

"Better lie down, then, and—forget me." He smiled down at her.

"I've never forgotten you, Jud. And now, seeing you again—I—"

Her face worked. She continued to look up at him, piteously. The appalling truth came to him then, and that part of him which had remained detached and aloof, watching, almost smiled at the irony. She cared for him. Out of her memories she had built up something to care for, something no more himself than she was the woman of his dreams; but with this difference, that she was clinging, woman-fashion, to the thing she had built, and he had watched it crumble before his eyes.

"Will you promise to go and rest?"

"Yes. If you say so."

She was acquiescent and humble. Her eyes were soft, faithful, childlike.

"I've suffered so, Jud."

"I know."

"You don't hate me, do you?"

"Why should I? Just remember this: while you were carrying this burden, I was happier than I'd ever been. I'll tell you about it some time."

She got up, and he perceived that she expected him again to take her in his arms. He felt ridiculous and resentful, and rather as though he was expected to kiss the hand that had beaten him, but when she came close to him he put an arm around her shoulders.

"Poor Bev!" he said. "We've made pretty much a mess of it, haven't we?"

He patted her and let her go, and her eyes followed him as he left the room. The elder brotherliness of that embrace had told her the truth as he could never have hurt her in words. She went back to the chair where he had sat, and leaned her cheek against it.

After a time she went slowly upstairs and into her room. When her maid came in she found her before the mirror of her dressing-table, staring at her reflection with hard, appraising eyes.

Leslie's partner, wandering into the hotel at six o'clock, found from the disordered condition of the room that Leslie had been back, had apparently bathed, shaved and made a careful toilet, and gone out again. Joe found himself unexpectedly at a loose end. Filled, with suppressed indignation he commenced to dress, getting out a shirt, hunting his evening studs, and lining up what he meant to say to Leslie over his defection.

Then, at a quarter to seven, Leslie came in, top-hatted and morning-coated, with a yellowing gardenia in his buttonhole and his shoes covered with dust.

"Hello, Les," Joe said, glancing up from a laborious struggle with a stud. "Been to a wedding?"

"Why?"

"You look like it."

"I made a call, and since then I've been walking."

"Some walk, I'd say," Joe observed, looking at him shrewdly. "What's wrong, Les? Fair one turn you down?"

"Go to hell," Leslie said irritably.

He flung off his coat and jerked at his tie. Then, with it hanging loose, he turned to Joe.

"I'm going to tell you something. I know it's safe with you, and I need some advice. I called on a woman this afternoon. You know who she is. Beverly Carlysle."

Joe whistled softly.

"That's not the point," Leslie declaimed, in a truculent voice. "I'm not defending myself. She's a friend; I've got a right to call there if I want to."

"Sure you have," soothed Joe.

"Well, you know the situation at home, and who Livingstone actually is. The point is that, while that poor kid at home is sitting around killing herself with grief, Clark's gone back to her. To Beverly Carlysle."

"How do you know?"

"Know? I saw him this afternoon, at her house."

He sat still, moodily reviewing the situation. His thoughts were a chaotic and unpleasant mixture of jealousy, fear of Nina, anxiety over Elizabeth, and the sense of a lost romantic adventure. After a while he got up.

"She's a nice kid," he said. "I'm fond of her. And I don't know what to do."

Suddenly Joe grinned.

"I see," he said. "And you can't tell her, or the family, where you saw him!"

"Not without raising the deuce of a row."

He began, automatically, to dress for dinner. Joe moved around the room, rang for a waiter, ordered orange juice and ice, and produced a bottle of gin from his bag. Leslie did not hear him, nor the later preparation of the cocktails. He was reflecting bitterly on the fact that a man who married built himself a wall against romance, a wall, compounded of his own new sense of responsibility, of family ties, and fear.

Joe brought him a cocktail.

"Drink it, old dear," he said. "And when it's down I'll tell you a few little things about playing around with ladies who have a past. Here's to forgetting 'em."

Leslie took the glass.

"Right-o," he said.

He went home the following day, leaving Joe to finish the business in New York. His going rather resembled a flight. Tossing sleepless the night before, he had found what many a man had discovered before him, that his love of clandestine adventure was not as strong as his caution. He had had a shock. True, his affair with Beverly had been a formless thing, a matter of imagination and a desire to assure himself that romance, for him, was not yet dead. True, too, that he had nothing to fear from Dick Livingstone. But the encounter had brought home to him the danger of this old-new game he was playing. He was running like a frightened child.

He thought of various plans. One of them was to tell Nina the truth, take his medicine of tears and coldness, and then go to Mr. Wheeler. One was to go to Mr. Wheeler, without Nina, and make his humiliating admission. But Walter Wheeler had his own rigid ideas, was uncompromising in rectitude, and would understand as only a man could that while so far he had been only mentally unfaithful, he had been actuated by at least subconscious desire.

His own awareness of that fact made him more cautious than he need have been, perhaps more self-conscious. And he genuinely cared for Elizabeth. It was, on the whole, a generous and kindly impulse that lay behind his ultimate resolution to tell her that her desertion was both wilful and cruel.

Yet, when the time came, he found it hard to tell her. He took her for a drive one evening soon after his return, forcibly driving off Wallie Sayre to do so, and eying surreptitiously now and then her pale, rather set face. He found a quiet lane and stopped the car there, and then turned and faced her.

"How've you been, little sister, while I've been wandering the gay white way?" he asked.

"I've been all right, Leslie."

"Not quite all right, I think. Have you ever thought, Elizabeth, that no man on earth is worth what you've been going through?"

"I'm all right, I tell you," she said impatiently. "I'm not grieving any more. That's the truth, Les. I know now that he doesn't intend to come back, and I don't care. I never even think about him, now."

"I see," he said. "Well, that's that."

But he had not counted on her intuition, and was startled to hear her say:

"Well? Go on."

"What do you mean, go on?"

"You brought me out here to tell me something."

"Not at all. I simply—"

"Where is he? You've seen him."

He tried to meet her eyes, failed, cursed himself for a fool. "He's alive and well, Elizabeth. I saw him in New York." It was a full minute before she spoke again, and then her lips were stiff and her voice strained.

"Has he gone back to her? To the actress he used to care for?"

He hesitated, but he knew he would have to go on.

"I'm going to tell you something, Elizabeth. It's not very creditable to me, but I'll have to trust you. I don't want to see you wasting your life. You've got plenty of courage and a lot of spirit. And you've got to forget him."

He told her, and then he took her home. He was a little frightened, for there was something not like her in the way she had taken it, a sort of immobility that might, he thought, cover heartbreak. But she smiled when she thanked him, and went very calmly into the house.

That night she accepted Wallie Sayre.

XLIII

Bassett was having a visitor. He sat in his chair while that visitor ranged excitedly up and down the room, a short stout man, well dressed and with a mixture of servility and importance. The valet's first words, as he stood inside the door, had been significant.

"I should like to know, first, if I am talking to the police."

"No—and yes," Bassett said genially. "Come and sit down, man. What I mean is this. I am a friend of Judson Clark's, and this may or may not be a police matter. I don't know yet."

"You are a friend of Mr. Clark's? Then the report was correct. He is still alive, sir?"

"Yes."

The valet got out a handkerchief and wiped his face. He was clearly moved.

"I am glad of that. Very glad. I saw some months ago, in a newspaper—where is he?"

"In New York. Now Melis, I've an idea that you know something about the crime Judson Clark was accused of. You intimated that at the inquest."

"Mrs. Lucas killed him."

"So she says," Bassett said easily.

The valet jumped and stared.

"She admits it, as the result of an accident. She also admits hiding the revolver where you found it."

"Then you do not need me."

"I'm not so sure of that."

The valet was puzzled.

"I want you to think back, Melis. You saw her go down the stairs, sometime before the shot. Later you were confident she had hidden the revolver, and you made a second search for it. Why? You hadn't heard her testimony at the inquest then. Clark had run away. Why didn't you think Clark had done it?"

"Because I thought she was having an affair with another man. I have always thought she did it."

Bassett nodded.

"I thought so. What made you think that?"

"I'll tell you. She went West without a maid, and Mr. Clark got a Swedish woman from a ranch near to look after her, a woman named Thorwald. She lived at her own place and came over every day. One night, after Mrs. Thorwald had started home, I came across her down the road near the irrigator's house, and there was a man with her. They didn't hear me behind them, and he was giving her a note for some one in the house."

"Why not for one of the servants?"

"That's what I thought then, sir. It wasn't my business. But I saw the same man later on, hanging about the place at night, and once I saw her with him—Mrs. Lucas, I mean. That was in the early evening. The gentlemen were out riding, and I'd gone with one of the maids to a hill to watch the moon rise. They were on some rocks, below in the canyon."

"Did you see him?"

"I think it was the same man, if that's what you mean. I knew something queer was going on, after that, and I watched her. She went out at night more than once. Then I told Donaldson there was somebody hanging round the place, and he set a watch."

"Fine. Now we'll go to the night Lucas was shot. Was the Thorwald woman there?"

"She had started home."

"Leaving Mrs. Lucas packing alone?"

"Yes. I hadn't thought of that. The Thorwald woman heard the shot and came back. I remember that, because she fainted upstairs and I had to carry her to a bed."

"I see. Now about the revolver."

"I located it the first time I looked for it. Donaldson and the others had searched the billiard room. So I tried the big room. It was under a chair. I left it there, and concealed myself in the room. She, Mrs. Lucas, came down late that night and hunted for it. Then she hid it where I got it later."

"I wish I knew, Melis, why you didn't bring those facts out at the inquest."

"You must remember this, sir. I had been with Mr. Clark for a long time. I knew the situation. And I thought that he had gone away that night to throw suspicion from her to himself. I was not certain what to do. I would have told it all in court, but it never came to trial."

Bassett was satisfied and fairly content. After the Frenchman's departure he sat for some time, making careful notes and studying them. Supposing the man Melis had seen to be Clifton

Hines, a good many things would be cleared up. Some new element he had to have, if Gregory's story were to be disproved, some new and different motive. Suppose, for instance...

He got up and paced the floor back and forward, forward and back. There was just one possibility, and just one way of verifying it. He sat down and wrote out a long telegram and then got his hat and carried it to the telegraph office himself. He had made his last throw.

He received a reply the following day, and in a state of exhilaration bordering on madness packed his bag, and as he packed it addressed it, after the fashion of lonely men the world over.

"Just one more trip, friend cowhide," he said, "and then you and I are going to settle down again to work. But it's some trip, old arm-breaker."

He put in his pajamas and handkerchiefs, his clean socks and collars, and then he got his revolver from a drawer and added it. Just twenty-four hours later he knocked at Dick's door in a boarding-house on West Ninth Street, found it unlocked, and went in. Dick was asleep, and Bassett stood looking down at him with an odd sort of paternal affection. Finally he bent down and touched his shoulder.

"Wake up, old top," he said. "Wake up. I have some news for you."

XLIV

To Dick the last day or two had been nightmares of loneliness. He threw caution to the winds and walked hour after hour, only to find that the street crowds, people who had left a home or were going to one, depressed him and emphasized his isolation. He had deliberately put away from him the anchor that had been Elizabeth and had followed a treacherous memory, and now he was adrift. He told himself that he did not want much. Only peace, work and a place. But he had not one of them.

He was homesick for David, for Lucy, and, with a tightening of the heart he admitted it, for Elizabeth. And he had no home. He thought of Reynolds, bent over the desk in his office; he saw the quiet tree-shaded streets of the town, and Reynolds, passing from house to house in the little town, doing his work, usurping his place in the confidence and friendship of the people; he saw the very children named for him asking: "Who was I named for, mother?" He saw David and Lucy gone, and the old house abandoned, or perhaps echoing to the laughter of Reynolds' children.

He had moments when he wondered what would happen if he took Beverly at her word. Suppose she made her confession, re-opened the thing, to fill the papers with great headlines, "Judson Clark Not Guilty. A Strange Story."

He saw himself going back to the curious glances of the town, never to be to them the same as before. To face them and look them down, to hear whispers behind his back, to feel himself watched and judged, on that far past of his. Suppose even that it could be kept out of the papers; Wilkins amiable and acquiescent, Beverly's confession hidden in the ruck of legal documents; and he stealing back, to go on as best he could, covering his absence with lies, and taking up his work again. But even that uneasy road was closed to him. He saw David and Lucy stooping to new and strange hypocrisies, watching with anxious old eyes the faces of their neighbors, growing defiant and hard as time went on and suspicion still followed him.

And there was Elizabeth.

He tried not to think of her, save as of some fine and tender thing he had once brushed as he passed by. Even if she still cared for him, he could, even less than David and Lucy, ask her to walk the uneasy road with him. She was young. She would forget him and marry Wallace Sayre. She would have luxury and gaiety, and the things that belong to youth.

He was not particularly bitter about that. He knew now that he had given her real love, something very different from that early madness of his, but he knew it too late...

He looked up at Bassett and then sat up.

"What sort of news?" he asked, his voice still thick with sleep.

"Get up and put some cold water on your head. I want you to get this."

He obeyed, but without enthusiasm. Some new clue, some hope revived only to die again, what did it matter? But he stopped by Bassett and put a hand on his shoulder.

"Why do you do it?" he asked. "Why don't you let me go to the devil in my own way?"

"I started this, and by Heaven I've finished it," was Bassett's exultant reply.

He sat down and produced a bundle of papers. "I'm going to read you something," he said. "And when I'm through you're going to put your clothes on and we'll go to the Biltmore. The Biltmore. Do you get it?"

Then he began to read.

"I, the undersigned, being of sound mind, do hereby make the following statement. I make the statement of my own free will, and swear before Almighty God that it is the truth. I am an illegitimate son of Elihu Clark. My mother, Harriet Burgess, has since married and is now known as Hattie Thorwald. She will confirm the statements herein contained.

"I was adopted by a woman named Hines, of the city of Omaha, whose name I took. Some years later this woman married and had a daughter, of whom I shall speak later.

"I attended preparatory school in the East, and was sent during vacations to a tutoring school, owned by Mr. Henry Livingstone. When I went to college Mr. Livingstone bought a ranch at Dry River, Wyoming, and I spent some time there now and then.

"I learned that I was being supported and sent to college from funds furnished by a firm of New York lawyers, and that aroused my suspicion. I knew that Mrs. Hines was not my mother. I finally learned that I was the son of Elihu Clark and Harriet Burgess.

"I felt that I should have some part of the estate, and I developed a hatred of Judson Clark, whom I knew. I made one attempt to get money from him by mail, threatening to expose his father's story, but I did not succeed.

"I visited my mother, Hattie Thorwald, and threatened to kill Clark. I also threatened Henry Livingstone, and his death came during a dispute over the matter, but I did not kill him. He fell down and hit his head. He had a weak heart.

"My foster-sister had gone on the stage, and Clark was infatuated with her. I saw him a number of times, but he did not connect me with the letter I had sent. My foster-sister's stage name is Beverly Carlysle.

"She married Howard Lucas and they visited the Clark ranch at Norada, Wyoming, in the fall of 1911. I saw my sister there several times, and as she knew the way I felt she was frightened. My mother, Hattie Thorwald, was a sort of maid to her, and together they tried to get me to go away."

Bassett looked up.

"Up to that point," he said, "I wrote it myself before I saw him." There was a note of triumph in his voice. "The rest is his."

"On the night Lucas was killed I was to go away. Bev had agreed to give me some money, for the piece had quit in June and I was hard up. She was going to borrow it from Jud Clark, and that set me crazy. I felt it ought to be mine, or a part of it anyhow.

"I was to meet my mother in the grounds, but I missed her, and I went to the house. I wasn't responsible for what I did. I was crazy, I guess. I saw Donaldson on the side porch, and beyond him were Lucas and Clark, playing roulette. It made me wild. I couldn't have played roulette that night for pennies.

"I went around the house and in the front door. What I meant to do was to walk into that room and tell Clark who I was. He knew me, and all I meant to do was to call Bev down, and mother, and make him sit up and take notice. I hadn't a gun on me.

"I swear I wasn't thinking of killing him then. I hated him like poison, but that was all. But I went into the living-room, and I heard Clark say he'd lost a thousand dollars. Maybe you don't get that. A thousand dollars thrown around like that, and me living on what Bev could borrow from him.

"That sent me wild. Lucas took a gun from him, just after that, and said he was going to put it in the other room. He did it, too. He put it on a table and started back. I got it and pointed it at Clark. I'd have shot him, too, but Bev came into the room.

"I want to exonerate Bev. She has been better than most sisters to me, and she has lied to try to save me. She came up behind me and grabbed my arm. Lucas had heard her, and he turned. I must have closed my hand on the trigger, for it went off and hit him.

"I was in the living-room when Donaldson ran in. I hid there until they were all gathered around Lucas and had quit running in, and then I got away. I saw my mother in the grounds later. I told her where the revolver was and that they'd better put it in the billiard room. I was afraid they'd suspect Bev.

"I have read the above statement and it is correct. I was legally adopted by Mrs. Alice Ford Hines, of Omaha, and use that signature. I generally use the name of Frederick Gregory, which I took when I was on the stage for a short time.

"(Signed) Clifton HINES."

Bassett folded up the papers and put them in the envelope. "I got that," he said, "at the point of a gun, my friend. And our friend Hines departed for the Mexican border on the evening train. I don't mind saying that I saw him off. He held out for a get-away, and I guess it's just as well."

He glanced at Dick, lying still and rigid on the bed.

"And now," he said. "I think a little drink won't do us any harm."

Dick refused to drink. He was endeavoring to comprehend the situation; to realize that Gregory, who had faced him with such sneering hate a day or so before, was his half-brother.

"Poor devil!" he said at last. "I wish to God I'd known. He was right, you know. No wonder—"

Sometime later he roused from deep study and looked at Bassett.

"How did you get the connection?"

"I saw Melis, and learned that Hines was in it somehow. He was the connecting link between Beverly Carlysle and the Thorwald woman. But I couldn't connect him with Beverly herself, except by a chance. I wired a man I knew in Omaha, and he turned up the second marriage, and a daughter known on the stage as Beverly Carlysle."

Bassett was in high spirits. He moved about the room immensely pleased with himself, slightly boastful.

"Some little stroke, Dick!" he said. "What price Mr. Judson Clark to-night, eh? It will be worth a million dollars to see Wilkins' face when he reads that thing."

"There's no mention of me as Livingstone in it, is there?"

"It wasn't necessary to go into that. I didn't know—Look here," he exploded, "you're not going to be a damned fool, are you?"

"I'm not going to revive Judson Clark, Bassett. I don't owe him anything. Let him die a decent death and stay dead."

"Oh, piffle!" Bassett groaned. "Don't start that all over again. Don't pull any Enoch Arden stuff on me, looking in at a lighted window and wandering off to drive a taxicab."

Suddenly Dick laughed. Bassett watched him, puzzled and angry, with a sort of savage tenderness.

"You're crazy," he said morosely. "Darned if I understand you. Here I've got everything fixed as slick as a whistle, and it took work, believe me. And now you say you're going to chuck the whole thing."

"Not at all," Dick replied, with a new ring in his voice. "You're right. I've been ten sorts of a fool, but I know now what I'm going to do. Take your paper, old friend, and for my sake go out and clear Jud Clark. Put up a headstone to him, if you like, a good one. I'll buy it."

"And what will you be doing in the meantime?"

Dick stretched and threw out his arms.

"Me?" he said. "What should I be doing, old man? I'm going home."

XLV

Lucy Crosby was dead. One moment she was of the quick, moving about the house, glancing in at David, having Minnie in the kitchen pin and unpin her veil; and the next she was still and infinitely mysterious, on her white bed. She had fallen outside the door of David's room, and lay there, her arms still full of fresh bath towels, and a fixed and intense look in her eyes, as though, outside the door, she had come face to face with a messenger who bore surprising news. Doctor Reynolds, running up the stairs, found her there dead, and closed the door into David's room.

But David knew before they told him. He waited until they had placed her on her bed, had closed her eyes and drawn a white coverlet over her, and then he went in alone, and sat down beside her, and put a hand over her chilling one.

"If you are still here, Lucy," he said, "and have not yet gone on, I want you to carry this with you. We are all right, here. Everybody is all right. You are not to worry."

After a time he went back to his room and got his prayer-book. He could hear Harrison Miller's voice soothing Minnie in the lower hall, and Reynolds at the telephone. He went back into the quiet chamber, and opening the prayer-book, began to read aloud.

"Now is Christ risen from the dead, and become the first fruits of them that slept—"

His voice tightened. He put his head down on the side of the bed.

He was very docile that day. He moved obediently from his room for the awful aftermath of a death, for the sweeping and dusting and clean curtains, and sat in Dick's room, not reading, not even praying, a lonely yet indomitable old figure. When his friends came, elderly men who creaked in and tried to reduce their robust voices to a decorous whisper, he shook hands with them and made brief, courteous replies. Then he lapsed into silence. They felt shut off and uncomfortable, and creaked out again.

Only once did he seem shaken. That was when Elizabeth came swiftly in and put her arms around him as he sat. He held her close to him, saying nothing for a long time. Then he drew a deep breath.

"I was feeling mighty lonely, my dear," he said.

He was the better for her visit. He insisted on dressing that evening, and on being helped down the stairs. The town, which had seemed inimical for so long, appeared to him suddenly to be holding out friendly hands. More than friendly hands. Loving, tender hands, offering service and affection and old-time friendship. It moved about sedately, in dark clothes, and came down the stairs red-eyed and using pocket-hand-kerchiefs, and it surrounded him with love and loving kindness.

When they had all gone Harrison Miller helped him up the stairs to where his tidy bed stood ready, and the nurse had placed his hot milk on a stand. But Harrison did not go at once.

"What about word to Dick, David?" he inquired awkwardly, "I've called up Bassett, but he's away. And I don't know that Dick ought to come back anyhow. If the police are on the job at all they'll be on the lookout now. They'll know he may try to come."

David looked away. Just how much he wanted Dick, to tide him over these bad hours, only David knew. But he could not have him. He stared at the glass of hot milk.

"I guess I can fight this out alone, Harrison," he said. "And Lucy will understand."

He did not sleep much that night. Once or twice he got up and tip-toed across the hall into Lucy's room and looked at her. She was as white as her pillow, and quite serene. Her hands, always a little rough and twisted with service, were smooth and rested.

"You know why he can't come, Lucy," he said once. "It doesn't mean that he doesn't care. You have to remember that." His sublime faith that she heard and understood, not the Lucy on the bed but the Lucy who had not yet gone on to the blessed company of heaven, carried him back to his bed, comforted and reassured.

He was up and about his room early. The odor of baking muffins and frying ham came up the stair-well, and the sound of Mike vigorously polishing the floor in the hall. Mixed with the odor of cooking and of floor wax was the scent of flowers from Lucy's room, and Mrs. Sayre's machine stopped at the door while the chauffeur delivered a great mass of roses.

David went carefully down the stairs and into his office, and there, at his long deserted desk, commenced a letter to Dick.

He was sitting there when Dick came up the street...

The thought that he was going home had upheld Dick through the days that followed Bassett's departure for the West. He knew that it would be a fight, that not easily does a man step out of life and into it again, but after his days of inaction he stood ready to fight. For David, for Lucy, and, if it was not too late, for Elizabeth. When Bassett's wire came from Norada, "All clear," he set out for Haverly, more nearly happy than for months. The very rhythm of the train sang: "Going home; going home."

At the Haverly station the agent stopped, stared at him and then nodded gravely. There was something restrained in his greeting, like the voices in the old house the night before, and Dick felt a chill of apprehension. He never thought of Lucy, but David... The flowers and ribbon at the door were his first intimation, and still it was David he thought of. He went cold and bitter, standing on the freshly washed pavement, staring at them. It was all too late. David! David!

He went into the house slowly, and the heavy scent of flowers greeted him. The hall was empty, and automatically he pushed open the door to David's office and went in. David was at the desk writing. David was alive. Thank God and thank God, David was alive.

"David!" he said brokenly. "Dear old David!" And was suddenly shaken with dry, terrible sobbing.

There was a great deal to do, and Dick was grateful for it. But first, like David, he went in and sat by Lucy's bed alone and talked to her. Not aloud, as David did, but still with that same queer conviction that she heard. He told her he was free, and that she need not worry about David, that he was there now to look after him; and he asked her, if she could, to help him with Elizabeth. Then he kissed her and went out.

He met Elizabeth that day. She had come to the house, and after her custom now went up, unwarned, to David's room. She found David there and Harrison Miller, and—it was a moment before she realized it—Dick by the mantel. He was greatly changed. She saw that. But she had no feeling of pity, nor even of undue surprise. She felt nothing at all. It gave her a curious, almost hard little sense of triumph to see that he had gone pale. She marched up to him and held out her hand, mindful of the eyes on her.

"I'm so very sorry, Dick," she said. "You have a sad home-coming."

Then she withdrew her hand, still calm, and turned to David.

"Mother sent over some things. I'll give them to Minnie," she said, her voice clear and steady. She went out, and they heard her descending the stairs.

She was puzzled to find out that her knees almost gave way on the staircase, for she felt calm and without any emotion whatever. And she finished her errand, so collected and poised that the two or three women who had come in to help stared after her as she departed.

"Do you suppose she's seen him?"

"She was in David's room. She must have."

Mindful of Mike, they withdrew into Lucy's sitting-room and closed the door, there to surmise and to wonder. Did he know she was engaged to Wallie Sayre? Would she break her engagement now or not? Did Dick for a moment think that he could do as he had done, go away and jilt a girl, and come back to be received as though nothing had happened? Because, if he did...

To Dick Elizabeth's greeting had been a distinct shock. He had not known just what he had expected; certainly he had not hoped to pick things up where he had dropped them. But there was a hard friendliness in it that was like a slap in the face. He had meant at least to fight to win back with her, but he saw now that there would not even be a fight. She was not angry or hurt. The barrier was more hopeless than that.

David, watching him, waited until Harrison had gone, and went directly to the subject.

"Have you ever stopped to think what these last months have meant to Elizabeth? Her own worries, and always this infernal town, talking, talking. The child's pride's been hurt, as well as her heart."

"I thought I'd better not go into that until after—until later," he explained. "The other thing was wrong. I knew it the moment I saw Beverly and I didn't go back again. What was the use? But—you saw her face, David. I think she doesn't even care enough to hate me."

"She's cared enough to engage herself to Wallace Sayre!"

After one astounded glance Dick laughed bitterly.

"That looks as though she cared!" he said. He had gone very white. After a time, as David sat silent and thoughtful, he said: "After all, what right had I to expect anything else? When you think that, a few days ago, I was actually shaken at the thought of seeing another woman, you can hardly blame her."

"She waited a long time."

Later Dick made what was a difficult confession under the circumstances.

"I know now—I think I knew all along, but the other thing was like that craving for liquor I told you about—I know now that she has always been the one woman. You'll understand that, perhaps, but she wouldn't. I would crawl on my knees to make her believe it, but it's too late. Everything's too late," he added.

Before the hour for the services he went in again and sat by Lucy's bed, but she who had given him wise counsel so many times before lay in her majestic peace, surrounded by flowers and infinitely removed. Yet she gave him something. Something of her own peace. Once more, as on the night she had stood at the kitchen door and watched him disappear in the darkness, there came the tug of the old familiar things, the home sense. Not only David now, but the house. The faded carpet on the stairs, the old self-rocker Lucy had loved, the creaking faucets in the bathroom, Mike and Minnie, the laboratory,—united in their shabby strength, they were home to him. They had come back, never to be lost again. Home.

Then, little by little, they carried their claim further. They were not only home. They were the setting of a dream, long forgotten but now vivid in his mind, and a refuge from the dreary present. That dream had seen Elizabeth enshrined among the old familiar things; the old house was to be a sanctuary for her and for him. From it and from her in the dream he was to go out in the morning; to it and to her he was to come home at night, after he had done a man's work.

The dream faded. Before him rose her face of the morning, impassive and cool; her eyes, not hostile but indifferent. She had taken herself out of his life, had turned her youth to youth, and forgotten him. He understood and accepted it. He saw himself as he must have looked to her, old and worn, scarred from the last months, infinitely changed. And she was young. Heavens, how young she was!...

Lucy was buried the next afternoon. It was raining, and the quiet procession followed Dick and the others who carried her light body under grotesquely bobbing umbrellas. Then he and David, and Minnie and Mike, went back to the house, quiet with that strange emptiness that follows a death, the unconscious listening for a voice that will not speak again, for a familiar footfall. David had not gone upstairs. He sat in Lucy's sitting-room, in his old frock coat and black tie, with a knitted afghan across his knees. His throat looked withered in his loose collar. And there for the first time they discussed the future.

"You're giving up a great deal, Dick," David said. "I'm proud of you, and like you I think the money's best where it is. But this is a prejudiced town, and they think you've treated Elizabeth badly. If you don't intend to tell the story—"

"Never," Dick announced, firmly. "Judson Clark is dead." He smiled at David with something of his old humor. "I told Bassett to put up a monument if he wanted to. But you're right about one thing. They're not ready to take me back. I've seen it a dozen times in the last two days."

"I never gave up a fight yet." David's voice was grim.

"On the other hand, I don't want to make it uncomfortable for her. We are bound to meet. I'm putting my own feeling aside. It doesn't matter—except of course to me. What I thought was— We might go into the city. Reynolds would buy the house. He's going to be married."

But he found himself up against the stone wall of David's opposition. He was too old to be uprooted. He liked to be able to find his way around in the dark. He was almost childish about it, and perhaps a trifle terrified. But it was his final argument that won Dick over.

"I thought you'd found out there's nothing in running away from trouble."

Dick straightened.

"You're right," he said. "We'll stay here and fight it out together."

He helped David up the stairs to where the nurse stood waiting, and then went on into his own bedroom. He surveyed it for the first time since his return with a sense of permanency and intimacy. Here, from now on, was to center his life. From this bed he would rise in the morning, to go back to it at night. From this room he would go out to fight for place again, and for the old faith in him, for confiding eyes and the clasp of friendly hands.

He sat down by the window and with the feeling of dismissing them forever retraced slowly and painfully the last few months; the night on the mountains, and Bassett asleep by the fire; the man from the cabin caught under the tree, with his face looking up, strangely twisted, from among the branches; dawn in the alfalfa field, and the long night tramp; the boy who had recognized him in Chicago; David in his old walnut bed, shrivelled and dauntless; and his own going out into the night, with Lucy in the kitchen doorway, Elizabeth and Wallace Sayre on the verandah, and himself across the street under the trees; Beverly, and the illumination of his freedom from the old bonds; Gregory, glib and debonair, telling his lying story, and later on, flying to safety. His half-brother!

All that, and now this quiet room, with David asleep beyond the wall and Minnie moving heavily in the kitchen below, setting her bread to rise. It was anti-climacteric, ridiculous, wonderful.

Then he thought of Elizabeth, and it became terrible.

After Reynolds came up he put on a dressing-gown and went down the stairs. The office was changed and looked strange and unfamiliar. But when he opened the door and went into the laboratory nothing had been altered there. It was as though he had left it yesterday; the microscope screwed to its stand, the sterilizer gleaming and ready. It was as though it had waited for him.

He was content. He would fight and he would work. That was all a man needed, a good fight, and work for his hands and brain. A man could live without love if he had work.

He sat down on the stool and groaned.

XLVI

One thing Dick knew must be done and got over with. He would have to see Elizabeth and tell her the story. He knew it would do no good, but she had a right to the fullest explanation he could give her. She did not love him, but it was intolerable that she should hate him.

He meant, however, to make no case for himself. He would have to stand on the facts. This thing had happened to him; the storm had come, wrought its havoc and passed; he was back, to start again as nearly as he could where he had left off. That was all.

He went to the Wheeler house the next night, passing the door twice before he turned in and rang the bell, in order that his voice might be calm and his demeanor unshaken. But the fact that Micky, waiting on the porch, knew him and broke into yelps of happiness and ecstatic wriggling almost lost him his self-control.

Walter Wheeler opened the door and admitted him.

"I thought you might come," he said. "Come in."

There was no particular warmth in his voice, but no unfriendliness. He stood by gravely while Dick took off his overcoat, and then led the way into the library.

"I'd better tell you at once," he said, "that I have advised Elizabeth to see you, but that she refuses. I'd much prefer—" He busied himself at the fire for a moment. "I'd much prefer to have her see you, Livingstone. But—I'll tell you frankly—I don't think it would do much good."

He sat down and stared at the fire. Dick remained standing. "She doesn't intend to see me at all?" he asked, unsteadily.

"That's rather out of the question, if you intend to remain here. Do you?"

"Yes."

An unexpected feeling of sympathy for the tall young man on the hearth rug stirred in Walter Wheeler's breast.

"I'm sorry, Dick. She apparently reached the breaking point a week or two ago. She knew you had been here and hadn't seen her, for one thing." He hesitated. "You've heard of her engagement?"

"Yes."

"I didn't want it," her father said drearily. "I suppose she knows her own business, but the thing's done. She sent you a message," he added after a pause. "She's glad it's cleared up and I believe you are not to allow her to drive you away. She thinks David needs you."

"Thank you. I'll have to stay, as she says."

There was another uncomfortable silence. Then Walter Wheeler burst out:

"Confound it, Dick, I'm sorry. I've fought your battles for months, not here, but everywhere. But here's a battle I can't fight. She isn't angry. You'll have to get her angle of it. I think it's something like this. She had built you up into a sort of superman. And she's—well, I suppose purity is the word. She's the essence of purity. Then, Leslie told me this to-night, she learned from him that you were back with the woman in the case, in New York."

And, as Dick made a gesture:

"There's no use going to him. He was off the beaten track, and he knows it. He took a chance, to tell her for her own good. He's fond of her. I suppose that was the last straw."

He sat still, a troubled figure, middle-aged and unhandsome, and very weary.

"It's a bad business, Dick," he said.

After a time Dick stirred.

"When I first began to remember," he said, "I wanted whisky. I would have stolen it, if I couldn't have got it any other way. Then, when I got it, I didn't want it. It sickened me. This other was the same sort of thing. It's done with."

Wheeler nodded.

"I understand. But she wouldn't, Dick."

"No. I don't suppose she would."

He went away soon after that, back to the quiet house and to David. Automatically he turned in at his office, but Reynolds was writing there. He went slowly up the stairs.

Ann Sayre was frankly puzzled during the next few days. She had had a week or so of serenity and anticipation, and although things were not quite as she would have had them,

Elizabeth too impassive and even Wallie rather restrained in his happiness, she was satisfied. But Dick Livingstone's return had somehow changed everything.

It had changed Wallie, too. He was suddenly a man, and not, she suspected, a very happy man. He came back one day, for instance, to say that he had taken a partnership in a brokerage office, and gave as his reason that he was sick of "playing round." She rather thought it was to take his mind off something.

A few days after the funeral she sent for Doctor Reynolds. "I caught cold at the cemetery," she said, when he had arrived and was seated opposite her in her boudoir. "I really did," she protested, as she caught his eye. "I suppose everybody is sending for you, to have a chance to talk."

"Just about."

"You can't blame us. Particularly, you can't blame me. I've got to know something, doctor. Is he going to stay?"

"I think so. Yes."

"Isn't he going to explain anything? He can't expect just to walk back into his practise after all these months, and the talk that's been going on, and do nothing about it."

"I don't see what his going away has to do with it. He's a good doctor, and a hard worker. When I'm gone—"

"You're going, are you?"

"Yes. I may live here, and have an office in the city. I don't care for general practise; there's no future in it. I may take a special course in nose and throat."

But she was not interested in his plans.

"I want to know something, and only you can tell me. I'm not curious like the rest; I think I have a right to know. Has he seen Elizabeth Wheeler yet? Talked to her, I mean?"

"I don't know. I'm inclined to think not," he added cautiously.

"You mean that he hasn't?"

"Look here, Mrs. Sayre. You've confided in me, and I know it's important to you. I don't know a thing. I'm to stay on until the end of the week, and then he intends to take hold. I'm in and out, see him at meals, and we've had a little desultory talk. There is no trouble between the two families. Mr. Wheeler comes and goes. If you ask me, I think Livingstone has simply accepted the situation as he found it."

"He isn't going to explain anything? He'll have to, I think, if he expects to practise here. There have been all sorts of stories."

"I don't know, Mrs. Sayre."

"How is Doctor David?" she asked, after a pause.

"Better. It wouldn't surprise me now to see him mend rapidly."

He met Elizabeth on his way down the hill, a strange, bright-eyed Elizabeth, carrying her head high and a bit too jauntily, and with a sort of hot defiance in her eyes. He drove on, thoughtfully. All this turmoil and trouble, anxiety and fear, and all that was left a crushed and tragic figure of a girl, and two men in an old house, preparing to fight that one of them might regain the place he had lost.

It would be a fight. Reynolds saw the village already divided into two camps, a small militant minority, aligned with Dick and David, and a waiting, not particularly hostile but intensely curious majority, who would demand certain things before Dick's reinstatement in their confidence.

Elizabeth Wheeler was an unconscious party to the division. It was, in a way, her battle they were fighting. And Elizabeth had gone over to the enemy.

Late that afternoon Ann Sayre had her first real talk with Wallie since Dick's return. She led him out onto the terrace, her shoulders militant and her head high, and faced him there.

"I can see you are not going to talk to me," she said. "So I'll talk to you. Has Dick Livingstone's return made any change between Elizabeth and you?"

"No."

"She's just the same to you? You must tell me, Wallace. I've been building so much."

She realized the change in him then more fully than ever for he faced her squarely and without evasion.

"There's no change in her, mother, but I think you and I will both have to get used to this: she's not in love with me. She doesn't pretend to be."

"Don't tell me it's still that man!"

"I don't know." He took a turn or two about the terrace. "I don't think it is, mother. I don't think she cares for anybody, that way, certainly not for me. And that's the trouble." He faced her again. "If marrying me isn't going to make her happy, I won't hold her to it. You'll have to support me in that, mother. I'm a pretty weak sister sometimes."

That appeal touched her as nothing had done for a long time. "I'll help all I can, if the need comes," she said, and turned and went heavily into the house.

XLVII

David was satisfied. The great love of his life had been given to Dick, and now Dick was his again. He grieved for Lucy, but he knew that the parting was not for long, and that from whatever high place she looked down she would know that. He was satisfied. He looked on his work and found it good. There was no trace of weakness nor of vacillation in the man who sat across from him at the table, or slammed in and out of the house after his old fashion.

But he was not content. At first it was enough to have Dick there, to stop in the doorway of his room and see him within, occupied with the prosaic business of getting into his clothes or out of them, now and then to put a hand on his shoulder, to hear him fussing in the laboratory again, and to be called to examine divers and sundry smears to which Dick attached impressive importance and more impressive names. But behind Dick's surface cheerfulness he knew that he was eating his heart out.

And there was nothing to be done. Nothing. Secretly David watched the papers for the announcement of Elizabeth's engagement, and each day drew a breath of relief when it did not come. And he had done another thing secretly, too; he did not tell Dick when her ring came back. Annie had brought the box, without a letter, and the incredible cruelty of the thing made David furious. He stamped into his office and locked it in a drawer, with the definite intention of saving Dick that one additional pang at a time when he already had enough to hear.

For things were going very badly. The fight was on.

It was a battle without action. Each side was dug in and entrenched, and waiting. It was an engagement where the principals met occasionally the neutral ground of the streets, bowed to each other and passed on.

The town was sorry for David and still fond of him, but it resented his stiff-necked attitude. It said, in effect, that when he ceased to make Dick's enemies his it was willing to be friends. But it said also, to each other and behind its hands, that Dick's absence was discreditable or it would be explained, and that he had behaved abominably to Elizabeth. It would be hanged if it would be friends with him.

It looked away, but it watched. Dick knew that when he passed by on the streets it peered at him from behind its curtains, and whispered behind his back. Now and then he saw, on his evening walks, that line of cars drawn up before houses he had known and frequented which indicated a party, but he was never asked. He never told David.

It was only when the taboo touched David that Dick was resentful, and then he was inclined to question the wisdom of his return. It hurt him, for instance, to see David give up his church, and reading morning prayer alone at home on Sunday mornings, and to see his grim silence when some of his old friends were mentioned.

Yet on the surface things were much as they had been. David rose early, and as he improved in health, read his morning paper in his office while he waited for breakfast. Doctor Reynolds had gone, and the desk in Dick's office was back where it belonged. In the mornings Mike oiled the car in the stable and washed it, his old pipe clutched in his teeth, while from the kitchen came the sounds of pans and dishes, and the odor of frying sausages. And Dick splashed in the shower, and shaved by the mirror with the cracked glass in the bathroom. But he did not sing.

The house was very quiet. Now and then the front door opened, and a patient came in, but there was no longer the crowded waiting-room, the incessant jangle of the telephone, the odor of pungent drugs and antiseptics.

When, shortly before Christmas, Dick looked at the books containing the last quarter's accounts, he began to wonder how long they could fight their losing battle. He did not mind for himself, but it was unthinkable that David should do without, one by one, the small luxuries of his old age, his cigars, his long and now errandless rambles behind Nettie.

He began then to think of his property, his for the claiming, and to question whether he had not bought his peace at too great a cost to David. He knew by that time that it was not fear, but pride, which had sent him back empty-handed, the pride of making his own way. And now and then, too, he felt a perfectly human desire to let Bassett publish the story as his vindication and then snatch David away from them all, to some luxurious haven where—that was the point at which he always stopped—where David could pine away in homesickness for them!

There was an irony in it that made him laugh hopelessly.

He occupied himself then with ways and means, and sold the car. Reynolds, about to be married and busily furnishing a city office, bought it, had it repainted a bright blue, and signified to the world at large that he was at the Rossiter house every night by leaving it at the curb. Sometimes, on long country tramps, Dick saw it outside a farmhouse, and knew that the boycott was not limited to the town.

By Christmas, however, he realized that the question of meeting their expenses necessitated further economies, and reluctantly at last they decided to let Mike go. Dick went out to the stable with a distinct sinking of the heart, while David sat in the house, unhappily waiting for the thing to be done. But Mike refused to be discharged.

"And is it discharging me you are?" he asked, putting down one of David's boots in his angry astonishment. "Well, then, I'm telling you you're not."

"We can't pay you any longer, Mike. And now that the car's gone—"

"I'm not thinking about pay. I'm not going, and that's flat. Who'd be after doing his boots and all?"

David called him in that night and dismissed him again, this time very firmly. Mike said nothing and went out, but the next morning he was scrubbing the sidewalk as usual, and after that they gave it up.

Now and then Dick and Elizabeth met on the street, and she bowed to him and went on. At those times it seemed incredible that once he had held her in his arms, and that she had looked up at him with loving, faithful eyes. He suffered so from those occasional meetings that he took to watching for her, so as to avoid her. Sometimes he wished she would marry Wallace quickly, so he would be obliged to accept what now he knew he had not accepted at all.

He had occasional spells of violent anger at her, and of resentment, but they died when he checked up, one after the other, the inevitable series of events that had led to the catastrophe. But it was all nonsense to say that love never died. She had loved him, and there was never anything so dead as that love of hers.

He had been saved one thing, however; he had never seen her with Wallie Sayre. Then, one day in the country while he trudged afoot to make one of his rare professional visits, they went

294

past together in Wallie's bright roadster. The sheer shock of it sent him against a fence, staring after them with an anger that shook him.

Late in November Elizabeth went away for a visit, and it gave him a breathing spell. But the strain was telling on him, and Bassett, stopping on his way to dinner at the Wheelers', told him so bluntly.

"You look pretty rotten," he said. "It's no time to go to pieces now, when you've put up your fight and won it."

"I'm all right. I haven't been sleeping. That's all."

"How about the business? People coming to their senses?"

"Not very fast," Dick admitted. "Of course it's a little soon."

After dinner at the Wheelers', when Walter Wheeler had gone to a vestry meeting, Bassett delivered himself to Margaret of a highly indignant harangue on the situation in general.

"That's how I see it," he finished. "He's done a fine thing. A finer thing by a damned sight than I'd do, or any of this town. He's given up money enough to pay the national debt—or nearly. If he'd come back with it, as Judson Clark, they wouldn't have cared a hang for the past. They'd have licked his boots. It makes me sick."

He turned on her.

"You too, I think, Mrs. Wheeler. I'm not attacking you on that score; it's human nature. But it's the truth."

"Perhaps. I don't know."

"They'll drive him to doing it yet. He came back to make a place for himself again, like a man. Not what he had, but what he was. But they'll drive him away, mark my words."

Later on, but more gently, he introduced the subject of Elizabeth.

"You can't get away from this, Mrs. Wheeler. So long as she stands off, and you behind her, the town is going to take her side. She doesn't know it, but that's how it stands. It all hangs on her. If he wasn't the man he is, I'd say his salvation hangs on her. I don't mean she ought to take him back; it's too late for that, if she's engaged. But a little friendliness and kindness wouldn't do any harm. You too. Do you ever have him here?"

"How can I, as things are?"

"Well, be friendly, anyhow," he argued. "That's not asking much. I suppose he'd cut my throat if he knew, but I'm a straight-to-the-mark sort of person, and I know this: what this house does the town will do."

"I'll talk to Mr. Wheeler. I don't know. I'll say this, Mr. Bassett. I won't make her unhappy. She has borne a great deal, and sometimes I think her life is spoiled. She is very different."

"If she is suffering, isn't it possible she cares for him?"

But Margaret did not think so. She was so very calm. She was so calm that sometimes it was alarming.

"He gave her a ring, and the other day I found it, tossed into a drawer full of odds and ends. I haven't seen it lately; she may have sent it back."

Elizabeth came home shortly before Christmas, undeniably glad to be back and very gentle with them all. She set to work almost immediately on the gifts, wrapping them and tying them with methodical exactness, sticking a tiny sprig of holly through the ribbon bow, and writing cards with neatness and care. She hung up wreaths and decorated the house, and when she was through with her work she went to her room and sat with her hands folded, not thinking. She did not think any more.

Wallie had sent her a flexible diamond bracelet as a Christmas gift and it lay on her table in its box. She was very grateful, but she had not put it on.

On the morning before Christmas Nina came in, her arms full of packages, and her eyes shining and a little frightened. She had some news for them. She hadn't been so keen about it, at first, but Leslie was like a madman. He was so pleased that he was ordering her that sable cape she had wanted so. He was like a different man. And it would be July.

Elizabeth kissed her. It seemed very unreal, like everything else. She wondered why Leslie should be so excited, or her mother crying. She wondered if there was something strange about her, that it should see so small and unimportant. But then, what was important? That one got up in the morning, and ate at intervals, and went to bed at night? That children came, and had to be fed and washed and tended, and cried a great deal, and were sick now and then?

She wished she could feel something, could think it vital whether Nina should choose pink or blue for her layette, and how far she should walk each day, and if the chauffeur drove the car carefully enough. She wished she cared whether it was going to rain to-morrow or not, or whether some one was coming, or not coming. And she wished terribly that she could care for Wallie, or get over the feeling that she had saved her pride at a cost to him she would not contemplate.

After a time she went upstairs and put on the bracelet. And late in the afternoon she went out and bought some wool, to make an afghan. It eased her conscience toward Nina. She commenced it that evening while she waited for Wallie, and she wondered if some time she would be making an afghan for a coming child of her own. Hers and Wallace Sayre's.

Suddenly she knew she would never marry him. She faced the future, with all that it implied, and she knew she could not do it. It was horrible that she had even contemplated it. It would be terrible to tell Wallie, but not as terrible as the other thing. She saw herself then with the same clearness with which she had judged Dick. She too, leaving her havoc of wrecked lives behind her; she too going along her headstrong way, raising hopes not to be fulfilled, and passing on. She too.

That evening, Christmas eve, she told Wallie she would not marry him. Told him very gently, and just after an attempt of his to embrace her. She would not let him do it.

"I don't know what's come over you," he said morosely. "But I'll let you alone, if that's the way you feel."

"I'm sorry, Wallie. It—it makes me shiver."

In a way he was prepared for it but nevertheless he begged for time, for a less unequivocal rejection. But he found her, for the first time, impatient with his pleadings.

"I don't want to go over and over it, Wallie. I'll take the blame. I should have done it long ago."

She was gentle, almost tender with him, but when he said she had spoiled his life for him she smiled faintly.

"You think that now. And don't believe I'm not sorry. I am. I hate not playing the game, as you say. But I don't think for a moment that you'll go on caring when you know I don't. That doesn't happen. That's all."

"Do you know what I think?" he burst out. "I think you're still mad about Livingstone. I think you are so mad about him that you don't know it yourself."

But she only smiled her cool smile and went on with her knitting. After that he got himself in hand, and—perhaps he still had some hope. It was certain that she had not flinched at Dick's name—told her very earnestly that he only wanted her happiness. He didn't want her unless she wanted him. He would always love her.

"Not always," she said, with tragically cold certainty. "Men are not like women; they forget."

She wondered, after he had gone, what had made her say that.

She did not tell the family that night. They were full of their own concerns, Nina's coming maternity, the wrapping of packages behind closed doors, the final trimming of the tree in the library. Leslie had started the phonograph, and it was playing "Stille Nacht, heilige Nacht."

Still night, holy night, and only in her was there a stillness that was not holy.

They hung up their stockings valiantly as usual, making a little ceremony of it, and being careful not to think about Jim's missing one. Indeed, they made rather a function of it, and Leslie demanded one of Nina's baby socks and pinned it up.

"I'm starting a bank account for the little beggar," he said, and dropped a gold piece into the toe. "Next year, old girl."

He put his arm around Nina. It seemed to him that life was doing considerably better than he deserved by him, and he felt very humble and contrite. He felt in his pocket for the square jeweler's box that lay there.

After that they left Walter Wheeler there, to play his usual part at such times, and went upstairs. He filled the stockings bravely, an orange in each toe, a box of candy, a toy for old time's sake, and then the little knickknacks he had been gathering for days and hiding in his desk. After all, there were no fewer stockings this year than last. Instead of Jim's there was the tiny one for Nina's baby. That was the way things went. He took away, but also He gave.

He sat back in his deep chair, and looked up at the stockings, ludicrously bulging. After all, if he believed that He gave and took away, then he must believe that Jim was where he had tried to think him, filling a joyous, active place in some boyish heaven.

After a while he got up and went to his desk, and getting pen and paper wrote carefully.

"Dearest: You will find this in your stocking in the morning, when you get up for the early service. And I want you to think over it in the church. It is filled with tenderness and with anxiety. Life is not so very long, little daughter, and it has no time to waste in anger or in bitterness. A little work, a little sleep, a little love, and it is all over.

"Will you think of this to-day?"

He locked up the house, and went slowly up to bed. Elizabeth found the letter the next morning. She stood in the bleak room, with the ashes of last night's fire still smoking, and the stockings overhead not festive in the gray light, but looking forlorn and abandoned. Suddenly her eyes, dry and fiercely burning for so long, were wet with tears. It was true. It was true. A little work, a little sleep, a little love. Not the great love, perhaps, not the only love of a man's life. Not the love of yesterday, but of to-day and to-morrow.

All the fierce repression of the last weeks was gone. She began to suffer. She saw Dick coming home, perhaps high with hope that whatever she knew she would understand and forgive. And she saw herself failing him, cold and shut away, not big enough nor woman enough to meet him half way. She saw him fighting his losing battle alone, protecting David but never himself; carrying Lucy to her quiet grave; sitting alone in his office, while the village walked by and stared at the windows; she saw him, gaining harbor after storm, and finding no anchorage there.

She turned and went, half blindly, into the empty street.

She thought he was at the early service. She did not see him, but she had once again the thing that had seemed lost forever, the warm sense of his thought of her.

He was there, in the shadowy back pew, with the grill behind it through which once insistent hands had reached to summon him. He was there, with Lucy's prayer-book in his hand, and none of the peace of the day in his heart. He knelt and rose with the others.

"O God, who makest us glad with the yearly remembrance of the birth of Thy Son—"

XLVIII

David was beaten; most tragic defeat of all, beaten by those he had loved and faithfully served.

He did not rise on Christmas morning, and Dick, visiting him after an almost untasted breakfast, found him still in his bed and questioned him anxiously.

"I'm all right," he asserted. "I'm tired, Dick, that's all. Tired of fighting. You're young. You can carry it on, and win. But I'll never see it. They're stronger than we are."

Later he elaborated on that. He had kept the faith. He had run with courage the race that was set before him. He had stayed up at night and fought for them. But he couldn't fight against them.

Dick went downstairs again and shutting himself in his office fell to pacing the floor. David was right, the thing was breaking him. Very seriously now he contemplated abandoning the town, taking David with him, and claiming his estate. They could travel then; he could get consultants in Europe; there were baths there, and treatments—

The doorbell rang. He heard Minnie's voice in the hall, not too friendly, and her tap at the door.

"Some one in the waiting-room," she called.

When he opened the connecting door he found Elizabeth beyond it, a pale and frightened Elizabeth, breathless and very still. It was a perceptible moment before he could control his voice to speak. Then:

"I suppose you want to see David. I'm sorry, but he isn't well to-day. He is still in bed."

"I didn't come to see David, Dick."

"I cannot think you want to see me, Elizabeth."

"I do, if you don't mind."

He stood aside then and let her pass him into the rear office.

But he was not fooled at all. Not he. He had been enough. He knew why she had come, in the kindness of heart. (She was so little. Good heavens, a man could crush her to nothing!) She had come because she was sorry for him, and she had brought forgiveness. It was like her. It was fine. It was damnable.

His voice hardened, for fear it might be soft.

"Is this a professional visit, or a Christmas call, Elizabeth? Or perhaps I shouldn't call you that."

"A Christmas call?"

"You know what I mean. The day of peace. The day—what do you think I'm made of, Elizabeth? To have you here, gentle and good and kind—"

He got up and stood over her, tall and almost threatening.

"You've been to church, and you've been thinking things over, I know. I was there. I heard it all, peace on earth, goodwill to men. Bosh. Peace, when there is no peace. Good will! I don't want your peace and good will."

She looked up at him timidly.

"You don't want to be friends, then?"

"No. A thousand times, no," he said violently. Then, more gently: "I'm making a fool of myself. I want your peace and good will, Elizabeth. God knows I need them."

"You frighten me, Dick," she said, slowly. "I didn't come to bring forgiveness, if that is what you mean. I came—"

"Don't tell me you came to ask it. That would be more than I can bear."

"Will you listen to me for a moment, Dick? I am not good at explaining things, and I'm nervous. I suppose you can see that." She tried to smile at him. "A—a little work, a sleep, a little love, that's life, isn't it?"

He was watching her intently.

"Work and trouble, and a long sleep at the end for which let us be duly thankful—that's life, too. Love? Not every one gets love."

Hopelessness and despair overwhelmed her. He was making it hard for her. Impossible. She could not go on.

"I did not come with peace," she said tremulously, "but if you don't want it—" She rose. "I must say this, though, before I go. I blame myself. I don't blame you. You are wrong if you think I came to forgive you."

She was stumbling toward the door.

"Elizabeth, what did bring you?"

She turned to him, with her hand on the door knob. "I came because I wanted to see you again."

He strode after her and catching her by the arm, turned her until he faced her.

"And why did you want to see me again? You can't still care for me. You know the story. You know I was here and didn't see you. You've seen Leslie Ward. You know my past. What you don't know—"

He looked down into her eyes. "A little work, a little sleep, a little love," he repeated. "What did you mean by that?"

"Just that," she said simply. "Only not a little love, Dick. Maybe you don't want me now. I don't know. I have suffered so much that I'm not sure of anything."

"Want you!" he said. "More than anything on this earth."

Bassett was at his desk in the office. It was late, and the night editor, seeing him reading the early edition, his feet on his desk, carried over his coffee and doughnuts and joined him.

"Sometime," he said, "I'm going to get that Clark story out of you. If it wasn't you who turned up the confession, I'll eat it."

Bassett yawned.

"Have it your own way," he said indifferently. "You were shielding somebody, weren't you? No? What's the answer?"

Bassett made no reply. He picked up the paper and pointed to an item with the end of his pencil.

"Seen this?"

The night editor read it with bewilderment. He glanced up.

"What's that got to do with the Clark case?"

"Nothing. Nice people, though. Know them both."

When the night editor walked away, rather affronted, Bassett took up the paper and reread the paragraph.

"Mr. and Mrs. Walter Wheeler, of Haverly, announce the engagement of their daughter, Elizabeth, to Doctor Richard Livingstone."

He sat for a long time staring at it.

The Case of Jennie Brice

CHAPTER I

We have just had another flood, bad enough, but only a foot or two of water on the first floor. Yesterday we got the mud shoveled out of the cellar and found Peter, the spaniel that Mr. Ladley left when he "went away". The flood, and the fact that it was Mr. Ladley's dog whose body was found half buried in the basement fruit closet, brought back to me the strange events of the other flood five years ago, when the water reached more than half-way to the second story, and brought with it, to some, mystery and sudden death, and to me the worst case of "shingles" I have ever seen.

My name is Pitman—in this narrative. It is not really Pitman, but that does well enough. I belong to an old Pittsburgh family. I was born on Penn Avenue, when that was the best part of town, and I lived, until I was fifteen, very close to what is now the Pittsburgh Club. It was a dwelling then; I have forgotten who lived there.

I was a girl in seventy-seven, during the railroad riots, and I recall our driving in the family carriage over to one of the Allegheny hills, and seeing the yards burning, and a great noise of shooting from across the river. It was the next year that I ran away from school to marry Mr. Pitman, and I have not known my family since. We were never reconciled, although I came back to Pittsburgh after twenty years of wandering. Mr. Pitman was dead; the old city called me, and I came. I had a hundred dollars or so, and I took a house in lower Allegheny, where, because they are partly inundated every spring, rents are cheap, and I kept boarders. My house was always orderly and clean, and although the neighborhood had a bad name, a good many theatrical people stopped with me. Five minutes across the bridge, and they were in the theater district. Allegheny at that time, I believe, was still an independent city. But since then it has allied itself with Pittsburgh; it is now the North Side.

I was glad to get back. I worked hard, but I made my rent and my living, and a little over. Now and then on summer evenings I went to one of the parks, and sitting on a bench, watched the children playing around, and looked at my sister's house, closed for the summer. It is a very large house: her butler once had his wife boarding with me—a nice little woman.

It is curious to recall that, at that time, five years ago, I had never seen my niece, Lida Harvey, and then to think that only the day before yesterday she came in her automobile as far as she dared, and then sat there, waving to me, while the police patrol brought across in a skiff a basket of provisions she had sent me.

I wonder what she would have thought had she known that the elderly woman in a calico wrapper with an old overcoat over it, and a pair of rubber boots, was her full aunt!

The flood and the sight of Lida both brought back the case of Jennie Brice. For even then, Lida and Mr. Howell were interested in each other.

This is April. The flood of 1907 was earlier, in March. It had been a long hard winter, with ice gorges in all the upper valley. Then, in early March, there came a thaw. The gorges broke up and began to come down, filling the rivers with crushing grinding ice.

There are three rivers at Pittsburgh, the Allegheny and the Monongahela uniting there at the Point to form the Ohio. And all three were covered with broken ice, logs, and all sorts of debris from the upper valleys.

A warning was sent out from the weather bureau, and I got my carpets ready to lift that morning. That was on the fourth of March, a Sunday. Mr. Ladley and his wife, Jennie Brice, had the parlor bedroom and the room behind it. Mrs. Ladley, or Miss Brice, as she preferred to be known, had a small part at a local theater that kept a permanent company. Her husband was in that business, too, but he had nothing to do. It was the wife who paid the bills, and a lot of quarreling they did about it.

I knocked at the door at ten o'clock, and Mr. Ladley opened it. He was a short man, rather stout and getting bald, and he always had a cigarette. Even yet, the parlor carpet smells of them.

"What do you want?" he asked sharply, holding the door open about an inch.

"The water's coming up very fast, Mr. Ladley," I said. "It's up to the swinging-shelf in the cellar now. I'd like to take up the carpet and move the piano."

"Come back in an hour or so," he snapped, and tried to close the door. But I had got my toe in the crack.

"I'll have to have the piano moved, Mr. Ladley," I said. "You'd better put off what you are doing."

I thought he was probably writing. He spent most of the day writing, using the wash-stand as a desk, and it kept me busy with oxalic acid taking ink-spots out of the splasher and the towels. He was writing a play, and talked a lot about the Shuberts having promised to star him in it when it was finished.

"Hell!" he said, and turning, spoke to somebody in the room.

"We can go into the back room," I heard him say, and he closed the door. When he opened it again, the room was empty. I called in Terry, the Irishman who does odd jobs for me now and then, and we both got to work at the tacks in the carpet, Terry working by the window, and I by the door into the back parlor, which the Ladleys used as a bedroom.

That was how I happened to hear what I afterward told the police.

Some one—a man, but not Mr. Ladley—was talking. Mrs. Ladley broke in: "I won't do it!" she said flatly. "Why should I help him? He doesn't help me. He loafs here all day, smoking and sleeping, and sits up all night, drinking and keeping me awake."

The voice went on again, as if in reply to this, and I heard a rattle of glasses, as if they were pouring drinks. They always had whisky, even when they were behind with their board.

"That's all very well," Mrs. Ladley said. I could always hear her, she having a theatrical sort of voice—one that carries. "But what about the prying she-devil that runs the house?"

"Hush, for God's sake!" broke in Mr. Ladley, and after that they spoke in whispers. Even with my ear against the panel, I could not catch a word.

The men came just then to move the piano, and by the time we had taken it and the furniture up-stairs, the water was over the kitchen floor, and creeping forward into the hall. I had never seen the river come up so fast. By noon the yard was full of floating ice, and at three that afternoon the police skiff was on the front street, and I was wading around in rubber boots, taking the pictures off the walls.

I was too busy to see who the Ladleys' visitor was, and he had gone when I remembered him again. The Ladleys took the second-story front, which was empty, and Mr. Reynolds, who was in the silk department in a store across the river, had the room just behind.

I put up a coal stove in a back room next the bathroom, and managed to cook the dinner there. I was washing up the dishes when Mr. Reynolds came in. As it was Sunday, he was in his slippers and had the colored supplement of a morning paper in his hand.

"What's the matter with the Ladleys?" he asked. "I can't read for their quarreling."

"Booze, probably," I said. "When you've lived in the flood district as long as I have, Mr. Reynolds, you'll know that the rising of the river is a signal for every man in the vicinity to stop work and get full. The fuller the river, the fuller the male population."

"Then this flood will likely make 'em drink themselves to death!" he said. "It's a lulu."

"It's the neighborhood's annual debauch. The women are busy keeping the babies from getting drowned in the cellars, or they'd get full, too. I hope, since it's come this far, it will come farther, so the landlord will have to paper the parlor."

That was at three o'clock. At four Mr. Ladley went down the stairs, and I heard him getting into a skiff in the lower hall. There were boats going back and forth all the time, carrying crowds of curious people, and taking the flood sufferers to the corner grocery, where they were lowering groceries in a basket on a rope from an upper window.

I had been making tea when I heard Mr. Ladley go out. I fixed a tray with a cup of it and some crackers, and took it to their door. I had never liked Mrs. Ladley, but it was chilly in the house with the gas shut off and the lower floor full of ice-water. And it is hard enough to keep boarders in the flood district.

She did not answer to my knock, so I opened the door and went in. She was at the window, looking after him, and the brown valise, that figured in the case later, was opened on the floor. Over the foot of the bed was the black and white dress, with the red collar.

When I spoke to her, she turned around quickly. She was a tall woman, about twenty-eight, with very white teeth and yellow hair, which she parted a little to one side and drew down over her ears. She had a sullen face and large well-shaped hands, with her nails long and very pointed.

"The 'she-devil' has brought you some tea," I said. "Where shall she put it?"

"'She-devil'!" she repeated, raising her eyebrows. "It's a very thoughtful she-devil. Who called you that?"

But, with the sight of the valise and the fear that they might be leaving, I thought it best not to quarrel. She had left the window, and going to her dressing-table, had picked up her nail-file.

"Never mind," I said. "I hope you are not going away. These floods don't last, and they're a benefit. Plenty of the people around here rely on 'em every year to wash out their cellars."

"No, I'm not going away," she replied lazily. "I'm taking that dress to Miss Hope at the theater. She is going to wear it in *Charlie's Aunt* next week. She hasn't half enough of a wardrobe to play leads in stock. Look at this thumb-nail, broken to the quick!"

If I had only looked to see which thumb it was! But I was putting the tea-tray on the wash-stand, and moving Mr. Ladley's papers to find room for it. Peter, the spaniel, begged for a lump of sugar, and I gave it to him.

"Where is Mr. Ladley?" I asked.

"Gone out to see the river."

"I hope he'll be careful. There's a drowning or two every year in these floods."

"Then I hope he won't," she said calmly. "Do you know what I was doing when you came in? I was looking after his boat, and hoping it had a hole in it."

"You won't feel that way to-morrow, Mrs. Ladley," I protested, shocked. "You're just nervous and put out. Most men have their ugly times. Many a time I wished Mr. Pitman was gone—until he went. Then I'd have given a good bit to have him back again."

She was standing in front of the dresser, fixing her hair over her ears. She turned and looked at me over her shoulder.

"Probably Mr. Pitman was a man," she said. "My husband is a fiend, a devil."

Well, a good many women have said that to me at different times. But just let me say such a thing to *them*, or repeat their own words to them the next day, and they would fly at me in a fury. So I said nothing, and put the cream into her tea.

I never saw her again.

CHAPTER II

There is not much sleeping done in the flood district during a spring flood. The gas was shut off, and I gave Mr. Reynolds and the Ladleys each a lamp. I sat in the back room that I had made into a temporary kitchen, with a candle, and with a bedquilt around my shoulders. The water rose fast in the lower hall, but by midnight, at the seventh step, it stopped rising and stood still. I always have a skiff during the flood season, and as the water rose, I tied it to one spindle of the staircase after another.

I made myself a cup of tea, and at one o'clock I stretched out on a sofa for a few hours' sleep. I think I had been sleeping only an hour or so, when some one touched me on the shoulder and I started up. It was Mr. Reynolds, partly dressed.

"Some one has been in the house, Mrs. Pitman," he said. "They went away just now in the boat."

"Perhaps it was Peter," I suggested. "That dog is always wandering around at night."

"Not unless Peter can row a boat," said Mr. Reynolds dryly.

I got up, being already fully dressed, and taking the candle, we went to the staircase. I noticed that it was a minute or so after two o'clock as we left the room. The boat was gone, not untied, but cut loose. The end of the rope was still fastened to the stair-rail. I sat down on the stairs and looked at Mr. Reynolds.

"It's gone!" I said. "If the house catches fire, we'll have to drown."

"It's rather curious, when you consider it." We both spoke softly, not to disturb the Ladleys. "I've been awake, and I heard no boat come in. And yet, if no one came in a boat, and came from the street, they would have had to swim in."

I felt queer and creepy. The street door was open, of course, and the lights going beyond. It gave me a strange feeling to sit there in the darkness on the stairs, with the arch of the front door like the entrance to a cavern, and see now and then a chunk of ice slide into view, turn around in the eddy, and pass on. It was bitter cold, too, and the wind was rising.

"I'll go through the house," said Mr. Reynolds. "There's likely nothing worse the matter than some drunken mill-hand on a vacation while the mills are under water. But I'd better look."

He left me, and I sat there alone in the darkness. I had a presentiment of something wrong, but I tried to think it was only discomfort and the cold. The water, driven in by the wind, swirled at my feet. And something dark floated in and lodged on the step below. I reached down and touched it. It was a dead kitten. I had never known a dead cat to bring me anything but bad luck, and here was one washed in at my very feet.

Mr. Reynolds came back soon, and reported the house quiet and in order.

"But I found Peter shut up in one of the third-floor rooms," he said. "Did you put him there?"

I had not, and said so; but as the dog went everywhere, and the door might have blown shut, we did not attach much importance to that at the time.

Well, the skiff was gone, and there was no use worrying about it until morning. I went back to the sofa to keep warm, but I left my candle lighted and my door open. I did not sleep: the dead cat was on my mind, and, as if it were not bad enough to have it washed in at my feet, about four in the morning Peter, prowling uneasily, discovered it and brought it in and put it on my couch, wet and stiff, poor little thing!

I looked at the clock. It was a quarter after four, and except for the occasional crunch of one ice-cake hitting another in the yard, everything was quiet. And then I heard the stealthy sound of oars in the lower hall.

I am not a brave woman. I lay there, hoping Mr. Reynolds would hear and open his door. But he was sleeping soundly. Peter snarled and ran out into the hall, and the next moment I heard Mr. Ladley speaking. "Down, Peter," he said. "Down. Go and lie down."

I took my candle and went out into the hall. Mr. Ladley was stooping over the boat, trying to tie it to the staircase. The rope was short, having been cut, and he was having trouble. Perhaps it was the candle-light, but he looked ghost-white and haggard.

"I borrowed your boat, Mrs. Pitman," he said, civilly enough. "Mrs. Ladley was not well, and I—I went to the drug store."

"You've been more than two hours going to the drug store," I said.

He muttered something about not finding any open at first, and went into his room. He closed and locked the door behind him, and although Peter whined and scratched, he did not let him in.

He looked so agitated that I thought I had been harsh, and that perhaps she was really ill. I knocked at the door, and asked if I could do anything. But he only called "No" curtly through the door, and asked me to take that infernal dog away.

I went back to bed and tried to sleep, for the water had dropped an inch or so on the stairs, and I knew the danger was over. Peter came, shivering, at dawn, and got on to the sofa with me. I put an end of the quilt over him, and he stopped shivering after a time and went to sleep.

The dog was company. I lay there, wide awake, thinking about Mr. Pitman's death, and how I had come, by degrees, to be keeping a cheap boarding-house in the flood district, and to having to take impudence from everybody who chose to rent a room from me, and to being called a she-devil. From that I got to thinking again about the Ladleys, and how she had said he was a fiend, and to doubting about his having gone out for medicine for her. I dozed off again at daylight, and being worn out, I slept heavily.

At seven o'clock Mr. Reynolds came to the door, dressed for the store. He was a tall man of about fifty, neat and orderly in his habits, and he always remembered that I had seen better days, and treated me as a lady.

"Never mind about breakfast for me this morning, Mrs. Pitman," he said. "I'll get a cup of coffee at the other end of the bridge. I'll take the boat and send it back with Terry."

He turned and went along the hall and down to the boat. I heard him push off from the stairs with an oar and row out into the street. Peter followed him to the stairs.

At a quarter after seven Mr. Ladley came out and called to me: "Just bring in a cup of coffee and some toast," he said. "Enough for one."

He went back and slammed his door, and I made his coffee. I steeped a cup of tea for Mrs. Ladley at the same time. He opened the door just wide enough for the tray, and took it without so much as a "thank you." He had a cigarette in his mouth as usual, and I could see a fire in the grate and smell something like scorching cloth.

"I hope Mrs. Ladley is better," I said, getting my foot in the crack of the door, so he could not quite close it. It smelled to me as if he had accidentally set fire to something with his cigarette, and I tried to see into the room.

"What about Mrs. Ladley?" he snapped.

"You said she was ill last night."

"Oh, yes! Well, she wasn't very sick. She's better."

"Shall I bring her some tea?"

"Take your foot away!" he ordered. "No. She doesn't want tea. She's not here."

"Not here!"

"Good heavens!" he snarled. "Is her going away anything to make such a fuss about? The Lord knows I'd be glad to get out of this infernal pig-wallow myself."

"If you mean my house—" I began.

But he had pulled himself together and was more polite when he answered. "I mean the neighborhood. Your house is all that could be desired for the money. If we do not have linen sheets and double cream, we are paying muslin and milk prices."

Either my nose was growing accustomed to the odor, or it was dying away: I took my foot away from the door. "When did Mrs. Ladley leave?" I asked.

"This morning, very early. I rowed her to Federal Street."

"You couldn't have had much sleep," I said dryly. For he looked horrible. There were lines around his eyes, which were red, and his lips looked dry and cracked.

"She's not in the piece this week at the theater," he said, licking his lips and looking past me, not at me. "She'll be back by Saturday."

I did not believe him. I do not think he imagined that I did. He shut the door in my face, and it caught poor Peter by the nose. The dog ran off howling, but although Mr. Ladley had been as fond of the animal as it was in his nature to be fond of anything, he paid no attention. As I started down the hall after him, I saw what Peter had been carrying—a slipper of Mrs. Ladley's. It was soaked with water; evidently Peter had found it floating at the foot of the stairs.

Although the idea of murder had not entered my head at that time, the slipper gave me a turn. I picked it up and looked at it—a black one with a beaded toe, short in the vamp and high-heeled, the sort most actresses wear. Then I went back and knocked at the door of the front room again.

"What the devil do you want now?" he called from beyond the door.

"Here's a slipper of Mrs. Ladley's," I said. "Peter found it floating in the lower hall."

He opened the door wide, and let me in. The room was in tolerable order, much better than when Mrs. Ladley was about. He looked at the slipper, but he did not touch it. "I don't think that is hers," he said.

"I've seen her wear it a hundred times."

"Well, she'll never wear it again." And then, seeing me stare, he added: "It's ruined with the water. Throw it out. And, by the way, I'm sorry, but I set fire to one of the pillow-slips—dropped asleep, and my cigarette did the rest. Just put it on the bill."

He pointed to the bed. One of the pillows had no slip, and the ticking cover had a scorch or two on it. I went over and looked at it.

"The pillow will have to be paid for, too, Mr. Ladley," I said. "And there's a sign nailed on the door that forbids smoking in bed. If you are going to set fire to things, I shall have to charge extra."

"Really!" he jeered, looking at me with his cold fishy eyes. "Is there any sign on the door saying that boarders are charged extra for seven feet of filthy river in the bedrooms?"

I was never a match for him, and I make it a principle never to bandy words with my boarders. I took the pillow and the slipper and went out. The telephone was ringing on the stair landing. It was the theater, asking for Miss Brice.

"She has gone away," I said.

"What do you mean? Moved away?"

"Gone for a few days' vacation," I replied. "She isn't playing this week, is she?"

"Wait a moment," said the voice. There was a hum of conversation from the other end, and then another man came to the telephone.

"Can you find out where Miss Brice has gone?"

"I'll see."

I went to Ladley's door and knocked. Mr. Ladley answered from just beyond.

"The theater is asking where Mrs. Ladley is."

"Tell them I don't know," he snarled, and shut the door. I took his message to the telephone.

Whoever it was swore and hung up the receiver.

All the morning I was uneasy—I hardly knew why. Peter felt it as I did. There was no sound from the Ladleys' room, and the house was quiet, except for the lapping water on the stairs and the police patrol going back and forth.

At eleven o'clock a boy in the neighborhood, paddling on a raft, fell into the water and was drowned. I watched the police boat go past, carrying his little cold body, and after that I was good for nothing. I went and sat with Peter on the stairs. The dog's conduct had been strange all morning. He had sat just above the water, looking at it and whimpering. Perhaps he was expecting another kitten or—

It is hard to say how ideas first enter one's mind. But the notion that Mr. Ladley had killed his wife and thrown her body into the water came to me as I sat there. All at once I seemed to see it all: the quarreling the day before, the night trip in the boat, the water-soaked slipper, his haggard face that morning—even the way the spaniel sat and stared at the flood.

Terry brought the boat back at half past eleven, towing it behind another.

"Well," I said, from the stairs, "I hope you've had a pleasant morning."

"What doing?" he asked, not looking at me.

"Rowing about the streets. You've had that boat for hours."

He tied it up without a word to me, but he spoke to the dog. "Good morning, Peter," he said. "It's nice weather—for fishes, ain't it?"

He picked out a bit of floating wood from the water, and showing it to the dog, flung it into the parlor. Peter went after it with a splash. He was pretty fat, and when he came back I heard him wheezing. But what he brought back was not the stick of wood. It was the knife I use for cutting bread. It had been on a shelf in the room where I had slept the night before, and now Peter brought it out of the flood where its wooden handle had kept it afloat. The blade was broken off short.

It is not unusual to find one's household goods floating around during flood-time. More than once I've lost a chair or two, and seen it after the water had gone down, new scrubbed and painted, in Molly Maguire's kitchen next door. And perhaps now and then a bit of luck would come to me—a dog kennel or a chicken-house, or a kitchen table, or even, as happened once, a month-old baby in a wooden cradle, that lodged against my back fence, and had come forty miles, as it turned out, with no worse mishap than a cold in its head.

But the knife was different. I had put it on the mantel over the stove I was using up-stairs the night before, and hadn't touched it since. As I sat staring at it, Terry took it from Peter and handed it to me.

"Better give me a penny, Mrs. Pitman," he said in his impudent Irish way. "I hate to give you a knife. It may cut our friendship."

I reached over to hit him a clout on the head, but I did not. The sunlight was coming in through the window at the top of the stairs, and shining on the rope that was tied to the banister. The end of the rope was covered with stains, brown, with a glint of red in them.

I got up shivering. "You can get the meat at the butcher's, Terry," I said, "and come back for me in a half-hour." Then I turned and went up-stairs, weak in the knees, to put on my hat and coat. I had made up my mind that there had been murder done.

CHAPTER III

I looked at my clock as I went down-stairs. It was just twelve-thirty. I thought of telephoning for Mr. Reynolds to meet me, but it was his lunch hour, and besides I was afraid to telephone from the house while Mr. Ladley was in it.

Peter had been whining again. When I came down the stairs he had stopped whimpering and was wagging his tail. A strange boat had put into the hallway and was coming back.

"Now, old boy!" somebody was saying from the boat. "Steady, old chap! I've got something for you."

A little man, elderly and alert, was standing up in the boat, poling it along with an oar. Peter gave vent to joyful yelps. The elderly gentleman brought his boat to a stop at the foot of the stairs, and reaching down into a tub at his feet, held up a large piece of raw liver. Peter almost went crazy, and I remembered suddenly that I had forgotten to feed the poor beast for more than a day.

"Would you like it?" asked the gentleman. Peter sat up, as he had been taught to do, and barked. The gentleman reached down again, got a wooden platter from a stack of them at his feet, and placing the liver on it, put it on the step. The whole thing was so neat and businesslike that I could only gaze.

"That's a well-trained dog, madam," said the elderly gentleman, beaming at Peter over his glasses. "You should not have neglected him."

"The flood put him out of my mind," I explained, humbly enough, for I was ashamed.

"Exactly. Do you know how many starving dogs and cats I have found this morning?" He took a note-book out of his pocket and glanced at it. "Forty-eight. Forty-eight, madam! And ninety-three cats! I have found them marooned in trees, clinging to fences, floating on barrels, and I have found them in comfortable houses where there was no excuse for their neglect. Well, I must be moving on. I have the report of a cat with a new litter in the loft of a stable near here."

He wiped his hands carefully on a fresh paper napkin, of which also a heap rested on one of the seats of the boat, and picked up an oar, smiling benevolently at Peter. Then, suddenly, he bent over and looked at the stained rope end, tied to the stair-rail.

"What's that?" he said.

"That's what I'm going to find out," I replied. I glanced up at the Ladleys' door, but it was closed.

The little man dropped his oar, and fumbling in his pockets, pulled out a small magnifying-glass. He bent over, holding to the rail, and inspected the stains with the glass. I had taken a fancy to him at once, and in spite of my excitement I had to smile a little.

"Humph!" he said, and looked up at me. "That's blood. Why did you *cut* the boat loose?"

"I didn't," I said. "If that is blood, I want to know how it got there. That was a new rope last night." I glanced at the Ladleys' door again, and he followed my eyes.

"I wonder," he said, raising his voice a little, "if I come into your kitchen, if you will allow me to fry a little of that liver. There's a wretched Maltese in a tree at the corner of Fourth Street that won't touch it, raw."

I saw that he wanted to talk to me, so I turned around and led the way to the temporary kitchen I had made.

"Now," he said briskly, when he had closed the door, "there's something wrong here. Perhaps if you tell me, I can help. If I can't, it will do you good to talk about it. My name's Holcombe, retired merchant. Apply to First National Bank for references."

"I'm not sure there *is* anything wrong," I began. "I guess I'm only nervous, and thinking little things are big ones. There's nothing to tell."

"Nonsense. I come down the street in my boat. A white-faced gentleman with a cigarette looks out from a window when I stop at the door, and ducks back when I glance up. I come in and find a pet dog, obviously overfed at ordinary times, whining with hunger on the stairs. As I prepare to feed him, a pale woman comes down, trying to put a right-hand glove on her left hand, and with her jacket wrong side out. What am I to think?"

I started and looked at my coat. He was right. And when, as I tried to take it off, he helped me, and even patted me on the shoulder—what with his kindness, and the long morning alone, worrying, and the sleepless night, I began to cry. He had a clean handkerchief in my hand before I had time to think of one.

"That's it," he said. "It will do you good, only don't make a noise about it. If it's a husband on the annual flood spree, don't worry, madam. They always come around in time to whitewash the cellars."

"It isn't a husband," I sniffled.

"Tell me about it," he said. There was something so kindly in his face, and it was so long since I had had a bit of human sympathy, that I almost broke down again.

I sat there, with a crowd of children paddling on a raft outside the window, and Molly Maguire, next door, hauling the morning's milk up in a pail fastened to a rope, her doorway being too narrow to admit the milkman's boat, and I told him the whole story.

"Humph!" he exclaimed, when I had finished. "It's curious, but—you can't prove a murder unless you can produce a body."

"When the river goes down, we'll find the body," I said, shivering. "It's in the parlor."

"Then why doesn't he try to get away?"

"He is ready to go now. He only went back when your boat came in."

Mr. Holcombe ran to the door, and flinging it open, peered into the lower hall. He was too late. His boat was gone, tub of liver, pile of wooden platters and all!

We hurried to the room the Ladleys had occupied. It was empty. From the window, as we looked out, we could see the boat, almost a square away. It had stopped where, the street being higher, a door-step rose above the flood. On the step was sitting a forlorn yellow puppy. As we stared, Mr. Ladley stopped the boat, looked back at us, bent over, placed a piece of liver on a platter, and reached it over to the dog. Then, rising in the boat, he bowed, with his hat over his heart, in our direction, sat down calmly, and rowed around the corner out of sight.

Mr. Holcombe was in a frenzy of rage. He jumped up and down, shaking his fist out the window after the retreating boat. He ran down the staircase, only to come back and look out the window again. The police boat was not in sight, but the Maguire children had worked their raft around to the street and were under the window. He leaned out and called to them.

"A quarter each, boys," he said, "if you'll take me on that raft to the nearest pavement."

"Money first," said the oldest boy, holding his cap.

But Mr. Holcombe did not wait. He swung out over the window-sill, holding by his hands, and lit fairly in the center of the raft.

"Don't touch anything in that room until I come back," he called to me, and jerking the pole from one of the boys, propelled the raft with amazing speed down the street.

The liver on the stove was burning. There was a smell of scorching through the rooms and a sort of bluish haze of smoke. I hurried back and took it off. By the time I had cleaned the pan, Mr. Holcombe was back again, in his own boat. He had found it at the end of the next street, where the flood ceased, but no sign of Ladley anywhere. He had not seen the police boat.

"Perhaps that is just as well," he said philosophically. "We can't go to the police with a wet slipper and a blood-stained rope and accuse a man of murder. We have to have a body."

"He killed her," I said obstinately. "She told me yesterday he was a fiend. He killed her and threw the body in the water."

"Very likely. But he didn't throw it here."

But in spite of that, he went over all the lower hall with his boat, feeling every foot of the floor with an oar, and finally, at the back end, he looked up at me as I stood on the stairs.

"There's something here," he said.

I went cold all over, and had to clutch the railing. But when Terry had come, and the two of them brought the thing to the surface, it was only the dining-room rug, which I had rolled up and forgotten to carry up-stairs!

At half past one Mr. Holcombe wrote a note, and sent it off with Terry, and borrowing my boots, which had been Mr. Pitman's, investigated the dining-room and kitchen from a floating plank; the doors were too narrow to admit the boat. But he found nothing more important than a rolling-pin. He was not at all depressed by his failure. He came back, drenched to the skin, about three, and asked permission to search the Ladleys' bedroom.

"I have a friend coming pretty soon, Mrs. Pitman," he said, "a young newspaper man, named Howell. He's a nice boy, and if there is anything to this, I'd like him to have it for his paper. He and I have been having some arguments about circumstantial evidence, too, and I know he'd like to work on this."

I gave him a pair of Mr. Pitman's socks, for his own were saturated, and while he was changing them the telephone rang. It was the theater again, asking for Jennie Brice.

"You are certain she is out of the city?" some one asked, the same voice as in the morning.

"Her husband says so."

"Ask him to come to the phone."

"He is not here."

"When do you expect him back?"

"I'm not sure he is coming back."

"Look here," said the voice angrily, "can't you give me any satisfaction? Or don't you care to?"

"I've told you all I know."

"You don't know where she is?"

"No, sir."

"She didn't say she was coming back to rehearse for next week's piece?"

"Her husband said she went away for a few days' rest. He went away about noon and hasn't come back. That's all I know, except that they owe me three weeks' rent that I'd like to get hold of."

The owner of the voice hung up the receiver with a snap, and left me pondering. It seemed to me that Mr. Ladley had been very reckless. Did he expect any one to believe that Jennie Brice had gone for a vacation without notifying the theater? Especially when she was to rehearse that week? I thought it curious, to say the least. I went back and told Mr. Holcombe, who put it down in his note-book, and together we went to the Ladleys' room.

The room was in better order than usual, as I have said. The bed was made—which was out of the ordinary, for Jennie Brice never made a bed—but made the way a man makes one, with the blankets wrinkled and crooked beneath, and the white counterpane pulled smoothly over the top, showing every lump beneath. I showed Mr. Holcombe the splasher, dotted with ink as usual.

"I'll take it off and soak it in milk," I said. "It's his fountain pen; when the ink doesn't run, he shakes it, and—"

"Where's the clock?" said Mr. Holcombe, stopping in front of the mantel with his note-book in his hand.

"The clock?"

I turned and looked. My onyx clock was gone from the mantel-shelf.

Perhaps it seems strange, but from the moment I missed that clock my rage at Mr. Ladley increased to a fury. It was all I had had left of my former gentility. When times were hard and I got behind with the rent, as happened now and then, more than once I'd been tempted to sell the clock, or to pawn it. But I had never done it. Its ticking had kept me company on many a lonely night, and its elegance had helped me to keep my pride and to retain the respect of my neighbors. For in the flood district onyx clocks are not plentiful. Mrs. Bryan, the saloon-keeper's wife, had one, and I had another. That is, I *had* had.

I stood staring at the mark in the dust of the mantel-shelf, which Mr. Holcombe was measuring with a pocket tape-measure.

"You are sure you didn't take it away yourself, Mrs. Pitman?" he asked.

"Sure? Why, I could hardly lift it," I said.

He was looking carefully at the oblong of dust where the clock had stood. "The key is gone, too," he said, busily making entries in his note-book. "What was the maker's name?"

"Why, I don't think I ever noticed."

He turned to me angrily. "Why didn't you notice?" he snapped. "Good God, woman, do you only use your eyes to cry with? How can you wind a clock, time after time, and not know the maker's name? It proves my contention: the average witness is totally unreliable."

"Not at all," I snapped, "I am ordinarily both accurate and observing."

"Indeed!" he said, putting his hands behind him. "Then perhaps you can tell me the color of the pencil I have been writing with."

"Certainly. Red." Most pencils are red, and I thought this was safe.

But he held his right hand out with a flourish. "I've been writing with a fountain pen," he said in deep disgust, and turned his back on me.

But the next moment he had run to the wash-stand and pulled it out from the wall. Behind it, where it had fallen, lay a towel, covered with stains, as if some one had wiped bloody hands on it. He held it up, his face working with excitement. I could only cover my eyes.

"This looks better," he said, and began making a quick search of the room, running from one piece of furniture to another, pulling out bureau drawers, drawing the bed out from the wall, and crawling along the base-board with a lighted match in his hand. He gave a shout of triumph finally, and reappeared from behind the bed with the broken end of my knife in his hand.

"Very clumsy," he said. "*Very* clumsy. Peter the dog could have done better."

I had been examining the wall-paper about the wash-stand. Among the ink-spots were one or two reddish ones that made me shiver. And seeing a scrap of note-paper stuck between the base-board and the wall, I dug it out with a hairpin, and threw it into the grate, to be burned later. It was by the merest chance there was no fire there. The next moment Mr. Holcombe was on his knees by the fireplace reaching for the scrap.

"*Never* do that, under such circumstances," he snapped, fishing among the ashes. "You might throw away valuable—Hello, Howell!"

I turned and saw a young man in the doorway, smiling, his hat in his hand. Even at that first glance, I liked Mr. Howell, and later, when every one was against him, and many curious things were developing, I stood by him through everything, and even helped him to the thing he wanted more than anything else in the, world. But that, of course, was later.

"What's the trouble, Holcombe?" he asked. "Hitting the trail again?"

"A very curious thing that I just happened on," said Mr. Holcombe. "Mrs. Pitman, this is Mr. Howell, of whom I spoke. Sit down, Howell, and let me read you something."

With the crumpled paper still unopened in his hand, Mr. Holcombe took his note-book and read aloud what he had written. I have it before me now:

"'Dog meat, two dollars, boat hire'—that's not it. Here. 'Yesterday, Sunday, March the 4th, Mrs. Pitman, landlady at 42 Union Street, heard two of her boarders quarreling, a man and his wife. Man's name, Philip Ladley. Wife's name, Jennie Ladley, known as Jennie Brice at the Liberty Stock Company, where she has been playing small parts.'"

Mr. Howell nodded. "I've heard of her," he said. "Not much of an actress, I believe."

"'The husband was also an actor, out of work, and employing his leisure time in writing a play.'"

"Everybody's doing it," said Mr. Howell idly.

"The Shuberts were to star him in this," I put in. "He said that the climax at the end of the second act—"

Mr. Holcombe shut his note-book with a snap. "After we have finished gossiping," he said, "I'll go on."

"'Employing his leisure time in writing a play—'" quoted Mr. Howell.

"Exactly. 'The husband and wife were not on good terms. They quarreled frequently. On Sunday they fought all day, and Mrs. Ladley told Mrs. Pitman she was married to a fiend. At four o'clock Sunday afternoon, Philip Ladley went out, returning about five. Mrs. Pitman carried their supper to them at six, and both ate heartily. She did not see Mrs. Ladley at the time, but heard her in the next room. They were apparently reconciled: Mrs. Pitman reports Mr. Ladley in high good humor. If the quarrel recommenced during the night, the other boarder, named Reynolds, in the next room, heard nothing. Mrs. Pitman was up and down until one o'clock, when she dozed off. She heard no unusual sound.

"'At approximately two o'clock in the morning, however, this Reynolds came to the room, and said he had heard some one in a boat in the lower hall. He and Mrs. Pitman investigated. The boat which Mrs. Pitman uses during a flood, and which she had tied to the stair-rail, was gone, having been cut loose, not untied. Everything else was quiet, except that Mrs. Ladley's dog had been shut in a third-story room.

310

"'At a quarter after four that morning Mrs. Pitman, thoroughly awake, heard the boat returning, and going to the stairs, met Ladley coming in. He muttered something about having gone for medicine for his wife and went to his room, shutting the dog out. This is worth attention, for the dog ordinarily slept in their room.'"

"What sort of a dog?" asked Mr. Howell. He had been listening attentively.

"A water-spaniel. 'The rest of the night, or early morning, was quiet. At a quarter after seven, Ladley asked for coffee and toast for one, and on Mrs. Pitman remarking this, said that his wife was not playing this week, and had gone for a few days' vacation, having left early in the morning.' Remember, during the night he had been out for medicine for her. Now she was able to travel, and, in fact, had started."

Mr. Howell was frowning at the floor. "If he was doing anything wrong, he was doing it very badly," he said.

"This is where I entered the case," said Mr. Holcombe, "I rowed into the lower hall this morning, to feed the dog, Peter, who was whining on the staircase. Mrs. Pitman was coming down, pale and agitated over the fact that the dog, shortly before, had found floating in the parlor down-stairs a slipper belonging to Mrs. Ladley, and, later, a knife with a broken blade. She maintains that she had the knife last night up-stairs, that it was not broken, and that it was taken from a shelf in her room while she dozed. The question is, then: Why was the knife taken? Who took it? And why? Has this man made away with his wife, or has he not?"

Mr. Howell looked at me and smiled. "Mr. Holcombe and I are old enemies," he said. "Mr. Holcombe believes that circumstantial evidence may probably hang a man; I do not." And to Mr. Holcombe: "So, having found a wet slipper and a broken knife, you are prepared for murder and sudden death!"

"I have more evidence," Mr. Holcombe said eagerly, and proceeded to tell what we had found in the room. Mr. Howell listened, smiling to himself, but at the mention of the onyx clock he got up and went to the mantel.

"By Jove!" he said, and stood looking at the mark in the dust. "Are you sure the clock was here yesterday?"

"I wound it night before last, and put the key underneath. Yesterday, before they moved up, I wound it again."

"The key is gone also. Well, what of it, Holcombe? Did he brain her with the clock? Or choke her with the key?"

Mr. Holcombe was looking at his note-book. "To summarize," he said, "we have here as clues indicating a crime, the rope, the broken knife, the slipper, the towel, and the clock. Besides, this scrap of paper may contain some information." He opened it and sat gazing at it in his palm. Then, "Is this Ladley's writing?" he asked me in a curious voice.

"Yes."

I glanced at the slip. Mr. Holcombe had just read from his note-book: "Rope, knife, slipper, towel, clock."

The slip I had found behind the wash-stand said "Rope, knife, shoe, towel. Horn—" The rest of the last word was torn off.

Mr. Howell was staring at the mantel. "Clock!" he repeated.

CHAPTER IV

It was after four when Mr. Holcombe had finished going over the room. I offered to make both the gentlemen some tea, for Mr. Pitman had been an Englishman, and I had got into the habit of having a cup in the afternoon, with a cracker or a bit of bread. But they refused. Mr. Howell said he had promised to meet a lady, and to bring her through the flooded district in a boat. He shook hands with me, and smiled at Mr. Holcombe.

"You will have to restrain his enthusiasm, Mrs. Pitman," he said. "He is a bloodhound on the scent. If his baying gets on your nerves, just send for me." He went down the stairs and stepped into the boat. "Remember, Holcombe," he called, "every well-constituted murder has two things: a motive and a corpse. You haven't either, only a mass of piffling details—"

"If everybody waited until he saw flames, instead of relying on the testimony of the smoke," Mr. Holcombe snapped, "what would the fire loss be?"

Mr. Howell poled his boat to the front door, and sitting down, prepared to row out.

"You are warned, Mrs. Pitman," he called to me. "If he doesn't find a body to fit the clues, he's quite capable of making one to fill the demand."

"Horn—" said Mr. Holcombe, looking at the slip again. "The tail of the 'n' is torn off— evidently only part of a word. Hornet, Horning, Horner—Mrs. Pitman, will you go with me to the police station?"

I was more than anxious to go. In fact, I could not bear the idea of staying alone in the house, with heaven only knows what concealed in the depths of that muddy flood. I got on my wraps again, and Mr. Holcombe rowed me out. Peter plunged into the water to follow, and had to be sent back. He sat on the lower step and whined. Mr. Holcombe threw him another piece of liver, but he did not touch it.

We rowed to the corner of Robinson Street and Federal—it was before Federal Street was raised above the flood level—and left the boat in charge of a boy there. And we walked to the police station. On the way Mr. Holcombe questioned me closely about the events of the morning, and I recalled the incident of the burned pillow-slip. He made a note of it at once, and grew very thoughtful.

He left me, however, at the police station. "I'd rather not appear in this, Mrs. Pitman," he said apologetically, "and I think better along my own lines. Not that I have anything against the police; they've done some splendid work. But this case takes imagination, and the police department deals with facts. We have no facts yet. What we need, of course, is to have the man detained until we are sure of our case."

He lifted his hat and turned away, and I went slowly up the steps to the police station. Living, as I had, in a neighborhood where the police, like the poor, are always with us, and where the visits of the patrol wagon are one of those familiar sights that no amount of repetition enabled any of us to treat with contempt, I was uncomfortable until I remembered that my grandfather had been one of the first mayors of the city, and that, if the patrol had been at my house more than once, the entire neighborhood would testify that my boarders were usually orderly.

At the door some one touched me on the arm. It was Mr. Holcombe again.

"I have been thinking it over," he said, "and I believe you'd better not mention the piece of paper that you found behind the wash-stand. They might say the whole thing is a hoax."

"Very well," I agreed, and went in.

The police sergeant in charge knew me at once, having stopped at my house more than once in flood-time for a cup of hot coffee.

"Sit down, Mrs. Pitman," he said. "I suppose you are still making the best coffee and doughnuts in the city of Allegheny? Well, what's the trouble in your district? Want an injunction against the river for trespass?"

"The river has brought me a good bit of trouble," I said. "I'm—I'm worried, Mr. Sergeant. I think a woman from my house has been murdered, but I don't know."

"Murdered," he said, and drew up his chair. "Tell me about it."

I told him everything, while he sat back with his eyes half closed, and his fingers beating a tattoo on the arm of his chair.

When I finished he got up and went into an inner room. He came back in a moment.

"I want you to come in and tell that to the chief," he said, and led the way.

All told, I repeated my story three times that afternoon, to the sergeant, to the chief of police, and the third time to both the others and two detectives.

The second time the chief made notes of what I said.

312

"Know this man Ladley?" he asked the others. None of them did, but they all knew of Jennie Brice, and some of them had seen her in the theater.

"Get the theater, Tom," the chief said to one of the detectives.

Luckily, what he learned over the telephone from the theater corroborated my story. Jennie Brice was not in the cast that week, but should have reported that morning (Monday) to rehearse the next week's piece. No message had been received from her, and a substitute had been put in her place.

The chief hung up the receiver and turned to me. "You are sure about the clock, Mrs. Pitman?" he asked. "It was there when they moved up-stairs to the room?"

"Yes, sir."

"You are certain you will not find it on the parlor mantel when the water goes down?"

"The mantels are uncovered now. It is not there."

"You think Ladley has gone for good?"

"Yes, sir."

"He'd be a fool to try to run away, unless—Graves, you'd better get hold of the fellow, and keep him until either the woman is found or a body. The river is falling. In a couple of days we will know if she is around the premises anywhere."

Before I left, I described Jennie Brice for them carefully. Asked what she probably wore, if she had gone away as her husband said, I had no idea; she had a lot of clothes, and dressed a good bit. But I recalled that I had seen, lying on the bed, the black and white dress with the red collar, and they took that down, as well as the brown valise.

The chief rose and opened the door for me himself. "If she actually left town at the time you mention," he said, "she ought not to be hard to find. There are not many trains before seven in the morning, and most of them are locals."

"And—and if she did not, if he—do you think she is in the house—or—or—the cellar?"

"Not unless Ladley is more of a fool than I think he is," he said, smiling. "Personally, I believe she has gone away, as he says she did. But if she hasn't—He probably took the body with him when he said he was getting medicine, and dropped it in the current somewhere. But we must go slow with all this. There's no use shouting 'wolf' yet."

"But—the towel?"

"He may have cut himself, shaving. It *has* been done."

"And the knife?"

He shrugged his shoulders good-naturedly.

"I've seen a perfectly good knife spoiled opening a bottle of pickles."

"But the slippers? And the clock?"

"My good woman, enough shoes and slippers are forgotten in the bottoms of cupboards year after year in flood-time, and are found floating around the streets, to make all the old-clothesmen in town happy. I have seen almost everything floating about, during one of these annual floods."

"I dare say you never saw an onyx clock floating around," I replied a little sharply. I had no sense of humor that day. He stopped smiling at once, and stood tugging at his mustache.

"No," he admitted. "An onyx clock sinks, that's true. That's a very nice little point, that onyx clock. He may be trying to sell it, or perhaps—" He did not finish.

I went back immediately, only stopping at the market to get meat for Mr. Reynolds' supper. It was after half past five and dusk was coming on. I got a boat and was rowed directly home. Peter was not at the foot of the steps. I paid the boatman and let him go, and turned to go up the stairs. Some one was speaking in the hall above.

I have read somewhere that no two voices are exactly alike, just as no two violins ever produce precisely the same sound. I think it is what they call the timbre that is different. I have, for instance, never heard a voice like Mr. Pitman's, although Mr. Harry Lauder's in a phonograph resembles it. And voices have always done for me what odors do for some people, revived forgotten scenes and old memories. But the memory that the voice at the head of the stairs brought back was not very old, although I had forgotten it. I seemed to hear again, all at once, the lapping of the water Sunday morning as it began to come in over the door-sill; the sound of Terry ripping up the parlor carpet, and Mrs. Ladley calling me a she-devil in the next room, in reply to this very voice.

But when I got to the top of the stairs, it was only Mr. Howell, who had brought his visitor to the flood district, and on getting her splashed with the muddy water, had taken her to my house for a towel and a cake of soap.

I lighted the lamp in the hall, and Mr. Howell introduced the girl. She was a pretty girl, slim and young, and she had taken her wetting good-naturedly.

"I know we are intruders, Mrs. Pitman," she said, holding out her hand. "Especially now, when you are in trouble."

"I have told Miss Harvey a little," Mr. Howell said, "and I promised to show her Peter, but he is not here."

I think I had known it was my sister's child from the moment I lighted the lamp. There was something of Alma in her, not Alma's hardness or haughtiness, but Alma's dark blue eyes with black lashes, and Alma's nose. Alma was always the beauty of the family. What with the day's excitement, and seeing Alma's child like this, in my house, I felt things going round and clutched at the stair-rail. Mr. Howell caught me.

"Why, Mrs. Pitman!" he said. "What's the matter?"

I got myself in hand in a moment and smiled at the girl.

"Nothing at all," I said. "Indigestion, most likely. Too much tea the last day or two, and not enough solid food. I've been too anxious to eat."

Lida—for she was that to me at once, although I had never seen her before—Lida was all sympathy and sweetness. She actually asked me to go with her to a restaurant and have a real dinner. I could imagine Alma, had she known! But I excused myself.

"I have to cook something for Mr. Reynolds," I said, "and I'm better now, anyhow, thank you. Mr. Howell, may I speak to you for a moment?"

He followed me along the back hall, which was dusk.

"I have remembered something that I had forgotten, Mr. Howell," I said. "On Sunday morning, the Ladleys had a visitor."

"Yes?"

"They had very few visitors."

"I see."

"I did not see him, but—I heard his voice." Mr. Howell did not move, but I fancied he drew his breath in quickly. "It sounded—it was not by any chance *you*?"

"I? A newspaper man, who goes to bed at three A.M. on Sunday morning, up and about at ten!"

"I didn't say what time it was," I said sharply.

But at that moment Lida called from the front hall.

"I think I hear Peter," she said. "He is shut in somewhere, whining."

We went forward at once. She was right. Peter was scratching at the door of Mr. Ladley's room, although I had left the door closed and Peter in the hall. I let him out, and he crawled to me on three legs, whimpering. Mr. Howell bent over him and felt the fourth.

"Poor little beast!" he said. "His leg is broken!"

He made a splint for the dog, and with Lida helping, they put him to bed in a clothes-basket in my up-stairs kitchen. It was easy to see how things lay with Mr. Howell. He was all eyes for her: he made excuses to touch her hand or her arm—little caressing touches that made her color heighten. And with it all, there was a sort of hopelessness in his manner, as if he knew how far the girl was out of his reach. Knowing Alma and her pride, I knew better than they how hopeless it was.

314

I was not so sure about Lida. I wondered if she was in love with the boy, or only in love with love. She was very young, as I had been. God help her, if, like me, she sacrificed everything, to discover, too late, that she was only in love with love!

CHAPTER V

Mr. Reynolds did not come home to dinner after all. The water had got into the basement at the store, he telephoned, one of the flood-gates in a sewer having leaked, and they were moving some of the departments to an upper floor. I had expected to have him in the house that evening, and now I was left alone again.

But, as it happened, I was not alone. Mr. Graves, one of the city detectives, came at half past six, and went carefully over the Ladleys' room. I showed him the towel and the slipper and the broken knife, and where we had found the knife-blade. He was very non-committal, and left in a half-hour, taking the articles with him in a newspaper.

At seven the door-bell rang. I went down as far as I could on the staircase, and I saw a boat outside the door, with the boatman and a woman in it. I called to them to bring the boat back along the hall, and I had a queer feeling that it might be Mrs. Ladley, and that I'd been making a fool of myself all day for nothing. But it was not Mrs. Ladley.

"Is this number forty-two?" asked the woman, as the boat came back.

"Yes."

"Does Mr. Ladley live here?"

"Yes. But he is not here now."

"Are you Mrs. Pittock?"

"Pitman, yes."

The boat bumped against the stairs, and the woman got out. She was as tall as Mrs. Ladley, and when I saw her in the light from the upper hall, I knew her instantly. It was Temple Hope, the leading woman from the Liberty Theater.

"I would like to talk to you, Mrs. Pitman," she said. "Where can we go?"

I led the way back to my room, and when she had followed me in, she turned and shut the door.

"Now then," she said without any preliminary, "where is Jennie Brice?"

"I don't know, Miss Hope," I answered.

We looked at each other for a minute, and each of us saw what the other suspected.

"He has killed her!" she exclaimed. "She was afraid he would do it, and—he has."

"Killed her and thrown her into the river," I said. "That's what I think, and he'll go free at that. It seems there isn't any murder when there isn't any corpse."

"Nonsense! If he has done that, the river will give her up, eventually."

"The river doesn't always give them up," I retorted. "Not in flood-time, anyhow. Or when they are found it is months later, and you can't prove anything."

She had only a little time, being due at the theater soon, but she sat down and told me the story she told afterward on the stand:

She had known Jennie Brice for years, they having been together in the chorus as long before as *Nadjy*.

"She was married then to a fellow on the vaudeville circuit," Miss Hope said. "He left her about that time, and she took up with Ladley. I don't think they were ever married."

"What!" I said, jumping to my feet, "and they came to a respectable house like this! There's never been a breath of scandal about this house, Miss Hope, and if this comes out I'm ruined."

"Well, perhaps they were married," she said. "Anyhow, they were always quarreling. And when he wasn't playing, it was worse. She used to come to my hotel, and cry her eyes out."

"I knew you were friends," I said. "Almost the last thing she said to me was about the black and white dress of hers you were to borrow for the piece this week."

"Black and white dress! I borrow one of Jennie Brice's dresses!" exclaimed Miss Hope. "I should think not. I have plenty of my own."

That puzzled me; for she had said it, that was sure. And then I remembered that I had not seen the dress in the room that day, and I went in to look for it. It was gone. I came back and told Miss Hope.

"A black and white dress! Did it have a red collar?" she asked.

"Yes."

"Then I remember it. She wore a small black hat with a red quill with that dress. You might look for the hat."

She followed me back to the room and stood in the doorway while I searched. The hat was gone, too.

"Perhaps, after all, he's telling the truth," she said thoughtfully. "Her fur coat isn't in the closet, is it?"

It was gone. It is strange that, all day, I had never thought of looking over her clothes and seeing what was missing. I hadn't known all she had, of course, but I had seen her all winter in her fur coat and admired it. It was a striped fur, brown and gray, and very unusual. But with the coat missing, and a dress and hat gone, it began to look as if I had been making a fool of myself, and stirring up a tempest in a teacup. Miss Hope was as puzzled as I was.

"Anyhow, if he didn't kill her," she said, "it isn't because he did not want to. Only last week she had hysterics in my dressing-room, and said he had threatened to poison her. It was all Mr. Bronson, the business manager, and I could do to quiet her."

She looked at her watch, and exclaimed that she was late, and would have to hurry. I saw her down to her boat. The river had been falling rapidly for the last hour or two, and I heard the boat scrape as it went over the door-sill. I did not know whether to be glad that the water was going down and I could live like a Christian again, or to be sorry, for fear of what we might find in the mud that was always left.

Peter was lying where I had put him, on a folded blanket laid in a clothes-basket. I went back to him, and sat down beside the basket.

"Peter!" I said. "Poor old Peter! Who did this to you? Who hurt you?" He looked at me and whined, as if he wanted to tell me, if only he could.

"Was it Mr. Ladley?" I asked, and the poor thing cowered close to his bed and shivered. I wondered if it had been he, and, if it had, why he had come back. Perhaps he had remembered the towel. Perhaps he would come again and spend the night there. I was like Peter: I cowered and shivered at the very thought.

At nine o'clock I heard a boat at the door. It had stuck there, and its occupant was scolding furiously at the boatman. Soon after I heard splashing, and I knew that whoever it was was wading back to the stairs through the foot and a half or so of water still in the hall. I ran back to my room and locked myself in, and then stood, armed with the stove-lid-lifter, in case it should be Ladley and he should break the door in.

The steps came up the stairs, and Peter barked furiously. It seemed to me that this was to be my end, killed like a rat in a trap and thrown out the window, to float, like my kitchen chair, into Mollie Maguire's kitchen, or to be found lying in the ooze of the yard after the river had gone down.

The steps hesitated at the top of the stairs, and turned back along the hall. Peter redoubled his noise; he never barked for Mr. Reynolds or the Ladleys. I stood still, hardly able to breathe. The door was thin, and the lock loose: one good blow, and—

The door-knob turned, and I screamed. I recall that the light turned black, and that is all I *do* remember, until I came to, a half-hour later, and saw Mr. Holcombe stooping over me. The door, with the lock broken, was standing open. I tried to move, and then I saw that my feet were propped up on the edge of Peter's basket.

"Better leave them up." Mr. Holcombe said. "It sends the blood back to the head. Half the damfool people in the world stick a pillow under a fainting woman's shoulders. How are you now?"

"All right," I said feebly. "I thought you were Mr. Ladley."

He helped me up, and I sat in a chair and tried to keep my lips from shaking. And then I saw that Mr. Holcombe had brought a suit case with him, and had set it inside the door.

"Ladley is safe, until he gets bail, anyhow," he said. "They picked him up as he was boarding a Pennsylvania train bound east."

"For murder?" I asked.

"As a suspicious character," he replied grimly. "That does as well as anything for a time." He sat down opposite me, and looked at me intently.

"Mrs. Pitman," he said, "did you ever hear the story of the horse that wandered out of a village and could not be found?"

I shook my head.

"Well, the best wit of the village failed to locate the horse. But one day the village idiot walked into town, leading the missing animal by the bridle. When they asked him how he had done it, he said: 'Well, I just thought what I'd do if I was a horse, and then I went and did it.'"

"I see," I said, humoring him.

"You *don't* see. Now, what are we trying to do?"

"We're trying to find a body. Do you intend to become a corpse?"

He leaned over and tapped on the table between us. "We are trying to prove a crime. I intend for the time to be the criminal."

He looked so curious, bent forward and glaring at me from under his bushy eyebrows, with his shoes on his knee—for he had taken them off to wade to the stairs—and his trousers rolled to his knees, that I wondered if he was entirely sane. But Mr. Holcombe, eccentric as he might be, was sane enough.

"Not *really* a criminal!"

"As really as lies in me. Listen, Mrs. Pitman. I want to put myself in Ladley's place for a day or two, live as he lived, do what he did, even think as he thought, if I can. I am going to sleep in his room to-night, with your permission."

I could not see any reason for objecting, although I thought it silly and useless. I led the way to the front room, Mr. Holcombe following with his shoes and suit case. I lighted a lamp, and he stood looking around him.

"I see you have been here since we left this afternoon," he said.

"Twice," I replied. "First with Mr. Graves, and later—"

The words died on my tongue. Some one had been in the room since my last visit there.

"He has been here!" I gasped. "I left the room in tolerable order. Look at it!"

"When were you here last?"

"At seven-thirty, or thereabouts."

"Where were you between seven-thirty and eight-thirty?"

"In the kitchen with Peter." I told him then about the dog, and about finding him shut in the room.

The wash-stand was pulled out. The sheets of Mr. Ladley's manuscript, usually an orderly pile, were half on the floor. The bed coverings had been jerked off and flung over the back of a chair.

Peter, imprisoned, *might* have moved the wash-stand and upset the manuscript—Peter had never put the bed-clothing over the chair, or broken his own leg.

"Humph!" he said, and getting out his note-book, he made an exact memorandum of what I had told him, and of the condition of the room. That done, he turned to me.

"Mrs. Pitman," he said, "I'll thank you to call me Mr. Ladley for the next day or so. I am an actor out of employment, forty-one years of age, short, stout, and bald, married to a woman I would like to be quit of, and I am writing myself a play in which the Shuberts intend to star me, or in which I intend the Shuberts to star me."

"Very well, Mr. Ladley," I said, trying to enter into the spirit of the thing, and, God knows, seeing no humor in it. "Then you'll like your soda from the ice-box?"

"Soda? For what?"

"For your whisky and soda, before you go to bed, sir."

"Oh, certainly, yes. Bring the soda. And—just a moment, Mrs. Pitman: Mr. Holcombe is a total abstainer, and has always been so. It is Ladley, not Holcombe, who takes this abominable stuff."

I said I quite understood, but that Mr. Ladley could skip a night, if he so wished. But the little gentleman would not hear to it, and when I brought the soda, poured himself a double portion. He stood looking at it, with his face screwed up, as if the very odor revolted him.

"The chances are," he said, "that Ladley—that I—having a nasty piece of work to do during the night, would—will take a larger drink than usual." He raised the glass, only to put it down. "Don't forget," he said, "to put a large knife where you left the one last night. I'm sorry the water has gone down, but I shall imagine it still at the seventh step. Good night, Mrs. Pitman."

"Good night, Mr. Ladley," I said, smiling, "and remember, you are three weeks in arrears with your board."

His eyes twinkled through his spectacles. "I shall imagine it paid," he said.

I went out, and I heard him close the door behind me. Then, through the door, I heard a great sputtering and coughing, and I knew he had got the whisky down somehow. I put the knife out, as he had asked me to, and went to bed. I was ready to drop. Not even the knowledge that an imaginary Mr. Ladley was about to commit an imaginary crime in the house that night could keep me awake.

Mr. Reynolds came in at eleven o'clock. I was roused when he banged his door. That was all I knew until morning. The sun on my face wakened me. Peter, in his basket, lifted his head as I moved, and thumped his tail against his pillow in greeting. I put on a wrapper, and called Mr. Reynolds by knocking at his door. Then I went on to the front room. The door was closed, and some one beyond was groaning. My heart stood still, and then raced on. I opened the door and looked in.

Mr. Holcombe was on the bed, fully dressed. He had a wet towel tied around his head, and his face looked swollen and puffy. He opened one eye and looked at me.

"What a night!" he groaned.

"What happened! What did you find?"

He groaned again. "Find!" he said. "Nothing, except that there was something wrong with that whisky. It poisoned me. I haven't been out of the house!"

So for that day, at least, Mr. Ladley became Mr. Holcombe again, and as such accepted ice in quantities, a mustard plaster over his stomach, and considerable nursing. By evening he was better, but although he clearly intended to stay on, he said nothing about changing his identity again, and I was glad enough. The very name of Ladley was horrible to me.

The river went down almost entirely that day, although there was still considerable water in the cellars. It takes time to get rid of that. The lower floors showed nothing suspicious. The papers were ruined, of course, the doors warped and sprung, and the floors coated with mud and debris. Terry came in the afternoon, and together we hung the dining-room rug out to dry in the sun.

As I was coming in, I looked over at the Maguire yard. Molly Maguire was there, and all her children around her, gaping. Molly was hanging out to dry a sodden fur coat, that had once been striped, brown and gray.

I went over after breakfast and claimed the coat as belonging to Mrs. Ladley. But she refused to give it up. There is a sort of unwritten law concerning the salvage of flood articles, and I had to leave the coat, as I had my kitchen chair. But it was Mrs. Ladley's, beyond a doubt.

I shuddered when I thought how it had probably got into the water. And yet it was curious, too, for if she had had it on, how did it get loose to go floating around Molly Maguire's yard? And if she had not worn it, how did it get in the water?

CHAPTER VI

The newspapers were full of the Ladley case, with its curious solution and many surprises. It was considered unique in many ways. Mr. Pitman had always read all the murder trials, and used to talk about the *corpus delicti* and writs of *habeas corpus*—*corpus* being the legal way, I believe, of spelling corpse. But I came out of the Ladley trial—for it came to trial ultimately—with only one point of law that I was sure of: that was, that it is mighty hard to prove a man a murderer unless you can show what he killed.

And that was the weakness in the Ladley case. There was a body, but it could not be identified.

The police held Mr. Ladley for a day or two, and then, nothing appearing, they let him go. Mr. Holcombe, who was still occupying the second floor front, almost wept with rage and despair when he read the news in the papers. He was still working on the case, in his curious way, wandering along the wharves at night, and writing letters all over the country to learn about Philip Ladley's previous life, and his wife's. But he did not seem to get anywhere.

The newspapers had been full of the Jennie Brice disappearance. For disappearance it proved to be. So far as could be learned, she had not left the city that night, or since, and as she was a striking-looking woman, very blond, as I have said, with a full voice and a languid manner, she could hardly have taken refuge anywhere without being discovered. The morning after her disappearance a young woman, tall like Jennie Brice and fair, had been seen in the Union Station. But as she was accompanied by a young man, who bought her magazines and papers, and bade her an excited farewell, sending his love to various members of a family, and promising to feed the canary, this was not seriously considered. A sort of general alarm went over the country. When she was younger she had been pretty well known at the Broadway theaters in New York. One way or another, the Liberty Theater got a lot of free advertising from the case, and I believe Miss Hope's salary was raised.

The police communicated with Jennie Brice's people—she had a sister in Olean, New York, but she had not heard from her. The sister wrote—I heard later—that Jennie had been unhappy with Philip Ladley, and afraid he would kill her. And Miss Hope told the same story. But—there was no *corpus*, as the lawyers say, and finally the police had to free Mr. Ladley.

Beyond making an attempt to get bail, and failing, he had done nothing. Asked about his wife, he merely shrugged his shoulders and said she had left him, and would turn up all right. He was unconcerned: smoked cigarettes all day, ate and slept well, and looked better since he had had nothing to drink. And two or three days after the arrest, he sent for the manuscript of his play.

Mr. Howell came for it on the Thursday of that week.

I was on my knees scrubbing the parlor floor, when he rang the bell. I let him in, and it seemed to me that he looked tired and pale.

"Well, Mrs. Pitman," he said, smiling, "what did you find in the cellar when the water went down?"

"I'm glad to say that I didn't find what I feared, Mr. Howell."

"Not even the onyx clock?"

"Not even the clock," I replied. "And I feel as if I'd lost a friend. A clock is a lot of company."

"Do you know what I think?" he said, looking at me closely. "I think you put that clock away yourself, in the excitement, and have forgotten all about it."

"Nonsense."

"Think hard." He was very much in earnest. "You knew the water was rising and the Ladleys would have to be moved up to the second floor front, where the clock stood. You went in there and looked around to see if the room was ready, and you saw the clock. And knowing that the Ladleys quarreled now and then, and were apt to throw things—"

"Nothing but a soap-dish, and that only once."

"—you took the clock to the attic and put it, say, in an old trunk."

"I did nothing of the sort. I went in, as you say, and I put up an old splasher, because of the way he throws ink about. Then I wound the clock, put the key under it, and went out."

"And the key is gone, too!" he said thoughtfully. "I wish I could find that clock, Mrs. Pitman."

"So do I."

"Ladley went out Sunday afternoon about three, didn't he—and got back at five?"

I turned and looked at him. "Yes, Mr. Howell," I said. "Perhaps *you* know something about that."

"I?" He changed color. Twenty years of dunning boarders has made me pretty sharp at reading faces, and he looked as uncomfortable as if he owed me money. "I!" I knew then that I had been right about the voice. It had been his.

"You!" I retorted. "You were here Sunday morning and spent some time with the Ladleys. I am the old she-devil. I notice you didn't tell your friend, Mr. Holcombe, about having been here on Sunday."

He was quick to recover. "I'll tell you all about it, Mrs. Pitman," he said smilingly. "You see, all my life, I have wished for an onyx clock. It has been my ambition, my *Great Desire*. Leaving the house that Sunday morning, and hearing the ticking of the clock up-stairs, I recognized that it was an *onyx* clock, clambered from my boat through an upper window, and so reached it. The clock showed fight, but after stunning it with a chair—"

"Exactly!" I said. "Then the thing Mrs. Ladley said she would not do was probably to wind the clock?"

He dropped his bantering manner at once. "Mrs. Pitman," he said, "I don't know what you heard or did not hear. But I want you to give me a little time before you tell anybody that I was here that Sunday morning. And, in return, I'll find your clock."

I hesitated, but however put out he was, he didn't look like a criminal. Besides, he was a friend of my niece's, and blood is thicker even than flood-water.

"There was nothing wrong about my being here," he went on, "but—I don't want it known. Don't spoil a good story, Mrs. Pitman."

I did not quite understand that, although those who followed the trial carefully may do so. Poor Mr. Howell! I am sure he believed that it was only a good story. He got the description of my onyx clock and wrote it down, and I gave him the manuscript for Mr. Ladley. That was the last I saw of him for some time.

That Thursday proved to be an exciting day. For late in the afternoon Terry, digging the mud out of the cellar, came across my missing gray false front near the coal vault, and brought it up, grinning. And just before six, Mr. Graves, the detective, rang the bell and then let himself in. I found him in the lower hall, looking around.

"Well, Mrs. Pitman," he said, "has our friend come back yet?"

"She was no friend of mine."

"Not *she*. Ladley. He'll be out this evening, and he'll probably be around for his clothes."

I felt my knees waver, as they always did when he was spoken of.

"He may want to stay here," said Mr. Graves. "In fact, I think that's just what he *will* want."

"Not here," I protested. "The very thought of him makes me quake."

"If he comes here, better take him in. I want to know where he is."

I tried to say that I wouldn't have him, but the old habit of the ward asserted itself. From taking a bottle of beer or a slice of pie, to telling one where one might or might not live, the police were autocrats in that neighborhood. And, respectable woman that I am, my neighbors' fears of the front office have infected me.

"All right, Mr. Graves," I said.

He pushed the parlor door open and looked in, whistling. "This is the place, isn't it?"

"Yes. But it was up-stairs that he—"

"I see. Tall woman, Mrs. Ladley?"

"Tall and blond. Very airy in her manner."

He nodded and still stood looking in and whistling. "Never heard her speak of a town named Horner, did you?"

"Horner? No."

"I see." He turned and wandered out again into the hall, still whistling. At the door, however, he stopped and turned. "Look anything like this?" he asked, and held out one of his hands, with a small kodak picture on the palm.

It was a snap-shot of a children's frolic in a village street, with some onlookers in the background. Around one of the heads had been drawn a circle in pencil. I took it to the gas-jet and looked at it closely. It was a tall woman with a hat on, not unlike Jennie Brice. She was looking over the crowd, and I could see only her face, and that in shadow. I shook my head.

"I thought not," he said. "We have a lot of stage pictures of her, but what with false hair and their being retouched beyond recognition, they don't amount to much." He started out, and stopped on the door-step to light a cigar.

"Take him on if he comes," he said. "And keep your eyes open. Feed him well, and he won't kill you!"

I had plenty to think of when I was cooking Mr. Reynolds' supper: the chance that I might have Mr. Ladley again, and the woman at Horner. For it had come to me like a flash, as Mr. Graves left, that the "Horn—" on the paper slip might have been "Horner."

CHAPTER VII

After all, there was nothing sensational about Mr. Ladley's return. He came at eight o'clock that night, fresh-shaved and with his hair cut, and, although he had a latch-key, he rang the door-bell. I knew his ring, and I thought it no harm to carry an old razor of Mr. Pitman's with the blade open and folded back on the handle, the way the colored people use them, in my left hand.

But I saw at once that he meant no mischief.

"Good evening," he said, and put out his hand. I jumped back, until I saw there was nothing in it and that he only meant to shake hands. I didn't do it; I might have to take him in, and make his bed, and cook his meals, but I did not have to shake hands with him.

"You, too!" he said, looking at me with what I suppose he meant to be a reproachful look. But he could no more put an expression of that sort in his eyes than a fish could. "I suppose, then, there is no use asking if I may have my old room? The front room. I won't need two."

I didn't want him, and he must have seen it. But I took him. "You may have it, as far as I'm concerned," I said. "But you'll have to let the paper-hanger in to-morrow."

"Assuredly." He came into the hall and stood looking around him, and I fancied he drew a breath of relief. "It isn't much yet," he said, "but it's better to look at than six feet of muddy water."

"Or than stone walls," I said.

He looked at me and smiled. "Or than stone walls," he repeated, bowing, and went into his room.

So I had him again, and if I gave him only the dull knives, and locked up the bread-knife the moment I had finished with it, who can blame me? I took all the precaution I could think of: had Terry put an extra bolt on every door, and hid the rat poison and the carbolic acid in the cellar.

Peter would not go near him. He hobbled around on his three legs, with the splint beating a sort of tattoo on the floor, but he stayed back in the kitchen with me, or in the yard.

It was Sunday night or early Monday morning that Jennie Brice disappeared. On Thursday evening, her husband came back. On Friday the body of a woman was washed ashore at Beaver, but turned out to be that of a stewardess who had fallen overboard from one of the Cincinnati packets. Mr. Ladley himself showed me the article in the morning paper, when I took in his breakfast.

"Public hysteria has killed a man before this," he said, when I had read it. "Suppose that woman had been mangled, or the screw of the steamer had cut her head off! How many people do you suppose would have been willing to swear that it was my—was Mrs. Ladley?"

"Even without a head, I should know Mrs. Ladley," I retorted.

He shrugged his shoulders. "Let's trust she's still alive, for my sake," he said. "But I'm glad, anyhow, that this woman had a head. You'll allow me to be glad, won't you?"

"You can be anything you want, as far as I'm concerned," I snapped, and went out.

Mr. Holcombe still retained the second-story front room. I think, although he said nothing more about it, that he was still "playing horse." He wrote a good bit at the wash-stand, and, from the loose sheets of manuscript he left, I believe actually tried to begin a play. But mostly he wandered along the water-front, or stood on one or another of the bridges, looking at the water and thinking. It is certain that he tried to keep in the part by smoking cigarettes, but he hated them, and usually ended by throwing the cigarette away and lighting an old pipe he carried.

On that Thursday evening he came home and sat down to supper with Mr. Reynolds. He ate little and seemed much excited. The talk ran on crime, as it always did when he was around, and Mr. Holcombe quoted Spencer a great deal—Herbert Spencer. Mr. Reynolds was impressed, not knowing much beyond silks and the National League.

"Spencer," Mr. Holcombe would say—"Spencer shows that every occurrence is the inevitable result of what has gone before, and carries in its train an equally inevitable series of results. Try to interrupt this chain in the smallest degree, and what follows? Chaos, my dear sir, chaos."

"We see that at the store," Mr. Reynolds would say. "Accustom a lot of women to a silk sale on Fridays and then make it toothbrushes. That's chaos, all right."

Well, Mr. Holcombe came in that night about ten o'clock, and I told him Ladley was back. He was almost wild with excitement; wanted to have the back parlor, so he could watch him through the keyhole, and was terribly upset when I told him there was no keyhole, that the door fastened with a thumb bolt. On learning that the room was to be papered the next morning, he grew calmer, however, and got the paper-hanger's address from me. He went out just after that.

Friday, as I say, was very quiet. Mr. Ladley moved to the back parlor to let the paper-hanger in the front room, smoked and fussed with his papers all day, and Mr. Holcombe stayed in his room, which was unusual. In the afternoon Molly Maguire put on the striped fur coat and went out, going slowly past the house so that I would be sure to see her. Beyond banging the window down, I gave her no satisfaction.

At four o'clock Mr. Holcombe came to my kitchen, rubbing his hands together. He had a pasteboard tube in his hand about a foot long, with an arrangement of small mirrors in it. He said it was modeled after the something or other that is used on a submarine, and that he and the paper-hanger had fixed a place for it between his floor and the ceiling of Mr. Ladley's room, so that the chandelier would hide it from below. He thought he could watch Mr. Ladley through it; and as it turned out, he could.

"I want to find his weak moment," he said excitedly. "I want to know what he does when the door is closed and he can take off his mask. And I want to know if he sleeps with a light."

"If he does," I replied, "I hope you'll let me know, Mr. Holcombe. The gas bills are a horror to me as it is. I think he kept it on all last night. I turned off all the other lights and went to the cellar. The meter was going around."

"Fine!" he said. "Every murderer fears the dark. And our friend of the parlor bedroom is a murderer, Mrs. Pitman. Whether he hangs or not, he's a murderer."

The mirror affair, which Mr. Holcombe called a periscope, was put in that day and worked amazingly well. I went with him to try it out, and I distinctly saw the paper-hanger take a cigarette from Mr. Ladley's case and put it in his pocket. Just after that, Mr. Ladley sauntered into the room and looked at the new paper. I could both see and hear him. It was rather weird.

"God, what a wall-paper!" he said.

CHAPTER VIII

That was Friday afternoon. All that evening, and most of Saturday and Sunday, Mr. Holcombe sat on the floor, with his eye to the reflecting mirror and his note-book beside him. I have it before me.

On the first page is the "dog meat—two dollars" entry. On the next, the description of what occurred on Sunday night, March fourth, and Monday morning, the fifth. Following that came a sketch, made with a carbon sheet, of the torn paper found behind the wash-stand:

And then came the entries for Friday, Saturday and Sunday. Friday evening:

6:30—Eating hearty supper.

7:00—Lights cigarette and paces floor. Notice that when Mrs. P. knocks, he goes to desk and pretends to be writing.

8:00—Is examining book. Looks like a railway guide.

8:30—It is a steamship guide.

8:45—Tailor's boy brings box. Gives boy fifty cents. Query. Where does he get money, now that J.B. is gone?

9:00—Tries on new suit, brown.

9:30—Has been spending a quarter of an hour on his knees looking behind furniture and examining base-board.

10:00—He has the key to the onyx clock. Has hidden it twice, once up the chimney flue, once behind base-board.

10:15—He has just thrown key or similar small article outside window into yard.

11:00—Has gone to bed. Light burning. Shall sleep here on floor.

11:30—He can not sleep. Is up walking the floor and smoking.

2:00 A.M.—Saturday. Disturbance below. He had had nightmare and was calling "Jennie!" He got up, took a drink, and is now reading.

8:00 A.M.—Must have slept. He is shaving.

12:00 M.—Nothing this morning. He wrote for four hours, sometimes reading aloud what he had written.

2:00 P.M.—He has a visitor, a man. Can not hear all—word now and then. "Llewellyn is the very man." "Devil of a risk—" "We'll see you through." "Lost the slip—" "Didn't go to the hotel. She went to a private house." "Eliza Shaeffer."

Who went to a private house? Jennie Brice?

2:30—Can not hear. Are whispering. The visitor has given Ladley roll of bills.

4:00—Followed the visitor, a tall man with a pointed beard. He went to the Liberty Theater. Found it was Bronson, business manager there. Who is Llewellyn, and who is Eliza Shaeffer?

4:15—Had Mrs. P. bring telephone book: six Llewellyns in the book; no Eliza Shaeffer. Ladley appears more cheerful since Bronson's visit. He has bought all the evening papers and is searching for something. Has not found it.

7:00—Ate well. Have asked Mrs. P. to take my place here, while I interview the six Llewellyns.

11:00—Mrs. P. reports a quiet evening. He read and smoked. Has gone to bed. Light burning. Saw five Llewellyns. None of them knew Bronson or Ladley. Sixth—a lawyer—out at revival meeting. Went to the church and walked home with him. He knows something. Acknowledged he knew Bronson. Had met Ladley. Did not believe Mrs. Ladley dead. Regretted I had not been to the meeting. Good sermon. Asked me for a dollar for missions.

9:00 A.M.—Sunday. Ladley in bad shape. Apparently been drinking all night. Can not eat. Sent out early for papers, and has searched them all. Found entry on second page, stared at it, then flung the paper away. Have sent out for same paper.

10:00 A.M.—Paper says: "Body of woman washed ashore yesterday at Sewickley. Much mutilated by flood débris." Ladley in bed, staring at ceiling. Wonder if he sees tube? He is ghastly.

That is the last entry in the note-book for that day. Mr. Holcombe called me in great excitement shortly after ten and showed me the item. Neither of us doubted for a moment that it was Jennie Brice who had been found. He started for Sewickley that same afternoon, and he probably communicated with the police before he left. For once or twice I saw Mr. Graves, the detective, sauntering past the house.

Mr. Ladley ate no dinner. He went out at four, and I had Mr. Reynolds follow him. But they were both back in a half-hour. Mr. Reynolds reported that Mr. Ladley had bought some headache tablets and some bromide powders to make him sleep.

Mr. Holcombe came back that evening. He thought the body was that of Jennie Brice, but the head was gone. He was much depressed, and did not immediately go back to the periscope. I asked if the head had been cut off or taken off by a steamer; he was afraid the latter, as a hand was gone, too.

It was about eleven o'clock that night that the door-bell rang. It was Mr. Graves, with a small man behind him. I knew the man; he lived in a shanty-boat not far from my house—a curious affair with shelves full of dishes and tinware. In the spring he would be towed up the Monongahela a hundred miles or so and float down, tying up at different landings and selling his wares. Timothy Senft was his name. We called him Tim.

Mr. Graves motioned me to be quiet. Both of us knew that behind the parlor door Ladley was probably listening.

"Sorry to get you up, Mrs. Pitman," said Mr. Graves, "but this man says he has bought beer here to-day. That won't do, Mrs. Pitman."

"Beer! I haven't such a thing in the house. Come in and look," I snapped. And the two of them went back to the kitchen.

"Now," said Mr. Graves, when I had shut the door, "where's the dog's-meat man?"

"Up-stairs."

"Bring him quietly."

I called Mr. Holcombe, and he came eagerly, note-book and all. "Ah!" he said, when he saw Tim. "So you've turned up!"

"Yes, sir."

"It seems, Mr. Dog's—Mr. Holcombe," said Mr. Graves, "that you are right, partly, anyhow. Tim here *did* help a man with a boat that night—"

"Threw him a rope, sir," Tim broke in. "He'd got out in the current, and what with the ice, and his not knowing much about a boat, he'd have kept on to New Orleans if I hadn't caught him—or Kingdom Come."

"Exactly. And what time did you say this was?"

"Between three and four last Sunday night—or Monday morning. He said he couldn't sleep and went out in a boat, meaning to keep in close to shore. But he got drawn out in the current."

"Where did you see him first?"

"By the Ninth Street bridge."

"Did you hail him?"

"He saw my light and hailed me. I was making fast to a coal barge after one of my ropes had busted."

"You threw the line to him there?"

"No, sir. He tried to work in to shore. I ran along River Avenue to below the Sixth Street bridge. He got pretty close in there and I threw him a rope. He was about done up."

"Would you know him again?"

"Yes, sir. He gave me five dollars, and said to say nothing about it. He didn't want anybody to know he had been such a fool."

They took him quietly up stairs then and let him look through the periscope. *He identified Mr. Ladley absolutely.*

When Tim and Mr. Graves had gone, Mr. Holcombe and I were left alone in the kitchen. Mr. Holcombe leaned over and patted Peter as he lay in his basket.

"We've got him, old boy," he said. "The chain is just about complete. He'll never kick you again."

But Mr. Holcombe was wrong, not about kicking Peter,—although I don't believe Mr. Ladley ever did that again,—but in thinking we had him.

I washed that next morning, Monday, but all the time I was rubbing and starching and hanging out, my mind was with Jennie Brice. The sight of Molly Maguire, next door, at the window, rubbing and brushing at the fur coat, only made things worse.

At noon when the Maguire youngsters came home from school, I bribed Tommy, the youngest, into the kitchen, with the promise of a doughnut.

"I see your mother has a new fur coat," I said, with the plate of doughnuts just beyond his reach.

"Yes'm."

"She didn't buy it?"

"She didn't buy it. Say, Mrs. Pitman, gimme that doughnut."

"Oh, so the coat washed in!"

"No'm. Pap found it, down by the Point, on a cake of ice. He thought it was a dog, and rowed out for it."

Well, I hadn't wanted the coat, as far as that goes; I'd managed well enough without furs for twenty years or more. But it was a satisfaction to know that it had not floated into Mrs. Maguire's kitchen and spread itself at her feet, as one may say. However, that was not the question, after all. The real issue was that if it was Jennie Brice's coat, and was found across the river on a cake of ice, then one of two things was certain: either Jennie Brice's body wrapped in the coat had been thrown into the water, out in the current, or she herself, hoping to incriminate her husband, had flung her coat into the river.

I told Mr. Holcombe, and he interviewed Joe Maguire that afternoon. The upshot of it was that Tommy had been correctly informed. Joe had witnesses who had lined up to see him rescue a dog, and had beheld his return in triumph with a wet and soggy fur coat. At three o'clock Mrs. Maguire, instructed by Mr. Graves, brought the coat to me for identification, turning it about for my inspection, but refusing to take her hands off it.

"If her husband says to me that he wants it back, well and good," she said, "but I don't give it up to nobody but him. Some folks I know of would be glad enough to have it."

I was certain it was Jennie Brice's coat, but the maker's name had been ripped out. With Molly holding one arm and I the other, we took it to Mr. Ladley's door and knocked. He opened it, grumbling.

"I have asked you not to interrupt me," he said, with his pen in his hand. His eyes fell on the coat. "What's that?" he asked, changing color.

"I think it's Mrs. Ladley's fur coat," I said.

He stood there looking at it and thinking. Then: "It can't be hers," he said. "She wore hers when she went away."

"Perhaps she dropped it in the water."

He looked at me and smiled. "And why would she do that?" he asked mockingly. "Was it out of fashion?"

"That's Mrs. Ladley's coat," I persisted, but Molly Maguire jerked it from me and started away. He stood there looking at me and smiling in his nasty way.

"This excitement is telling on you, Mrs. Pitman," he said coolly. "You're too emotional for detective work." Then he went in and shut the door.

When I went down-stairs, Molly Maguire was waiting in the kitchen, and had the audacity to ask me if I thought the coat needed a new lining!

It was on Monday evening that the strangest event in years happened to me. I went to my sister's house! And the fact that I was admitted at a side entrance made it even stranger. It happened in this way:

Supper was over, and I was cleaning up, when an automobile came to the door. It was Alma's car. The chauffeur gave me a note:

"DEAR MRS PITMAN—I am not at all well, and very anxious. Will
you come to see me at once? My mother is out to dinner, and I am
alone. The car will bring you. Cordially,
"LIDA HARVEY."

I put on my best dress at once and got into the limousine. Half the neighborhood was out watching. I leaned back in the upholstered seat, fairly quivering with excitement. This was Alma's car; that was Alma's card-case; the little clock had her monogram on it. Even the flowers in the flower holder, yellow tulips, reminded me of Alma—a trifle showy, but good to look at! And I was going to her house!

I was not taken to the main entrance, but to a side door. The queer dream-like feeling was still there. In this back hall, relegated from the more conspicuous part of the house, there were even pieces of furniture from the old home, and my father's picture, in an oval gilt frame, hung over my head. I had not seen a picture of him for twenty years. I went over and touched it gently.

"Father, father!" I said.

Under it was the tall hall chair that I had climbed over as a child, and had stood on many times, to see myself in the mirror above. The chair was newly finished and looked the better for its age. I glanced in the old glass. The chair had stood time better than I. I was a middle-aged woman, lined with poverty and care, shabby, prematurely gray, a little hard. I had thought my father an old man when that picture was taken, and now I was even older. "Father!" I whispered again, and fell to crying in the dimly lighted hall.

Lida sent for me at once. I had only time to dry my eyes and straighten my hat. Had I met Alma on the stairs, I would have passed her without a word. She would not have known me. But I saw no one.

Lida was in bed. She was lying there with a rose-shaded lamp beside her, and a great bowl of spring flowers on a little stand at her elbow. She sat up when I went in, and had a maid place a chair for me beside the bed. She looked very childish, with her hair in a braid on the pillow, and her slim young arms and throat bare.

"I'm so glad you came!" she said, and would not be satisfied until the light was just right for my eyes, and my coat unfastened and thrown open.

"I'm not really ill," she informed me. "I'm—I'm just tired and nervous, and—and unhappy, Mrs. Pitman."

"I am sorry," I said. I wanted to lean over and pat her hand, to draw the covers around her and mother her a little,—I had had no one to mother for so long,—but I could not. She would have thought it queer and presumptuous—or no, not that. She was too sweet to have thought that.

"Mrs. Pitman," she said suddenly, "*who was* this Jennie Brice?"

"She was an actress. She and her husband lived at my house."

"Was she—was she beautiful?"

"Well," I said slowly, "I never thought of that. She was handsome, in a large way."

"Was she young?"

"Yes. Twenty-eight or so."

"That isn't very young," she said, looking relieved. "But I don't think men like very young women. Do you?"

"I know one who does," I said, smiling. But she sat up in bed suddenly and looked at me with her clear childish eyes.

"I don't want him to like me!" she flashed. "I—I want him to hate me."

"Tut, tut! You want nothing of the sort."

"Mrs. Pitman," she said, "I sent for you because I'm nearly crazy. Mr. Howell was a friend of that woman. He has acted like a maniac since she disappeared. He doesn't come to see me, he has given up his work on the paper, and I saw him to-day on the street—he looks like a ghost."

That put me to thinking.

"He might have been a friend," I admitted. "Although, as far as I know, he was never at the house but once, and then he saw both of them."

"When was that?"

"Sunday morning, the day before she disappeared. They were arguing something."

She was looking at me attentively. "You know more than you are telling me, Mrs. Pitman," she said. "You—do you think Jennie Brice is dead, and that Mr. Howell knows—who did it?"

"I think she is dead, and I think possibly Mr. Howell suspects who did it. He does not *know*, or he would have told the police."

"You do not think he was—was in love with Jennie Brice, do you?"

"I'm certain of that," I said. "He is very much in love with a foolish girl, who ought to have more faith in him than she has."

She colored a little, and smiled at that, but the next moment she was sitting forward, tense and questioning again.

"If that is true, Mrs. Pitman," she said, "who was the veiled woman he met that Monday morning at daylight, and took across the bridge to Pittsburgh? I believe it was Jennie Brice. If it was not, who was it?"

"I don't believe he took any woman across the bridge at that hour. Who says he did?"

"Uncle Jim saw him. He had been playing cards all night at one of the clubs, and was walking home. He says he met Mr. Howell face to face, and spoke to him. The woman was tall and veiled. Uncle Jim sent for him, a day or two later, and he refused to explain. Then they forbade him the house. Mama objected to him, anyhow, and he only came on sufferance. He is a college man of good family, but without any money at all save what he earns.. And now—"

I had had some young newspaper men with me, and I knew what they got. They were nice boys, but they made fifteen dollars a week. I'm afraid I smiled a little as I looked around the room, with its gray grass-cloth walls, its toilet-table spread with ivory and gold, and the maid in attendance in her black dress and white apron, collar and cuffs. Even the little nightgown Lida was wearing would have taken a week's salary or more. She saw my smile.

"It was to be his chance," she said. "If he made good, he was to have something better. My Uncle Jim owns the paper, and he promised me to help him. But—"

So Jim was running a newspaper! That was a curious career for Jim to choose. Jim, who was twice expelled from school, and who could never write a letter without a dictionary beside him! I had a pang when I heard his name again, after all the years. For I had written to Jim from Oklahoma, after Mr. Pitman died, asking for money to bury him, and had never even had a reply.

"And you haven't seen him since?"

"Once. I—didn't hear from him, and I called him up. We—we met in the park. He said everything was all right, but he couldn't tell me just then. The next day he resigned from the paper and went away. Mrs. Pitman, it's driving me crazy! For they have found a body, and they think it is hers. If it is, and he was with her—"

"Don't be a foolish girl," I protested. "If he was with Jennie Brice, she is still living, and if he was *not* with Jennie Brice—"

"If it was *not* Jennie Brice, then I have a right to know who it was," she declared. "He was not like himself when I met him. He said such queer things: he talked about an onyx clock, and said he had been made a fool of, and that no matter what came out, I was always to remember that he had done what he did for the best, and that—that he cared for me more than for anything in this world or the next."

"That wasn't so foolish!" I couldn't help it; I leaned over and drew her nightgown up over her bare white shoulder. "You won't help anything or anybody by taking cold, my dear," I said. "Call your maid and have her put a dressing-gown around you."

I left soon after. There was little I could do. But I comforted her as best I could, and said good night. My heart was heavy as I went down the stairs. For, twist things as I might, it was clear that in some way the Howell boy was mixed up in the Brice case. Poor little troubled Lida! Poor distracted boy!

I had a curious experience down-stairs. I had reached the foot of the staircase and was turning to go back and along the hall to the side entrance, when I came face to face with Isaac, the old colored man who had driven the family carriage when I was a child, and whom I had seen, at intervals since I came back, pottering around Alma's house. The old man was bent and feeble; he came slowly down the hall, with a bunch of keys in his hand. I had seen him do the same thing many times.

He stopped when he saw me, and I shrank back from the light, but he had seen me. "Miss Bess!" he said. "Foh Gawd's sake, Miss Bess!"

"You are making a mistake, my friend," I said, quivering. "I am not 'Miss Bess'!"

He came close to me and stared into my face. And from that he looked at my cloth gloves, at my coat, and he shook his white head. "I sure thought you was Miss Bess," he said, and made no further effort to detain me. He led the way back to the door where the machine waited, his head shaking with the palsy of age, muttering as he went. He opened the door with his best manner, and stood aside.

"Good night, ma'am," he quavered.

I had tears in my eyes. I tried to keep them back. "Good night," I said. "Good night, *Ikkie*."

It had slipped out, my baby name for old Isaac!

"Miss Bess!" he cried. "Oh, praise Gawd, it's Miss Bess again!"

He caught my arm and pulled me back into the hall, and there he held me, crying over me, muttering praises for my return, begging me to come back, recalling little tender things out of the past that almost killed me to hear again.

But I had made my bed and must lie in it. I forced him to swear silence about my visit; I made him promise not to reveal my identity to Lida; and I told him—Heaven forgive me!—that I was well and prosperous and happy.

Dear old Isaac! I would not let him come to see me, but the next day there came a basket, with six bottles of wine, and an old daguerreotype of my mother, that had been his treasure. Nor was that basket the last.

CHAPTER IX

The coroner held an inquest over the headless body the next day, Tuesday. Mr. Graves telephoned me in the morning, and I went to the morgue with him.

I do not like the morgue, although some of my neighbors pay it weekly visits. It is by way of excursion, like nickelodeons or watching the circus put up its tents. I have heard them threaten the children that if they misbehaved they would not be taken to the morgue that week!

I failed to identify the body. How could I? It had been a tall woman, probably five feet eight, and I thought the nails looked like those of Jennie Brice. The thumb-nail of one was broken short off. I told Mr. Graves about her speaking of a broken nail, but he shrugged his shoulders and said nothing.

There was a curious scar over the heart, and he was making a sketch of it. It reached from the center of the chest for about six inches across the left breast, a narrow thin line that one could hardly see. It was shaped like this:

I felt sure that Jennie Brice had had no such scar, and Mr. Graves thought as I did. Temple Hope, called to the inquest, said she had never heard of one, and Mr. Ladley himself, at the inquest, swore that his wife had had nothing of the sort. I was watching him, and I did not think he was lying. And yet—the hand was very like Jennie Brice's. It was all bewildering.

Mr. Ladley's testimoney at the inquest was disappointing. He was cool and collected: said he had no reason to believe that his wife was dead, and less reason to think she had been drowned; she had left him in a rage, and if she found out that by hiding she was putting him in an unpleasant position, she would probably hide indefinitely.

To the disappointment of everybody, the identity of the woman remained a mystery. No one with such a scar was missing. A small woman of my own age, a Mrs. Murray, whose daughter, a stenographer, had disappeared, attended the inquest. But her daughter had had no such scar, and had worn her nails short, because of using the typewriter. Alice Murray was the missing girl's name. Her mother sat beside me, and cried most of the time.

One thing was brought out at the inquest: the body had been thrown into the river *after* death. There was no water in the lungs. The verdict was "death by the hands of some person or persons unknown."

Mr. Holcombe was not satisfied. In some way or other he had got permission to attend the autopsy, and had brought away a tracing of the scar. All the way home in the street-car he stared at the drawing, holding first one eye shut and then the other. But, like the coroner, he got nowhere. He folded the paper and put it in his note-book.

"None the less, Mrs. Pitman," he said, "that is the body of Jennie Brice; her husband killed her, probably by strangling her; he took the body out in the boat and dropped it into the swollen river above the Ninth Street bridge."

"Why do you think he strangled her?"

"There was no mark on the body, and no poison was found."

"Then if he strangled her, where did the blood come from?"

"I didn't limit myself to strangulation," he said irritably. "He may have cut her throat."

"Or brained her with my onyx clock," I added with a sigh. For I missed the clock more and more.

He went down in his pockets and brought up a key. "I'd forgotten this," he said. "It shows you were right—that the clock was there when the Ladleys took the room. I found this in the yard this morning."

It was when I got home from the inquest that I found old Isaac's basket waiting. I am not a crying woman, but I could hardly see my mother's picture for tears.—Well, after all, that is not the Brice story. I am not writing the sordid tragedy of my life.

That was on Tuesday. Jennie Brice had been missing nine days. In all that time, although she was cast for the piece at the theater that week, no one there had heard from her. Her relatives had had no word. She had gone away, if she had gone, on a cold March night, in a striped black and white dress with a red collar, and a red and black hat, without her fur coat, which she had worn all winter. She had gone very early in the morning, or during the night. How had she gone? Mr. Ladley said he had rowed her to Federal Street at half after six and had brought the boat back. After they had quarreled violently all night, and when she was leaving him, wouldn't he have allowed her to take herself away? Besides, the police had found no trace of her on an early train. And then at daylight, between five and six, my own brother had seen a woman with Mr. Howell, a woman who might have been Jennie Brice. But if it was, why did not Mr. Howell say so?

Mr. Ladley claimed she was hiding, in revenge. But Jennie Brice was not that sort of woman; there was something big about her, something that is found often in large women—a lack of spite. She was not petty or malicious. Her faults, like her virtues, were for all to see.

In spite of the failure to identify the body, Mr. Ladley was arrested that night, Tuesday, and this time it was for murder. I know now that the police were taking long chances. They had no strong motive for the crime. As Mr. Holcombe said, they had provocation, but not motive, which is different. They had opportunity, and they had a lot of straggling links of clues, which in the total made a fair chain of circumstantial evidence. But that was all.

That is the way the case stood on Tuesday night, March the thirteenth.

Mr. Ladley was taken away at nine o'clock. He was perfectly cool, asked me to help him pack a suit case, and whistled while it was being done. He requested to be allowed to walk to the jail, and went quietly, with a detective on one side and I think a sheriff's officer on the other.

Just before he left, he asked for a word or two with me, and when he paid his bill up to date, and gave me an extra dollar for taking care of Peter, I was almost overcome. He took the manuscript of his play with him, and I remember his asking if he could have any typing done in the jail. I had never seen a man arrested for murder before, but I think he was probably the coolest suspect the officers had ever seen. They hardly knew what to make of it.

Mr. Reynolds and I had a cup of tea after all the excitement, and were sitting at the dining-room table drinking it, when the bell rang. It was Mr. Howell! He half staggered into the hall when I opened the door, and was for going into the parlor bedroom without a word.

"Mr. Ladley's gone, if you want him," I said. I thought his face cleared.

"Gone!" he said. "Where?"

"To jail."

He did not reply at once. He stood there, tapping the palm of one hand with the forefinger of the other. He was dirty and unshaven. His clothes looked as if he had been sleeping in them.

"So they've got him!" he muttered finally, and turning, was about to go out the front door without another word, but I caught his arm.

"You're sick, Mr. Howell," I said. "You'd better not go out just yet."

"Oh, I'm all right." He took his handkerchief out and wiped his face. I saw that his hands were shaking.

"Come back and have a cup of tea, and a slice of home-made bread."

He hesitated and looked at his watch. "I'll do it, Mrs. Pitman," he said. "I suppose I'd better throw a little fuel into this engine of mine. It's been going hard for several days."

He ate like a wolf. I cut half a loaf into slices for him, and he drank the rest of the tea. Mr. Reynolds creaked up to bed and left him still eating, and me still cutting and spreading. Now that I had a chance to see him, I was shocked. The rims of his eyes were red, his collar was black, and his hair hung over his forehead. But when he finally sat back and looked at me, his color was better.

"So they've canned him!" he said.

"Time enough, too," said I.

He leaned forward and put both his elbows on the table. "Mrs. Pitman," he said earnestly, "I don't like him any more than you do. But he never killed that woman."

"Somebody killed her."

"How do you know? How do you know she is dead?"

Well, I didn't, of course—I only felt it.

"The police haven't even proved a crime. They can't hold a man for a supposititious murder."

"Perhaps they can't but they're doing it," I retorted. "If the woman's alive, she won't let him hang."

"I'm not so sure of that," he said heavily, and got up. He looked in the little mirror over the sideboard, and brushed back his hair. "I look bad enough," he said, "but I feel worse. Well, you've saved my life, Mrs. Pitman. Thank you."

"How is my—how is Miss Harvey?" I asked, as we started out. He turned and smiled at me in his boyish way.

"The best ever!" he said. "I haven't seen her for days, and it seems like centuries. She—she is the only girl in the world for me, Mrs. Pitman, although I—" He stopped and drew a long breath. "She is beautiful, isn't she?"

"Very beautiful," I answered. "Her mother was always—"

"Her mother!" He looked at me curiously.

"I knew her mother years ago," I said, putting the best face on my mistake that I could.

"Then I'll remember you to her, if she ever allows me to see her again. Just now I'm *persona non grata*."

"If you'll do the kindly thing, Mr. Howell," I said, "you'll *forget* me to her."

He looked into my eyes and then thrust out his hand.

"All right," he said. "I'll not ask any questions. I guess there are some curious stories hidden in these old houses."

Peter hobbled to the front door with him. He had not gone so far as the parlor once while Mr. Ladley was in the house.

They had had a sale of spring flowers at the store that day, and Mr. Reynolds had brought me a pot of white tulips. That night I hung my mother's picture over the mantel in the dining-room, and put the tulips beneath it. It gave me a feeling of comfort; I had never seen my mother's grave, or put flowers on it.

CHAPTER X

I have said before that I do not know anything about the law. I believe that the Ladley case was unusual, in several ways. Mr. Ladley had once been well known in New York among the people who frequent the theaters, and Jennie Brice was even better known. A good many lawyers, I believe, said that the police had not a leg to stand on, and I know the case was watched with much interest by the legal profession. People wrote letters to the newspapers, protesting against Mr. Ladley being held. And I believe that the district attorney, in taking him before the grand jury, hardly hoped to make a case.

But he did, to his own surprise, I fancy, and the trial was set for May. But in the meantime, many curious things happened.

In the first place, the week following Mr. Ladley's arrest my house was filled up with eight or ten members of a company from the Gaiety Theater, very cheerful and jolly, and well behaved. Three men, I think, and the rest girls. One of the men was named Bellows, John Bellows, and it turned out that he had known Jennie Brice very well.

From the moment he learned that, Mr. Holcombe hardly left him. He walked to the theater with him and waited to walk home again. He took him out to restaurants and for long street-car rides in the mornings, and on the last night of their stay, Saturday, they got gloriously drunk together—Mr. Holcombe, no doubt, in his character of Ladley—and came reeling in at three in the morning, singing. Mr. Holcombe was very sick the next day, but by Monday he was all right, and he called me into the room.

"We've got him, Mrs. Pitman," he said, looking mottled but cheerful. "As sure as God made little fishes, we've got him." That was all he would say, however. It seemed he was going to New York, and might be gone for a month. "I've no family," he said, "and enough money to keep me. If I find my relaxation in hunting down criminals, it's a harmless and cheap amusement, and—it's my own business."

He went away that night, and I must admit I missed him. I rented the parlor bedroom the next day to a school-teacher, and I found the periscope affair very handy. I could see just how much gas she used; and although the notice on each door forbids cooking and washing in rooms, I found she was doing both: making coffee and boiling an egg in the morning, and rubbing out stockings and handkerchiefs in her wash-bowl. I'd much rather have men as boarders than women. The women are always lighting alcohol lamps on the bureau, and wanting the bed turned into a cozy corner so they can see their gentlemen friends in their rooms.

Well, with Mr. Holcombe gone, and Mr. Reynolds busy all day and half the night getting out the summer silks and preparing for remnant day, and with Mr. Ladley in jail and Lida out of the city—for I saw in the papers that she was not well, and her mother had taken her to Bermuda—I had a good bit of time on my hands. And so I got in the habit of thinking things over, and trying to draw conclusions, as I had seen Mr. Holcombe do. I would sit down and write things out as they had happened, and study them over, and especially I worried over how we could have found a slip of paper in Mr. Ladley's room with a list, almost exact, of the things we had discovered there. I used to read it over, "rope, knife, shoe, towel, Horn—" and get more and more bewildered. "Horn"—might have been a town, or it might not have been. There *was* such a town, according to Mr. Graves, but apparently he had made nothing of it. *Was* it a town that was meant?

The dictionary gave only a few words beginning with "horn"—hornet, hornblende, hornpipe, and horny—none of which was of any assistance. And then one morning I happened to see in the personal column of one of the newspapers that a woman named Eliza Shaeffer, of Horner, had day-old Buff Orpington and Plymouth Rock chicks for sale, and it started me to puzzling again. Perhaps it had been Horner, and possibly this very Eliza Shaeffer—

I suppose my lack of experience was in my favor, for, after all, Eliza Shaeffer is a common enough name, and the "Horn" might have stood for "hornswoggle," for all I knew. The story of the man who thought of what he would do if he were a horse, came back to me, and for an hour or so I tried to think I was Jennie Brice, trying to get away and hide from my rascal of a husband. But I made no headway. I would never have gone to Horner, or to any small town, if I had wanted to hide. I think I should have gone around the corner and taken a room in my own neighborhood, or have lost myself in some large city.

It was that same day that, since I did not go to Horner, Horner came to me. The bell rang about three o'clock, and I answered it myself. For, with times hard and only two or three roomers all winter, I had not had a servant, except Terry to do odd jobs, for some months.

There stood a fresh-faced young girl, with a covered basket in her hand.

"Are you Mrs. Pitman?" she asked.

"I don't need anything to-day," I said, trying to shut the door. And at that minute something in the basket cheeped. Young women selling poultry are not common in our neighborhood. "What have you there?" I asked more agreeably.

"Chicks, day-old chicks, but I'm not trying to sell you any. I—may I come in?"

It was dawning on me then that perhaps this was Eliza Shaeffer. I led her back to the dining-room, with Peter sniffing at the basket.

"My name is Shaeffer," she said. "I've seen your name in the papers, and I believe I know something about Jennie Brice."

Eliza Shaeffer's story was curious. She said that she was postmistress at Horner, and lived with her mother on a farm a mile out of the town, driving in and out each day in a buggy.

On Monday afternoon, March the fifth, a woman had alighted at the station from a train, and had taken luncheon at the hotel. She told the clerk she was on the road, selling corsets, and was much disappointed to find no store of any size in the town. The woman, who had registered as Mrs. Jane Bellows, said she was tired and would like to rest for a day or two on a farm. She was told to see Eliza Shaeffer at the post-office, and, as a result, drove out with her to the farm after the last mail came in that evening.

Asked to describe her—she was over medium height, light-haired, quick in her movements, and wore a black and white striped dress with a red collar, and a hat to match. She carried a small brown valise that Miss Shaeffer presumed contained her samples.

Mrs. Shaeffer had made her welcome, although they did not usually take boarders until June. She had not eaten much supper, and that night she had asked for pen and ink, and had written a letter. The letter was not mailed until Wednesday. All of Tuesday Mrs. Bellows had spent in her room, and Mrs. Shaeffer had driven to the village in the afternoon with word that she had been crying all day, and bought some headache medicine for her.

On Wednesday morning, however, she had appeared at breakfast, eaten heartily, and had asked Miss Shaeffer to take her letter to the post-office. It was addressed to Mr. Ellis Howell, in care of a Pittsburgh newspaper!

That night when Miss Eliza went home, about half past eight, the woman was gone. She had paid for her room and had been driven as far as Thornville, where all trace of her had been lost. On account of the disappearance of Jennie Brice being published shortly after that, she and her mother had driven to Thornville, but the station agent there was surly as well as stupid. They had learned nothing about the woman.

Since that time, three men had made inquiries about the woman in question. One had a pointed Vandyke beard; the second, from the description, I fancied must have been Mr. Graves. The third without doubt was Mr. Howell. Eliza Shaeffer said that this last man had seemed half frantic. I brought her a photograph of Jennie Brice as "Topsy" and another one as "Juliet". She said there was a resemblance, but that it ended there. But of course, as Mr. Graves had said, by the time an actress gets her photograph retouched to suit her, it doesn't particularly resemble her. And unless I had known Jennie Brice myself, I should hardly have recognized the pictures.

Well, in spite of all that, there seemed no doubt that Jennie Brice had been living three days after her disappearance, and that would clear Mr. Ladley. But what had Mr. Howell to do with it all? Why had he not told the police of the letter from Horner? Or about the woman on the bridge? Why had Mr. Bronson, who was likely the man with the pointed beard, said nothing about having traced Jennie Brice to Horner?

I did as I thought Mr. Holcombe would have wished me to do. I wrote down on a clean sheet of note-paper all that Eliza Shaeffer said: the description of the black and white dress, the woman's height, and the rest, and then I took her to the court-house, chicks and all, and she told her story there to one of the assistant district attorneys.

The young man was interested, but not convinced. He had her story taken down, and she signed it. He was smiling as he bowed us out. I turned in the doorway.

"This will free Mr. Ladley, I suppose?" I asked.

"Not just yet," he said pleasantly. "This makes just eleven places where Jennie Brice spent the first three days after her death."

"But I can positively identify the dress."

"My good woman, that dress has been described, to the last stilted arch and Colonial volute, in every newspaper in the United States!"

That evening the newspapers announced that during a conference at the jail between Mr. Ladley and James Bronson, business manager at the Liberty Theater, Mr. Ladley had attacked Mr. Bronson with a chair, and almost brained him.

CHAPTER XI

Eliza Shaeffer went back to Horner, after delivering her chicks somewhere in the city. Things went on as before. The trial was set for May. The district attorney's office had all the things we had found in the house that Monday afternoon—the stained towel, the broken knife and its blade, the slipper that had been floating in the parlor, and the rope that had fastened my boat to the staircase. Somewhere—wherever they keep such things—was the headless body of a woman with a hand missing, and with a curious scar across the left breast. The slip of paper, however, which I had found behind the base-board, was still in Mr. Holcombe's possession, nor had he mentioned it to the police.

Mr. Holcombe had not come back. He wrote me twice asking me to hold his room, once from New York and once from Chicago. To the second letter he added a postscript:

"Have not found what I wanted, but am getting warm. If any news, address me at Des Moines, Iowa, General Delivery.   H."

It was nearly the end of April when I saw Lida again. I had seen by the newspapers that she and her mother were coming home. I wondered if she had heard from Mr. Howell, for I had not, and I wondered, too, if she would send for me again.

But she came herself, on foot, late one afternoon, and the school-teacher being out, I took her into the parlor bedroom. She looked thinner than before, and rather white. My heart ached for her.

"I have been away," she explained. "I thought you might wonder why you did not hear from me. But, you see, my mother—" she stopped and flushed. "I would have written you from Bermuda, but—my mother watched my correspondence, so I could not."

No. I knew she could not. Alma had once found a letter of mine to Mr. Pitman. Very little escaped Alma.

"I wondered if you have heard anything?" she asked.

"I have heard nothing. Mr. Howell was here once, just after I saw you. I do not believe he is in the city.

"Perhaps not, although—Mrs. Pitman, I believe he is in the city, hiding!"

"Hiding! Why?"

"I don't know. But last night I thought I saw him below my window. I opened the window, so if it were he, he could make some sign. But he moved on without a word. Later, whoever it was came back. I put out my light and watched. Some one stood there, in the shadow, until after two this morning. Part of the time he was looking up."

"Don't you think, had it been he, he would have spoken when he saw you?"

She shook her head. "He is in trouble," she said. "He has not heard from me, and he—thinks I don't care any more. Just look at me, Mrs. Pitman! Do I look as if I don't care?"

She looked half killed, poor lamb.

"He may be out of town, searching for a better position," I tried to comfort her. "He wants to have something to offer more than himself."

"I only want him," she said, looking at me frankly. "I don't know why I tell you all this, but you are so kind, and I *must* talk to some one."

She sat there, in the cozy corner the school-teacher had made with a portière and some cushions, and I saw she was about ready to break down and cry. I went over to her and took her hand, for she was my own niece, although she didn't suspect it, and I had never had a child of my own.

But after all, I could not help her much. I could only assure her that he would come back and explain everything, and that he was all right, and that the last time I had seen him he had spoken of her, and had said she was "the best ever." My heart fairly yearned over the girl, and I think she felt it. For she kissed me, shyly, when she was leaving.

With the newspaper files before me, it is not hard to give the details of that sensational trial. It commenced on Monday, the seventh of May, but it was late Wednesday when the jury was finally selected. I was at the court-house early on Thursday, and so was Mr. Reynolds.

The district attorney made a short speech. "We propose, gentlemen, to prove that the prisoner, Philip Ladley, murdered his wife," he said in part. "We will show first that a crime was committed; then we will show a motive for this crime, and, finally, we expect to show that the body washed ashore at Sewickley is the body of the murdered woman, and thus establish beyond doubt the prisoner's guilt."

Mr. Ladley listened with attention. He wore the brown suit, and looked well and cheerful. He was much more like a spectator than a prisoner, and he was not so nervous as I was.

Of that first day I do not recall much. I was called early in the day. The district attorney questioned me.

"Your name?"

"Elizabeth Marie Pitman."

"Your occupation?"

"I keep a boarding-house at 42 Union Street."

"You know the prisoner?"

"Yes. He was a boarder in my house."

"For how long?"

"From December first. He and his wife came at that time."

"Was his wife the actress, Jennie Brice?"

"Yes, sir."

"Were they living together at your house the night of March fourth?"

"Yes, sir."

"In what part of the house?"

"They rented the double parlors down-stairs, but on account of the flood I moved them up-stairs to the second floor front."

"That was on Sunday? You moved them on Sunday?"

"Yes, sir."

"At what time did you retire that night?"

"Not at all. The water was very high. I lay down, dressed, at one o'clock, and dropped into a doze."

"How long did you sleep?"

"An hour or so. Mr. Reynolds, a boarder, roused me to say he had heard some one rowing a boat in the lower hall."

"Do you keep a boat around during flood times?"

"Yes, sir."

"What did you do when Mr. Reynolds roused you?"

"I went to the top of the stairs. My boat was gone."

"Was the boat secured?"

"Yes, sir. Anyhow, there was no current in the hall."

"What did you do then?"

"I waited a time and went back to my room."

"What examination of the house did you make—if any?"

"Mr. Reynolds looked around."

"What did he find?"

"He found Peter, the Ladleys' dog, shut in a room on the third floor."

"Was there anything unusual about that?"

"I had never known it to happen before."

"State what happened later."

"I did not go to sleep again. At a quarter after four, I heard the boat come back. I took a candle and went to the stairs. It was Mr. Ladley. He said he had been out getting medicine for his wife."

"Did you see him tie up the boat?"

"Yes."

"Did you observe any stains on the rope?"

"I did not notice any."

"What was the prisoner's manner at that time?"

"I thought he was surly."

"Now, Mrs. Pitman, tell us about the following morning."

"I saw Mr. Ladley at a quarter before seven. He said to bring breakfast for one. His wife had gone away. I asked if she was not ill, and he said no; that she had gone away early; that he had rowed her to Federal Street, and that she would be back Saturday. It was shortly after that that the dog Peter brought in one of Mrs. Ladley's slippers, water-soaked."

"You recognized the slipper?"

"Positively. I had seen it often."

"What did you do with it?"

"I took it to Mr. Ladley."

"What did he say?"

"He said at first that it was not hers. Then he said if it was, she would never wear it again—and then added—because it was ruined."

"Did he offer any statement as to where his wife was?"

"No, sir. Not at that time. Before, he had said she had gone away for a few days."

"Tell the jury about the broken knife."

"The dog found it floating in the parlor, with the blade broken."

"You had not left it down-stairs?"

"No, sir. I had used it up-stairs, the night before, and left it on a mantel of the room I was using as a temporary kitchen."

"Was the door of this room locked?"

"No. It was standing open."

"Were you not asleep in this room?"

"Yes."

"You heard no one come in?"

"No one—until Mr. Reynolds roused me."

"Where did you find the blade?"

"Behind the bed in Mr. Ladley's room."

"What else did you find in the room?"

"A blood-stained towel behind the wash-stand. Also, my onyx clock was missing."

"Where was the clock when the Ladleys were moved up into this room?"

"On the mantel. I wound it just before they came up-stairs."

"When you saw Mrs. Ladley on Sunday, did she say she was going away?"

"No, sir."

"Did you see any preparation for a journey?"

"The black and white dress was laid out on the bed, and a small bag. She said she was taking the dress to the theater to lend to Miss Hope."

"Is that all she said?"

"No. She said she'd been wishing her husband would drown; that he was a fiend."

I could see that my testimony had made an impression.

CHAPTER XII

The slipper, the rope, the towel, and the knife and blade were produced in court, and I identified them all. They made a noticeable impression on the jury. Then Mr. Llewellyn, the lawyer for the defense, cross-examined me.

"Is it not true, Mrs. Pitman," he said, "that many articles, particularly shoes and slippers, are found floating around during a flood?"

"Yes," I admitted.

"Now, you say the dog found this slipper floating in the hall and brought it to you. Are you sure this slipper belonged to Jennie Brice?"

"She wore it. I presume it belonged to her."

"Ahem. Now, Mrs. Pitman, after the Ladleys had been moved to the upper floor, did you search their bedroom and the connecting room down-stairs?"

"No, sir."

"Ah. Then, how do you know that this slipper was not left on the floor or in a closet?"

"It is possible, but not likely. Anyhow, it was not the slipper alone. It was the other things *and* the slipper. It was—"

"Exactly. Now, Mrs. Pitman, this knife. Can you identify it positively?"

"I can."

"But isn't it true that this is a very common sort of knife? One that nearly every housewife has in her possession?"

"Yes, sir. But that knife handle has three notches in it. I put the notches there myself."

"Before this presumed crime?"

"Yes, sir."

"For what purpose?"

"My neighbors were constantly borrowing things. It was a means of identification."

"Then this knife is yours?"

"Yes."

"Tell again where you left it the night before it was found floating down-stairs."

"On a shelf over the stove."

"Could the dog have reached it there?"

"Not without standing on a hot stove."

"Is it not possible that Mr. Ladley, unable to untie the boat, borrowed your knife to cut the boat's painter?"

"No painter was cut that I heard about The paper-hanger—"

"No, no. The boat's painter—the rope."

"Oh! Well, he might have. He never said."

"Now then, this towel, Mrs. Pitman. Did not the prisoner, on the following day, tell you that he had cut his wrist in freeing the boat, and ask you for some court-plaster?"

"He did not," I said firmly.

"You have not seen a scar on his wrist?"

"No." I glanced at Mr. Ladley: he was smiling, as if amused. It made me angry. "And what's more," I flashed, "if he has a cut on his wrist, he put it there himself, to account for the towel."

I was sorry the next moment that I had said it, but it was too late. The counsel for the defense moved to exclude the answer and I received a caution that I deserved. Then:

"You saw Mr. Ladley when he brought your boat back?"

"Yes."

"What time was that?"

"A quarter after four Monday morning."

"Did he come in quietly, like a man trying to avoid attention?"

"Not particularly. It would have been of no use. The dog was barking."

"What did he say?"

"That he had been out for medicine. That his wife was sick."

"Do you know a pharmacist named Alexander—Jonathan Alexander?"

"There is such a one, but I don't know him."

I was excused, and Mr. Reynolds was called. He had heard no quarreling that Sunday night; had even heard Mrs. Ladley laughing. This was about nine o'clock. Yes, they had fought in the afternoon. He had not overheard any words, but their voices were quarrelsome, and once he heard a chair or some article of furniture overthrown. Was awakened about two by footsteps on the stairs, followed by the sound of oars in the lower hall. He told his story plainly and simply. Under cross-examination admitted that he was fond of detective stories and had tried to write one himself; that he had said at the store that he would like to see that "conceited ass" swing, referring to the prisoner; that he had sent flowers to Jennie Brice at the theater, and had made a few advances to her, without success.

My head was going round. I don't know yet how the police learned it all, but by the time poor Mr. Reynolds left the stand, half the people there believed that he had been in love with Jennie Brice, that she had spurned his advances, and that there was more to the story than any of them had suspected.

Miss Hope's story held without any alteration under the cross-examination. She was perfectly at ease, looked handsome and well dressed, and could not be shaken. She told how Jennie Brice had been in fear of her life, and had asked her, only the week before she disappeared, to allow her to go home with her—Miss Hope. She told of the attack of hysteria in her dressing-room, and that the missing woman had said that her husband would kill her some day. There was much wrangling over her testimony, and I believe at least a part of it was not allowed to go to the jury. But I am not a lawyer, and I repeat what I recall.

"Did she say that he had attacked her?"

"Yes, more than once. She was a large woman, fairly muscular, and had always held her own."

"Did she say that these attacks came when he had been drinking?"

"I believe he was worse then."

"Did she give any reason for her husband's attitude to her?"

"She said he wanted to marry another woman."

There was a small sensation at this. If proved, it established a motive.

"Did she know who the other woman was?"

"I believe not. She was away most of the day, and he put in his time as he liked."

"Did Miss Brice ever mention the nature of the threats he made against her?"

"No, I think not."

"Have you examined the body washed ashore at Sewickley?"

"Yes—" in a low voice.

"Is it the body of Jennie Brice?"

"I can not say."

"Does the remaining hand look like the hand of Jennie Brice?"

"Very much. The nails are filed to points, as she wore hers."

"Did you ever know of Jennie Brice having a scar on her breast?"

"No, but that would be easily concealed."

"Just what do you mean?"

"Many actresses conceal defects. She could have worn flesh-colored plaster and covered it with powder. Also, such a scar would not necessarily be seen."

"Explain that."

"Most of Jennie Brice's décolleté gowns were cut to a point. This would conceal such a scar."

Miss Hope was excused, and Jennie Brice's sister from Olean was called. She was a smaller woman than Jennie Brice had been, very lady-like in her manner. She said she was married and living in Olean; she had not seen her sister for several years, but had heard from her often. The witness had discouraged the marriage to the prisoner.

"Why?"

"She had had bad luck before."

"She had been married before?"

"Yes, to a man named John Bellows. They were in vaudeville together, on the Keith Circuit. They were known as The Pair of Bellows."

I sat up at this for John Bellows had boarded at my house.

"Mr. Bellows is dead?"

"I think not. She divorced him."

"Did you know of any scar on your sister's body?"

"I never heard of one."

"Have you seen the body found at Sewickley?"

"Yes"—faintly.

"Can you identify it?"

"No, sir."

A flurry was caused during the afternoon by Timothy Senft. He testified to what I already knew—that between three and four on Monday morning, during the height of the flood, he had seen from his shanty-boat a small skiff caught in the current near the Ninth Street bridge. He had shouted encouragingly to the man in the boat, running out a way on the ice to make him hear. He had told him to row with the current, and to try to steer in toward shore. He had followed close to the river bank in his own boat. Below Sixth Street the other boat was within rope-throwing distance. He had pulled it in, and had towed it well back out of the current. The man in the boat was the prisoner. Asked if the prisoner gave any explanation—yes, he said he couldn't sleep, and had thought to tire himself rowing. Had been caught in the current before he knew it. Saw nothing suspicious in or about the boat. As they passed the police patrol boat, prisoner had called to ask if there was much distress, and expressed regret when told there was.

Tim was excused. He had made a profound impression. I would not have given a dollar for Mr. Ladley's chance with the jury, at that time.

CHAPTER XIII

The prosecution produced many witnesses during the next two days: Shanty-boat Tim's story withstood the most vigorous cross-examination. After him, Mr. Bronson from the theater corroborated Miss Hope's story of Jennie Brice's attack of hysteria in the dressing-room, and told of taking her home that night.

He was a poor witness, nervous and halting. He weighed each word before he said it, and he made a general unfavorable impression. I thought he was holding something back. In view of what Mr. Pitman would have called the denouement, his attitude is easily explained. But I was puzzled then.

So far, the prosecution had touched but lightly on the possible motive for a crime—the woman. But on the third day, to my surprise, a Mrs. Agnes Murray was called. It was the Mrs. Murray I had seen at the morgue.

I have lost the clipping of that day's trial, but I remember her testimony perfectly.

She was a widow, living above a small millinery shop on Federal Street, Allegheny. She had one daughter, Alice, who did stenography and typing as a means of livelihood. She had no office, and worked at home. Many of the small stores in the neighborhood employed her to send out their bills. There was a card at the street entrance beside the shop, and now and then strangers brought her work.

Early in December the prisoner had brought her the manuscript of a play to type, and from that time on he came frequently, sometimes every day, bringing a few sheets of manuscript at a time. Sometimes he came without any manuscript, and would sit and talk while he smoked a cigarette. They had thought him unmarried.

On Wednesday, February twenty-eighth, Alice Murray had disappeared. She had taken some of her clothing—not all, and had left a note. The witness read the note aloud in a trembling voice:

"DEAR MOTHER: When you get this I shall be married to Mr. Ladley.

Don't worry. Will write again from N.Y. Lovingly,

"ALICE."

From that time until a week before, she had not heard from her daughter. Then she had a card, mailed from Madison Square Station, New York City. The card merely said:

"Am well and working. ALICE."

The defense was visibly shaken. They had not expected this, and I thought even Mr. Ladley, whose calm had continued unbroken, paled.

So far, all had gone well for the prosecution. They had proved a crime, as nearly as circumstantial evidence could prove a crime, and they had established a motive. But in the identification of the body, so far they had failed. The prosecution "rested," as they say, although they didn't rest much, on the afternoon of the third day.

The defense called, first of all, Eliza Shaeffer. She told of a woman answering the general description of Jennie Brice having spent two days at the Shaeffer farm at Horner. Being shown photographs of Jennie Brice, she said she thought it was the same woman, but was not certain. She told further of the woman leaving unexpectedly on Wednesday of that week from Thornville. On cross-examination, being shown the small photograph which Mr. Graves had shown me, she identified the woman in the group as being the woman in question. As the face was in shadow, knew it more by the dress and hat: she described the black and white dress and the hat with red trimming.

The defense then called me. I had to admit that the dress and hat as described were almost certainly the ones I had seen on the bed in Jennie Brice's room the day before she disappeared. I could not say definitely whether the woman in the photograph was Jennie Brice or not; under a magnifying-glass thought it might be.

Defense called Jonathan Alexander, a druggist who testified that on the night in question he had been roused at half past three by the prisoner, who had said his wife was ill, and had purchased a bottle of a proprietary remedy from him. His identification was absolute.

The defense called Jennie Brice's sister, and endeavored to prove that Jennie Brice had had no such scar. It was shown that she was on intimate terms with her family and would hardly have concealed an operation of any gravity from them.

The defense scored that day. They had shown that the prisoner had told the truth when he said he had gone to a pharmacy for medicine that night for his wife; and they had shown that a woman, answering the description of Jennie Brice, spent two days in a town called Horner, and had gone from there on Wednesday after the crime. And they had shown that this woman was attired as Jennie Brice had been.

That was the way things stood on the afternoon of the fourth day, when court adjourned.

Mr. Reynolds was at home when I got there. He had been very much subdued since the developments of that first day of the trial, sat mostly in his own room, and had twice brought me a bunch of jonquils as a peace-offering. He had the kettle boiling when I got home.

"You have had a number of visitors," he said. "Our young friend Howell has been here, and Mr. Holcombe has arrived and has a man in his room."

Mr. Holcombe came down a moment after, with his face beaming.

"I think we've got him, Mrs. Pitman," he said. "The jury won't even go out of the box."

But further than that he would not explain. He said he had a witness locked in his room, and he'd be glad of supper for him, as they'd both come a long ways. And he went out and bought some oysters and a bottle or two of beer. But as far as I know, he kept him locked up all that night in the second-story front room. I don't think the man knew he was a prisoner. I went in to turn down the bed, and he was sitting by the window, reading the evening paper's account of the trial—an elderly gentleman, rather professional-looking.

Mr. Holcombe slept on the upper landing of the hall that night, rolled in a blanket—not that I think his witness even thought of escaping, but the little man was taking no chances.

At eight o'clock that night the bell rang. It was Mr. Howell. I admitted him myself, and he followed me back to the dining-room. I had not seen him for several weeks, and the change in him startled me. He was dressed carefully, but his eyes were sunken in his head, and he looked as if he had not slept for days.

Mr. Reynolds had gone up-stairs, not finding me socially inclined.

"You haven't been sick, Mr. Howell, have you?" I asked.

"Oh, no, I'm well enough, I've been traveling about. Those infernal sleeping-cars—"

His voice trailed off, and I saw him looking at my mother's picture, with the jonquils beneath.

"That's curious!" he said, going closer. "It—it looks almost like Lida Harvey."

"My mother," I said simply.

"Have you seen her lately?"

"My mother?" I asked, startled.

"No, Lida."

"I saw her a few days ago."

"Here?"

"Yes. She came here, Mr. Howell, two weeks ago. She looks badly—as if she is worrying."

"Not—about me?" he asked eagerly.

"Yes, about you. What possessed you to go away as you did? When my—bro—when her uncle accused you of something, you ran away, instead of facing things like a man."

"I was trying to find the one person who could clear me, Mrs. Pitman." He sat back, with his eyes closed; he looked ill enough to be in bed.

"And you succeeded?"

"No."

I thought perhaps he had not been eating and I offered him food, as I had once before. But he refused it, with the ghost of his boyish smile.

"I'm hungry, but it's not food I want. I want to see *her*," he said.

I sat down across from him and tried to mend a table-cloth, but I could not sew. I kept seeing those two young things, each sick for a sight of the other, and, from wishing they could have a minute together, I got to planning it for them.

"Perhaps," I said finally, "if you want it very much—"

"Very much!"

"And if you will sit quiet, and stop tapping your fingers together until you drive me crazy, I might contrive it for you. For five minutes," I said. "Not a second longer."

He came right over and put his arms around me.

"Who are you, anyhow?" he said. "You who turn to the world the frozen mask of a Union Street boarding-house landlady, who are a gentlewoman by every instinct and training, and a girl at heart? Who are you?"

"I'll tell you what I am," I said. "I'm a romantic old fool, and you'd better let me do this quickly, before I change my mind."

He freed me at that, but he followed to the telephone, and stood by while I got Lida. He was in a perfect frenzy of anxiety, turning red and white by turns, and in the middle of the conversation taking the receiver bodily from me and holding it to his own ear.

She said she thought she could get away; she spoke guardedly, as if Alma were near, but I gathered that she would come as soon as she could, and, from the way her voice broke, I knew she was as excited as the boy beside me.

She came, heavily coated and veiled, at a quarter after ten that night, and I took her back to the dining-room, where he was waiting. He did not make a move toward her, but stood there with his very lips white, looking at her. And, at first, she did not make a move either, but stood and gazed at him, thin and white, a wreck of himself. Then:

"Ell!" she cried, and ran around the table to him, as he held out his arms.

The school-teacher was out. I went into the parlor bedroom and sat in the cozy corner in the dark. I had done a wrong thing, and I was glad of it. And sitting there in the darkness, I went over my own life again. After all, it had been my own life; I had lived it; no one else had shaped it for me. And if it was cheerless and colorless now, it had had its big moments. Life is measured by big moments.

If I let the two children in the dining-room have fifteen big moments, instead of five, who can blame me?

CHAPTER XIV

The next day was the sensational one of the trial. We went through every phase of conviction: Jennie Brice was living. Jennie Brice was dead. The body found at Sewickley could not be Jennie Brice's. The body found at Sewickley *was* Jennie Brice's. And so it went on.

The defense did an unexpected thing in putting Mr. Ladley on the stand. That day, for the first time, he showed the wear and tear of the ordeal. He had no flower in his button-hole, and the rims of his eyes were red. But he was quite cool. His stage training had taught him not only to endure the eyes of the crowd, but to find in its gaze a sort of stimulant. He made a good witness, I must admit.

He replied to the usual questions easily. After five minutes or so Mr. Llewellyn got down to work.

"Mr. Ladley, you have said that your wife was ill the night of March fourth?"

"Yes."

"What was the nature of her illness?"

"She had a functional heart trouble, not serious."

"Will you tell us fully the events of that night?"

"I had been asleep when my wife wakened me. She asked for a medicine she used in these attacks. I got up and found the bottle, but it was empty. As she was nervous and frightened, I agreed to try to get some at a drug store. I went down-stairs, took Mrs. Pitman's boat, and went to several stores before I could awaken a pharmacist."

"You cut the boat loose?"

"Yes. It was tied in a woman's knot, or series of knots. I could not untie it, and I was in a hurry."

"How did you cut it?"

"With my pocket-knife."

"You did not use Mrs. Pitman's bread-knife?"

"I did not."

"And in cutting it, you cut your wrist, did you?"

"Yes. The knife slipped. I have the scar still."

"What did you do then?"

"I went back to the room, and stanched the blood with a towel."

"From whom did you get the medicine?"

"From Alexander's Pharmacy."

"At what time?"

"I am not certain. About three o'clock, probably."

"You went directly back home?"

Mr. Ladley hesitated. "No," he said finally. "My wife had had these attacks, but they were not serious. I was curious to see how the river-front looked and rowed out too far. I was caught in the current and nearly carried away."

"You came home after that?"

"Yes, at once. Mrs. Ladley was better and had dropped asleep. She wakened as I came in. She was disagreeable about the length of time I had been gone, and would not let me explain. We—quarreled, and she said she was going to leave me. I said that as she had threatened this before and had never done it, I would see that she really started. At daylight I rowed her to Federal Street."

"What had she with her?"

"A small brown valise."

"How was she dressed?"

"In a black and white dress and hat, with a long black coat."

"What was the last you saw of her?"

"She was going across the Sixth Street bridge."

"Alone?"

"No. She went with a young man we knew."

There was a stir in the court room at this.

"Who was the young man?"

"A Mr. Howell, a reporter on a newspaper here."

"Have you seen Mr. Howell since your arrest?"

"No, sir. He has been out of the city."

I was so excited by this time that I could hardly hear. I missed some of the cross-examination. The district attorney pulled Mr. Ladley's testimony to pieces.

"You cut the boat's painter with your pocket-knife?"

"I did."

"Then how do you account for Mrs. Pitman's broken knife, with the blade in your room?"

"I have no theory about it. She may have broken it herself. She had used it the day before to lift tacks out of a carpet."

That was true; I had.

"That early Monday morning was cold, was it not?"

"Yes. Very."

"Why did your wife leave without her fur coat?"

"I did not know she had until we had left the house. Then I did not ask her. She would not speak to me."

"I see. But is it not true that, upon a wet fur coat being shown you as your wife's, you said it could not be hers, as she had taken hers with her?"

"I do not recall such a statement."

"You recall a coat being shown you?"

"Yes. Mrs. Pitman brought a coat to my door, but I was working on a play I am writing, and I do not remember what I said. The coat was ruined. I did not want it. I probably said the first thing I thought of to get rid of the woman."

I got up at that. I'd held my peace about the bread-knife, but this was too much. However, the moment I started to speak, somebody pushed me back into my chair and told me to be quiet.

"Now, you say you were in such a hurry to get this medicine for your wife that you cut the rope, thus cutting your wrist."

"Yes. I have the scar still."

"You could not wait to untie the boat, and yet you went along the river-front to see how high the water was?"

"Her alarm had excited me. But when I got out, and remembered that the doctors had told us she would never die in an attack, I grew more composed."

"You got the medicine first, you say?"

"Yes."

"Mr. Alexander has testified that you got the medicine at three-thirty. It has been shown that you left the house at two, and got back about four. Does not this show that with all your alarm you went to the river-front first?"

"I was gone from two to four," he replied calmly. "Mr. Alexander must be wrong about the time I wakened him. I got the medicine first."

"When your wife left you at the bridge, did she say where she was going?"

"No."

"You claim that this woman at Horner was your wife?"

"I think it likely."

"Was there an onyx clock in the second-story room when you moved into it?"

"I do not recall the clock."

"Your wife did not take an onyx clock away with her?"

Mr. Ladley smiled. "No."

The defense called Mr. Howell next. He looked rested, and the happier for having seen Lida, but he was still pale and showed the strain of some hidden anxiety. What that anxiety was, the next two days were to tell us all.

"Mr. Howell," Mr. Llewellyn asked, "you know the prisoner?"

"Slightly."

"State when you met him."

"On Sunday morning, March the fourth. I went to see him."

"Will you tell us the nature of that visit?"

"My paper had heard he was writing a play for himself. I was to get an interview, with photographs, if possible."

"You saw his wife at that time?"

"Yes."

"When did you see her again?"

"The following morning, at six o'clock, or a little later. I walked across the Sixth Street bridge with her, and put her on a train for Horner, Pennsylvania."

"You are positive it was Jennie Brice?"

"Yes. I watched her get out of the boat, while her husband steadied it."

"If you knew this, why did you not come forward sooner?"

"I have been out of the city."

"But you knew the prisoner had been arrested, and that this testimony of yours would be invaluable to him."

"Yes. But I thought it necessary to produce Jennie Brice herself. My unsupported word—"

"You have been searching for Jennie Brice?"

"Yes. Since March the eighth."

"How was she dressed when you saw her last?"

"She wore a red and black hat and a black coat. She carried a small brown valise."

"Thank you."

The cross-examination did not shake his testimony. But it brought out some curious things. Mr. Howell refused to say how he happened to be at the end of the Sixth Street bridge at that hour, or why he had thought it necessary, on meeting a woman he claimed to have known only twenty-four hours, to go with her to the railway station and put her on a train.

The jury was visibly impressed and much shaken. For Mr. Howell carried conviction in every word he said; he looked the district attorney in the eye, and once when our glances crossed he even smiled at me faintly. But I saw why he had tried to find Jennie Brice, and had dreaded testifying. Not a woman in that court room, and hardly a man, but believed when he left the stand, that he was, or had been, Jennie Brice's lover, and as such was assisting her to leave her husband.

"Then you believe," the district attorney said at the end,—"you believe, Mr. Howell, that Jennie Brice is living?"

"Jennie Brice was living on Monday morning, March the fifth," he said firmly.

"Miss Shaeffer has testified that on Wednesday this woman, who you claim was Jennie Brice, sent a letter to you from Horner. Is that the case?"

"Yes."

"The letter was signed 'Jennie Brice'?"

"It was signed 'J.B.'"

"Will you show the court that letter?"

"I destroyed it."

"It was a personal letter?"

"It merely said she had arrived safely, and not to let any one know where she was."

"And yet you destroyed it?"

"A postscript said to do so."

"Why?"

"I do not know. An extra precaution probably."

"You were under the impression that she was going to stay there?"

"She was to have remained for a week."

"And you have been searching for this woman for two months?"

He quailed, but his voice was steady. "Yes," he admitted.

He was telling the truth, even if it was not all the truth. I believe, had it gone to the jury then, Mr. Ladley would have been acquitted. But, late that afternoon, things took a new turn. Counsel for the prosecution stated to the court that he had a new and important witness, and got permission to introduce this further evidence. The witness was a Doctor Littlefield, and proved to be my one-night tenant of the second-story front. Holcombe's prisoner of the night before took the stand. The doctor was less impressive in full daylight; he was a trifle shiny, a bit bulbous as to nose and indifferent as to finger-nails. But his testimony was given with due professional weight.

"You are a doctor of medicine, Doctor Littlefield?" asked the district attorney.

"Yes."

"In active practise?"

"I have a Cure for Inebriates in Des Moines, Iowa. I was formerly in general practise in New York City."

"You knew Jennie Ladley?"

"I had seen her at different theaters. And she consulted me professionally at one time in New York."

"You operated on her, I believe?"

"Yes. She came to me to have a name removed. It had been tattooed over her heart."

"You removed it?"

"Not at once. I tried fading the marks with goat's milk, but she was impatient. On the third visit to my office she demanded that the name be cut out."

"You did it?"

"Yes. She refused a general anesthetic and I used cocaine. The name was John—I believe a former husband. She intended to marry again."

A titter ran over the court room. People strained to the utmost are always glad of an excuse to smile. The laughter of a wrought-up crowd always seems to me half hysterical.

"Have you seen photographs of the scar on the body found at Sewickley? Or the body itself?"

"No, I have not."

"Will you describe the operation?"

"I made a transverse incision for the body of the name, and two vertical ones—one longer for the *J*, the other shorter, for the stem of the *h*. There was a dot after the name. I made a half-inch incision for it."

"Will you sketch the cicatrix as you recall it?"

The doctor made a careful drawing on a pad that was passed to him. The drawing was much like this.

Line for line, dot for dot, it was the scar on the body found at Sewickley.

"You are sure the woman was Jennie Brice?"

"She sent me tickets for the theater shortly after. And I had an announcement of her marriage to the prisoner, some weeks later."

"Were there any witnesses to the operation?"

"My assistant; I can produce him at any time."

That was not all of the trial, but it was the decisive moment. Shortly after, the jury withdrew, and for twenty-four hours not a word was heard from them.

CHAPTER XV

After twenty-four hours' deliberation, the jury brought in a verdict of guilty. It was a first-degree verdict. Mr. Howell's unsupported word had lost out against a scar.

Contrary to my expectation, Mr. Holcombe was not jubilant over the verdict. He came into the dining-room that night and stood by the window, looking out into the yard.

"It isn't logical," he said. "In view of Howell's testimony, it's ridiculous! Heaven help us under this jury system, anyhow! Look at the facts! Howell knows the woman: he sees her on Monday morning, and puts her on a train out of town. The boy is telling the truth. He has nothing to gain by coming forward, and everything to lose. Very well: she was alive on Monday. We know where she was on Tuesday and Wednesday. Anyhow, during those days her gem of a husband was in jail. He was freed Thursday night, and from that time until his rearrest on the following Tuesday, I had him under observation every moment. He left the jail Thursday night, and on Saturday the body floated in at Sewickley. If it was done by Ladley, it must have been done on Friday, and on Friday he was in view through the periscope all day!"

Mr. Reynolds came in and joined us. "There's only one way out that I see," he said mildly. "Two women have been fool enough to have a name tattooed over their hearts. No woman ever thought enough of me to have *my* name put on her."

"I hope not," I retorted. Mr. Reynold's first name is Zachariah.

But, as Mr. Holcombe said, all that had been proved was that Jennie Brice was dead, probably murdered. He could not understand the defense letting the case go to the jury without their putting more stress on Mr. Howell's story. But we were to understand that soon, and many other things. Mr. Holcombe told me that evening of learning from John Bellows of the tattooed name on Jennie Brice and of how, after an almost endless search, he had found the man who had cut the name away.

At eight o'clock the door-bell rang. Mr. Reynolds had gone to lodge, he being an Elk and several other things, and much given to regalia in boxes, and having his picture in the newspapers in different outlandish costumes. Mr. Pitman used to say that man, being denied his natural love for barbaric adornment in his every-day clothing, took to the different fraternities as an excuse for decking himself out. But this has nothing to do with the door-bell.

It was old Isaac. He had a basket in his hand, and he stepped into the hall and placed it on the floor.

"Evening, Miss Bess," he said. "Can you see a bit of company to-night?"

"I can always see you," I replied. But he had not meant himself. He stepped to the door, and opening it, beckoned to some one across the street. It was Lida!

She came in, her color a little heightened, and old Isaac stood back, beaming at us both; I believe it was one of the crowning moments of the old man's life—thus to see his Miss Bess and Alma's child together.

"Is—is he here yet?" she asked me nervously.

"I did not know he was coming." There was no need to ask which "he." There was only one for Lida.

"He telephoned me, and asked me to come here. Oh, Mrs. Pitman, I'm so afraid for him!" She had quite forgotten Isaac. I turned to the school-teacher's room and opened the door. "The woman who belongs here is out at a lecture," I said. "Come in here, Ikkie, and I'll find the evening paper for you.

"'Ikkie'!" said Lida, and stood staring at me. I think I went white.

"The lady heah and I is old friends," Isaac said, with his splendid manner. "Her mothah, Miss Lida, her mothah—"

But even old Isaac choked up at that, and I closed the door on him.

"How queer!" Lida said, looking at me. "So Isaac knew your mother? Have you lived always in Allegheny, Mrs. Pitman?"

"I was born in Pittsburgh," I evaded. "I went away for a long time, but I always longed for the hurry and activity of the old home town. So here I am again."

Fortunately, like all the young, her own affairs engrossed her. She was flushed with the prospect of meeting her lover, tremulous over what the evening might bring. The middle-aged woman who had come back to the hurry of the old town, and who, pushed back into an eddy of the flood district, could only watch the activity and the life from behind a "Rooms to Let" sign, did not concern her much. Nor should she have.

Mr. Howell came soon after. He asked for her, and going back to the dining-room, kissed her quietly. He had an air of resolve, a sort of grim determination, that was a relief from the half-frantic look he had worn before. He asked to have Mr. Holcombe brought down, and so behold us all, four of us, sitting around the table—Mr. Holcombe with his note-book, I with my mending, and the boy with one of Lida's hands frankly under his on the red table-cloth.

"I want to tell all of you the whole story," he began. "To-morrow I shall go to the district attorney and confess, but—I want you all to have it first. I can't sleep again until I get it off my chest. Mrs. Pitman has suffered through me, and Mr. Holcombe here has spent money and time—"

Lida did not speak, but she drew her chair closer, and put her other hand over his.

"I want to get it straight, if I can. Let me see. It was on Sunday, the fourth, that the river came up, wasn't it? Yes. Well, on the Thursday before that I met you, Mr. Holcombe, in a restaurant in Pittsburgh. Do you remember?"

Mr. Holcombe nodded.

"We were talking of crime, and I said no man should be hanged on purely circumstantial evidence. You affirmed that a well-linked chain of circumstantial evidence could properly hang a man. We had a long argument, in which I was worsted. There was a third man at the table—Bronson, the business manager of the Liberty Theater."

"Who sided with you," put in Mr. Holcombe, "and whose views I refused to entertain because, as publicity man for a theater, he dealt in fiction rather than in fact."

"Precisely. You may recall, Mr. Holcombe, that you offered to hang any man we would name, given a proper chain of circumstantial evidence against him?"

"Yes."

"After you left, Bronson spoke to me. He said business at the theater was bad, and complained of the way the papers used, or would not use, his stuff. He said the Liberty Theater had not had a proper deal, and that he was tempted to go over and bang one of the company on the head, and so get a little free advertising.

"I said he ought to be able to fake a good story; but he maintained that a newspaper could smell a faked story a mile away, and that, anyhow, all the good stunts had been pulled off. I agreed with him. I remember saying that nothing but a railroad wreck or a murder hit the public very hard these days, and that I didn't feel like wrecking the Pennsylvania Limited.

"He leaned over the table and looked at me. 'Well, how about a murder, then?' he said. 'You get the story for your paper, and I get some advertising for the theater. We need it, that's sure.'

"I laughed it off, and we separated. But at two o'clock Bronson called me up again. I met him in his office at the theater, and he told me that Jennie Brice, who was out of the cast that week, had asked for a week's vacation. She had heard of a farm at a town called Horner, and she wanted to go there to rest.

"'Now the idea is this,' he said. 'She's living with her husband, and he has threatened her life more than once. It would be easy enough to frame up something to look as if he'd made away with her. We'd get a week of excitement, more advertising than we'd ordinarily get in a year; you get a corking news story, and find Jennie Brice at the end, getting the credit for that. Jennie gets a hundred dollars and a rest, and Ladley, her husband, gets, say, two hundred.'

"Mr. Bronson offered to put up the money, and I agreed. The flood came just then, and was considerable help. It made a good setting. I went to my city editor, and got an assignment to interview Ladley about this play of his. Then Bronson and I went together to see the Ladleys on Sunday morning, and as they needed money, they agreed. But Ladley insisted on fifty dollars a week extra if he had to go to jail. We promised it, but we did not intend to let things go so far as that.

"In the Ladleys' room that Sunday morning, we worked it all out. The hardest thing was to get Jennie Brice's consent; but she agreed, finally. We arranged a list of clues, to be left around, and Ladley was to go out in the night and to be heard coming back. I told him to quarrel with his wife that afternoon,—although I don't believe they needed to be asked to do it,—and I suggested also the shoe or slipper, to be found floating around."

"Just a moment," said Mr. Holcombe, busy with his note-book. "Did you suggest the onyx clock?"

"No. No clock was mentioned. The—the clock has puzzled me."

"The towel?"

"Yes. I said no murder was complete without blood, but he kicked on that—said he didn't mind the rest, but he'd be hanged if he was going to slash himself. But, as it happened, he cut his wrist while cutting the boat loose, and so we had the towel."

"Pillow-slip?" asked Mr. Holcombe.

"Well, no. There was nothing said about a pillow-slip. Didn't he say he burned it accidentally?"

"So he claimed." Mr. Holcombe made another entry in his book.

348

"Then I said every murder had a weapon. He was to have a pistol at first, but none of us owned one. Mrs. Ladley undertook to get a knife from Mrs. Pitman's kitchen, and to leave it around, not in full view, but where it could be found."

"A broken knife?"

"No. Just a knife."

"He was to throw the knife into the water?"

"That was not arranged. I only gave him a general outline. He was to add any interesting details that might occur to him. The idea, of course, was to give the police plenty to work on, and just when they thought they had it all, and when the theater had had a lot of booming, and I had got a good story, to produce Jennie Brice, safe and well. We were not to appear in it at all. It would have worked perfectly, but we forgot to count on one thing—Jennie Brice hated her husband."

"Not really hated him!" cried Lida.

"*Hated* him. She is letting him hang. She could save him by coming forward now, and she won't do it. She is hiding so he will go to the gallows."

There was a pause at that. It seemed too incredible, too inhuman.

"Then, early that Monday morning, you smuggled Jennie Brice out of the city?"

"Yes. That was the only thing we bungled. We fixed the hour a little too late, and I was seen by Miss Harvey's uncle, walking across the bridge with a woman."

"Why did you meet her openly, and take her to the train?"

Mr. Howell bent forward and smiled across at the little man. "One of your own axioms, sir," he said. "Do the natural thing; upset the customary order of events as little as possible. Jennie Brice went to the train, because that was where she wanted to go. But as Ladley was to protest that his wife had left town, and as the police would be searching for a solitary woman, I went with her. We went in a leisurely manner. I bought her a magazine and a morning paper, asked the conductor to fix her window, and, in general, acted the devoted husband seeing his wife off on a trip. I even"—he smiled—"I even promised to feed the canary."

Lida took her hands away. "Did you kiss her good-by?" she demanded.

"Not even a chaste salute," he said. His spirits were rising. It was, as often happens, as if the mere confession removed the guilt. I have seen little boys who have broken a window show the same relief after telling about it.

"For a day or two Bronson and I sat back, enjoying the stir-up. Things turned out as we had expected. Business boomed at the theater. I got a good story, and some few kind words from my city editor. Then—the explosion came. I got a letter from Jennie Brice saying she was going away, and that we need not try to find her. I went to Horner, but I had lost track of her completely. Even then, we did not believe things so bad as they turned out to be. We thought she was giving us a bad time, but that she would show up.

"Ladley was in a blue funk for a time. Bronson and I went to him. We told him how the thing had slipped up. We didn't want to go to the police and confess if we could help it. Finally, he agreed to stick it out until she was found, at a hundred dollars a week. It took all we could beg, borrow and steal. But now—we have to come out with the story anyhow."

Mr. Holcombe sat up and closed his note-book with a snap. "I'm not so sure of that," he said impressively. "I wonder if you realize, young man, that, having provided a perfect defense for this man Ladley, you provided him with every possible inducement to make away with his wife? Secure in your coming forward at the last minute and confessing the hoax to save him, was there anything he might not have dared with impunity?"

"But I tell you I took Jennie Brice out of town on Monday morning."

"*Did you*?" asked Mr. Holcombe sternly.

But at that, the school-teacher, having come home and found old Isaac sound asleep in her cozy corner, set up such a screaming for the police that our meeting broke up. Nor would Mr. Holcombe explain any further.

Mr. Holcombe was up very early the next morning. I heard him moving around at five o'clock, and at six he banged at my door and demanded to know at what time the neighborhood rose: he had been up for an hour and there were no signs of life. He was more cheerful after he had had a cup of coffee, commented on Lida's beauty, and said that Howell was a lucky chap.

"That is what worries me, Mr. Holcombe," I said. "I am helping the affair along and—what if it turns out badly?"

He looked at me over his glasses. "It isn't likely to turn out badly," he said. "I have never married, Mrs. Pitman, and I have missed a great deal out of life."

"Perhaps you're better off: if you had married and lost your wife—" I was thinking of Mr. Pitman.

"Not at all," he said with emphasis. "It's better to have married and lost than never to have married at all. Every man needs a good woman, and it doesn't matter how old he is. The older he is, the more he needs her. I am nearly sixty."

I was rather startled, and I almost dropped the fried potatoes. But the next moment he had got out his note-book and was going over the items again. "Pillow-slip," he said, "knife *broken*, onyx clock—wouldn't think so much of the clock if he hadn't been so damnably anxious to hide the key, the discrepancy in time as revealed by the trial—yes, it is as clear as a bell. Mrs. Pitman, does that Maguire woman next door sleep all day?"

"She's up now," I said, looking out the window.

He was in the hall in a moment, only to come to the door later, hat in hand. "Is she the only other woman on the street who keeps boarders?"

"She's the only woman who doesn't," I snapped. "She'll keep anything that doesn't belong to her—except boarders."

"Ah!"

He lighted his corn-cob pipe and stood puffing at it and watching me. He made me uneasy: I thought he was going to continue the subject of every man needing a wife, and I'm afraid I had already decided to take him if he offered, and to put the school-teacher out and have a real parlor again, but to keep Mr. Reynolds, he being tidy and no bother.

But when he spoke, he was back to the crime again: "Did you ever work a typewriter?" he asked.

What with the surprise, I was a little sharp. "I don't play any instrument except an egg-beater," I replied shortly, and went on clearing the table.

"I wonder—do you remember about the village idiot and the horse? But of course you do, Mrs. Pitman; you are a woman of imagination. Don't you think you could be Alice Murray for a few moments? Now think—you are a stenographer with theatrical ambitions: you meet an actor and you fall in love with him, and he with you."

"That's hard to imagine, that last."

"Not so hard," he said gently. "Now the actor is going to put you on the stage, perhaps in this new play, and some day he is going to marry you."

"Is that what he promised the girl?"

"According to some letters her mother found, yes. The actor is married, but he tells you he will divorce the wife; you are to wait for him, and in the meantime he wants you near him; away from the office, where other men are apt to come in with letters to be typed, and to chaff you. You are a pretty girl."

"It isn't necessary to overwork my imagination," I said, with a little bitterness. I had been a pretty girl, but work and worry—

"Now you are going to New York very soon, and in the meantime you have cut yourself off from all your people. You have no one but this man. What would you do? Where would you go?"

"How old was the girl?"

"Nineteen."

"I think," I said slowly, "that if I were nineteen, and in love with a man, and hiding, I would hide as near him as possible. I'd be likely to get a window that could see his going out and coming in, a place so near that he could come often to see me."

"Bravo!" he exclaimed. "Of course, with your present wisdom and experience, you would do nothing so foolish. But this girl was in her teens; she was not very far away, for he probably saw her that Sunday afternoon, when he was out for two hours. And as the going was slow that day, and he had much to tell and explain, I figure she was not far off. Probably in this very neighborhood."

During the remainder of that morning I saw Mr. Holcombe, at intervals, going from house to house along Union Street, making short excursions into side thoroughfares, coming back again and taking up his door-bell ringing with unflagging energy. I watched him off and on for two hours. At the end of that time he came back flushed and excited.

"I found the house," he said, wiping his glasses. "She was there, all right, not so close as we had thought, but as close as she could get."

"And can you trace her?" I asked.

His face changed and saddened. "Poor child!" he said. "She is dead, Mrs. Pitman!"

"Not she—at Sewickley!"

"No," he said patiently. "That was Jennie Brice."

"But—Mr. Howell—"

"Mr. Howell is a young ass," he said with irritation. "He did not take Jennie Brice out of the city that morning. He took Alice Murray in Jennie Brice's clothing, and veiled."

Well, that is five years ago. Five times since then the Allegheny River, from being a mild and inoffensive stream, carrying a few boats and a great deal of sewage, has become, a raging destroyer, and has filled our hearts with fear and our cellars with mud. Five times since then Molly Maguire has appropriated all that the flood carried from my premises to hers, and five times have I lifted my carpets and moved Mr. Holcombe, who occupies the parlor bedroom, to a second-floor room.

A few days ago, as I said at the beginning, we found Peter's body floating in the cellar, and as soon as the yard was dry, I buried him. He had grown fat and lazy, but I shall miss him.

Yesterday a riverman fell off a barge along the water-front and was drowned. They dragged the river for his body, but they did not find him. But they found something—an onyx clock, with the tattered remnant of a muslin pillow-slip wrapped around it. It only bore out the story, as we had known it for five years.

The Murray girl had lived long enough to make a statement to the police, although Mr. Holcombe only learned this later. On the statement being shown to Ladley in the jail, and his learning of the girl's death, he collapsed. He confessed before he was hanged, and his confession, briefly, was like this:

He had met the Murray girl in connection with the typing of his play, and had fallen in love with her. He had never cared for his wife, and would have been glad to get rid of her in any way possible. He had not intended to kill her, however. He had planned to elope with the Murray girl, and awaiting an opportunity, had persuaded her to leave home and to take a room near my house.

Here he had visited her daily, while his wife was at the theater.

They had planned to go to New York together on Monday, March the fifth. On Sunday, the fourth, however, Mr. Bronson and Mr. Howell had made their curious proposition. When he accepted, Philip Ladley maintained that he meant only to carry out the plan as suggested. But the temptation was too strong for him. That night, while his wife slept, he had strangled her.

I believe he was frantic with fear, after he had done it. Then it occurred to him that if he made the body unrecognizable, he would be safe enough. On that quiet Sunday night, when Mr. Reynolds reported all peaceful in the Ladley room, he had cut off the poor wretch's head and had tied it up in a pillow-slip weighted with my onyx clock!

It is a curious fact about the case that the scar which his wife incurred to enable her to marry him was the means of his undoing. He insisted, and I believe he was telling the truth, that he did not know of the scar: that is, his wife had never told him of it, and had been able to conceal it. He thought she had probably used paraffin in some way.

In his final statement, written with great care and no little literary finish, he told the story in detail: of arranging the clues as Mr. Howell and Mr. Bronson had suggested; of going out in the boat, with the body, covered with a fur coat, in the bottom of the skiff: of throwing it into the current above the Ninth Street bridge, and of seeing the fur coat fall from the boat and carried beyond his reach; of disposing of the head near the Seventh Street bridge: of going to a drug store, as per the Howell instructions, and of coming home at four o'clock, to find me at the head of the stairs.

Several points of confusion remained. One had been caused by Temple Hope's refusal to admit that the dress and hat that figured in the case were to be used by her the next week at the theater. Mr. Ladley insisted that this was the case, and that on that Sunday afternoon his wife had requested him to take them to Miss Hope; that they had quarreled as to whether they should be packed in a box or in the brown valise, and that he had visited Alice Murray instead. It was on the way there that the idea of finally getting rid of Jennie Brice came to him. And a way—using the black and white striped dress of the dispute.

Another point of confusion had been the dismantling of his room that Monday night, some time between the visit of Temple Hope and the return of Mr. Holcombe. This was to obtain the scrap of paper containing the list of clues as suggested by Mr. Howell, a clue that might have brought about a premature discovery of the so-called hoax.

To the girl he had told nothing of his plan. But he had told her she was to leave town on an early train the next morning, going as his wife; that he wished her to wear the black and white dress and hat, for reasons that he would explain later, and to be veiled heavily, that to the young man who would put her on the train, and who had seen Jennie Brice only once, she was to be Jennie Brice; to say as little as possible and not to raise her veil. Her further instructions were simple: to go to the place at Horner where Jennie Brice had planned to go, but to use the name of "Bellows" there. And after she had been there for a day or two, to go as quietly as possible to New York. He gave her the address of a boarding-house where he could write her, and where he would join her later.

He reasoned in this way: That as Alice Murray was to impersonate Jennie Brice, and Jennie Brice hiding from her husband, she would naturally discard her name. The name "Bellows" had been hers by a previous marriage and she might easily resume it. Thus, to establish his innocence, he had not only the evidence of Howell and Bronson that the whole thing was a gigantic hoax; he had the evidence of Howell that he had started Jennie Brice to Horner that Monday morning, that she had reached Horner, had there assumed an incognito, as Mr. Pitman would say, and had later disappeared from there, maliciously concealing herself to work his undoing.

In all probability he would have gone free, the richer by a hundred dollars for each week of his imprisonment, but for two things: the flood, which had brought opportunity to his door, had brought Mr Holcombe to feed Peter, the dog. And the same flood, which should have carried the headless body as far as Cairo, or even farther on down the Mississippi, had rejected it in an eddy below a clay bluff at Sewickley, with its pitiful covering washed from the scar.

Well, it is all over now. Mr Ladley is dead, and Alice Murray, and even Peter lies in the yard. Mr Reynolds made a small wooden cross over Peter's grave, and carved "Till we meet again" on it. I dare say the next flood will find it in Molly Maguire's kitchen.

Mr Howell and Lida are married. Mr Howell inherited some money, I believe, and what with that and Lida declaring she would either marry him in a church or run off to Steubenville, Ohio, Alma had to consent. I went to the wedding and stood near the door, while Alma swept in, in lavender chiffon and rose point lace. She has not improved with age, has Alma. But Lida? Lida, under my mother's wedding veil, with her eyes like stars, seeing no one in the church in all that throng but the boy who waited at the end of the long church aisle-I wanted to run out and claim her, my own blood, my more than child.

I sat down and covered my face. And from the pew behind me some one leaned over and patted my shoulder.

"Miss Bess!" old Isaac said gently. "Don't take on, Miss Bess!"

He came the next day and brought me some lilies from the bride's bouquet, that she had sent me, and a bottle of champagne from the wedding supper. I had not tasted champagne for twenty years!

That is all of the story. On summer afternoons sometimes, when the house is hot, I go to the park and sit. I used to take Peter, but now he is dead. I like to see Lida's little boy; the nurse knows me by sight, and lets me talk to the child. He can say "Peter" quite plainly. But he does not call Alma "Grandmother." The nurse says she does not like it. He calls her "Nana."

Lida does not forget me. Especially at flood-times, she always comes to see if I am comfortable. The other day she brought me, with apologies, the chiffon gown her mother had worn at her wedding. Alma had never worn it but once, and now she was too stout for it. I took it; I am not proud, and I should like Molly Maguire to see it.

Mr. Holcombe asked me last night to marry him. He says he needs me, and that I need him.

I am a lonely woman, and getting old, and I'm tired of watching the gas meter; and besides, with Peter dead, I need a man in the house all the time. The flood district is none too orderly. Besides, when I have a wedding dress laid away and a bottle of good wine, it seems a pity not to use them.

I think I shall do it.

THE END

Manufactured by Amazon.ca
Bolton, ON

10743507R00195